HADRIAN'S TOMB.

THE HISTORICAL ROMANCES OF
GEORG EBERS

THE EMPEROR

Translated from the German by
Clara Bell

BIGELOW, BROWN & CO., Inc.
New York

TO MY DEAR FRIEND AND COLLEAGUE

OTTO STOBBE

FAITHFUL ALIKE IN HAPPINESS AND IN SADNESS,

IN HOURS GRAVE OR GAY,

I DEDICATE THIS BOOK IN UNALTERABLE

AFFECTION AND REGARD

GEORG EBERS

PREFACE.

——

It is now fourteen years since I planned the story related in these volumes, the outcome of a series of lectures which I had occasion to deliver on the period of the Roman dominion in Egypt. But the pleasures of inventive composition were forced to give way to scientific labors, and when I was once more at leisure to try my wings with increase of power I felt more strongly urged to other flights. Thus it came to pass that I did not take the time of Hadrian for the background of a tale till after I had dealt with the still later period of the early monastic move in "Homo Sum." Since finishing that romance my old wish to depict, in the form of a story, the most important epoch of the history of that venerable nation to which I have devoted nearly a quarter century of my life, has found its fulfilment. I have endeavored to give a picture of the splendor of the Pharaonic times in "Uarda," of the subjection of Egypt to the new Empire of the Persians in "An Egyptian Princess," of the Hellenic period under the Lagides in "The Sisters," of the Roman dominion and the early growth of Christianity in "The Emperor," and of the anchorite spirit—in the deserts and rocks of the Sinaitic Peninsula—in "Homo Sum." Thus the present work is the last of which the scene will be laid in Egypt.

This series of romances will not only have introduced the reader to a knowledge of the history of man-

ners and culture in Egypt, but will have facilitated his
comprehension of certain dominant ideas which stirred
the mind of the Ancients. How far I may have succeeded
in rendering the color of the times I have described and in
producing pictures that realize the truth, I myself cannot
venture to judge; for since even present facts are differently reflected in different minds, this must be still
more emphatically the case with things long since past
and half-forgotten. Again and again, when historical
investigation has refused to afford me the means of
resuscitating some remotely ancient scene, I have been
obliged to take counsel of imagination and remember
the saying that ' the Poet must be a retrospective Seer,'
and could allow my fancy to spread her wings, while I
remained her lord and knew the limits up to which I
might permit her to soar. I considered it my lawful
privilege to paint much that was pure invention, but
nothing that was not possible at the period I was representing. A due regard for such possibility has always set
the bounds to fancy's flight; wherever existing authorities
have allowed me to be exact and faithful I have always
been so, and the most distinguished of my fellow-pro-
fessors in Germany, England, France and Holland, have
more than once borne witness to this. But, as I need
hardly point out, poetical and historical truth are not
the same thing; for historical truth must remain, as far
as possible, unbiassed by the subjective feeling of the
writer, while poetical truth can only find expression
through the medium of the artist's fancy.

As in my last two romances, so in "The Emperor,"
I have added no notes: I do this in the pleasant conviction of having won the confidence of my readers by
my historical and other labors. Nothing has encour-

aged me to fresh imaginative works so much as the fact
that through these romances the branch of learning
that I profess has enlisted many disciples whose names
are now mentioned with respect among Egyptologists.
Every one who is familiar with the history of Hadrian's
time will easily discern by trifling traits from what
author or from which inscription or monument the minor
details have been derived, and I do not care to interrupt the course of the narrative and so spoil the pleasure
of the larger class of readers.   It would be a happiness
to me to believe that this tale deserves to be called a
real work of art, and, as such, its first function should
be to charm and elevate the mind.   Those who at the
same time enrich their knowledge by its study ought
not to detect the fact that they are learning.

Those who are learned in the history of Alexandria
under the Romans may wonder that I should have
made no mention of the Therapeutai on Lake Mareotis.
I had originally meant to devote a chapter to them, but
Lucä's recent investigations led me to decide on leaving it unwritten.   I have given years of study to the
early youth of Christianity, particularly in Egypt, and it
affords me particular satisfaction to help others to realize
how, in Hadrian's time, the pure teaching of the Saviour,
as yet little sullied by the contributions of human minds,
conquered—and could not fail to conquer—the hearts of
men.   Side by side with the triumphant Faith I have set
that noble blossom of Greek life and culture—Art—
which in later ages, Christianity absorbed in order to
dress herself in her beautiful forms.   The statues and
bust of Antinous which remain to us of that epoch,
show that the drooping tree was still destined to put
forth new leaves under Hadrian's rule.

The romantic traits which I have attributed to the character of my hero, who travelled throughout the world, climbing mountains to rejoice in the splendor of the rising sun, are authentic. One of the most difficult tasks I have ever set myself was to construct from the abundant but essentially contradictory accounts of Hadrian a human figure in which I could myself at all believe; still, how gladly I set to work to do so! There was much to be considered in working out this narrative, but the story itself has flowed straight from the heart of the writer; I can only hope it may find its way to that of the reader.

LEIPZIG, November, 1880.

GEORG EBERS.

THE EMPEROR.

CHAPTER I.

THE morning twilight had dawned into day, and
the sun had risen on the first of December of the year
of our Lord 129, but was still veiled by milk-white
mists which rose from the sea, and it was cold.

Kasius, a mountain of moderate elevation, stands
on a tongue of land that projects from the coast between the south of Palestine and Egypt. It is washed
on the north by the sea which, on this day, is not
gleaming, as is its wont, in translucent ultramarine; its
more distant depths slowly surge in blue-black waves,
while those nearer to shore are of quite a different hue,
and meet their sisters that lie nearer to the horizon in a
dull greenish-grey, as dusty plains join darker lava-
beds. The northeasterly wind, which had risen as the
sun rose, now blew more keenly, wreaths of white foam
rode on the crests of the waves, though these did not
beat wildly and stormily on the mountain-foot, but
rolled heavily to the shore in humped ridges, endlessly
long, as if they were of molten lead. Still the clear
bright spray splashed up when the gulls dipped their
pinions in the water as they floated above it, hither and
thither, restless and uttering shrill little cries, as though
driven by terror.

Three men were walking slowly along the causeway

which led from the top of the hill down into the valley,
but it was only the eldest, who walked in front of the
other two, who gave any heed to the sky, the sea, the
g⋯¹ls, and the barren plain that lay silent at his feet.
He stopped, and as soon as he did so, the others followed his example.   The landscape below him seemed
to rivet his gaze, and it justified the disapproval with
which he gently shook his head, which was somewhat
sunk into his beard.   A narrow strip of desert stretched
westward before him as far as the eye could reach,
dividing two levels of water.   Along this natural dyke
a caravan was passing, and the elastic feet of the camels
fell noiselessly on the road they trod.   The leader,
wrapped in his white mantle, seemed asleep, and the
camel-drivers to be dreaming; the dull-colored eagles
by the road-side did not stir at their approach.   To the
right of the stretch of flat coast along which the road
ran from Syria to Egypt, lay the gloomy sea, overhung
by grey clouds; to the left lay the desert, a strange and
mysterious feature in the landscape, of which the eye
could not see the end, either to the east or to the west,
and which looked here like a stretch of snow, there like
standing water, and again like a thicket of rushes.

The eldest of our travellers gazed constantly towards
heaven or into the distance; the second, a slave who
carried rugs and cloaks on his broad shoulders, never
took his eyes off his master; and the third, a young,
free-man, looked wearily and dreamily down the road.

A broad path, leading to a stately temple, crossed
that which led from the summit of the mountain to the
coast, and the bearded pedestrian turned up it; but he
followed it only for a few steps, then he turned his
head with a dissatisfied air, muttered a few unintelligible

words into his beard, turned round and hastily retraced
his steps to the narrow way, down which he went towards the valley. His young companion followed him
without raising his head or interrupting his reverie, as
if he were his shadow, but the slave lifted his cropped
fair head and a stolen smile crossed his lips as on the
left hand side of the Kasius road he caught sight of a
black kid, and close beside it an old woman who, at
the approach of the three men covered her wrinkled
face in alarm with her dark blue veil.

"That is the reason then!" said the slave to himself
with a nod, and blowing a kiss into the air to a black-
haired girl who crouched at the old woman's feet. But
she, for whom the greeting was intended, did not observe this mute courtship, for her eyes followed the
travellers, and especially the young man, as if spellbound. As soon as the three were far enough off not
to hear her, the girl asked with a shiver, as if some
desert-spectre had passed by—and in a low voice:
"Grandmother, who was that?"

The old woman raised her veil, laid her hand on
her grandchild's mouth, and whispered:

"It was he."

"The Emperor?"

The old woman answered with a significant nod,
but the girl squeezed herself up, against her grandmother, with vehement curiosity stretching out her
dusky head to see better, and asked softly: "The
young one?"

"Silly child! the one in front with a grey beard."

"He? Oh, I wish the young one was the Emperor!"

It was in fact Hadrian, the Roman Emperor, who

walked on in silence before his escort, and it seemed as though his advent had given life to the desert, for as he approached the reed-swamp, the kites flew up in the air, and from behind a sand-hill on the edge of the broader road which Hadrian had avoided, came two men in priestly robes. They both belonged to the temple of Baal of Kariotis, a small structure of solid stone, which faced the sea, and which the Emperor had yesterday visited.

"Do you think he has lost his way?" said one to the other, in the Phœnician tongue.

"Hardly," was the answer. "Mastor said that he could always find a road again by which he had once gone, even in the dark."

"And yet he is gazing more at the clouds than at the road."

"Still, he promised us yesterday."

"He promised nothing for certain," interrupted the other.

"Indeed he did; at parting he called out—and I heard him distinctly: 'Perhaps I shall return and consult your oracle.'"

"Perhaps."

"I think he said 'probably.'"

"Who knows whether some sign he has seen up in the sky may not have turned him back; he is going to the camp by the sea."

"But the banquet is standing ready for him in our great hall."

"He will find what he needs down there. Come, it is a wretched morning, and I am being frozen."

"Wait a little longer—look there."

"What?"

" He does not even wear a hat to cover his grey hair."

" He has never yet been seen to travel with anything on his head."

" And his grey cloak is not very imperial looking."

" He always wears the purple at a banquet."

" Do you know who his walk and appearance remind me of ?"

" Who ?"

" Of our late high-priest, Abibaal ; he used to walk in that ponderous, meditative way, and wear a beard like the Emperor's."

" Yes, yes—and had the same piercing grey eye."

" He too used often to gaze up at the sky. They have both the same broad forehead, too ; but Abibaal's nose was more aquiline, and his hair curled less closely."

" And our governor's mouth was grave and dignified, while Hadrian's lips twitch and curl at all he says and hears, as if he were laughing at it all."

" Look, he is speaking now to his favorite—Antonius I think they call the pretty boy."

" Antinous, not Antonius. He picked him up in Bithynia, they say."

" He is a beautiful youth."

" Incomparably beautiful ! What a figure and what a face ! Still, I cannot wish that he were my son."

" The Emperor's favorite !"

" For that very reason. Why, he looks already as if he had tried every pleasure, and could never know any farther enjoyment."

———

On a little level close to the sea-shore, and sheltered by crumbling cliffs from the east wind, stood a number

of tents.   Between them fires were burning, round which
were gathered groups of Roman soldiers and imperial
servants.   Half-naked boys, the children of the fishermen and camel-drivers who dwelt in this wilderness,
were running busily hither and thither, feeding the
flames with dry stems of sea-grass and dead desert-
shrubs; but though the blaze flew high, the smoke did
not rise, but driven here and there by the squalls of
wind, swirled about close to the ground in little clouds,
like a flock of scattered sheep.   It seemed as though it
feared to rise in the grey, damp, uninviting atmosphere.

    The largest of the tents, in front of which Roman
sentinels paced up and down, two and two, on guard,
was wide open on the side towards the sea.   The slaves
who came out of the broad door-way with trays on their
cropped heads—loaded with gold and silver vessels,
plates, wine-jars, goblets, and the remains of a meal—
had to hold them tightly with both hands that they
might not be blown over.

    The inside of the tent was absolutely unadorned.
The Emperor lay on a couch near the right wall, which
was blown in and bulged by the wind; his bloodless lips
were tightly set, his arms crossed over his breast, and
his eyes half closed.   But he was not asleep, for he
often opened his mouth and smacked his lips, as if
tasting the flavor of some viand.   From time to time
he raised his eyelids—long, finely wrinkled, and blue-
veined—turning his eyes up to heaven or rolling them
to one side and then downwards towards the middle of
the tent.   There, on the skin of a huge bear trimmed
with blue cloth, lay Hadrian's favorite Antinous.   His
beautiful head rested on that of the beast, which had
been slain by his sovereign, and its skull and skin

skilfully preserved, his right leg, supported on his left knee, he flourished freely in the air, and his hands were caressing the Emperor's bloodhound, which had laid its sage-looking head on the boy's broad, bare breast, and now and then tried to lick his soft lips to show its affection. But this the youth would not allow; he playfully held the beast's muzzle close with his hands or wrapped its head in the end of his mantle, which had slipped back from his shoulders.

The dog seemed to enjoy the game, but once when Antinous had drawn the cloak more tightly round its head and it strove in vain to be free from the cloth that impeded its breathing, it set up a loud howl, and this doleful cry made the Emperor change his attitude and cast a glance of displeasure at the boy lying on the bear-skin; but only a glance, not a word of blame. And soon the expression, even of his eyes, changed, and he fixed them on the lads's figure with a gaze of loving contemplation, as though it were some noble work of art that he could never tire of admiring. And truly the Immortals had moulded this child of man to such a type; every muscle of that throat, that chest, those arms and legs was a marvel of softness and of power; no human countenance could be more regularly chiselled. Antinous observing that his master's attention had been attracted to his play with the dog, let the animal go and turned his large, but not very brilliant, eyes on the Emperor.

"What are you doing here?" asked Hadrian kindly.

"Nothing," said the boy.

"No one can do nothing. Even if we fancy we have succeeded in doing nothing we still continue to

2

think that we are unoccupied, and to think is a good deal."

"But I cannot even think."

"Every one can think; besides you were not doing nothing, for you were playing."

"Yes, with the dog." With these words Antinous stretched out his legs on the ground, pushed away the dog, and raised his curly head on both hands.

"Are you tired?" asked the Emperor.

"Yes."

"We both kept watch for an equal portion of the night, and I, who am so much older, feel quite wide awake."

"It was only yesterday that you were saying that old soldiers were the best for night-watches."

The Emperor nodded, and then said:

"At your age while we are awake we live three times as fast as at mine, and so we need to sleep twice as long. You have every right to be tired. To be sure it was not till three hours after midnight that we climbed the mountain, and how often a supper party is not over before that."

"It was very cold and uncomfortable up there."

"Not till after the sun had risen."

"Ah! before that you did not notice it, for till then you were busy thinking of the stars."

"And you only of yourself—very true."

"I was thinking of your health too when that cold wind rose before Helios appeared."

"I was obliged to await his rising."

"And can you discern future events by the way and manner of the rising of the sun?"

Hadrian looked in surprise at the speaker, shook his

head in negation, looked up at the top of the tent, and after a long pause said, in abrupt sentences, with frequent interruptions:

"Day is the present merely, and the future is evolved out of darkness; the corn grows from the clods of the field; the rain falls from the darkest clouds; a new generation is born of the mother's womb; the limbs recover their vigor in sleep. And what is begotten of the darkness of death—who can tell?"

When, after saying this, the Emperor had remained for some time silent, the youth asked him:

"But if the sunrise teaches you nothing concerning the future why should you so often break your night's rest and climb the mountain to see it?"

"Why? Why?" repeated Hadrian, slowly and meditatively, stroking his grizzled beard; then he went on as if speaking to himself:

"That is a question which reason fails to answer, before which my lips find no words; and, if I had them at my command, who among the rabble would understand me? Such questions can best be answered by means of parables. Those who take part in life are actors, and the world is their stage. He who wants to look tall on it wears the cothurnus, and is not a mountain the highest vantage ground that a man can find for the sole of his foot? Kasius there is but a hill, but I have stood on greater giants than he, and seen the clouds rise below me, like Jupiter on Olympus."

"But you need climb no mountains to feel yourself a god," cried Antinous; "the godlike is your title— you command and the world must obey. With a mountain beneath his feet a man is nearer to heaven no doubt than he is on the plain."

"Well?"

"I dare not say what came into my mind."

"Speak out."

"I knew a little girl who when I took her on my shoulder would stretch out her arms and exclaim, 'I am so tall!' She fancied that she was taller than I then, and yet was only little Panthea."

"But in her own conception of herself, it was she who was tall, and that decides the issue, for to each of us a thing is only that which it seems to us. It is true they call me godlike, but I feel every day, and a hundred times a day, the limitations of the power and nature of man, and I cannot get beyond them. On the top of a mountain I cease to feel them; there I feel as if I were great, for nothing is higher than my head, far or near. And when, as I stand there, the night vanishes before my eyes, when the splendor of the young sun brings the world into new life for me, by restoring to my consciousness all that just before had been engulfed in gloom, then a deeper breath swells my breast, and my lungs fill with the purer and lighter air of the heights. Up there, alone and in silence, no hint can reach me of the turmoil below, and I feel myself one with the great aspect of nature spread before me. The surges of the sea come and go, the tree-tops in the forest bow and rise, fog and mist roll away and part asunder hither and thither, and up there I feel myself so merged with the creation that surrounds me that often it even seems as though it were my own breath that gives it life. Like the storks and the swallows, I yearn for the distant land, and where should the human eye be more likely to be permitted, at least in fancy, to discern the remote goal than from the summit of a mountain?

The limitless distance which the spirit craves for seems there to assume a form tangible to the senses, and the eye detects its border line. My whole being feels not merely elevated, but expanded, and that vague longing which comes over me as soon as I mix once more in the turmoil of life, and when the cares of state demand my strength, vanishes. But you cannot understand it, boy. These are things which no other mortal can share with me."

"And it is only to me that you do not scorn to reveal them!" cried Antinous, who had turned round to face the Emperor, and who with wide eyes had not lost one word.

"You?" said Hadrian, and a smile, not absolutely free from mockery, parted his lips. "From you I should no more have a secret than from the Cupid by Praxiteles, in my study at Rome."

The blood mounted to the lad's cheeks and dyed them flaming crimson. The Emperor observed this and said kindly:

"You are more to me than the statue, for the marble cannot blush. In the time of the Athenians Beauty governed life, but in you I can see that the gods are pleased to give it a bodily existence, even in our own days, and to look at you reconciles me to the discords of existence. It does me good. But how should I expect to find that you understand me; your brow was never made to be furrowed by thought; or did you really understand one word of all I said?"

Antinous propped himself on his left arm, and lifting his right hand, he said emphatically:

"Yes."

"And which," asked Hadrian.

"I know what longing is."

"For what?"

"For many things."

"Tell me one."

"Some enjoyment that is not followed by depression. I do not know of one."

"That is a desire you share with all the youth of Rome, only they are apt to postpone the reaction. Well, and what next?"

"I cannot tell you."

"What prevents your speaking openly to me?"

"You, yourself did."

"I?"

"Yes, you; for you forbid me to speak of my home, my mother, and my people."

The Emperor's brow darkened, and he answered sternly:

"I am your father and your whole soul should be given to me."

"It is all yours," answered the youth, falling back on to the bear-skin, and drawing the pallima closely over his shoulders, for a gust blew coldly in at the side of the tent, through which Phlegon, the Emperor's private secretary, now entered and approached his master. He was followed by a slave with several sealed rolls under his arms.

"Will it be agreeable to you, Caesar, to consider the despatches and letters that have just arrived?" asked the official, whose carefully-arranged hair had been tossed by the sea-breeze.

"Yes, and then we can make a note of what I was able to observe in the heavens last night. Have you the tablets ready?"

"I left them in the tent set up especially for the work, Caesar."

"The storm has become very violent."

"It seems to blow from the north and east both at once, and the sea is very rough. The Empress will have a bad voyage."

"When did she set out?"

"The anchor was weighed towards midnight. The vessel which is to fetch her to Alexandria is a fine ship, but rolls from side to side in a very unpleasant manner."

Hadrian laughed loudly and sharply at this, and said:

"That will turn her heart and her stomach upside down. I wish I were there to see—but no, by all the gods, no! for she will certainly forget to paint this morning; and who will construct that edifice of hair if all her ladies share her fate. We will stay here to-day, for if I meet her soon after she has reached Alexandria she will be undiluted gall and vinegar."

With these words Hadrian rose from his couch, and waving his hand to Antinous, went out of the tent with his secretary.

A third person standing at the back of the tent had heard the Emperor's conversation with his favorite; this was Mastor, a Sarmatian of the race of the Taryges. He was a slave, and no more worthy of heed than the dog which had followed Hadrian, or than the pillows on which the Emperor had been reclining. The man, who was handsome and well grown, stood for some time twisting the ends of his long red moustache, and stroking his round, closely-cropped head with his hands; then he drew the open chiton together over his broad breast, which seemed to gleam from the remarkable whiteness of the skin. He never took his eyes off Antinous, who had turned over, and covering his face with his hands had buried them in the bear's hairy mane.

Mastor had something he wanted to say to him, but he dared not address him for the young favorite's demeanor could not be reckoned on. Often he was ready to listen to him and talk with him as a friend, but often, too, he repulsed him more sharply than the haughtiest upstart would repel the meanest of his servants. At last the slave took courage and called the lad by his name, for it seemed less hard to submit to a scolding than to smother the utterance of a strong, warm feeling, unimportant as it might be, which was formed in words in his mind. Antinous raised his head a little on his hands and asked:

" What is it ?"

" I only wanted to tell you," replied the Sarmatian, " that I know who the little girl was that you so often took upon your shoulders. It was your little sister, was it not, of whom you were speaking to me lately ?"

The lad nodded assent, and then once more buried his head in his hands, and his shoulders heaved so violently that it would seem that he was weeping. Mastor remained silent for a few minutes, then he went up to Antinous and said:

"You know I have a son and a little daughter at home, and I am always glad to hear about little girls. We are alone and if it will relieve your heart ——"

"Let me alone, I have told you a dozen times already about my mother and little Panthea," replied Antinous, trying to look composed.

"Then do so confidently for the thirteenth," said the

slave. "In the camp and in the kitchen I can talk
about my people as much as I like. But you—tell me,
what do you call the little dog that Panthea made a
scarlet cloak for?"

"We called it Kallista," cried Antinous wiping his
eyes with the back of his hand. "My father would not
allow it but we persuaded my mother. I was her favorite, and when I put my arms round her and looked at
her imploringly she always said 'yes' to anything I
asked her."

A bright light shone in the boy's weary eyes; he had
remembered a whole wealth of joys which left no depression behind them.

CHAPTER II.

ONE of the palaces built in Alexandria by the
Ptolemaic kings stood on the peninsula called Lochias
which stretched out into the blue sea like a finger pointing northwards; it formed the eastern boundary of the
great harbor. Here there was never any lack of vessels
but to-day they were particularly numerous, and the
quay-road paved with smooth blocks of stone, which
led from the palatial quarter of the town—the Bruchiom
as it was called—which was bathed by the sea, to the
spit of land was so crowded with curious citizens on
foot and in vehicles, that all conveyances were obliged
to stop in their progress before they had reached the
private harbor reserved for the Emperor's vessels.

But there was something out of the common to be
seen at the landing-place, for there lying under the

shelter of the high mole were the splendid triremes, gal-
leys, long boats and barges which had brought Hadrian's
wife and the suite of the imperial couple to Alexandria.
A very large vessel with a particularly high cabin on
the after deck and having the head of a she-wolf on the
lofty and boldly-carved prow excited the utmost attention. It was carved entirely in cedar wood, richly
decorated with bronze and ivory, and named the Sabina.
A young Alexandrian pointed to the name written in
gold letters on the stern, nudging his companion and
saying with a laugh:

"Sabina has a wolf's head then!"

"A peacock's would suit her better. Did you see
her on her way to the Caesareum?" replied the other.

"Alas! I did," said the first speaker, but he said no
more perceiving, close behind him, a Roman lictor who
bore over his left shoulder his fasces, a bundle of elm-
rods skilfully tied together, and who, with a wand in
his right-hand and the assistance of his comrades, was
endeavoring to part the crowd and make room for the
chariot of his master, Titianus, the imperial prefect,
which came slowly in the rear. This high official had
overheard the citizens' heedless words, and turning to
the man who stood beside him, while with a light fling
he threw the end of his toga into fresh folds, he said:

"An extraordinary people! I cannot feel annoyed
with them, and yet I would rather walk from here to
Canopus on the edge of a knife than on that of an
Alexandrian's tongue."

"Did you hear what the stout man was saying
about Verus?"

"The lictor wanted to take him up, but nothing is
to be done with them by violence. If they had to pay

only a sesterce for every venomous word, I tell you Pontius, the city would be impoverished and our treasury would soon be fuller than that of Gyges at Sardis."

"Let them keep their money," cried the other, the chief architect of the city, a man of about thirty years of age with highly-arched brows and eager piercing eyes; and grasping the roll he held in his hand with a strong grip, he continued.

"They know how to work, and sweat is bitter. While they are busy they help each other, in idleness they bite each other, like unbroken horses harnessed to the same pole. The wolf is a fine brute, but if you break out his teeth he becomes a mangy hound."

"You speak after my own heart," cried the prefect. "But here we are, eternal gods! I never imagined anything so bad as this. From a distance it always looked handsome enough!"

Titianus and the architect descended from the chariot, the former desired a lictor to call the steward of the palace, and then he and his companion inspected first the door which led into it. It looked fine enough with its double columns which supported a lofty pediment, but, all the same, it did not present a particularly pleasing aspect, for the stucco had, in several places, fallen from the walls, the capitals of the marble columns were lamentably injured and the tall doors, overlaid with metal, hung askew on their hinges. Pontius inspected every portion of the door-way with a keen eye and then, with the prefect, went into the first court of the palace, in which, in the time of the Ptolemies, the tents had stood for ambassadors, secretaries, and the officers in waiting on the king. There they met with an unexpected hindrance, for across the paved court-yard, where the grass grew in tufts, and tall thistles were in bloom, a number of ropes were stretched aslant from the little house in which dwelt the gate-keeper; and on these ropes were hung newly-washed garments of every size and shape.

"A pretty residence for an Emperor," sighed Titi- anus, shrugging his shoulders, but stopping the lictor, who had raised his fasces to cut the ropes.

"It is not so bad as it looks," said the architect positively. "Gate-keeper! hi, gate-keeper! Where is the lazy fellow hiding himself?"

While he called out and the lictor hurried forward into the interior of the palace, Pontius went towards the gate-keeper's lodge, and having made his way in a stooping attitude through the damp clothes, there he stood still. Ever since he had come in at the gate annoyance and vexation had been stamped on his countenance, but now his large mouth spread into a smile, and he called to the prefect in an undertone:

"Titianus, just take the trouble to come here."

The elderly dignitary, whose tall figure exceeded that of the architect in height by a full head, did not find it quite so easy to pass under the ropes with his head bent down; but he did it with good humor, and while carefully avoiding pulling down the wet linen, he called out:

"I am beginning to feel some respect for children's shirts; one can at any rate get through them without breaking one's spine. Oh! this is delicious—quite de- licious!"

This exclamation was caused by the sight which the architect had invited the prefect to come and enjoy, and which was certainly droll enough. The front of the

gate-keeper's house was quite grown over with ivy
which framed the door and window in its long runners.
Amidst the greenery hung numbers of cages with star-
lings, blackbirds, and smaller singing-birds. The wide
door of the little house stood open, giving a view into a
tolerably spacious and gaily-painted room. In the
background stood a clay model of an Apollo of admirable workmanship; above, and near this, the wall
was hung with lutes and lyres of various size and form.

In the middle of the room, and near the open door,
was a table, on which stood a large wicker cage containing several nests of young goldfinches, and with
green food twined among the osiers. There were, too,
a large wine-jar and an ivory goblet decorated with fine
carving. Close to the drinking-vessels, on the stone
top of the table, rested the arm of an elderly woman
who had fallen asleep in the arm-chair in which she sat.
Notwithstanding the faint grey moustache that marked
her upper-lip and the pronounced ruddiness of her forehead and cheeks, she looked pleasant and kind. She
must have been dreaming of something that pleased
her, for the expression of her lips and of her eyes—one
being half open and the other closely shut—gave her a
look of contentment. In her lap slept a large grey cat,
and by its side—as though discord never could enter
this bright little abode which exhaled no savor of poverty, but, on the contrary, a peculiar and fragrant scent—
lay a small shaggy dog, whose snowy whiteness of coat
could only be due to the most constant care. Two
other dogs, like this one, lay stretched on the floor at
the old lady's feet, and seemed no less soundly asleep.

As the prefect came up, the architect pointed to this
study of still-life, and said in a whisper:

"If we had a painter here it would make a lovely little picture."

"Incomparable," answered Titianus, "only the vivid scarlet on the dame's cheeks seems to me suspicious, considering the ample proportions of the wine-jar at her elbow."

"But did you ever see a calmer, kindlier, or more contented countenance?"

"Baucis must have slept like that when Philemon allowed himself leave of absence for once! or did that devoted spouse always remain at home?"

"Apparently he did. Now, peace is at an end."

The approach of the two friends had waked one of the little dogs. He gave tongue, and his companion immediately jumped up and barked as if for a wager. The old woman's pet sprang out of her lap, but neither his mistress nor the cat let themselves be disturbed by the noise, and slept on.

"A watcher among a thousand!" said the architect, laughing.

"And this phalanx of dogs which guard the palace of a Caesar," added Titianus, "might be vanquished with a blow. Take heed, the worthy matron is about to wake."

The dame had in fact been disturbed by the barking. She sat up a little, lifted her hands, and then, half singing, half muttering a few words, she sank back again in her chair.

"This is delicious!" cried the prefect. "'Begone dull care' she sang in her sleep. How may this rare specimen of humanity look when she is awake?"

"I should be sorry to drive the old lady out of her nest!" said the architect unrolling his scroll.

"You shall touch nothing in the little house," cried the prefect eagerly. "I know Hadrian; he delights in such queer things and queer people, and I will wager he will make friends with the old woman in his own way. Here at last comes the steward of this palace."

The prefect was not mistaken; the hasty step he had heard was that of the official they awaited. At some little distance they could already hear the man, panting as he hurried up, and as he came, before Titianus could prevent him, he had snatched down the cords that were stretched across the court and flung all the washing on the ground. As soon as the curtain had thus dropped which had divided him from the Emperor's representative and his companion, he bowed to the former as low as the rotund dimensions of his person would allow; but his hasty arrival, the effort of strength he had made, and his astonishment at the appearance of the most powerful personage in the Nile Province in the building entrusted to his care, so utterly took away his breath—of which he at all times was but "scant"—that he was unable even to stammer out a suitable greeting. Titianus gave him a little time, and then, after expressing his regret at the sad plight of the washing, now strewn upon the ground, and mentioning to the steward the name and position of his friend Pontius, he briefly explained to him that the Emperor wished to take up his abode in the palace now in his charge; that he—Titianus—was cognizant of the bad condition in which it then was, and had come to take council with him and the architect as to what could be done in the course of a few days to make the dilapidated residence habitable for Hadrian, and to repair, at

any rate, the more conspicuous damage. He then desired the steward to lead him through the rooms.

"Directly—at once," answered the Greek, who had
attained his present ponderous dimensions through
many years of rest: "I will hasten to fetch the keys."
And as he went, puffing and panting, he re-arranged
with his short, fat fingers the still abundant hair on the
right side of his head. Pontius looked after him.

"Call him back, Titianus," said he. "We disturbed him in the midst of curling his hair; only one
side was done when the lictor called him away, and I
will wager my own head that he will have the other
side frizzled before he comes back. I know your true
Greek!"

"Well, let him," answered Titianus. "If you have
taken his measure rightly he will not be able to give his
attention without reserve to our questions till the other
half of his hair is curled. I know, too, how to deal
with a Hellene."

"Better than I, I perceive," said the architect in a
tone of conviction. "A statesman is used to deal with
men as we do with lifeless materials. Did you see the
fat fellow turn pale when you said that it would be but
a few days before the Emperor would make his entry
here? Things must look well in the old house there.
Every hour is precious, and we have lingered here too
long."

The prefect nodded agreement and followed the
architect into the inner court of the palace. How
grand and well-proportioned was the plan of this immense building through which the steward Keraunus,
who returned with his fine curls complete all round,
now led the Romans. It stood on an artificial hill in

the midst of the peninsula of Lochias, and from many a window and many a balcony there were lovely prospects of the streets and open squares, the houses, palaces and public buildings of the metropolis, and of the harbor, swarming with ships. The outlook from Lochias was rich, gay and varied to the south and west, but east and north from the platform of the palace of the Ptolemies, the gaze fell on the never-wearying prospect of the eternal sea, limited only by the vault of heaven. When Hadrian had sent a special messenger from Mount Kasius to desire his prefect Titianus to have this particular building prepared for his reception, he knew full well what advantages its position offered; it was the part of his officials to restore order in the interior of the palace, which had remained uninhabited from the time of Cleopatra's downfall. He gave them for the purpose eight, or perhaps nine, days—little more than a week. And in what a condition did Titianus and Pontius find this now dilapidated and plundered scene of former magnificence—the sweat pouring from their foreheads with their exertions as they inspected and sketched, questioned and made notes of it all.

The pillars and steps in the interior were tolerably well preserved, but the rain had poured in through the open roofs of the banqueting and reception-halls, the fine mosaic pavements had started here and there, and in other places a perfect little meadow had grown in the midst of a hall, or an arcade; for Octavianus Augustus, Tiberius, Vespasian, Titus and a whole series of prefects, had already carefully removed the finest of the mosaics from the famous palace of the Ptolemies, and carried them to Rome or to the provinces, to decorate their town houses or country villas. In the same way

3

the best of the statues were gone, with which a few
centuries previously the art-loving Lagides had decorated this residence—besides which they had another,
still larger, on the Bruchiom.

In the midst of a vast marbled hall stood an
elegantly-wrought fountain, connected with the fine
aqueduct of the city. A draught of air rushed through
this hall, and in stormy weather switched the water
all over the floor, now robbed of its mosaics, and
covered, wherever the foot could tread, with a thin,
dark green, damp and slippery coating of mossy plants
and slime. It was here that Keraunus leaned breathless against the wall, and, wiping his brow, panted
rather than said : " At last, this is the end !"

The words sounded as if he meant his own end and
not that of their excursion through the palace, and it
seemed like a mockery of the man himself when Pontius
unhesitatingly replied with decision :

" Good, then we can begin our re-examination here,
at once."

Keraunus did not contradict him, but, as he remembered the number of stairs to be climbed over
again, he looked as if sentence of death had been
passed upon him.

" Is it necessary that I should remain with you during the rest of your labors, which must be principally
directed to details ?" asked the prefect of the architect.

" No," answered Pontius, " provided you will take
the trouble to look at once at my plan, so as to inform
yourself on the whole of what I propose, and to give
me full powers to dispose of men and means in each
case as it arises."

" That is granted," said Titianus. " I know that

Pontius will not demand a man or a sesterce more or less than is needed for the purpose."

The architect bowed in silence and Titianus went on.

" But above all things, do you think you can accomplish your task in eight days and nine nights ?"

" Possibly, at a pinch ; and if I could only have four days more at my disposal, most probably."

",Then all that is needed is to delay Hadrian's arrival by four days and nights."

" Send some interesting people—say the astronomer Ptolemaeus, and Favorinus, the sophist, who await him here—to meet him at Pelusium. They will find some way of detaining him there."

" Not a bad idea ! We will see. But who can reckon on the Empress's moods ? At any rate, consider that you have only eight days to dispose of."

" Good."

" Where do you hope to be able to lodge Hadrian ?"

" Well, a very small portion of the old building is, strictly speaking, fit to use."

"Of that, I regret to say, I have fully convinced myself," said the prefect emphatically, and turning to the steward, he went on in a tone less of stern reproof than of regret.

"It seems to me, Keraunus, that it would have been your duty to inform me earlier of the ruinous condition of the building."

"I have already lodged a complaint," replied the man, "but I was told in answer to my report that there were no means to apply to the purpose."

"I know nothing of these things," cried Titianus.

"When did you forward your petition to the prefect's office ?"

"Under your predecessor, Haterius Nepos."

"Indeed," said the prefect with a drawl.

"So long ago. Then, in your place, I should have repeated my application every year, without any reference to the appointment of a new prefect. However, we have now no time for talking. During the Emperor's residence here, I shall very likely send one of my subordinates to assist you !"

Titianus turned his back on the steward, and asked the architect :

"Well, my good Pontius, what part of the palace have you your eye upon ?"

"The inner halls and rooms are in the best repair."

"But they are the last that can be thought of," cried Titianus. "The Emperor is satisfied with everything in camp, but where fresh air and a distant prospect are to be had, he must have them."

"Then let us choose the western suite; hold the plan my worthy friend."

The steward did as he was desired, the architect took his pencil and made a vigorous line in the air above the left side of the sketch, saying :

"This is the west front of the palace which you see from the harbor. From the south you first come into the lofty peristyle, which may be used as an ante-chamber; it is surrounded with rooms for the slaves and body-guard. The next smaller sitting-rooms by the side of the main corridor we may assign to the officers and scribes, in this spacious hypæthral hall—the one with the Muses—Hadrian may give audience and the guests may assemble there whom he may admit to eat at his table in this broad peristyle. The smaller and well-preserved rooms, along this long passage leading to the steward's house, will do for the pages, secretaries and other attendants on Caesar's person, and this long saloon, lined with fine porphyry and green marble, and adorned with the beautiful frieze in bronze will, I fancy, please Hadrian as a study and private sitting-room."

"Admirable!" cried Titianus, "I should like to show your plan to the Empress."

"In that case, instead of eight days I must have as many weeks," said Pontius coolly.

"That is true," answered the prefect laughing. "But tell me, Keraunus, how comes it that the doors are wanting to all the best rooms?"

"They were of fine thyra wood, and they were wanted in Rome."

"I must have seen one or another of them there," muttered the prefect.

"Your cabinet-workers will have a busy time, Pontius."

"Nay, the hanging-makers may be glad; wherever we can we will close the door-ways with heavy curtains."

"And what will you do with this damp abode of fogs, which, if I mistake not, must adjoin the dining-hall?"

"We will turn it into a garden filled with ornamental foliage."

"That is quite admissable—and the broken statues?"

"We will get rid of the worst."

"The Apollo and the nine Muses stand in the room you intend for an audience-hall—do they not?"

" Yes."

" They are in fairly good condition, I think."

" Urania is wanting entirely," said the steward, who was still holding the plan out in front of him.

" And what became of her?" asked Titianus, not without excitement.

" Your predecessor, the prefect Haterius Nepos, took a particular fancy to it and carried it with him to Rome."

" Why Urania of all others?" cried Titianus angrily. " She, above all, ought not to be missing from the hall of audience of Caesar the pontiff of heaven! What is to be done?"

"It will be difficult to find an Urania ready-made as tall as her sisters, and we have no time to search one out, a new one must be made."

" In eight days?"

" And eight nights."

" But my good friend, only to get the marble—"

" Who thinks of marble? Papias will make us one of straw, rags and gypsum—I know his magic hand— and in order that the others may not be too unlike their new-born sister they shall be whitewashed."

" Capital—but why choose Papias when we have Harmodius?"

" Harmodius takes art in earnest, and we should have the Emperor here before he had completed his sketches. Papias works with thirty assistants at any-thing that is ordered of him, so long as it brings him money. His last things certainly amaze me, particularly the Hygyeia for Dositheus the Jew, and the bust of Plutarch put up in the Caesareum, they are full of grace and power. But who can distinguish what is his work

and what that of his scholars? Enough, he knows
how things should be done; and if a good sum is to be
got by it he will hew you out a whole sea-fight in marble in five days."

"Then give Papias the commission — but the
hapless mutilated pavements — what will you do with
them?"

"Gypsum and paint must mend them," said Pontius, "and where that will not do, we must lay carpets
on the floor in the Eastern fashion. Merciful night!
how dark it is growing; give me the plan Keraunus
and provide us with torches and lamps for to-day, and
the next following ones must have twenty-four hours
apiece, full measure. I must ask you for half a dozen
trustworthy slaves Titianus; I shall want them for
messengers. What are you standing there for man?
Lights, I said. You have had half a lifetime to rest
in, and when Caesar is gone you will have as many
more years for the same laudable purpose—"

As he spoke the steward had silently gone off, but
the architect did not spare him the end of the sentence;
he shouted after him:

"Unless by that time you are smothered in your
own fat. Is it Nile-mud or blood that runs in that
huge mortal's veins?"

"I am sure I do not care," said the prefect, "so
long as the glorious fire that flows in yours only holds
out till the work is done. Do not allow yourself to be
overworked at first, nor require the impossible of your
strength, for Rome and the world still expect great
things of you. I can now write in perfect security to
the Emperor that all will be ready for him in Lochias,
and as a farewell speech, I can only say, it is folly to be

discouraged if only Pontius is at hand to support and assist me."

CHAPTER III.

THE prefect ordered the lictors, who were awaiting him with his chariot, to hasten to his house, and to conduct to Pontius several most worthy slaves, familiar with Alexandria—some of whom he named—and at the same time to send the architect a good couch with pillows and coverlets, and to despatch a good meal and fine wine to the old palace at Lochias. Then he mounted his chariot and drove through the Bruchiom along the shore to the great edifice known as the Caesareum. He got on but slowly, for the nearer he approached ·his destination the denser was the crowd of inquisitive citizens, who stood closely packed round the vast circumference of the building. Quite from a distance the prefect could see a bright light; it rose to heaven from the large pans of pitch which were placed on the towers on each side of the tall gate of the Caesareum which faced the sea. To the right and left of this gate stood a tall obelisk, and on each of these, men were lighting lamps which had been attached to the sides and placed on the top, on the previous day.

"In honor of Sabina," said the prefect to himself. "All that this Pontius does is thoroughly done, and there is no more complete sinecure than the supervision of his arrangements."

Fully persuaded of this he did not think it necessary to go up to the illuminated door-way which led into

the temple erected by Octavian in honor of Julius
Caesar; on the contrary, he directed the charioteer to
stop at a door built in the Egyptian style, which faced
the garden of the palace of the Ptolemies, and which
led to the imperial residence that had been built by the
Alexandrians for Tiberius, and had been greatly extended and beautified under the later Caesars. A sacred
grove divided it from the temple of Caesar, with which
it communicated by a covered colonnade. Before this
door there were several chariots and horses, and a
whole host of slaves, black and white, were in atten-
dance with their masters' litters. Here lictors kept back
the sight-seeking crowd, officers were lounging against
the pillars, and the Roman guard were just assembling
with a clatter of arms, to the sound of a trumpet within
the door, to await their dismissal.

Everything gave way respectfully before the chariot
of the prefect, and as Titianus walked through the illuminated arcades of the Caesareum, passing by the mas-
terpieces of statuary placed there, and the rows of
pictures—and reached the halls in which the library of
the palace was kept, he could not help thinking of all
the care and trouble which with the assistance of Pontius, he had for months devoted to rendering this
palace which had not been used since Titus had set out
for Judaea, fit quarters for Hadrian's reception. The
Empress now lived in the rooms intended for her husband, and decorated with the choicest works of art;
and Titianus reflected with regret that, after Sabina had
once become aware of their presence there, it would be
quite impossible to transfer them to Lochias. At the
door of the splendid room which he had intended for
Hadrian he was met by Sabina's chamberlain who

undertook to conduct him at once into the presence of his mistress.

The roof of the hall in which the prefect found the Empress, in summer was open to the sky; but at this, season was suitably covered in by a movable copper roof, partly to keep off the rain of the Alexandrian winter, and partly too because, even in the warmer season Sabina was wont to complain of cold; but beneath it a wide opening allowed the air free entrance and exit. As Titianus entered the room a comfortable warmth and subtle perfume met his senses; the warmth was produced by stoves of a peculiar form standing in the middle of the room; one of these represented Vulcan's forge. Brightly glowing charcoal lay in front of the bellows which were worked by an automaton, at short regular intervals, while the god and his assistants modelled in brass, stood round the genial fire with tongs and hammers. The other stove was a large silver bird's-nest, in which likewise charcoal was burning. Above the glowing fuel a phœnix, also in brass, and in the likeness of an eagle, seemed striving to soar heavenwards. Besides these a number of lamps lighted the saloon, which in truth looked too large for the number of people assembled in it, and which was lavishly furnished with gracefully-formed seats, couches, and tables, vases of flowers and statues.

The prefect and Pontius had intended a quite different room to serve for smaller assemblies, and had fitted it up suitably for the purpose, but the Empress had .preferred the great hall to the smaller room. The venerable and nobly-born statesman was filled with vexation, nay, with an embarrassment that made him feel estranged, when he had to glance round the room to find the persons in it, collected, as they were, into small knots. He could hear nothing but hushed voices; here an unintelligible murmur and there a suppressed laugh, but from no one a frank speech or full utterance. For a moment he felt as if he had found admittance to the abode of whispering calumny, and yet he knew why here no one dared to speak out or above a murmur. Loud voices hurt the Empress, and a clear voice was a misery to her, and yet few men possessed so loud and penetrating a chest voice as her husband, who was not wont to lay restraint upon himself for any human being, not even for his wife.

Sabina sat on a large divan, more like a couch than a chair; her feet were buried in the shaggy fell of a buffalo, and her knees and ankles wrapped round with down-cushions covered with silk. Her head she held very upright, and it was difficult to imagine how her slender throat could support it, loaded as it was with strings of pearls and precious stones which were braided in the tall structure of her reddish-gold hair, that was arranged in long cylindrical curls pinned closely side by side. The Empress's thin face looked particularly small under the mass of natural and artificial adornment which towered above her brow. Beautiful she could never have been, even in her youth, but her features were regular, and the prefect confessed to himself as he looked at Sabina's face, marked as it was with minute wrinkles and touched up with red and white, that the sculptor who a few years previously had been commissioned to represent her as *Venus Victrix* might very well have given the goddess a certain amount of resemblance to the imperial model. If only her eyes, which were

The Emperor. I.

absolutely bereft of lashes, had not been quite so small
and keen—in spite of the dark lines painted round
them—and if only the sinews in her throat had not
stood out quite so conspicuously from the flesh which
formerly had covered them!

With a deep bow Titianus took the Empress's right
hand, covered with rings; but she withdrew it quickly
from that of her husband's friend and relative, as if she
feared that the carefully-cherished limb—useless as it was
for any practical purpose, a mere toy among hands—
might suffer some injury, and wrapped it and her arm
in her upper-robe.   But she returned the prefect's
friendly greeting with all the warmth at her command.
Though formerly at Rome she had been accustomed to
see Titianus every day at her house, this was their first
meeting in Alexandria; for the previous day, exhausted
by the sufferings of her sea-voyage, she had been carried in a closed litter to the Caesareum, and this morning
she had declined to receive his visit, as her whole time
was given up to her physicians, bathing-women, and
coiffeurs.

" How can you survive in this country ?" she said in
a low but harsh voice, which always made the hearer
feel that it was that of a dull, fractious, childless
woman.   " At noon the sun burns you up, and in the
evening it is so cold—so intolerably cold!"   As she
spoke she drew her robe closer round her, but Titianus,
pointing to the stoves in the middle of the hall, said:

" I hoped we had succeeded in cutting the bow-
strings of the Egyptian winter, and it is but a feeble
weapon."

" Still young, still imaginative, still a poet!" said the
Empress wearily.   " I saw your wife a couple of hours

since. Africa seems to suit her less well; I was shocked
to see Julia, the handsome matron, so altered. She
does not look well."

" Years are the foe of beauty."

" Frequently they are, but true beauty often resists
their attacks."

" You are yourself the living proof of your assertion."

" That is as much as to say that I am growing old."

" Nay—only that you know the secret of remaining
beautiful."

" You are a poet !" murmured the Empress with a
twitch of her thin under-lip.

" Affairs of state do not favor the Muses."

" But I call any man a poet who sees things more
beautiful than they are, or who gives them finer names
than they deserve—a poet, a dreamer, a flatterer—for it
comes to that."

" Ah! modesty can always find words to repel even
well-merited admiration."

" Why this foolish bandying of words ?" sighed
Sabina, flinging herself back in her chair. " You have
been to school under the hair-splitting logicians in the
Museum here, and I have not. Over there sits Favorinus, the sophist; I dare say he is proving to Ptolemaeus that the stars are mere specks of blood in our eyes,
which we choose to believe are in the sky. Florus, the
historian, is taking note of this weighty discussion;
Pancrates, the poet, is celebrating the great thoughts of
the philosopher. As to what part the philologist there
can find to take in this important event you know better than I. What is the man's name ?"

" Apollonius."

"Hadrian has nick-named him 'the obscure.' The more difficult it is to understand the discourses of these gentlemen the more highly are they esteemed."

"One must dive to obtain what lies at the bottom of the water—all that floats on the surface is borne by the waves, a plaything for children. Apollonius is a very learned man."

"Then my husband ought to leave him among his disciples and his books. It was his wish that I should invite these people to my table. Florus and Pancrates I like—not the others."

"I can easily relieve you of the company of Favorinus and Ptolemaeus; send them to meet the Emperor."

"To what end?"

"To entertain him."

"He has his plaything with him," said Sabina, and her thin lips curled with an expression of bitter contempt.

"His artistic eye delights in the beauty of Antinous, which is celebrated, but which it has not yet been my privilege to see."

"And you are very anxious to see this marvel?"

"I cannot deny it."

"And yet you want to postpone your meeting with Caesar?" said Sabina, and a keen glance of inquiry and distrust twinkled in her little eyes.

"Why do you want to delay my husband's arrival?"

"Need I tell you," said Titianus eagerly, "how greatly I shall rejoice to see once more my sovereign, the companion of my youth, the greatest and wisest of men, after a separation of four years? What would I not give if he were here already! And yet I would rather that he should arrive in fourteen days than in eight."

" What reason can you have ?"

" A mounted messenger brought me a letter to-day in which the Emperor tells me that he proposes to in-habit the old palace at Lochias, and not the Caesareum."

At these words Sabina's forehead clouded, her gaze, dark and blank, was fixed on her lap, and biting her under-lip, she muttered:

" Because *I* am *here*."

Titianus made as though he had not heard these words, and continued in an easy tone:

" There he has a wide outlook into the distance, which is what he has loved from his youth up. But the old building is much dilapidated, and though I have already begun to exert all the forces at my com-mand, with the assistance of our admirable architect, Pontius, to restore a portion of it at any rate, and make it a habitable and not too uncomfortable residence, the time is too short to do anything thoroughly worthy—"

" I wish to see my husband here, and the sooner the better," interrupted the Empress with decision. Then she turned towards the row of pillars which stood by the right-hand wall of the hall, and which were at some distance from her couch, calling out " Verus." But her voice was so weak that it did not reach the person addressed, so turning to the prefect, she said: " I beg of you to call Verus to me, the praetor Lucius Aurelius Verus." Titianus immediately obeyed.

As he entered the hall he had already exchanged friendly greetings with the man to whom the Empress wished to speak. He now did not succeed in attracting his attention till he stood close at his elbow, for he formed the centre of a small group of men and women who were hanging on his words. What he was saying in a subdued voice must have been extraordinarily diverting, for it could be seen that his hearers were making the greatest efforts to keep their suppressed laughter from breaking out into a shout that would shake the very hall, a noise the Empress detested. When the prefect came up to Verus, a young girl, whose pretty head was crowned by a perfect thicket of little ringlets, was just laying her hand on his arm and saying:

"Nay—that is too much; if you go on like this, for the future whenever you speak I shall stop my ears with my hands, as sure as my name is Balbilla."

"And as sure as you are descended from King Antiochus," added Verus bowing.

"Always the same," laughed the prefect, nodding to the audacious jester.

"Sabina wants to speak to you."

"Directly, directly," said Verus. "My story is a true one, and you all ought to be grateful to me for having released you from that tedious philologer who has now button-holed my witty friend Favorinus. I like your Alexandria, Titianus; still it is not a great capital like Rome. The people have not yet learned not to be astonished; they are perpetually in amazement. When I go out driving—"

"Your runners ought to fly before you with roses in their hair and wings on their shoulders like Cupids."

"In honor of the Alexandrian ladies?"

"As if the Roman ladies in Rome, and the fair Greeks at Athens," interrupted Balbilla.

"The praetor's runners go faster than Parthian horses," cried the Empress's chamberlain. "He has named them after the winds."

"As they deserve," added Verus "Come, Titianus." He laid his hand in a confidential manner on the arm of the prefect, to whom he was related; and as they went towards Sabina he whispered in his ear:

"I can keep her waiting as if I were the Emperor."

Favorinus who had been engaged in talk with Ptolemaeus, the astronomer, Apollonius, and the philosopher and poet Pancrates in another part of the hall, looked after the two men and said:

"A handsome couple. One the personification of imperial and dignified Rome; the other with his Hermes-like figure."

"The other"—interrupted the philologist with stern displeasure, "the other is the very incarnation of the haughtiness, the luxury pushed to insanity, and the infamous depravity of the metropolis. That dissipated ladies'-man."

"I will not defend his character," said Favorinus in his pleasant voice, and with an elegance in his pronunciation of Greek which delighted even the grammarian. "His ways and doings are disgraceful; still you must allow that his manners are tinged with the charm of Hellenic beauty, that the Charites kissed him at his birth, and though, by the stern laws of virtue we must condemn him, he deserves to be crowned with praise and garlands from the point of view of the feeling for beauty."

"Oh! for the artist who wants a model he is a choice morsel."

4

"The Athenian judges acquitted Phryne because she was beautiful."

"They did wrong."

"Hardly in the eyes of the gods, whose fairest works must deserve our respect."

"Still poison may be kept in the most beautiful vessels."

"And yet body and soul always to a certain extent correspond."

"And can you dare to call the handsóme Verus the admirable Verus ?"

"No, but the reckless Lucius Aurelius Verus is at the same time the gayest and pleasantest of all the Romans, free alike from spite or carefulness, he troubles himself with no doctrines of virtue, and as when a thing pleases him, he desires to possess it, he endeavors to give pleasure to every one else."

"He has wasted his pains so far as I am concerned."

"I do as he wishes."

The last words both of the philologer and the sophist were spoken somewhat louder than was usual in the presence of the Empress. Sabina, who had just told the praetor which residence her husband had decided on inhabiting, drew up her shoulders and pinched her lips as if in pain, while Verus turned a face of indignation—a face which was manly in spite of all the delicacy and regularity of the features—on the two speakers, and his fine bright eyes caught the hostile glance of Apollonius.

An intimation of aversion to his person was one of the things which to him were past endurance; he hastily passed his hand through his blue-black hair, which was only slightly grizzled at the temples and flowed uncurled, but in soft waving locks round his head, and said, not heeding Sabina's question as to his opinion of her husband's latest instructions:

"He is a repulsive fellow, that wrangling logician; he has an evil eye that threatens mischief to us all, and his trumpet voice cannot hurt you more than it does me. Must we endure him at table with us every day?"

"So Hadrian desires."

"Then I shall start for Rome," said Verus decidedly. "My wife wants to be back with her children, and as praetor, it is more fitting that I should stay by the Tiber than by the Nile."

The words were spoken as lightly as though they were nothing more than a proposition to go to supper, but they seemed to agitate the Empress deeply, for her head, which had seemed almost a fixture during her conversation with Titianus, now shook so violently that the pearls and jewels rattled in the erection of curls. There she sat for some seconds staring into her lap.

Verus stooped to pick up a gem that had fallen from her hair, and as he did so she said hastily:

"You are right. Apollonius is intolerable. Let us send him to meet my husband."

"Then I will remain," answered Verus, as pleased as a wilful boy who has got his own way.

"Fickle as the wind," murmured Sabina, threatening him with her finger. "Show me the stone—it is one of the largest and finest; you may keep it."

When an hour later, Verus quitted the hall with the prefect, Titianus said:

"You have done me a service cousin, without know-

ing it.   Now can you contrive that Ptolemaeus and
Favorinus shall go with Apollonius to meet the Emperor at Pelusium?"

"Nothing easier" was the answer.

And the same evening the prefect's steward conveyed to Pontius the information that he might count
on having probably fourteen days for his work, instead
of eight or nine only.

CHAPTER IV.

In the Caesareum, where the Empress dwelt, the
lights were extinguished one after another; but in the
palace of Lochias they grew more numerous and
brighter.   In festal illuminations of the harbor pitch
cressets on the roof, and long rows of lamps that accu-
mulated architectonic features of the noble structure,
were always kindled; but inside it, no blaze so brilliant
had ever lighted it within the memory of man.   The
harbor watchmen at first gazed anxiously up at Lochias,
for they feared that a fire must have broken out in the
old palace; they were soon reassured however, by one
of the prefect's lictors, who brought them a command
to keep open the harbor gates that night, and every
night till the Emperor should have arrived, to all who
might wish to proceed from Lochias to the city, or
from the city to the peninsula, under the orders of
Pontius the architect.   And till long past midnight
not a quarter of an hour passed in which the people
whom the architect had summoned to his aid were
not knocking at the harbor gates, which, though not

locked were all guarded. The little house belonging
to the gate-keeper was also brightly lighted up; the
birds and cats belonging to the old woman whom
the prefect and his companions had found slumbering by her wine-jar, were now fast asleep, but the little
dogs still flew loudly yelping into the yard each time
a new-comer entered by the open gate.

"Come, Aglaia, what will folks think of you? Thalia, my beauty, behave like a good dog; come here,
Euphrosyne, and don't be so silly!" cried the old lady
in a voice which was both pleasant and peremptory, as
she stood—wide awake now—behind her table, folding
together the dried clothes. The little barking beasts
who were thus endowed with the names of the three
Graces did not trouble themselves much about her affectionate admonitions; to their sorrow, for it happened
more than once to each of them, when they had got
under the feet of some new-comer, to creep, whining
and howling, into the house again to seek consolation
from their mistress, who would pick up the sufferer and
soothe it with kisses and coaxing.

The old lady was no longer alone, for in the background, on a long and narrow couch which stood in
front of the statue of Apollo, lay a tall, lean man, wearing a red chiton. A little lamp hanging from the ceiling
threw a dull light on him and on the lute he was playing. To the faint sound of the instrument, which was
rather a large one, and which he had propped on the
pillow by his side, he was singing, or rather murmuring
a long ditty. Twice, thrice, four times he repeated it
in the same way.

Now and again he suddenly let his voice sound more
loudly—and though his hair was quite grey his voice

was not unpleasing—and sang a few phrases full of
expression and with artistic delivery; and then, when
the dogs barked too vehemently, he would spring up,
and with his lute in his left-hand and a long pliable rat-
tan in his right, he would rush into the court-yard, shout
the names of the dogs, and raise his cane as if he would
kill them; but he always took care not to hit them,
only to beat on the pavement near them. When, returning from such an excursion, he stretched himself
again on his couch, the old woman, pointing to the
hanging-lamp which the impatient creature often
knocked with his head, would call out, "Euphorion,
mind the oil."

And he each time answered with the same threatening gesture and the same glare in his black eyes:

"The little brutes!"

The singer had been diligently practising his musical
exercises for about an hour, when the dogs rushed into
the court-yard, not barking this time, but yelping loudly
with joy. The old woman laid aside the washing and
listened, but the tall man said:

"As many birds come flying before the Emperor as
gulls before a storm. If only they would leave us in
peace—"

"Hark, that is Pollux; I know by the dogs," said
the woman, hastening as fast as she could over the
threshold and out to meet him. But the expected visitor was already at the door. He picked up the three
four-footed Graces who leaped round him, one after the
other by the skin of the neck, and gave each a tap on
its nose. Then, seeing the old woman, he took her
head between his hands, and kissed her forehead, saying, "Good-evening, little Mother," and shook hands

with the singer, adding, "How are you, great, big
Father?"

"You are as big as I am," replied the man thus
addressed, and he drew the younger man towards him,
and laid one of his broad hands on his own grey head
and the other on that of his first-born, with its wealth of
brown hair.

"As if we were cast in the same mould," cried the
youth; and in fact he was very like his father— like, no
doubt, as a noble hunter is like a worn-out hack— as
marble is like limestone—as a cedar is like a fir-tree.
Both were remarkably tall, had thick hair, dark eyes,
and strongly aquiline noses, exactly of the same shape;
but the cheerful brightness which irradiated the countenance of the youth had certainly not been inherited
from the lute-player, but from the little woman who
looked up into his face and patted his arm.

But whence did he derive the powerful, but inde-
scribable something which gave nobility to his head,
and of which it was impossible to say whether it lay in
his eye, or in the lofty brow, arched so differently to
that of either parent?

"I knew you would come," cried his mother. "This
afternoon I dreamed it, and I can prove that I expected
you, for there, on the brazier, stands the stewed cabbage
and sausage waiting for you."

"I cannot stay now," replied Pollux. "Really, I
cannot, though your kind looks would persuade me
and the sausage winks at me out of the cabbage-pan.
My master, Papias, is gone on ahead, and in the palace
there we are to work wonders in less time than it
generally takes to consider which end the work should
be begun at."

"Then I will carry the cabbage into the palace for you," said Doris, standing on tip-toe to hold a sausage to the lips of her tall son. Pollux bit off a large mouthful and said, as he munched it:

"Excellent! I only wish that the thing I am to construct up there may turn out as good a statue as this savory cylinder—now fast disappearing—was a superior and admirable sausage."

"Have another?" said Doris.

"No mother; and you must not bring the cabbage either. Up to midnight not a minute must be lost, and if I then leave off for a little while you must by that time be dreaming of all sorts of pleasant things."

"I will carry you the cabbage then," said his father, "for I shall not be in bed so early at any rate. The hymn to Sabina, composed by Mesomedes, is to be performed with the chorus, as soon as the Empress visits the theatre, and I am to lead the upper part of the old men, who grow young again at the sight of her. The rehearsal is fixed for to-morrow, and I know nothing about it yet. Old music, note for note, is ready and safe in my throat, but new things—new things!"

"It is according to circumstances," said Pollux, laughing.

"If only they would perform your father's Satyr-play, or his Theseus!" cried Doris.

"Only wait a little, I will recommend him to Caesar as soon as he is proud to call me his friend, as the Phidias of the age. Then, when he asks me 'Who is the happy man who begot you?' I will answer: 'It is Euphorion, the divine poet and singer; and my mother, too, is a worthy matron, the gate-keeper of your palace,

Doris, the enchantress, who turns dingy clothes into snow-white linen."

These last words the young artist sang in a fine and powerful voice to a mode invented by his father.

" If only you had been a singer !" exclaimed Euphorion.

" Then I should have enjoyed the prospect," retorted Pollux, " of spending the evening of my life as your successor in this little abode."

" And now for wretched pay, you plant the laurels with which Papias crowns himself !" answered the old man shrugging his shoulders.

" His hour is coming, too," cried Doris, " his merit will be recognized; I saw him in my dreams, with a great garland on his curly head !"

" Patience, father—patience," said the young man, grasping his father's hand. " I am young and strong, and do all I can. Here, behind this forehead, good ideas are seething; what I have succeeded in carrying out by myself, has at any rate brought credit and fame to others, although it is all far from resembling the ideal of beauty that here—here—I seem to see far away and behind a cloud; still I feel that if, in a moment of kindness, Fortune will but shed a few fresh drops of dew on it all I shall, at any rate, turn out something better than the mere ill-paid right-hand of Papias, who, without me does not know what he ought to do, or how to do it."

" Only keep your eyes open and work hard," cried Doris.

" It is of no use without luck," muttered the singer, shrugging his shoulders.

The young artist bid his parents good-night, and

was about to leave, but his mother detained him to
show him the young goldfinches, hatched only the day
before. Pollux obeyed her wish, not merely to please
her, but because he liked to watch the gay little bird
that sat warming and sheltering her nestlings. Close
to the cage stood the huge wine-jar and his mother's
cup, decorated by his own hand. His eye fell on these,
and he pushed them aside in silence. Then, taking
courage, he said, laughing: " The Emperor will often
pass by here, mother; give up celebrating your Dionysiac festival. How would it do if you filled the jar
with one-fourth wine and three-fourths water ? It does
not taste badly."

" Spoiling good gifts," replied his mother.

" One-fourth wine—to please me," Pollux entreated,
taking his mother by the shoulders and kissing her forehead.

" To please you, you great boy !" said Doris, as her
eyes filled with tears. " Why for you, if I must, I
would drink nothing but wretched water.   Euphorion
you may finish what is left in the jar presently."

––––––––––

Pontius had already begun his labors, at first with
aid only of his assistants who had followed him on
foot. Measuring, estimating, sending short notes and
writing figures, names and suggestions on the plan, and
on his folding wax-tablets, he was not idle for an instant,
though frequently interrupted by the appointed superintendents of the workshops and manufactures in
Lochias, whose co-operation he required. They only
came at this late hour because they were called upon
by the prefect's orders.

Papias, the sculptor, introduced himself among the látest, though Pontius had written to him with his own hand that he had to communicate to him a very remunerative and particularly pressing commission for the Emperor, which might, perhaps, be taken in hand that very night. The matter in question was a statue of Urania, which must be completed in eight days by the same method which Papias had introduced at the last festival of Adonis, and to the scale which he, Pontius, indicated, in the palace of Lochias itself. With regard to several works of restoration which had to be carried out with equal rapidity, and as to the price to be paid, they could agree at the same time and place.

The sculptor was a man of foresight and did not appear on the scene alone but with his best assistant, Pollux, the son of the worthy couple at the gate, and several slaves who dragged after him sundry trunks and carts loaded with tools, boards, clay, gypsum and other raw materials of his art. On the road to Lochias he had informed the young sculptor of the business in hand, and had told him in a condescending tone that he would be permitted to try his skill in reconstructing the Urania. At the gate he had permitted Pollux to greet his parents, and had gone alone into the palace to open his bargain with the architect without the presence of witnesses.

The young artist perfectly understood his master. He knew that he would be expected to carry out the statue of Urania, while his task-master, after making some trifling alterations in the completed work, would declare that it was his own. Pollux had for two years been obliged, more than once, to put up with similar treatment; and now, as usual, he submitted to this dishonest manœuvre because, under his master there was plenty to do, and the delight of work was to him the greatest he could have.

Papias, to whom he had gone early as an apprentice and to whom he owed the knowledge he possessed, was no miser, still Pollux needed money, not for himself alone but because he had taken on himself the charge of a widowed sister and her children as if they were his own family. He was always glad to take some comfort into the narrow home of his parents, who were poor, and to maintain his younger brother Teuker—who had devoted himself to the same art—during the years of his apprenticeship. Again and again he had thought of telling his master that he should start on his own footing and earn laurels for himself, but what then would become of those who relied on his help, if he gave up his regular earnings and if he got no commissions when there were so many unknown beginners eager for them ? Of what avail were all his ability and the most honest good-will if no opportunity offered for his executing his work in noble materials ? With his own means he certainly was in no position to do so.

While he was talking to his parents Papias had opened his transactions with the architect. Pontius explained to the sculptor what was required and Papias listened attentively; he never interrupted the speaker, but only stroked his face from time to time, as if to make it smoother than it was already, though it was shaved with peculiar care and formed and colored like a warm mask; meanwhile draping the front of his rich blue toga, which he wore in the fashion of a Roman senator, into fresh folds.

But when Pontius showed him, at the end of the

rooms destined for the Emperor, the last of the statues to be restored, and which needed a new arm, Papias said decisively:

" It cannot be done."

" That is a rash verdict," replied the architect. " Do you not know the proverb, which, being such a good one, is said to have been first uttered by more than one sage: 'That it shows more ill-judgment to pronounce a thing impossible than to boast that we can achieve a task however much it may seem to transcend our powers.'"

Papias smiled and looked down at his gold-embroidered shoes as he said:

" It is more difficult to us sculptors to imagine ourselves waging Titanic warfare against the impossible, than it is to you who work with enormous masses. I do not yet see the means which would give me courage to begin the attack."

" I will tell you," replied Pontius quickly and decidedly. " On your side good-will, plenty of assistants and night-watchers; on ours, the Caesar's approval and plenty of gold."

After this the transaction came to a prompt and favorable issue, and the architect could but express his entire approbation, in most cases, of the sculptor's judicious and well-considered suggestions.

" Now I must go home," concluded Papias. " My assistants will proceed at once with the necessary preparations. The work must be carried on behind screens, so that no one may disturb us or hinder us with remarks."

Half an hour later a scaffolding was already erected in the middle of the hall where the Urania was to stand.

It was concealed from public gaze by thick linen stretched on tall wooden frames, and behind these screens Pollux was busied in framing a small model in wax, while his master had returned home to make arrangements for the labors of the following day.

It wanted only an hour of midnight, and still the supper sent to the palace for the architect by the prefect remained untouched. Pontius was hungry enough, but before attacking the meal that a slave had set out on a marble table—the roast meat which looked so inviting, the orange-red crayfish, the golden-brown pasty and the many-hued fruits—he conceived it his duty to inspect the rooms to be restored. It was needful to see whether the slaves who had been set, in the first place to clean out all the rooms, were being intelligently directed by the men set over them, whether they were doing their duty and had all that they required; they had got some hours to work, then they were to rest and to begin again at sunrise, reinforced by other laborers both slave and free.

More and better lighting was universally demanded, and when, in the hall of the Muses, the men who were cleaning the pavement and scraping the columns loudly clamored for torches and lamps, a young man's head peered over the screen which shut in the place reserved for the restoration of the Urania, and a lamentable voice cried out:

" My Muse, with her celestial sphere, is the guardian of star-gazers and is happiest in the dark—but not till she is finished. To form her we must have light and more light—and when it is lighter here the voice of the people down there, which does not sound very delightful up in this hollow space, will diminish somewhat also. Give light, then, O, men! Light for my goddess, and for your scrubbers and scourers."

Pontius looked up smiling at Pollux, who had uttered this appeal, and answered:

"Your cry of distress is fully justified, my friend. But do you really believe in the power of light to diminish noise?"

"At any rate," replied Pollux, "where it is absent, that is to say in the dark, every noise seems redoubled."

"That is true, but there are other reasons for that," answered the architect. "To-morrow in an interval of work we will discuss these matters. Now I will go to provide you with lamps and lights."

"Urania, the protectress of the fine arts, will be beholden to you," cried Pollux as the architect went away.

Pontius meanwhile sought his chief foreman to ask him whether he had delivered his orders to Keraunus, the palace-steward, to come to him, and to put the cressets and lamps commonly used for the external illuminations, at the service of his workmen.

"Three times," was the answer "have I been myself to the man, but each time he puffed himself out like a frog and answered me not a word, but only sent me into a little room with his daughter—whom you must see, for she is charming—and a miserable black slave, and there I found these few wretched lamps that are now burning."

"Did you order him to come to me?"

"Three hours ago, and again a second time, when you were talking with Papias."

The architect turned his back upon the foreman in

angry haste, unrolled the plan of the palace, quickly found upon it the abode of the recalcitrant steward, seized a small red-clay lamp that was standing near him, and being quite accustomed to guide himself by a plan, went straight through the rooms, which were not a few, and by a long corridor from the hall of the Muses, to the lodging of the negligent official. An unclosed door led him into a dark ante-chamber followed by another room, and finally into a large, well-furnished apartment. All these door-ways, into what seemed to be at once the dining and sitting-room of the steward, were bereft of doors, and could only be closed by stuff curtains, just now drawn wide open. Pontius could therefore look in, unhindered and unperceived, at the table on which a three-branched bronze lamp was standing between a dish and some plates. The stout man was sitting with his rubicund moon-face towards the architect, who, indignant as he was, would have gone straight up to him with swift decision, if, before entering the second room, a low but pitiful sob had not fallen on his ear.

The sob proceeded from a slight young girl who came forward from a door beyond the sitting-room, and who now placed a platter with a loaf on the table by the steward.

"Come, do not cry, Selene," said the steward, breaking the bread slowly and with an evident desire to soothe his child.

"How can I help crying," said the girl. "But to-morrow morning let me buy a piece of meat for you; the physician forbade you to eat bread."

"Man must be filled," replied the fat man, "and meat is dear. I have nine mouths to fill, not counting the slaves. And where am I to get the money to fill us all with meat ?"

" We need none, but for you it is necessary."

" It is of no use, child. The butcher will not trust us any more, the other creditors press us, and at the end of the·month we shall have just ten drachmae left us."

The girl turned pale, and asked in anxiety :

" But, father, it was only to-day that you showed me the three gold pieces which you said had been given you as a present out of the money distributed on the arrival of the Empress."

The steward absently rolled a piece of bread-crumb between his fingers and said :

" I spent that on this fibula with an incised onyx— and as cheap as dirt, I can tell you. If Caesar comes he must see who and what I am; and if I die any one will give you twice as much for it as I paid. I tell you the Empress's money was well laid out on the thing."

Selene made no answer, but she sighed deeply, and her eye glanced at a quantity of useless things which her father had acquired and brought home because they were cheap, while she and her seven sisters wanted the most necessary things.

" Father," the girl began again after a short silence, " I ought not to go on about it, but even if it vexes you, I must—the architect, who is settling all the work out there, has sent for you twice already."

" Be silent!" shouted the fat man, striking his hand on the table. " Who is this Pontius, and who am I !"

" You are of a noble Macedonian family, related perhaps even to the Ptolemies; you have your seat in the Council of the Citizens—but do, this time, be conde-

5

scending and kind. The man has his hands full, he is tired out."

"Nor have I been able to sit still the whole day, and what is fitting, is fitting. I am Keraunus the son of Ptolemy, whose father came into Egypt with Alexander the Great, and helped to found this city, and every one knows it. Our possessions were diminished; but it is for that very reason that I insist on our illustrious blood being recognized. Pontius sends to command the presence of Keraunus! If it were not infuriating it would be laughable—for who is this man, who? I have told you his father was a freedman of the former prefect Claudius Balbillus, and by the favor of the Roman his father rose and grew rich. He is the descendant of slaves, and you expect that I shall be his obedient humble servant, whenever he chooses to call me?"

"But father, my dear father, it is not the son of Ptolemy, but the palace-steward that he desires shall go to him."

"Mere chop-logic!—you have nothing to say, not a step do I take to go to him."

The girl clasped her hands over her face, and sobbed loudly and pitifully. Keraunus started up and cried out, beside himself.

"By great Serapis. I can bear this no longer. What are you whimpering about?"

The girl plucked up courage and going up to the indignant man she said, though more than once interrupted by tears.

"You must go father—indeed you must. I spoke to the foreman, and he told me coolly and decidedly that the architect was placed here in Caesar's name,

and that if you do not obey him you will at once be
superseded in your office. And if that were to happen,
if that—O father, father, only think of blind Helios and
poor Berenice! Arsinoe and I could earn our bread,
but the little ones—the little ones."

With these words the girl fell on her knees lifting
her hands in entreaty to her obstinate parent. The
blood had mounted to the man's face and eyes, and
pressing his hand to his purple forehead he sank back
in his chair as if stricken with apoplexy. His daughter
sprang up and offered him the cup full of wine and
water which was standing on the table; but Keraunus
pushed it aside with his hands, and panted out, while
he struggled for breath :

"Supersede me—in my place—turn me out of this
palace! Why there, in that ebony trunk, lies the re-
script of Euergetes which confers the stewardship of this
residence on my ancestor Philip, and as a hereditary
dignity in his family. Now Philip's wife had the honor
of being the king's mistress—or, as some say, his
daughter. There lies the document, drawn up in red
and black ink on yellow papyrus and ratified with the
seal and signature of Euergetes the Second. All the
princes of the Lagides have confirmed it, all the Roman
prefects have respected it, and now—now."

"But father" said the girl interrupting her father, and
wringing her hands in despair, "you still hold the place
and if you will only give in."

"Give in, give in," shrieked the corpulent steward
shaking his fat hands above his blood-shot face. "I will
give in—I will not bring you all to misery—for my
children's sake I will allow myself to be ill-treated and
down-trodden, I will go—I will go directly. Like the

pelican I will feed my children with my heart's blood.
But you ought to know what it costs me, to humiliate
myself thus; it is intolerable to me, and my heart is
breaking—for the architect, the architect has trampled
upon me as if I were his servant; he wished—I heard
him with these ears—he shrieked after me a villanous
hope that I might be smothered in my own fat—and
the physician has told me I may die of apoplexy!
Leave me, leave me. I know those Romans are capable of anything. Well—here I am; fetch me my saffron-colored pallium, that I wear in the council, fetch me
my gold fillet for my head. I will deck myself like a
beast for sacrifice, and I will show him—"

Not a word of this harangue had escaped the ears
of the architect who had been at first indignant and
then moved to laughter, and withal it had touched his
heart. A sluggish and torpid character was repugnant
to his vigorous nature, and the deliberate and indifferent
demeanor of the stout steward, on an occasion which
had prompted him and all concerned to act as quickly
and energetically as possible, had brought words to his
lips which he now wished that he had never spoken.
It is true that the steward's false pride had roused his
indignation, and who can listen calmly to any comment
on a stain on his birth? But the appeal of this miserable father's daughter had gone to his heart. He pitied
the fatuous simpleton whom, with a turn of his hand,
he could reduce to beggary, and who had evidently
been far more deeply hurt by his words than Pontius
had been by what he had overheard, and so he followed
the kindly impulse of a noble nature to spare the unfortunate.

He rapped loudly with his knuckles on the inside

of the door-post of the ante-room, coughed loudly, and then said, bowing deeply to the steward on the threshold of the sitting-room :

" Noble Keraunus—I have come, as beseems me, to pay you my respests. Excuse the lateness of the hour, but you can scarcely imagine how busy I have been since we parted."

Keraunus had at first started at the late visitor, then he stared at him in consternation. He now went towards him, stretched out both hands as if suddenly relieved of a nightmare, and a bright expression of such warm and sincere satisfaction overspread his countenance that Pontius wondered how he could have failed to observe what a well-cut face this fat original had.

" Take a seat at our humble table," said Keraunus. " Go Selene and call the slaves. Perhaps there is yet a pheasant in the house, a roast fowl or something of the kind—but the hour, it is true, is late."

" I am deeply obliged to you," replied the architect, smiling. " My supper is waiting for me in the hall of the Muses, and I must return to my work-people. I should be grateful to you if you would accompany me. We must consult together as to the lighting of the rooms, and such matters are best discussed over a succulent roast and a flask of wine."

" I am quite at your service," said Keraunus with a bow.

" I will go on ahead," said the architect, " but first will you have the goodness to give all that you have in the way of cressets, lights and lamps to the slaves, who, in a few minutes, shall await your orders at your door."

When Pontius had departed, Selene exclaimed with a deep sigh:

"Oh! what a fright I have had! I will go now and find the lamps. How terribly it might have ended."

"It is well that he should have come," murmured Keraunus. "Considering his birth and origin, the architect is certainly a well-bred man."

CHAPTER V.

PONTIUS had gone to the steward's room, with a frowning brow, but it was with a smile on his strongly-marked lips, and a brisk step that he returned to his work-people. The foreman came to meet him with looks of enquiry as he said. "The steward was a little offended and with reason; but now we are capital friends and he will do what he can in the matter of lighting."

In the hall of the Muses he paused outside the screen, behind which Pollux was working, and called out:

"Friend sculptor, listen to me, it is high time to have supper."

"It is, indeed," replied Pollux, "else it will be break-fast."

"Then lay aside your tools for a quarter of an hour and help me and the palace-steward to demolish the food that has been sent me."

"You will need no second assistant if Keraunus is there. Food melts before him like ice before the sun."

"Then come and save him from an overloaded stomach."

"Impossible, for I am just now dealing most unmercifully with a bowl full of cabbage and sausages. My mother had cooked that food of the gods and my father has brought it in to his first-born son."

"Cabbage and sausages!" repeated the architect, and his tone betrayed that his hungry stomach would fain have made closer acquaintance with the savory mess.

"Come in here," continued Pollux, "and be my guest. The cabbage has experienced the process which is impending over this palace—it has been warmed up."

"Warmed-up cabbage is better than freshly-cooked, but the fire over which we must try to make this palace enjoyable again, burns too hotly and must be too vigorously stirred. The best things have been all taken out, and cannot be replaced."

"Like the sausages, I have fished out of my cabbages," laughed the sculptor. "After all I cannot invite you to be my guest, for it would be a compliment to this dish if I were now to call it cabbage with sausages. I have worked it like a mine, and now that the vein of sausages is nearly exhausted, little remains but the native soil in which two or three miserable fragments remain as memorials of past wealth. But my mother shall cook you a mess of it before long, and she prepares it with incomparable skill."

"A good idea, but you are my guest."

"I am replete."

"Then come and spice our meal with your good company."

"Excuse me, sir; leave me rather here behind my

screen. In the first place, I am in a happy vein, and on the right track ; I feel that something good will come of this night's work."

" And to-morrow—"

" Hear me out."

" Well."

" You would be doing your other guest an ill-ser-vice by inviting me."

" Do you know the steward then ?"

" From my earliest youth, I am the son of the gate-keeper of the palace."

" Oh, ho! then you came from that pretty little lodge with the ivy and the birds, and the jolly old lady."

" She is my mother—and the first time the butcher kills she will concoct for you and me a dish of sausages and cabbage without an equal."

" A very pleasing prospect."

" Here comes a hippopotamus—on closer inspec-tion Keraunus, the steward."

" Are you his enemy ?"

" I, no ; but he is mine—yes," replied Pollux. " It is a foolish story. When we sup together don't ask me about it if you care to have a jolly companion. And do not tell Keraunus that I am here, it will lead to no good."

" As you wish, and here are our lamps too."

" Enough to light the nether world," exclaimed Pol-lux, and waving his hand to the architect in farewell he vanished behind the screens to devote himself entirely to his model.

———

It was long past midnight, and the slaves who had set

to work with much zeal had finished their labors in the hall of the Muses. They were now allowed to rest for some hours on straw that had been spread for them in another wing of the building. The architect himself wished to take advantage of this time to refresh himself by a short sleep, for the exertions of the morrow, but between this intention and its fulfilment an obstacle was interposed, the preposterous dimensions namely of his guest. He had invited the steward on purpose to give him his fill of meat, and Keraunus had shown himself amenable to encouragement in this respect. But after the last dish had been removed the steward thought that good manners demanded that he should honor his entertainer by his illustrious presence, and at the same time the prefect's good wine loosened the tongue of the man, who was not usually communicative.

First he spoke of the manifold infirmities which tormented him and endangered his life, 'and when Pontius, to divert his talk into other channels, was so imprudent as to allude to the Council of Citizens, Keraunus gave full play to his eloquence, and, while he emptied cup after cup of wine, tried to lay down the reasons which had made him and his friends decide on staking everything in order to deprive the members of the extensive community of Jews in the city of their rights as citizens, and to expel them, if possible, from Alexandria. So warm was his zeal that he totally forgot the presence of the architect, and his humble origin, and declared to be indispensable, that even the descendants of freed-slaves should be disenfranchised.

Pontius saw in the steward's inflamed eyes and cheeks that it was the wine which spoke within him, and he made no answer; and determined that the rest he needed should not be thus abridged, he rose from table and briefly excusing himself he retired to the room in which the couch had been prepared for him. After he had undressed he desired his slave to see what Keraunus was about, and soon received the reassuring information that the steward was fast asleep and snoring.

"Only listen," said the slave, to confirm his report. "You can hear him grunting and snuffing as far as this. I pushed a cushion under his head, for otherwise, so full as he is, the stout gentleman might come to some harm."

Love is a plant which springs up for many who have never sown it, and grows into a spreading tree for many who have neither fostered nor tended it. How little had Keraunus ever done to win the heart of his daughter, how much on the contrary which could not fail to overshadow and trouble her young life. And yet Selene, whose youth—for she was but nineteen—needed repose and to whom the evening with the reprieve of sleep brought more pleasure than the morning with its load of cares and labor, sat by the three-branched lamp and watched, and tormented herself more and more as it grew later and later, at her father's long absence. About a week before the strong man had suddenly lost consciousness; only, it is true, for a few minutes, and the physician had told her that though he appeared to be in superabundant health, the attack indicated that he must follow his prescriptions strictly and avoid all kinds of excess. A single indiscretion, he had declared, might swiftly and suddenly cut the thread of his existence. After her father had gone out in obedience to the architect's invitation, Selene had brought out her youngest brothers' and sisters' garments, in order to mend them. Her sister Arsinoe, who was her junior by two years, and whose fingers were as nimble as her own, might indeed have helped her, but she had gone to bed early and was sleeping by the children who could not be left untended at night. Her female slave, who had been in her grandmother's service, ought to have assisted her; but the old half-blind negress saw even worse by lamp-light than by daylight, and after a few stitches could do no more. Selene sent her to bed and sat down alone to her work.

For the first hour she sewed away without looking up, considering, meanwhile, how she could best contrive to support the family till the end of the month on the few drachmae she could dispose of. As it got later she grew wearier and wearier, but still she sat at the work, though her pretty head often sank upon her breast. She must await her father's return, for a potion prepared by the physician stood waiting for him, and she feared he would forget it if she did not remind him.

By the end of the second hour sleep overcame her, and she felt as if the chair she was sitting on was giving way under her, and as if it was sinking at first slowly and then quicker and quicker, into a deep abyss that opened beneath her. Looking up for help in her dream, she could see nothing but her father's face, which looked aside with indifference. As her dream went on she called him and called him again, but for a long time he did not seem to hear her. At last he looked down at her and when he perceived her he smiled, but instead of helping her he picked up stones and clods from the edge of the gulf and threw them on her hands with which she had clutched the brambles and roots that grew out of the rift of the rocks. She

entreated him to cease, implored him, shrieked to him
to spare her, but not a muscle moved in the face above
her; it seemed set in a vacant smile, and even his heart
was dead too, for he ruthlessly flung down now a pebble,
now a clod, one after the other, till her hands were
losing their last feeble hold and she was on the point of
falling into the fatal gulf below. Her own cry of terror
aroused her, but during the brief process of returning
from her dream to actuality, she saw through swiftly
parting mists—only for an instant, and yet quite plainly
—the tall grass of a meadow, spangled with ox-eye
daisies, white and gold, with violet-hued blue bells and
scarlet poppies, among which she was lying as in a
soft green bed, while near the sward lay a sparkling
blue lake and behind it rose beautiful swelling hills,
with red cliffs, and green groves, and meadows bright
in the clear sunshine. A clear sky, across which a
soft breeze gently blew light silvery flakes of cloud, bent
over the lovely but fleeting picture, which she could not
compare with anything she had ever seen near her own
home.

She had only slept for a short time, but when, once
more thoroughly awake, she rubbed her eyes, she
thought her dream must have lasted for hours.

One flame of the three-branched lamp had flickered
into extinction and the wick of another was beginning
to waste. She hastily put it out with a pair of tongs
that hung by a chain, and then after pouring fresh oil
into the lamp that was still burning she carried the light
into her father's sleeping room.

He had not yet returned. She was seized with a
mortal terror. Had the architect's wine bereft him of
his senses? Had he on his way back to his rooms been

seized with a fresh attack of giddiness? In spirit she
saw the heavy man incapable of raising himself, dying
perhaps where he had fallen.

No choice remained to her; she must go at once to
the hall of the Muses and see what had happened to her
father, pick him up, give him help or—if he still were
feasting—endeavor to tempt him back by any excuse she
could find. Everything was at stake; her father's life
and with it maintenance and shelter for eight helpless
creatures.

The December night was stormy, a keen and bitter
wind blew through the ill-closed opening in the roof of
the room as Selene, before she began her expedition, tied
a handkerchief over her head and threw over her shoulders a white mantle which had been worn by her dead
mother. In the long corridor which lay between her
father's rooms and the front portion of the palace, she
had to screen the flickering light of the little lamp with
her left hand, carrying it in her right; the flame blown
about by the draught and her own figure were mirrored
here and there in the polished surface of the dark marble. The thick sandals she had tied on to her feet
roused loud echoes in the empty rooms as they fell on
the stone pavements, and terror possessed Selene's anxious soul. Her fingers trembled as they held the lamp
and her heart beat audibly as, with bated breath, she
went through the cupolaed hall in which Ptolemy Euergetes ' the fat ' was said, some years ago, to have murdered his own son, and in which even a deep breath
roused an echo.

But even in this room she did not forget to look to
the right and left for her father. She breathed a sigh
of relief when she perceived a streak of light which

shone through the gaping rift of a cracked side-door of
the hall of the Muses and fell in a broken reflection on
the floor and the wall of the last room through which
she had to pass. She now entered the large hall which
was dimly lighted by the lamps behind the sculptor's
screen, and by several tapers, now burnt down low.
These were standing on a table knocked together out
of blocks of wood and planks at the extreme end of the
hall, and behind this her father was sound asleep.

The deep notes brought out of the sleeper's broad
chest, were echoed in a very uncanny way from the bare
walls of the vast empty room, and she was frightened by
them and still more by the long black shadows of the
pillars, that lay, like barriers, across her path. She stood
listening in the middle of the hall and soon recognized
in the alarming tones a sound that was only too familiar.
Without a moment's hesitation she started to run, and
hastened to the sleeper, shook him, pushed him, called
him, sprinkled his forehead with water, and appealed
to him by the tenderest names with which her sister
Arsinoe was wont to coax him. When, in spite of all
this, he neither spoke nor stirred, she flung the full light
of the lamp on his face. Then she thought she perceived that a bluish tinge had overspread his bloated
features, and she broke into the deep, agonized, weeping which, a few hours previously had touched the
architect's heart.

There was a sudden stir behind the screens which
enclosed the sculptor and the work in progress. Pollux had been working for a long time with zeal and
pleasure, but at last the steward's snoring had begun to
disturb him. The body of the Muse had already taken
a definite form and he could begin to work out the head

with the earliest dawn of day. He now dropped his arms wearily, for as soon as he ceased to create with his whole heart and mind he felt tired, and saw plainly that without a model he could do nothing satisfactory with the drapery of his Urania. So he pulled his stool up to a great chest full of gypsum to get a little repose by leaning against it.

But sleep avoided the artist who was too much excited by his rapid night's work, and as soon as Selene opened the door he sat upright and peeped through an opening between the frames of his place of retirement. When he saw the tall draped figure in whose hand a lamp was trembling, when he watched her cross the spacious hall, and then suddenly stand still, he was not a little startled, but this did not hinder him from noting every step of the nocturnal spectre with far more curiosity than alarm. Then, when Selene looked round her, and the lamp illuminated her face, he recognized the steward's daughter, and immediately knew what she must be seeking.

Her vain attempts to rouse the sleeper, though somewhat pathetic, had in them at the same time something irresistibly ludicrous, and Pollux felt sorely tempted to laugh. But as soon as Selene began to weep so bitterly he hastily pushed apart two of the laths of the screen, went up and called her name, at first softly not to frighten her, and then more loudly. When she turned her head he begged her warmly not to be alarmed for he was no ghost, only a very humble and ordinary mortal, in fact—as she might see—nothing more, alas!, than the son of Euphorian, the gate-keeper, good for nothing as yet, but treading the path to something better.

"You, Pollux?" asked the girl with surprise.

"The very man. But you—can I help you?"

"My poor father," sobbed Selene. "He does not stir, he is immovable—and his face—oh! merciful gods."

"A man who snores is not dead," said the sculptor.

"But the doctor told him—"

"He is not even ill! Pontius only gave him stronger wine to drink than he is used to. Let him be; he is sleeping with the pillow under his neck, as comfortably as a child. When he began just now to trumpet a little too loud I whistled as loud as a plover, for that often silences a snorer; but I could more easily have made those stone Muses dance than have roused him."

"If only we could get him to bed."

"Well, if you have four horses at hand."

"You are as bad as you ever were!"

"A little less so, Selene, only you must become accustomed again to my way of speaking. This time I only mean that we two together are not strong enough to carry him away."

"But what can I do, then? The doctor said—"

"Never mind the doctor. The complaint your father is suffering from is one I know well. It will be gone to-morrow, perhaps by sundown, and the only pain it will leave behind, he will feel under his wig. Only leave him to sleep."

"But it is so cold here."

"Take my cloak and cover him with that."

"Then you will be frozen."

"I am used to it. How long has Keraunus had dealings with the doctor?"

Selene related the accident that had befallen her

father and how justified were her fears. The sculptor listened to her in silence and then said in a quite altered tone:

"I am truly sorry to hear it. Let us put some cold water on his forehead, and until the slaves come back again I will change the wet cloth every quarter of an hour. Here is a jar and a handkerchief—good, they might have been left on purpose. Perhaps, too, it will wake him, and if not the people shall carry him to his own rooms."

"Disgraceful, disgraceful!" sighed the girl.

"Not at all; the high-priest of Serapis even is sometimes unwell. Only let me see to it."

"It will excite him afresh if he sees you. He is so angry with you—so very angry."

"Omnipotent Zeus, what harm have I done you, fat father! The gods forgive the sins of the wise, and a man will not forgive the fault committed by a stupid lad in a moment of imprudence."

"You mocked at him."

"I set a clay head that was like him on the shoulders of the fat Silenus near the gate, that had lost its own head. It was my first piece of independent work."

"But you did it to vex my father."

"Certainly not, Selene; I was delighted with the joke and nothing more."

"But you knew how touchy he is."

"And does a wild boy of fifteen ever reflect on the consequences of his audacity? If he had but given me a thrashing his annoyance would have discharged itself like thunder and lightning, and the air would have been clear again. But, as it was, he cut the face

6

off the work with a knife, and deliberately trod the
pieces under foot as they lay on the ground. He gave
me one single blow—with his thumb—which I still
feel, it is true, and then he treated me and my parents
with such scorn, so coldly and hardly, with such bitter
contempt—"

"He never is really violent, but wrath seems to eat
him inwardly, and I have rarely seen him so angry as
he was that time."

"But if he had only settled the account with me on
the spot! but my father was by, and hot words fell like
rain, and my mother added her share, and from that
time there has been utter hostility between our little
house and you up here. What hurt me most was that
you and your sister were forbidden to come to see us
and to play with me."

"That has spoilt many pleasant hours for me,
too."

"It was nice when we used to dress up in my
father's theatrical finery and cloaks."

"And when you made us dolls out of clay."

"Or when we performed the Olympian games."

"I was always the teacher when we played at
school with our little brothers and sisters."

"Arsinoe gave you most trouble."

"Oh! and what fun when we went fishing!"

"And when we brought home the fishes and mother
gave us meal and raisins to cook them."

"Do you remember the festival of Adonis, and
how I stopped the runaway horse of that Numidian
officer?"

"The horse had knocked over Arsinoe, and when
we got home mother gave you an almond-cake."

" And your ungrateful sister bit a great piece out of it and left me only a tiny morsel. Is Arsinoe as pretty as she promised to become ? It is two years since I last saw her; at our place we never have time to leave work till it is dark. For eight months I had to work for the master at Ptolemais, and often saw the old folks but once in the month."

" We go out very little, too, and we are not allowed to go into your parents' house. My sister—"

" Is she pretty ?"

" Yes, I think she is. Whenever she can get hold of a piece of ribbon she plaits it in her hair, and the men in the street turn round to look at her. She is sixteen now."

" Sixteen ! What, little Arsinoe ! Why, how long then is it since your mother died ?"

" Four years and eight months."

" You remember the date very exactly; such a mother is not easily forgotten, indeed. She was a good woman and a kinder I never met. I know, too, that she tried to mollify your father's feeling, but she could not succeed, and then she need must die !"

" Yes," said Selene gloomily. " How could the gods decree it ! They are often more cruel than the hardest hearted man."

" Your poor little brothers and sisters !"

The girl bowed her head sadly and Pollux stood for some time with his eyes fixed on the ground. Then he raised his head and exclaimed :

" I have something for you that will please you."

" Nothing ever pleases me now she is dead."

" Yes, yes indeed," replied the young sculptor eagerly. " I could not forget the good soul, and once

in my idle moments I modelled her bust from memory.
To-morrow I will bring it to you."

"Oh!" cried Selene, and her large heavy eyes
brightened with a sunny gleam.

" Now, is not it true, you are pleased ?"

" Yes indeed, very much. But when my father
learns that it is, you who have given me the portrait—"

" Is he capable of destroying it ?"

" If he does not destroy it, he will not suffer it in
the house as soon as he knows that you made it."

Pollux took the handkerchief from the steward's
head, moistened it afresh, and exclaimed as he re-
arranged it on the forehead of the sleeping man :

" I have an idea. All that matters is that my bust
should serve to remind you often of your mother; the
bust need not stand in your rooms. The busts of the
women of the house of Ptolemy stand on the rotunda,
which you can see from your balcony, and which you
can pass whenever you please; some of them are badly
mutilated and must be got rid of. I will undertake to
restore the Berenice and put your mother's head on her
shoulders. Then you have only to go out and look at
her. Will that do ?"

" Yes, Pollux; you are a good man."

" So I told you just now. I am beginning to improve. But time—time! if I am to undertake to repair
Berenice I must begin by saving the minutes."

" Go back to your work now; I know how to apply
a wet compress only too well."

With these words Selene threw back her mantle
over her shoulders so as to leave her hands free for use,
and stood with her slender figure, her pale face, and the

fine broadly-flowing folds of rich stuff, like a statue in the eyes of the young sculptor.

"Stop—stay so—just so," cried Pollux to the astonished girl, so loudly and eagerly that she was startled.

"Your cloak hangs with a wonderfully-free flow from your shoulders—in the name of all the gods do not touch it. If only I might model from it I should in a few minutes gain a whole day for our Berenice. I will wet the handkerchief at intervals in the pauses."

Without waiting for Selene's answer the sculptor hastened into his nook and returned first with one of the lamps he worked by in each hand, and some small tools in his mouth, and then fetched his wax model which he placed on the outer side of the table, behind which the steward was sleeping. The tapers were put out, the lamps pushed aside, and raised or lowered, and when at last a tolerably suitable light was procured Pollux threw himself on a stool, straddled his legs, craned his head forward as far as his neck would allow, looking, with his hooked nose, like a vulture that strives to descry his distant prey—cast his eyes down, raised them again to take in something fresh, and after a long gaze looked down again while his fingers and nails moved over the surface of the wax-figure, sinking into the plastic material, applying new pieces to apparently complete portions, removing others with a decided nip and rounding them off with bewildering rapidity to use them for a fresh purpose.

He seemed to be seized with cramp in his hands, but still under his knotted brow his eye shone earnest, resolute and calm, and yet full of profound and speechless inspiration. Selene had said not a word that per-

mitted his using her as a model; but, as if his enthusiasm was infectious, she remained motionless, and
when, as he worked, his gaze met hers she could detect
the stern earnestness which at this moment possessed
her eager companion.

Neither of them opened their lips for some time.
At last he stood back from his work, stooping low to
look first at Selene and then at his statuette with keen
examination from head to foot; and then, drawing a
deep breath, and rubbing the wax over with his finger,
he said:

"There, that is how it must go! Now I will wet
your father's handkerchief and then we can go on
again. If you are tired you can rest."

She availed herself but little of this permission and
presently he began work again. As he proceeded carefully to replace some folds of her drapery which had
fallen out of place, she moved her foot as if to draw
back, but he begged her earnestly to stand still and
she obeyed his request.

Pollux now used his fingers and modelling tools
more calmly; his gaze was less wistful and he began to
talk again.

"You are very pale," he said. "To be sure the
lamp-light and a sleepless night have something to do
with it."

"I look just the same by daylight, but I am not ill."

"I thought Arsinoe would have been like your
mother, but now I see many features of her face in
yours again. The oval of their form is the same and,
in both, the line of the nose runs almost straight to the
forehead; you have her eyes and the same bend of the
brow, but your mouth is smaller and more sharply cut,

and she could hardly have made such a heavy knot of
her hair. I fancy, too, that yours is lighter than hers."

"As a girl she must have had still more hair, and
perhaps she may have been as fair as I was—I am
brown now."

"Another thing you inherit from her is that your
hair, without being curly, lies upon your head in such
soft waves."

"It is easy to keep in order."

"Are not you taller than she was?"

"I fancy so, but as she was stouter she looked
shorter. Will you soon have done?"

"You are getting tired of standing?"

"Not very."

"Then have a little more patience. Your face reminds me more and more of our early years; I should
be glad to see Arsinoe once more. I feel at this moment as if time had moved backwards a good piece.
Have you the same feeling?"

Selene shook her head.

"You are not happy?"

"No."

"I know full well that you have very heavy duties
to perform for your age."

"Things go as they may."

"Nay, nay. I know you do not let things go hap-
hazard. You take care of your brothers and sisters like
a mother."

"Like a mother!" repeated Selene, and she smiled a
bitter negative.

"Of course a mother's love is a thing by itself, but
your father and the little ones have every reason to be
satisfied with yours."

"The little ones are perhaps, and Helios who is blind, but Arsinoe does what she can."

"You certainly are not content, I can hear it in your voice, and you used formerly to be as merry and happy as your sister, though perhaps not so saucy."

"Formerly—"

"How sadly that sounds! And yet you are handsome, you are young, and life lies before you."

"But what a life!"

"Well, what?" asked the sculptor, and taking his hands from his work he looked ardently at the fair pale girl before him and cried out fervently: "A life which might be full of happiness and satisfied affection."

The girl shook her head in negation and answered coldly:

"'Love is joy,' says the Christian woman who superintends us at work in the papyrus factory, and since my mother died I have had no love. I enjoyed all my share of happiness once for all in my childhood, now I am content if only we are spared the the worst misfortunes. Otherwise I take what each day brings, because I can not do otherwise. My heart is empty, and if I ever feel anything keenly, it is dread. I have long since ceased to expect any thing good of the future."

"Girl!" exclaimed Pollux. "Why, what has been happening to you? I do not understand half of what you are saying. How came you in the papyrus factory?"

"Do not betray me," begged Selene. "If my father were to hear of it."

"He is asleep, and what you confide to me no one will ever hear of again."

"Why should I conceal it? I go every day with

Arsinoe for two hours to the manufactory, and we work
there to earn a little money."

" Behind your father's back ?"

" Yes, he would rather that we should starve than
allow it. Every day I feel the same loathing for the
deceit; but we could not get on without it, for Arsinoe
thinks of nothing but herself, plays draughts with my
father, curls his hair, plays with the children as if they
were dolls, but it is my part to take care of them."

"And you, you say, have no share of love. Hap-
pily· no one believes you, and I least of all. Only
lately my mother was telling me about you, and I
thought you were a girl who might turn out just such a
wife as a woman ought to be."

" And now ?"

" Now, I know it for certain."

" You may be mistaken."

" No, no ! your name is Selene, and you are as gentle as the kindly moonlight; names, even, have their
significance."

" And my blind brother who has never even seen
the light is called Helios !" answered the girl.

Pollux had spoken with much warmth, but Selene's
last words startled him and checked the effervescence
of his feelings. Finding he did not answer her bitter
exclamation, she said, at first coolly, but with increasing
warmth:

"You are beginning to believe me, and you are
right, for what I do for the children is not done out of
love, or out of kindness, or because I set their welfare
above my own. I have inherited my father's pride, and
it would be odious to me if my brothers and sisters
went about in rags, and people thought we were as poor

and helpless as we really are. What is most horrible
to me is sickness in the house, for that increases the
anxiety I always feel and swallows up my last coin; the
children must not perish for want of it. I do not want
to make myself out worse than I am; it grieves me too
to see them drooping. But nothing that I do brings me
happiness—at most it moderates my fears. You ask
what I am afraid of?—of everything, everything that
can happen to me, for I have no reason to look forward
to anything good. When there is a knock, it may be a
creditor; when people look at Arsinoe in the street, I
seem to see dishonor lurking round her; when my father
acts against the advice of the physician I feel as if
we were standing already roofless in the open street.
What is there that I can do with a happy mind? I
certainly am not idle, still I envy the woman who can
sit with her hands in her lap and be waited on by
slaves, and if a golden treasure fell into my possession,
I would never stir a finger again, and would sleep every
day till the sun was high and make slaves look after
my father and the children. My life is sheer misery.
If ever we see better days I shall be astonished, and
before I have got over my astonishment it will all be
over."

The sculptor felt a cold chill, and his heart which
had opened wide to his old playfellow shrank again
within him. Before he could find the right words of
encouragement which he sought, they heard in the hall,
where the workmen and slaves were sleeping, the blast
of a trumpet intended to awake them. Selene started,
drew her mantle more closely round her, begged Pollux
to take care of her father, and to hide the wine-jar which
was standing near him from the work-people and then,

forgetting her lamp, she went hastily toward the door by which she had entered. Pollux hurried after her to light the way and while he accompanied her as far as the door of her rooms, by his warm and urgent words which appealed wonderfully to her heart, he extracted from her a promise to stand once more in her mantle as his model.

A quarter of an hour later the steward was safe in bed and still sleeping soundly, while Pollux, who had stretched himself on a mattress behind his screen, could not for a long time cease to think of the pale girl with her benumbed soul. At last sleep overcame him too, and a sweet dream showed him pretty little Arsinoe, who but for him must infallibly have been killed by the Numidian's restive horse, taking away her sister Selene's almond-cake and giving it to him. The pale girl submitted quietly to the robbery and only smiled coldly and silently to herself.

CHAPTER VI.

ALEXANDRIA was in the greatest excitement.

The Emperor's visit now immediately impending had tempted the busy hive of citizens away from the common round of life in which, day after day,—swarming, hurrying, pushing each other on, or running each other down—they raced for bread and for the means of filling their hours of leisure with pleasures and amusements. The unceasing wheel of industry to-day had pause in the factories, workshops, storehouses and courts of justice, for all sorts and conditions of

men were inspired by the same desire to celebrate
Hadrian's visit with unheard-of splendor. All that the
citizens could command of inventive skill, of wealth,
and of beauty was called forth to be displayed in the
games and processions which were to fill up a number
of days. The richest of the heathen citizens had·
undertaken the management of the pieces to be performed in the Theatre, of the mock fight on the lake,
and of the sanguinary games in the Amphitheatre; and
so great was the number of opulent persons that many
more were prepared to pay for smaller projects, for
which there was no opening. Nevertheless the arrangements for certain portions of the procession, in which
even the less wealthy were to take a share, the erection
of the building in the Hippodrome, the decorations
in the streets, and the preparations for entertaining
the Roman visitors absorbed sums so large that they
seemed extravagant even to the prefect Titianus, who
was accustomed to see his fellow-officials in Rome
squander millions.

As the Emperor's viceroy it behoved him to give his
assent to all that was planned to feast his sovereign's eye
and ear. On the whole, he left the citizens of the great
town free to act as they would; but he had, more than
once, to exert a decided opposition to their overdoing
the thing; for though the Emperor might be able to
endure a vast amount of pleasure, what the Alexandrians originally proposed to provide for him to see and
hear would have exhausted the most indefatigable
human energy.

That which gave the greatest trouble, not merely to
him, but also to the masters of the revels chosen by
the municipality, were the never-dormant hostility be

tween the heathen and the Jewish sections of the inhabitants, and the processions, since no division chose
to come last, nor would any number be satisfied to be
only the third or the fourth.

It was from a meeting, where his determined intervention had at last brought all these preliminaries to
a decision beyond appeal, that Titianus proceeded to
the Caesareum to pay the Empress the visit which she
expected of him daily. He was glad to have come to
some conclusion, at any rate provisionally, with regard
to these matters, for six days had slipped away since
the works had been begun in the palace of Lochias,
and Hadrian's arrival was nearing rapidly.

He found Sabina, as usual, on her divan, but on
this occasion the Empress was sitting upright on her
cushions. She seemed quite to have got over the
fatigues of the sea-voyage, and in token that she felt
better she had applied more red to her cheeks and lips
than three days ago, and because she was to receive a
visit from the sculptors, Papias and Aristeas, she had
had her hair arranged as it was worn in the statue of
Venus Victrix, with whose attributes she had, five years
previously—though not, it is true, without some resistance—been represented in marble. When a copy of
this statue had been erected in Alexandria, an evil
tongue had made a speech which was often repeated
among the citizens.

"This Aphrodite is triumphant to be sure, for all
who see her make haste to fly; she should be called
' Cypris the scatterer.' "

Titianus was still under the excitement of the embittered squabbles and unpleasing exhibitions of character at which he had just been present when he

entered the presence of the Empress, whom he found in a small room with no one but the chamberlain and a few ladies-in-waiting. To the prefect's respectful inquiries after her health, she shrugged her shoulders and replied :

" How should I be ? If I said well it would not be true ; if I said ill, I should be surrounded with pitiful faces, which are not pleasant to look at. After all we must endure life. Still, the innumerable doors in these rooms will be the death of me if I am compelled to remain here long."

Titianus glanced at the two doors of the room in which the Empress was sitting, and began to express his regrets at their bad condition, which had escaped his notice; but Sabina interrupted him, saying :

" You men never do observe what hurts us women. Our Verus is the only man who can feel and understand,—who can divine it, as I might say. There are five and thirty doors in my rooms! I had them counted—five and thirty! If they were not old and made of valuable wood I should really believe they had been made as a practical joke on me."

" Some of them might be supplemented with curtains."

" Oh! never mind—a few miseries, more or less in my life do not matter. Are the Alexandrians ready at last with their preparations ?"

" I am sure I hope so," said the prefect with a sigh. 'They are bent on giving all that is their best; but in the endeavor to outvie each other every one is at war with his neighbor, and I still feel the effects of the odious wrangling which I have had to listen to for hours, and that I have been obliged to check again and again with threats of 'I shall be down upon you.'"

" Indeed," said the Empress with a pinched smile, as if she had heard some thing that pleased her.

" Tell me something about your meeting. I am bored to death, for Verus, Balbilla and the others have asked for leave of absence that they may go to inspect the work doing at Lochias; I am accustomed to find that people would rather be any where than with me. Can I wonder then that my presence is not enough to enable a friend of my husband's to forget a little annoyance—the impression left by some slight misunderstanding? But my fugitives are a long time away; there must be a great deal that is beautiful to be seen at Lochias."

The prefect suppressed his annoyance and did not express his anxiety lest the architect and his assistants should be disturbed, but began in the tone of the messenger in a tragedy:

" The first quarrel was fought over the order of the procession."

" Sit a little farther off," said Sabina pressing her jewelled right-hand on her ear, as if she were suffering pain in it. The prefect colored slightly, but he obeyed the desire of Caesar's wife and went on with his story, pitching his voice in a somewhat lower key than before:

" Well, it was about the procession, that the first breach of the peace arose."

" I have heard that once already," replied the lady, yawning. " I like processions."

" But," said the prefect, a man in the beginning of the sixties—and he spoke with some irritation, "here as in Rome and every where else, where they are not con-

trolled by the absolute will of a single individual, processions are the children of strife, and they bring forth
strife, even when they are planned in honor of a festival
of Peace."

"It seems to annoy you that they should be organized in honor of Hadrian?"

"You are in jest; it is precisely because I care particularly that they should be carried out with all possible splendor, that I am troubling myself about them in
person, even as to details; and to my great satisfaction
I have been able even to subdue the most obstinate;
still it was scarcely my duty—"

"I fancied that you not only served the state but
were my husband's friend."

"I am proud to call myself so."

"Aye—Hadrian has many, very many friends since
he has worn the purple. Have you got over your ill-
temper Titianus? You must have become very touchy.
Poor Julia has an irritable husband!"

"She is less to be pitied than you think," said Titianus with dignity, "for my official duties so entirely
claim my time that she is not often likely to know what
disturbs me. If I have forgotten to dissimulate my
vexation before you, I beg you to pardon me, and
to attribute it to my zeal in securing a worthy reception
for Hadrian."

"As if I had scolded you! But to return to your
wife—as I understand she shares the fate I endure. We
poor women have nothing to expect from our husbands,
but the stale leavings that remain after business has absorbed the rest! But your story—go on with your story."

"The worst moments I had at all were given me by
the bad feeling of the Jews towards the other citizens."

"I hate all these infamous sects—Jews, Christians or whatever they are called! Do they dare to grudge their money for the reception of Caesar?"

"On the contrary Alabarchos, their wealthy chief, has offered to defray all the cost of the Naumachia and his co-religionist Artemion."

"Well, take their money, take their money."

"The Greek citizens feel that they are rich enough to pay all the expenses, which will amount to many millions of sesterces, and they wish to exclude the Jews, if possible, from all the processions and games."

"They are perfectly right."

"But allow me to ask you whether it is just to prohibit half the population of Alexandria doing honor to their Emperor!"

"Oh! Hadrian will, with pleasure, dispense with the honor. Our conquering heroes have thought it redounded to their glory to be called Africanus, Germanicus and Dacianus, but Titus refused to be called Judaicus when he had destroyed Jerusalem."

"That was because he dreaded the remembrance of the rivers of blood which had to be shed in order to break the fearfully obstinate resistance of that nation. The besieged had to be conquered limb by limb, and finger by finger, before they would make up their minds to yield."

"Again you are speaking half poetically, or have these people elected you as their advocate?"

"I know them and make every effort to secure them justice, just as much as any other citizen of this country which I govern in the name of the Empire and of Caesar. They pay taxes as well as the rest of the Alexandrians; nay more, for there are many wealthy men among them

7

who are honorably prominent in trade, in professions, learning and art, and I therefore mete to them the same measure as to the other inhabitants of this city. Their superstition offends me no more than that of the Egyptians."

"But it really is above all measure. At Aelia Capitolina which Hadrian had decorated with several buildings, they refused to sacrifice to the statues of Zeus and Hera. That is to say they scorn to do homage to me and my husband!"

"They are forbidden to worship any other divinity than their own God. Aelia rose up on the very soil where their ruined Jerusalem had stood, and the statues of which you speak stand in their holy places."

"What has that to do with us?"

"You know that even Caius* could not reduce them by placing his statue in the Holy of Holies of their temple; and Petronius, the governor, had to confess that to subdue them meant to exterminate them."

"Then let them meet with the fate they deserve, let them be exterminated!" cried Sabina.

"Exterminated?" asked the prefect. "In Alexandria they constitute nearly half of the citizens, that is to say several hundred thousand of obedient subjects, exterminated!"

"So many?" asked the Empress in alarm." But that is frightful. Omnipotent Jove! supposing that mass were to revolt against us! No one ever told me of this danger. In Cyrenaica, and at Salamis in Cyprus, they killed their fellow-citizens by thousands."

"They had been provoked to extremities and they were superior to their oppressors in force."

* Caligula.

"And in their own land one revolt after another is organized."

"By reason of the sacrifices of which we were speaking."

"Tinnius Rufus is at present the legate in Palestine. He has a horribly shrill voice—but he looks like a man who will stand no trifling, and will know how to quell the venomous brood."

"Possibly" replied Titianus. "But I fear that he will never attain his end by mere severity; and if he should he will have depopulated his province."

"There are already too many men in the empire."

"But never enough good and useful citizens."

"Outrageous contemners of the gods and useless citizens!"

"Here in Alexandria, where many have accommodated themselves to Greek habits of life and thought, and where all have adopted the Greek tongue, they are undoubtedly good citizens, and wholly devoted to Caesar."

"Do they take part in the rejoicings?"

"Yes, as far as the Greek citizens will allow them."

"And the arrangement of the water-fight?"

"That will not be given over to them, but Artemion will be permitted to supply the wild beasts for the games in the Amphitheatre."

"And he was not avaricious about it?"

"So far from it that you will be astonished. The man must know the secret of Midas, of turning stones into gold."

"And are there many like him among your Jews?"

"A good number."

"Then I wish that they would attempt a revolt, for if this led to the destruction of the rich ones, their gold, at any rate, would remain."

"Meanwhile I will try and keep them alive, as being good rate-payers."

"And does Hadrian share your wish?"

"Without doubt."

"Your successor may perhaps bring him to another mind."

"He always acts according to his own judgment, and for the present I am in office," answered Titianus haughtily.

"And may the God of the Jews long preserve you in it!" retorted Sabina scornfully.

CHAPTER VII.

BEFORE Titianus could open his lips to reply, the principal door of the room was opened cautiously but widely, and the praetor Lucius Aurelius Verus, his wife Domitia Lucilla, the young Balbilla and, last of all, Annaeus Florus, the historian, entered. All four were in the best spirits, and immediately after the preliminary greetings, were eager to report what they had seen at Lochias; but Sabina waved silence with her hand, and breathed out:

"No, no; not at present. I feel quite exhausted. This long waiting, and then—my smelling-bottle, Verus. Leukippe, bring me a cup of water with some fruit-syrup—but not so sweet as usual."

The Greek slave-girl hastened to execute this command, and the Empress, as she waved an elegant bottle, carved in onyx, under her nostrils, went on:

"It is a little eternity—is it not, Titianus, that we have been discussing state affairs? You all know how frank I am and that I cannot be silent when I meet with perverse opinions. While you have been away I have had much to hear and to say; it would have exhausted the strength of the strongest. I only wonder you don't find me more worn out, for what can be more excruciating for a woman than to be obliged to enter the lists for manly decisiveness against a man who is defending a perfectly antagonistic view? Give me the water, Leukippe."

While the Empress drank the syrup with tiny sips, twitching her thin lips over it, Verus went up to the prefect and asked him in an under tone:

"You were a long while alone with Sabina, cousin?"

"Yes," replied Titianus, and he set his teeth as he spoke and clenched his fist so hard that the praetor could not misunderstand, and replied in a low voice:

"She is much to be pitied, and particularly just now she has hours—"

"What sort of hours?" asked Sabina taking the cup from her lips.

"These," replied Verus quickly, "in which I am not obliged to occupy myself in the senate or with the affairs of state. To whom do I owe them but to you?"

With these words he approached the mature beauty, and taking the goblet out of her hand with affectionate subservience, as a son might wait on his honored and suffering mother, he gave it to the Greek slave. The Empress bowed her thanks again and again to the praetor with much affability, and then said, with a slight infusion of cheerfulness in her tones:

"Well—and what is there to be seen at Lochias?"

"Wonderful things," answered Balbilla readily and clasping her little hands. "A swarm of bees, a colony of ants, have taken possession of the palace. Hands black, white and brown—more than we could count, are busy there and of all the hundreds of workmen which are astir there, not one got in the way of another, for one little man orders and manages them all, just as the prescient wisdom of the gods guides the stars through the 'gracious and merciful night' so that they may never push or run against each other."

"I must put in a word on behalf of Pontius the architect," interposed Verus. "He is a man of at least average height."

"Let us admit it to satisfy your sense of justice," returned Balbilla. "Let us admit it—a man of average height, with a papyrus-roll in his right-hand and a stylus in the left, controls them. Now, does my way of stating it please you better?"

"It can never displease me," answered the praetor.

"Let Balbilla go on with her story," commanded the Empress.

"What we saw was chaos," continued the girl, "still in the confusion we could divine the elements of an orderly creation in the future; nay, it was even visible to the eye."

"And not unfrequently stumbled over with the foot," laughed the praetor. "If it had been dark, and if the laborers had been worms, we must have trodden half of them to death—they swarmed so all over the pavement."

" What were they doing ?"

" Every thing," answered Balbilla quickly. " Some were polishing damaged pieces, others were laying new bits of mosaic in the empty places from which it had formerly been removed, and skilled artists were painting colored figures on smooth surfaces of plaster. Every pillar and every statue was built round with a scaffolding reaching to the ceiling on which men were climbing and crowding each other just as the sailors 'climb into the enemy's ships in the Naumachia."

The girl's pretty cheeks had flushed with her eager reminiscence of what she had seen, and, as she spoke, moving her hands with expressive gestures, the tall structure of curls which crowned her small head shook from side to side.

" Your description begins to be quite poetical," said the Empress, interrupting her young companion. " Perhaps the Muse may even inspire you with verse."

" All the Pierides," said the praetor, " are represented at Lochias. We saw eight of them, but the ninth, that patroness of the arts, who protects the stargazer, the lofty Urania, has at present, in place of a head—allow me to leave it to you to guess divine Sabina ?"

"Well—what ?"

"A wisp of straw."

"Alas," sighed the Empress. "What do you say, Florus ? Are there not among your learned and verse-spinning associates certain men who resemble this Urania?"

" At any rate," replied Florus, "we are more prudent than the goddess, for we conceal the contents of our heads in the hard nut of the skull, and under a more or less abundant thatch of hair.   Urania displays her straw openly."

"That almost sounds," said Balbilla laughing and pointing to her abundant locks, "as if I especially needed to conceal what is covered by my hair."

"Even the Lesbian swan was called the fair-haired," replied Florus.

"And you are our Sappho," said the praetor's wife, drawing the girl's arm to her bosom.

"Really! and will you not write in verse all that you have seen to-day?" asked the Empress.

Balbilla looked down on the ground a minute and then said brightly: "It might inspire me, everything strange that I meet with prompts me to write verse."

" But follow the counsel of Apollonius the philologer," advised Florus.   "You are the Sappho of our day, and therefore you should write in the ancient Aeolian dialect and not Attic Greek."   Verus laughed, and the Empress, who never was strongly moved to laughter, gave a short sharp giggle, but Balbilla said eagerly:

"Do you think that I could not acquire it and do so?   To-morrow morning I will begin to practise myself in the old Aeolian forms."

"Let it alone," said Domitia Lucilla; "your simplest songs are always the prettiest."

"No one shall laugh at me!" declared Balbilla pertinaciously.   "In a few weeks I will know how to use the Aeolian dialect, for I can do anything I am determined to do—anything, anything."

"What a stubborn little head we have under our curls!" exclaimed the Empress, raising a graciously threatening finger.

"And what powers of apprehension," added Florus.

"Her master in language and metre told me his best pupil was a woman of noble family and a poetess besides—Balbilla in short."

The girl colored at the words, and said with pleased excitement :

"Are you flattering me or did Hephaestion really say that?"

"Woe is me!" cried the praetor, "for Hephaestion was my master too, and I am one of the masculine scholars beaten by Balbilla. But it is no news to me, for the Alexandrian himself told me the same thing as Florus."

"You follow Ovid and she Sappho," said Florus; "you write in Latin and she in Greek. Do you still always carry Ovid's love-poems about with you?"

"Always," replied Verus, "as Alexander did his Homer."

"And out of respect for his master your husband endeavors, by the grace of Venus, to live like him," added Sabina, addressing herself to Domitia Lucilla.

The tall and handsome Roman lady only shrugged her shoulders slightly in answer to this not very kindly-meant speech; but Verus said, while he picked up Sabina's silken coverlet, and carefully spread it over her knees:

"My happiest fortune consists in this: that *Venus Victrix* favors me. But we are not yet at the end of our story; our Lesbian swan met at Lochias with another rare bird, an artist in statuary."

"How long have the sculptors been reckoned among birds?" asked Sabina. "At the utmost can they be compared to woodpeckers."

"When they work in wood," laughed Verus. "Our

artist, however, is an assistant of Papias, and handles noble materials in the grand style. On this occasion, however, he is building a statue out of a very queer mixture of materials."

"Verus may very well call our new acquaintance a bird," interrupted Balbilla, "for as we approached the screen behind which he is working he was whistling a tune with his lips, so pure and cheery, and loud, that it rang through the empty hall above all the noise of the workmen. A nightingale does not pipe more sweetly. We stood still to listen till the merry fellow, who had no idea that we were by, was silent again; and then hearing the architect's voice, he called to him over the screen. 'Now we must clap Urania's head on; I saw it clearly in my mind and would have had it finished with a score of touches, but Papias said he had one in the workshop. I am curious to see what sort of a sugar-plum face, turned out by the dozen, he will stick on my torso—which will please me, at any rate, for a couple of days. Find me a good model for the bust of the Sappho I am to restore. A thousand gadflies are buzzing in my brain—I am so tremendously excited! What I am planning now will come to something!'"

Balbilla, as she spoke the last words, tried to mimic a man's deep voice, and seeing the Empress smile she went on eagerly.

"It all came out so fresh, from a heart full to bursting of happy vigorous creative joy, that it quite fired me, and we all went up to the screen and begged the sculptor to let us see his work."

"And you found?" asked Sabina.

"He positively refused to let us into his retreat," replied the praetor; "but Balbilla coaxed the permission out of him, and the tall young fellow seems to have really learnt something. The fall of the drapery that covers the Muse's figure is perfectly thought out with reference to possibility—rich, broadly handled, and at the same time of surprising delicacy. Urania has drawn her mantle closely round her, as if to protect herself from the keen night-air while gazing at the stars. When he has finished his Muse, he is to repair some mutilated busts of women; he was fixing the head of a finished Berenice to-day, and I proposed to him to take Balbilla as the model for his Sappho."

"A good idea" said the Empress. "If the bust is successful I will take him with me to Rome."

"I will sit to him with pleasure," said the girl. "The bright young fellow took my fancy."

"And Balbilla his," added the praetor's wife; he gazed at her as a marvel, and she promised him that, with your permission, she would place her face at his disposal for three hours to-morrow."

"He begins with the head," interposed Verus. "What a happy man is an artist such as he! He may turn about her head, or lay her peplum in folds without reproof or repulse, and to-day when we had to get past bogs of plaster, and lakes of wet paint, she scarcely picked up the hem of her dress, and never once allowed me—who would so willingly have supported her—to lift her over the worst places."

Balbilla reddened and said angrily:

"Really Verus, in good earnest, I will not allow you to speak to me in that way, so now you know it once for all; I have so little liking for what is not clean that I find it quite easy to avoid it without assistance."

"You are too severe," interrupted the Empress with

a hideous smile. "Do not you think Domitia Lucilla,
that she ought to allow your husband to be of service
to her?"

"If the Empress thinks it right and fitting," replied
the lady raising her shoulders, and with an expressive
movement of her hands. Sabina quite took her meaning, and suppressing another yawn she said angrily:

"In these days we must be indulgent toward a husband who has chosen Ovid's amatory poems as his
faithful companion. What is the matter Titianus?"

While Balbilla had been relating her meeting with
the sculptor Pollux, a chamberlain had brought in to
the prefect an important letter, admitting of no delay.
The state official had withdrawn to the farther side of
the room with it, had broken the strong seal and had
just finished reading it, when the Empress asked her
question.

Nothing of what went on around her escaped
Sabina's little eyes, and she had observed that while the
governor was considering the document addressed to
him he had moved uneasily. It must contain something of importance.

"An urgent letter," replied Titianus, "calls me home.
I must take my leave, and I hope ere long to be able
to communicate to you something agreeable."

"What does that letter contain?"

"Important news from the provinces," said Titianus.

"May I inquire what?"

"I grieve to say that I must answer in the negative.
The Emperor expressly desired that this matter should
be kept secret. Its settlement demands the promptest
haste, and I am therefore unfortunately obliged to quit
you immediately."

Sabina returned the prefect's parting salutations with icy coldness and immediately desired to be conducted to her private rooms to dress herself for supper.

Balbilla escorted her, and Florus betook himself to the "Olympian table," the famous eating-house kept by Lycortas, of whom he had been told wonders by the epicures at Rome.

When Verus was alone with his wife he went up in a friendly manner and said:

"May I drive you home again?"

Domitia Lucilla had thrown herself on a couch, and covered her face with her hands, and she made no reply.

"May I?" repeated the praetor. As his wife persisted in her silence, he went nearer to her, laid his hand on her slender fingers that concealed her face, and said:

"I believe you are angry with me!" She pushed away his hand, with a slight movement, and said:

"Leave me."

"Yes, unfortunately I must leave you. Business takes me into the city and I will—"

"You will let the young Alexandrians, with whom you revelled through the night, introduce you to new fair ones—I know it."

"There are in fact women here of incredible charm," replied Verus quite coolly. "White, brown, copper-colored, black—and all delightful in their way. I could never be tired of admiring them."

"And your wife?" asked Lucilla, facing him, sternly.

"My wife? yes, my fairest. Wife is a solemn title of honor and has nothing to do with the joys of life. How could I mention your name in the same hour with those of the poor children who help me to beguile an idle hour."

Domitia Lucilla was used to such phrases, and yet
on this occasion they gave her a pang. But she concealed it, and crossing her arms she said resolutely and
with dignity:

"Go your way—through life with your Ovid, and
your gods of love, but do not attempt to crush innocence under the wheels of your chariot."

. "Balbilla do you mean," asked the praetor with a
loud laugh. "She knows how to take care of herself
and has too much spirit to let herself get entangled in
erotics. The little son of Venus has nothing to say to
two people who are such good friends as she and I are."

" May I believe you ?"

" My word for it, I ask nothing of her but a kind
word," cried he, frankly offering his hand to his wife.
Lucilla only touched it lightly with her fingers and said :

" Send me back to Rome. I have an unutterable
longing to see my children, particularly the boys."

" It cannot be," said Verus. " Not at present; but
in a few weeks, I hope."

" Why not sooner ?"

" Do not ask me."

" A mother may surely wish to know why she is
separated from her baby in the cradle."

" That cradle is at present in your mother's house,
and she is taking care of our little ones. Have patience,
a little longer for that which I am striving after, for you,
and for me, and not last, for our son, is so great, so
stupendously great and difficult that it might well outweigh years of longing."

Verus spoke the last words in a low tone, but with
a dignity which characterized him only in decisive
moments, but his wife, even before he had done speak-

ing, clasped his right-hand in both of hers and said in a
low frightened voice:

"You aim at the purple?"

He nodded assent.

"That is what it means then!"

"What?"

"Sabina and you—"

"Not on that account only; she is hard and sharp
to others, but to me she has shown nothing but kindness, ever since I was a boy."

"She hates me."

"Patience, Lucilla; patience! The day is coming
when the daughter of Nigrinus, the wife of Caesar, and
the former Empress—but I will not finish. I am, as
you know, warmly attached to Sabina, and sincerely
wish the Emperor a long life."

"And he will adopt."

"Hush!—he is thinking of it, and his wife wishes
it."

"Is it likely to happen soon?"

"Who can tell at this moment what Caesar may
decide on in the very next hour. But probably his
decision may be made on the thirtieth of December."

"Your birthday."

"He asked what day it was, and he is certainly
casting my horoscope, for the night when my mother
bore me—"

"The stars then are to seal our fate?"

"Not they alone. Hadrian must also be inclined
to read them in my favor."

"How can I be of use to you?"

"Show yourself what you really are in your intercourse with the Emperor."

"Thank you for those words—and I beg you do not provoke me any more. If it might yet be something more than a mere post of honor to be the wife of Verus, I would not ask for the new dignity of becoming wife to Caesar."

"I will not go into the town to-day; I will stay with you. Now are you happy?"

"Yes, yes," cried she, and she raised her arm to throw it round her husband's neck, but he held her aside and whispered:

"That will do. The idyllic is out of place in the race for the purple."

CHAPTER VIII.

TITIANUS had ordered his charioteer to drive at once to Lochias. The road led past the prefect's palace, his residence on the Bruchiom, and he paused there; for the letter which lay hidden in the folds of his toga, contained news, which, within a few hours, might put him under the necessity of not returning home till the following morning. Without allowing himself to be detained by the officials, subalterns, or lictors, who were awaiting his return to make communications, or to receive his orders, he went straight through the ante-room and the large public rooms for men, to find his wife in the women's apartments which looked upon the garden. He met her at the door of her room, for she had heard his step approaching and came out to receive him.

"I was not mistaken," said the matron with sincere

pleasure. "How pleasant that you have been released so early to-day. I did not expect you till supper was over."

"I have come only to go again," replied Titianus, entering his wife's room. "Have some bread brought to me and a cup of mixed wine; why—really! here stands all I want ready as if I had ordered it. You are right, I was with Sabina a shorter time than usual; but she exerted herself in that short time to utter as many sour words as if we had been talking for half a day. And in five minutes I must quit you again, till when?—the gods alone know when I shall return. It is hard even to speak the words, but all our trouble and care, and all poor Pontius' zeal and pains-taking labor are in vain."

As he spoke the prefect threw himself on a couch; his wife handed him the refreshment he had asked for, and said, as she passed her hand over his grey hair:

"Poor man! Has Hadrian then determined after all to inhabit the Caesareum?"

"No. Leave us, Syra — you shall see directly. Please read me Caesar's letter once more. Here it is."

Julia unfolded the papyrus, which was of elegant quality, and began:

"Hadrian to his friend Titianus, the Governor of Egypt. The deepest secrecy—Hadrian greets Titianus, as he has so often done for years at the beginning of disagreeable business letters, and only with half his heart. But to-morrow he hopes to greet the dear friend of his youth, his prudent vicegerent, not merely with his whole soul, but with hand and tongue. And now to be more explicit, as follows: I come to-morrow morning, the fifteenth of December, towards evening,

S

to Alexandria, with none but Antinous, the slave
Mastor, and my private secretary, Phlegon. We land
at Lochias, in the little harbor, and you will know my
ship by a large silver star at the prow. If night should
fall before I arrive there, three red lanterns at the end
of the mast shall inform you of the friend that is approaching. I have sent home the learned and witty
men whom you sent to meet me, in order to detain me,
and gain time for the restoration of the old nest in
which I had a fancy to roost with Minerva's birds—
which have not, I hope, all been driven out of it—in
order that Sabina and her following may not lack entertainment, nor the famous gentlemen themselves be un-
necessarily disturbed in their labors. I need them not.
If perchance it was not you who sent them, I ask your
pardon. An error in this matter would certainly involve
some humiliation, for it is easier to explain what has
happened than to foresee what is to come. Or is the
reverse the truth? I will indemnify the learned men
for their useless journey by disputing this question with
them and their associates in the Museum. The rapid
movement to which the philologer was prompted on
my account will prolong his existence; he bristles with
learning at the tip of every hair, and he sits still more
than is good for him.

"We shall arrive in modest disguise and will sleep at
Lochias; you know that I have rested more than once
on the bare earth, and, if need be, can sleep as well on
a mat as on a couch. My pillow follows at my heels—
my big dog, which you know; and some little room,
where I can meditate undisturbed on my designs for
next year, can no doubt be found.

"I entreat you to keep my secret strictly. To none

,—man nor woman—and I beseech you as urgently as friend or Caesar ever besought a favor—let the least suspicion of my arrival be known. Nor must the smallest preparation betray whom it is you receive. I cannot command so dear a friend as Titianus, but I appeal to his heart to carry out my wishes.

"I rejoice to see you again; what delight I shall find in the whirl of confusion that I hope to find at Lochias. You shall take me to see the artists, who are, no doubt, swarming in the old castle, as the architect Claudius Venator from Rome, who is to assist Pontius with his advice. But this Pontius, who carried out such fine works for Herodes Atticus, the rich Sophist, met me at his house, and will certainly recognize me. Tell him, therefore, what I propose doing. He is a serious and trustworthy man, not a chatterbox or scatter-brained simpleton who loses his head. Thus you may take him into the secret, but not till my vessel is in sight. May all be well with you."

"Well, what do you say to that?" asked Titianus, taking the letter from his wife's hand. "Is it not more than vexatious—our work was going on so splendidly."

"But," said Julia thoughtfully and with a meaning smile. "Perhaps it might not have been finished in time. As matters now stand it need not be complete, and Hadrian will see the good intention all the same. I am glad about the letter, for it takes a great responsibility off your otherwise overloaded shoulders."

"You always see the right side," cried the prefect. "It is well that I came home, for I can await Caesar with a much lighter heart. Let me lock up the letter, and then farewell. This parting is for some hours from you, and from all peace for many days."

Titianus gave her his hand. She held it firmly and said :

" Before you go I must confess to you that I am very proud."

" You have every right to be."

" But you have not said a word to me about keeping silence."

" Because you have kept other tests—still, to be sure, you are a woman, and a very handsome one besides."

" An old grandmother, with grey hair !"

" And still more upright and more charming than a thousand of the most admired younger beauties."

" You are trying to convert my pride into vanity, in my old age."

" No, no ! I was only looking at you with an examining eye, as our talk led me to do, and I remembered that Sabina had lamented that handsome Julia was not looking well. But where is there another woman of your age with such a carriage, such unwrinkled features, so clear a brow, such deep kind eyes, such beautifully-polished arms—"

" Be quiet," exclaimed his wife. " You make me blush."

" And may I not be proud that a grandmother, who is a Roman, as my wife is, can find it so easy to blush ? You are quite different from other women."

" Because you are different from other men."

" You are a flatterer ; since all our children have left us, it is as if we were newly married again."

" Ah ! the apple of discord is removed."

" It is always over what he loves best that man is most prompt to be jealous. But now, once more, fare- well."

Titianus kissed his wife's forehead and hurried towards the door; Julia called him back and said:

"One thing at any rate we can do for Caesar. I send food every day down to the architect at Lochias, and to-day there shall be three times the quantity."

"Good; do so."

"Farewell, then."

"And we shall meet again, when it shall please the gods and the Emperor."

————

When the prefect reached the appointed spot, no vessel with a silver star was to be seen.

The sun went down and no ship with three red lanterns was visible.

The harbor-master, into whose house Titianus went, was told that he expected a great architect from Rome, who was to assist Pontius with his counsel in the works at Lochias, and he thought it quite intelligible that the governor should do a strange artist the honor of coming to meet him; for the whole city was well aware of the incredible haste and the lavish outlay of means that were being given to the restoration of the ancient palace of the Ptolemies as a residence for the Emperor.

While he was waiting, Titianus remembered the young sculptor Pollux, whose acquaintance he had made, and his mother in the pretty little gate-house. Well disposed towards them as he felt, he sent at once to old Doris, desiring her not to retire to rest early that evening, since he, the prefect, would be going late to Lochias.

"Tell her, too, as from yourself and not from me," Titianus instructed the messenger, "that I may very

likely look in upon her. She may light up her little
room and keep it in order."

No one at Lochias had the slightest suspicion of
the honor which awaited the old palace.

After Verus had quitted it with his wife and Balbilla, and when he had again been at work for about
an hour the sculptor Pollux came out of his nook,
stretching himself, and called out to Pontius, who was
standing on a scaffold:

"I must either rest or begin upon something new.
One cures me of fatigue as much as the other. Do
you find it so?"

"Yes, just as you do," replied the architect, as he
continued to direct the work of the slave-masons, who
were fixing a new Corinthian capital in the place of an
old one which had been broken.

"Do not disturb yourself," Pollux cried up to him.
"I only request you to tell my master Papias when he
comes here with Gabinius, the dealer in antiquities, that
he will find me at the rotunda that you inspected with
me yesterday. I am going to put the head on to the
Berenice; my apprentice must long since have completed his preparations; but the rascal came into the
world with two left-hands, and as he squints with one
eye everything that is straight looks crooked to him,
and—according to the law of optics—the oblique looks
straight. At any rate, he drove the peg which is to
support the new head askew into the neck, and as no
historian has recorded that Berenice ever had her neck
on one side, like the old color-grinder there, I must
see to its being straight myself. In about half an hour,
as I calculate, the worthy Queen will no longer be one
of the headless women."

"Where did you get the new head?" asked Pontius.

"From the secret archives of my memory," replied Pollux. "Have you seen it?"

"Yes."

"And do you like it?"

"Very much."

"Then it is worthy to live," sang the sculptor, and, as he quitted the hall, he waved his left-hand to the architect, and with his right-hand stuck a pink, which he had picked in the morning, behind his ear.

At the rotunda his pupil had done his business better than his master could have expected, but Pollux was by no means satisfied with his own arrangements. His work, like several others standing on the same side of the platform, turned its back on the steward's balcony, and the only reason why he had parted with the portrait of Selene's mother, of which he was so fond, was that his playfellow might gaze at the face whenever she chose. He found, however, to his satisfaction, that the busts were held in their places on their tall pedestals only by their own weight, and he then resolved to alter the historical order of the portrait-heads by changing their places, and to let the famous Cleopatra turn her back upon the palace, so that his favorite bust might look towards it.

In order to carry out this purpose then and there, he called some slaves up to help him in the alteration. This gave rise, more than once, to a warning cry, and the loud talking and ordering on this spot, for so many years left solitary and silent, attracted an inquirer, who, soon after the apprentice had begun his work, had shown herself on the balcony, but who had soon retreated after casting a glance at the dirty lad, splashed from head to foot with plaster. This time, however, she remained to watch, following every movement of Pollux as he directed the slaves; though, all the time and whatever he was doing, he turned his back upon her.

At last the portrait-head had found its right position, shrouded still in a cloth to preserve it from the marks of workmen's hands. With· a deep breath the artist turned full on the steward's house, and immediately a clear merry voice called out:

"What, tall Pollux! It really is tall Pollux; how glad I am !"

With these words the girl on the balcony loudly clapped her hands; and as the sculptor hailed her in return, and shouted:

"And you are little Arsinoe, eternal gods! What the little thing has come to !" She stood on tip-toe to seem taller, nodded at him pleasantly, and laughed out:

"I have not done growing yet; but as for you, you look quite dignified with the beard on your chin, and your eagle's nose. Selene did not tell me till to-day that you were living down there with the others."

The artist's eyes were fixed on the girl, as if spellbound. There are poetic natures in which the imagination immediately transmutes every new thing that strikes the eyes or the intelligence, into a romance, or rapidly embodies it in verse; and Pollux, like many of his calling, could never set his eyes on a fine human form and face, without instantly associating them with his art.

"A Galatea—a Galatea without an equal !" thought he, as he stood with his eyes fixed on Arsinoe's face and figure. "Just as if she had this instant risen from the sea—that form is just as fresh, and joyous, and healthy; and her little curls wave back from her brow as if they were still floating on the water; and now as she stoops, how full and supple is every movement. It is like a daughter of Nereus following the line of the waves as they rise into crests and dip again into watery valleys. She is like Selene and her mother in the shape of her head and the Greek cut of her face, but the elder sister is like the statue of Prometheus before it had a soul, and Arsinoe is like the Master's work after the celestial fire coursed through her veins."

The artist had felt and thought all this out in a few seconds, but the girl found her speechless admirer's silence too long, and exclaimed impatiently:

"You have not yet offered me any proper greeting. What are you doing down there?"

"Look here," he replied, lifting the cloth from the portrait, which was a striking likeness.

Arsinoe leaned far over the parapet of the balcony, shaded her eyes with her hand and was silent for more than a minute. Then she suddenly cried out loudly and exclaiming:

"Mother—it is my mother!" She flew into the room behind her.

"Now she will call her father and destroy all poor Selene's comfort," thought Pollux, as he pushed the heavy marble bust on which his gypsum head was fixed, into its right place.

"Well, let him come. We are the masters here now, and Keraunus dare not touch the Emperor's property." He crossed his arms and stood gazing at the bust, muttering to himself:

"Patchwork—miserable patchwork. We are cobbling up a robe for the Emperor out of mere rags; we are upholsterers and not artists. If it were only for

Hadrian, and not for Diotima and her children, not another finger would I stir in the place."

The path from the steward's residence led through some passages and up a few steps to the rotunda, on which the sculptor was standing, but in little more than a minute from Arsinoe's disappearance from the balcony she was by his side. With a heightened color she pushed the sculptor away from his 'work and put herself in the place where he had been standing, to be able to gaze at her leisure at the beloved features. Then she exclaimed again :

" It is mother—mother !" and the bright tears ran over her cheeks, without restraint from the presence of the artist, or the laborers and slaves whom she had flown past on her way, and who stared at her with as much alarm as if she were possessed.

Pollux did not disturb her. His heart was softened as he watched the tears running down the cheeks of this light-hearted child, and he could not help reflecting that goodness was indeed well rewarded when it could win such tender and enduring love as was cherished for the poor dead mother on the pedestal before him.

After looking for some time at the sculptor's work Arsinoe grew calmer, and turning to Pollux she asked:

" Did you make it ?"

" Yes," he replied, looking down.

" And entirely from memory ?"

" To be sure."

" Do you know what ?"

" Well."

" This shows that the Sibyl at the festival of Adonis was right when she sang in the Jalemus that the gods did half the work of the artist."

"Arsinoe!" cried Pollux, for her words made him feel as if a hot spring were seething in his heart, and he gratefully seized her hand; but she drew it away, for her sister Selene had come out on the balcony and was calling her.

It was for his elder playfellow and not for Arsinoe that Pollux had set his work in this place, but, just now, her gaze fell like a disturbing chill on his excited mood.

"There stands your mother's portrait," he called up to the balcony in an explanatory tone, pointing to the bust.

"I see it," she replied coldly. "I will look at it presently more closely. Come up Arsinoe, father wants to speak to you."

Again Pollux stood alone.

As Selene withdrew into the room, she gently shook her pale head, and said to herself:

"'It was to be for me,' Pollux said; something for me, for once—and even this pleasure is spoilt."

CHAPTER IX.

THE palace-steward, to whom Selene had called up his younger daughter, had just returned from the meeting of the citizens; and his old black slave, who always accompanied him when he went out, took the saffron-colored pallium from his shoulders, and from his head the golden circlet, with which he loved to crown his curled hair when he quitted the house. Keraunus still looked heated, his eyes seemed more prominent than usual and large drops of sweat stood upon his brow,

when his daughter entered the room where he was.
He absently responded to Arsinoe's affectionate greeting with a few unmeaning words, and before making
the important communication he had to disclose to his
daughters, he walked up and down before them for
some time, puffing out his fat cheeks and crossing his
arms. Selene was alarmed, and Arsinoe had long been
out of patience, when at last he began :

" Have you heard of the festivals which are to be
held in Caesar's honor ?"

Selene nodded and her sister exclaimed :

" Of course we have ! Have you secured places
for us on the seats kept for the town council ?"

" Do not interrupt me," the steward crossly ordered
his daughter. " There is no question of staring at them.
All the citizens are required to allow their daughters
to take part in the grand things that are to be carried
out, and we all were asked how many girls we had."

" And how are we to take part in the show ?" cried
Arsinoe, joyfully clapping her hands.

" I wanted to withdraw before the summons was
proclaimed, but Tryphon, the shipwright, who has a
workshop down by the King's Harbor, held me back
and called out to the assembly that his sons said that I
had two pretty young daughters. Pray how did he
know that ?"

With these words the steward lifted his grey brows
and his face grew red to the roots of his hair. Selene
shrugged her shoulders, but Arsinoe said :

" Tryphon's shipyard lies just below and we often
pass it ; but we do not know him or his sons. Have
you ever seen them Selene ? At any rate it is polite of
him to speak of us as pretty."

" Nobody need trouble themselves about your appearance unless they want to ask my permission to
marry you," replied the steward with a growl.

" And what did you say to Tryphon ?" asked
Selene.

" I did as I was obliged. Your father is steward of
a palace which at present belongs to Rome and the
Emperor; hence I must receive Hadrian as a guest in
this, the dwelling of my fathers, and therefore I, less
than any other citizen—cannot withhold my share in
the honors which the city council has decreed shall be
paid to him."

" Then we really may," said Arsinoe, and she went
up to her father to give him a coaxing pat. But
Keraunus was not in the humor to accept caresses; he
pushed her aside with an angry " Leave me alone,"
and then went on:

" If Hadrian were to ask me ' Where are your
daughters on the occasion of the festival ?' and if I had
to reply, ' They were not among the daughters of the
noble citizens,' it would be an insult to Caesar, to
whom in fact I feel very well disposed. All this I had
to consider, and I gave your names and promised to
send you to the great Theatre to the assembly of young
girls. There you will be met by the noblest matrons
and maidens of the city, and the first painters and
sculptors will decide to what part of the performance
your air and appearance are best fitted."

" But, father," cried Selene, " we cannot show ourselves in such an assembly in our common garments,
and where are we to find the money to buy new
ones ?"

" We can quite well show ourselves by any other

girls, in clean, white woollen dresses, prettily smartened
with fresh ribbons," declared Arsinoe, interposing between her father and her sister.

"It is not that which troubles me," replied the
steward; "it is the costumes, the costumes! It is only
the daughters of the poorer citizens who will be paid
by the council, and it would be a disgrace to be numbered among the poor—you understand me, children."

"I will not take part in the procession," said Selene
resolutely, but Arsinoe interrupted her.

"It is inconvenient and horrible to be poor, but it
certainly is no disgrace! The most powerful Romans
of ancient times, regarded it as honorable to die poor.
Our Macedonian descent remains to us even if the
state should pay for our costumes."

"Silence," cried the steward. "This is not the
first time that I have detected this low vein of feeling
in you. Even the noble may submit to the misfortunes
entailed by poverty, but the advantages it brings with
it he can never enjoy unless he resigns himself to—
being so no longer."

It had cost the steward much trouble to give due
expression to this idea, which he did not recollect to
have heard from another, which seemed new to him,
and which nevertheless fully represented what he felt;
and he slowly sank, with all the signs of exhaustion,
into a couch which formed a divan round a side recess
in the spacious sitting-room.

In this room Cleopatra might have held with Antony those banquets of which the unequalled elegance
and refinement had been enhanced by every grace of
art and wit. On the very spot where Keraunus now
reclined the dining-couch of the famous lovers had

probably stood; for, though the whole hall had a care-
fully-laid pavement, in this recess there was a mosaic of
stones of various colors of such beauty and delicacy of
finish that Keraunus had always forbidden his children
to step upon it. This, it is true, was less out of regard
for the fine work of art than because his father had
always prohibited his doing so, and his father again
before him. The picture represented the marriage of
Peleus and Thetis, and the divan only covered the
outer border of the picture, which was decorated with
graceful little Cupids.

Keraunus desired his daughter to fetch him a cup
of wine, but she mixed the juice of the grape with a
judicious measure of water. After he had half drunk
the diluted contents of the goblet, with many faces of
disgust, he said:

"Would you like to know what each of your dresses
will cost if it is to be in no respect inferior to those of
the others?"

"Well," said Arsinoe anxiously.

"About seven hundred drachmae;* Philinus, the
tailor, who is working for the theatre, tells me it will be
impossible to do anything well for less."

"And you are really thinking of such insane ex-
travagance," cried Selene. "We have no money, and
I should like to know the man who would lend us any
more."

The steward's younger daughter looked doubtfully
at the tips of her fingers and was silent, but her eyes
swimming in tears betrayed what she felt. Keraunus
was rejoiced at the silent consent which Arsinoe seemed
to accord to his desire to let her take part in the dis-

---

* Rather less than £24, or 115 dollars.

play at whatever cost. He forgot that he had just reproached her for her low sentiments, and said:

" The little one always feels what is right. As for you, Selene, I beg you to reflect seriously that I am your father, and that I forbid you to use this admonishing tone to me; you have accustomed yourself to it with the children and to them you may continue to use it. Fourteen hundred drachmae certainly, at the first thought of it, seems a very large sum, but if the material and the trimming required are bought with judgment, after the festival we may very likely sell it back to the man with profit."

" With profit!" cried Selene bitterly, " not half is to be got for old things—not a quarter! And even if you turn me out of the house—I will not help to drag us into deeper wretchedness; I will take no part in the performances."

The steward did not redden this time, he was not even violent; on the contrary, he simply raised his head and compared his daughters as they stood—not without an infusion of satisfaction. He was accustomed to love his daughters in his own way, Selene as the useful one, and Arsinoe as the beauty; and as on this occasion all he cared for was to satisfy his vanity, and as this end could be attained through his younger daughter alone, he said:

" Stay with the children then, for all I care. We will excuse you on the score of weak health, and certainly, child, you do look extremely pale. I would far rather find the means for the little one only."

Two sweet dimples again began to show in Arsinoe's cheeks, but Selene's lips were as white as her bloodless cheeks as she exclaimed:

"But, father—father! neither the baker nor the butcher has had a coin paid him for the last two months, and you will squander seven hundred drachmae!"

"Squander!" cried Keraunus indignantly, but still in a tone of disgust rather than anger. "I have already forbidden you to speak to me in that way. The richest of our noble youths will take part in the games; Arsinoe is handsome and perhaps one of them may choose her for his wife. And do you call it squandering, when a father does his utmost to find a suitable husband for his daughter. After all, what do you know of what I may possess?"

"We have nothing, so I cannot know of it," cried the girl beside herself.

"Indeed!" drawled Keraunus with an embarrassed smile. "And is that nothing which lies in the cupboard there, and stands on the cornice shelf? For your sakes I will part with these—the onyx fibula, the rings, the golden chaplet, and the girdle of course."

"They are of mere silver-gilt!" Selene interrupted, ruthlessly. "All my grandfather's real gold you parted with when my mother died."

"She had to be cremated and buried as was due to our rank," answered Keraunus; "but I will not think now of those melancholy days."

"Nay, do think of them, father."

"Silence! All that belongs to my own adornment of course I cannot do without, for I must be prepared to meet Caesar in a dress befitting my rank; but the little bronze Eros there must be worth something, Plutarch's ivory cup, which is beautifully carved, and above all, that picture; its former possessor was con-

vinced that it had been painted by Apelles himself here
in Alexandria. You shall know at once what these
little things are worth, for, as the gods vouchsafed, on
my way home I met, here in the palace, Gabinius of
Nicaea, the dealer in such objects. He promised me
that when he had done his business with the architect
he would come to me to inspect my treasures, and to
pay money down for anything that might suit him. If
my Apelles pleases him, he will give ten talents for that
alone, and if he buys it for only the half, or even the
tenth of that sum, I will make you enjoy yourself for
once, Selene."

"We will see," said the pale girl, shrugging her
shoulders, and her sister exclaimed:

"Show him the sword too, that you always declared belonged to Caesar, and if he gives you a good
sum for it you will buy me a gold bracelet."

"And Selene shall have one, too. But I have the
very slenderest hopes of the sword, for a connoisseur
would hardly pronounce it genuine. But I have other
things, many others. Hark! that is Gabinius, no
doubt. Quick, Selene, throw the chiton round me
again. My chaplet, Arsinoe. A well-to-do man always gets a higher price than a poor one. I have
ordered the slave to await him in the ante-room; it is
always done in the best houses."

The curiosity dealer was a small, lean man, who,
by prudence and good luck, had raised himself to be
one of the most esteemed of his class and a rich man.
Having matured his knowledge by industry and experience, he knew better than any man how to distinguish what was good from what was indifferent or
bad, what was genuine from what was spurious. No

one had a keener eye; but he was abrupt in his dealings
with those from whom he had nothing to gain. In circumstances where there was profit in view, he could, to
be sure, be polite even to subservience and show inexhaustible patience. He commanded himself so far as
to listen with an air of conviction to the steward as he
told him in a condescending tone that he was tired of
his little possessions, that he could just as well keep
them as part with them; he merely wanted to show
them to him as a connoisseur and would only part with
them if a good round sum were offered for what was in
fact idle capital. One piece after another passed
through the dealer's slender fingers, or was placed before him that he might contemplate it; but the man
spoke not, and only shook his head as he examined
every fresh object. And when Keraunus told him
whence this or that specimen of his treasures had been
obtained, he only murmured—" Indeed " or " Really,"
" Do you think so?" After the last piece of property
had passed through his hands, the steward asked:

" Well, what do you think of them ? "

The beginning of the sentence was spoken confidently, the end almost in fear, for the dealer only
smiled and shook his head again before he said:

" There are some genuine little things among them,
but nothing worth speaking of. I advise you to keep
them, because you have an affection for them, while I
could get very little by them."

Keraunus avoided looking towards Selene, whose
large eyes, full of dread, had been fixed on the dealer's
lips; but Arsinoe, who had followed his movements
with no less attention, was less easily discouraged, and
pointing to her father's Apelles, she said:

" And that picture, is that worth nothing ?"

" It grieves me that I cannot tell so fair a damsel that it is inestimably valuable," said the dealer, stroking his gray whiskers. " But we have here only a very feeble copy. The original is in the Villa belonging to Phinius on the Lake of Larius, and which he calls Cothurnus. I have no use whatever for this piece."

" And this carved cup ?" asked Keraunus. " It came from among the possessions of Plutarch, as I can prove, and it is said to have been the gift of the Emperor Trajan."

" It is the prettiest thing in your collection," replied Gabinius; " but it is amply paid for with four hundred drachmae."

" And this cylinder from Cyprus, with the elegant incised work ?" The steward was about to take up the polished crystal, but his hand was trembling with agitation and pushed instead of lifting it from the table. It rolled away on the floor and across the smooth mosaic picture as far as the couches. Keraunus was about to stoop to pick it up, but his daughters both held him back, and Selene cried out :

"Father, you must not; the physician strictly forbade it."

While the steward pushed the girls away grumbling, the dealer had gone down on his knees to pick up the cylinder, but it seemed to cost the slightly-built man much less effort to stoop than to get up again, for some minutes had elapsed before he once more stood on his feet, in front of Keraunus. His countenance had put on an expression of eager attention, and he once more took up the painting attributed to Apelles, sat down with it on the couch, and appeared wholly absorbed in the contemplation of the picture, which hid his face from the bystanders.

But his eye was not resting on the work before him, but on the marriage-scene at his feet, in which he detected each moment some fresh and unique beauty. As the dealer sat there for some minutes with the little picture on his knee, the steward's face brightened, Selene drew a deep breath, and Arsinoe went up to her father to cling to his arm and whisper in his ear:

" Do not let him have the Apelles cheap—remember my bracelet."

Gabinius now rose, glanced at the various objects lying on the table and said in a much shorter and more business-like tone than before:

" For all these things I can give you—wait a minute—twenty—seventy—four hundred—four hundred and fifty—I can give you six hundred and fifty drachmae, not a sesterce more !"

" You are joking," cried Keraunus.

" Not a sesterce more," answered the other coldly.

" I do not want to make anything, but you as a business man will understand that I do not wish to buy with a certain prospect of loss. As regards the Apelles—"

" Well ?"

" It may be of some value to me, but only under certain conditions. The case is quite different as regards buying pictures. Your two young damsels know of course that my line of business leads me to admire and value all that is beautiful, but still I must request you to leave me alone with your father for a little while. I want to speak with him about this curious painting."

Keraunus signed to his daughters, who immediately

left the room. Before the door was closed upon them
the dealer called after them :

"It is already growing dark, might I ask you to
send me as bright a light as possible by one of your
slaves."

"What about the picture ?" asked Keraunus.

"Till the light is brought let us talk of something
else," said Gabinius.

"Then take a seat on the couch," said Keraunus.
"You will be doing me a pleasure and perhaps yourself
as well."

As soon as the two men were seated on the divan,
Gabinius began :

"Those little things which we have collected with
particular liking, we do not readily part with—that I
know by long experience. Many a man who has come
into some property after he has sold all his little antiquities has offered me ten times the price I have paid
him to get them back again, generally in vain, unfortunately. Now, what is true of others is true of you,
and if you had not been in immediate need of money
you would hardly have offered me these things."

"I must entreat you," began the steward, but the
dealer interrupted him, saying :

"Even the richest are sometimes in want of ready
money; no one knows that better than I, for I—I
must confess—have large means at my command. Just
at present it would be particularly easy for me to free
you from all embarrassment."

"There stands my Apelles," exclaimed the steward.
"It is yours if you make a bid that suits me."

"The light—here comes the light !" exclaimed Gabinius, taking from the slave's hand the three-branched

lamp which Selene had hastily supplied with a fresh wick, and he placed it, while he murmured to Keraunus, " By your leave," down on the centre of the mosaic. The steward looked at the man on his left hand, with puzzled inquiry, but Gabinius heeded him not but went down on his knees again, felt the mosaic over with his hand, and devoured the picture of the marriage of Peleus with his eyes.

" Have you lost anything?" asked Keraunus.

" No—nothing whatever. There in the corner— now I am satisfied. Shall I place the lamp there, on the table? So—and now to return to business."

" I beg to do so, but I may as well begin by telling you that in my case it is a question not of drachmae but of Attic talents."*

" That is a matter of course, and I will offer you five; that is to say a sum for which you could buy a handsome roomy house."

Once more the blood mounted to the steward's head ; for a few minutes he could not utter a word, for his heart thumped violently; but presently he so far controlled himself as to be able to answer. This time, at any rate, he was determined to seize Fortune by the forelock and not to be taken advantage of, so he said:

" Five talents will not do; bid higher."

" Then let us say six."

" If you say double that we are agreed."

" I cannot put it beyond ten talents; why, for that sum you might build a small palace."

" I stand out for twelve."

" Well, be it so, but not a sesterce more."

" I cannot bear to part with my splendid work of

* The Attic talent was worth about £200, or 1,000 dollars.

art," sighed·Keraunus. "But I will take your offer, and give you my Apelles."

"It is not that picture I am dealing for," replied Gabinius. "It is of trifling value, and you may continue to enjoy the possession of it. It is another work of art in this room that I wish to have, and which has hitherto seemed to you scarcely worth notice. I have discovered it, and one of my rich customers has asked me to find him just such a thing."

"I do not know what it is."

"Does everything in this room belong to you?"

"Whom else should it belong to?"

"Then you may dispose of it as you please?"

"Undoubtedly."

"Very well, then—the twelve Attic talents which I offer you are to be paid for the picture that is under our feet."

"The mosaic! that? It belongs to the palace."

"It belongs to your residence, and that, I heard you say yourself, has been inhabited for more than a century by your forefathers. I know the law; it pronounces that everything which has remained in undisputed possession in one family, for a hundred years, becomes their property."

"This mosaic belongs to the palace."

"I assert the contrary. It is an integral portion of your family dwelling, and you may freely dispose of it."

"It belongs to the palace."

"No, and again no; you are the owner. To-morrow morning early you shall receive twelve Attic talents in gold, and, with the help of my son, later in the day I will take up the picture, pack it, and when it grows dark, carry it away. Procure a carpet to cover the empty place for the present. As to the secrecy of the transaction—I must of course insist on it as strongly—and more so—than yourself."

"The mosaic belongs to the palace," cried the stew-ard, this time in a louder voice, "Do you hear? it be-longs to the palace, and whoever dares touch it, I will break his bones."

As he spoke Keraunus stood up, his huge chest panting, his cheeks and forehead dyed purple, and his fist, which he held in the dealer's face, was trembling.

Gabinius drew back startled, and said:

"Then you will not have the twelve talents!"

"I will—I will!" gasped Keraunus, "I will show you how I beat those who take me for a rogue. Out of my sight, villain, and let me hear not another word about the picture, and the robbery in the dark, or I will send the prefect's lictors after you and have you thrown into irons, you rascally thief!"

Gabinius hurried to the door, but he there turned round once more to the groaning and gasping colos-sus, and cried out, as he stood on the threshold:

"Keep your rubbish! we shall have more to say to each other yet."

When Selene and Arsinoe returned to the sitting-room they found their father breathing hard and sitting on the couch, with his head drooping forward. Much alarmed, they went close up to him, but he exclaimed quite coherently:

"Water—a drink of water!—the thief!—the scoun-drel!"

Though hardly pressed, it had not cost him a strug-gle or a pang to refuse what would have placed him and his children in a position of ease; and yet he would not have hesitated to borrow it, aye, or twice the sum, from rich or poor, though he knew full certainly that he would never be in a position to restore it. Nor was he even proud of what he had done; it seemed to him quite natural in a Macedonian noble. It was to him altogether out of the pale of possibility that he should entertain the dealer's proposition for an instant.

But where was he to get the money for Ansinoe's outfit? how could he keep the promise given at the meeting?

He lay meditating on the divan for an hour; then he took a wax tablet out of a chest and began to write a letter on it to the prefect. He intended to offer the precious mosaic picture which had been discovered in his abode, to. Titianus for the Emperor, but he did not bring his composition to an end, for he became involved in high-flown phrases. At last he doubted whether it would do at all, flung the unfinished letter back into the chest, and disposed himself to sleep.

CHAPTER X.

WHILE anxiety and trouble were brooding over the steward's dwelling, while dismay and disappointment were clouding the souls of its inhabitants, the hall of the Muses was merry with feasting and laughter.

Julia, the prefect's wife, had supplied the architect at Lochias with a carefully-prepared meal, sufficient to fill six hungry maws, and Pontius' slave—who had received it on its arrival and had unpacked it dish after dish, and set them out on the humblest possible table—

haJ then hastened to fetch his master to inspect all these marvels of the cook's art. The architect shook his head as he contemplated the superabundant blessing, and muttered to himself:

"Titianus must take me for a crocodile, or rather for two crocodiles," and he went to the sculptor's little tabernacle, where Papias the master was also, to invite the two men to share his supper.

Besides them he asked two painters, and the chief mosaic worker of the city, who all day long had been busied in restoring the old and faded pictures on the ceilings and pavements, and under the influence of good wine and cheerful chat they soon emptied the dishes and bowls and trenchers. A man who for several hours has been using his hands or his mind, or both together, waxes hungry, and all the artists whom Pontius had brought together at Lochias had now been working for several days almost to the verge of exhaustion. Each had done his best, in the first place, no doubt, to give satisfaction to Pontius, whom all esteemed, and to himself; but also in the hope of giving proof of his powers to the Emperor and of showing him how things could be done in Alexandria. When the dishes had been removed and the replete feasters had washed and dried their hands, they filled their cups out of a jar of mixed wine, of which the dimensions answered worthily to the meal they had eaten. One of the painters then proposed that they should hold a regular drinking-bout, and elect Papias, who was as well known as a good table orator as he was as an artist, to be the leader of the feast. However, the master declared that he could not accept the honor, for that it was due to the worthiest of their company; to the man namely,

who, only a few days since, had entered this empty
palace and like a second Deucalion had raised up
illustrious artists, such as he then saw around him in
great numbers, and skilled workmen by hundreds, not
out of plastic stone but out of nothing. And then—
while declaring that he understood the use of the
hammer and chisel better than that of the tongue, and
that he had never studied the art of making speeches—
he expressed his wish that Pontius would lead the revel,
in the most approved form.

But he was not allowed to get to the end of this
evidence of his skill, for Euphorion the door-keeper of
the palace, Euphorion the father of Pollux, ran hastily
into the hall of the Muses with a letter in his hand
which he gave to the architect.

"To be read without an instant's delay," he added,
bowing with theatrical dignity to the assembled artists.
"One of the prefect's lictors brought this letter, which,
if my wishes be granted, brings nothing that is unwelcome. Hold your noise you little blackguards or I
will be the death of you."

These words, which so far as the tone was concerned, formed a somewhat inharmonious termination
to a speech intended for the ears of great artists, were
addressed to his wife's four-footed Graces who had
followed him against his wish, and were leaping round
the table barking for the slender remains of the consumed food.

Pontius was fond of animals and had made friends
with the old woman's pets, so, as he opened the prefect's letter, he said:

"I invite the three little guests to the remains of
our feast. Give them anything that is fit for them,

Euphorion, and whatever seems to you most suitable to your own stomach you may put into it."

While the architect first rapidly glanced through the letter and then read it carefully, the singer had collected a variety of good morsels for his wife's favorites on a plate, and finally carried the last remaining pasty, with the dish on which it reposed, to the vicinity of his own hooked nose.

" For men or for dogs?" he asked his son, as he pointed to it with a rigid finger.

" For the gods!" replied Pollux. " Take it to mother; she will like to eat ambrosia for once."

" A jolly evening to you!" cried the singer, bowing to the artists who were emptying their cups, and he quitted the hall with his pasty and his dogs. Before he had fairly left the hall with his long strides, Papias, whose speech had been interrupted, once more raised his wine-cup and began again:

" Our Deucalion, our more than Deucalion—"

" Pardon me," interrupted Pontius. " If I once more stop your discourse which began so promisingly; this letter contains important news and our revels must be over for the night. We must postpone our symposium and your drinking-speech."

" It was not a drinking-speech, for if ever there was a moderate man—" Papias began. But Pontius stopped him again, saying:

" Titianus writes me word that he proposes coming to Lochias this evening. He may arrive at any moment; and not alone, hut with my fellow-artist, Claudius Venator from Rome, who is to assist me with his advice."

" I never even heard his name," said Papias, who

was wont to trouble himself as little about the persons
as about the works of other artists.

"I wonder at that," said Pontius, closing the double
tablets which announced the Emperor's advent.

"Can he do anything?" asked Pollux.

"More than any one of us," replied Pontius. "He
is a mighty man."

"That is splendid!" exclaimed Pollux. "I like to
see great men. When one looks me in the eye I always
feel as if some of his superabundance overflowed into
me, and irresistibly I draw myself up and think how fine
it would be if one day I might reach as high as that
man's chin."

"Beware of morbid ambition," said Papias to his
pupil in a warning voice. "It is not the man who
stands on tiptoe, but he who does his duty diligently,
that can attain anything great."

"He honestly does his," said the architect rising,
and he laid his hand on the young sculptor's shoulder.
"We all do; to-morrow by sunrise each must be at his
post again. For my colleague's sake it will be well that
you should all be there in good time."

The artists rose, expressing their thanks and regrets.

"You will not escape the continuation of this evening's entertainment," cried one of the painters, and Papias, as he parted from Pontius, said:

"When we next meet I will show you what I understand by a drinking-speech. It will do perhaps for
your Roman guest. I am curious to hear what he will
say about our Urania. Pollux has done his share of
the work very well, and I have already devoted an
hour's work to it, which has improved it. The more
humble our material, the better I shall be pleased if the

work satisfies Caesar; he himself has tried his hand at sculpture."

" If only Hadrian could hear that !" cried one of the painters. " He likes to think himself a great artist—one of the foremost of our time. It is said that he caused the life of the great architect, Apollodorus—who carried out such noble works for Trajan—to be extinguished— and why ? because formerly that illustrious man had treated the imperial bungler as a mere dabbler, and would not accept his plan for the temple of Venus at Rome."

" Mere talk !" answered Pontius to this accusation. Apollodorus died in prison, but his incarceration had little enough to do with the Emperor's productions— excuse me, gentlemen, I must once more look through the sketches and plans."

The architect went away, but Pollux continued the conversation that had been begun by saying :

" Only I cannot understand how a man who prac- tises so many arts at once as Hadrian does, and at the same time looks after the state and its government, who is a passionate huntsman and who dabbles in every kind of miscellaneous learning, contrives, when he wants to practise one particular form of art, to recall all his five senses into the nest from which he has let them fly, here, there, and everywhere. The inside of . his head must be like that salad-bowl—which we have reduced to emptiness—in which Papias discovered three sorts of fish, brown and white meat, oysters and five other substances."

" And who can deny," added Papias, " that if talent is the father, and meat the mother of all productiveness, practice must be the artist's teacher ! Since Hadrian took to sculpture and painting it has become the universal fashion here to practise these arts, and among the wealthier youth who come to my workroom, many have very good abilities; but not one of them brings anything to any good issue, because so much of their time is taken up by the gymnasium, the bath, the quail-fights, the suppers, and I know not what besides, so that they do nothing by way of practice."

" True," said a painter. " Without the restraint and worry of apprenticeship no one can ever rise to happy and independent creativeness; and in the schools of rhetoric or in hunting or fighting no one can study drawing. It is not till a pupil has learned to sit steady and worry himself over his work for six hours on end that I begin to believe he will ever do any good work. Have you any of you seen the Emperor's work ?"

" I have," answered a mosaic worker. " Many years ago Hadrian sent a picture to me that he had painted; I was to make a mosaic from it. It was a fruit piece. Melons, gourds, apples, and green leaves. The drawing was but so-so, and the color impossibly vivid, still the composition was pleasing from its solidity and richness. And after all, when one sees it, one cannot but feel that such superfluity is better than meagreness and feebleness. The larger fruits, especially under the exuberant sappy foliage, were so huge that they might have been grown in the garden of luxury itself, still the whole had a look of reality. I mitigated the colors somewhat in my transcript; you may still see a copy of the picture at my house, it hangs in the studio where my men draw. Nealkes, the rich hanging-maker, has had a tapestry woven from it which Pontius proposes to use as a hanging for a wall of the work-room, but I have made a fine frame on purpose for it."

" Say rather for its designer."

" Or yet rather," added the most loquacious of the painters, " for the visit he may possibly pay your workshops."

" I only wish the Emperor may come to ours too! I should like to sell him my picture of Alexander saluted by the priests in the temple of Jupiter Ammon."

" I hope that when you agree about the price you will remember we are partners," said his fellow-artist smugly.

" I will follow your example strictly," replied the other.

" Then you will certainly not be a loser," cried Papias, " for Eustorgius is fully aware of the worth of his works. And if Hadrian is to order works from every master whose art he dabbles in, he will require a fleet on purpose to carry his purchases to Rome."

" It is said," continued Eustorgius, laughing, " that he is a painter among poets, a sculptor among painters, an astronomer among musicians, and a sophist among artists—that is to say, that he pursues every art and science with some success as his secondary occupation."

As he spoke the last words Pontius returned to the table where the artists were standing round the wine-jar; he had heard the painter's last remark and interrupted him by saying:

" But my friend you forget that he is a monarch among monarchs—and not merely among those of to-day—in the fullest meaning of the word. Each of us separately can produce something better and more perfect in his own line; but how great is the man who by

10

earnestness and skill can even apprehend everything
that the mind has ever been able to conceive of, or
the creative spirit of the artist to embody! I know
him, and I know that he loves a really thorough
master, and tries to encourage him with princely liberality. But his ears are everywhere, and he promptly
becomes the implacable enemy of those who provoke
his resentment. So bridle your restive Alexandrian
tongues, and let me tell you that my colleague from
Rome is in the closest intimacy with Hadrian. He is
of the same age, resembles him greatly, and repeats to
him everything that he hears said about him. So cease
talking about Caesar and pass no severer judgments on
dilettanti in the purple than on your wealthy pupils,
who paint and chisel for the mere love of it, and for
whom you find it so easy to lisp out 'charming,' or
'wonderfully pretty,' or 'remarkably nice.' Take my
warning in good part, you know I mean it well."

He spoke the last words with a cordial, manly feeling, of which his voice was peculiarly capable, and
which was always certain to secure him the confidence
even of the recalcitrant.

The artists exchanged greetings and hand-shakings
and left the hall; a slave carried away the wine-jar and
wiped the table, on which Pontius proceeded to lay out
his sketches and plans. But he was not alone, for
Pollux was soon at his side, and with a comical expression of pathos and laying his finger on his nose, he
said:

"I have come out of my cage to say something
more to you."

"Well ?"

"The hour is approaching when I may hope to re-

pay the beneficent deeds, which, at various times, you
have done to my interior. My mother will to-morrow
morning, set before you that dish of cabbage. It could
not be done sooner, because the only perfect sausage-
maker, the very king of his trade, prepares these savory
cylinders only once a week. A few hours ago he completed the making of the sausages, and to-morrow
morning my mother will warm up for our breakfasts the
noble mess, which she is preparing for us this evening—
for, as I have told you, it is in its warmed-up state that
it is the ideal of its kind. What will follow by way of
sweets we shall owe again to my mother's art; but the
cheering and invigorating element—I mean the wine
that ' drives dull care away,' we owe to my sister."

" I will come," said Pontius, " if my guest leaves
me an hour free, and I shall enjoy the excellent dish.
But what does a gay bird like you know of dull care ?"

" The words fit into the metre," replied Pollux. " I
inherit from my father—who, when he is not gate-keep-
ing, sings and recites—a troublesome tendency whenever anything incites me to drift into rhythm."

" But to-day you have been more silent than usual,
and yet you seemed to me to be extraordinarily content.
Not your face only, but your whole length—a good
measure—from the sole of your foot to the crown of
your head was like a brimming cask of satisfaction."

" Well, there is much that is lovely in this world !"
cried Pollux, stretching himself comfortably and lifting
his arms with his hands clasped far above his head towards heaven.

" Has anything specially pleasant happened to
you ?"

" There is no need for that ! Here I live in excellent company, the work progresses, and—well, why should I deny it? There was something specially to mark to-day; I met an old acquaintance again."

"An old one?"

"I have already known her sixteen years; but when I first saw her she was in swaddling clothes."

"Then this venerable damsel friend is more than sixteen, perhaps seventeen! Is Eros the friend of the happy, or does happiness only follow in his train?" As the architect thoughtfully said these words to him-self, Pollux listened attentively to a noise outside, and said:

"Who can be passing out there at this hour? Do you not hear the bark of a big dog mingle with the snapping of the three Graces?"

"It is Titianus conducting the architect from Rome," replied Pontius excitedly.

"I will go to meet him. But one thing more my friend, you too have an Alexandrian tongue. Beware of laughing at the Emperor's artistic efforts in the presence of this Roman. I repeat it: the man who is now coming is superior to us all, and there is nothing more repellant to me than when a small man assumes a strutting air of importance because he fancies he has discovered in some great man a weak spot where his own little body happens to be sound. The artist I am expecting is a grand man, but the Emperor Hadrian is a grander. Now retire behind your screens, and to-morrow morning I will be your guest."

CHAPTER XI.

PONTIUS threw his pallium over the chiton he commonly wore at his work and went forward to meet the sovereign of the world, whose arrival had been announced to him in the prefect's letter. He was perfectly calm, and if his heart beat a little faster than usual, it was only because he was pleased once more to meet the wonderful man whose personality had made a deep impression on him before.

In the happy consciousness of having done all that lay in his power and of deserving no blame, he went through the ante-chambers and chief entrance of the palace into the fore-court, where a crowd of slaves were busied by torch-light in laying new marble slabs. Neither these workmen nor their overseers had paid any heed to the barking of the dogs and the loud talking which had for some little time been audible in the vicinity of the gate-keeper's lodge; for a special rate of payment had been promised to the laborers and their foremen if they should have finished a set piece of the new pavement by a certain hour, to the satisfaction of the architect. No one who heard the deep man's-voice ring through the court from the doorway guessed to whom it belonged.

The Emperor had been delayed by adverse winds and had not run into the harbor till a little before midnight.

Titianus, who was watching for him, he greeted as an old friend with heartfelt warmth, and with him and

Antinous he stepped into the prefect's chariot, while
Phlegon the secretary, Hermogenes his physician, and
Mastor with the luggage, among which were their camp-
beds, were to follow in another vehicle. The harbor
watchmen hastened to array themselves indignantly to
oppose the chariot, as it rolled noisily along the street,
and the huge dog that destroyed the peace of the night
with its baying; but as soon as they recognized Titianus
they respectfully made way. The gate-keeper and his
wife, obedient to the prefect's warning, had remained
up, and as soon as the singer heard the chariot approaching which bore the Emperor, he hastened to
open the palace-gates. The broken-up pavement and
the swarms of men engaged in repairing it, obliged
Titianus and his companions to quit the chariot here and
to pass close to the little gate-house. Hadrian, whose
observation nothing ever escaped which came in his
way and seemed worth noticing, stood still before Euphorion's door and looked into the comfortable little
room, with its decoration of flowers and birds and the
statue of Apollo; while dame Doris in her newest garments, stood on the threshold to watch for the prefect.
And Titianus greeted her warmly, for he was wont
whenever he came to Lochias to exchange a few merry
or wise words with her. The little dogs had already
crept into their basket, but as soon as they caught
sight of a strange dog they rushed past their mistress
into the open air, and dame Doris found herself
obliged, while she returned the kindly greeting of her
patron, to shout at Euphrosyne, Thalia and Aglaia
more than once by their pretty names.

"Splendid, splendid!" cried Hadrian, pointing into
the little house. "An idyl, a perfect idyl. Who would

have expected to find such a smiling nook of peace in the most restless and busy town in the empire."

"I and Pontius were equally surprised at this little nest, and we therefore left it untouched," said the prefect.

"Intelligent people understand each other, and I owe you thanks for preserving this little home," answered the Emperor. "What an omen, what a favorable, in every way favorable augury, it offers me. The Graces receive me here into these old walls, Aglaia, Thalia and Euphrosyne !"

"Good luck to you, Master," old Doris called out to the prefect.

"We come late," said Hadrian.

"That does not matter," said the old woman. "Here at Lochias for the last week we have quite forgotten to distinguish day from night, and a blessing can never come too late."

"I have brought with me to-day an illustrious guest," said Titianus. "The great Roman architect Claudius Venator. He only disembarked a few minutes since."

"Then a draught of wine will do him good. We have in the house some good white Marcotic from my daughter's garden by the lake. If your friend will do us humble folks so much honor, I beg he will step into our room ; it is clean, is it not sir ? and the cup I will give him to drink it out of would not disgrace the Emperor himself. Who knows what you will find up in the midst of all the muddle yonder ?"

"I will accept your invitation with pleasure," answered Hadrian. "I can see by your face that you have a pleasure in entertaining us, and any one might envy you your little house."

"When the climbing-rose and the honey-suckle are out it is much prettier," said Doris, as she filled the cup. "Here is some water for mixing."

The Emperor took the cup carved by Pollux, looked at it with admiration, and before putting it to his lips said:

"A masterpiece, dame; what would Caesar find to drink out of here where the gate-keeper uses such a treasure? Who executed this admirable work, pray?"

"My son carved it for me in his spare time."

"He is a highly-skilled sculptor," Titianus explained.

When the Emperor had half emptied the cup with much satisfaction he set it on the table, and said:

"A very noble drink! I thank you, mother."

"And I you, for styling me mother: there is no better title a woman can have who has brought up good children; and I have three who need never be ashamed to be seen."

"I wish you all luck with them, good little mother," replied the Emperor. "We shall meet again, for I am going to spend some days at Lochias."

"Now, in all this bustle?" asked Doris.

"This great architect," said Titianus, in explanation, "is to advise and help our Pontius."

"He needs no help!" cried the old woman. "He is a man of the best stamp. His foresight and energy, my son says, are incomparable. I have seen him giving his orders myself, and I know a man when I see him!"

"And what particularly pleased you in him?" asked Hadrian, who was much amused with the shrewd old woman's freedom.

"He never for a moment loses his temper in all the

hurry, never speaks a word too much or too little; he
can be stern when it is necessary, but he is kind to his
inferiors. What his merits are as an artist I am not
capable of judging, but I am quite certain that he is a
just and able man."

"I know him myself," replied Caesar, "and you
describe him rightly; but he seemed to me sterner than
he has shown himself to you."

"Being a man he must be able to be severe; but
he is so only when it is necessary, and how kind he can
be he shows himself every day. A man grows to the
mould of his own mind when he is a great deal alone;
and this I have noticed, that a man who is repellant
and sharp to those beneath him is not in himself anything really great; for it shows that he considers it
necessary to guard against the danger of being looked
upon as of no more consequence than the poorer folks
he deals with. Now, a man of real worth knows that
it can be seen in his bearing, even when he treats one
of us as an equal. Pontius does so, and Titianus, and
you who are his friend, no less. It is a good thing
that you should have come—but, as I said before, the
architect up there can do very well without you."

"You do not seem to rate my capacity very highly,
and I regret it, for you have lived with your eyes open
and have learned to judge men keenly."

Doris looked shrewdly at the Emperor with her
kindly glance, as if taking his mental measure, and then
answered confidently:

"You—you are a great man too—it is quite pos-
sible that you might see things that would escape
Pontius. There are a few choice souls whom the
Muses particularly love and you are one of them."

" What leads you to suppose so ?"

" I see it in your gaze—in your brow."

" You have the gift of divination, then ?"

" No, I am not one of that sort; but I am the mother of two sons on whom also the Immortals have bestowed the special gift, which I cannot exactly describe. It was in them I first saw it, and wherever I have met with it since in other men and artists—they have been the elect of their circle.   And you too—I could swear to it, that you are foremost of the men among whom you live."

" Do not swear lightly," laughed the Emperor. " We will meet and talk together again little mother, and when I depart I will ask you again whether you have not been deceived in me.   Come now, Telemachus, the dame's birds seem to delight you very much."

These words were addressed to Antinous, who had been going from cage to cage contemplating the feathered pets, all sleeping snugly, with much curiosity and pleasure.

" Is that your son ?" asked Doris.

" No, dame, he is only my pupil; but I feel as if he were my son."

" He is a beautiful lad !"

" Why, the old lady still looks after the young men !"

" We do not give that up till we are a hundred or till the Parcae cut the thread of life."

" What a confession !"

" Let me finish my speech.—We never cease to take pleasure in seeing a handsome young fellow, but so long as we are young we ask ourselves what he may have in store for us, and as we grow old we are perfectly satisfied to be able to show him kindness. Listen young master. You will always find me here if you want anything in which I can serve you. I am like a snail and very rarely leave my shell."

"Till our next meeting," cried Hadrian, and he and his companions went out into the court.

There the difficulty was to find a footing on the disjointed pavement. Titianus went on in front of the Emperor and Antinous, and so but few words of friendly pleasure could be exchanged by the monarch and his vicegerent on the occasion of their meeting again. Hadrian stepped cautiously forward, his face wearing meanwhile a satisfied smile. The verdict passed by the simple shrewd woman of the people had given him far greater pleasure than the turgid verse in which Mesomedes and his compeers were wont to sing his praises, or the flattering speeches with which he was loaded by the sophists and rhetoricians.

The old woman had taken him for no more than an artist; she could not know who he was, and yet she had recognized—or had Titianus been indiscreet? Did she know or suspect whom she was talking to? Hadrian's deeply suspicious nature was more and more roused; he began to fancy that the gate-keeper's wife had learnt her speech by heart, and that her welcome had been preconcerted; he suddenly paused and desired the prefect to wait for him, and Antinous to remain behind with the dog. He turned round, retraced his steps to the gate-house and slipped close up to it in a very unprincely way. He stood still by the door of the little house which was still open, and listened to the conversation between Doris and her husband.

"A fine tall man," said Euphorion, "he is a little like the Emperor."

"Not a bit," replied Doris. "Only think of the full-length statue of Hadrian in the garden of the Paneum; it has a dissatisfied satirical expression, and the architect has a grave brow, it is true, but pure friendly kindness lights up his features. It is only the beard that reminds you of the one when you look at the other. Hadrian might be very glad if he were like the prefect's guest."

"Yes, he is handsomer—how shall I say it—more like the gods than that cold marble figure," Euphorion declared. "A grand noble, he is no doubt, but still an artist too; I wonder whether he could be induced by Pontius or Papias or Aristeas or one of the great painters to take the part of Calchas the soothsayer in our group at the festival? He would perform it in quite another way than that dry stick Philemon the ivory carver. Hand me my lute; I have already forgotten again the beginning of the last verse. Oh! my wretched memory! Thank you."

Euphorion loudly struck the strings and sang in a voice that was still tolerably sweet and very well trained:

"'Sabina hail! Oh Sabina!—Hail; victorious hail to the conquering goddess Sabina!' If only Pollux were here he would remind me of the right words. 'Hail; victorious hail, to the thousandfold Sabina!'—That is nonsense. 'Hail, hail! divine hail to thee O all-conquering Sabina.' No it was not that either. If a crocodile would only swallow this Sabina I would give him that hot cake in yonder dish with pleasure, for his pudding. But stay—I have it. 'Hail, a thousand-fold hail to the conquering goddess Sabina!'"

Hadrian had heard all he wanted; while Euphorion went on repeating his line a score or more of times to impress it on his recalcitrant memory. Caesar turned his back on the gate-house, and while he and his companions picked their way not without difficulty through the workmen who squatted here and there and everywhere on the ground, he clapped Titianus more than once on his shoulder, and after he had been received and welcomed by Pontius, he exclaimed:

" I bless my decision to come here now! I have had a good evening, a quite delightful evening."

The Emperor had not felt so cheerful and free from care for years as on this occasion, and when in spite of the late hour he found the workmen still busy everywhere, and saw all that had already been restored in the old palace and what was being done for its renovation, the restless man could not resist expressing his satisfaction, and exclaimed to Antinous:.

" Here we may see that even in our sordid times miracles may be wrought by good-will, industry, and skill. Explain to me my good Pontius how you were able to construct that enormous scaffold."

CHAPTER XII.

MORE pleasant hours were to follow on the amusing arrival of the Emperor at his half-finished residence at Lochias that night. Pontius proposed to him to inspect several well-preserved rooms, which had in the first instance been reserved for the gentlemen of his suite ; and one of these with an open outlook on the harbor, the town, and the island of Antirrhodus he suggested should be provisionally furnished for the Emperor's reception. Thanks to the architect's foresight, to Mastor's practised hand, and to the numbers of men employed in the palace who were accustomed to all kinds of service—provision was soon made for the night, for Hadrian and his companions. The comfortable couch which the prefect had sent to Lochias for Pontius was carried into the Emperor's sleeping-room, and the camp-beds for Antinous and the suite were soon set up in the other rooms. Tables, pillows, and various household vessels which had already been sent in from the manufactories of Alexandria, and which stood packed in bales and cases in the large central court of the palace were soon taken out, and so far as they were applicable for use were carried into the hastily-arranged rooms. Even before Hadrian, under the prefect's guidance, had reached the last room in which restorations were being carried out, Pontius was ready with his arrangements, and could assure the Emperor that to-night he would find a good bed and very tolerable quarters, and that by to-morrow he should have a really elegantly-furnished room.

"Charming, quite delightful," cried the Emperor, as he entered his room. "One might fancy you had some industrious demons at your command. Pour some water over my hands, Mastor, and then to supper ! I am as hungry as a beggar's dog."

"I think we shall find all you need," replied Titianus, while Hadrian washed his hands and his bearded face.

"Have you eaten all that I sent down to Lochias to-day, my dear Pontius ? "

"Alas! we have," sighed Pontius.

"But I gave orders that a supper for five should be sent."

"It sufficed for six hungry artists," answered the architect, "if only I could have guessed for whom the food was intended! And now what is to be done? There are wine and bread still in the hall of the Muses, meanwhile——"

"That must satisfy us," said the Emperor, as he wiped his face. "In the Dacian war, in Numidia, and often when out hunting, I have been glad if only one or the other was to be obtained."

Antinous, who was very hungry and tired, made a melancholy face at these words of his master, and Hadrian perceiving it, added with a smile:

"But youth needs something more to live upon than bread and wine. You pointed out to me just now the residence of the palace-steward. Might we not find there a morsel of meat or cheese, or something of the kind?"

"Hardly," replied Pontius "for the man stuffs his fat stomach and his eight children with bread and porridge. But an attempt will at any rate be worth making."

"Then send to him; but conduct us at once to the hall where the Muses have preserved some bread and wine for me and these good fellows, though they do not always provide them for their disciples."

Pontius at once conducted the Emperor into the hall. On the way thither, Hadrian asked:

"Is the steward so miserably paid that he is forced to content himself with such meagre fare?"

"He has a residence rent free, and two hundred drachmae a month."

"That is not so very little. What is the man's name, and of what kith and kin is he?"

"He is called Keraunus, and is of ancient Macedonian descent. His ancestors from time immemorial have held the office he now fills, and he even supposes himself to be related to the extinct royal dynasty through the mistress of some one of the Lagides. Keraunus sits in the town council and never stirs out in the streets without his slave, who is one of the sort which the merchants in the slave market throw into the bargain with the buyer. He is as fat as a stuffed pig, dresses like a senator, loves antiquities and curiosities, for which he will let himself be cheated of his last coin, and bears his poverty with more of pride than of dignity; and still he is an honorable man, and can be made useful, if he is taken on the right side."

"Altogether a queer fellow. And you say he is fat, is he jolly?"

"As far from it as possible."

"Ah, people who are fat and cross are my aversion. What is this by way of an erection?"

"Behind that screen works Papias' best scholar. His name is Pollux, and he is the son of the couple who keep the gate-house. You will be pleased with him."

"Call him here," said the Emperor.

But before the architect could comply with his desire the sculptor's head had appeared above the screen. The young man had heard the approaching voices and steps; he greeted the prefect respectfully from his elevated position, and after satisfying his curiosity was about to spring down from the stool on which he had climbed when Pontius called to him that Claudius

Venator, the architect from Rome, wished to make his acquaintance.

"That is very kind in him, and still more kind in you," Pollux answered from above, "since it is only from you that he can know that I exist beneath the moon, and use the hammer and chisel. Allow me to descend from my four-legged cothurnus, for at present you are forced to look up to me, and from all I have heard of your talents from Pontius, nothing can be more absolutely the reverse of what it ought to be."

"Nay, stop where you are," answered Hadrian. "We, as fellow-artists, may waive ceremony.—What are you doing in there?"

"I will push the screen back in a moment and show you our Urania. It is very good for an artist to hear the opinion of a man who thoroughly understands the thing."

"Presently, friend—presently; first let me enjoy a scrap of bread, for the severity of my hunger might very possibly influence my judgment."

As he was speaking the architect offered the Emperor a salver with bread, salt, and a cup of wine, which his own slave had carried to him. When Pollux observed this modest meal, he called out:

"That is prisoners' fare, Pontius; have we nothing better in the house than that?"

"Possibly you yourself assisted in demolishing the dainty dishes I had sent down for the architect," cried Titianus, pretending to threaten him.

"You are defacing a fair memory," sighed the sculptor, with mock melancholy. "But, by Hercules, I did my fair share of the work of destruction. If only now—but stay! I have an idea worthy of Aristotle

11

himself! that breakfast, to which I invited you to-
morrow morning, most noble Pontius, is all ready at
my mother's, and can be warmed up in a few minutes.
Do not be alarmed, worthy sir, but the dish in question
is cabbage with sausages—a mess which, like the soul
of an Egyptian, possesses at the instant of resurrection,
nobler qualities than when it first sees the light."

"Excellent," cried Hadrian. "Cabbage and sausages!" He wiped his full lips with his hand, smiling
with gratification, and he broke into a hearty laugh of
amusement as he heard a loud "Ah!" of satisfaction
from Antinous, who drew nearer to the canvas screen.
"There is another whose mouth waters and whose
imagination revels in a happy future," said the Emperor
to the prefect, pointing to his favorite.

But he had misinterpreted the lad's exclamation, for
it was the mere name of the dish—which his mother
had often set on the table of his humble home in Bithynia—which reminded him of his native country and his
childhood, and transplanted him in thought back into
their midst. It was a swift leap at his heart, and not
merely the pleasant watering of his gums, that had
forced the "Ah" to his lips. Still, he was glad to see
his native dish again, and would not have exchanged it
against the richest banquet. Pollux had meanwhile
come out of his nook, and said:

"In a quarter of an hour I shall set before you the
breakfast which has been turned into a supper. Miti-
gate your worst hunger with some bread and salt,
and then my mother's cabbage-stew will not only
satisfy you, but will be enjoyed with calm appreci-
ation."

"Greet dame Doris from me," Hadrian called after

the sculptor; and when Pollux had quitted the hall he turned to Titianus and Pontius and said :

"What a splendid young fellow. I am curious to see what he can do as an artist."

"Then follow me," replied Pontius, leading the way.

"What do you say to this Urania? Papias made the head of the Muse, but the figure and the drapery Pollux formed with his own hand in a few days."

The imperial artist stood in front of the statue, with his arms crossed, and remained there for some time in silence. Then he nodded his bearded head approvingly, and said gravely :

"A well-considered work, and carried out with re-markable freedom; this mantle drawn over the bosom would not disgrace a Phidias. All is broad, character-istic and true. Did the young artist work from the model here at Lochias?"

"I have seen no model, and I believe that he evolved the whole figure out of his head," replied Pontius.

"Impossible, perfectly impossible," cried the Em-peror, in the tone of a man who knows well what he is talking about. "Such lines, such forms not Praxiteles himself could have invented. He must have seen them, have formed them as he stood face to face with the living copy. We will ask him. What is to be made out of that newly-set-up mass of clay?"

"Possibly the bust of some princess of the house of the Lagides. To-morrow you shall see a head of Berenice by our young friend, which seems to me to be one of the best things ever done in Alexandria."

"And is the lad a proficient in magic?" asked

Hadrian. "It seems to me simply impossible that he
should have completed this statue and a woman's bust
in these few days."

Pontius explained to the Emperor that Pollux had
mounted the head on a bust already to hand, and as he
answered his questions without reserve, he revealed to
him what stupendous exertions of the arts had been
called into requisition to give the dilapidated palace a
suitable and, in its kind, even brilliant appearance. He
frankly confessed that here he was working only for
effect, and talked to Hadrian exactly as he would have
discussed the same subject with any other fellow-artist.

While the Emperor and the architect were thus
eagerly conversing, and the prefect was hearing from
Phlegon, the secretary, all the experience of their journey, Pollux reappeared in the hall of the Muses accompanied by his father. The singer carried before him a
steaming mess, fresh cakes of bread, and the pasty
which a few hours previously he had carried home to his
wife from the architect's table. Pollux held to his
breast a tolerably large two-handled jar full of Mareotic
wine, which he had hastily wreathed with branches of
ivy.

A few minutes later the Emperor was reclining on a
mattress that had been laid for him, and was making
his way valiantly through the savory mess. He was in
the happiest humor; he called Antinous and his secretary, heaped abundant portions with his own hand on
their plates, which he bade them hold out to him,
declaring as he did so that it was to prevent their fishing
the best of the sausages out of the cabbage for themselves. He also spoke highly of the Mareotic wine.

When they came to opening the pasty the expression

of his face changed ; he frowned and asked the prefect
in a suspicious tone, severely and sternly :

"How came these people by such a pasty as this ?"

"Where did you get it from ?" asked the prefect of
the singer.

"From the banquet which the architect gave to the
artists here," answered Euphorion. "The bones were
given to the Graces and this dish, which had not been
touched, to me and my wife. She devoted it with
pleasure to Pontius' guest."

Titianus laughed and exclaimed :

"This then accounts for the total disappearance of
the handsome supper which we sent down to the architect. This pasty—allow me to look at it—this pasty
was prepared by a recipe obtained from Verus. He
invited us to breakfast yesterday and instructed my cook
how to prepare it."

"No Platonist ever propagated his master's doctrines
with greater zeal than Verus does the merits of this
dish," said the Emperor, who had recovered his good
humor as soon as he perceived that no artful preparation for his arrival was to be suspected in this matter.
"What follies that spoilt child of fortune can commit ! Does he still insist on cooking with his own
hands ?"

"No, not quite that," replied the prefect. "But he
had a couch placed for him in the kitchen on which he
stretched himself at full length and told my cook exactly
how to prepare the pasty, of which you are—I should
say, of which the Emperor is particularly fond. It consists of pheasant, ham, cow's udder and a baked crust."

"I am quite of Hadrian's opinion," laughed the
Emperor. doing all justice to the excellent pie. "You

entertain me splendidly my friend, and I am very much
your debtor. What did you say your name is young
man ?"

" Pollux."

"Your Urania, Pollux, is a fine piece of work, and
Pontius says you executed the drapery without a model.
I said, and I repeat, that it is simply impossible."

"You judge rightly, a young girl stood for it."

The Emperor glanced at the architect, as much as
to say, I knew it ! Pontius asked in astonishment :

" When ?   I have never seen a female form within
these walls."

"Recently."

" But I have never quitted Lochias for a minute.   I
have never gone to rest before midnight, and have been
on my legs again long before sunrise."

"But still there were several hours between your
going to sleep, and waking up again," replied Pollux.

" Ah, youth—youth!" exclaimed the Emperor, and a
satirical smile played upon his lips.   " Part Damon and
Phyllis by iron doors, and they will find their way to
each other through the key-hole."

Euphorion looked seriously at his son, the architect
shook his head and refrained from further questions, but
Hadrian rose from his couch, dismissed Antinous and
his secretary to bed, requested Titianus to go home and
to give his wife his kindly greetings, and then desired
Pollux to conduct him within this screen, since he himself was not tired and was accustomed to do with only
a few hours sleep.

The young sculptor was strongly attracted by this
commanding personage.   It had not escaped him
that the gray-bearded stranger greatly resembled the

Emperor; but Pontius had prepared him for the likeness, and in fact there was much in the eyes and mouth
of the Roman architect that he had never traced in any
portrait of Hadrian 'Imperator.' And as they stood
before his scarcely-finished statue his respect increased
for the new visitor to Lochias; for, with earnest frankness, he pointed out to him certain faults, and while
praising the merits of the rapidly-executed figure he
explained in a few brief and pithy phrases his own conception of the ideal Urania. Then shortly but clearly,
he stated his views as to how the plastic artist must deal
with the problems of his art.

The young man's heart beat faster, and more than
once he turned hot and cold by turns as he heard things
uttered by the bearded lips of this imposing man, in a
rich voice and in lucid phrases, which he had often
divined or vaguely felt, but for which, while learning,
observing, and working, he had never sought expression
in words. And how kindly the great master took up
his timid observations, how convincingly he answered
them. Such a man as this he had never met, never
had he bowed with such full consent before the superiority and sovereign power of another mind.

The second hour after midnight had begun, when
Hadrian, standing before the rough-cast clay bust, asked
Pollux:

" What is this to be ? "

" A portrait of a girl."

" Probably of the complaisant model who ventures
into Lochias at night ? "

" No ; a lady of rank will sit to me."

" An Alexandrian ? "

" Oh, no. A beauty in the train of the Empress."

" What is her name ?   I know all the Roman ladies."
" Balbilla."

" Balbilla ?   There are many of that name.   What is she like, the lady you mean ? " asked Hadrian, with a cunning glance of amusement.

"That is easier to ask than to answer," replied the artist, who, seeing his gray-bearded companion smile, recovered his gay vivacity   " But stay—you have seen a peacock spread its tail—now only imagine that every eye in the train of Hera's bird was a graceful round curl, and that in the middle of the circle there was a charming, intelligent girl's face, with a merry little nose, and a rather too high forehead, and you will have the portrait of the young damsel who has graciously permitted me to model from her person."

Hadrian laughed heartily, threw off his cloak, and exclaimed :

" Stand aside—I know your maiden—and if I mean a different one you shall tell me."

While he was still speaking he had plunged his powerful hands into the yielding clay, and kneading and pinching like a practised modeller, wiping off and pressing on, he formed a woman's face with a towering structure of curls, which resembled Babilla, but which reproduced every conspicuous peculiarity with such whimsical exaggeration that Pollux could not contain his delight.   When at last Hadrian stepped back from the happy caricature and called upon him to say whether that were not indeed the Roman lady, Pollux exclaimed :

" It is as surely she, as you are not merely a great architect, but an admirable sculptor.   The thing is coarse, but unmistakably characteristic."

The Emperor himself seemed to enjoy his artistic joke hugely, for he looked at it, and laughed again and again. Pontius, however, seemed to view it differently; he had listened with eager sympathy to the conversation between Hadrian and the sculptor, and had watched the former as he began his work; but as it went on he turned away, for he hated that distortion of fine forms, which he often found that the Egyptians took a special delight in. It was positively painful to him to see a graceful, highly-gifted and defenceless creature, to whom, too, he felt himself bound by ties of gratitude, mocked at in this way by such a man as Hadrian. He had only to-day met Balbilla for the first time, but he had heard from Titianus that she was staying at the Caesareum with the Empress, and the prefect had also told him that she was the granddaughter of that same governor, Claudius Balbillus, who had granted freedom to his own grandfather, a learned Greek slave.

He had met her with grateful sympathy and devotion; her bright and lively nature had delighted him, and at each thoughtless word she uttered he would have liked to give her some warning sign, as though she were near to him through some tie of blood, or some old established friendship that might warrant his right to do so. The defiant, half gallant way in which Verus, the dissipated lady-killer, had spoken to her had enraged him and filled him with anxiety, and long after the illustrious visitors had left Lochias he had thought of her again and again, and had resolved, if it were possible, to keep a watchful eye on the descendant of the benefactor of his family. He felt it as a sacred duty to shelter and protect her, seeming to him as she did, an airy, pretty, defenceless song-bird.

The Emperor's caricature had the same effect on his feelings as though some one had insulted and scorned, before his eyes, something that ought to be regarded as sacred. And there stood the monarch, a man no longer young, gazing at his performance and never weary of the amusement it afforded him. It pained Pontius keenly, for like all noble natures, he could not bear to discover anything mean or vulgar in a man to whom he had always looked up as to a strong exceptional character. As an artist Hadrian ought not to have vilified beauty, as a man he ought not to have insulted unprotected innocence.

In the soul of the architect, who had hitherto been one of the Emperor's warmest admirers, a slight aversion began to dawn, and he was glad, when, at last, Hadrian decided to withdraw to rest.

The Emperor found in his room every requisite he was accustomed to use, and while his slave undressed him, lighted his night-lamp and adjusted his pillows, he said :

" This is the best evening I have enjoyed for years— Is Antinous comfortably in bed ? "

" As much so as in Rome."

" And the big dog ? "

" I will lay his rug in the passage at your door."

" Has he had any food ?"

" Bones, bread and water."

" I hope you have had something to eat this evening."

"I was not hungry, and there was plenty of bread and wine."

" To-morrow we shall be better supplied. Now, good-night. Weigh your words for fear you should be·

tray me. A few days here undisturbed would be delightful ! "

With these words the Emperor turned over on his
couch and was soon asleep.

Mastor, too, lay down to rest after he had spread a rug
for the dog in the corridor outside the Emperor's sleeping-room. His head rested on a curved shield of stout
cowhide under which lay his short sword ; the bed was
but a hard one, but Mastor had for years been used to
rest on nothing better, and still had enjoyed the dreamless slumbers of a child; but to-night sleep avoided
him, and from time to time he pressed his hand on his
wearily open eyes to wipe away the salt dew which rose
to them again and again. For a long time he had re-
strained these tears bravely enough, for the Emperor
liked to see none but cheerful faces among his servants;
nay, he had once said that it was in consequence of his
bright eyes that he had entrusted to him the care of his
person. Poor, cheerful Mastor ! He was nothing but
a slave, still he had a heart which lay open to joy and
suffering, to pleasure and trouble, to hatred and to love.

In his childhood his native village had fallen into the
hands of the foes of his race. He and his brother had
been carried away as slaves, first into Asia Minor, and
then as they were both particularly pretty fair-haired
boys, to Rome. There they had been bought for the
Emperor; Mastor had been chosen to wait on Hadrian's
person, his brother had been put to work in the gardens.
Nothing was lacking to either except his liberty; nothing
tormented them but their longing for their native home,
and even this altogether faded away after he had married the pretty little daughter of a superintendent of the
gardens, a slave like himself. She was a lively little

woman with sparkling eyes, whom no one could pass by without noticing.

The slave's duties left him but little time to enjoy the society of his pretty partner and of the two children she bore him, but the consciousness of possessing them made him happy when he followed his master to the chase, or in the journeys through the empire. Now, for seven months he had heard nothing of his family; but a short letter had reached him at Pelusium, which had been sent with the despatches for the Emperor from Ostia to Egypt. He could not read, and in consequence of the Emperor's rapid travelling, it was not till he reached Lochias, that he was put in possession of its contents.

Before going to rest Antinous had read him the letter, which had been written for his brother by a public scribe, and its contents were enough to wreck the heart even of a slave. His pretty little wife had fled from her home and from the Emperor's service to follow a Greek ship's captain across the world; his eldest child, a boy, the darling of his heart, was dead; and his fair-haired tender little Tullia, with her pearly teeth, her round little arms, and her pretty tiny fingers that had often tried to pull his close-cropped hair, and had fondly stroked and patted it, had been carried off to the miserable refuge, under whose squalid roof the children of deceased slaves were reared. Only two hours since, and in fancy he had possessed a home, and a group of human beings, whom he could love. Now, this was all over and with however hard a hand the deepest woes might fall on him, he might not sob or groan aloud, or even roll from side to side as again and again he was violently prompted to do, for his lord slept lightly and the least noise might wake him. At sunrise he must appear before the Emperor as cheerful as usual, and yet he felt as if he must himself perish miserably as his happiness had done. His heart was bursting with anguish, still he neither groaned nor stirred.

CHAPTER XIII.

THE night had been almost as sleepless to Keraunus' daughter Selene as it had been to the hapless slave. Her father's vain wish to let Arsinoe take a part with the daughters of the wealthier citizens had filled the girl's heart with fresh terrors. It was the final blow which would demolish the structure of their social existence, standing as it did on quaking ground, and which must fling her family and herself into disgrace and want. When their last treasure of any value was sold, and the creditors could no longer be put off, particularly during the Emperor's presence in the city, when they should try to sell up all her father's little property, or to carry him off to a debtor's prison, was it not then as good as certain that some one else would be appointed to fill his place, and that she and the other children would fall into misery? And there lay Arsinoe by her side, and slept with as calm and deep a breath as blind Helios and the other little ones.

Before going to bed she had tried with all the fervency and eloquence of which she was mistress, to persuade, entreat, and implore the heedless girl to refuse as postively as she herself had refused to take any part in the processions; but Arsinoe had at first repulsed her

crossly, and finally had defiantly declared that means
might yet very likely be found, and that what her father
permitted, Selene had no right to interfere in, still less to
forbid.   And when afterwards she saw Arsinoe sleeping
so calmly by her side, she felt as if she would like to
shake her; but she was so accustomed to bear all the
troubles of the family alone, and to be unkindly repelled by her sister whenever she attempted to ad-
monish her, that she forbore.

Arsinoe had a good and tender heart; but she was
young, pretty, and vain.   With affectionate persuasion
she might be won over to anything, but Selene, whenever she remonstrated with her, made her feel her
superiority over herself, acquired from her care of the
family and her maternal character.   Thus, not a day
passed without some quarrelling and tears between these
two sisters who were so dissimilar, and yet, both so well
disposed.   Arsinoe was always the first to offer her
hand for a reconciliation, but Selene would rarely have
a kinder answer ready to her affectionate advances than,
" Let be," or " Oh yes, I know !" and their outward intercourse bore an aspect of coolness, which was easily
worked up to an outbreak of hostile speeches.   Hundreds of times they would go to bed without wishing
each other ' good-night,' and still more often would
they avoid any morning greeting when they first met in
the day.

Arsinoe liked talking, but in Selene's presence she
was taciturn; there were few things in which Selene
took pleasure, while her sister delighted in every thing
which can charm youth.   It was the steward's eldest
daughter who attended to the daily needs of the children, their food and clothes; it was the second who

superintended their games, and their dolls. The eldest watched and taught them with anxious care, detecting in every little fault the germ of some evil tendency in the future, while the other enticed them into follies, it is true, but opened their minds to joyous impressions, and attained more by kisses and kind words than Selene could by fault-finding. The children would call Selene when they wanted her, but would fly to Arsinoe as soon as they saw her. Their hearts were hers, and Selene felt this bitterly; it seemed to her to be unjust, for she saw clearly that her sister could reap, from mere frivolous play in her idle hours, a sweeter reward than she could earn by the anxiety, trouble and exhausting toil, in which she often spent her nights.

But children are not unjust in this way. It is true that they keep an account in their heart and not in their head. Those who give them the warmth of affection they pay back most honestly.

On this particular night it was not, it is certain, with very sisterly feelings that Selene looked at the sleeping Arsinoe, and the words on the girl's lips as she had dropped asleep, had sounded very unkind; but, nevertheless, they felt warmly towards each other, and any one who should have attempted to say a word against the one in the presence of the other would soon have found out how close a bond held together these two hearts, dissimilar as they were. But no girl of nineteen can pass a night altogether without sleeping, however sadly she may turn and turn over and over again in her bed. So slumber overmastered Selene every now and then for a quarter of an hour, and each time she dreamed of her sister.

Once she saw Arsinoe dressed out like a queen, fol-

lowed by beggar children and pelted with bad words—
then she saw her on the rotunda below the balcony
romping with Pollux, and in their bold sport they broke
her mother's bust.   At last she dreamed that she herself was playing—as in the days of her childhood—in
the gate-keeper's garden with the sculptor.   They were
making cakes of sand together, and Arsinoe jumped on
the cakes as soon as they were made, and trod them
all into dust.

The pretty pale girl had for a long time ceased to
know the refreshing, dreamless, sound sleep of youth,
for the sweetest slumbers are more apt to seek out those
who by day have some rest, than those who are worn
out by fatigue, and evening after evening Selene was
one of these.   Every night she had dreams, but to-
night they were almost exclusively sad in character, and
so terrifying that she woke herself repeatedly with her
own groaning, or disturbed Arsinoe's peaceful sleep by
loud cries.

These cries did not disturb her father, he—to-night,
as every night—had begun to snore soon after he had
gone to rest, never to cease till it was time to rise again.

Selene was always busy in the house before any
one, even before the slaves; and the approach of day
this time seemed to the sleepless girl a real release.
When she rose it was still perfectly dark, but she knew
that the rising of the December sun could not be long
to wait for.

Without paying any heed to the sleepers, or making
any special effort to tread noiselessly, or to do what she
had to do without disturbing them, she lighted her little
lamp, at the night-lamp, washed herself, arranged her
hair, and then knocked at the doors of the old slaves.

As soon as they had yawned out " directly," or a sleepy " very well," she went into her father's room and took his jug to fetch him fresh water in it. The best well in the palace was on a small terrace on the west side; it was supplied by the city aqueducts, and was constructed of five marble monsters, bearing up on twisted fish-tails a huge shell, in which sat a bearded river-god. Their horse-shaped heads poured water into a vast basin, which, in the lapse of centuries, had grown full of a green and filmy vegetation.

In order to reach this fountain, Selene had to go along the corridor where lay the rooms occupied by the Emperor and his followers. She only knew that an architect from Rome had taken up his quarters at Lochias, for, some time after midnight, she had been to get out meat and salt for him, but in what rooms the strangers had been lodged no one had told her. But this morning as she followed the path she was accustomed to tread day by day at the same hour, she felt an anxious shiver. She felt as if everything were not quite the same as usual, and just as she had set her foot on the top step of the flight leading to the corridor, she raised her lamp to discover whence came the sound she thought she could hear, she perceived in the gloom a fearful something, which as she approached it resembled a dog, and which was larger—much larger—than a dog should be.

Her blood ran cold with terror; for a few moments she stood as if spellbound, and was only conscious that the growling and snarling that she heard meant mischief and threatening to herself. At last she found strength to turn to fly, but at the same instant a loud and furious bark echoed behind her and she heard the monster's

12

quick leaps as he flew after her along the stone pavement.

She felt a violent shock, the pitcher flew out of her
hand and was shattered into a thousand fragments, and
she sank to the ground under the weight of a warm,
rough, heavy mass.   Her loud cries of alarm resounded
from the hard bare walls, and roused the sleepers and
brought them to her side.

"See what it is," cried Hadrian to his slave, who
had immediately sprung up and seized his shield and
sword.

"The dog has attacked a woman who wanted to
come this way," replied Mastor.

"Hold him off, but do not beat him," the Emperor
shouted after him.   "Argus has only done his duty."

The slave hastened down the passage as fast as possible, loudly calling the dog by his name.   But another
had been beforehand and had dragged him off his victim, and this was Antinous, whose room was close to
the scene of action, and who, as soon as he had heard
the dog's bark and Selene's scream, had hurried to hold
back the brute which was really dangerous when on
guard and in the dark.

When Mastor appeared the lad had just succeeded
in dragging the dog away from Selene, who was lying
on the stairs leading to the corridor.   Before Antinous
could reach her Argus was standing over her gnashing
his teeth and growling.   Argus, who was quickly quieted
by his friends' tone of kindly admonition, stood aside
silent and with his head down, while Antinous knelt by
the senseless girl on whom the pale light of early dawn
fell through a wide window.   The boy looked with
alarm on her pale face, lifted her helpless arm, and

sought on her light-colored dress for any trace of blood
that might have been drawn, but in vain.   After he
had assured himself that she still breathed, and that her
lips moved, he called to Mastor :

" Argus seems only to have pulled her down, not to
have wounded her ; she has lost consciousness however.
Go quickly into my room and bring me the blue phial
out of my medicine-case and a cup of water."

The slave whistled to the hound and obeyed the
order as quickly as possible.

Meanwhile Antinous remained on his knees by the
senseless girl, and ventured to raise her head with its
long soft weight of hair.   How beautiful were those
marble-white, and nobly-cut features ! How touching did
the silent accent of pain that lay on her lips seem to
him, and how happy was the spoilt darling of the Emperor, who was loved by all who saw him, to be able to
be tender and helpful, unasked !

" Wake up, oh ! wake up!" he cried to Selene—and
when still she did not move, he repeated more urgently
and tenderly, " Pray, pray wake up."

But she did not hear him, and remained motionless
even when, with a slight blush, he drew over her
shoulder her peplum, which the dog had torn away.
Now Mastor returned with the water and the blue
phial, and gave them to the Bithynian. While Antinous
laid the girl's head in his lap, the slave was hurrying
away, saying: " Caesar called me."

The lad moistened Selene's forehead with the revi-
ving fluid, made her inhale the strong essence which the
phial contained, and cried again loud and earnestly,
" Wake, wake."—And presently her lips parted, showing her small, white teeth, and then she slowly raised

the lids which had veiled her eyes. With a deep sigh
of relief he set the cup and the phial on the ground so
as to support her when she slowly began to raise herself; but, scarcely had he turned his face towards her,
when she sprang up suddenly and violently, and flinging both her arms round his neck, cried out :

"Save me, Pollux, save me! The monster is devouring me." Antinous much startled, seized the girl's
arms to release himself from their embrace, but, she had
already freed him and sunk back on to the ground.
The next moment she was shivering violently as if from
an attack of fever; again she threw up her hands,
pressed them to her temples, and gazed with terror and
bewilderment into the face that bent above her.

"What is it? Who are you?" she asked, in a low
voice.

He rose quickly, and while he supported her as she
attempted to rise and stand upon her feet, he said :

"The gods be praised that you are still alive. Our
big hound threw you down—and he has terrible teeth."

Selene was now standing up, and face to face with
the boy at whose last words she shuddered again.

"Do you feel any pain?" asked Antinous, anxiously.

"Yes," she said, dully.

"Did he bite you?"

"I think not—pick up that pin, it has fallen out of
my dress."

The Bithynian obeyed her behest, and while the
girl re-fastened her peplum over her shoulders she
asked him again :

"Who are you? How came the dog in our
palace?"

"He belongs—he belongs to us. We arrived late last night, and Pontius put us ———"

"Then you are with the architect from Rome ?"

"Yes, but who are you ?"

"Selene is my name, I am the daughter of the palace-steward."

"And who is Pollux, whom you were calling to help you when you recovered your senses ?"

"What does that matter to you ?"

Antinous colored,. and answered in confusion:

"I was startled when you suddenly roused up, with his name so loudly on your lips, when I brought you back to life with water and this essence."

"Well, I was roused—and now I can walk again. People who bring furious dogs into a strange place, should know how to take better care of them. Tie the dog up safely, for the children—my little brothers and sisters—come this way when they want to go out. Thank you for your help—and my pitcher ?"

As she spoke she looked down on the remains of the pretty jar, which was one her mother had particularly valued. When she saw the fragments lying on the ground, she gave a deep sob, but she shed no tears. Then she exclaimed angrily: "It is infamous !"

With these words she turned her back on Antinous and returned to her father's room, using her left foot, however, with caution, for it was very painful.

The young Bithynian gazed in silence at Selene's tall, slight form, he felt prompted to follow her, to say to her how very sorry he was for the mischance that had befallen her, and that the hound belonged not to him but to another man; but he dared not. Long after she had disappeared from sight he stood on the same spot. At last he collected his senses, and slowly went back to his room, where he sat on his couch with his eyes fixed dreamily on the ground, till the Emperor's call roused him from his reverie.

Selene had hardly vouchsafed Antinous a glance. She was in pain not merely in her left foot, but also in the back of her head where she found there was a deep cut; but her thick hair had staunched the blood that flowed from the wound. She felt very tired, and the loss of her pretty jug, which must also be replaced by another, vexed her far more than the beauty of the favorite had charmed her.

She slowly and wearily entered the sitting-room, where her father was by this time waiting for her and his water. He was accustomed to have it regularly at the same hour, and as Selene was absent longer than usual, he could think of no better way of filling up the time than by grumbling and scolding to himself; when, at last, his daughter appeared on the threshold, he at once perceived that she had no jug, and said crossly:

"And am I to have no water to-day?"

Selene shook her head, sank into a seat, and began to cry softly.

"What is the matter?" asked her father.

"The pitcher is broken," she said sadly.

"You should take better care of such expensive things," scolded her father. "You are always complaining of want of money, and at the same time you break half our belongings."

"I was thrown down," answered Selene, drying her eyes.

"Thrown down! by whom?" asked the steward, slowly rising.

" By the architect's big dog—the architect who came
last night from Rome, and to whom we gave that meat
and salt in the middle of the night. He slept here, at
Lochias."

" And he set his dog on my child ! " shouted Keraunus, with an angry glare.

" The hound was alone in the passage when I went
there."

" Did it bite you ? "

" No, but it pulled me down, and stood over me,
and gnashed its teeth—oh ! it was horrible."

" The cursed, vagabond scoundrel ! " growled the
steward, " I will teach him how to behave in a strange
house ! "

" Let him be," said Selene, as she saw her father
about to don the saffron cloak.

" What is done cannot be undone, and if quarrels
and dissentions come of it, it will make you ill."

" Vagabonds ! impudent rascals ! who fill my palace
with quarrelsome curs," muttered Keraunus without
listening to his daughter, and as he settled the folds of his
pallium he growled " Arsinoe ! why is it that girl never
hears me."

When she appeared he desired her to heat the irons
to curl his hair.

" They are ready by the fire," answered Arsinoe.
" Come into the kitchen with me."

Keraunus followed her, and had his locks curled
and scented, while his younger children stood round
him waiting for the porridge which Selene usually prepared for them at this hour.

Keraunus responded to their morning greetings with
nods as friendly as Arsinoe's tongs, which held his head

tightly by the hair, would allow. It was only the blind Helios, a pretty boy of six, that he drew to his side and gave a kiss on his cheek. He loved this child, who, though deprived of the noblest of the senses, was always merry and contented, with peculiar tenderness. Once he even laughed aloud when the child clung to his sister, as she brandished the tongs, and said:

"Father, do you know why I am sorry I cannot see?"

"Well?" said his father.

"Because I should so like to see you for once with the beautiful curls which Arsinoe makes with the irons."

But the steward's mirth was checked when his daughter, pausing in her labors, said half in jest, but half in earnest:

"Have you thought any more about the Emperor's arrival, father? I smarten and dress you so fine every day—but to-day you ought to think of dressing me."

"We will see about it," said Keraunus evasively.

"Do you know," said Arsinoe, after a short pause, as she twisted the last lock in the freshly-heated tongs, "I thought it all over last night again. If we cannot succeed any way in scraping together the money for my dress, we can still——"

"Well?"

"Even Selene can say nothing against it."

"Against what?"

"But, you will be angry!"

"Speak out."

"You pay taxes like the rest of the citizens."

"What has that to do with it?"

"Well then, we are justified in expecting something from the city."

" What for ? "

" To pay for my dress for the festival which is got
up for the Emperor, not by an individual, but by the
citizens as a body. We could not accept alone, but it
is folly to refuse what a rich municipality offers. That
is neither more nor less than making them a present."

" You be silent," cried Keraunus, really furious, and
trying in vain to remember the argument with which,
only yesterday, he had refused the same suggestion.
" Be silent, and wait till I begin to talk about such matters."

Arsinoe flung the tongs on the hearth with so much
annoyance that they fell on the stone with a loud clatter; but her father quitted the kitchen and returned to
the sitting-room. There he found Selene lying on a
couch, and the old slave-woman, who had tied a wet
handkerchief round the girl's head, pressing another to
her bare left foot.

" Wounded ! " cried Keraunus, and his eyes rolled
slowly from right to left and from left to right.

" Look at the swelling ! " cried the old woman in
broken Greek, raising Selene's snow-white foot in her
black hands for her father to see. " Thousands of fine
ladies have hands that are not so small. Poor, poor
little foot," and as she spoke the old woman pressed it
to her lips.

Selene pushed her aside, and said, turning to her
father :

" The cut on my head is nothing to speak of, but
the muscles and veins here at the ancle are swelled and
my leg hurts me rather when I tread. When the dog
threw me down I must have hit it against the stone
step."

"It is outrageous!" cried Keraunus, the blood again mounting to his head, "only wait and I will show them what I think of their goings on."

"No, no," entreated Selene, "only beg them politely to shut up the dog, or to chain it, so that it may not hurt the children."

Her voice trembled with anxiety as she spoke the words, for the dread, which, she knew not why, had so long been tormenting her lest her father should lose his place, seemed to affect her more than ever to-day.

"What! civil words after what has now happened?" cried Keraunus indignantly, and as if something quite unheard of had been suggested to him.

"Nay, nay, say what you mean," shrieked the old woman. "If such a thing had occurred to your father he would have fallen on the strange builder with a good thrashing."

"And his son Keraunus will not let him off," declared the steward, quitting the room without heeding Selene's entreaty not to let himself be provoked.

In the ante-chamber he found his old slave whom he ordered to take a stick and go before him to announce him to Pontius' guest, the architect, who was lodging in the rooms in the wing near the fountain. This was the elegant thing to do, and by this means the black slave would meet the big dog before his master who held him and all dogs in the utmost abhorrence. As he approached his destination he found himself quite in the humor to speak his mind to the stranger who had come here with a ferocious hound to tear the members of his family.

CHAPTER XIV.

HADRIAN had slept most comfortably; only a few hours it is true, but they had sufficed to refresh his spirit. He was now in his sitting-room and had gone to the window, which took up more than half the extent of the long west wall of the room, and opened on the sea. The wide opening, which extended downwards to within a few spans of the floor, was finished at either side by a tall pillar of fine reddish-brown porphyry, fleeked with white, and crowned with gilt Corinthian capitals.

Against one of these the Emperor was leaning stroking the blood-hound, whose prompt and vigorous watchfulness had pleased him greatly. What did he care for the terrors the dog might have caused a mere girl?

By the other pillar stood Antinous; he had placed his right foot on the low window-sill, and with his chin resting on his hand and his elbow on his knee, his figure was well within the room.

"This, Pontius, is really a first-rate man," said Hadrian, pointing to a tapestry hanging across the narrow end of the room. "This hanging was copied from a fruit-piece that I painted some time since, and had executed here in mosaic. Yesterday this room was not even intended for my use, thus the hanging must have been put up between our arrival and this morning. And how many other beautiful things I see around me! The whole place looks habitable, and the eye finds an abundance of objects on which it can rest with pleasure."

"Have you examined that magnificent cushion?" asked Antinous; "and the bronze figures, there in the corner, look to me far from bad."

"They are admirable works," said Hadrian. "Still, I would do without them with pleasure rather than miss this window. Which is the bluer, the sky or the sea? And what a delicious spring breeze fans us here, in the middle of December. Which are the more delightful to contemplate, the innumerable ships in the harbor, which communicate between this flowery land and other countries, and bless it with wealth, or the buildings which attract the eye in whichever direction it turns. It is difficult to know whether most to admire their stately dimensions or the beauty of their forms."

"And what is that long, huge dyke, which connects the island with the mainland? Only look! There is a huge trireme passing under one of the wide arches, on which it is supported—and there comes another."

"That is the great viaduct, called by the Alexandrians the Heptastadion, because it is said to be seven stadia in length; and in the upper portion it carries a stone water-course—as an elder tree has in it a vein of pith—which supplies water to the island of Pharos."

"What a pity it is," said Antinous, "that we cannot overlook from here the whole of the structure with the men and the vehicles that swarm upon it like busy ants. That little island and the narrow tongue of land that runs out into the harbor with the tall slender building at the end of it, half hide it."

"But they serve to vary the picture," replied the **Emperor.** "Cleopatra often dwelt in the little castle on the island with its harbor, and in that tall tower on the northern side of the peninsula, round which, just now, the blue waves are playing, while the gulls and pigeons fly happily over it—there Antony retreated after the fight of Actium."

"To forget his disgrace!" exclaimed Antinous.

"He named it his Timonareum, because he hoped there to remain unmolested by other human beings, like the wise misanthrope of Athens. How would it be if I called Lochias my Timonareum?"

"No man need try to hide fame and greatness."

"Who told you that it was shame that led Antony to hide himself in that place?" asked the imperial sophist; "he proved often enough, at the head of his cavalry, that he was a brave soldier; and though at Actium, when all was still going well, he let his ship be turned, it was out of no fear of swords and spears, but because Fate compelled him to subjugate his strong will to the wishes of a woman with whose destiny his was linked."

"Then do you excuse his conduct?"

"I only seek to account for it, and never, for a moment, could allow myself to believe that shame ever prompted a single act in Antony. I—do you suppose I could ever blush? Nay, we cease to feel shame when we have lived to feel such profound contempt for the world."

"But why then should Marc Antony have shut himself up, in yonder sea-washed prison?"

"Because, to every true man, who has dissipated whole years of his life with women, jesters and flatterers, a moment comes of satiety and loathing. In such an hour he feels that of all the men under the lights of heaven, he, himself, is the only one with whom it is worth his while to commune. After Actium, this was what Antony felt, and he quitted the society of men in order to find himself for once in good company."

"It is that, no doubt, which drives you now and again into solitude."

"No doubt—but you are always allowed to follow me."

"Then you regard me as better than others," exclaimed Antinous joyfully.

"As more beautiful at any rate," replied Hadrian kindly. "Ask me some more questions."

But Antinous needed a few minutes pause before he could comply with this desire. At last he recollected himself and proceeded to inquire why most of the vessels were moored in the harbor beyond the Heptastadion, known as Eunostus. The entrance there was less dangerous than that between the Pharos and the point of Lochias which led into the eastern landing-places. And then Hadrian could give him information as to every building in the city about which his companion evinced any curiosity. But when the Emperor had pointed out the Soma, under which rested the remains of Alexander the Great, he became thoughtful, and said, as if to himself:

"The Great—We may well envy the young Macedonian; not the mere name of Great, for many of small worth have had it bestowed on them, but because he really earned it!"

There was not a question put by the handsome Bithynian that Hadrian could not answer; Antinous followed all his explanations with growing astonishment, exclaiming at last:

" How perfectly well you know this place—and yet you never were here before."

" It is one of the greatest pleasures of travelling," replied Hadrian, " that on our journeys we come to know many things in their actuality of which we have formed an idea from books and narratives. This requires us to compare the reality with the pictures in our own minds, seen with the inward eye, before we saw the reality. It is to me a far smaller pleasure to be surprised by something new and unexpected than to make myself more closely acquainted with something I know already sufficiently to deem it worthy to be known better. Do you understand what I mean ? "

" To be sure I do. We hear of a thing, and when we afterwards see it we ask ourselves whether we have conceived of it rightly. But I always picture people or places which I hear much praised, as much more beautiful than I ever find the reality."

" The balance of difference, which is to the disadvantage of reality," answered Hadrian, " stands not so much to its discredit, as to the credit of the eager and beautifying power of your youthful imagination. I— I—" and the Emperor stroked his beard and gazed out into the distance. " I learn by experience that the older I grow, the more often I find it possible so to imagine men, places, and things that I have not seen as that when I meet them in real life for the first time, I feel justified in fancying that I have known them long since, visited them, and beheld them with my bodily eyes. Here, for instance, I feel as if I saw nothing new, but only gazed once more at what has long been familiar. But that is no wonder, for I know my Strabo, and have heard and read a hundred accounts of this city. Still there are many things which are quite strange to me, and yet as they come before me make me feel as if I had seen or known them long ago."

" I have felt something like that," said Antinous. "Can our souls have ever lived in other bodies, and sometimes recall the impressions made in that former existence ? " Favorinus once told me that some great philosopher, Plato, I think, asserts that before we are born our souls are wafted about in the firmament that they may contemplate the earth on which they are destined subsequently to dwell.   Favorinus says too——"

" Favorinus ! " cried Hadrian, evasively. " That graceful elocutionist has plenty of skill in giving new and captivating forms to the thoughts of the great philosophers ; but he has not been able to surprise the secret of his own soul—besides, he talks too much, and he cannot dispense with the excitement of life."

" Still you have recognized the phenomenon, but you disapprove of Favorinus' explanation of it ? "

" Yes, for I have met men and things as old acquaintances which never saw the light till long after I was born. Possibly my own interpretation may not adapt itself to the consciousness of all—but in myself, I know for certain, there dwells a mysterious something which stirs and works in me independently of myself, which enters into me, and takes its departure at its will. Call it as you will, my Daimon, or even my Genius— the name matters not. Nor will this 'something' always come at my bidding, while it often possesses me when I least expect it.   In those moments when it stirs within me, I am master of much which is peculiar to the experience and potentiality of that hour. What is known to that Daimon always appears to me the very same when I actually meet it. Thus Alexandria is not unknown to me, because my Genius has seen it in his flights. It has learnt and done much, both in me and for me ; a hundred times, face to face with my own finished works I have asked myself: ' Is it possible that you—Hadrian—your mother's son—can have achieved this ? What then is the mysterious power that aided you to do it ? ' Now I also recognize it, and can see it work in others. The man in whom it dwells soon excels his fellows, and it is most manifest in artists. Or is it that mere common men become great artists simply because the Genius selects them as his temple to dwell in ? Do you follow me, boy ? "

"Not altogether," replied Antinous, and his large eyes which had sparkled brightly so long as he gazed with the Emperor on the city, were now cast down and fixed wearily on the ground. " Do not be angry with me, my Lord, but I shall never understand such things as these, for there is no man with whom your Genius, as you term it, has less concern than with me. Thoughts of my own have I none, and it is difficult to me to fol- low the thoughts of others; indeed I should like to know how I am ever to do anything right. When I want to work, to work something out, no Daimon helps my soul; no—it feels quite helpless, and drifts into dreaminess. And if I ever do complete anything, I am obliged to own to myself that I certainly might have been able to do it better."

" Self-knowledge," laughed Hadrian, " is the climax of wisdom. A man has done something if he has only added a ' thing of beauty ' to the joys of a friend's im- agination ; what others do by hard work you do by mere existence. Be quiet, Argus ! " For, while he

13

was speaking, the hound had risen, and had gone snarling to the door. In spite of his master's orders he broke into a loud bark when he heard a steady knock at the door. Hadrian looked round in bewilderment, and asked: "Where is Mastor?"

Antinous shouted the slave's name into the Emperor's bedroom, which was next to the living-room, but in vain. "He generally is always at hand, and as brisk as a lark, but to-day he looked as if in a dream, and while he was dressing me he first let my shoe fall out of his hand and then my brooch."

"I read him yesterday a letter from Rome. His young wife has gone away with a ship's captain."

"We may wish him joy of being free again."

"It does not seem to afford him any satisfaction."

"Oh! a handsome lad like my body-slave can find as many substitutes as he likes."

"But he has not done so. For the present he is still smarting under his loss."

"How wise! There, some one is knocking again. Just see who ventures—but to be sure any one has a right to knock, for at Lochias I am not the Emperor, but a simple private gentleman. Lie down Argus, are you crazy, old fellow? Why the dog maintains my dignity better than I do, and he does not seem altogether to like the architect's part I am playing."

Antinous had already raised his hand to lift the handle, when the door was gently opened from outside, and the steward's slave stood on the threshold. The old negro presented a lamentable spectacle. The Emperor's dignified and awe-compelling figure, and his favorite's rich garments made him feel embarrassed, and the hound's threatening growl filled him with such terror that he huddled his lean negro-legs together, and, as far as its length would allow, tried to cover them for protection with his threadbare tunic.

Hadrian gazed in astonishment at this image of fear, and then asked :

" Well ! what do you want, fellow ? "

The slave attempted to advance a step or two, but at a loud command from Hadrian he stood still, and as he looked down at his flat feet, he ruefully scratched his short-cropped grey hair, some of which had fallen off and left a bald patch.

" Well," repeated Hadrian, in a tone which was any- thing rather than encouraging, as he relaxed his hold on the hound's collar in a somewhat suspicious manner. The slave's bent knees began to quake, and holding out his broad palm to the grey-bearded gentleman, who seemed to him hardly less alarming than the dog, he began to stammer out in fearfully-mutilated Greek the speech which his master had repeated to him several times, and which set forth that he had come " into the presence of the architect, Claudius Venator, of Rome, to announce the visit of his master, a member of the town-council, a Macedonian, and a Roman citizen, Keraunus, the son of Ptolemy, steward of the once royal but now imperial palace at Lochias."

Hadrian unrelentingly allowed the poor wretch to finish his speech, rubbing his hands with amusement, while the sweat of anguish stood on the old slave's face, and to prolong the delightful joke, he took good care not to help the miserable old man when his unaccus- tomed tongue came to some insuperable difficulty. When, at length, the negro had finished the pompous announcement, Hadrian said, kindly:

"Tell your master he may come in."

Scarcely had the slave left the room, when the sovereign, turning to his favorite, exclaimed:

"This is a delicious joke! What will the Jupiter be like, when the eagle is such a bird as this!"

Keraunus was not long to wait for. While pacing up and down the passage outside the Emperor's room, his bad humor had risen considerably, for he took it as a slight on the part of the architect, that he should allow him—whose birth and dignities 'he would have learnt from his slave—to wait several minutes, each of which seemed to him a quarter of an hour. His expectation too, that the Roman would come to conduct him in person into his apartment was by no means fulfilled, for the slave's message was briefly—"He may come in."

"Did he say *may*? Did he not say 'please to come in, or have the goodness to come in?'" asked the steward.

"'He may come in'—was what he said," replied the slave. Keraunus grunted out, "Well!" set his gold circlet straight on his head which he held very upright, crossed his arms over his broad chest with a sigh, and ordered the black man:

"Open the door."

The steward crossed the threshold with much dignity: then, not to commit any breach of courtesy, he bowed low, and was about to begin to utter his reprimand in cutting terms, when a glance at the Emperor and at the splendid decoration which the room had undergone since the day previous, not to mention the very unpleasant growling of the big dog, prompted him to strike a milder string. His slave had followed him and had sought a safe corner near the door, between the wall of the room and a couch, but he himself, conquering his alarm at the dog, went forward some distance into the room. The Emperor had seated himself on the window-sill; he pressed his foot lightly on the head of the dog, and gazed at Keraunus as at some remarkable curiosity. His eye thus met that of the steward and made him clearly understand that he had to do with a greater personage than he had expected. There was something imposing in the person of the man who sat before him; for this very reason, however, his pride stood on tiptoe, and he asked in a tone of swaggering dignity, though not so sharply and abruptly as he had intended.

"Am I standing before the new visitor to Lochias, the architect Claudius Venator of Rome?"

"You are—standing—" replied the Emperor, with a roguish side glance at Antinous.

"You have met with a friendly reception to this palace. Like my fathers, who have enjoyed the stewardship of it for centuries, I know how to exercise the sacred duties of hospitality."

"I am surprised to hear of the high antiquity of your family and bow to your pious sentiments," answered Hadrian, in the same tone as the steward. "What farther may I learn from you?"

"I did not come here to relate history," said Keraunus, whose gall rose as he thought he detected a mocking smile on the stranger's lips. "I did not come here to tell stories, but to complain that you, as a warmly-welcomed guest, show so little anxiety to protect your host from injury."

"How is that?" asked Hadrian, rising from his seat

and signing to Antinous to hold back the hound, which manifested a peculiar aversion to the steward. It no doubt detected that he had come to show no special friendliness to his owner.

"Is that dangerous dog, gnashing its teeth there, your property?" asked Keraunus.

"Yes."

"This morning it threw down my daughter and smashed a costly pitcher, which she is fond of carrying to fetch water in the dawn."

"I heard of that misadventure," said Hadrian, "and I would give much if I could undo it. The vessel shall be amply made good to you."

"I beg you not to add insult to the injury, we have suffered by your fault. A father whose daughter has been knocked down and hurt—"

"Then, Argus actually bit her?" cried Antinous, horrified.

"No," Keraunus replied. "But as she fell her head and foot have been injured, and she is suffering much pain."

"That is very sad," said Hadrian, "and as I am not ignorant of the healing art, I will gladly try to help the poor girl."

"I pay a professional leech, who attends me and mine," replied the steward, in a repellant tone, "and I came hither to request—or, to be frank with you—to require—"

"What?"

"First, that my pardon shall be asked."

"That, the artist, Claudius Venator, is always ready to do when any one has suffered damage by his fault. What has happened—I repeat it—grieves me sincerely, and I beg you tell the maiden to whom the accident happened, that her pain is mine. What more do you desire?"

The steward's features had calmed down at these last words, and he answered with less excitement than before:

"I must request you to chain up your dog, or to shut it up, or in some way to keep it from mischief."

"That is pretty strong!" cried the Emperor.

"It is only a reasonable demand, and I must stand by it," replied Keraunus decidedly. "Neither I—nor my children's lives are safe, so long as this wild beast is prowling about at pleasure."

Hadrian had, ere now, erected monuments to deceased favorites, both dogs and horses, and his faithful Argus was no less dear to him, than other four-footed companions have been to other childless men; hence the queer fat man's demand seemed to him so audacious and monstrous, that he indignantly exclaimed:

"Folly!—the dog shall be watched, but nothing farther."

"You will chain him up," replied Keraunus, with an angry glare, "or some one will be found who will make him harmless forever."

"That will be an evil attempt for the cowardly murderer!" cried Hadrian. "Eh! Argus, what do you think?"

At these words the dog drew himself up, and would have sprung at the steward's throat if his master and Antinous had not held him back.

Keraunus felt that the dog had threatened him, but at this instant he would have let himself be torn by him without wincing, so completely was he overmastered by the fury born of his injured pride.

" And am I—I too, to be hunted down by a dog, in this house ? " he cried defiantly, setting his left fist on his hip. " Every thing has its limits, and so has my patience with a guest who, in spite of his ripe age forgets due consideration. I will inform the prefect Titianus of your proceedings here, and when the Emperor arrives he shall know———"

" What ? " laughed Hadrian.

" The way you behave to me."

" Till then the dog shall stay where it is, and really under due restraint. But I can tell you man, that Hadrian is as much a friend of dogs as I am—and fonder of me than even of dogs."

" We will see," growled Keraunus, " I or the dog !"

" I am afraid it will be the dog then."

" And Rome will see a fresh revolt," cried Keraunus, rolling his eyes. " You took Egypt from the Ptolemies."

" And with very good reason—besides that is a stale old story."

" Justice is never stale, like a bad debt."

" At any rate it perishes with persons it concerns ; there have been no Lagides left here—how many years ? "

" So you believe, because it suits your ends to believe it," replied the steward. " In the man who stands before you flows the blood of the Macedonian rulers of this country. My eldest son bears the name of Ptolemaeus Helios—that borne by the last of the Lagides, who perished as you pretend."

"Dear, good, blind Helios!" interrupted the black slave; for he was accustomed to avail himself of the hapless child's name as a protection, when Keraunus was in a doubtful humor.

"Then the last descendant of the Ptolemies is blind!" laughed the Emperor. "Rome may ignore his claims. But I will inform the Emperor how dangerous a pretender this roof yet harbors."

"Denounce me, accuse me, calumniate me!" cried the steward, contemptuously. "But I will not let myself be trodden on. Patience—patience! you will live to know me yet."

"And you, the blood-hound," replied Hadrian, "if you do not this instant quit the room with your mouthing crow——"

Keraunus signed to his slave, and without greeting his foe in any way, turned his back upon him. He paused for a moment at the door of the room and cried out to Hadrian:

"Rely upon this, I shall complain to the Council and write to Caesar how you presume to behave to a Macedonian citizen."

As soon as the steward had quitted the room, Hadrian freed the dog, which flew raging at the door which was closed between him and the object of his aversion. Hadrian ordered him to be quiet, and then turning to his companion, he exclaimed:

"A perfect monster of a man! to the last degree ridiculous, and at the same time repulsive. How his rage seethed in him, and yet could not break out fairly and thoroughly. I am always on my guard with such obstinate fools. Pay attention to my Argus, and remember, we are in Egypt, the land of poison, as

Homer long since said. Mastor must keep his eyes open—Here he is at last."

CHAPTER XV.

AFTER the Emperor's body-slave had started up to go to the aid of Selene, who was attacked by his sovereign's dog, something had happened to him which he could not forget; he had received an impression which he could not wipe out, and words and tones had stirred his mind and soul which incessantly echoed in them, so that it was in a preoccupied and half-dreamy way that he had done his master those little services which he was accustomed to perform every morning, briskly and with complete attention.

Summer and winter Mastor was accustomed to leave his master's bedroom before sunrise to prepare everything that Hadrian could need when he rose from his slumbers. There was the gold plating to clean on the narrow greaves and the leather straps which belonged to his master's military boots, his clothes to air and to perfume with the slight, hardly perceptible scent that he liked, but the preparations for Hadrian's bath were what took up most of his time. At Lochias there were not as yet—as there were in the imperial palace at Rome—properly-filled baths; still his servant knew that here, as there, his master would use a due abundance of water. He had been told that if he required anything for his master he was to apply to Pontius. Him he found, without seeking him, outside the room meant for Hadrian's sitting-room, to which, while the Em-

peror still slept, he was endeavoring, with the help of
his assistants, to give a comfortable and pleasing aspect.
The architect referred the slave to the workmen who
were busy laying the pavement in the forecourt of the
palace; these men would carry in for him as much
water as ever he could need. The body-servant's position relieved him of such humble duties, still, when on
the chase, when travelling, or as need arose, he was
accustomed to perform them unasked, and very willingly.

The sun had not yet risen when he went out into
the court, a number of slaves were lying on their
mats asleep, others had camped round a fire and were
waiting for their early broth, which was being stirred
with wooden sticks by an old man and a boy. Mastor
would not disturb either group; he went up to a party
of workmen, who seemed to be talking together, and
yet remained attentive to the speech of an old man
who was evidently telling them a story.

The poor fellow's heart was heavy and his mind was
little bent on tales and amusements. All life was embittered. The services required of him usually seemed
to him of paramount importance, beyond everything
else; but to-day it was different. He had an obscure
feeling as though fate herself had released him from
all his duties, as if misfortune had cut the bonds which
bound him to his service to the Emperor, and had
made him an isolated and lonely being. It even came
into his head whether he should not take in his hand
all the gold pieces given him sometimes by Hadrian, or
which the wealthy folks who wished to be the foremost
of those introduced into the Emperor's presence, after
waiting in the antechamber, had flung to him or slipped

into his hand—make his escape and carouse away all
that he possessed in the taverns of the great city, in
wine and the gay company of women. It was all the
same to him what might happen to him.

If he were caught he would probably be flogged to
death ; but he had had kicks and blows in plenty before
he had got into the Emperor's service, nay, when he was
brought to Rome he had once even been hunted with
dogs. If he lost his life, after all what would it matter ?
He would have done with it then, once for all, and the
future offered him no prospect but perpetual fatigue in
the service of a restless master, anxiety and contempt.
He was a thoroughly good-hearted being who could
not bear to hurt any one, and who found it equally hard
to disturb a fellow-man in his pleasures or amusement.
He felt particularly disinclined to do so just now, for
a wounded soul is keenly alive to the moods and feelings
of others; so, as he approached the group of workmen,
from among whom he proposed to choose his water-
carrier, he determined that he would not interrupt the
story-teller, on whose lips the gaze of his audience was
riveted with interest.

The glare of the blaze under the soup-kettle fell full
on the speaker's face. He was an old laborer, but his
long hair proclaimed him a freeman. His abundant
white beard induced Mastor to suppose that he must be
a Jew or a Phœnician, but there was nothing remarkable in the old man, who was dressed in a poor and
scanty tunic, excepting his peculiarly brilliant eyes,
which were immovably fixed on the heavens, and the
oblique position in which he held his head, supporting
it on the left side with his raised hands.

" And now," said the speaker, dropping his arms,

"let us go back to our labors, my brethren. 'In the
sweat of thy face shalt thou eat bread,' it is written. It
is often hard to us old men to heave stones, and bend
our stiff backs for so long together, but we are nearer
than you younger ones to the happy future. Life is
not easy to all of us, but it is we who labor and are
heavy laden—we above all others—that the Lord has
bidden to be his guests, and not last among us the
slaves."

"Come unto me all ye that labor and are heavy
laden, and I will refresh you," interrupted one of the
younger men repeating the words of Christ.

"Yea, thus saith the Saviour," said the old man approvingly, "and he surely then was thinking of us. I
said just now our load is not light, but how much
heavier was the burden he took upon him of his own
free will to release us from woe. Every one must work,
nay even Caesar himself, but he who could dwell in the
glory of his Father let himself be mocked and scorned
and spit in the face, let the crown of thorns be pressed
on his suffering head, bore his heavy cross, sinking
under its weight, and endured a death of. torment, and
all for our sakes, without a murmur. But he suffered
not in vain, for God accepted the sacrifice of his Son,
and did his will and said, 'All that believe on Him
should not perish, but have everlasting life.' And though
a new and weary day is now beginning, and though it
should be followed by a thousand wearier still, though
death is the end of life—still we believe in our Redeemer, we have God's word bidding us out of sorrows
and sufferings into his Heaven, promising us for a brief
time of misery in this world, endless ages of joy.—Now
go to work. Our sturdy friend Krates will work for

you dear Knakias until your finger is healed. When
the bread is distributed remember, each of you, the
children of our poor deceased brother Philammon.
You, poor Gibbus, will find your labors bitter to-day.
This man's master, my dear brethren, sold both his
daughters yesterday to a dealer from Smyrna; but if
you never see them again in Egypt, or in any other
country, my friend, you will meet them in the home of
your Heavenly Father—of that you may rest assured.
Our life on earth is but a pilgrimage, and Heaven is the
goal, and the Guide who teaches us never to miss the
way, is our Saviour. Weariness and toil, sorrow and
suffering are easy to bear, to him who knows that when
the solemn hour is near, the King of Kings shall throw
open his dwelling-place, and invite him to enter as a
favored guest to inhabit there, where all we have loved
have found joy and rest."

" Come unto me all ye that labor and are heavy
laden, and I will refresh you," said a man's loud voice
again from the circle that sat round the old man.   The
old man stood up, signed to a boy who distributed the
bread in equal shares to the workmen, and took up a
jar with handles, out of which he filled a large wooden
cup with wine.

Not a word of this discourse had escaped Mastor,
and the often repeated verse, " Come unto me all ye
that labor," dwelt in his mind like the invitation of a
hospitable friend bidding him to happy days of freedom
and enjoyment. A distant gleam shone through the
weight of his troubles, seeming to promise the dawn of
a new day, and he reverently went up to the old man,
in the first place to ask him if he was the overseer of the
workmen who stood round him.

"I am," replied the old man, and as soon as he learnt what Mastor required as a commission from the controlling architect, he pointed out some young slaves who quickly brought the water that he needed.

Pontius met the Emperor's servant and his water-carriers and remarked, loudly enough for Mastor to understand him, to Pollux who was with him:

"The architect's servant is getting Christians to wait upon his master to-day. They are regular and sober workmen who do their duty silently and well."

While Mastor was giving his master towels, and helping to dry and dress him, he was far less attentive than usual, for he could not get the words he had heard from the overseer's lips out of his mind. He had not understood them all, but he had fully comprehended that there was a kind and loving God who had suffered in his own person the utmost torments, who was especially gracious to the poor, the miserable, and the bondsman, and who promised to refresh them and comfort them, and to re-unite them to those who had once been dear to them. "Come unto me," sounded again and again in his ears, and struck so warmly to his heart that he could not help thinking first of his mother, who, so many a time, when he was a child, had called to him only to clasp him in her arms as he ran towards her, and to press him to her heart. Just so had he often called his poor little dead son, and the feeling that there could be any one who might still call to him— the forsaken lonely man—with loving words to release him from his griefs, to reunite him to his mother, his father, and all the dear ones left behind in his lost and distant home, took half the bitterness from his pain.

He was accustomed to listen to all that was said in

the Emperor's presence, and year by year he had learnt
to understand more of what he heard.   He had often
heard the Christians discussed, and usually as deluded
but dangerous fools.   Many of his fellow-slaves, too,
he had heard called Christian idiots, but still not unfrequently very reasonable men, and sometimes even Hadrian himself, had taken the part of the Christians.

This was the first time that Mastor had heard from
their own lips what they believed and hoped, and now,
while fulfilling his duties he could hardly bear the delay
before he could once more seek out the old pavement-
worker, to enquire of him, and to have the hopes confirmed which his words had aroused in his soul.

No sooner had Hadrian and Antinous gone into
the living-room than Mastor had hastened off across
the court to find the Christians.   There he tried to
open a conversation with the overseer concerning his
faith, but the old man answered that there was a season
for everything; just now he could not interrupt the
work, but that he might come again after sundown, and
that he then would tell him of Him who had promised
to refresh the sorrow-laden.

Mastor thought no more of making his escape.
When he appeared again in his master's presence there
was such a sunny light in his blue eyes that Hadrian
left the angry words he had prepared for him unspoken,
and cried to Antinous, laughing and pointing to the
slave:

" I really believe the rascal has consoled himself
already, and found a new mate.   Let us, too, follow the
precept of Horace, so far as we may, and enjoy the
present day.   The poet may let the future go as it will,
but I cannot, for, unfortunately, I am the Emperor."

"And Rome may thank the gods that you are," replied Antinous.

"What happy phrases the boy hits upon sometimes," said Hadrian with a laugh, and he stroked the lad's brown curls. "Now till noon I must work with Phlegon and Titianus, whom I am expecting, and then perhaps we may find something to laugh at. Ask the tall sculptor there behind the screens, at what hour Balbilla is to sit to him for her bust. We must also inspect the architect's work, and that of the Alexandrian artists by daylight ; that, their zeal has well deserved."

Hadrian retired to the room where his private secretary had ready for him the despatches and papers for Rome and the provinces, which the Emperor was required to read and to sign. Antinous remained alone in the sitting- room, and for an hour he continued to gaze at the ships which came to anchor in the harbor, or sailed out of the roads, and amused himself with watching the swift boats which swarmed round the larger vessels, like wasps round ripe fruit. He listened to the songs of the sailors, and the music of the fluteplayers, to the measured beat of the oars, which came up from the triremes in the private harbor of the Emperor as they went out to sea. Even the pure blue of the sky and the warmth of the delicious morning were a pleasure to him, and he asked himself whether the smell of tar, which pervaded the seaport, were agreeable or not.

Presently as the sun mounted in the sky, its bright sphere dazzled him ; he left the window with a yawn, stretched himself on a couch, and stared absently up at the ceiling of the room without thinking of the subject which the faded picture on it was intended to represent.

14

Idleness had long since grown to be the occupation of his life; but accustomed to it as he was, he was sometimes conscious of its dark attendant shadow—ennui—as of a disagreeable and intrusive interruption to the enjoyment of life. Generally in such lonely hours of idle reverie his thoughts reverted to his belongings in Bithynia, of whom he never dared to speak before the Emperor, or perhaps of the hunting excursions he had made with Hadrian, of the slaughtered game, of the fish he—an experienced angler—had caught, or such like. What the future might bring him troubled him not, for to the love of creativeness, to ambition—to all, in short, that bore any resemblance to a passionate excitement his soul had, so far, remained a stranger. The admiration which was universally excited by his beauty gave him no pleasure, and many a time he felt as though it was not worth while to stir a limb or draw a breath. Almost everything he saw was indifferent to him excepting a kind word from the lips of the Emperor, whom he regarded as great above all other men, whom he feared as Destiny incarnate, and to whom he felt himself bound as intimately as the flower to the tree, the blossom that must die when the stem is broken, on which it flaunts as an ornament and a grace.

But, to-day, as he flung himself on the divan his visions took a new direction. He could not help thinking of the pale girl whom he had saved from the jaws of the blood-hound—of the white cold hand which for an instant had clung to his neck—of the cold words with which she had afterwards repelled him.

Antinous began to long violently to see Selene. That same Antinous, to whom in all the cities he had visited with the Emperor, and in Rome particularly, the noble fair ones had sent branches of flowers and tender letters, and who nevertheless, since the day when he left his home, had never felt for any woman or girl half so tender a sentiment, as for the hunter the Emperor had given him, or for the big dog. This girl stood before his memory like breathing marble. Perchance the man might be doomed to death who should rest on her cold breast, but such a death must be full of ecstasy, and it seemed to him that it would be far more blissful to die with the blood frozen in his veins, than of the too rapid throbbing of his heart.

"Selene," he murmured, now and again, with soft hesitation; a strange unrest foreign to his calm nature seemed to propagate itself through all his limbs, and he who commonly would be stretched on a couch for hours without stirring, lost in dreams, now sprang up and paced the room, sighing deeply, and with long strides.

It was a passionate longing for Selene that drove him up and down, and his wish to see her again crystallized into resolve, and prompted him to contrive the ways and means of meeting her once more before the Emperor's return.

Simply to invade her father's lodging without farther ceremony, seemed to him out of the question, and yet he was certain of finding her there, since her injured foot would of course keep her at home. Should he once more go to the steward with a request for bread and salt? But he dared not ask anything of Keraunus in Hadrian's name after the scene which had so recently taken place. Should he go there to carry her a new pitcher in the place of the broken one? But that would only freshly enrage the arrogant official.

Should he—should he—should he not? But no,

it was quite impossible—still, that no doubt—that was
the right idea. In his medicine-chest there were a few
extracts which had been given to him by the Emperor;
he would offer her one of these to dilute with water and
apply to her bruised foot. And this act of sympathy
could not displease even his master, who liked to
prove his healing art on the sick or suffering. He at
once called Mastor, and desired him to take charge of
the hound which had followed his steps as he paced
the room, then he went into his sleeping-room, took out
a phial of a most costly essence, which Hadrian had given
him on his last birthday, and which had formerly belonged
to Trajan's wife, Kotina, and then proceeded to the
steward's rooms. On the steps where he had found
Selene, he found the black slave with some children.
The old man had sat down there and got no farther for
fear of the Roman's dog. Antinous went up to him and
begged him to guide him to his master's quarters, and
the negro·immediately showed him the way, opened
the door of the antechamber, and pointing to the
living-room said :

"There—but Keraunus is absent."

Without troubling himself any further about Antinous
the slave went back to the children, but the Bithynian
stood irresolute, with his flask in his hand, for besides
Selene's voice he heard that of another girl and the
deeper tones of a man. He was still hesitating when
Arsinoe's loud exclamation of "Who's there?" obliged
him to advance.

In the sitting-room Selene was standing dressed in
a long light-colored robe with a veil over her head, as if
prepared to go out, but Arsinoe was perched on the edge
of a table, in such a way as that the tips of her toes only

touched the ground, and on the table lay a quantity of old-fashioned things. Before her stood a Phœnician, of middle age, holding in his hand a finely-carved cup; apparently he was in treaty for it with the young girl.

Kéraunus had been again to-day to a dealer in curiosities, but he had not found him at home, so he had left word at his shop that Hiram might call upon him in his rooms at Lochias, where he could show him several valuable rarities. The Phœnician had arrived before the return of the steward himself, who had been detained at a meeting of the town council, and Arsinoe was displaying' her father's treasures, whose beauties she was extolling with much eloquence. Hiram unfortunately offered a no higher price than Gabinius, whom the steward had sent off so indignantly the previous evening.

Selene had been convinced from the first of the bootlessness of the attempt, and was now anxious to bring the transaction to a speedy conclusion, as the hour was approaching when she and Arsinoe had to go to the papyrus factory. To her sister's refusal to accompany her, and to the old slave-woman's entreaty that she would rest her foot, at any rate for to-day, she had responded only with a resolute, "I am going."

The appearance of the youth on the scene occasioned the girls some embarrassment. Selene recognized him at once, Arsinoe thought him handsome but awkward, while the curiosity-dealer gazed at him in perfect admiration, and was the first to offer him a greeting. Antinous returned it, bowed to the sisters, and then said turning to Selene:

"We heard that your head was cut, and your foot hurt, and as we were guilty of your mishap, we venture

to offer you this phial which contains a good remedy
for such injuries."

"Thank you," replied the girl.   "But I feel already
so well that I shall try to go out."

"That you certainly ought not to do," said Antinous,
beseechingly.

"I must," replied Selene, gravely.

"Then, at any rate, take the phial to use for a
lotion when you return.   Ten drops in such a cup as
that, full of water."

"I can try it when I come in."

"Do so, and you will see how healing it is.   You
are not vexed with us any longer?"

"No."

"I am glad of that!" cried the boy, fixing his large
dreamy eyes on Selene with silent passion.   This gaze
displeased her, and she said more coldly than before to
the Bithynian.

"To whom shall I give the phial when I have used
the stuff in it?"

"Keep it, pray keep it," begged Antinous.   "It is
pretty, and will be twice as precious in my eyes when
it belongs to you."

"It is pretty—but I do not wish for presents."

"Then destroy it when you have done with it.   You
have not forgiven us our dog's bad behavior, and we
are sincerely sorry that our dog——"

"I am not vexed with you.   Arsinoe pour the
medicine into a saucer."

The steward's younger daughter immediately
obeyed, and noticing as she did so, how pretty the
phial was, sparkling with various colors, she said
frankly enough.

"If my sister will not have it, give it to me. How can you make such a pother about nothing, Selene?"

"Take it," said Antinous, looking anxiously at the ground, for it had now just occurred to him how highly the Emperor had valued this little bottle, and that he might possibly ask him some time what had become of it. Selene shrugged her shoulders, and drawing her veil round her head, she exclaimed, with a glance of annoyance at her sister.

"It is high time!"

"I am not going to-day," replied Arsinoe, defiantly, "and it is folly for you to walk a quarter of a mile with your swollen foot."

"It would be wiser to take some care of it," observed the dealer, politely, and Antinous anxiously added:

"If you increase your own suffering you will add to our self-reproach."

"I must go," Selene repeated resolutely, "and you with me, sister."

It was not out of mere wilfulness that she spoke, it was bitter necessity, that forced her to utter the words. To-day, at any rate, she must not miss going to the papyrus factory, for the week's wages for her work and Arsinoe's were to be paid. Besides, the next day, and for four days after, the workshops and counting-house would be closed, for the Emperor had announced to the wealthy proprietor his intention of visiting them, and in his honor various dilapidations in the old rooms were to be repaired, and various decorations added to the bare-looking building. Hence, to remain away from the works to-day meant, not merely the loss of a week's pay, but the sacrifice of twelve days, since it had been announced to the work-people, that as a token of rejoicing, and in honor of the imperial visit, full pay would be given for the unemployed days; and Selene needed money to maintain the family, and must therefore persist in her intention.

When she saw that Arsinoe showed no sign of accompanying her, she once more asked with stern determination:

"Are you coming?—Yes, or no."

"No," cried Arsinoe, defiantly, and sitting farther on the table.

"Then I am to go alone?"

"You are to stay here."

Selene went close up to her sister and looked at her enquiringly and reproachfully; but Arsinoe adhered to her refusal. She pouted like a sulky child, and slapping the hand on which she was leaning three times on the table, she repeated, "No—no—no."

Selene called to the old slave-woman, and desired her to remain in the sitting-room till her father should return, greeted the dealer politely, and Antinous with a careless nod, and then left the room. The lad had followed her, and they both met the children. Selene pulled their dresses straight, and strictly enjoined them not to go near the corridor on account of the strange dog. Antinous stroked the blind boy's pretty curly head, and then, as Selene was about to descend the stairs, he asked her:

"May I help you?"

"Yes," said the girl, for at the very first step an acute pain in the ancle checked her, and she put out her arm to the young man that he might support her elbow on his hand. But her answer would assuredly have been "no," if she had had the smallest feeling of liking for the Emperor's favorite ; but she bore the image of another in her heart, and did not even perceive that Antinous was beautiful. The Bithynian's heart, on the other hand, had never beaten so violently as during the brief moments when he was permitted to hold Selene's arm. He felt intoxicated, while he was alive to the fact that during the descent of the few steps she was suffering great pain.

"Stay at home, and spare yourself!" he begged her once more in a trembling voice.

"You worry me!" she said, in a tone of vexation. "I must go, and it is not far."

"May I accompany you?"

She laughed aloud and answered somewhat scornfully :

"Certainly not. Only conduct me through the corridor that the dog may not attack me again, then go where you will—but not with me."

He obeyed when at the end of the passage where it opened into a large hall, he bid her farewell, and she thanked him with a few friendly words.

There were two ways out from her father's rooms into the road, one led through the rotunda where the Ptolemaic Queens were placed, and across several terraces up and down steps through the forecourt ; the other, on a level all the way, through the rooms and halls of the palace. She was forced to choose the latter, for it would have been impossible for her with her aching foot to clamber up a number of steps without help and down them again, but she came to this conclusion much against her will, for she knew what numbers of men were engaged in the works of restoration ; and to get through them safely it struck her that she might ask her old playfellow to escort her through the crowd of workmen and rough slaves as far as his parent's gate-house. But she did not easily decide on this course, for, since the afternoon when Pollux had shown her mother's bust to Arsinoe before showing it to her, she had felt a grudge towards the sculptor, who so lately before had touched and opened her weary and loveless soul; and this sore feeling had not diminished, but had rather increased with time. At every hour of the day, and whatever she was occupied in, she could not help repeating to herself, that she had every reason to be vexed with him.

She had stood to him a second time as a model for his work, had spoken to him many times, and when last they parted had promised to allow him this very evening to study once more the folds of her mantle. With what pleasure she had looked forward to each meeting with Pollux, how truly lovable she had thought him on every fresh occasion; how frankly he too, expressed his pleasure as often as they met! They had talked of all sorts of things, even of love, and how eager he had been when he told her that the only thing she needed to make her happy was a good husband who would succor and comfort her as she deserved, and as he spoke he had looked at his own strong hands while she had turned red, and had thought to herself that if he liked it she would willingly make the experiment of enjoying life heartily by his side.

It seemed to her as though they belonged to each other, as if she had been born for him alone, and he for her. Why then yesterday had he shown Arsinoe her mother's bust before her?

Well, now she would ask him plainly whether he had placed it on the rotunda for her or for her sister, and let him see she was not pleased. She must tell him, too, that she could not stand as his model that evening; if only on account of her foot that would be impossible.

With increasing pain and effort she crossed the threshold of the hall of the Muses, and went up to the screen behind which her friend was concealed. He was not alone, for she heard voices within—and it was not a man but a woman who was with him; she could hear her clear laugh at some distance. When she came close up to the screen to call Pollux, the woman, who was certainly sitting to him as a model, spoke louder than before, and called out merrily:

" But this is delicious! I am to let you fulfil the office of my maid, what audacity these artists have !"

" Say yes," begged the artist, in the gay and cordial tone which more than once had helped to ensnare Selene's heart. " You are beautiful, Balbilla, but if you would allow me, you might be far handsomer than you are even."

And again there was a merry laugh behind the screen. The pleasant voice must have hurt poor Selene acutely for she drew up her shoulders, and her fair features were stamped with an expression of keen suffering, and she pressed both hands over her heart as she went on past the screen and her handsome flirting playfellow, limping across the courtyard and into the road.

What tortured the poor child so cruelly ? The poverty of her house, and her bodily pain, which increased at every step, or her numbed and sore heart, betrayed of her newly-blossoming, last, and fairest hope ?

CHAPTER XVI.

USUALLY when Selene went out walking, many people looked at her with admiration, but to-day a couple of street-boys composed her escort. They ran after her calling out impudently, 'dot, and go one,' and tried ruthlessly to snatch at the loosely-tied sandal on her injured foot, which tapped the pavement at every step. While Selene was thus making her way with cruel pain, satisfaction and happiness had visited Arsinoe; for hardly had Selene and Antinous quitted her father's apartments, when Hiram begged her to show him the little bottle which the handsome youth had just given her. The dealer turned it over and over in the sunlight, tested its ring, tried to scratch it with the stone in his ring, and then muttered, "Vasa Murrhina."

The words did not escape the girl's sharp ears, and she had heard her father say that the costliest of all the ornamental vessels with which the wealthy Romans were wont to decorate their reception-rooms, were those called Vasa Murrhina; so she explained to him at once, that she knew what high prices were paid for such vases, and that she had no mind to sell it cheaply. He began to bid, she laughingly demanded ten times the price, and after a long battle between the dealer and the owner, fought now half in jest, and now in grave earnest, the Phœnician said:

"Two thousand drachmae; not a sesterce more."

"That is not enough by a long way, but then—it is yours."

"I would hardly have given half to a less fair customer."

"And I only let you have it because you are such a polite man."

"I will send you the money before sundown."

At these words the girl, who had been radiant with surprise and delight, and who would have liked to throw her arms round the bald-headed merchant's neck, or round that of her old slave, who was even less attractive, or for that matter, would have embraced the world—the triumphant girl became thoughtful; her father would certainly come home ere long, and she could 'not conceal from herself that he would disapprove of the whole proceeding, and would probably send the phial back to the young man, and the money to the dealer. She herself would never have asked the stranger for the bottle if she had had the slightest suspicion of its value; but now it certainly belonged to her, and if she had given it back again she would have given no one any pleasure; on the contrary, she would have offended the stranger, and probably have lost the greatest pleasure that she had ever enjoyed.

What was to be done now? She was still perched on the table; she had taken her left foot in her right hand, and sitting in this quaint position, she looked down on the ground as gravely as if she were trying to find an idea, or a way out of the difficulty, in the pattern on the floor.

The dealer for a moment amused himself in studying her bewilderment, which he thought charming—only wishing that his son, a young painter, were standing in his place. At last he broke the silence however, saying:

" Your father, perhaps, will not agree to our bargain; and yet it is for him you want the money ?"

" Who says so ?"

" Would he have offered me his own treasures if he had not wanted money ?"

" It is only—I can only—" stammered Arsinoe, who was unaccustomed to falsehood—" I would merely not confess to him——"

" I myself saw how innocently you came by the phial," said the dealer, " and Keraunus never need know anything about such a trifle. Fancy yourself, that you have broken it, and that the pieces are lying at the bottom of the sea. Which of all these things does your father value least ?"

" This old sword of Antony," answered the child, her face brightening once more. " He says it is much too long, and too slender to be what it pretends to be. For my part I do not believe that it is a sword at all, but a roasting-spit."

" I shall apply it to that very purpose to-morrow morning in my kitchen," said the dealer, "but I offer you two thousand drachmae for it, and will take it with me and send you the amount in a few hours. Will that do ? "

Arsinoe dropped her foot, glided from the table, and instead of answering, clapped her hands with glee.

" Only tell him," continued Hiram, " that I am able just now to pay so much for this kind of thing, because Caesar is certain to look about him for the things that belonged to Julius Caesar, Marc Antony, Octavianus, Augustus, and other great Romans who have lived in Egypt. The old woman there may bring the spit after me. My slave is waiting outside, and can

hide it under his chiton as far as my kitchen door, for
if he carried it openly the connoisseurs passing by might
covet the priceless treasure, and we must protect ourselves from the evil eye."

The dealer laughed, took the little bottle into his
own keeping, gave the sword to the old woman, and
then took a friendly leave of the young girl.

As soon as Arsinoe was alone, she flew into the bedroom to put on her sandals, threw her veil over her
head, and hastened to the papyrus manufactory. Selene
must know of the unexpected good fortune that had befallen her, and all of them, and then she would have the
poor girl carried home in a litter, for there were always
plenty for hire on the quay.

Things did not always go smoothly—very often very
unsmoothly and stormily between the sisters, but still
anything of importance that happened to Arsinoe,
whether it were good or evil, she must at once tell Selene.

Ye gods! what happiness! She could take her
place among the daughters of the great citizens in the
processions, no less richly apparelled than they, and still
there would remain a nice little sum for her father and
sister; and the work in the factory, the nasty dirty work,
which she hated and loathed, would be at an end, it
was to be hoped, for ever.

The old slave was still sitting on the steps with the
children ; Arsinoe tossed them up one after the other,
and whispered in each child's ear :

"Cakes this evening!" and she kissed the blind
child's eyes, and said :

"You may come with me, dear little man. I will
find a litter for Selene and put you in, and you will be
carried home like a little prince."

The little blind boy threw his arms up with delight, exclaiming: "Through the air, and without falling."

While she was still holding him in her arms, her father came up the steps that led from the rotunda to the passage, his face streaming with heat and excitement; and after wiping his brow and panting to regain his breath, he said:

"Hiram, the curiosity-dealer, met me just outside, with the sword that belonged to Antony; and you sold it to him for two thousand drachmae! you little fool!"

"But, father, you would have given the old spit for a pasty and a draught of wine," laughed Arsinoe.

"I?" cried Keraunus. "I would have had three times the sum for that venerable relic, for which Caesar will give its weight in silver; however, sold is sold. And yet—and yet, the thought that I no longer possess the sword of Antony, will give me many sleepless nights."

"If this evening we set you down to a good dish of meat, sleep will soon follow," answered Arsinoe, and she took the handkerchief out of her father's hand, and coaxingly wiped his temples, going on vivaciously: "We are quite rich folks, father, and will show the other citizens' daughters what we can do."

"Now you shall both take part in the festival," said Keraunus, decidedly. "Caesar shall see that I shun no sacrifice in his honor, and if he notices you, and I bring my complaint against that insolent architect before him——"

"You must let that pass," begged Arsinoe, "if only poor Selene's foot is well by that time."

"Where is she?"

"Gone out."

"Then her foot cannot be so very bad. She will soon come in, it is to be hoped."

"Probably—I mean to fetch her with a litter."

"A litter?" said Keraunus, in surprise. "The two thousand drachmae have turned the girl's head."

"Only on account of her foot. It was hurting her so much when she went out."

"Then why did she not stay at home? As usual she has wasted an hour to save a sesterce, and you, neither of you have any time to spare."

"I will go after her at once."

"No—no, you at any rate, must remain here, for in two hours the matrons and maidens are to meet at the theatre."

"In two hours! but mighty Serapis, what are we to put on?"

"It is your business to see to that," replied Keraunus, "I myself will have the litter you spoke of, and be carried down to Tryphon, the ship-builder. Is there any money left in Selene's box?" Arsinoe went into her sleeping-room, and said, as she returned:

"This is all—six pieces of two drachmae."

"Four will be enough for me," replied the steward, but after a moment's reflection he took the whole half-dozen.

"What do you want with the ship-builder?" asked Arsinoe.

"In the Council," replied Keraunus, "I was worried again about you girls. I said one of my daughters was ill, and the other must attend upon her; but this would not do, and I was asked to send the one who was well. Then I explained that you had no mother, that we lived a retired life for each other, and that I

15

could not bear the idea of sending my daughter alone, and without any protectress to the meeting So then Tryphon said that it would give his wife pleasure to take you to the theatre with her own daughter. This I half accepted, but I declared at once that you would not go, if your elder sister were not better. I could not give any positive consent—you know why." " Oh, blessings on Antony and his noble spit!" cried Arsinoe. " Now everything is settled, and you can tell the ship-builder we shall go. Our white dresses are still quite good, but a few ells of new light blue ribbon for my hair, and of red for Selene's, you must buy on the way, at Abibaal, the Phœnician's."

"Very good."

" I will see at once to both the dresses—but, to be sure, when are we to be ready ? "

'· In two hours."

" Then, do you know what, dear old father ? "

" Well ? "

" Our old woman is half blind, and does everything wrong. Do let me go down to dame Doris at the gate-house, and ask her to help me. She is so clever and kind, and no one irons so well as she does."

" Silence ! " cried the steward, angrily, interrupting his daughter. " Those people shall never again cross my threshold."

" But look at my hair ; only look at the state it is in," cried Arsinoe, excitedly, and thrusting her fingers into her thick tresses which she pulled into disorder. " To do that up again, plait it with new ribbons, iron our dresses, and sew on the brooches—why the Empress' ladies-maid could not do all that in two hours."

"Doris shall never cross this threshold," repeated Keraunus, for all his answer.

"Then tell the tailor Hippias to send me an assistant; but that will cost money."

"We have it, and can pay," replied Keraunus, proudly, and in order not to forget his commissions he muttered to himself while he went to get a litter:

"Hippias the tailor, blue ribbon, red ribbon, and Tryphon the ship-builder."

The tailor's nimble apprentice helped Arsinoe to arrange her dress and Selene's, and was never weary of praising the sheen and silkiness of Arsinoe's hair, while she twisted it with ribbons, built it up and twisted it at the back so gracefully with a comb, that it fell in a thick mass of artfully-curled locks down her neck and back. When Keraunus came back, he gazed with justifiable pride at his beautiful child; he was immensely pleased, and even chuckled softly to himself as he laid out the gold pieces which were brought to him by the curiosity-dealer's servant, and set them in a row and counted them. While he was thus occupied, Arsinoe went up to him and asked laughing: "Hiram has not cheated me then?" Keraunus desired her not to disturb him, and added:

"Think of that sword, the weapon of the great Antony, perhaps the very one with which he pierced his own breast.—Where can Selene be?"

"An hour, an hour and a half had slipped by, and when the fourth half-hour was well begun, and still his eldest daughter did not return, the steward announced that they must set out, for that it would not do to keep the ship-builder's wife waiting. It was a sincere grief to Arsinoe to be obliged to go without Selene. She had

made her sister's dress look as nice as her own, and had
laid it carefully on the divan near the mosaic pavement.
She had taken a great deal of trouble. Never before
had she been out in the streets alone, and it seemed impossible to enjoy anything without the companionship
and supervision of her absent sister. But her father's assertion, that Selene would have a place gladly found for
her, even later, among the maidens, reassured the girl
who was overflowing with joyful expectation.

Finally she perfumed herself a little with the fragrant
extract which Keraunus was accustomed to use before
going to the council, and begged her father to order
the old slave-woman to go and buy the promised cakes
for the little ones during her absence. The children had
all gathered round her, admiring her ' with loud ohs!
and ahs! as if she were some wondrous incarnation, not
to be too nearly approached, and on no account to be
touched. The elaborate dressing of her hair would
not allow of her stooping over them as usual. She
could only stroke little Helios' curls, saying: "To-
morrow you shall have a ride in the air, and perhaps
Selene will tell you a pretty story by-and-bye."

Her heart beat faster than usual as she stepped into
the litter, which was wating for her just in front of the
gate-house. Old Doris looked at her from a distance with
pleasure, and while Keraunus stepped out into the street
to call a litter for himself, the old woman hastily cut the
two finest roses from her bush, and pressing her fingers
to her lips with a sly smile, put them into the girl's
hand.

Arsinoe felt as if it were in a dream that she went to
the ship-builder's house, and from thence to the theatre,
and on her way she fully understood, for the first time,

that alarm and delight may find room side by side in
a girl's mind, and that one by no means hinders the
existence of the other.

Fear and expectation so completely overmastered
her, that she neither saw nor heard what was going on
around her; only once she noticed a young man with a
garland on his head, who, as he passed her, arm in arm
with another, called out to her gaily: "Long live
beauty!"

From that moment she kept her eyes fixed on her
lap and on the roses dame Doris had given her. The
flowers reminded her of the kind old woman's son, and
she wondered whether tall Pollux had perhaps seen her
in her finery. That, she would have liked very much;
and after all, it was not at all impossible, for, of course,
since Pollux had been working at Lochias he must often
have gone to his parents. Perhaps even he had himself
picked the roses for her, but had not dared to give them
to her as her father was so near.

CHAPTER XVII.

But the young sculptor had not been at the gate-
house when Arsinoe went by. He had thought of her
often enough since meeting her again by the bust of her
mother; but on this particular afternoon his time and
thoughts were fully claimed by another fair damsel. Balbilla had arrived at Lochias about noon, accompanied, as
was fitting, by the worthy Claudia, the not wealthy widow
of a senator, who for many years had filled the place of
lady-in-attendance and protecting companion to the

rich fatherless and motherless girl. At Rome, she conducted Balbilla's household affairs with as much sense
and skill as satisfaction in the task. Still she was not
perfectly content with her lot, for her ward's love of
travelling, often compelled her to leave the metropolis,
and in her estimation, there was no place but Rome
where life was worth living. A visit to Baiae for bath-
ing, or in the winter months a flight to the Ligurian coast,
to escape the cold of January and February—these she
could endure; for she was certain there to find, if not
Rome, at any rate Romans; but Balbilla's wish to venture in a tossing ship, to visit the torrid shores of Africa,
which she pictured to herself as a burning oven, she had
opposed to the utmost. At last, however, she was
obliged to put a good face on the matter, for the Empress herself expressed so decidedly her wish to take
Balbilla with her to the Nile, that any resistance would
have been unduteous. Still; in her secret heart, she
could not but confess to herself that her high-spirited
and wilful foster-child—for so she loved to call Balbilla
—would undoubtedly have carried out her purpose
without the Empress' intervention.

Balbilla had come to the palace, as the reader knows,
to sit for her bust.

When Selene was passing by the screen which concealed her playfellow and his work from her gaze, the
worthy matron had fallen gently asleep on a couch,
and the sculptor was exerting all his zeal to convince
the noble damsel that the size to which her hair was
dressed was an exaggeration, and that the superincum-
bence of such a mass must disfigure the effect of the
delicate features of her face. He implored her to remember in how simple a style the great Athenian mas-.

ters, at the best period of the plastic arts, had taught
their beautiful models to dress their hair, and requested
her to do her own hair in that manner next day, and to
come to him before she allowed her maid to put a single
lock through the curling-tongs; for to-day, as he said,
the pretty little ringlets would fly back into shape, like the
spring of a fibula when the pin was bent back. Balbilla
contradicted him with gay vivacity, protested against
his desire to play the part of lady's maid, and defended
her style of hair-dressing on the score of fashion.

"But the fashion is ugly, monstrous, a pain to one's
eyes!" cried Pollux. "Some vain Roman lady must
have invented it, not to make herself beautiful, but to
be conspicuous."

"I hate the idea of being conspicuous by my appearance," answered Balbilla. "It is precisely by following the fashion, however conspicuous it may be, that
we are less remarkable than when we carefully dress far
more simply and plainly—in short, differently to what
it prescribes. Which do you regard as the vainer, the
fashionably-dressed young gentleman on the Canopic
way, or the cynical philosopher with his unkempt hair, his
carefully-ragged cloak over his shoulders, and a heavy
cudgel in his dirty hands?"

"The latter, certainly," replied Pollux. "Still he
is sinning against the laws of beauty which I desire to
win you over to, and which will survive every whim of
fashion, as certainly as Homer's Iliad will survive the
ballad of a street-singer, who celebrates the last murder
that excited the mob of this town.—Am I the first artist
who has attempted to represent your face?"

"No," said Balbilla, with a laugh. "Five Roman
artists have already experimented on my head."

" And did any one of their busts satisfy you ? "

" Not one seemed to me better than utterly bad."

" And your pretty face is to be handed down to posterity in five-fold deformity ? "

" Ah ! no—I had them all destroyed."

" That was very good of them ! " cried Pollux, eagerly. Then turning with a very simple gesture to the bust before him he said :   " Hapless clay, if the lovely lady whom thou art destined to resemble will not sacrifice the chaos of her curls, thy fate will undoubtedly be that of thy predecessors."

The sleeping matron was roused by this speech. " You were speaking," she said, " of the broken busts of Balbilla ? "

"Yes," replied the poetess.

" And perhaps this one may follow them," sighed Claudia.   " Do you know what lies before you in that case ? "

" No, what ? "

" This young lady knows something of your art."

" I learnt to knead clay a little of Aristaeus," interrupted Balbilla.

" Aha ! because Caesar set the fashion, and in Rome it would have been conspicuous not to dabble in sculpture."

" Perhaps."

" And she tried to improve in every bust all that particularly displeased her," continued Claudia.

" I only began the work for the slaves to finish," Balbilla threw in, interrupting her companion.   " Indeed, my people became quite expert in the work of destruction."

" Then my work may, at any rate, hope for a short

agony and speedy death," sighed Pollux. "And it is true—all that lives comes into the world with its end already preordained."

"Would an early demise of your work pain you much?" asked Balbilla.

"Yes, if I thought it successful; not if I felt it to be a failure."

"Any one who keeps a bad bust," said Balbilla, "must feel fearful lest an undeservedly bad reputation is handed down to future generations."

"Certainly! but how then can you find courage to expose yourself for the sixth time to a form of calumny that it is difficult to counteract?"

"Because I can have anything destroyed that I choose," laughed the spoilt girl. "Otherwise sitting still is not much to my taste."

"That is very true," sighed Claudia. "But from you I expect something strikingly good."

"Thank you," said Pollux, "and I will take the utmost pains to complete something that may correspond to my own expectations of what a marble portrait ought to be, that deserves to be preserved to posterity."

"And those expectations require—?"

Pollux considered for a moment, and then he replied:

"I have not always the right words at my command, for all that I feel as an artist. A plastic presentment, to satisfy its creator, must fulfil two conditions; first it must record for posterity in forms of eternal resemblance all that lay in the nature of the person it represents; secondly, it must also show to posterity what the art of the time when it was executed, was capable of"

" That is a matter of course—but you are forgetting your own share."

" My own fame you mean ? "

" Certainly."

" I work for Papias and serve my art, and that is enough ; meanwhile Fame does not trouble herself about me, nor do I trouble myself about her."

" Still, you will put your name on my bust ? "

" Why not ? "

" You are as prudent as Cicero."

" Cicero ? "

" Perhaps you would hardly know old Tullius' wise remark that the philosophers who wrote of the vanity of writers put their names to their books all the same."

" Oh ! I have no contempt for laurels, but I will not run after a thing which could have no value for me, unless it came unsought, and because it was my due."

" Well and good ; but your first condition could only be fulfilled in its widest sense if you could succeed in making yourself acquainted with my thoughts and feelings, with the whole of my inmost mind."

" I see you and talk to you," replied Pollux.

Claudia laughed aloud, and said :

" If instead of two sittings of two hours you were to talk to her for twice as many years you would always find something new in her.   Not a week passes in which Rome does not find in her something to talk about. That restless brain is never quiet, but her heart is as good as gold, and always and everywhere the same."

" And did you suppose that that was new to me ?" asked Pollux.   " I can see the restless spirit of my model in her brow and in her mouth, and her nature is revealed in her eyes."

"And in my snub-nose?" asked Balbilla.

"It bears witness to your wonderful and whimsical notions, which astonish Rome so much."

"Perhaps you are one more that works for the hammer of the slaves," laughed Balbilla.

"And even if it were so," said Pollux, "I should always retain the memory of this delightful hour."

Pontius the architect here interrupted the sculptor, begging Balbilla to excuse him for disturbing the sitting; Pollux must immediately attend to some business of importance, but in ten minutes he would return to his work. No sooner were the two ladies alone, than Balbilla rose and looked inquisitively round and about the sculptor's enclosed work-room; but her companion said:

"A very polite young man, this Pollux, but rather too much at his ease, and too enthusiastic."

"An artist," replied Balbilla, and she proceeded to turn over every picture and tablet with the sculptor's studies in drawing, raised the cloth from the wax model of the Urania, tried the clang of the lute which hung against one of the canvas walls, was here, there, and everywhere, and at last stood still in front of a large clay model, placed in a corner of the studio, and closely wrapped in cloths.

"What may that be?" asked Claudia.

"No doubt a half-finished new model."

Balbilla felt the object in front of her with the tips of her fingers, and said: "It seems to me to be a head. Something remarkable at any rate. In these close-covered dishes we sometimes find the best meat. Let us unveil this shrouded portrait."

"Who knows what it may be?" said Claudia, as she

loosened a twist in the cloths which enveloped the bust.
There are often very remarkable things to be seen in
such workshops.

"Hey, what, it is only a woman's head! I can feel
it," cried Balbilla.

"But you can never tell," the older lady went on, un-
tying a knot. "These artists are such unfettered, unac-
countable beings."

"Do you lift the top, I will pull here," and a
moment later the young Roman stood face to face with
the caricature which Hadrian had moulded on the previous evening, in all its grimacing ugliness. She recognized herself in it at once, and at the first moment,
laughed loudly, but the longer she looked at the disfigured likeness, the more vexed, annoyed and angry
she became. She knew her own face, feature
for feature, all that was pretty in it, and all that
was plain, but this likeness ignored everything in her
face that was not unpleasing, and this it emphasized
ruthlessly, and exaggerated with a refinement.of spite-
fulness. The head was hideous, horrible, and yet it was
hers. As she studied it in profile, she remembered what
Pollux had declared he could read in her features, and
deep indignation rose up in her soul.

Her great inexhaustible riches, which allowed her
the reckless gratification of every whim, and secured
consideration, even for her follies, had not availed to
preserve her from many disappointments which other
girls, in more modest circumstances, would have been
spared. Her kind heart and open hand had often been
abused, even by artists, and it was self-evident to her,
that the man who could make this caricature, who had
so enjoyed exaggerating all that was unlovely in her

face, had wished to exercise his art on her features, not
for her own sake, but for that of the high price she
might be inclined to pay for a flattering likeness. She
had found much to please her in the young sculptor's
fresh and happy artist nature, in his frank demeanor and
his honest way of speech. She felt convinced that Pollux, more readily than anybody else, would understand
what it was that lent a charm to her face, which was in
no way strictly beautiful, a charm which could not be
disputed in spite of the coarse caricature which stood
before her.

She felt herself the richer by a painful experience, indignant, and offended. Accustomed as she was to give
prompt utterance even to her displeasure, she exclaimed hotly, and with tears in her eyes:

"It is shameful, it is base. Give me my wraps
Claudia. I will not stay an instant longer to be the
butt of this man's coarse and spiteful jesting."

"It is unworthy," cried the matron, "so to insult a
person of your position. It is to be hoped our litters
are waiting outside."

Pontius had overheard Balbilla's last words. He
had come into the work-place without Pollux, who was
still speaking to the prefect, and he said gravely as he
approached Balbilla:

"You have every reason to be angry, noble lady.
This thing is an insult in clay, malicious, and at the same
time coarse in every detail; but it was not Pollux who
did it, and it is not right to condemn without a
trial."

"You take your friend's part!" exclaimed Balbilla.

"I would not tell a lie for my own brother."

"You know how to give your words the aspect of

an honorable meaning in serious matters, as he does in jest."

"You are angry and unaccustomed to bridle your tongue," replied the architect. "Pollux, I repeat it, did not perpetrate the caricature, but a sculptor from Rome."

"Which of them? I know them all."

"I may not name him."

"There—you see.—Come away Claudia."

"Stay," said Pontius, decisively. "If you were any one but yourself, I would let you go at once in your anger, and with the double charge on your conscience of doing an injustice to two well-meaning men. But as you are the granddaughter of Claudius Balbillus, I feel it to be due to myself to say, that if Pollux had really made this monstrous bust he would not be in this palace now, for I should have turned him out and thrown the horrid object after him. You look surprised—you do not know who I am that can address you so."

"Yes, yes," cried Balbilla, much mollified, for she felt assured that the man who stood before her, as un- flinching as if he were cast in bronze, and with an earn- est frown, was speaking the truth, and that he must have some right to speak to her with such unwonted de- cision. "Yes indeed, you are the principal architect of the city; Titianus, from whom we have heard of you, has told us great things of you; but how am I to ac- count for your special interest in me?"

"It is my duty to serve you—if necessary, even with my life."

"You," said Balbilla, puzzled. "But I never saw you till yesterday."

"And yet you may freely dispose of all that I have

and am, for my grandfather was your grandfather's
slave."

"I did not know"—said Balbilla, with increasing confusion.

"Is it possible that your noble grandfather's instruc-
tor, the venerable Sophinus, is altogether forgotten.
Sophinus, whom your grandfather freed, and who continued to teach your father also."

"Certainly not—of course not," cried Balbilla.
"He must have been a splendid man, and very learned
besides."

"He was my father's father," said Pontius.

"Then you belong to our family," exclaimed Balbilla, offering him a friendly hand.

"I thank you for those words," answered Pontius.
"Now, once more, Pollux had nothing to, do with that
image."

"Take my cloak, Claudia," said the girl.   "I will sit
again to the young man."

"Not to-day—it would spoil his work," replied Pontius.   "I beg of you to go, and let the annoyance you
so vehemently expressed die out some where else.   The
young sculptor must not know that you have seen this
caricature, it would occasion him much embarrassment.
But if you can return to-morrow in a calmer and more
happy humor, with your lively spirit tuned to a softer
key, then Pollux will be able to make a likeness which
may satisfy the granddaughter of Claudius Balbillus."

"And, let us hope, the grandson of his learned
teacher also," answered Balbilla, with a kindly farewell
greeting, as she went with her companion towards the
door of the hall of the Muses, where her slaves were
waiting.   Pontius escorted her so far in silence, then he

returned to the work-place, and safely wrapped the caricature up again in its cloths.

As he went out into the hall again, Pollux hurried up to meet him, exclaiming:

"The Roman architect wants to speak to you, he is a grand man!"

"Balbilla was called away, and bid me greet you," replied Pontius. "Take that thing away for fear she should see it. It is coarse and hideous." •

A few moments later he stood in the presence of the Emperor, who expressed the wish to play the part of listener while Balbilla was sitting. When the architect, after begging him not to let Pollux know of the incident, told him of what had occurred in the screened-off studio, and how angry the young Roman lady had been at the caricature, which was certainly very offensive, Hadrian rubbed his hands and laughed aloud with delight. Pontius ground his teeth, and then said very earnestly:

"Balbilla seems to me a merry-hearted girl, but of a noble nature. I see no reason to laugh at her."

Hadrian looked keenly into the daring architect's eyes, laid his hand on his shoulder, and replied with a certain threatening accent in his deep voice:

"It would be an evil moment for you, or for any one, who should do so in my presence. But age may venture to play with edged tools, which children may not even touch."

CHAPTER XVIII.

SELENE entered the gate-way in the endlessly-long walk of sun-dried bricks which enclosed the wide space where stood the court-yards, water-tanks and huts, belonging to the great papyrus manufactory of Plutarch, where she and her sister were accustomed to work. She could generally reach it in a quarter of an hour, but to-day it had taken more than four times as long and she herself did not know how she had managed to hold herself up, and to walk—limp—stumble along, in spite of the acute pain she was suffering. She would willingly have clung to every passer-by, have held on to every slow passing vehicle, to every beast of burden that overtook her—but man and beast mercilessly went on their way, without paying any heed to her. She got many a push from those who were hurrying by and who scarcely turned round to look at her, when from time to time she stopped to sink for a moment on to the nearest door-step, or some low cornice or bale of goods; to dry her eyes, or press her hand to her foot, which was now swollen to a great size, hoping, as she did so, to be able to forget, under the sense of a new form of pain, the other unceasing and unendurable torment, at least for a few minutes.

The street boys who had run after her, and laughed at her, ceased pursuing her when they found that she constantly stopped to rest. A woman with a child in her arms once asked her, as she stopped to rest a minute on a threshold, whether she wanted anything, but walked

16

on when Selene shook her head and made no other
answer.

Once she thought she must give up altogether, when
suddenly the street was filled with jeering boys and inquisitive men and women—for Verus, the superb Verus,
came by in his chariot, and what a chariot! The Alexandrian populace were accustomed to see much that
was strange in the busy streets of their crowded city ;
but this vehicle attracted every eye, and excited astonishment, admiration and mirth, wherever it appeared, and
not unfrequently the bitterest ridicule.   The handsome
Roman stood in the middle of his gilt chariot, and himself
drove the four white horses, harnessed abreast; on his
head he wore a wreath, and across his breast, from one
shoulder, a garland of roses.   On the foot-board of the
quadriga sat two children, dressed as Cupids; their
little legs dangled in the air, and they each held, attached
by a long gilt wire, a white dove which fluttered in front
of Verus.

The dense and hurrying crowd, crushed Selene re-
morselessly against the wall; instead of looking at the
wonderful sight she covered her face with her hands to
hide the distortion of pain in her features; still she just saw
the splendid chariot, the gold harness on the horses, and
the figure of the insolent owner glide past her, as if in a
dream that was blurred by pain, and the sight infused
into her soul, that was already harassed by pain and anxiety, a feeling of bitter aversion, and the envious thought
that the mere trappings of the horses of this extravagant
prodigal would suffice to keep her and her family above
misery for a whole year.

By the time the chariot had turned the next corner,
and the crowd had followed it, she had almost fallen to

the ground. She could not take another step, and looked round for a litter, but, while generally there was no lack of them, in this spot, to-day there was not one to be seen. The factory was only a few hundred steps farther, but in her fancy they seemed like so many stadia. Presently some of the workmen and women from the factory came by, laughing and showing each other their wages, so the payment must be now going on. A glance at the sun showed her how long she had already been on her way, and remined her of the purpose of her walk.

With the exertion of all her strength, she dragged herself a few steps farther; then, just as her courage was again beginning to fail, a little girl came running towards her who was accustomed to wait upon the workers at the table where Selene and Arsinoe were employed, and who held in her hand a pitcher. She called the dusky little Egyptian, and said:

" Hathor, pray come back to the factory with me. I cannot walk any farther, my foot is so dreadfully painful ; but if I lean a little on your shoulder, I shall get on better."

" I cannot," said the child. ‚ " If I make haste home I shall have some dates," and she ran on.

Selene looked after her, and an inward voice, against which she had had to rebel before to-day, asked her why she of all people must be a sufferer for others, when they thought only of themselves, and with a heavy sigh, she made a fresh attempt to proceed on her way.

When she had gone a few steps, neither seeing nor hearing anything that passed her, a girl came up to her, and asked her timidly, but kindly, what was the matter. It was a leaf-joiner who sat opposite to her at the works, a poor, deformed creature, who, nevertheless, plied her nimble fingers contentedly and silently, and who at first had taught Selene and Arsinoe many useful tricks of working. The girl offered her crooked shoulder un-asked as a support to Selene, and measured her steps to those of the sufferer with as much nicety as if she felt everything that Selene herself did ; thus, without speaking, they reached the door of the factory; there, in the first court-yard the little hunchback made Selene sit down on one of the bundles of papyrus-stems which lay all about the place, by the side of the tanks in which the plants were dipped to freshen them, and arranged in order, built up into high heaps, according to the locali-ties whence they were brought. After a short rest, they went on through the hall in which the triangular green stems were sorted, according to the quality of the white pith they contained. The next rooms, in which men stripped the green sheath from the pith, and the long galleries where the more skilled hands split the pith with sharp knives into long moist strips about a finger wide, and of different degrees of fineness, seemed to Selene to grow longer the farther she went, and to be absolutely interminable.

Generally the pith-splitters sat here in long rows, each at his own little table, on each side of a gangway left for the slaves, who carried the prepared material to the drying-house ; but, to-day, most of them had left their places and stood chatting together and packing up their wooden clips, knives, and sharpening-stones. Half way down this room Selene's hand fell from her com-panion's shoulder, she turned giddy, and said in a low tone:

" I can go no farther—"

The little hunchback held her up as well as she could, and though she herself was far from strong, she succeeded in dragging, rather than carrying, Selene to an empty couch and in laying her upon it. A few workmen gathered around the senseless girl, and brought some water, then when she opened her eyes again, and they found that she belonged to the rooms where the prepared papyrus-leaves were gummed together, some of them offered to carry her thither, and before Selene could consent they had taken up the bench and lifted it with its light burden. Her damaged foot hung down, and gave the poor girl such pain that she cried out, and tried to raise the injured limb and hold her ankle in her hand; her comrade helped by taking the poor little foot in her own hand, and supporting it with tender and cautious care.

As she thus went by, carried, as it were, in triumph by the men, and borne high in the air, every one turned to look at her, and the suffering girl felt this rather as if she were some criminal being carried through the streets to exhibit her disgrace to the citizens. But when she found herself in the large rooms where, in one place men, and in another the most skilled of the women and girls were employed in laying the narrow strips of papyrus crosswise over each other, and gumming them together, she had recovered strength enough to pull her veil over her face which she held down. Arsinoe, and she herself, in order to remain unrecognized had always been accustomed to walk through these rooms closely veiled, and not to lay their wraps aside till they reached the little room where they sat with about twenty other women to glue the sheets together.

Every one looked at her with curious enquiry. Her

foot certainly hurt her, the cut in her head was burning, and she felt altogether intensely miserable; still there was room and to spare in her soul for the false pride that she inherited from her father, and for the humiliating consciousness that she was regarded by these people as one of themselves.

In the room in which she worked, none but free women were employed, but more than a thousand slaves worked in the factory and she would as soon have eaten with beasts without plate or spoon, as have shared a meal with them. At one time, when every thing in their house seemed going to ruin, it was her own father who had suggested the papyrus factory to her attention, by telling her, with indignation, that the daughter of an impoverished citizen had degraded herself and her whole class by devoting herself to working in the papyrus factory to earn money. She was pretty well paid, to be sure, and in answer to Selene's enquiry, he had stated the amount she earned and mentioned the name of the rich manufacturer to whom she had sold her social standing for gold.

Soon after this Selene had gone alone to the factory, had discussed all that was necessary with the manager, and had then begun, with Arsinoe, to work regularly in the factory where they now for two years had spent some hours of every day in gumming the papyrus-leaves together.

How many a time at the beginning of a new week, or when under the influence of a special fit of aversion to her work, had Arsinoe refused to go with her ever again to the factory; how much persuasive eloquence had she expended, how many new ribbons had she bought, how often had she consented to allow her to go to some spectacle, which consumed half a week's wages, to induce Arsinoe to persist in her work, or to avert the fulfilment of her threat to tell her father, whither her daily walk—as she called it—tended.

When Selene, who had been carried as far as the door of her own work-room, was sitting once more in her usual place in front of the long table on which she worked, and where hundreds of prepared papyrus strips were to be joined together, she felt scarcely able to raise the veil from her face. She drew the uppermost sheets towards her, dipped the brush in the gum-jar, and began to touch the margin of the leaf with it—but in the very act, her strength forsook her, the brush fell from her fingers, she dropped her hands on the table and her face in her hands, and began to cry softly.

While she sat thus, her tears slowly flowing, her shoulders heaving, and her whole body shaken with shuddering sobs, a woman who sat opposite to her, beckoned to the deformed girl, and after whispering to her a few words grasped her hand firmly and warmly and looked straight into her eyes with her own, which though lustreless were clear and steady; then the little hunchback silently took Arsinoe's vacant place by Selene, and pushed the smaller half of the papyrus leaves over to the woman, and both set diligently to work on the gumming.

They had been thus occupied for some time when Selene at last raised her head and was about to take up her brush again. She looked round for it and perceived her companion, whom she had not even thanked for her helpfulness, busily at work in Arsinoe's seat. She looked at her neighbor with eyes still full of tears, and as the girl, who was wholly absorbed in her task, did not notice her gaze, Selene said in a tone of surprise rather than kindliness.

"This is my sister's place; you may sit here to-day, but when the factory opens again she must sit by me again."

"I know, I know," said the workwoman shyly. "I am only finishing your sheets because I have no more of my own to do, and I can see how badly your foot is hurting you."

The whole transaction was so strange and novel to Selene that she did not even understand her neighbor's meaning, and she only said, with a shrug:

"You may earn all you can, for aught I can do; I cannot do anything to-day."

Her deformed companion colored and looked up doubtfully at her opposite neighbor, who at once laid aside her brush and said, turning to Selene:

"That is not what Mary means, my child. She is doing one-half of your day's task and I am doing the other, so that your suffering foot may not deprive you of your day's pay."

"Do I look so very poor then?" exclaimed Keraunus' daughter, and a faint crimson tinged her pale cheeks.

"By no means, my child," replied the woman. "You and your sister are evidently of good family—but pray let us have the pleasure of being of some help to you."

"I do not know—" Selene stammered.

"If you saw that it hurt me to stoop when the wind blows the strips of papyrus on to the floor, would you not willingly pick them up for me?" continued the woman. "What we are doing for you is neither less

nor yet much more than that. In a few minutes we
shall have finished and then we can follow the others,
for every one else has left. I am the overseer of the
room, as you know, and must in any case remain here
till the last workwoman has gone."

Selene felt full well that she ought to be grateful for
the kindness shown her by these two women, and yet
she had a sense of having a deed of almsgiving forced
upon her acceptance, and she answered quickly, still
with the blood mounting to her cheeks. "I am very
grateful for your good intentions, of course, very grateful; but here each one must work for herself, and it
would ill-become me to allow you to give me the
money you have earned."

The girl spoke these words with a decisiveness
which was not free from arrogance, but this did not disturb the woman's gentle equanimity—"widow Hannah," as she was called by the workwomen—and fixing
the calm gaze of her large eyes on Selene, she answered
kindly:

"We have been very happy to work for you, dear
daughter, and a divine Sage has said that it is more
blessed to give than to receive. Do you understand
all that that means? In our case it is as much as to say
that it makes kind-hearted folks much happier to do
others a pleasure than to receive good gifts. You said
just now that you were grateful; do you want now to
spoil our pleasure?"

"I do not quite understand—" answered Selene.

"No?" interrupted widow Hannah. "Then only
try for once to do some one a pleasure with sincere and
heartfelt love, and you will see how much good it does
one, how it opens the heart and turns every trouble to

a pleasure. Is it not true Mary, we shall be sincerely obliged to Selene if only she will not spoil the pleasure we have had in working for her ?"

"I have been so glad to do it," said the deformed girl, "and there—now I have finished."

"And I too," said the widow, pressing the last leaf on to its fellow with a cloth, and then adding her pile of finished sheets to Mary's.

"Thank you very much," murmured Selene, with downcast eyes, and rising from her seat, but she tried to support herself on her lame foot and this caused her such pain, that with a low cry, she sank back on the stool. The widow hastened to her side, knelt down by her, took the injured foot with tender care in her delicate and slender hands, examined it attentively, felt it gently, and then exclaimed with horror :

"Good Lord! and did you walk through the streets with a foot in this state?" and looking up at Selene she said affectionately. "Poor child, poor child! it must have hurt you! Why the swelling has risen above your sandal-straps. It is frightful! and yet—do you live far from this ?"

"I can get home in half an hour."

"Impossible! First let me see on my tablets how much the paymaster owes you that I may go and fetch it, and then we will soon see what can be done with you. Meanwhile you sit still daughter dear, and you Mary rest her foot on a stool and undo the straps very gently from her ankle. Do not be afraid my child, she has soft, careful hands." As she spoke she rose and kissed Selene on her forehead and eyes, and Selene clung to her and could only say with swimming eyes, and a voice trembling with feeling :

" Dame Hannah, dear widow Hannah."

As the warm sunshine of an October day reminds the traveller of the summer that is over, so the widow's words and ways brought back to Selene the long lost love and care of her good mother; and something soothing mingled in the bitterness of the pain she was suffering. She looked gratefully at the kind woman and obediently sat still; it was such a comfort once more to obey an order, and to obey willingly—to feel herself a child again and to be grateful for loving care.

Hannah went away, and Mary knelt down in front of Selene to loosen and remove the straps which were half buried in the swelled muscles. She did it with the greatest caution, but her fingers had hardly touched her, when Selene shrank back with a groan, and before she could undo the sandal, the patient had fainted away. Mary fetched some water and bathed her brow, and the burning wound in her head, and by the time Selene had once more opened her eyes, dame Hannah had returned. When the widow stroked her thick soft hair, Selene looked up with a smile and asked: " Have I been to sleep ?"

" You shut your eyes my child," replied the widow. " Here are your wages and your sister's, for twelve days; do not move, I will put it in your little bag. Mary has not succeeded in loosening your sandal, but the physician who is paid to attend on the factory people will be here directly, and will order what is proper for your poor foot. The manager is having a litter fetched for you.—Where do you live ?"

" We ?" cried Selene, alarmed. " No, no, I must go home."

"But my child you cannot walk farther than the court-yard even if we both help you."

"Then let me get a litter out in the street. My father—no one must know—I cannot."

Hannah signed to Mary to leave them, and when she had shut the door on the deformed girl, she brought a stool, sat down opposite to Selene, laid a hand on the knee that was not hurt, and said:

"Now, dear girl, we are alone. I am no chatter-box, and will certainly not betray your confidence. Tell me quietly who you belong to. Tell me—you believe that I mean well by you?"

"Yes," replied Selene, looking the widow full in the face—a regularly-cut face, set in abundant smooth brown hair, and with the stamp of genuine and heart-felt goodness. "Yes—you remind me of my mother."

"Well, I might be your mother."

"I am nineteen years old already."

"Already," replied Hannah, with a smile. "Why my life has been twice as long as yours. I had a child, too, a boy; and he was taken from me when he was quite little. He would be a year older than you now, my child—is your mother still alive?"

"No," said Selene, with her old dry manner, that had become a habit. "The gods have taken her from us. She would have been, like you, not quite forty now, and she was as pretty and as kind as you are. When she died she left seven children besides me, all little, and one of them blind. I am the eldest, and do what I çan for them, that they may not be starved."

"God will help you in the loving task."

"The gods!" exclaimed Selene, bitterly. "They

let them grow up, the rest I have to see to—oh! my foot, my foot!"

" Yes, we will think of that before anything else. Your father is alive ? "

" Yes."

" And he is not to know that you work here ? " Selene shook her head.

" He is in moderate circumstances, but of good family ? "

" Yes."

" Here, I think, is the doctor. Well ? May I know your father's name ? I must if I am to get you safe home."

" I am the daughter of Keraunus, the steward of the palace, and we have rooms there, at Lochias," Selene answered, with rapid decision, but in a low whisper, so that the physician, who just then opened the room door, might not hear her. " No one, and least of all, my father, must know that I work here."

The widow made a sign to her to be easy, greeted the grey-haired leech who came in with his assistant; and then, while the old man examined the injured limb, and cut the straps with a sharp pair of scissors, she bathed the girl's face and cut head with a wet handkerchief, supported the poor child in her arms, and, when the pain seemed too much for her, kissed her pale cheeks.

Many sighs from the bottom of her heart, and many shrill little cries betrayed how intense was the pain Selene was enduring. When at length, her delicate and graceful foot—distorted just now by the extensive swelling—was freed from the bands and straps, and the ankle had been felt and pressed in every direction by the leech, he exclaimed, turning to the assistant who stood ready to lend a helping hand:

"Look here, Hippolytus, the girl came along the streets with her ankle in this state. If any one else had told me of such a thing, I should have desired him to keep his lies to himself. The fibula is broken at the joint, and with this injured limb the child has walked farther than I could trust myself at all without my litter. By Sirius! child, if you are not crippled for life it will be a miracle."

Selene had listened with closed eyes, and exhausted almost to unconsciousness; but at his last words she slightly shrugged her shoulders with a faint smile of scorn on her lips.

"You think nothing of being lame!" said the old man, who let no gesture of his patient escape him. "That, of course, is your affair, but it is mine to see that you do not become a cripple in my hands. The opportunity for working a miracle is not given to one of us every day, and happily for me, you yourself bring a powerful coadjutor to help me. I do not mean a lover or anything of that kind, though you are much too pretty, but your lovely, vigorous, healthy youth. The hole in your head is hotter than it need be—keep it properly cool with fresh water. Where do you live, child?"

"Almost half an hour from here," said Hannah, answering for Selene.

"She cannot be taken so far as that, even in a litter, at present," said the old man.

"I must go home!" cried Selene, resolutely, and trying to sit up.

"Nonsense," exclaimed the physician. "I must

forbid your moving at all. Lie still, and be patient and obedient, or your foolish joke will come to a bad end; fever has already set in, and it will increase by the evening. It has nothing much to do with the leg, but all the more with the inflamed scalp-wound. Do you think," he added, turning to the widow, "that perhaps a bed could be made here on which she might lie, and remain here till the factory reopens?"

"I would rather die," shrieked Selene, trying to draw away her foot from the leech.

"Be still—be still, my dear child," said the good woman, soothingly. "I know where I can take you. My house is in a garden belonging to Paulina, the widow of Pudeus, near this and close to the sea; it is not above a thousand paces off, and there you will have a soft couch and tender care. A good litter is waiting, and I should think——"

"Even that is a good distance," said the old man. "However, she cannot possibly be better cared for than by you, dame Hannah. Let us try it then, and I will accompany you to lash those accursed bearers' skins if they do not keep in step."

Selene made no attempt to resist these orders, and willingly drank a potion which the old man gave her; but she cried to herself as she was lifted into the litter and her foot was carefully propped on pillows.

In the street, which they soon reached through a side door, she again almost lost consciousness, and half awake but half as in a dream, she heard the leech's voice as he cautioned the bearers to walk carefully, and saw the people, and vehicles, and horsemen pass her on their way. Then she saw that she was being carried through a large garden, and at last she dimly perceived

that she was being laid on a bed. From that moment
every thing was merged in a dream, though the frequent
convulsions of pain that passed over her features and
now and then a rapid movement of her hand to the cut
in her head, showed that she was not altogether
oblivious to the reality of her sufferings.

Dame Hannah sat by the bed, and carried out the
physician's instructions with exactness; he himself did
not leave his patient till he was perfectly satisfied with
her bed and her position. Mary stayed with the
widow helping her to wet handkerchiefs and to make
bandages out of old linen.

When Selene began to breathe more calmly Hannah
beckoned her assistant to come close to her and asked
in a low voice.

"Can you stay here till early to-morrow, we must
take it in turns to watch her, most likely for several
nights—how hot this wound on her head is!"

"Yes, I can stay, only I must tell my mother that
she may not be frightened."

"Quite right, and then you may undertake another
commission for I cannot leave the poor child just
now."

"Her people will be anxious about her."

"That is just where you must go; but no one besides us two must know who she is. Ask for Selene's
sister and tell her what has happened; if you see her
father tell him that I am taking care of his daughter,
and that the physician strictly forbids her moving or
being moved. But he must not know that Selene is
one of us workers, so do not say a word about the
factory before him. If you find neither Arsinoe nor
her father at home, tell any one that opens the door to

you that I have taken the sick child in, and did it gladly. But about the workshop, do your hear, not a word. One thing more, the poor girl would never have come down to the factory in spite of such pain, unless her family had been very much in need of her wages; so just give these drachmae to some one and say, as is perfectly true, that we found them about her person."

CHAPTER XIX. ·

PLUTARCH was one of the richest citizens of Alexandria, and the owner of the papyrus manufactory where Selene and Arsinoe worked; and he had of his own free will offered to provide for the "suitable" entertainment of the wives and daughters of his fellow-citizens, who were, this very day, to assemble in one of the smaller theatres of the city. Every one that knew him, knew too that "suitable" with him meant as much as to say imperial splendor.

The ship-builder's daughter had prepared Arsinoe for grand doings, but by the time she had reached the entrance only of the theatre her expectations were exceeded, for as soon as she gave her father's name and her own, a boy, who looked out from an arbor of flowers gave her a magnificent bunch of flowers, and another, who sat perched on a dolphin, handed her, as a ticket of admission, a finely-cut ornament of ivory mounted in gold, with a pin, by which the invited owner was intended to fix it like a brooch in her peplum; and at each entrance to the theatre, the

17

ladies, as they came in, had a similar present made them.

The passage leading to the auditorium was full of perfume, and Arsinoe, who had already visited this theatre two or three times, hardly recognized it, it was so gaily decorated with colored scarfs. And who had ever seen ladies and young girls filling the best places instead of men, as was the case to-day? Indeed the citizens' daughters were in general not permitted to see a theatrical peformance at all, unless on very special and exceptional occasions. She looked up with a smile at the empty topmost rows of the cheapest seats of the semicircular auditorium, as one looks at an old play-fellow one had outgrown by a head, for it was there—when she had occasionally been permitted to dip into their scanty common purse—that she had almost fainted many a time, with pleasure, fear, or sympathy, though the draught so high up and under the open heaven which was the only roof, was incessantly blowing; and in summer the discomforts were even greater from the awning which shaded the amphitheatre on the sunny side. The wide breadths of canvas were managed by means of stout ropes, and when these were pulled through the rings they rode in, they made a screech which compelled the bearer to stop his ears; and often it was necessary to duck his head not to be hit by the heavy ropes or by the awning itself. But Arsinoe only remembered these things to-day as a butterfly sporting in the sun may remember the hideous pupa-case that it has burst and left behind it.

Radiant with happy excitement, she was led to her seat with her young companion, the black-haired daughter of the shipwright. She perceived indeed that numerous eyes turned upon her, but that only added to her pleasure, for she knew that she could well bear looking at, and there could be no greater pleasure, as she thought, than to give pleasure to a multitude.

To-day at any rate! For those who were looking at her were the chief citizens of Alexandria; they stood on the stage, and among them stood kind tall Pollux, waving his hand to her. She could not keep her feet quiet, but she did contrive to keep her arms still by crossing them in front of her, so that they might not betray how excited she was.

This distribution of parts had already begun, for, by waiting for Selene, she had come in almost half an hour too late. As soon as she saw that the eyes that had been attracted to herself as she entered the theatre had turned to other objects she herself looked round her. She was sitting on a bench at the lowest and narrowest end of one of the wedge-shaped sections of seats, which grew wider at the upper end, and which were divided from each other by gangways for those who came and went, thus forming the semicircular area of the audi-torium.

Here she was surrounded only by young girls and women who were to have a part or place in the performances. The places for these interested persons were divided from the stage by a space for the orchestra, whence the stage was easily reached by steps up which the chorus were wont to mount to it.

Behind Arsinoe, in the larger circular rows, sat the parents and husbands of the performers, among whom Keraunus, in his saffron robe, had taken a place, besides a considerable number of sight-loving matrons and older citizens who had accepted Plutarch's invitation.

Among the young women and girls Arsinoe saw
several whose beauty struck her, but she admired them
ungrudgingly, and it never came into her head to compare herself with them, for she knew very accurately
that she was pretty, and that even here she had nothing
to conceal, and this was enough for her.

The many-voiced hum which incessantly buzzed in
her ears, and the perfume which rose from the attar in
the orchestra had something intoxicating in them. Her
gaze round the assembled multitude could not disturb
any one, and her companion had found some friends
with whom she was chattering and laughing. Other
ladies and young girls sat staring silently in front of
them, or studying the appearance of the rest of the audience, male and female ; while others again concentrated
their whole attention on the stage. Arsinoe soon followed this example, nor was this solely on account of
Pollux who, by the prefect's orders, had been enlisted
among the artists to whom the arrangement of the display was entrusted, in spite of the objections of his master Papias. More than once before had she seen the afternoon sun shine as brightly into the theatre as it did
to-day, and the blue sky overarching it without a cloud,
but with what different feelings did she now direct her
gaze to the raised level behind the orchestra. The background, it is true, was the same as usual, the pillared
front of a palace built entirely of colored marbles, and
ornamented with gold ; but on this occasion fresh garlands of fragrant flowers hung gracefully between the
pilasters and across from column to column. Several
artists, the first of the city, with tablets and styla in their
hands were moving about among fifty girls and ladies,
and Plutarch himself, and the gentlemen with him, com-

posed, as it were a grand chorus which sometimes divided, and sometimes stood all together.

On the right side of the stage were three purple-covered couches. On one of them sat Titianus, the prefect, who, like the artists, used his pencil; with him was his wife Julia. On another reclined Verus, at full length, and as usual, crowned with roses; the third was for Plutarch, but was unoccupied. The praetor did not hesitate to interrupt any speaker, as though he were the host of the entertainment, and many of his remarks were followed by loud applause, or approving laughter.

The face and figure of the wealthy Plutarch, which could never be forgotten, were not altogether strange to Arsinoe, for, a few days previously he had shown himself for the first time in many years in his papyrus factory, with an architect to settle with him how the courts and rooms could best be cleaned and decorated for the reception of the Emperor; and on this occasion he had gone into the room where she worked and had pinched her cheek with a few roguish and flattering words.

There he was, walking across the stage. He was an old man, said to be about seventy years of age, his legs were half-paralyzed, and they nevertheless moved with a series of incessant and rapid but unvoluntary jerks under his heavy bowed body, and he was supported on either hand by a tall young fellow. His nobly-formed head, must have been in his youth, of extraordinary beauty. Now his head was covered by a wig of long brown hair, his eyebrows and lashes were darkly dyed, his cheeks daubed with red and white paint, which gave his countenance a fixed expression, as if he had been stricken in the very act of smiling. On his curls he wore a wreath of rare flowers in long racemes. An

abundance of red and white roses stuck out from the
front folds of his ample toga, and were held in their
place by gold brooches, sparkling with precious stones
of large size. The hems of his mantle were all edged
with rose-buds, and each was fastened in with an emer-
ald that shone like some bright insect. The young
men who supported him seemed like a portion of himself; he took no more heed of them than if they had
been crutches, and they needed not command to tell
them where he wished to go, where to stand still, and
where to rest.   .

At a distance his face was like that of a youth, but
seen close it looked like a painted plaster mask, with
regular features and large movable eyes.

Favorinus, the sophist, had said of him that one
might cry over his handsome locomotive corpse, if one
were not obliged to laugh at it, and it was said that he
had himself declared that he would force his faithless
youth to remain with him. The Alexandrians called
him the Adonis with six legs, on account of the lads
who supported him, and without whom no one ever
saw him and who always accompanied him when he
went out. The first time he heard this nickname he
remarked: "They had better have called me six-
handed;" and in fact he had a thoroughly good heart,
he was liberal and benevolent, took fatherly care of his
work-people, treated his slaves well, enriched those
whom he set free, and from time to time distributed large
sums among the people in money and in grain.

Arsinoe looked compassionately on the poor old
man who could not buy back his youth with all his
money and all his art.

In the supercilious man who at once came up to Plu-

tarch she recognized the art-dealer Gabinius to whom
her father had shown the door, on account of the mosaic
picture in their sitting-room, but their conversation was
interrupted, for the distribution of the women's part for
the group of Alexander's entry into Babylon, was now
about to take place; about fifty girls and young women
were sent away from the stage and went down into the
orchestra. The Exegetes, the highest official in the town,
now came forward and took a new list out of the hand of
Papias the sculptor. After rapidly casting an eye on
this, he handed it to a herald who followed him, who
proclaimed to all the assembly :

"In the name of the most noble Exegetes I request
your attention, all you ladies here assembled, the wives
and daughters of Macedonians and of Roman citizens.
We now come to a distribution of the characters in our
representation of the life and history of the great Macedonian, of the 'Marriage of Alexander and Roxana,'
and I hereby request those among you to come upon
the stage whom our artists have selected to take part in
this scene in the procession." After this exordium he
shouted in a deep and resonant voice a long list of
names, and while this was going on every other sound
was hushed in the wide amphitheatre.

Even on the stage all was still ; only Verus whispered
a few remarks to Titianus, and the curiosity-dealer spoke
into Plutarch's ear, long sentences with the stringent
emphasis which was peculiar to him; and the old man
answered sometimes with an assenting nod, and sometimes with a deprecatory motion of his hands.

Arsinoe listened with suspended breath to the
herald's proclamation ; she started and colored all over,
with her eyes fixed on the bunch of flowers in her hand,

when she heard from the stage loudly uttered and plain to be heard by all present:

"Arsinoe, the second daughter of Keraunus, the Macedonian and a Roman citizen."

The ship-builder's daughter had already been called before her, and had immediately left her seat, but Arsinoe waited modestly till some older ladies rose. She then joined them and went among the last members of the little procession which went down to the orchestra and from thence up the steps for the chorus, on to the stage.

There the ladies and young girls were placed in two ranks, and looked at with amiable consideration by the artists. Arsinoe was not long in perceiving that these gentlemen looked at her longer and more often than at the others; and then, after the masters of the festival had gone aside in groups to discuss the matter they looked at her constantly and were talking, she felt sure, about her. Nor did it escape her that she had become the centre of many glances from the lookers-on who were sitting in the theatre, and it occurred to her that on several sides people were pointing at her with their fingers. She did not know which way she should look and began to feel bashful; still she was pleased at being remarked by so many people, and as she stood looking at the ground out of sheer embarrassment to hide the delight she felt, Verus, who had gone up to the group of artists, called out, putting his hand on the prefect's arm.

"Charming—charming! a Roxana that might have sprung straight out of the picture."

Arsinoe heard these words, and guessing that they referred to her she became more confused than ever,

while her awkward smile gradually changed to an expression of joyful but anxious expectation of a delight
which was almost painful in its magnitude.

Now one of the artists pronounced her name, and
as she ventured to raise her eyes to see if it were not
Pollux who had spoken, she observed the wealthy
Plutarch who, with his two living crutches and Gabinius, the lean curiosity-dealer, was inspecting the ranks
of her companions. Presently he had come quite close
to her, and as he was helped towards her with tottering
steps, he dug the dealer in the ribs and said, kissing the
back of his hand, and winking his great eyes: " I know
—I know ! It is not easily forgotten. Ivory and red
coral ! "

Arsinoe started, the blood left her cheeks, and all
satisfaction fled from her heart when the old man came
to a stand-still in front of her, and said kindly:

"Ah ! ah ! a bud out of the papyrus factory among
all these proud roses and lilies. Ah ! ah ! out of my
work-rooms to join my assembly ! Never mind—never
mind, beauty is everywhere welcome. I do not
ask how you got here. I am only glad that you are
here."

Arsinoe covered part of her face with her hand, but
he tapped her white arm three times with his middle
finger, and then tottered on laughing to himself. The
dealer had caught Plutarch's words, and asked him,
when they had gone a few steps from Arsinoe, with
eager indignation:

" Did I hear you rightly ? a workwoman in your
factory, and here among our daughters ? "

" So it is—two busy hands among so many idle
ones," said the old man, gaily.

"Then she must have forced her way in, and must be turned out."

"Certainly she shall not.—Why, she is charm ing."

"It is revolting! here, in this assembly!"

"Revolting?" interrupted Plutarch. "Oh dear, no! we must not be too particular. And how are we to obtain mere children from you antiquity-mongers?" Then he added pleasantly:

"This lovely creature must I should think, delight your fine sense of beauty; or are you afraid that she may seem better suited to the part of Roxana than your own charming daughter? Only listen to the men up there! Let us see what is going on."

These words referred to a loud discussion which had arisen close by the couches of the prefect and Verus, the praetor. They, and with them most of the painters and sculptors present, were of opinion that Arsinoe would be a wonderfully effective Roxana; they maintained that her face and figure answered perfectly to those of the Bactrian princes as they were represented by Action, whose picture was, to a certain extent, to serve as the basis of the living group. Only Papias and two of his fellow-artists, declared against this choice, and eagerly asserted that among all the damsels present one, and one alone, was worthy to appear before the Emperor as Alexander's bride, and that one was Praxilla, the daughter of Gabinius. All three were in close business relations with the father of the young girl, who was tall, and slim, and certainly very lovely, and they wanted to do a pleasure to the rich and knowing purchaser. Their zeal even assumed a tone of vehemence, when the dealer, following in the wake of Plutarch,

joined the group of disputants, and they were certain of
being heard by him.

"And who is this girl yonder?" asked Papias, pointing to Arsinoe. as the two came up. "Nothing can be
said against her beauty, but she is dressed less than
simply, and wears no kind of ornament worth speaking
of—it is a thousand to one against her parents being in
a position to provide her with such a rich dress, and
such costly jewels as Roxana certainly ought to display
when about to be married to Alexander. The Asiatic
princess must appear in silk, gold and precious stones.
Now my friend here will be able so to dress his Praxilla
that the splendor of her attire might have astonished
the great Macedonian himself, but who is the father of
that pretty child who is satisfied with the blue ribbon
in her hair, her two roses, and her little white frock?"

"Your reflections are just, Papias," interrupted the
dealer, with dry incisiveness. "The girl you are speaking of is quite out of the question. I do not say so for
my daughter's sake, but because everything in bad taste
is odious to me; it is hardly conceivable how such a
young thing could have had the audacity to force herself in here. A pretty face, to be sure, opens locks and
bars. She is—do not be too much startled—she is
nothing more than a work-girl in the papyrus factory of
our excellent host, Plutarch."

"That is not the truth," Pollux interrupted, indignantly, as he heard this assertion.

"Moderate your tongue, young man," replied the
dealer. "I can call you to witness, noble Plutarch."

"Let her be whom she may," answered the old
man, with annoyance. "She is very like one of my
workwomen, but even if she had come straight here

from the gumming-table with such a face and such a figure, she is perfectly in place here and everywhere. That is my opinion."

"Bravo! my fine friend!" cried Verus, nodding to the old man. "Caesar will be far better pleased with such a paragon of charmers as that sweet creature, than with all your old writs of citizenship and heavy purses."

"That is true," the prefect said, confirming this statement. "And I dare swear she is a free maiden, and not a slave. But you stood up for her friend Pollux— what do you know about her?"

"That she is the daughter of Keraunus, the palace-steward, and that I have known her from her childhood," answered the youthful artist emphatically. "He is a Roman citizen, and of an old Macedonian house as well."

"Perhaps even of royal descent," added Titianus, laughing.

"I know the man," answered the dealer hastily. "He is an impecunious insolent old fool."

"I should think," interrupted Verus with lofty composure, but rather as being bored, than as reproving the irritated speaker, "it seems to me—that this is hardly the place to conduct a discussion as to the nature and disposition of the fathers of all those ladies and young girls."

"But he is poor," cried the dealer angrily. "A few days since he offered to sell me his few miserable curiosities, but really I could not—"

"We are sorry for your sake if the transaction was unsuccessful," Verus again interposed, this time with excessive politeness. "Now, first let us decide on the

persons and afterwards on the costumes. The father of
the girl is a Roman citizen then ?"

"A member of the council, and in his way a man
of position," replied Titianus.

"And I," added his wife Julia, "have taken a great
fancy to the sweet little maid, and if the principal part
is given to her, and her noble father is without adequate
means, as you assert my friend, I will undertake to provide for her costume. Caesar will be charmed with
such a Roxana."

The dealer's clients were silent, he himself was
trembling with disappointment and vexation, and his
fury rose to the utmost when Plutarch, whom till then
he thought he had won over to his daughter's side, tried
to bow his bent old body before dame Julia, and said
with a graceful gesture of regret :

"My old eyes have deceived me again on this occasion. The little girl is very like one of my workwomen; very like—but I see now that there is a certain something which the other lacks. I have done her
an injustice and remain her debtor. Permit, me, noble
lady to add the ornaments to the dress you provide for
our Roxana. I may be lucky enough to find something
pretty for her. A sweet child! I shall go at once and
beg her forgiveness and tell her what we propose. May
I do so noble Julia? Have I your permission gentlemen ?"

In a very few minutes it was known all over the
stage, and soon after all through the amphitheatre, that
Arsinoe, the daughter of Keraunus, had been selected to
represent the character of Roxana.

"But who was Keraunus ?"

"How was it that the children of the most illus-

trious and wealthy citizens had been overlooked in as-
signing this most prominent part ?"

"This was just what might be expected when every
thing was left to those reckless artists !"

"And where was a poor little girl like that to find
the talents which it would cost to procure the costume
of an Asiatic princess, Alexander's bride ?"

"Plutarch, and the prefect's wife had undertaken
that."

"A mere beggar."

"How well the family jewels would have suited our
daughters !"

"Do we want to show Caesar nothing but a few
silly pretty faces ?—and not something of our wealth
and taste ?"

"Supposing Hadrian asks who this Roxana is, and
had to be told that a collection had to be made to get
her a proper costume."

"Such things never could happen anywhere but in
Alexandria."

"Every one wants to know whether she worked in
Plutarch's factory.—They say it is not true—but the
painted old villain still loves a pretty face. He smug-
gled her in, you may be sure; where there is smoke
there is fire, and it is beyond a doubt that she gets
money from the old man."

"What for ?"

Ah ! you had better enquire of a priest of Aphrodite.
It is nothing to laugh at, it is scandalous, audacious !"

Thus and on this wise ran the comments with which
the announcement of Arsinoe's preferment to the part
of Roxana was received, and hatred and bitter animos-
ity had grown up in the souls of the dealer and his

daughter. Praxilla was selected as a companion to Alexander's bride, and she yielded without objecting, but on her way homewards she nodded assent when her father said:

"Let things go on now as they may, but a few hours before the performance begins, I will send them word that you are ill."

The selection of Arsinoe had however, on the other hand, given pleasure as well as pain. Up in the middle places in the amphitheatre sat Keraunus, his legs far apart, his face glowing, panting and choking with sheer delight, and too haughty to draw in his feet even when the brother of the archidikastes tried to squeeze by his bulky person which filled two seats at once. Arsinoe, whose sharp ears had not failed to catch the dealer's remonstrances, and the words in which brave Pollux had taken her part, had, at first, felt dying of shame and terror, but now she felt as though she could fly on the wings of her delight. She had never been so happy in her life, and when she got out with her father, in the first dark street she threw her arms round his neck, kissed both his cheeks, and then told him how kind the lady Julia, the prefect's wife had been to her, and that she had undertaken, with the warmest friendliness, to have her costly dress made for her.

Keraunus had no objection to offer, and, strange to say, he did not consider it beneath his dignity to allow Arsinoe to be supplied with jewels by the wealthy manufacturer.

"People have seen," he said, pathetically, "that we need not shrink from doing as much as other citizens do, but to dress a Roxana as befits a bride would cost millions, and I am very willing to confess to my friends

that I have not millions. Where the costume comes
from is all the same, be that as it may you will still
stand the first of all the maidens in the city, and I am
pleased with you for that, my child. To-morrow will
be the last meeting, and then perhaps Selene too, may
have a prominent part given to her. Happily we are
able to dress her as befits. When will the prefect's wife
fetch you ? "

"To-morrow about noon."

"Then early to-morrow buy a nice new dress."

"Will there not be enough for a new bracelet too ?"
asked Arsinoe, coaxingly. "This one of mine is too
narrow and trumpery."

"You shall have one, for you have deserved it," replied Keraunus, with dignity. "But you must have
patience till the day after to-morrow; to-morrow the
goldsmiths will be closed on account of the festival."

Arsinoe had never seen her father so cheerful and
talkative as he was to-day, and yet the walk from the
theatre to Lochias was not a very short one, and it was
long past the early hour at which he was accustomed
to retire to bed.

By the time the father and daughter reached the
palace it was already tolerably late, for, after Arsinoe
had quitted the stage, suitable representatives of parts
had been selected for three other scenes from the life of
Alexander, by the light of torches, lamps and tapers;
and before the assemblage broke up, Plutarch's guests
were entertained with wine, fruit, syrups, sweet cakes,
oyster pasties, and other delicacies. The steward had
fallen with good will on the noble drink and excellent
food, and when he was replete, he was wont to be in a
better humor, and after a modicum of wine, in a more

cheerful mood than usual. Just now he was content
and kind, for although he had done all that lay in his
power, the entertainment had not lasted long enough,
for him to arrive at a state of intoxication which could
make him surly, or to overload his digestion. Towards
the end of their walk, he turned thoughtful and said:

" To-morrow the council does not sit on account
of the festival, and that is well; all the world will con-
gratulate me, question me, and notice me, and the gild-
ing on my circlet is quite shabby; and in some places
the silver shines through. Your outfit will now cost
nothing, and it is quite necessary that before the next
meeting I should go to a goldsmith and exchange that
wretched thing for- one of real gold. A man should
show what he is."

He spoke the words pompously, and Arsinoe eagerly acquiesced, and only begged him, as they went in at
the open door, to leave enough for Selene's costume;
he laughed quietly to himself, and said:

" We need no longer be so very cautious. I should
like to know who the Alexander will be who will be
the first to ask for my Roxana as his wife. Rich old
Plutarch's only son already has a seat in the council,
and has not yet taken a wife. He is no longer very
young, but he is a fine man still."

The radiant father's dream of the future was interrupted by Doris, who came out of the gate-house and
called him by his name. Keraunus stood still. When
the old woman went on:

" I must speak with you." He answered, repellently:

" But I shall not listen to you—neither now nor at
any time."

" It was certainly not for my pleasure," retorted
18

Doris, " that I called to you; I have only to tell you that you will not find your daughter Selene at home."

"What do you say?" cried Keraunus.

" I say that the poor girl with her damaged foot could at last walk no farther, and that she had to be carried into a strange house where she is being taken care of."

" Selene!" cried Arsinoe, falling from all her clouds of happiness, startled and grieved — " do you know where she is ? "

Before Doris could reply, Keraunus stormed out :

" It is all the fault of the Roman architect and his raging beast of a dog. Very good! very good! now Caesar will certainly help me to my rights. He will give a lesson to those who throw Roxana's sister into a sick-bed, and hinder her from taking any part in the processions. Very good! very good indeed!"

" It is sad enough to cry over!" said the gate-keeper's wife, indignantly. " Is this the thanks she gets for all her care of her little brothers and sisters ! Only to think that a father can speak so, when his best child is lying with a broken leg, helpless among strangers!"

" With a broken leg," whimpered Arsinoe.

" Broken!" repeated Keraunus slowly, and now sincerely anxious. " Where can I find her ? "

" At dame Hannah's little house at the bottom of the garden belonging to the widow of Pudeus."

" Why did they not bring her here ? "

" Because the physician forbade it. She is in a fever, but she is well cared for. Hannah is one of the Christians. I cannot bear the people, but they know how to nurse the sick better than any one."

" With Christians ! my child is with Christians ! "

shrieked Keraunus, beside himself. "At once Arsinoe, at once come with me; Selene shall not stay a moment longer among that accursed rabble. Eternal gods! besides all our other troubles this disgrace too!"

"Nay, it is not so bad as that," said Doris soothingly. "There are very estimable folks even among the Christians. At any rate they are certainly honorable, for the poor hunch-backed creature who first brought the bad news gave me this little bag of money which dame Hannah had found in Selene's pocket."

Keraunus took his daughter's hard-won wages as contemptuously as though he was quite accustomed to gold, and thought nothing of mere wretched silver; but Arsinoe began to cry at the sight of the drachmae, for she knew it was for the sake of that money that Selene had left her home, and could divine what frightful pain she must have suffered on the way.

"Honorable this, and honorable that!" cried Keraunus, as he tied up his money-bag. "I know well enough how shameless are the goings on in assemblies of that stamp; kissing and hugging slaves! quite the right sort of thing for my daughter! Come Arsinoe, let us find a litter at once!"

"No, no!" exclaimed Doris eagerly. "For the present you must leave her in peace. I should be glad to conceal it from you as a father—but the physician declared it might cost her her life if she were not left just now in perfect quiet. No one goes to any kind of assembly with a burning wound in the head, a high fever and a broken leg.—Poor dear child!"

Keraunus stood silent in grave consternation, while Arsinoe exclaimed through her tears:

"But I must go to her, I must see her Doris."

" That I cannot blame you for, my pretty one," said the old woman. I have already been to the house of the Christians, but they would not let me in to see the patient. With you it is rather different as you are her sister."

" Come father," begged Arsinoe, " first let us see to the children, and then you shall come with me to see Selene. Oh! why did I not go with her. Oh! if she should die."

CHAPTER XX.

KERAUNUS and his daughter reached their rooms less quickly than usual, for the steward dreaded a fresh attack from the blood-hound, which, to-night however, was sharing Antinous' room. They found the old slave-woman up, and in great excitement, for she loved Selene, she was frightened at her absence, and in the children's sleeping-room all was not as it should be.

Arsinoe went without delay to see the little ones, but the black woman remained with her master, and told him with many tears, while he exchanged his saffron-colored pallium for an old cloak, that the joy of her heart, little blind Helios had been ill, and could not sleep, even after she had given him some of the drops which Keraunus himself was accustomed to take.

" Idiotic animal!" exclaimed Keraunus, " to give my medicine to the child," and he kicked off his new shoes to replace them with shabbier ones. " If you were younger I would have you flogged."

" But you did say the drops were good," stammered the old woman.

" For me," shouted the steward, and without fastening his shoe-straps round his ankles, so that they flapped and pattered on the ground, he hurried off into the children's room. There sat his darling blind child, his 'heir' as he liked to call him, with his pretty, fair, curly head resting on Arsinoe's breast. The child recognized his step, and began his little lament :

" Selene was away, and I was frightened, and I feel so sick, so sick."

The steward laid his hand on the child's forehead, and feeling how hot it was he began to walk restlessly up and down by the little bed.

"That is just how it always happens," he said. "When one misfortune comes another always follows. Look at him Arsinoe. Do you remember how the fever took poor Berenice ? Sickness, uneasiness, and a burning head.—Have you any pain in your head my boy ?"

" No," answered Helios, "but I feel so sick."

The steward opened the child's little shirt to see if he had any spots on his breast, but Arsinoe said, as she bent over him :

" It is nothing much, he has only overloaded his stomach. The stupid old woman gives him every thing he asks for, and she let him have half of the currant cake, which we sent her to fetch before we went out."

" But his head is burning," repeated Keraunus.

" He will be quite well again by to-morrow morning," replied Arsinoe. " Our poor Selene needs us far more than he does. Come father. The old woman can stay with him."

"I want Selene to come," whimpered the child.
"Pray, pray, do not leave me alone again."

"Your old father will stay with you my pet," said
Keraunus tenderly, for it cut him to the soul to see this
child suffer. "You none of you know what this boy
is to us all."

"He will soon go to sleep," Arsinoe asserted. "Do
let us go, or it will be too late."

"And leave the old woman to commit some other
stupid blunder?" cried Keraunus. "It is my duty to
stay with the poor little boy. You can go to your sister
and take the old woman with you."

"Very good, and to-morrow early I will come back."

"To-morrow morning?" said Keraunus surprised.
"No, no, that will not do. Doris said just now that
Selene will be well nursed by the Christians. Only see
how she is, give her my love, and then come back."

"But father—"

"Besides you must remember that the prefect's wife
expects you to-morrow at noon to choose the stuff for
your dress, and you must not look as if you had been
sitting up all night."

"I will rest a little while in the morning."

"In the morning? And how about curling my hair?
And your new frock? And poor little Helios?—No
child, you are only just to see Selene and then come
back again. Early in the morning too the holiday will
have begun, and you know what goes on then; the old
woman would be of no use to you in the throng. Go
and see how Selene is, you are not to stay."

"I will see —"

"Not a word about seeing—you come home again.
I desire it; in two hours you are to be in bed."

Arsinoe shrugged her shoulders, and two minutes later she was standing with the old slave-woman in front of the gate-house.

A broad beam of light still fell through the half-open door of the bowery little room, so Euphorion and Doris had not retired to rest and could at once open the palace-gate for her. The Graces set up a bark as Arsinoe crossed the threshold of her old friends' house, but they did not leave their cushion for they soon recognized her.

It was several years since Arsinoe, in obedience to her father's strict prohibition had set foot in the snug little house, and her heart was deeply touched as she saw again all the surroundings she had loved as a child, and had not forgotten as she grew into girlhood. There were the birds, the little dogs, and the lutes on the wall near the Apollo. On worthy dame Doris' table there had always been something to eat, and there, now, stood a lovely, golden-brown cake, by the side of the wine-jar. How often as a child had she sneaked in to beg a sweet morsel, how often to see whether tall Pollux were not there, Pollux, whose bold devices and original suggestions, gave his work and his play alike, the stamp of genius, and lent them a peculiar charm. And there sat her saucy playfellow in person, his legs stretched at full length in front of him, and talking eagerly. Arsinoe heard him relating the end of the history of her being chosen for Roxana, and caught her own name, graced with such epithets as brought the blushes to her cheeks, and gave her double pleasure be-cause he could not guess that she could overhear them. From a boy he had grown to a man, and a fine man, and a great artist—but he was still the old kind and audacious Pollux.

The sudden leap with which he sprang from his seat
to welcome her, the frank laughter with which he several
times interrupted her speech, the childlike loving way
in which he held his arm round his little mother while
he greeted her, and asked why she was going out so late,
the winning, touching tone of his voice as he expressed
his regret at Selene's mishaps—all went home to Arsinoe
as a thing known and loved, of which she had long been
deprived, and she clung to the two strong hands he
held out to her. If at that moment he had taken her
up, and clasped her to his heart before the very eyes of
Euphorion and his mother she really would have been
incapable of resisting him.

It was with a heavy heart that Arsinoe had gone
into dame Doris, but in the gate-keeper's house there
reigned an atmosphere in which care and anxiety could
not breathe, and the light-hearted girl's vision of her sister as tormented with pain and threatened with danger
was changed in a wonderfully short time to that of a sufferer comfortably in bed, with only a severely-injured
foot. In the place of consuming anxiety she felt only
hearty sympathy, and this sounded in her voice as she
begged the singer Euphorion to open the gate for her,
because she wanted to go out with her slave-woman
to ascertain how Selene was.

Doris soothed her, repeating her assurance that the
patient would be nursed with the utmost care in dame
Hannah's hands ; still, she thought her wish to see her
sister very justifiable, and eagerly seconded Pollux
when he entreated Arsinoe to accept his escort ; for the
festival would be beginning soon after midnight, the
streets would be full of rough and impudent people, and
a bunch of feathers would be about as much use against

the drunken slaves as her black scarecrow, who had
been falling into decrepitude even before she had done
the stupidest deed of her life and roused the steward's
anger against herself.

So they went along the dark streets which grew full
of people the farther they went, side by side in silence.
Presently Pollux said :

"Put your arm through mine; you ought to feel
that I am protecting you, and I—I should like to feel
at every step that I have found you once more, and am
allowed to be near you—so sweet a creature."

The words did not sound impertinent, on the contrary, they sounded very much in earnest, and the sculptor's deep voice trembled with emotion as he spoke them
with deep tenderness. They knocked at the door of
the girl's heart with the urgent hand of love; she unhesitatingly put her hand through his arm and answered
softly :

"You will take care of me now."

"Yes," said he, and he took her little hand, which
rested on his right arm, in his left hand. She did not
draw it away, and after they had gone on thus for a few
paces he sighed and said:

"Do you know how I feel ? "

"Well ! "

"Nay, I myself cannot put it into words. Rather
as if I had triumphed in the Olympian games, or as if
Caesar had invested me with the purple!—But who
cares for the wealth or the purple ! You are hanging
on my arm, and I have hold of your hand; compared
with this, all is as nought. If it were not for the people
about I—I do not know what I could do."

She looked up at him with happy content, but he

lifted her hand to his lips and pressed it to them long
and fervently. Then he let it go again and said, with a
sigh that came up from the bottom of his heart:

"Oh Arsinoe, my sweet Arsinoe, how I love you!"

As the words came softly yet hotly from his lips the
girl clasped his arm closely to her bosom, leaned her
head on his shoulder, looked up at him with a wide-
eyed, tender gaze, and said softly:

"Oh Pollux, I am so happy, the world is so good!"

"Nay, I could hate it!" cried the sculptor. "To
hear this—and to have an old mother wide awake at
home, and to be obliged to walk steadily on in a street
crowded with men—it is unendurable! I shall not hold
out much longer—sweetest of girls—here it is quiet and
dark."

Yes, in a little nook made by two contiguous houses,
and into which Pollux drew Arsinoe, it was pitch dark,
as he hastily pressed his first kiss on her innocent lips;
but in their hearts it was light—radiant sunshine.

She had thrown her arms round his neck and would
willingly have clung to him till day should end; but
they heard the approach of a noisy procession of slaves.
These unfortunate creatures began soon after midnight
singing and shouting so as to avail themselves to the ex-
tremest limit of the holiday, which released them for a
short time from their tasks and duties; Pollux knew well
how unbounded the license of their pleasures could be,
and as he walked on with Arsinoe he enjoined her to
keep with him as close as possible to the houses.

"How jolly they are!" he said pointing to the
merry-makers. "Their masters will wait on themselves
a little to-day, and the best day in the year is just beginning for them, but for us the best day in all our lives."

"Yes, yes," cried Arsinoe, and she clasped his strong arm with both her hands.

Then they both laughed merrily, for Pollux had noticed that the old slave-woman had gone on past them with her head sunk on her breast, and was following another pair.

"I will call her," Arsinoe said.

"No, no, let her be," said the artist. "The couple in front certainly require her protection more than we do."

"But how could she possibly mistake that little man for you?" laughed Arsinoe.

"I wish I were a little smaller," replied Pollux with a sigh. "Only picture to yourself the vast amount of burning love and tormenting longing that can be contained in so large a body as mine!" She slapped him on the arm, and to punish her he hastily pressed his lips on her forehead.

"Don't—think of the people," she said reprovingly, but he gaily answered:

"It is not a misfortune to be envied."

Here the streets came to an end, and they found themselves in front of the garden belonging to Pudeus' widow; Pollux knew it, for Paulina who owned it was the sister of Pontius, the architect, who himself owned a magnificent house in the city. But could it be possible? Had invisible hands brought them here already? The gate of the enclosure was locked. Pollux roused a porter, told him what he wanted, and was conducted by him with Arsinoe to a part of the grounds where a bright light shone out from dame Hannah's little abode, for he had had instructions to admit the sick girl's friends even during the night.

A crescent moon lighted the paths, which were strewed with shells; the shrubs and trees in the garden threw sharply-defined shadows on their gleaming whiteness, the sea sparkled brightly, and as soon as the porter had left the happy young pair together, and they found themselves in a shadowy alley, Pollux said, opening his arms to the girl:

"Now—one more kiss, just for a remembrance, while I wait."

"Not now," begged Arsinoe. "I am no longer happy since we came in here. I cannot help thinking of poor Selene."

"I have not a word to say against that," replied Pollux submissively. "Then when waiting is over may I have my reward?"

"No, no, now, at once," cried Arsinoe throwing herself on his breast, and then she hurried towards the house.

He followed her, and when she paused in front of a brightly-lighted window on the ground floor, he stopped also. They both looked in on a lofty and spacious room, kept in the most perfect order and cleanliness; it had one door only opening on the roofless forecourt of the house; the walls of the room were plainly painted of a light green color, and the only ornament it contained was one piece of carved work over the door.

On the farther side stood the bed on which Selene was lying; a few paces from it sat the deformed girl asleep, while dame Hannah softly went up to the patient with a wet compress in her hand which she carefully laid on her head.

Pollux touched Arsinoe and whispered to her:

"Your sister lies there in her sleep like an Ariadne

deserted by Dionysus. How wretched she will feel
when she comes to herself."

"She looks to me less pale than usual."

·· Look now, how she bends her arm, and what a
lovely attitude as she puts her hand to her head !"

"Go—" said Arsinoe. "You ought not to be spy-
ing here."

"Directly, directly—but if you were lying there no
power should stir me from the spot. How carefully
Hannah lifts the wet wrapper from her poor broken
ankle. You could not touch your eye more gently
than the good woman handles Selene's foot."

"Go back, she is looking straight this way."

"What a wonderful face ! It would do for a Pene-
lope, but there is something singular in her eyes. Now
if I had to make another star-gazing Urania, or a Sappho full of the deity, and with eyes fixed on the heavens
in poetic rapture, that is what I would put into her !
She is no longer young, but how pure her face is ! It is
like a sky when the wind has swept it clear of clouds."

"Seriously you must go now," said Arsinoe drawing
away her hand, which he had again taken. Pollux saw
that his praise of another woman's beauty annoyed her,
and he said soothingly :

"Be easy child. You have not your match here in
Alexandria, no, nor so far as Greek is spoken. A perfectly clear sky is certainly not the most beautiful to my
taste. Pure light, and pure blue, give no satisfaction to
the artist, it is only behind a few moving clouds, lighted
up by changing gleams of gold and silver, that the firmament has any true charm, and though your face too
is like heaven to me it does not lack sweet movement,
never twice alike. Now this matron—"

"Only look," interrupted Arsinoe, "how tenderly dame Hannah bends over Selene, and now she is gently kissing her brow. No mother could tend her own daughter more lovingly. I have known her for a long time; she is good, very good; it is hardly credible for she is a Christian."

"The cross up there over the door," said Pollux "is the token by which these extraordinary people recognize each other."

"And what is signified by the dove and fish and anchor round it?" asked Arsinoe.

"They are emblems of the mysteries of the Christians," replied Pollux. "I do not understand them; the things are wretchedly painted; the adherents of the crucified God contemn all art, and particularly my branch of it, for they hate all images of the gods."

"And yet among such blasphemers we find such good men; I will go in at once; Hannah is wetting another handkerchief."

"And how unwearied and kind she looks as she does it; still there is something strange, deserted, and graceless in this large bare room. I should not like to live there."

"Have you noticed the faint scent of lavender that comes through the window?"

"Long since—there your sister is moving and has opened her eyes—now she has shut them again."

"Go back into the garden and wait till I come," Arsinoe commanded him decidedly. "I will only see how Selene is going on; I will not stop long for my father wishes me to return soon, and no one can nurse her better than Hannah!"

The girl drew her hand out of her lover's and knocked

at the door of the little house; it was opened and the widow herself led Arsinoe to the bedside of her sister.

Pollux at first sat a while on a bench in the garden, but soon sprang up and paced with long steps the path he had previously trodden with Arsinoe. A stone table across the path, brought him to a stand-still, and he took a fancy for leaping it. The third time he came up to it he sprang over it with a long jump. But no sooner had he done the frolicsome deed than he paused, shook his head at himself and muttered to himself: " Like a boy!"—He felt indeed like a happy child. But as he waited he became calmer and graver. He acknowledged to himself, with sincere thankfulness, that he had now found the ideal woman, of whom he had dreamed in his hours of best inspiration, and that she was his, wholly and alone. And after all, what was he? A poor rascal who had many mouths to fill, and was no more than two fingers of his master's hand. This must be altered. He would not reduce his sister's comforts in any way but he must break with Papias, and stand henceforth on his own feet. His courage mounted fast, and when at last, Arsinoe returned from her sister, he had resolved that he must first finish Balbilla's bust with all diligence in his own workshop, and that then he would model his beloved; these two female heads he could not fail in. Caesar must see them, they must be exhibited, and already in his mind's eye, he saw himself refusing order after order, and accepting only the most splendid where all were good.

Arsinoe went home comforted. Selene's sufferings were certainly less than she had pictured them; she did not wish to be nursed by any one besides dame Hannah. She might perhaps have a little fever, but any one who was capable of discussing every little question of house-keeping, and all that related to the children could not be—as Arsinoe thought while she walked back through the garden, leaning on the artist's arm —really and properly ill.

"It must revive and delight her to have Roxana for a sister!" cried Pollux; but his pretty companion shook her head and said: "She is always so odd; what most delights me is averse to her."

"Well Selene is of course the moon, and you are the sun."

"And what are you?" asked Arsinoe.

"I am tall Pollux, and to-night I feel as if I might some day be great Pollux."

"If you succeed I shall grow with you."

"That will be your right, since it is only through you that I can ever succeed in that which I propose to do."

"And how should a simple little thing, such as I am, be able to help an artist?"

"By living, and by loving him," cried the sculptor, lifting her up in his arms before she could prevent him.

Outside the garden-gate the old slave-woman was sitting asleep. She had learnt from the porter that her young mistress had been admitted with her companion, but she herself had been forbidden to enter the grounds. A curbstone had served her for a seat, and as she waited her eyes had closed, in spite of the increasing noise in the street. Arsinoe did not waken her, but asked Pollux, with a roguish laugh:

"We shall find our way alone, shall we not?"

"If Eros does not lead us astray," answered the

artist. And so, as they went on their way, they jested and exchanged little tender speeches.

The nearer they got to Lochias and to the main lines of traffic which intersected at right angles the Canopic way—the widest and longest road in the city—the fuller was the stream of people that flowed onwards in· the direction in which they were going; but this circumstance favored them, for those who wish to be unobserved, when they cannot be absolutely alone, have only to mix with the crowd. As they were borne towards the focus and centre of the festive doings, they clung closely together, she to him, and he to her, so that they might not be torn apart by any of the rushing and tumultuous processions of excited Thracian women who, faithful to their native usages, came storming by with a young bull, on this particular night of the year, that following the shortest day. They had hardly gone a hundred paces beyond the Moon-street when they heard proceeding from it a wild roving song of tipsy jollity, and loud above it the sound of drums and pipes, cymbals and noisy shouting, and at the same time in the King's-street, a road which crossed the Bruchiom and opened on Lochias, a merry troup came towards them.

At their head, among other acquaintances, came Teuker, the gem-cutter, the younger brother of Pollux. Crowned with ivy, and flourishing a thyrsus he came dancing on, and behind him, leaping and shouting, a train of men and women, all excited to the verge of folly, singing, holloo-ing, and dancing.

Garlands of vine, ivy and asphodel fluttered from a hundred heads; poplar, lotus, and laurel wreaths over-hung their heated brows; panther-skins, deer and goat-skins hung from their bare shoulders and waved in the

19

wind as their bearers hurried onwards. This procession
had been first formed by some artists and rich youths
returning with some women from a banquet, with a
band of music ; every one who met this festal party had
joined it or had been forced to enlist with it. Respectable .citizens and their wives, laborers, maid-servants.
slaves, soldiers and sailors, officers, women flute-players,
artisans, ship-captains, the whole chorus of a theatre
invited by a friend of art, excited women who dragged
with them a goat that was to be slaughtered to Dionysus—none had been able to resist the temptation to join
the procession. It turned down the Moon-street, keeping to the middle of the road which was planted with
elms, and had on each side of it a raised foot-way,
which at this time of night no one used. How clear
was the sound of the double-pipes, how bravely the girls
hit the calf-skin of the tambourines with their soft fists,
how saucily the wind tossed and tangled the dishevelled
hair of the riotous women and played with the smoke
of the torches which were wielded in the air by audacious youths, disguised as Pan or as Satyrs, and shouting
as they went.

Here a girl, holding her tambourine high in the air,
rattled the little bells on its hoop, as she flew along, as
violently as though she wanted to shake the hollow
metal balls out of their frame, and send them whistling
through the air on their own account—there, side by
side with his comrades, who were excited almost to
madness, a handsome lad came skipping along in elaborately graceful leaps, but carrying over his arm, with
comic care, a long bull's-tail that he had tied on, and
blowing alternately up and down the short scale from
the shortest to the longest of the reeds composing his

panpipes. Through the noisy crowd as they rushed by, sounded, now and again, a loud roar, that might as easily have been caused by pain as joy; but it was each time hastily drowned in mad laughter, extravagant singing and jubilant music.

Old and young, great and small, all in short that came near this rabble train, were carried off with irresistible force to follow it with shouts of triumph. Even Pollux and Arsinoe had for some time ceased to walk soberly side by side, but moved their feet, laughingly in time to the merry measure.

" How nice it sounds," cried the artist. " I could dance and be merry too Arsinoe, dance and make merry with you like a madman !"

Before she could find time to say ' yes ' or 'no,' he shouted a loud " Io, Io, Dionysus," and flung her up in the air. She too was caught by the spirit of the thing, and waving her hand above her head she joined in his shout of triumph, and let him drag her along to a corner of the Moon-street where a seller of garlands offered her wares for sale. There she let him wreathe her with ivy, she stuck a laurel wreath on his head, twisted a streamer of ivy round his neck and breast, and laughed loudly as she flung a large silver coin into the flower-woman's lap and clung tightly to his arm. It was all done in swift haste without reflection, as if in a fit of intoxication, and with trembling hands.

The procession was drawing to an end. Six women and girls in wreaths closed it, walking arm in arm with loud singing. Pollux drew his sweetheart behind this jovial crew, threw his arm around Arsinoe once more, while she put hers round him, and then both of them stepped out in a brisk dance-step flinging their arms

left free, throwing back their heads, shouting and singing loudly, and forgetting all that surrounded them ; they
felt as though they were bound to each other by a glory
of sunbeams, while some god lifted them above the earth
and bore them up through a realm of delight and joy
beyond the myriad stars and through the translucent
ether; thus they let themselves be led away through
the Moon-street into the Canopic way and so back to
the sea, and as far as the temple of Dionysus.

There they paused breathless and it suddenly struck
them that he was Pollux and she Arsinoe, and that she
must get back again to her father and the children.

" Come home," she said softly, and as she spoke she
dropped her arm and began to gather up her loosened
hair.

" Yes, yes," he said as if in a dream. He released
her, struck his hand against his brow, and turning to the
open cella of the temple he said :

" Long have I known that thou art mighty O Dionysus, and that thou O Aphrodite art lovely, and that
thou art sweet O Eros ! but how inestimable your gifts,
that I have learnt to-day for the first time."

" We were indeed full of the deity," said Arsinoe. " But
here comes another procession and I must go home."

" Then let us go by the Little Harbor," answered
Pollux.

" Yes—I must pick the leaves out of my hair and
no one will see us there."

" I will help you—"

" No, you are not to touch me," said Arsinoe decidedly. She grasped her abundant soft and shiny hair,
and cleared it of the leaves that had got entangled in it,
as tiny beetles do in a double flower. Finally she hid her

hair under her veil, which had slipped off her head long since, but, almost by a miracle, had caught and remained hanging on the brooch of her peplum. Pollux stood looking at her, and overmastered by the passion that possessed him, he exclaimed:

"Eternal gods! how I love you! Till now my soul has been like a careless child, to-day it is grown to heroic stature.—Wait—only wait, it will soon learn to use its weapons."

"And I will help it in the fight," she said happily, as she put her hand through his arm again, and they hurried back to the old palace, dancing rather than walking.

The late December sun was already giving warning of his approaching rising by cold yellowish-grey streaks in the sky as Pollux and his companion entered the gate, which had long since been opened for the workmen. In the hall of the Muses they took a first farewell, in the passage leading to the steward's room, a second—sad and yet most happy; but this was but a short one for the gleam of a lamp made them start apart, and Arsinoe instantly fled.

The disturber was Antinous who was waiting here for the Emperor who was still gazing at the stars from the watch-tower Pontius had erected for him. As she vanished he turned to Pollux and said gaily:

"I need your forgiveness for I have disturbed you in an interview with your sweetheart."

"She will be my wife," said the sculptor proudly.

"So much the better!" replied the favorite, and he drew a deep breath, as though the artist's words had re-l.eved his mind of a burden. "Ah! so much the better. Can you tell me where to find the fair Arsinoe's sister?"

"To be sure," replied the artist, and he felt pleased
that the young Bythinian should cling to his arm.
Within the next hour, Pollux, from whose lips there
flowed a stream of eager and enthusiastic words, like
water from a spring, had completely won the heart of
the Emperor's favorite.

The girl found both her father and Helios, who no
longer looked like a sick patient—fast asleep.   The old
slave-woman came in a few mintes after her, and when at
last, after unbinding her hair, Arsinoe threw herself on her
bed she fell asleep instantly, and in her dreams found herself once more by the side of her Pollux, while they
both were flying to the sound of drums, flutes, and
cymbals high above the dusty ways of earth, like leaves
swept on by the wind.

CHAPTER XXI.

THE steward awoke soon after sunrise.   He had
slept no less soundly, it is true, in his arm-chair than in
his bed, but he did not feel refreshed, and his limbs
ached.

In the living-room everything was in the same disorder as on the previous evening, and this annoyed him,
for he was accustomed to find his room in order when
he entered it in the morning.   On the table, surrounded
by flies, stood the remains of the children's supper, and
among the bread crusts and plates lay his own ornaments and his daughter's!   Wherever he turned he saw
articles of dress and other things out of their place.

The old slave-woman came in yawning, her woolly

grey hair hung in disorder about her face, and her eyes seemed fixed, her feet carried her unsteadily here and there.

"You are drunk," cried Keraunus; nor was he mistaken, for when the old woman had waked up, sitting by the house of Pudeus, and had learned from the gatekeeper that Arsinoe had quitted the garden, she had gone into a tavern with other slave-women. When her master seized her arm and shook her, she exclaimed with a stupid grin on her wet lips:

"It is the feast-day. Every one is free, to-day is the feast."

"Roman nonsense!" interrupted the steward. "Is my breakfast ready?"

While the old woman stood muttering some inaudible words, the slave came into the room and said:

"To-day is a general holiday, may I go out too?"

"Oh that would suit me admirably!" cried the steward. "This monster drunk, Selene sick, and you running about the streets."

"But no one stops at home to-day," replied the slave timidly.

"Be off then!" cried Keraunus. "Walk about from now till midnight! Do as you please, only do not expect me to keep you any longer. You are still fit to turn the hand-mill, and I dare say I can find a fool to give me a few drachmae for you."

"No, no, do not sell me," groaned the old man, raising his hands in entreaty; Keraunus however would not hear him, but went on angrily:

"A dog at least remains faithful to his master, but you slaves eat him out of house and home, and when he most needs you, you want to run about the streets."

" But I will stay," howled the old man.

" Nay, do as you please. You have long been like
a lame horse which makes its rider a butt for the laughter
of children. When you go out with me every one looks
round as if I had a stain on my pallium. And then
the mangy dog wants to keep holiday, and stick himself up among the citizens !"

" I will stay here, only do not sell me !" whimpered
the miserable old man, and he tried to take his master's
hand ; but the steward shoved him off, and desired him
to go into the kitchen and light a fire, and throw some
water on the old woman's head to sober her. The
slave pushed his companion out of the room, while
Keraunus went into his daughter's bedroom to rouse
her.

There was no light in Arsinoe's room but that
which could creep in through a narrow opening just below the ceiling; the slanting rays fell directly on the
bed up to which Keraunus went. There lay his daughter
in sound sleep ; her pretty head rested on her uplifted
right arm, her unbound brown hair flowed like a stream
over her soft round shoulders and over the edge of the
little bed. He had never seen the child look so pretty,
and the sight of her really touched his heart, for Arsinoe
reminded him of his lost wife, and it was not vain pride
merely, but a movement of true paternal love, which
involuntarily transformed his earnest wish that the gods
might leave him this child and let her be happy, into an
unspoken but fervent prayer.

He was not accustomed to waking his daughter
who was always up and busy before he was, and he
could hardly bear to disturb his darling's sweet sleep;
but it had to be done, so he called Arsinoe by her name,

shook her arm and said, as at last she sat up and looked at him enquiringly :

"It is I, get up, remember what has to be done to-day."

"Yes—yes," she said yawning, "but it is so early yet !"

"Early," said Keraunus, smiling. "My stomach says the contrary. The sun is already high, and I have not yet had my porridge."

"Make the old woman cook it."

"No, no, my child—you must get up. Have you forgotten whom you are to represent? And my hair is to be curled, and the prefect's wife, and then your dress."

"Very well—go; I do not care the least bit about Roxana and all the dressing-up."

"Because you are not yet quite awake," laughed the steward. "How did this ivy-leaf get into your hair ?"

Arsinoe colored, put her hand to the spot indicated by her father, and said reluctantly :

"Out of some bough or another, but now go that I may get up."

"In a minute—tell me how did you find Selene ?"

"Not so very bad—but I will tell you all about that afterwards. Now I want to be alone." ·

When, half an hour later, Arsinoe brought her father his porridge he gazed at the child in astonishment. Some extraordinary change seemed to have come over his daughter. Something shone in her eyes that he had never observed before, and that gave her childlike features an importance and significance that almost startled him. While she was making the porridge, Keraunus, with the slave's help, had taken the children up and dressed them; now they were all sitting at breakfast; Helios among them fresh and blooming. Now, while Arsinoe told her father all about Selene, and the nursing she was having at dame Hannah's hands, Keraunus kept his eyes fixed on her, and when she noticed this and asked impatiently what there was peculiar in her appearance to-day, he shook his head and answered:

" What strange things are girls ! A great honor has been done you. You are to represent the bride of Alexander, and pride and delight have changed you wonderfully in a single night—but I think to your disadvantage.

" Folly," said Arsinoe reddening, and stretching herself with fatigue she threw herself back on a couch. She did not feel weary exactly, for the lassitude she felt in every limb had a peculiar pleasure in it. She felt as if she had come out of a hot bath, and since her father had roused her she seemed to hear, again and again, the sound of the inspiriting music which she had followed arm in arm with Pollux. Now and again she smiled, now and again she gazed straight before her, and at the same time she said to herself that if at this very moment her lover were to ask her, she would not lack strength to fling herself at once, with him, once more into the mad whirl. Yes—she felt perfectly fresh ! only her eyes burned a little; and if Keraunus fancied he saw anything new in his daughter it must be the glowing light which now lurked in them along with the playful sparkle he had always seen there.

When breakfast was over the slave took the children out, and Arsinoe had begun to curl her father's hair, when Keraunus put on his most dignified attitude and said ponderously :

" My child."

The girl dropped the heated tongs and calmly asked.
" Well"—fully prepared to hear one of the wonderful
propositions which Selene was wont to oppose.

" Listen to me attentively."

Now, what Keraunus was about to say had only
occurred to him an hour since when he had spoiled his
slave's desire to go out ; but as he said it he pressed his
hand to his forehead assuming the expression of a
meditative philosopher.

" For a long time I have been considering a very
important matter. Now I have come to a decision
and I will confide it to you. We must buy a new man-
slave."

" But father !" cried Arsinoe, " think what it will cost
you. If we have another man to feed—"

" There is no question of that," replied Keraunus.
" I will exchange the old one for a younger one that
I need not be ashamed to be seen with. Yesterday I
told you that henceforth we shall attract greater attention than hitherto, and really if we appear with that
black scarecrow at our heels in the streets or elsewhere—"

" Certainly we cannot make much show with
Sebek," interrupted Arsinoe, " but we can leave him at
home for the future."

"Child, child !" exclaimed Keraunus reproachfully,
" will you never remember who and what we are. How
would it beseem us to appear in the streets without a
slave ?"

The girl shrugged her shoulders, and put it to her
father that Sebek was an old piece of family property,
that the little ones were fond of him because he cared

for them like a nurse, that a new slave would cost a great deal and would only be driven by force to many services which the old one was always ready and willing to fulfil.

But Arsinoe preached to deaf ears. Selene was not there; secure from her reproaches and as anxious as a spoiled boy for the thing that was denied him, Keraunus adhered to his determination to exchange the faithful old fellow for a new and more showy slave. Not for a moment did he think of the miserable fate that threatened the decrepit creature, who had grown old in his house, if he were to sell him; but he still had a feeling that it was not quite right to spend the last money that had chanced to come into the house, on a thing that really and truly was not in any way necessary. The more justifiable Arsinoe's doubts seemed to be and the more loudly did an inward voice warn him not to offer this fresh sacrifice to his vain-gloriousness, the more firmly and desperately did he defend his wish to do so; and as he fought for the thing he desired, it acquired in his eyes a semblance of necessity and a number of reasons suggested themselves which made it appear both justifiable and easy of attainment.

There was money in hand; after Arsinoe's being chosen for the part of Roxana he might expect to be able to borrow more; it was his duty to appear with due dignity that he might not scare off the illustrious son-in-law of whom he dreamed, and in the extremity of need he could still fall back on his collection of rarities. The only thing was to find the right purchaser; for, if the sword of Antony had brought him so much, what would not some amateur give him for the other, far more valuable, objects.

Arsinoe turned red and white as her father referred again and again to the bargain she had made; but she dared not confess the truth, and she rued her falsehood all the more bitterly the more clearly she saw with her own sound sense, that the honor which had fallen upon her yesterday, threatened to develop all her father's weaknesses in an absolutely fatal manner.

To-day she would have been amply satisfied with pleasing Pollux, and she would, without a regret have transferred to another her part with all the applause and admiration it would procure her, and which, only yesterday, had seemed to her so inestimably precious. This she said; but Keraunus would not take the assertion in earnest, laughed in her face, went off into mysterious allusions to the wealth which could not fail to come into the house and—since an obscure consciousness told him that it would be becoming him to prove that it was not solely personal vanity and self-esteem that influenced all his proceedings—he explained that he had made up his mind to a great sacrifice and would be content on the coming occasion to wear his gilt fillet and not buy a pure gold one. By this act of self-denial he fancied he had acquired a full right to devote a very pretty little sum to the acquisition of a fine-looking slave. Arsinoe's entreaties were unheeded, and when she began to cry with grief at the prospect of losing her old house-mate he forbid her crossly to shed a tear for such a cause, for it was very childish, and he would not be pleased to conduct her with red eyes to meet the prefect's wife.

During the course of this argument his hair had got itself duly curled, and he now desired Arsinoe to arrange her own hair nicely and then to accompany him.

They would buy a new dress and peplum, go to see Se-lene, and then be carried to the prefect's.

Only yesterday he had thought it too bold a step to use a litter, and to-day he was already considering the propriety of hiring a chariot.

No sooner was he alone than a new idea occurred to him. The insolent architect should be taught that he was not the man to be insulted and injured with impunity. So he cut a clean strip of papyrus off a letter that lay in his chest, and wrote upon it the following words:

"Keraunus, the Macedonian, to Claudius Venator, the architect, of Rome : "

"My eldest daughter, Selene, is by your fault, so severely hurt that she is in great danger, is kept to her bed and suffers frightful pain. My other children are no longer safe in their father's house, and I therefore require you, once more, to chain up your dog. If you refuse to accede to this reasonable demand I will lay the matter before Caesar. I can tell you that circumstances have occurred which will determine Hadrian to punish any insolent person who may choose to neglect the respect due to me and to my daughters."

When Keraunus had closed this letter with his seal he called the slave and said coldly :

" Take this to the Roman architect, and then fetch two litters ; make haste, and while we are out take good care of the children. To-morrow or next day you will be sold. To whom ? That must depend on how you behave during the last hours that you belong to us."

The negro gave a loud cry of grief that came from the depth of his heart, and flung himself on the ground at the steward's feet. His cry did indeed pierce his

master's soul—but Keraunus had made up his mind not
to let himself be moved nor to yield. But the negro
clung more closely to his knees, and when the children,
attracted to the spot by their poor old friend's lamentation, cried loudly in unison, and little Helios began to
pat and stroke the little remains of the negro's woolly
hair, the vain man felt uneasy about the heart, and to
protect himself against his own weakness he cried out
loudly and violently :

"Now, away with you, and do as you are ordered
or I will find the whip."

With these words he tore himself loose from the
miserable old man who left the room with his head
hanging down, and who soon was standing at the door
of the Emperor's rooms with the letter in his hand.
Hadrian's appearance and manner had filled him with
terror and respect, and he dared not knock at the door.
After he had waited for some time, still with tears in his
eyes, Mastor came into the passage with the remains of
his master's breakfast. The negro called to him and held
out the steward's letter, stammering out lamentably :

"From Keraunus, for you master."

"Lay it here on the tray," said the Sarmatian.
"But what has happened to you, my old friend ? you
are wailing most pitifully and look miserable. Have
you been beaten ?"

The negro shook his head and answered, whimpering : "Keraunus is going to sell me."

"There are better masters than he."

"But Sebek is old, Sebek is weak—he can no longer
lift and pull, and with hard work he will certainly die."

"Has life been so easy and comfortable then at the
steward's ?"

"Very little wine, very little meat, very much hunger," said the old man.

"Then you must be glad to leave him."

"No, no," groaned Sebek.

"You foolish old owl," said Mastor. "Why do you care then for that grumpy niggard?"

The negro did not answer for some time, then his lean breast heaved and fell, and, as if the dam were broken through that had choked his utterance, he burst out with a mixture of loud sobs:

"The children, the little ones, our little ones. They are so sweet; and our little blind Helios stroked my hair because I was to go away, here—just here he stroked it"—and he put his hand on a perfectly bald place—"and now Sebek must go and never see them all again, just as if they were all dead."

And the words rolled out and with difficulty, as if carried on in the flood of his tears. They went to Mastor's heart, rousing the memory of his own lost children and a strong desire to comfort his unhappy comrade.

"Poor fellow!" he said, compassionately. "Aye, the children! they are so small, and the door into one's heart is so narrow—and they dance in at it a thousand times better and more easily than grown-up folks. I, too, have lost dear children, and they were my own, too. I can teach any one what is meant by sorrow—but I know too now where comfort is to be found."

With these words Mastor held the tray he was carrying on his hip with his right hand, while he put the left on the negro's shoulder and whispered to him:

"Have you ever heard of the Christians?"

Sebek nodded eagerly as if Mastor were speaking of

a matter of which he had heard great things and expected much, and Mastor went on in a low voice:

"Come early to-morrow before sunrise to the pavement-workers in the court, and there you will hear of
One who comforts the weary and heavy-laden."

The Emperor's servant once more took his tray in
both hands and hurried away, but a faint gleam of hope
had lighted up in the old slave's eyes. He expected no
happiness, but perhaps there might be some way of
bearing the sorrows of life more easily.

Mastor as soon he had given his tray to the kitchen
slaves—who were now busy again in the palace at Lochias—returned to his lord and gave him the steward's
letter. It was an ill-chosen hour for Keraunus, for the
Emperor was in a gloomy mood. He had sat up till
morning, had rested scarcely three hours, and now, with
knitted brows, was comparing the results of his night's
observation of the starry sky with certain astronomical
tables which lay spread out before him. Over this
work he frequently shook his head which was covered
with crisp waves of hair; nay—he once flung the pencil, with which he was working his calculations, down
on the table, leaned back in his seat and covered his
eyes with both hands. Then again he began to write
fresh numbers, but his new results seemed to be no
more satisfactory than the former one.

The steward's letter had been for a long time lying
before him when at last it again caught his attention as
he put out his hand for another document. Needing
some change of ideas he tore it open, read it and flung
it from him with annoyance. At any other time he
would have expressed some sympathy with the suffering girl, have laughed at the ridiculous man, and have

20

thought out some trick to tease or to terrify; but just now the steward's threats made him angry and increased his dislike for him.

Tired of the silence around him he called to Antinous, who sat gazing dreamily down on the harbor; the youth immediately approached his master. Hadrian looked at him and said, shaking his head :

"Why you too look as if some danger were threatening you. Is the sky altogether overcast?"

"No my lord, it is blue over the sea, but towards the south the black clouds are gathering."

"Towards the south?" said Hadrian thoughtfully. "Any thing serious can hardly threaten us from that quarter.—But it comes, it is near, it is upon us before we suspect it."

"You sat up too long, and that has put you out of tune."

"Out of tune?" muttered Hadrian to himself. "And what is tune? That subtle harmony or discord is a condition which masters all the emotions of the soul at once; and not without reason—to-day my heart is paralyzed with anxiety."

"Then you have seen evil signs in the heavens?"

"Direful signs !"

"You wise men believe in the stars," replied Antinous. "No doubt you are right, but my weak head cannot understand what their regular courses have to do with my inconstant wanderings."

"Grow gray," replied the Emperor, "learn to comprehend the universe with your intellect, and not till then speak of these things for not till then will you discern that every atom of things created, and the greatest as well as the least, is in the closest bonds with

every other; that all work together, and each depends
on all. All that is or ever will be in nature, all that
we men feel, think or do, all is dependent on eternal and
immutable causes; and these causes have each their
Daimon who interposes between us and the divinity and
is symbolized in golden characters on the vault of
heaven. The letters are the stars, whose orbits are as
unchanging and everlasting as are the first causes of all
that exists or happens."

"And are you quite sure that you never read wrongly
in this great record?" asked Antinous.

"Even I may err," replied Hadrian. "But this
time I have not deceived myself. A heavy misfortune
threatens me. It is a strange, terrible and extraordinary
coincidence!"

"What?"

"From that accursed Antioch—whence nothing
good has ever come to me—I have received the saying of an oracle which foretells that, that—why should
I hide it from you—in the middle of the year now
about to begin some dreadful misfortune shall fall upon
me, as lightning strikes the traveller to the earth; and to-
night—look here. Here is the house of Death, here
are the planets—but what do you know of such things?
Last night—the night in which once before such terrors
were wrought, the stars confirmed the fatal oracle with
as much naked plainness, as much unmistakable certainty as if they had tongues to shout the evil forecast
in my ear. It is hard to walk on with such a goal in prospect. What may not the new year bring in its course?"

Hadrian sighed deeply, but Antinous went close up
to him, fell on his knees before him and asked in a tone
of childlike humility :

"May I, a poor foolish lad, teach a great and wise man how to enrich his life with six happy months?"

The Emperor smiled, as though he knew what was coming, but his favorite felt encouraged to proceed.

"Leave the future to the future," he said. "What must come will come, for the gods themselves have no power agaist Fate. When evil is approaching it casts its black shadow before it; you fix your gaze on it and let it darken the light of day. I saunter dreamily on my way and never see misfortune till it runs up against me and falls upon me unawares—"

"And so you are spared many a gloomy day," interrupted Hadrian.

"That is just what I would have said."

"And your advice is excellent, for you and for every other loiterer through the gay fair-time of an idle life," replied the Emperor, "but the man whose task it is to bear millions in safety and over abysses, must watch the signs around him, look out far and near, and never dare close his eyes, even when such terrors loom as it was my fate to see during the past night."

As he spoke, Phlegon, the Emperor's private secretary, came in with letters just received from Rome, and approached his master. He bowed low, and taking up Hadrian's last words he said:

"The stars disquiet you, Caesar?"

"Well, they warn me to be on my guard," replied Hadrian.

"Let us hope that they lie," cried the Greek, with cheerful vivacity. "Cicero was not altogether wrong when he doubted the arts of Astrology."

"He was a mere talker!" said the Emperor, with a frown.

" But," asked Phlegon, " would it not be fair that
if the horoscopes cast for Cneius or Caius, let us say,
were alike, to expect that Cneius or Caius must have
the same temperament and the same destiny through
life if they had happened to be born in the same hour ?"

" Always the old commonplaces, the old silly objections !" interrupted Hadrian, vexed to the verge of rage.
" Speak when you are spoken to, and do not trouble
yourself about things you do not understand and which
do not concern you. Is there anything of importance
among these papers ? "

Antinous gazed at his sovereign in astonishment ;
why should Phlegon's objections make him so furious
when he had answered his so kindly ?

Hadrian paid no farther heed to him, but read the
despatches one after another, hastily but attentively,
wrote brief notes on the margins, signed a decree with
a firm hand, and, when his work was finished desired
the Greek to leave him. Hardly was he alone with
Antinous when the loud cries and jovial shouting of a
large multitude came to their ears through the open window.

" What does this mean ?" he asked Mastor, and as
soon as he had been informed that the workmen and
slaves had just been let out to give themselves up to the
pleasures of their holiday, he muttered to himself:

" These creatures can riot, shout, dress themselves
with garlands, forget themselves in a debauch—and I,
I whom all envy—I spoil my brief span of life with
vain labors, let myself be tormented with consuming
cares—I—" here he broke off and cried in quite an
altered tone :

" Ha! ha! Antinous, you are wiser than I. Let us

leave the future to the future. The feast-day is ours
too ; let us take advantage of this day of freedom. We
too will throw ourselves into the holiday whirlpool—
disguised, I as a satyr, and you as a young faun or
something of the kind; we will drain cups, wander
round the city and enjoy all that is enjoyable."

" Oh !" exclaimed Antinous, joyfully clapping his
hands.

" Evoe Bacche !" cried Hadrian, tossing up his cup
that stood on his table. You are free till this evening,
Mastor, and you my boy, go and talk to Pollux, the
sculptor. He shall be our guide and he will provide
us with wreaths and some mad disguise. ·I must see
drunken men, I must laugh with the jolliest before I am
Caesar again. Make haste, my friend, or new cares
will come to spoil my holiday mood."

CHAPTER XXII.

ANTINOUS and Mastor at once quitted the Emperor's room; in the corridor the lad beckoned the slave
to him and said in a low voice :

" You can hold your tongue I know, will you do
me a favor ?"

"Three sooner than one," replied the Sarmatian.

" You are free to-day—are you going into the city ?"

" I think so."

" You are not known here, but that does not matter. Take these gold pieces and in the flower-market
buy with one of them the most beautiful bunch of flowers
you can find, with another you may make merry, and

out of the remainder spend a drachma in hiring an ass.
The driver will conduct you to the garden of Pudeus'
widow where stands the house of dame Hannah ; you
remember the name ?"

" Dame Hannah and the widow of Pudeus."

"And at the little house, not the big one, leave the
flowers for the sick Selene."

"The daughter of the fat steward, who was attacked
by our big dog ?" asked Mastor, curiously.

"She or another," said Antinous, impatiently, "and
when they ask you who sent the flowers, say ' the friend
at Lochias,' nothing more. You understand."

The slave nodded and said to himself:

" What ! you too—oh ! these women."

Antinous signed to him to be silent, impressed on
him in a few hasty words that he was to be discreet and
to pick out the very choicest flowers, and then betook
himself into the hall of the Muses to seek Pollux.
From him he had learnt where to find the suffering Selene, of whom he could not help thinking incessantly
and wherever he might be. He did not find the sculptor in his screened-off nook ; prompted by a wish to
speak to his mother, Pollux had gone down to the gate-
house where he was now standing before her and frankly
narrating, with many eager gestures of his long arms,
all that had occurred on the previous night. His story
flowed on like a song of triumph, and when he described how the holiday procession had carried away
Arsinoe and himself, the old woman jumped up from her
chair and clapping her fat little hands, she exclaimed :

" Ah ! that is pleasure, that is happiness ! I remember flying along with your father in just the same way
thirty years ago."

"And since thirty years," Pollux interposed. "I can still remember very well how at one of the great Diony- siac festivals, fired by the power of the god, you rushed through the streets with a deer-skin over your shoulders."

"That was delightful—lovely!" cried Doris with sparkling eyes. "But thirty years since it was all differ- ent, very different. I have told you before now how I went with our maid-servant into the Canopic way to the house of my aunt Archidike to look on at the great pro- cession. I had not far to go for we lived near the Theatre, my father was stage-manager and yours was one of the chief singers in the chorus. We hurried along, but all sorts of people stopped us, and drunken men wanted to joke with me."

"Ah, you were as sweet as a rose-bud then," her son interrupted.

"As a rose-bud, yes, but not like your lovely rose," said the old woman. "At any rate I looked nice enough for the men in disguise—fauns and satyrs— and were the cynic hypocrites in their ragged cloaks, to think it worth while to look at me and to take a rap on the knuckles when they tried to put an arm round me or to steal a kiss, I did not care for the handsom- est of them, for Euphorion had done for me with his fiery glances—not with words for I was very strictly kept and he had never been able to get a chance to speak to me. At the corner of the Canopic way and the Market street we could get no farther, for the crowd had blocked the way and were howling and storming as they stared at a party of Klodones and other Mænads, who in their sacred fury were tearing a goat to pieces with their teeth. I shuddered at the spectacle, but I must need stare with

the rest and shout and halloo as they did. My maid, who
I held on to tightly, was seized with the frenzy and dragged me into the middle of the circle close up to the
bleeding sacrifice. Two of the possessed women sprang
upon us, and I felt one clasping me tightly and trying to
throw me down. It was a horrible moment but I defended myself bravely and had succeeded in keeping on
my feet when your father sprang forward, set me free
and led me away. What happened after I could not
tell you now; it was one of those wild happy dreams
in which you must hold your heart with both hands for
fear it should crack with joy, or fly out and away up
to the sky and in the very eye of the sun. Late in the
evening I got home and a week after I was Euphorion's
wife."

"We have exactly followed your example," said
Pollux, " and if Arsinoe grows to be like my dear old
woman I shall be quite satisfied."

"Happy and contented," replied Doris. " Keep
you health, snap your fingers at care and sorrow, do
your duty on work-days and drink till you are jolly in
honor of the god on holidays, and then all will be well.
Those who do all they are able and enjoy as much as they
can get, make good use of their lives and need feel no
remorse in their last hours. What is past is done for, and
when Atropos cuts our thread some one else will stand
in our place and joys will begin all over again. May
the gods bless you!"

"You are right," said Pollux embracing his mother,
"and two together can turn the work out of hand more
lightly and enjoy the pleasures of existence better than
each alone—can they not?"

"I am sure of it; and you have chosen the right

mate," cried the old woman. " You are a sculptor and
used to simple things ; you need no riches, only a
sweet face which may every day rejoice your heart, and
that you have found."

" There is nowhere a sweeter or a lovelier," said
Pollux.

" No, that there is not," continued Doris. " First I
cast my eyes on Selene. She need not be ashamed to
show herself either, and she is a pattern for girls; but
then as Arsinoe grew older, whenever she passed this
way I thought to myself: 'that girl is growing up for
my boy,' and now that you have won her I feel as if I
were once more as young as your sweetheart herself.
My old heart beats as happily as if the little Loves were
touching it with their wings and rosy fingers. If my
feet had not grown so heavy with constantly standing
over the hearth and at washing—really and truly I could
take Euphorion by the arm and dance through the
streets with him to-day."

"Where is father ?"

" Out singing."

" In the morning ! where ?"

" There is some sect that are celebrating their mysteries.   They pay well and he had to sing dismal
hymns for them behind a curtain ; the wildest stuff, in
which he does not follow a word, and that I do not understand a half of."

" It is a pity for I wanted to speak to him."

" He will not be back till late."

" There is plenty of time."

" So much the better, otherwise I might have told
him what you had to say."

" Your advice is as good as his. I think of giving

up working under Papias and standing on my own feet."

"You are quite right; the Roman architect told me yesterday that a great future was open to you."

"There are only my poor sister and the children to be considered. If, during the first few months I should find myself falling short—"

"We will manage to pull through. It is high time that you yourself should reap from what you sow."

"So it seems to me, for my own sake and Arsinoe's; if only Keraunus—"

"Aye—there will be a battle to fight with him."

"A hard one, a hard one," sighed Pollux. "The thought of the old man troubles my happiness."

"Folly!" cried Doris. "Avoid all useless anxiety. It is almost as injurious as remorse gnawing at your heart. Take a workshop of your own, do some great work in a joyful spirit, something to astonish the world, and I will wager anything that the old fool of a steward will only be vexed to think that he destroyed the first work of the celebrated Pollux, instead of treasuring it in his cabinet of curiosities. Just imagine that no such person exists in the world and enjoy your happiness."

"I will stick to that."

"One thing more my lad: take good care of Arsinoe. She is young and inexperienced and you must not persuade her to do anything you would advise her not to do if she were betrothed to your brother instead of to yourself."

Doris had not done speaking when Antinous came into the gate-house and delivered the commands of the architect Claudius Venator, to escort him through the city. Pollux hesitated with his answer, for he had still much to do in the palace, and he hoped to see Arsinoe again in the course of the day. After such a morning what could noon and evening be to him without her? Dame Doris noticed his indecision and cried:

"Yes, go; the festival is for pleasure, besides, the architect can perhaps advise you on many points, and recommend you to his friends."

"Your mother is right," said Antinous. "Claudius Venator can be very touchy, but he can also be grateful, and I wish you sincerely well—"

"Good then, I will come," Pollux interposed while the Bithynian was still speaking, for he felt himself strongly attracted by Hadrian's imposing personality and considered that under the circumstances, it might be very desirable to revel with him for a while.

"I will come, but first I must let Pontius know that I am going to fly from the heat of the fray for a few hours to-day."

"Leave that to Venator," replied the favorite, "and you must find some amusing disguise and procure masks for him and for me and, if you like, for yourself too. He wants to join the revel as a satyr and I in some other disguise."

"Good," replied the sculptor. "I will go at once and order what is requisite. A quantity of dresses for the Dionysiac processions are lying in our workshop and in half an hour I will be back with the things."

"But pray make haste," Antinous begged him. "My master cannot bear to be kept waiting, and besides—one thing—"

At these words Antinous had grown embarrassed and had gone quite close up to the artist. He laid his

hand on his shoulder and said in a low voice but im-
pressively : ·

"Venator stands very near to Caesar. Beware of
saying anything before him that is not in Hadrian's
favor."

"Is your master Caesar's spy ?" asked Pollux, looking suspiciously at Antinous. "Pontius has already
given me a similar warning, and if that is the case—"

"No, no," interrupted the lad hastily. "Anything
but that ; but the two have no secrets from each other
and Venator talks a good deal—cannot hold his
tongue—"

"I thank you and will be on my guard."

"Aye do so—I mean it honestly." The Bithynian
held out his hand to the artist with an expression of
warm regard on his handsome features and with an indescribably graceful gesture. Pollux took it heartily,
but dame Doris, whose old eyes had been fixed as if
spellbound on Antinous, seized her son's arm and quite
excited by the sight of his beauty cried out :

"Oh ! what a splendid creature ! moulded by the
gods ! sacred to the gods ! Pollux, boy ! you might almost think one of the immortals had come down to
earth."

"Look at my old woman!" exclaimed Pollux laughing, "but in truth friend, she has good reasons for her
ecstasies, I could follow her example."

"Hold him fast, hold him fast !" cried Doris. "It
he only will let you take his likeness you can show the
world a thing worth seeing."

"Will you ?" interrupted Pollux turning to Hadrian's
favorite.

"I have never yet been able to keep still for any

artist," said Antinous. " But I will do any thing you
wish to please you. It only vexes me that you too
should join in the chorus with the rest of the world.
Farewell for the present, I must go back to my master."

As soon as the youth had left the house Doris exclaimed:

" Whether a work of art is good for any thing or not
I can only guess at, but as to what is beautiful that I
know as well as any other woman in Alexandria. If
that boy will stand as your model you will produce
something that will delight men and turn the heads of
the women, and you will be sought after even in a
workshop of your own. Eternal gods ! such beauty as
that is sublime. Why are there no means of preserving
such a face and such a form from old age and wrinkles ?"

" I know the means, mother," said Pollux, as he
went to the door. " It is called Art: to her it is given
to bestow eternal youth on this mortal Adonis."

The old woman glanced at her son with pardona-
ble pride, and confirmed his words by an assenting
nod. While she fed her birds, with many coaxing
words, and made one which was a special favorite pick
crumbs from her lips, the young sculptor was hurrying
through the streets with long steps.

He was greeted as he went with many a cross word,
and many exclamations rose from the crowd he left behind him, for he pushed his way by the weight of his
tall person and his powerful arms, and saw and heard,
as he went, little enough of what was going around
him. He thought of Arsinoe, and between whiles of
Antinous and of the attitude in which he best might represent him—whether as hero or god.

In the flower-market, near the Gymnasium, he was

for a moment roused from his reverie by a picture which
struck him as being unusual and which riveted his gaze,
as did every thing exceptional that came under his eyes.
On a very small dark-colored donkey sat a tall, well-
dressed slave, who held in his right hand a nosegay of
extraordinary size and beauty. By his side walked a
smartly dressed-up man with a splendid wreath, and a
comic mask over his face followed by two garden-gods
of gigantic stature, and four graceful boys. In the
slave, Pollux at once recognized the servant of Claudius
Venator, and he fancied he must have seen the masked
gentlemen too before now, but he could not remember
where, and did not trouble himself to retrace him in his
mind. At any rate, the rider of the donkey had just
heard something he did not like, for he was looking
anxiously at his bunch of flowers.

After Pollux had hurried past this strange party
his thoughts reverted to other, and to him far nearer
and dearer subjects. But Mastor's anxious looks were
not without a cause, for the gentleman who was talking to him was no less a person than Verus, the praetor, who was called by the Alexandrians the sham Eros.
He had seen the Emperor's body-slave a hundred
times about his person; he therefore recognized him
at once, and his presence here in Alexandria led him
directly to the simple and correct inference that his
master too must be in the city. The praetor's curiosity
was roused, and he at once proceeded to ply the poor
fellow with bewildering cross-questions. When the
donkey-rider shortly and sharply refused to answer,
Verus thought it well to reveal himself to him, and the
slave lost his confident demeanor when he recognized
the grand gentleman, the Emperor's particular friend.

He lost himself in contradictory statements, and although
he did not directly admit it, he left his interrogator in
the certainty that Hadrian was in Alexandria.

It was perfectly evident that the beautiful nosegay,
which had attracted the praetor's attention to Mastor
could not belong to himself. What could be its destination? Verus recommenced his questioning, but the
Sarmatian would betray nothing, till Verus tapped him
lightly first on one cheek and then on the other, and
said gaily:

"Mastor, my worthy friend Mastor, listen to me.
I will make you certain proposals, and you shall nod
your head, towards that of the estimable beast with two
pairs of legs on which you are mounted, as soon as one
of them takes your fancy."

"Let me go on my way," the slave implored, with
growing anxiety.

"Go, by all means, but I go with you," retorted
Verus, "until I have hit on the thing that suits you.
A great many plans dwell in my head, as you will see.
First I must ask you, shall I go to your master and tell
him that you have betrayed his presence in Alexandria?"

"Sir, you will never do that!" cried Mastor.

"To proceed then. Shall I and my following hang
on to your skirts and stay with you till nightfall, when
you and your steed must return home? You decline—
with thanks! and very wisely, for the execution of this
project would be equally unpleasant to you and to me,
and would probably get you punished. Whisper to
me then, softly, in my ear, where your master is lodging, and from whom and to whom you are carrying
those flowers; as soon as you have agreed to that pro-
posal I will let you go on alone, and will show you

that I care no more for my gold pieces here, in Alexandria, than I do in Italy."

"Not gold—certainly I will not take gold!" cried Mastor.

"You are an honest fellow," replied Verus in an altered tone, "and you know of me,that I treat my servants well and would rather be kind to folks than hard upon them. So satisfy my curiosity without any fear, and I will promise you in return, that not a soul, your master least of all, shall ever know from me what you tell me." Mastor hesitated a little, but as he could not but own to himself that he would be obliged at last to yield to the stronger will of this imperious man, and as moreover he knew that the haughty and extravagant praetor was in fact one of the kindest of masters, he sighed deeply and whispered :

"You will not be the ruin of a poor wretch like me, that I know, so I will tell you, we are living at Lochias."

"There," exclaimed Verus clapping his hands. "And now as to the flowers ?"

"Mere trifling."

"Is Hadrian then in a merry mood?"

"Till to-day he was very gay—but since last night—"

"Well ?"

"You know yourself what he is when he has seen bad signs in the sky."

"Bad signs," said Verus gravely. "And yet he sends flowers ?"

"Not he, can you not guess ?"

"Antinous ?"

Mastor nodded assent.

21

"Only think," laughed Verus. "Then he too is beginning to think it better worth while to admire than to be admired. And who is the fair one who has succeeded in waking up his slumbering heart?"

"Nay—I promised him not to chatter."

"And I promise you the same. My powers of re serve are far greater than my curiosity even."

"Be content, I beseech you with what you already know."

"But to know half is less endurable than to know nothing."

"Nay—I cannot tell you."

"Then am I to begin with fresh suggestions, and all over again?"

"Oh! my lord. I beg you, entreat you—"

"Out with the word, and I go on my way, but if you persist in refusing—"

"Really and truly it only concerns a white-faced girl whom you would not even look at."

"A girl—indeed!"

"Our big dog threw the poor thing down."

"In the street?"

"No, at Lochias. Her father is Keraunus the palace-steward."

"And her name is Arsinoe?" asked Verus with undisguised concern, for he had a pleasant recollection of the beautiful child who had been selected to fill the part of Roxana.

"No, her name is Selene; Arsinoe indeed is her younger sister."

"Then you bring these flowers from Lochias?"

"She went out, and she could not get back home again; she is now lying in the house of a stranger."

" Where ?"

" That must be quite indifferent to you "

" By no means, quite the contrary. I beg you to tell me the whole truth."

" Eternal gods ! what can you care about the poor sick creature ?"

" Nothing whatever; but I must know whither you are riding."

" Down by the sea. I do not know the house, but the donkey driver—"

" Is it far from here ?"

" About half an hour yet," said the lad.

" A good way then," replied Verus. " And Hadrian is particularly anxious to remain unknown."

"Certainly."

" And you his body-servant, who are known to numbers of others here from Rome, like myself, you propose to ride half a mile through the streets where every creature that can stand or walk is swarming, with a large nosegay in your hand which attracts every body's attention. Oh Mastor that is not wise !"

The slave started, and seeing at once that Verus was right, he asked in alarm :

" What then can I do ?"

" Get off your donkey," said the praetor. " Disguise yourself and make merry to your heart's content with these gold pieces."

" And the flowers ?"

" I will see to that."

"You will ? I may trust you; and never betray to Antinous what you compelled me to do ?"

" Positively not."

" There—there are the flowers, but I cannot take the gold."

" Then I shall fling it among the crowd. Buy yourself a garland, a mask and some wine, as much as you can carry. Where is the girl to be found?"

" At dame Hannah's. She lives in a little house in a garden belonging to the widow of Pudeus. And whoever gives it to her is to say that it is sent by the friend at Lochias."

" Good. Now go, and take care that no one recognizes you. Your secret is mine, and the friend at Lochias shall be duly mentioned."

Mastor disappeared in the crowd. Verus put the nosegay into the hands of one of the garden-gods that followed in his train, sprang laughing on to the ass, and desired the driver to show him the way. At the corner of the next street, he met two litters, carried with difficulty through the crowd by their bearers. In the first sat Keraunus, whose saffron-colored cloak was conspicuous from afar, as fat as Silenus the companion of Dionysus, but looking very sullen. In the second sat Arsinoe, looking gaily about her, and so fresh and pretty that the Roman's easily-stirred pulses beat more rapidly.

Without reflecting, he took the flowers from the hand of the garden-god—the flowers intended for Selene—laid them on the girl's litter, and said:

" Alexander greets Roxana, the fairest of the fair."

Arsinoe colored, and Verus, after watching her for some time as she was carried onwards, desired one of his boys to follow her litter, and to join him again in the flower-market, where he would wait, to inform him whither she had gone.

The messenger hurried off, and Verus, turning his ass's head soon reached a semicircular pillared hall on the shady side of a large open space, under which the better sort of gardeners and flower dealers of the city exposed their gay and fragrant wares to be sold by pretty girls. To-day every stall had been particularly well supplied, but the demand for wreaths and flowers had steadily increased from an early hour, and although Verus had all that he could find of fresh flowers arranged and tied together, still the nosegay, though much larger, was not half so beautiful as that intended for Selene, and for which he substituted it.

Now this annoyed the Roman. His sense of justice prompted him to make good the loss he had inflicted on the sick girl. Gay ribbons were wound round the stalks of the flowers, and the long ends floated in the air, so Verus took a brooch from his dress and stuck it into the bow which ornamented the stem of the nosegay; then he was satisfied, and as he looked at the stone set in a gold border—an onyx on which was engraved Eros sharpening his arrows—he pictured to himself the pleasure, the delight of the girl that the handsome Bithynian loved, as she received the beautiful gift.

His slaves, natives of Britain, who were dressed as garden-gods, were charged with the commission to proceed to dame Hannah's under the guidance of the donkey-driver to deliver the nosegay to Selene from ' the friend at Lochias,' and then to wait for him outside the house of Titianus, the prefect; for thither, as he had ascertained from his swift-footed messenger, had Keraunus and his daughter been carried.

Verus needed a longer time than the boy, to make his way through the crowd. At the door of the pre-

fect's residence he laid aside his mask, and in an anteroom where the steward was sitting on a couch waiting for his daughter, he arranged his hair and the folds
of his toga, and was then conducted to the lady Julia
with whom he hoped, once more, to see the charming
Arsinoe.

But in the reception-room, instead of Arsinoe he
found his own wife and the poetess Balbilla and her
companion. He greeted the ladies gaily, amiably and
gracefully, as usual, and then, as he looked enquiringly
round the large room without concealing his disappointment, Balbilla came up to him and asked him in a low
voice :

" Can you be honest, Verus ?"

" When circumstances allow it, yes."

" And will they allow it here ?"

" I should suppose so."

" Then answer me truly. Did you come here for
Julia's sake, or did you come——"

" Well ?"

" Or did you expect to find the fair Roxana with the
prefect's wife ?"

" Roxana ?" asked Verus, with a cunning smile.
" Roxana ! Why she was the wife of Alexander the
Great, and is long since dead, but I care only for the
living, and when I left the merry tumult in the streets
it was simply and solely——"

" You excite my curiosity."

" Because my prophetic heart promised me, fairest
Balbilla, that I should find you here."

" And that you call honest !" cried the poetess, hit-
ting the praetor a blow with the stick of the ostrich-
feather fan she held in her hand. " Only listen, Lucilla,

your husband declares he came here for my sake."
The praetor looked reproachfully at the speaker, but she
whispered:

"Due punishment for a dishonest man." Then, raising her voice, she said:

"Do you know, Lucilla, that if I remain unmarried,
your husband is not wholly innocent in the matter."

"Alas! yes, I was born too late for you," interrupted Verus, who knew very well what the poetess was
about to say.

"Nay — no misunderstanding!" cried Balbilla.
"For how can a woman venture upon wedlock when
she cannot but fear the possibility of getting such a husband as Verus."

"And what man," retorted the praetor, "would ever
be so bold as to court Balbilla, could he hear how cruelly she judges an innocent admirer of beauty?"

"A husband ought not to admire beauty—only the
one beauty who is his wife."

"Ah Vestal maiden," laughed Verus. "I am meanwhile punishing you by withholding from you a great
secret which interests us all. No, no, I am not going to
tell—but I beg you my lady wife to take her to task,
and teach her to exercise some indulgence so that
her future husband may not have too hard a time
of it."

"No woman can learn to be indulgent," replied
Lucilla. "Still we practise indulgence when we have no
alternative, and the criminal requires us to make al-
lowance for him in this thing or the other."

Verus made his wife a bow and pressed his lips
on her arm, then he asked. "And where is dame
Julia?"

"She is saving the sheep from the wolf," replied Balbilla.

"Which means— ?"

"That as soon as you were announced she carried off little Roxana to a place of safety."

"No, no," interrupted Lucilla. "The tailor was waiting in an inner room to arrange the charming child's costume. Only look at the lovely nosegay she brought to Julia. And do you deny my right to share your secret?"

"How could I?" replied Verus.

"He is very much in need of your making allowances!" laughed Balbilla, while the praetor went up to his wife and told her in a whisper what he had learnt from Mastor. Lucilla clasped her hands in astonishment, and Verus cried to the poetess:

"Now you see what a satisfaction your cruel tongue has deprived you of?"

"How can you be so revengeful most estimable Verus," said the lady coaxingly. "I am dying of curiosity."

"Live but a few days longer fair Balbilla, for my sake," replied the Roman, "and the cause of your early death will be removed."

"Only wait, I will be revenged!" cried the girl threatening him with her finger, but Lucilla led her away saying:

"Come now, it is time we should give Julia the benefit of our advice."

"Do so," said Verus. "Otherwise I am afraid my visit to-day would seem opportune to no one.—Greet Julia from me."

As he went away he cast a glance at the nosegay

which Arsinoe had given away as soon as she had received it from him, and he sighed : " As we grow old we have to learn wisdom."

END OF VOL. I.

THE EMPEROR.

CHAPTER I.

DAME HANNAH had watched by Selene till sunrise
and indefatigably cooled both her injured foot and the
wound in her head. The old physician was not dissatisfied with the condition of his patient, but ordered
the widow to lie down for a time and to leave the care
of her for a few hours to her young friend. When
Mary was alone with the sick girl and had laid the fresh
cold handkerchief in its place, Selene turned her face
towards her and said:

"Then you were at Lochias yesterday. Tell me
how you found them all there. Who guided you to
our lodgings and did you see my little brother and
sisters?"

"You are not yet quite free of fever, and I do not
know how much I ought to talk to you—but I would
with all my heart."

The words were spoken kindly and there was a deep
loving light in the eyes of the deformed girl as she said
them. Selene excited not merely her sympathy and pity,
but her admiration too, for she was so beautiful, so
totally different from herself, and in every little service
she rendered her, she felt like some despised beggar
whom a prince might have permitted to wait upon him.
Her hump had never seemed to her so bent, nor her

brown skin so ugly at any other time as it did to-day, when side by side with this symmetrical and delicate girlish form, rounded to such tender contours.

But Mary felt not the smallest movement of envy. She only felt happy to help Selene, to serve her, to be allowed to gaze at her although she was a heathen. During the night too, she had prayed fervently that the Lord might graciously draw to himself this lovely, gentle creature, that He might permit her to recover, and fill her soul with the same love for the Saviour that gave joy to her own. More than once she had longed to kiss her, but she dared not, for it seemed to her as though the sick girl were made of finer stuff than she herself.

Selene felt tired, very tired, and as the pain diminished, a comfortable sense stole over her of peace and respite in the silent and loving homeliness of her surroundings; a feeling that was new and very soothing, though it was interrupted, now and again, by her anxiety for those at home. Dame Hannah's presence did her good, for she fancied she recognized in her voice something that had been peculiar to her mother's, when she had played with her and pressed her with special affection to her heart.

In the papyrus factory, at the gumming-table, the sight of the little hunchback had disgusted Selene, but here she observed what good eyes she had, and how kind a voice, and the care with which Mary lifted the compress from her foot—as softly, as if in her own hands she felt the pain that Selene was suffering—and then laid another on the broken ankle, aroused her gratitude, Her sister Arsinoe was a vain and thorough Alexandrian girl, and she had nicknamed the poor thing after

the ugliest of the Hellenes who had besieged Troy.
"Dame Thersites," and Selene herself had often repeated it.   Now she forgot the insulting name altogether, and met the objections of her nurse by saying:

"The fever cannot be much now; if you tell me
something I shall not think so constantly of this atro-
cious pain.   I am longing to be at home.   Did you
see the children?"

"No, Selene.   I went no farther than the entrance
of your dwelling, and the kind gate-keeper's wife told
me at once that I should find neither your father nor
your sister, and that your slave-woman was gone out to
buy cakes for the children."

"To buy them!" exclaimed Selene in astonishment.

"The old woman told me too that the way to your
apartments led through several rooms in which slaves
were at work, and that her son, who happened to be
with her, should accompany me, and so he did, but the
door was locked, and he told me I might entrust his
mother with my commission.   I did so, for she looked
as if she were both judicious and kind."

"That she is."

"And she is very fond of you, for when I told her
of your sufferings the bright tears rolled down her
cheeks, and she praised you as warmly, and was as much
troubled as if you had been her own daughter."

"You said nothing about our working in the factory?" asked Selene anxiously.

"Certainly not, you had desired me not to mention
it.   I was to say everything that was kind to you from
the old lady."

For several minutes the two girls were silent, then
Selene asked:

22

"Did the gate-keeper's son who accompanied you also hear of the disaster that had befallen me?"

"Yes, on the way to your rooms he was full of fun and jokes, but when I told him that you had gone out with your damaged foot and now could not get home again, and were being treated by the leech, he was very angry and used blasphemous language."

"Can you remember what he said?"

"Not perfectly, but one thing I still recollect. He accused his gods of having created a beautiful work only to spoil it, nay he abused them—" Mary looked down as she spoke, as if she were repeating something ill to tell, but Selene colored slightly with pleasure, and exclaimed eagerly, as if to outdo the sculptor in abuse:

"He is quite right, the powers above act in such a way—"

"That is not right," said the deformed girl reprovingly.

"What?" asked the patient. "Here you live quietly to yourselves in perfect peace and love. Many a word that I heard dame Hannah say has stuck in my mind, and I can see for myself that you act as kindly as you speak. The gods no doubt are good to you!"

"God is for each and all."

"What!" exclaimed Selene with flashing eyes. "For those whose every pleasure they destroy? For the home of eight children whom they rob of their mother? For the poor whom they daily threaten to deprive of their bread-winner?"

"For them too, there is a merciful God," interrupted dame Hannah who had just come into the room. "I will lead you to the loving Father in Heaven who cares for us all as if we were His children; but not now—you must rest and neither talk nor hear of anything that can excite your fevered blood. Now I will rearrange the pillow under your head. Mary will wet a fresh compress and then you must try to sleep."

"I cannot," replied Selene, while Hannah shook her pillows and arranged them carefully. "Tell me about your God who loves us."

"By-and-bye, dear child. Seek Him and you will find Him, for of all His children He loves them best who suffer."

"Those who suffer?" asked Selene, in surprise. "What has a God in his Olympian joys to do with those who suffer?"

"Be quiet, child," interrupted Hannah, patting the sick girl with a soothing hand, "you soon will learn how God takes care of you and that Another loves you."

"Another," muttered Selene, and her cheeks turned crimson.

She thought at once of Pollux, and asked herself why the story of her sufferings should have moved him so deeply if he were not in love with her. Then she began to seek some colorable ground for what she had heard as she went past the screen behind which he had been working. He had never told her plainly that he loved her. Why should he, an artist and a bright, high-spirited young fellow, not be allowed to jest with a pretty girl, even if his heart belonged to another. No, she was not indifferent to him: that she had felt that night when she had stood as his model, and now—as she thought— could guess, nay, feel sure of, from Mary's story.

The longer she thought of him, the more she began to long to see him whom she had loved so dearly even

22

as a child.   Her heart had never yet beat for any other man, but since she had met Pollux again in the hall of the Muses, his image had filled her whole soul, and what she now felt must be love—could be nothing else. Half awake, but half asleep, she pictured him to herself, entering this quiet room, sitting down by the head of her couch, and looking with his kind eyes into hers. Ah! and how could she help it—she sat up and opened her arms to him.

"Lie still, my child, lie still," said Hannah.   "It is not good for you to move about so much."

Selene opened her eyes, but only to close them again and to dream for some time longer till she was startled from her rest by loud voices in the garden.   Hannah left the room, and her voice presently mingled with those of the other persons outside, and when she returned her cheeks were flushed and she could not find fitting words in which to tell her patient what she had to say.

"A very big man, in the most outrageous dress," she said at last, "wanted to be let in; when the gate-keeper refused, he forced his way in.   He asked for you."

"For me," said Selene, blushing.

"Yes, my child, he brought a large and beautiful nosegay of flowers, and said 'your friend at Lochias sends you his greeting.'"

"My friend at Lochias?" murmured thoughtfully Selene to herself.   Then her eyes sparkled with gladness, and she asked quickly:

"You said the man who brought the flowers was very tall."

"He was."

"Oh please, dame Hannah, let me see the flowers?"
cried Selene, trying to raise herself.

"Have you a lover, child?" asked the widow.

"A lover?—no, but there is a young man with
whom we always used to play when we were quite little
—an artist, a kind, good man—and the nosegay must
be from him."

Hannah looked with sympathy at the girl, and signing to Mary she said:

"The nosegay is a very large one. You may see it,
but it must not remain in the room; the smell of so many
flowers might do you harm."

Mary rose from her seat at the head of the bed, and
whispered to the sick girl:

"Is that the tall gate-keeper's son?" Selene nodded, smiling, and as the women went away she changed
her position from lying on one side, stretched herself out
on her back, pressed her hand to her heart, and looked
upwards with a deep sigh. There was a singing in her
ears, and flashes of colored light seemed to dance before her closed eyes. She drew her breath with difficulty,
but still it seemed as though the air she drew in was
full of the perfume of flowers.

Hannah and Mary carried in the enormous bunch
of flowers. Selene's eyes shone more brightly, and she
clasped her hands in admiration. Then she made them
show her the lovely, richly-tinted and fragrant gift, first
on one side and then on the other, burried her face in
the flowers, and secretly kissed the delicate petals of a
lovely, half-opened rose-bud. She felt as if intoxicated,
and the bright tears flowed in slow succession down her
cheeks. Mary was the first to detect the brooch stuck
into the ribbons that tied the stems of the flowers. She

unfastened it and showed it to Selene, who hastily took
it out of her hand. Blushing deeper and deeper, she fixed
her eyes on the intaglio carved on the stone of the love-
god sharpening his arrows. She felt her pain no more
pain, she felt quite well, and at the same time glad, proud,
too happy. Dame Hannah noted her excitement with
much anxiety; she nodded to Mary and said :

"Now my daughter, this must do; we will place the
flowers outside the window so that you may see them."

"Already," said Selene, in a regretful tone, and she
broke off a few violets and roses from the crowded mass.

When she was alone again, she laid the flowers down
and once more tenderly contemplated the figures on the
handsome gem. It had no doubt been engraved by
Teuker, the brother of Pollux. How fine the carving
was, how significant the choice of the subject represented!
Only the heavy gold setting disturbed the poor child,
who for so many years had had to stint and contrive
with her money. She said to herself that it was wrong
of the young fellow, who, besides being poor, had to support his sister, to rush into such an outlay for her. But
his gift gave her none the less pleasure, out of her own
possessions nothing would have seemed too precious to
give him. She would teach him to be saving by-and-
bye.

The women presently returned after they had with
much trouble set up the nosegay outside the window,
and they renewed the wet handkerchief without speaking. She did not in the least want to talk, she was listening with so much pleasure to the fair promises which
her fancy was making, and wherever she turned her eyes
they fell on something she could love. The flowers on
her bed, the brooch in her hand, the nosegay outside the

window, and never dreaming that another—not the man
she loved—could have sent it to her, another for whom
she cared even less than for the Christians who walked
up and down in Paulina's garden, under her window.
There she lay, full of sweet contentment and secure of a
love that had never been hers—of possessing the heart
of a man who never once thought of her, but who, only
a few hours since, had rushed off with her sister, intoxicated with joy and delight.   Poor Selene!

And her next dreams were of untroubled happiness,
but the minutes flew after each other, each bringing her
nearer to waking—and what a waking!

Her father had not come, as he had intended, to see
her before going to the prefect's house with Arsinoe.
His desire to conduct his daughter to Julia in a dress
worthy of her prospects had detained him a long time,
and even then he had not succeeded in his object.   All
the weavers, and the shops were closed, for every work-
man, whether slave or free, was taking part in the festivities, and when the hour fixed by the prefect drew near,
his daughter was still sitting in her litter, in her simple
white dress and her modest peplum, bound with blue
ribbon, which looked even more insignificant by day
than in the evening.

The nosegay which had been given to Arsinoe by
Verus gave her much pleasure, for a girl is always pleased
with beautiful flowers—nay, they have something in common.   As she and her father approached the prefect's
house Arsinoe grew frightened, and her father could not
conceal his vexation at being obliged to take her to the
lady Julia in so modest a garb.   Nor was his gloomy
humor at all enlivened when he was left to wait in the
anteroom while Julia and the wife of Verus, aided by

Balbilla chose for his daughter the finest colored and costliest stuffs of the softest wool, silk, and delicate bombyx tissue. This sort of occupation has this peculiarity, that the longer time it takes the more assistance is needed, and the steward had to submit to wait fully two hours in the prefect's anteroom, which gradually grew fuller and fuller of clients and visitors. At last Arsinoe came back all glowing and full of the beautiful things that were to be prepared for her.

Her father rose slowly from his easy seat, and as she hastened towards him the door opened, and through it came Plutarch, freshly wreathed, freshly decked with flowers which were fastened to the breast-folds of his pallium, and lifted into the room by his two human crutches. Every one rose as he came in, and when Keraunus saw that the chief lawyer of the city, a man of ancient family, bowed before him, he did likewise. Plutarch's eyesight was stronger than his legs were, and where a pretty woman was to be seen, it was always very keen. He perceived Arsinoe as soon as he had crossed the threshold and waved both hands towards her, as if she were an old and favorite acquaintance.

The sweet child had quite bewitched him; in his younger days he would have given anything and everything to win her favor; now he was satisfied to make his favor pleasing to her; he touched her playfully two or three times on the arm and said gaily:

"Well pretty Roxana, has dame Julia done well with the dresses?"

"Oh! they have chosen such pretty, such really lovely things!" exclaimed the girl:

"Have they?" said Plutarch, to conceal by speech

the fact that he was meditating on some subject;
"Have they? and why should they not?"

Arsinoe's washed dress had caught the old man's eye,
and remembering that Gabinius the curiosity-dealer had
that very morning been to him to enquire whether Arsinoe were not in fact one of his work-girls, and to repeat
his statement that her father was a beggarly toady, full
of haughty airs, whose curiosities, of which he contemptuously mentioned a few, were worth nothing, Plutarch
was hastily asking himself how he could best defend his
pretty protegé against the envious tongues of her rivals;
for many spiteful speeches of theirs had already come
to his ears.

"Whatever the noble Julia undertakes is always admirably done," he said aloud, and he added in a whisper: "The day after to-morrow when the goldsmiths
have opened their workshops again, I will see what I
can find for you. I am falling in a heap, hold me up
higher Antaeus and Atlas. So.—Yes, my child you
look even better from up here than from a lower level.
Is the stout man standing behind you your father?"

"Yes."

"Have you no mother?"

"She is dead."

"Oh!" said Plutarch in a tone of regret. Then
turning to the steward he said:

"Accept my congratulations on having such a daughter Keraunus. I hear too that you have to supply a
mother's place to her."

"Alas sir! she is very like my poor wife, since her
death I live a joyless life."

"But I hear that you take pleasure in collecting rare
and beautiful objects. This is a taste we have in com-

mon. Are you inclined to part with the cup that belonged to my namesake Plutarch?   It must be a fine
piece of work from what Gabinius tells me."

"That it is," replied the steward proudly.   "It was
a gift to the philosopher from Trajan; beautifully carved
in ivory. I cannot bear to part with such a gem but,"
and as he spoke he lowered his voice.   "I am under
obligations to you, you have taken charge of my
daughter's outfit and to offer you some return I
will—"

"That is quite out of the question," interrupted Plutarch, who knew men, and who saw from the steward's
pompous pretentiousness that the dealer had done him
no injustice in describing him as overbearing.   "You
are doing me an honor by allowing me to contribute
what I can towards decorating our Roxana.   I beg you
to send me the cup, and whatever price you put upon it,
I, of course, shall pay, that is quite understood."

Keraunus had a brief internal conflict with himself.
If he had not so sorely needed money, if he had not so
keenly desired to see a young and comely slave walking
behind him, he would have adhered to his purpose of
presenting the cup to Plutarch; as it was he cleared his
throat, looked at the ground, and said with an embarrassed manner and without a trace of his former
confidence:

"I remain your debtor, and it seems you do not
wish this business to be mixed up with other matters.
Well then, I had two thousand drachmae for a sword
that belonged to Antony."

"Then certainly," interrupted Plutarch, "the cup,
the gift of Trajan, must be worth double, particularly
to me who am related to the illustrious owner.   May

I offer you four thousand drachmae for your precious possession ?"

"I am anxious to oblige you, and so I say yes," replied the steward with much dignity, and he squeezed Arsinoe's little finger, for she was standing close to him. Her hand had for some time been touching his in token of warning that he should adhere to his first intention of making the cup a present to Plutarch.

As the pair, so unlike each other, quitted the ante-room, Plutarch looked after them with a meaning smile and thought to himself: "That is well done. How little pleasure I generally have from my riches! How often when I see a sturdy porter I would willingly change places with him! But to-day I am glad to have as much money as I could wish. Sweet child! She must have a new dress of course for the sake of appearance, but really her beauty did not suffer from the washed-out rag of a dress. And she belongs to me, for I have seen her at the factory among the workwomen, of that I am certain."

Keraunus had gone out with his daughter and once outside the prefect's house, he could not help chuckling aloud, while he patted his daughter on the shoulder, and whispered to her:

"I told you so child! we shall be rich yet, we shall rise in life again and need not be behind the other citizens in any thing."

"Yes, father, but it is just because you believe that, that you ought to have given the cup to the old man."

"No," replied Keraunus, "business is business, but by and bye I will repay him tenfold for all he does for you now, by giving him my painting by Apelles. And

Julia shall have the pair of sandal-straps set with cut-gems that came off a sandal of Cleopatra's."

Arsinoe looked down, for she knew what these treasures were worth, and said:

" We can consider all that later."

Then she and her father got into the litters that had been waiting for them, and without which Keraunus thought he could no longer exist, and they were carried to the garden of Pudeus' widow.

Their visit came to interrupt Selene's blissful dreams. Keraunus behaved with icy coldness to dame Hannah, for it afforded him a certain satisfaction to make a display of contempt for every thing Christian. When he expressed his regret that Selene should have been obliged to remain in her house, the widow replied:

" She is better here than in the street, at any rate."

And when Keraunus went on to say that he would take nothing as a gift and would pay her for her care of his daughter, Hannah answered:

" We are happy to do all we can for your child, and Another will reward us."

" That I certainly forbid," exclaimed the steward wrathfully.

" We do not understand each other," said the Christian pleasantly. " I do not allude to any mortal being, and the reward we work for is not gold and possessions, but the happy consciousness of having mitigated the sufferings of a fellow-creature."

Keraunus shrugged his shoulders, and after desiring Selene to ask the physician when she might be taken home, he went away.

" I will not leave you here an instant longer than is necessary," he said as urgently as though she were in

some infected house; he kissed her forehead, bowed to
Hannah as loftily as though he had just bestowed an
alms upon her, and departed, without listening to
Selene's assurances that she was extremely happy and
comfortable with the widow.

The ground had long burnt under his feet, and the
money in his pocket, he was now possessed of ample
means to acquire a good new slave, perhaps, if he threw
old Sebek into the bargain, they might even suffice to
procure him a handsome Greek, who might teach the
children to read and write. He could direct his first
attention to the external appearance of the new member
of his household, if he were a scholar as well, he would
feel justified in the high price he expected to be obliged
to pay for him.

As Keraunus approached the slave-market he said,
not without some conscious emotion at his own paternal
devotion:

"All for the credit of the house, all, and only, for the
children."

Arsinoe carried out her intention of staying with
Selene; her father was to fetch her on his way home.
After he was gone, Hannah and Mary left the two sisters together, for they supposed that they must wish to
discuss a variety of things without the presence of
strangers.

As soon as the girls were alone Arsinoe began:

"Your cheeks are rosy, Selene, and you look cheerful—ah! and I, I am so happy—so happy!"

"Because you are to fill the part of Roxana?"

"That is very nice too, and who would have thought
only yesterday morning that we should be so rich to-
day. We hardly know what to do with all the money."

"We?"

"Yes, for father has sold two objects out of his collection for six thousand drachmae."

"Oh!" cried Selene clasping her hands, "then we can pay our most pressing debts."

"To be sure, but that is not nearly all."

"No?"

"Where shall I begin? Ah! Selene, my heart is so full. I am tired, and yet I could dance and sing and shout all day and all the night through till to-morrow. When I think how happy I am, my head turns, and I feel as if I must use all my self-control to keep myself from turning giddy. You do not know yet how you feel when the arrow of Eros has pierced you. Ah! I love Pollux so much, and he loves me too."

At these words all the color fled from Selene's cheeks, and her pale lips brought out the words:

"Pollux? The son of Euphorion, Pollux the sculptor?"

"Yes, our dear, kind, tall Pollux!" cried Arsinoe. "Now prick up your ears, and you shall hear how it all came to pass. Last night on our way to see you he confessed how much he loved me, and now you must advise me how to win over my father to our side, and very soon too. By-and-bye he will of course say yes, for Pollux can do anything he wants, and some day he will be a great man, as great as Papias, and Aristaeus, and Kealkes all put together. His youthful trick with that silly caricature—but how pale you are, Selene!"

"It is nothing—nothing at all—a pain—go on," said Selene.

"Dame Hannah begged me not to let you talk much."

"Only tell me everything; I will be quiet."

"Well, you have seen the lovely head of mother that he made," Arsinoe went on. "Standing by that we saw each other and talked for the first time after long years, and I felt directly that there was not a dearer man than he in the whole world, wide as it is. And he fell in love too with a stupid little thing like me. Yesterday evening he came here with me; and then as I went home, taking his arm in the dark through the streets, then— Oh, Selene, it was splendid, delightful! You cannot imagine!—Does your foot hurt you very much, poor dear? Your eyes are full of tears."

"Go on, tell me all, go on."

And Arsinoe did as she was desired, sparing the poor girl nothing that could widen and deepen the wound in her soul. Full of rapturous memories she described the place in the streets where Pollux had first kissed her. The shrubs in the garden where she had flung herself into his arms, her blissful walk in the moonlight, and all the crowd assembled for the festival, and finally how, possessed by the god, they had together joined the procession, and danced through the streets. She described, with tears in her eyes, how painful their parting had been, and laughed again, as she told how an ivy leaf in her hair had nearly betrayed everything to her father. So she talked and talked, and there was something that intoxicated her in her own words.

How they were affecting Selene she did not observe. How could she know that it was her narrative and no other suffering which made her sister's lips quiver so sorrowfully? Then, when she went on to speak of the splendid garments which Julia was having made for her, the suffering girl listened with only half an ear, but her attention revived when she heard how much old Plutarch had offered for the ivory cup, and that her father proposed to exchange their old slave for a more active one.

"Our good black mouse-catching old stork looks shabby enough it is true," said Arsinoe, "still I am very sorry he should go away. If you had been at home, perhaps father would have waited to consider."

Selene laughed drily, and her lips curled scornfully as she said:

"That is the way! go on! two days before you are turned out of house and home you ride in a chariot and pair!"

"You always see the worst side," said Arsinoe with annoyance. "I tell you it will all turn out far better and nicer and more happily than we expect. As soon as we are a little richer we will buy back the old man, and keep him and feed him till he dies."

Selene shrugged her shoulders, and her sister jumped up from her seat with her eyes full of tears. She had been so happy in telling how happy she was that she firmly believed that her story must bring brightness into the gloom of the sick girl's soul, like sunshine after a dark night; and Selene had nothing to give her but scornful words and looks. If a friend refuses to share in joys it is hardly less wounding than if he were to abandon us in trouble.

"How you always contrive to embitter my happiness!" cried Arsinoe. "I know very well that nothing that I can do can ever be right in your eyes; still, we are sisters, and you need not set your teeth and grudge your words, and shrug your shoulders when I tell you of things which, even a stranger, if I were to confide them to her, would rejoice over with me. You are so cold and heartless! I dare say you will betray me to my father—"

But Arsinoe did not finish her sentence, for Selene looked up at her with a mixture of suffering and alarm, and said:

"I cannot be glad—I am in too much pain." As she spoke the tears ran down her cheeks and as soon as Arsinoe saw them she felt a return of pity for the sick girl, bent over and kissed her cheeks once, twice, thrice; but Selene pushed her aside and murmured piteously:

"Leave me—pray leave me; go away, I can bear it no longer." She turned her face to the wall, sobbing aloud. Arsinoe attempted once more to show her some marks of affection, but her sister pushed her away still more decidedly, crying out loudly, as if in desperation:

" I shall die if you do not leave me alone."

And the happier girl, whose best offerings were thus disdained by her only female friend, went weeping away to · await her father's return outside the door of the widow's house.

When Hannah went to lay fresh handkerchiefs on Selene's wounds she saw that she had been crying, but she did not enquire into the reason of her tears. Towards evening the widow explained to her patient that she must leave her alone for half an hour, for that she and Mary were going out to pray to their God with their brethren and sisters, and they would pray for her also.

" Leave me, only leave me," said Selene, " as it is, so it is—there are no gods."

"Gods?" replied Hannah. " No. But there is one good and loving Father in Heaven, and you soon shall learn to know him."

23

"I know him, well!" muttered the sick girl with keen
irony.

No sooner was she alone than she sat up in bed, and
flung the flowers, which had been lying on it, far from
her across the room, twisted the pin of the brooch till it
was broken, and did not stir a finger to save the gold
setting and engraved stone when they fell between the
bed and wall of the room.   Then she lay staring at the
ceiling, and did not stir again.   It was now quite dark.
The lilies and honeysuckle in the great nosegay outside
the window began to smell more strongly, and their perfume forced itself inexorably on her senses, rendered
painfully acute by fever.   She perceived it at every
breath she drew, and not for a minute would it let her
forget her wrecked happiness, and the wretchedness of
her heart, till the heavy sweetness of the flowers became
more unendurable than the most pungent odor, and she
drew the coverlet over her head to escape this new torment; but she soon cast it off again, for she thought she
should be suffocated under it.   An intolerable restless-
ness took possession of her, while the pain in her injured
foot throbbed madly, the cut in her head seemed to burn,
and her temples beat with an agonizing headache that
contracted the muscles of her eyes.   Every nerve in her
body, every thought of her brain was a separate torture,
and at the same time she felt herself without a stay, without protection, and wholly abandoned to some cruel influence, which tossed and tore her soul as the storm
tosses the crowns of the palm-trees.

Without tears, incapable of lying still and yet punished for the slightest movement by some fresh pain,
racked in every joint, not strong enough in her bewilderment to carry through a single connected thought,

and yet firmly convinced that the perfume she was forced
to inhale at every breath was poisoning her—destroying
her—driving her mad—she lifted her damaged foot out
of bed, dragged the other after it, and sat up on her couch
regardless of the pain she felt, and the warnings of the
physician.   Her long hair fell dishevelled over her face,
her arms, and her hands, in which she held her aching
head; and in this new attitude the excitement of her
brain and heart took fresh development.

She sat gazing at the floor with a freezing gaze, and
bitter enmity towards her sister, hatred towards Pollux,
contempt for her father's miserable weakness, and her
own utter blindness, rang wild changes in her soul.
Outside all lay in peaceful calm, and from the house in
which Paulina lived the evening breeze now and again
bore the pure tones of a pious hymn upon her ear.   Selene never heeded it, but as the same air wafted the
scent of the flowers in her face even stronger than before,
she clutched her hair in her fingers and pulled it so violently that she actually groaned with the pain she gave
herself.

The question as to whether her hair was less abundant and beautiful than her sister's suddenly occurred
to her, and like a flash in the darkness the wish shot
through her soul that she could fling Arsinoe to the
ground by the hair, with the hand which was now hurting herself.

That perfume! that horrible perfume!

She could bear it no longer.   She stood up on her
uninjured foot, and with very short steps she dragged
herself half crying to the window, and flung the nosegay with the great jar of burnt clay down on to the
ground.   The vessel was broken.—It had cost poor

23

Hannah many hardly-saved pieces not long since. Selene stood on one foot, leaning, to recover herself, against the right-hand post of the window-opening, and there she could hear more distinctly than from her couch, the voice of the waves as they broke on the stone quay just behind dame Hannah's little house. The child of the Lochias was familiar with their tones, but the clashing and gurgling of the cool, moist element against the stones had never affected her before as they did now. Her fevered blood was on fire, her foot was burning, her head was hot, and hatred seemed to consume her soul as in a slow fire; she felt as if every wave that broke upon the sea-wall was calling out to her: "I am cool, I am moist, I can extinguish the flame that is consuming you. I can refresh and revive you."

What had the world to offer her but new torment and new misery? But the sea—the blue dark sea was wide, and cold, and deep, and its waves promised her in insidious tones to relieve her at once of the rage of her fever, and of the burden of her life. Selene did not pause, did not reflect; she remembered neither the children whom she had so long cared for as a mother, nor her father, whose comfort and support she was—vague voices in her brain seemed to be whispering to her that the world was evil and cruel, and the abode of all the torment and care that gnawed at her heart. She felt as if she had been plunged to the temples in a pool of fire, and, like some poor wretch whose garments have been caught by the flames, she had an instinct to fly to the water, at the bottom of which she might hope to find the fulfilment of her utmost longing, sweet cold death, in which all is forgotten.

Groaning and tottering she pushed her way through

the door into the garden and hobbled down to the sea, grasping her temples in her hands.

CHAPTER II.

THE Alexandrians were a stiff-necked generation. Only some phenomenal sight far transcending their every-day experience could avail to make them turn their heads to stare at it, but just now there was something to look at, at every moment and in every street of the city. To-day too each one thought only of himself and of his own pleasure. Some particularly pretty, tall, or well-dressed figure would give rise to a smile or an exclamation of approval, but before one sight had been thoroughly enjoyed the inquisitive eye was seeking a fresh one.

Thus it happened that no one paid any special attention to Hadrian and his companions who allowed themselves to be unresistingly carried along the streets by the current of the crowd; and yet each one of them was, in his way, a remarkable object. Hadrian was dressed as Silenus, Pollux as a faun. Both wore masks and the disguise of the younger man was as well suited to his pliant and vigorous figure as that of the elder to his powerful stately person. Antinous followed his master, dressed as Eros. He wore a crimson mantle and was crowned with roses, while the silver quiver on his shoulder and the bow in his hand clearly symbolized the god he was intended to represent. He too wore a mask, but his figure attracted many gazers, and many a greeting of "Long live the god of love" or "Be

gracious to me oh! son of Aphrodite" was spoken as
he passed.

Pollux had obtained all the things requisite for these
disguises from the store of drapery belonging to his master. Papias had been out, but the young man did not
deem it necessary to ask his consent, for he and the
other assistants had often used the things for similar pur-
poses with his full permission. Only as he took the
quiver intended for Antinous, Pollux hesitated a little
for it was of solid silver and had been given to his master by the wife of a wealthy corn-dealer, whom he had
represented in marble as Artemis equipped for the chase.

"The Roman's handsome companion," thought the
young artist as he placed the costly object in with the
others in a basket, which a squinting apprentice was to
carry behind him.—"The Roman's handsome companion must be made a splendid Eros—and before sunrise
the useless thing will be hanging on its hook again."

Indeed Pollux had not much time to admire the
splendid appearance of the god of love he had so richly
adorned, for the Roman architect was possessed by such
thirst for knowledge and such inexhastible curiosity as to
the minutest details that even Pollux who was born in
Alexandria, and had grown up there with his eyes very
wide open, was often unabie to answer his indefatigable
questioning.

The grey-bearded master wanted to see every thing
and to be informed on every subject. Not content with
making acquaintance with the main streets and squares
the public sites and buildings, he peeped into the handsomest of the private houses and asked the names, rank
and fortunes of the owners. The decided way in which
he told Pollux the way he wished to be conducted

proved to the artist that he was thoroughly familiar with the plan of the city. And when the sagacious and enlightened man expressed his approval, nay his admiration of the broad clean streets of the town, the handsome open places, and particularly handsome buildings which abounded on all sides, the young Alexandrian who was proud of his city was delighted.

First Hadrian made him lead him along the seashore by the Bruchiom to the temple of Poseidon, where he performed some devotions, then he looked into the garden of the palace and the courts of the adjoining museum. The Caesareum with its Egyptian gateway excited his admiration no less than the theatre, surrounded with pillared arcades in stories, and decorated with numerous statues. From thence deviating to the left they once more approached the sea to visit the great Emporium, to see the forest of masts of Eunostus, and the finely-constructed quays. They left the viaduct known as the Heptastadion to their right and the harbor of Kibotus, swarming with small merchant craft, did not detain them long.

Here they turned backs on the sea following a street which led inland through the quarter called Khakotis inhabited only by native Egyptians, and here the Roman found much to see that was noteworthy. First he and his companions met a procession of the priests who serve the gods of the Nile valley, carrying reliquaries and sacred vessels, with images of the gods and sacred animals, and tending towards the Serapeum which towered high above the streets in the vicinity. Hadrian did not visit the temple, but he inspected the chariots which carried people along an inclined road which led up the hill on which was the sanctuary, and watched devotees on foot who mounted by an endless flight of steps constructed on purpose; these grew wider towards the top, terminating in a platform where four mighty pillars bore up a boldly-curved cupola. Nothing looked down upon the temple-building which with its halls, galleries and rooms rose behind this huge canopy.

The priests with their white robes, the meagre, half-naked Egyptians with their pleated aprons and head-cloths, the images of beasts and the wonderfully-painted houses in this quarter of the city, particularly attracted Hadrian's attention and made him ask many questions, not all of which could Pollux answer.

Their walk which now took them farther and farther from the sea extended to the extreme south of the town and the shores of lake Mareotis. Nile boats and vessels of every form and size lay at anchor in this deep and sheltered inland sea; here the sculptor pointed out to Hadrian the canal through which goods were conveyed to the marine fleet which had been brought down the river to Alexandria. And he pointed out to the Roman the handsome country-houses and well-tended vineyards on the shores of the lake.

" The bodies in this city ought to thrive," said Hadrian meditatively. " For here are two stomachs and two mouths by which they absorb nourishment; the sea, I mean, and this lake."

" And the harbors in each," added Pollux.

" Just so; but now it is time we should turn about," replied Hadrian, and the party soon took a road leading eastward; they walked without pause through the quiet streets inhabited by the Christians, and finally through the Jews' quarter. In the heart of this quarter many houses were shut up, and there were no signs to

be seen of the gay doings which crowded on the sense
and fancy in the heathen part of the town, for the
stricter among the Hebrews held sternly aloof, from the
holiday festivities in which most of their nation and
creed who dwelt among the Greeks, took part.

For a third time Hadrian and his companions
crossed the Canopic way which formed the main artery
of the city and divided it into the northern and southern halves, for he wished to look down from the hill of
the Paneum on the combined effect as a whole of all
that he had seen in detail. The carefully-kept gardens
which surrounded this elevation swarmed with men,
and the spiral path which led to the top was crowded
with women and children, who came here to see the
most splendid spectacle of the whole day, which closed
with performances in all the theatres in the town. Before the Emperor and his escort could reach the Paneum
itself the crowd suddenly packed more closely and began exclaiming among themselves, " Here they come!"
" They are early to-day! " " Here they are!"

Lictors with their fasces over their shoulders were
clearing the broad roadway, which led from the prefect's
on the Bruchiom to the Paneum, with their staves and
paying no heed to the mocking and witty speeches
addressed to them by the mob wherever they appeared.
One woman, as she was driven back by a Roman
guardian of the peace, cried scornfully, " Give me your
rods for my children and do not use them on unoffend-
ing citizens."

" There is an axe hidden among the faggots," added
an Egyptian letter-writer in a warning voice.

" Bring it here," cried a butcher. " I can use it to
slaughter my beasts."

The Romans as they heard these bandied words
felt the blood mounting to their faces, but the prefect,
who knew his Alexandrians well, had counselled them
to be deaf; to see everything but to hear nothing.
Now there appeared a cohort of the Twelfth Legion,
who were quartered in garrison in Egypt, in their richest arms and holiday uniforms. Behind them came two
files of particularly tall lictors wearing wreaths, and
they were followed by several hundred wild beasts,
leopards and panthers, giraffes, gazelles, antelopes, and
deer, all led by dark-colored Egyptians. Then came a
richly-dressed and much be-wreathed Dionysian chorus
with the sound of tambourines and lyres, double flutes
and triangles, and finally, drawn by ten elephants and
twenty white horses, a large ship, resting on wheels and
gilt from stem to stern, representing the vessel in which
the Tyrrhenian pirates were said to have carried off the
young Dionysus when they had seen the black-haired
hero on the shore in his purple garments. But the mis-
creants—so the myth went on to say—were not allowed
long to rejoice in their violence, for hardly had the ship
reached the open sea when the fetters dropped from
the god, vines entwined the sails in sudden luxuriance,
tendrils encumbered the oars and rudder, heavy grapes
clustered round the ropes, and ivy clung to the mast
and shrouded the seats and sides of the vessel. Dionysus is equally powerful on sea and on land; in the
pirates' ship he assumed the form of a lion, and the
pirates, filled with terror, flung themselves into the sea,
and in the form of dolphins followed their lost bark.

All this Titianus had caused to be represented just as
the Homeric hymns described it, out of slight materials,
but richly and elegantly decorated, in order to provide a

feast for the eyes of the Alexandrians, with the intention
of riding in it himself, with his wife and the most illustrious of the Romans who formed the Empress' suite, to
enjoy all the holiday doings in the chief streets of the
city. Young and old, great and small, men and women,
Greeks, Romans, Jews, Egyptians, foreigners dark and
fair, with smooth hair or crisp wool, crowded with equal
eagerness to the edge of the roadway to see the gorgeous boat.

Hadrian, far more anxious to see the show than his
younger but less excitable favorite, pushed into the
front rank, and as Antinous was trying to follow him, a
Greek boy, whom he had shoved aside, snatched his
mask from his face, threw himself on the ground, and
slipped nimbly off with his booty. When Hadrian
looked round for the Bithynian, the ship—in which the
prefect was standing between the images of the Emperor and Empress, while Julia, Balbilla, and her companion, and other Roman lords and ladies were sitting
in it—had come quite near to them. His sharp eye
had recognized them all, and fearing that the lad's un-
covered face would betray them he cried out:

"Turn round and get into the crowd again." The
favorite immediately obeyed, and only too glad to
escape from the crowd, which was a thing he detested,
he sat down on a bench close to the Paneum, and
looked dreamily at the ground while he thought of
Selene and the nosegay he had sent her, neither seeing
nor hearing anything of what was going on around him.

When the gaudy ship left the gardens of the Paneum
and turned into the Canopic way, the crowd pursued it
in a dense mass, hallooing and shouting. Like a torrent
suddenly swelled by a storm it rushed on, surging and

growing at each moment, and carrying with it even
those who tried to resist its force. Thus even Hadrian
and Pollux were forced to follow in its wake, and it was
not till they found themselves in the broad Canopic way
that they were able to come to a stand-still. The broad
roadway of this famous street was bordered on each
side by a long vista of colonnade, and it extended
from one end of the city to the other. There were
hundreds of the Corinthian columns which supported
the roof that covered the footway, and near to one of
these the Emperor and Pollux succeeded at last in
effecting a halt and taking breath.

Hadrian's first thought was for his favorite, and
being averse to venturing himself once more to mix
with the crowd, he begged the sculptor to go and seek
him and conduct him safely.

" Will you wait for me here ?" asked Pollux.

" I have known a pleasanter halting place," sighed
the Emperor.

" So have I," answered the artist. " But that tall
door there, wreathed round with boughs of poplar and
ivy, leads into a cook-shop where the gods themselves
might be content to find themselves."

" Then I will wait there."

" But I warn you to eat as much as you can, for the
' Olympian table ' as kept by Lykortas, the Corinthian,
is the dearest eating-house in the whole city. None
but the richest are his guests."

" Very good," laughed Hadrian. " Only find my
assistant a new mask and bring him back to me. It
will not ruin me quite, even if I pay for a supper for all
three of us, and on a holiday one expects to spend
something."

"I hope you may not live to repent," retorted Pollux. "But a long fellow like me is a good trencherman, and can do his part with the wine-jar."

"Only show me what you can do," cried Hadrian after him as Pollux hurried off. "I owe you a supper at any rate, for that cabbage stew of your mother's."

While Pollux went to seek the Bithynian in the vicinity of the Paneum, the Emperor entered the eating-house, which the skill of the cook had made the most frequented and fashionable in Alexandria. The place in which most of the customers of the house dined, consisted of a large open hall, surrounded by arcades which were roofed in on three of its sides and closed by a wall on its fourth; in these arcades stood couches, on which the guests reclined singly, or in couples, or in larger groups, and ordered the dishes and liquors which the serving slaves, pretty boys with curling hair and handsome dresses, placed before them on low tables. Here all was noise and bustle; at one table an epicure devoted himself silently to the enjoyment of some carefully-prepared delicacy, at another a large circle of men seemed to be talking more eagerly than they either eat or drank, and from several of the smaller rooms behind the wall at the back of the hall came sounds of music and song, and the bold laughter of men and women.

The Emperor asked for a private room, but they were all occupied, and he was requested to wait a little while, for that one of the adjoining rooms would very soon be vacant. He had taken off his mask, and though he was not particularly afraid of being recognized in his disguise he chose a couch that was screened by a broad pillar in one of the arcades at the inner side of the court, and which, now that evening was beginning to fall was already in obscurity. There he ordered, first some wine and then some oysters to begin with; while he was eating these he called one of the superintendents and discussed with him the details of the supper he wished presently to be served to himself and his two guests. During this conversation the bustling host came to make his bow to his new customer, and seeing that he had to do with a man fully conversant with all the pleasures of the table, he remained ·to attend on him, and entered with special zeal into Hadrian's various requirements.

There was, too, plenty to be seen in the court, which roused the curiosity of the most inquisitive and enquiring man of his time. In the large space enclosed by the arcades, and under the eyes of the guests, on gridirons and hearths, on spits and in ovens the various dishes were prepared which were served up by the slaves. The cooks prepared their savory messes on large, clean tables, and the scene of their labors, which, though enclosed by cords was open to public gaze was surrounded by a small market, where however only the choicest of wares were displayed.

Here in tempting array was every variety of vegetable reared on Greek or Egyptian soil; here speckless fruits of every size and hue were set out, and there ready-baked, shining, golden-brown pasties were displayed. Those containing meat, fish or the mussels of Canopus were prepared in Alexandria itself, but others containing fruit or the leaves of flowers were brought from Arsinoe on the shores of Lake Moeris, for in that neighborhood the cultivation of fruit and horticulture generally were pursued with the greatest success. Meat of all sorts lay or hung in suitable places; there were juicy hams from Cyrene, Italian sausages and uncooked joints of various slaughtered beasts. By them lay or hung game and poultry in select abundance, and a large part of the court was taken up by a tank in which the choicest of the scaly tribes of the Nile, and of the lakes of Northern Egypt, were swimming about as well as the Muraena and other fish of Italian breed. Alexandrian crabs and the mussels, oysters, and cray-fish of Canopus and Klysma were kept alive in buckets or jars. The smoked meats of Mendes and the neighborhood of Lake Moeris hung on metal pegs, and in a covered but well-aired room, sheltered from the sun lay freshly-imported fish from the Mediterranean and Red Sea. Every guest at the 'Olympian table' was allowed here to select the meat, fruit, asparagus, fish, or pasty which he desired to have cooked for him. The host, Lykortas, pointed out to Hadrian an old gentleman who was busy in the court that was so prettily decorated with still-life, engaged in choosing the raw materials of a banquet he wished to give some friends in the evening of this very day.

"It is all very nice and extremely good," said Hadrian, "but the gnats and flies which are attracted by all those good things are unendurable, and the strong smell of food spoils my appetite."

"It is better in the side-rooms," said the host. "In the one kept for you the company is now preparing to depart. In behind here the sophists Demetrius and Pancrates are entertaining a few great men from Rome, rhetoricians or philosophers or something of the kind. Now they are bringing in the fine lamps and they have been sitting and talking at that table ever since breakfast. There come the guests out of the side room. Will you take it?"

"Yes," said Hadrian. "And when a tall young man ,
comes to ask for the architect Claudius Venato., from
Rome, bring him in to me."

"An architect then, and not a sophist or a rhetorician," said mine host, looking keenly at the Emperor.

"Silenus,—a philosopher!"

"Oh the two vociferous friends there go about even
on other days naked and with ragged cloaks thrown over
their lean shoulders.   To-day they are feeding at the ex-
pense of rich Josephus."

"Josephus! he must be a Jew and yet he is making
a large hole in the ham."

"There would be more swine in Cyrene if there were
no Jews; they are Greeks like ourselves, and eat everything that is good."

Hadrian went into the vacant room, lay down on a
couch that stood by the wall, and urged the slaves who
were busied in removing the dishes and vessels used by
his predecessors, and which were swarming with flies.
As soon as he was alone he listened to the conversation
which was being carried on between Favorinus, Florus,
and their Greek guests.   He knew the two first very
well, and not a word of what they were saying escaped
his keen ear.

Favorinus was praising the Alexandrians in a loud
voice, but in flowing and elegantly-accented Greek.
He was a native of Arelas* in Gaul, but no Hellene of
them all could pour forth a purer flow of the language
of Demosthenes than he.   The self-reliant, keen, and
vivacious natives of the African metropolis were far more
to his taste than the Athenians; these dwelt only in, and
for, the past ; the Alexandrians rejoiced in the present.

* Arles.

Here an independent spirit still survived, while on the shores of the Ilissus there were none but servile souls who made a merchandise of learning, as the Alexandrians did of the products of Africa˙ and the treasures of India. Once when he had fallen into disgrace with Hadrian, the Athenians had thrown down his statue, and the favor or disfavor of the powerful weighed with him more than intellectual greatness, valuable labors, and true merit.

Florus agreed with Favorinus on the whole, and declared that Rome must be freed from the intellectual influence of Athens; but Favorinus did not admit this; he opined that it was very difficult for any one who had left youth behind him, to learn anything new, thus referring, with light irony, to the famous work in which Florus had attempted to divide the history of Rome into four periods, corresponding to the ages of man, but had left out old age, and had treated only of childhood, youth, and manhood. Favorinus reproached him with overestimating the versatility of the Roman genius, like his friend Fronto, and underrating the Hellenic intellect.

Florus answered the Gaulish orator in a deep voice, and with such a grand flow of words, that the listening Emperor would have enjoyed expressing his approbation, and could not help considering the question as to how many cups of wine his usually placid fellow-countryman might have taken since breakfast to be so excited. When Florus tried to prove that under Hadrian's rule Rome had risen to the highest stage of its manhood, his friend, Demetrius, of Alexandria, interrupted him, and begged him to tell him something about the Emperor's person. Florus willingly acceded to this request, and sketched a brilliant picture of the administrative talent, the learning, and the capability of the Emperor.

" There is only one thing," he cried eagerly, "that I cannot approve of; he is too little at Rome, which is now the core and centre of the world. He must need see every thing for himself, and he is always wandering restlessly through the provinces. I should not care to change with him!"

" You have expressed the same ideas in verse," said Favorinus.

" Oh! a jest at supper-time. So long as I am in Alexandria and waiting on Caesar I can make myself very comfortable every day at the ' Olympian table ' of this admirable cook."

" But how runs your poem ?" asked Pancrates.

" I have forgotten it, and it deserved no better fate," replied Florus.

" But I," laughed the Gaul, " remember the beginning. The first lines, I think, ran thus :

> " ' Let others envy Caesar's lot ;
> To wander through Britannia's dales
> And be snowed up in Scythian vales
> Is Caesar's taste—I'd rather not?' "

As he heard these words Hadrian struck his fist into the palm of his left hand, and while the feasters were hazarding guesses as to why he was so long in coming to Alexandria, he took out the folding tablet he was in the habit of carrying in his money-bag, and hastily wrote the following lines on the wax face of it :

> ' Let others envy Florus' lot ;
> To wander through the shops for drink,
> Or, into foolish dreaming sink
> In a cook-shop, where sticky flies
> Buzz round him till he shuts his eyes—
> Is Florus' taste—I'd rather not ?*'

* From verses by Hadrian and Florus, preserved in Spartianus.

Hardly had he ended the lines, muttering them to himself with much relish as he wrote, when the waiter showed in Pollux. The sculptor had failed to find Antinous, and suggested that the young man had probably gone home; he also begged that he might not be detained long at supper, for he had met his master Papias, who had been extremely annoyed by his long absence. Hadrian was no longer satisfied with the artist's society, for the conversation in the next room was to him far more attractive than that of the worthy young fellow. He himself was anxious to quit the meal soon, for he felt restless and uneasy. Antinous could no doubt easily find his way to Lochias, but recollections of the evil omens he had observed in the heavens last night flitted across his soul like bats through a festal hall, marring the pleasure on which he again tried to concentrate it, in order to enjoy his hours of liberty.

. Even Pollux was not so light-hearted as before. His long walk had made him hungry, and he addressed himself so vigorously to the excellent dishes which rapidly followed each other by his entertainer's orders, and emptied the cup with such unfailing diligence, that the Emperor was astonished: but the more he had to think about, the less did he talk.

Pollux, to be sure, had had his answer ready for his master, and without considering how easy it would have been to part from him in kindness, he had shortly and roundly quitted his service. Now indeed he stood on his own feet, and he was longing to tell Arsinoe and his parents of what he had done.

During the course of the meal his mother's advice recurred to his mind: to do his best to win the favor and good will of the architect whose guest he was; but

24

he set it aside, for he was accustomed to owe all he
gained to his own exertions, and though he still keenly
felt in Hadrian the superiority of a powerful mind, their
expedition through the city had not brought him any
nearer to the Roman. Some insurmountable barrier
stood fixed between himself and this restless, inquisitive
man, who required so many answers that no one else
had time to ask a question, and who when he was silent
looked · so absorbed and unapproachable that no one
would have ventured to disturb him. The bold young
artist had, however, tried now and again to break
through the fence, but each time, he had at once been
seized with a feeling, of which he could not rid himself,
that he had done something awkward and unbecoming.
He felt in his intercourse with the architect as a noble dog
might feel that sported with a lion, and such sport could
come to no good. Thus, for various reasons, host and
guest were well content when the last dish was removed.

Before Pollux left the room the Emperor gave him
the tablets with the verses and begged him, with a meaning smile, to desire the gate-keeper at the Caesareum to
give them to Annaeus Florus the Roman. He once
more urgently charged the sculptor to look about for his
young friend and, if he should find him at Lochias, to
tell him that he, Claudius Venator, would return home
ere long. Then the artist went his way.

Hadrian still sat a long time listening to the talk
close by; but after waiting for above an hour to hear
some fresh mention made of himself, he paid his reckoning and went out into the Canopic way, now brilliantly
lighted. There he mingled with the revellers, and
walked slowly onward, seeking suspiciously and anxiously for his vanished favorite.

CHAPTER III.

ANTINOUS, searching for his master, had wandered about in the crowd. Whenever he saw any figures of exceptional stature he followed them, but each time only to discover that he had entered on a false track. Long and persistent effort was not in his nature, so as soon as he began to get tired, he gave up the search and sat down again on a stone bench in the garden of the Paneum.

Two cynic philosophers, with unkempt hair, tangled beards, and ragged cloaks flung over their shivering bodies, sat down by him and fell into loud and contemptuous abuse of the deference shown, ' in these days,' to external things and vulgar joys, and of the wretched sensualists who regarded pleasure and splendor, rather than virtue, as the aim and end of existence. In order to be heard by the by-standers they spoke in loud tones, and the elder of the two, flourished his knotted stick as viciously, as though he had to defend himself against an attack. Antinous felt much disgusted by the hideous appearance, the coarse manners, and shrill voices of these persons, and when he rose—as the cynics' diatribe seemed especially directed against him— they scoffed at him as he went, mocking at his costume and his oiled and perfumed hair. The Bithynian made no reply to this abuse. It was odious to him, but he thought it might perhaps have amused Caesar.

He wandered on without thinking; the street in which he presently found himself must no doubt lead

to the sea, and if he could once find himself on the
shore he could not fail to make his way to Lochias.
By the time it was growing dark he was once more
standing outside the little gate-house, and there he
learnt from Doris that the Roman and her son had not
yet returned.

What was he to do alone in the vast empty palace ?
Were not the very slaves free to-day ? Why should not
he too for once enjoy life independently and in his own
way ? Full of the pleasant sense of being his own
master and at liberty to walk in a road of his own
choosing, he went onwards, and when he presently
passed by the stall of a flower-seller, he began once
more to think eagerly of Selene and the nosegay, which
must long since have reached her hands.

He had heard from Pollux in the morning that the
steward's daughter was being tended by Christians in a
little house not far from the sea-shore ; indeed the sculptor himself had been quite excited as he told Antinous
that he himself had peeped into the lighted room and
had seen her. ' A glorious creature' he had called her,
and had said that she had never looked more beautiful
than in a recumbent attitude on her bed.

Antinous recalled all this and determined to venture
on an attempt to see again the maiden whose image
filled his heart and brain.

It was now dark and the same light which had allowed of the sculptor's seeing Selene's features might
this evening reveal them to him also. Full of passionate excitement, he got into the first litter he met with.
The swarthy bearers were far too slow for his longing,
and more than once he flung to them as much money
as they were wont to earn in a week, to urge them to a

brisker pace. At last he reached his destination; but seeing that several men and women robed in white, were going into the garden, he desired the bearers to carry him farther. Close to a dark narrow lane which bounded the widow's garden-plot on the east and led directly to the sea, he desired them to stop, got out of the litter and bid the slaves wait for him. At the garden door he still found two men dressed in white, and one of the cynic philosophers who had sat by him on the bench near the Paneum. He paced impatiently up and down, waiting till these people should have disappeared, and thus passing again and again under the light of the torches that were stuck up by the gate.

The dry cynic's prominent eyes were everywhere at once, and as soon as he perceived the peripatetic Bithynian he flung up his arm, exclaiming, as he pointed to him with a long, lean, stiff forefinger—half to the Christians with whom he had been talking and half to the lad himself:

" What does he want. That fop! that over-dressed minion! I know the fellow ; with his smooth face and the silver quiver on his shoulder he believes he is Eros in person. Be off with you, you house-rat. The women and girls in here know how to protect themselves against the sort who parade the streets in rose-colored draperies. Take yourself off, or you will make acquaintance with the noble Paulina's slaves and dogs. Hi! gate-keeper, here ! keep an eye on this fellow."

Antinous made no answer, but slowly went back to his litter.

" To-morrow perhaps, if I cannot manage it to-night," he thought to himself as he went ; and he never thought of any other means of attaining his end, much as he longed for it. A hindrance that came in his way ceased to be a hindrance as soon as he had left it behind him, and after this reflection he acted on this occasion as on many former ones. The litter was no longer standing where he had left it; the bearers had carried it into the lane leading to the sea, for the only little abode which stood on the eastern side of it belonged to a fisherman whose wife sold thin potations of Pelusium beer.

Antinous went down the green alley overarched with boughs of fig, to call the negroes who were sitting in the dull light of a smoky oil-lamp. Here it was dark, but at the end of the alley the sea shone and sparkled in the moonlight; the splashing of the waves tempted him onwards and he loitered down to the stone-bound shore. There he spied a boat dancing on the water between two piles and it came into his head that it might be possible to see the house where Selene was sleeping, from the sea.

He undid the rope which secured the boat without any difficulty; he seated himself in it, laid aside the quiver and bow, pushed off with one of the oars that lay at the bottom of the boat and pulled with steady strokes towards the long path of light where the moon touched the crest of each dancing wavelet with unresting tremulous flecks of silver.

There lay the widow's garden. In that small white house must the fair pale Selene be sleeping, but though he rowed hither and thither, backwards and forwards, he could not succeed in discovering the window of which Pollux had spoken. Might it not be possible to find a spot where he could disembark and then make his way into the garden? He could see two little boats, but they lay in a narrow walled canal and this was closed by an iron railing. Beyond, was a terrace projecting into the sea, and surrounded by an elegant balustrade of little columns, but it rose straight out of the sea on smooth high walls. But there—what was that gleaming under the two palm-trees which, springing from the same root, had grown together tall and slender —was not that a flight of marble steps leading down to the sea?

Antinous dipped his right oar in the waves with a practised hand to alter the head of the boat and was in the act of pulling his hand up to make his stroke against the pressure of the waves—but he did not complete the movement, nay he counteracted the stroke by a dexterous reverse action; a strange vision arrested his attention. On the terrace, which lay full in the bright moonlight, there appeared a white-robed figure with long floating hair.

How strangely it moved! It went now to one side and now to the other, then again it stood still and clasped its head in its hands. Antinous shuddered, he could not help thinking of the Daimons of which Hadrian so often spoke. They were said to be of half-divine and half-human nature, and sometimes appeared in the guise of mortals.

Or was Selene dead and was the white figure her wandering shade? Antinous clutched the handles of the oars, now merely floating on the water, and bending forward gazed fixedly and with bated breath at the mysterious being which had now reached the balustrade of the terrace, now—he saw quite plainly—covered its face with both hands, leaned far over the parapet, and now—

As a star falls through the sky on a clear night, as a
fruit drops from the tree in autumn, the white form of
the girl dropped from the terrace. A loud cry of anguish
broke the silence of the night which veiled the world,
and almost at the same instant the water splashed and
gurgled up, and the moonbeams, cold and bright as
ever, were mirrored in the thousand drops that flew up
from its surface.

Was this Antinous, the indolent dreamer, who so
promptly plunged his oars in the water, pulled a powerful stroke, and then, when in a few seconds after her
fall, the form of the drowning girl came to the surface
again quite close to the boat, flung aside the oar that
was in his way ? Leaning far over the edge of the boat
he seized the floating garment of the drowning creature
—it was a woman, no Daimon nor shade—and drew her
towards him. He succeeded in raising her high out of
the waves, but when he tried to pull her fairly out of her
watery bed, the weight, all on one side of the boat, was
too great; it turned over and Antinous was in the sea.

The Bithynian was a good swimmer. Before the
white form could sink a second time he had caught at
it once more with his right hand and taking care that
her head should not again touch the surface of the water,
he swam with his left arm and legs towards the spot
where he remembered he had seen the flight of steps.
As soon as his feet felt the ground he lifted the girl in
both arms and a groan of relief broke from his lips as
he saw the marble steps close below him. He went up
them without hesitation, and then, with a swift elastic
step, carried his dripping and senseless burden to the
terrace where he had observed that there were benches.
The wide floor of the sea-terrace, paved with smooth

flags of marble, was brightly lighted by the broad moon-
shine, and the whiteness of the stone reflected and
seemed to increase the light. There stood the benches
which Antinous had seen from afar.

He laid his burden on the first he came to, and a
thrill of thankful joy warmed his shivering body when
the rescued woman uttered a low cry of pain which told
him that he had not toiled in vain. He gently slipped
his arm between the hard elbow of the marble seat and
her head, to give it a somewhat softer resting-place.
Her abundant hair fell in clammy tresses, covering her
face like a thick but fine veil; he parted it to the right
and left and then—then he sank on his knees by her
side as if a sudden bolt had fallen from the blue sky
above them; for the features were hers, Selene's, and the
pale girl before whom he was kneeling was she herself,
the woman he loved.

Almost beside himself and trembling in every limb,
he drew her closer to him and put his ear against her
mouth to listen whether he had not deceived himself,
whether she had not indeed fallen a victim to the waves
or whether some warm breath were passing the portals
of her lips.

Yes she breathed! she was alive! Full of thankful
ecstasy he pressed his cheek to hers. Oh! how cold
she was, icy, cold as death!

The torch of life was flickering, but he would not—
could not—must not let it die out: and with all the care,
rapidity and decision of the most capable man, he once
more raised her, lifted her in both arms as if she were a
child, and carried her straight to the house whose white
walls he could see gleaming among the shrubs behind
the terrace. The little lamp was still burning in dame

Hannah's room, which Selene had so lately quitted; in front of the window through which the dim light came to mingle with the moonbeams, lay the flowers whose perfume had so troubled the suffering girl, and with them Hannah's clay jar, all still strewn on the ground.

Was this nosegay his gift? Very likely.

But the lamp-lighted room into which he now looked could be none other than the sick-room, which he recognized from the sculptor's account. The house-door was open and even that of the room in which he had seen the bed was unfastened; he pushed it open with his foot, entered the room, and laid Selene on the vacant couch.

There she lay as if dead; and as he looked at her immovable features, hallowed to solemnity by sorrow and suffering, his heart was touched with an ineffable solicitude, sympathy and pity; and, as a brother might bend over a sleeping sister, he bent over Selene and kissed her forehead. She moved, opened her eyes, gazed into his face—but her glance was so full of horror, so vague, glassy and bewildered, that he drew back with a shudder, and with hands uplifted could only stammer out: "Oh! Selene, Selene! do you not know me?" and as he spoke he looked anxiously in the face of the rescued girl; but she seemed not to hear him and nothing moved but her eyes which slowly followed his every movement.

"Selene!" he cried again, and seizing her inanimate hand which hung down, he pressed it passionately to his lips.

Then she gave a loud cry, a violent shiver shook her in every limb, she turned aside with sighs and groans, and at the same instant the door was opened, the little

deformed girl entered the room and gave a shrill scream
of terror as she saw Antinous standing by the side of
her friend.

The lad himself started and, like a thief who has
been caught in the act, he fled out into the night, through
the garden, and as far as the gate which led into the
street without being stopped by any one. Here the
gate-keeper met him, but he threw him aside with a
powerful fling, and while the old man—who had grown
gray in his office—caught hold of his wet chiton he tore
the door open and ran on, dragging his pursuer with him
for some paces. Then he flew down the street with
long steps as if he were racing in the Gymnasium, and
soon he felt that his pursuer, in whose hand he had left
a piece of his garment, had given up the chase.

The gate-keeper's outcry had mingled with the pious
hymns of the assembled Christians in Paulina's villa, and
some of them had hurried out to help capture the disturber of the peace. But the young Bithynian was
swifter than they and might consider himself perfectly
safe when once he had succeeded in mixing with a festal
procession. Half-willingly and half-perforce, he followed
the drunken throng which was making its way from the
heart of the city towards the lake, where, on a lonely
spot on the shore to the east of Nikropolis, they were to
celebrate certain nocturnal mysteries. The goal of the
singing, shouting, howling mob with whom Antinous
was carried along, was between Alexandria and Canopus
and far enough from Lochias; thus it fell out that it was
long past midnight when Hadrian's favorite, dirty, out
of breath, and his clothes torn, at last appeared in the
presence of his master.

CHAPTER IV.

HADRIAN had expected Antinous many hours since, and the impatience and vexation which had been long seething in him were reflected plainly enough in his sternly-bent brow and the threatening fire of his eye.

"Where have you been?" he imperiously asked.

"I could not find you, so I took a boat and went out on the lake."

"That is false."

Antinous did not answer, but merely shrugged his shoulders.

"Alone?" asked the Emperor more gently.

"Alone."

"And for what purpose?"

"I was gazing at the stars."

"You!"

"And may I not, for once, tread in your footsteps?"

"Why not indeed? The lights of heaven shine for the foolish as well as for the wise. Even asses must be born under a good or an evil star. One donkey serves a hungry grammarian and feeds on used-up papyrus, while another enters the service of Caesar and is fattened up, and finds time to go star-gazing at night. What a state you are in."

"The boat upset and I fell into the water."

Hadrian was startled, and observing his favorite's tangled hair in which the night wind had dried the salt water, and his torn chiton, he anxiously exclaimed:

"Go this instant and let Mastor dry you and anoint

you. He too came back with a bruised hand and red
eyes. Everything is upside down this accursed evening.
—You look like a slave that has been hunted by
dogs. Drink a few cups of wine and then lie down."

" I obey your orders, great Caesar."

"So formal? The donkey simile vexed you."

"You used always to have a kind word for me."

"Yes, yes, and I shall have them again, I shall have
them again. Only not to-night—go to bed."

Antinous left him, but the Emperor paced his room,
up and down with long steps, his arms crossed over his
breast and his eyes fixed on the ground. His super-
stitious soul had been deeply disturbed by a series of
evil signs which he had not only seen the previous night
in the sky, but had also met on his way to Lochias, and
which seemed to be beginning to be fulfilled already.

He had left the eating house in an evil humor, the
bad omens made him anxious, and though on his arrival at home he had done one or two things which he already regretted, this had certainly not been due to any
adverse Daimons but to the brooding gloom of his
clouded mind. Eternal circumstances, it is true, had led
to his being witness to an attack made by the mob on
the house of a wealthy Israelite, and it was attributable
to a vexatious accident that at this juncture, he should
have met Verus, who had observed and recognized him.
Yes, the Spirits of evil were abroad this day, but his
subsequent experiences and deeds upon reaching Lochias, would certainly not have taken place on any
more fortunate day, or, to be more exact, if he had been
in a calmer frame of mind; he himself alone was in
fault, he alone, and no spiteful accident, nor malicious
and tricky Daimon. Hadrian, to be sure, attributed to

these sprites all that he had done, and so considered it irremediable; an excellent way, no doubt, of exonerating oneself from a burdensome duty, or from repairing some injustice, but conscience is a register in which a mysterious hand inexorably enters every one of our deeds, and in which all that we do is ruthlessly called by its true name.   We often succeed, it is true, in effacing the record for a longer or a shorter period, but often, again, the letters on the page shine with an uncanny light, and force the inward eye to see them and to heed them.

On this particular night Hadrian felt himself compelled to read the catalogue of his actions and among them he found many a sanguinary crime, many a petty action unworthy of a far meaner soul than he; still the record commemorated many duties strictly fulfilled, much honest work, an unceasing struggle towards high aims, and an unwearied effort to feel his way intellectually, to the most remote and exalted limits possible to the human mind and comprehension.

In this hour Hadrian thought of none but his evil deeds, and vowed to the gods—whom he mocked at with his philosophical friends, and to whom he nevertheless addressed himself whenever he felt the insufficiency of his own strength and means—to build a temple here, to offer a sacrifice there, in order to expiate old crimes and divert their malice. He felt like a great man must who is threatened with the disfavor of his superiors, and who hopes to propitiate them with gifts.   The haughty Roman quailed at the thought of unknown dangers, but he was far from feeling the wholesome pangs of repentance.

Hardly an hour since he had forgotten himself and

had disgracefully abused his power over a weaker creature, and now he was vexed at having behaved so and not otherwise; but it never entered his head to humiliate his pride or, by offering some compensation to the offended party, tacitly to confess the injustice he had committed. Often he deeply felt his human weakness, but he was quite capable of believing in the sacredness of his imperial person, and this he always found most easy when he had trodden under foot some one who had been rash enough to insult him, or not to acknowledge his superiority. And was it not on the contemners of the gods that their heaviest punishments fell?

To-day the terrestrial Jupiter had again crushed into the earth with his thunderbolts, an overbold mortal, and this time the son of the worthy gate-keeper was his victim. The sculptor certainly had been so unlucky as to touch Hadrian in his most sensitive spot, but a cordially benevolent feeling is not easily converted into a relentless opposition if we are not ourselves—as was the case with the Emperor—accustomed to jump from one mood to the other, are not conscious—as he was—of having it in our power directly to express our good-will or our aversion in action.

The sculptor's capacities had commanded the Emperor's esteem, his fresh and independent nature had at first suited and attracted him, but even during the walk together through the streets, the young man's uncompromising manner of treating him as an equal had become unpleasing to him. In his workshop he saw in Pollux only the artist, and delighted in his original and dashing powers; but out of it, and among men of a commoner stamp, from whom he was accustomed to meet with deference, the young man's speech and demeanor seemed unbecoming, bold, and hard to be endured. In the eating-house the huge eater and drinker, who laughingly pressed him to do his part, so as not to make a present to the landlord, had filled Hadrian with repulsion. And after this, when Hadrian had returned to Lochias, out of humor and rendered apprehensive by evil omens, and even then had not found his favorite, he impatiently paced up and down the hall of the Muses and would not deign to offer a greeting to the sculptor, who was noisily occupied behind his screens.

Pollux had passed quite as bad an evening as the Emperor. When, in his desire to see Arsinoe once more, he penetrated to the door of the steward's apartment, Keraunus had stopped his way, and sent him about his business with insulting words. In the hall of the Muses he had met his master, and had had a quarrel with him, for Papias, to whom he repeated his notice to quit, had grown angry, and had desired him then and there to sort out his own tools, and to return those that belonged to him, his master, and for the future to keep himself as far as possible from Papias' house, and from the works in progress at Lochias. On this, hard words had passed on both sides, and when Papias had left the palace and Pollux went to seek Pontius the architect, in order to discuss his future plans with him, he learnt that he too had quitted Lochias a short time before, and would not return till the following morning.

After brief reflection he determined to obey the orders of Papias and to pack his own tools together. Without paying any heed to Hadrian's presence he began to toss some of the hammers, chisels, and wooden modelling tools into one box, and others into another, doing it as recklessly as though he were minded to punish the unconscious tools as adverse creatures who had turned against him.

At last his eye fell on Hadrian's bust of Balbilla. The hideous caricature at which he had laughed only yesterday, made him angry now, and after gazing at it thoughtfully for a few minutes his blood boiled up furiously, he hastily pulled a lath out of the partition and struck at the monstrosity with such fury that the dry clay flew in pieces, and the fragments were strewed far and wide about the workshop. The wild noise behind the sculptor's screen made the Emperor pause in his walk to see what the artist was doing; he looked on at the work of destruction, unobserved by Pollux, and as he looked the blood mounted to his head; he knit his brows in anger, a blue vein in his forehead swelled and stood out, and ominous lines appeared above his brow. The great master of state-craft could more easily have borne to hear himself condemned as a ruler than to see his work of art despised. A man who is sure of having done some thing great can smile at blame, but he, who is not confident in himself has reason to dread it, and is easily drawn into hating the critic who utters it. Hadrian was trembling with fury, he doubled his first as he lifted it in Pollux's face, and going close up to him asked in a threatening tone :

"What do you mean by that ?"

The sculptor glanced round at the Emperor and answered, raising his stick for another blow :

" I am demolishing this caricature for it enrages me."

" Come here," shouted Hadrian, and clutching the girdle which confined the artist's chiton, in his strong sinewy hand, he dragged the startled sculptor in front of

25

his Urania wrenched the lath out of his hand, struck the bust of the scarcely-finished statue off the body, exclaiming as he did so, in a voice that mimicked Pollux :

"I am demolishing this bungler's work for it enrages me !"

The artist's arms fell by his side; astonished and infuriated he stared at the destroyer of his handiwork, and cried out :

"Madman! this is enough. One blow more and you will feel the weight of my fists."

Hadrian laughed aloud, a cold hard laugh, flung the lath at Pollux's feet and said :

"Judgment against judgment—it is only fair."

"Fair ?" shrieked Pollux, beside himself. "Your wretched rubbish, which my squinting apprentice could have done as well as you, and this figure born in a moment of inspiration! Shame upon you ! Once more, if you touch the Urania again I warn you, you shall learn——"

"Well, what ?"

"That in Alexandria grey hairs are only respected so long as they deserve it."

Hadrian folded his arms, stepped quite close up to Pollux, and said :

"Gently, fellow, if you value your life."

Pollux stepped back before the imposing personage that stood before him, and, as it were scales, fell from his eyes. The marble statue of the Emperor in the Caesareum represented the sovereign in this same attitude. The architect, Claudius Venator, was none other than Hadrian.

The young artist turned pale and said with bowed head, and in low voice as he turned to go :

" Right is always on the side of the strongest. Let me go. I am nothing but a poor artist—you are something very different. I know you now; you are Caesar."

" I am Caesar," snarled ·Hadrian, " and if you think more of yourself as an artist than of me, I will show you which of us two is the sparrow, and which the eagle."

" You have the power to destroy, and I only desire—"

" The only person here who has a right to desire is myself," cried the Emperor, " and I desire that you shall never enter this palace again, nor ever come within sight of me so long as I remain here. What to do with your kith and kin I will consider. Not another word ! Away with you, I say, and thank the gods that I judge the misdeed of a miserable boy more mercifully than you dared to do in judging the work of a greater man than yourself, though you knew that he had done it in an idle hour with a few hasty touches. Be off, fellow ; my slaves will finish destroying your image there, for it deserves no better fate, and because—what was it you said just now ? I remember—and because it enrages me."

A bitter laugh rang after the lad as he quitted the hall. At the entrance, which was perfectly dark, he found his master, Papias, who had not missed a word of what had passed between him and the Emperor. As Pollux went into his mother's house he cried out :

" Oh mother, mother, what a morning, and what an evening. Happiness is only the threshold to misery."

CHAPTER V.

WHILE Pollux and his mother, who was much grieved,
waited for Euphorion's return, and while Papias was
ingratiating himself with the Emperor by pretending
still to believe that Hadrian was nothing more than
Claudius Venator, the architect, Aurelius Verus, nick·
named by the Alexandrians, " the sham Eros " had lived
through strange experiences.

In the afternoon he had visited the Empress, in the
hope of persuading her to look on at the gay doings of
the people, even if incognito; but Sabina was out of
spirits, declared herself unwell, and was quite sure that
the noise of the rabble would be the death of her.
Having, as she said, so vivacious a reporter as Verus,
she might spare herself from exposing her own person
to the dust and smell of the town, and the uproar of
men.   As soon as Lucilla begged her husband to
remember his rank and not to mingle with the excited
multitude, at any rate after dark, the Empress strictly
enjoined him to see with his own eyes everything that
could be worth notice in the festival, and more particularly to give attention to everything that was peculiar to
Alexandria and not to be seen in Rome.

After sunset Verus had first gone to visit the veterans of the Twelfth Legion who had been in the field
with him against the Numidians, and to whom he gave
a dinner at an eating-house, as being his old fellow·
soldiers.   For above an hour he sat drinking with the
brave old fellows; then, quitting them, he went to look

at the Canopic way by night, as it was but a few paces
thither from the scene of his hospitality. It was brilliantly lighted with tapers, torches, and lamps, and
the large houses behind the colonnades were gaudy
with rich hangings; only the handsomest and stateliest
of them all had no kind of decoration. This was the
abode of the Jew Apollodorus.

In former years the finest hangings had decorated
his windows, which had been as gay with flowers and
lamps as those of the other Israelites who dwelt in the
Canopic way, and who were wont to keep the festival
in common with their heathen fellow-citizens as jovially
as though they were no less zealous to do homage to
Dionysus. Apollodorus had his own reasons for keeping aloof on this occasion from all that was connected
with the holiday doings of the heathen. Without
dreaming that his withdrawal could involve him in any
danger, he was quietly sitting in his house, which was
so splendidly furnished as to seem fitted for some
princely Greek rather than for a Hebrew. This was
especially the case with the men's living-room, in which
Apollodorus sat, for the pictures on the walls and pavement of this beautiful hall—of which the roof, which
was half open, was supported on columns of the finest
porphyry—represented the loves of Eros and Psyche;
while between the pillars stood busts of the greatest
heathen philosophers, and in the background a fine
statue of Plato was conspicuous. Among all the Greeks
and Romans there was the portrait of only one Jew,
and this was that of Philo, whose intellectual and delicate features greatly resembled those of the most illustrious of his Greek companions.

In this splendid room, lighted by silver lamps, there

was no lack of easy couches, and on one of these Apollodorus was reclining; a fine-looking man of fifty, with his mild but shrewd eyes fixed on a tall and aged fellow-Israelite who was pacing up and down in front of him and talking eagerly; the old man's hands too were never still, now he used them in eager gesture, and again stroked his long white beard. On an easy seat opposite to the master of the house sat a lean young man with pale and very regular finely-cut features, black hair and a black beard; he sat with his dark glowing eyes fixed on the ground, tracing lines and circles on the pavement with the stick he held in his hand, while the excited old man, his uncle, urgently addressed Apollodorus in a vehement but fluent torrent of words. Apollodorus, however, shook his head from time to time at his speech and frequently met him with a brief contradiction.

It was easy to see that what he was listening to touched him painfully, and that the two diametrically different men were fighting a battle which could never lead to any satisfactory issue. For, though they both used the Greek tongue and confessed the same religion, all they felt and thought was grounded on views, as widely dissimilar as though the two men had been born in different spheres. When two opponents of such different calibre meet, there is a great clatter of arms but no bloody wounds are dealt and neither rout nor victory can result.

It was on account of this old man and his nephew that Apollodorus had forborne to-day to decorate his house, for the Rabbi Gamaliel, who had arrived only the day before from Palestine, and had been welcomed by his Alexandrian relatives, condemned every form of

communion with the gentiles, and would undoubtedly
have quitted the residence of his host if he had ventured
to adorn it in honor of the feast-day of the false gods.
Gamaliel's nephew, Rabbi Ben Jochai, enjoyed a reputation little inferior to that of his father, Ben Akiba. The
elder was the greatest sage and expounder of the law—
the son the most illustrious astronomer and the most
skilled interpreter of the mystical significance of the
position of the heavenly bodies, among the Hebrews.

It redounded greatly to the honor of Apollodorus
that he should be privileged to shelter under his roof
the sage Gamaliel and the famous son of so great a
father, and in his hours of leisure he loved to occupy
himself with learned subjects, so he had done his utmost
to make their stay in his house in every way agreeable
to them. He had bought, on purpose for them, a kitchen
slave, himself a strict Jew and familiar with the requirements of the Levitical law as to food, who during their
stay was to preside over the mysteries of the hearth,
instead of the Greek cook who usually served him,
so that none but clean meat should be prepared according to the Jewish ritual. He had forbidden his
grown-up sons to invite any of their Greek friends into
the house during the visit of the illustrious couple or to
discuss the festival; they were also enjoined to avoid
using the names of the gods of the heathen in their conversation—but he himself was the first to sin against
this prohibition.

He, like all the Hebrews of good position in Alexandria, had acquired Greek culture, felt and thought in
Greek modes, and had remained a Jew only in name;
for though they still believed in the one God of their
fathers instead of in a crowd of Olympian deities, the

One whom they worshipped was no longer the almighty
and jealous God of their nation, but the all-pervading
plasmic and life-giving Spirit with whom the Greeks had
become familiar through Plato.

Every hour that they had spent in each other's company had widened the gulf between Apollodorus and
Gamaliel, and the relations of the Alexandrian to the
sage had become almost intolerable, when he learnt that
the old man—who was related to himself—had come to
Egypt with his nephew, in order to demand the daughter of Apollodorus in marriage. But the fair Ismene
was not in the least disposed to listen to this grave and
bigoted suitor. The home of her people was to her a
barbarous land, the young astronomer filled her with
alarm, and besides all this her heart was already engaged; she had given it to the son of Alabarchos, who
was the Superior of all the Israelites in Egypt, and this
young man possessed the finest horse in the whole city,
with which he had won several races in the Hippodrome,
and he also had distinguished her above all the maidens.
To him, if to any one, would she give her hand, and she
had explained herself to this effect to her father when he
informed her of Ben Jochai's suit, and Apollodorus, who
had lost his wife several years before, had neither the
wish nor the power to put any pressure on his pretty
darling.

To be sure the temporizing nature of the man rendered it very difficult to him to give a decided no to his
venerable old friend; but it had to be done sooner or
later, and the present evening seemed to him an appropriate moment for this unpleasant task.

He was alone with his guests. His daughter had
gone to the house of a friend to look on at the gay doings

in the street, his three sons were out, all the slaves had leave to enjoy their holiday till midnight; nothing was likely to disturb them, and so, after many warm expressions of his deep respect, he found courage to confess to them that he could not support Ben Jochai's pretensions. His child, he said, clung too fondly to Alexandria to wish to quit it, and his learned young friend would be but ill suited with a wife who was accustomed to freer manners and habits, and could hardly feel herself at ease in a home where the laws of her fathers were strictly observed, and in which therefore no kind of freedom of life would be tolerated.

Gamaliel let the Alexandrian speak to the end, but then, as his nephew was beginning to argue against their host's hesitancy, the old man abruptly interrupted him. Drawing up his figure, which was a little bent, to its full height, and passing his hand among the blue veins and fine wrinkles that marked his high forehead, he began:

"Our house was decimated in our wars against the Romans, and among the daughters of our race Ben Akiba found not one in Palestine who seemed to him worthy to marry his son. But the report of the good fortune of the Alexandrian branch of our family had reached Judea, and Ben Akiba thought that he would do like our father Abraham, and he sent me, his Eliezer, into a strange land to win the daughter of a kinsman to wife for his Isaac. Now, who and what the young man is, and the esteem in which he and his father are held by men—"

"I know well," interrupted Apollodorus, "and my house has never been so highly honored as in your visit."

"And notwithstanding," continued the Rabbi, "we must return home as we came; and indeed this will not

only suit you best, but us too, and my brother, whose
ambassador I am, for after what I have learnt from you
within this last hour we must in any case withdraw our
suit. Do not interrupt me! Your Ismene scorns to
veil her face, and no doubt it is a very pretty one to look
upon—you have trained her mind like that of a man, and
so she seeks to go her own way. That may be all very
well for a Greek woman, but in the house of Ben Akiba
the woman must obey her husband's will, as the ship
obeys the helm, and have no will of her own; her husband's will always coincides with what the law commands, which you yourself learnt to obey."

" We recognize its excellence," replied Apollodorus,
" but even if all the laws which Moses received on Sinai
were binding on all mortals alike, the various ordinances
which were wisely laid down for the regulation of the
social life of our fathers, are not universally applicable
for the children of our day. And least of all can we observe them here, where, though true to our ancient faith,
we live as Greeks among Greeks."

" That I perceive," retorted Gamaliel, " for even the
language—that clothing of our thoughts—the language
of our fathers and of the scriptures, you have abandoned for another, sacrificed to another."

" You and your nephew also speak Greek."

" We do it here, because the heathen, because you
and yours, no longer understand the tongue of Moses
and the prophets."

" But wherever the Great Alexander bore his arms
Greek is spoken ; and does not the Greek version of the
scriptures, translated by the seventy interpreters under
the direct guidance of our God, exactly reproduce the
Hebrew text ?"

" And would you exchange the stone engraved by Bryasis that you wear on your finger, and showed me yesterday with so much pride, for a wax impression of the gem ?"

"The language of Plato is not an inferior thing; it is as noble as the costliest sapphire."

" But ours came to us from the lips of the Most High. What would you think of a child that, disdaining the tongue of its father listened only to that of its neighbors and made use of an interpreter to be able to understand its parents' commands ?"

" You are speaking of parents who have long since left their native land. The ancestor need not be indignant with his descendants when they use the language of their new home, so long as they continue to act in accordance with his spirit."

"We must live not merely in accordance with the spirit, but by the words of the Most High, for not a syllable proceeds from His lips in vain. The more exalted the spirit of a discourse is, the more important is every word and syllable. One single letter often changes the meaning of whole sentences.—What a noise the people outside are making ! The wild tumult penetrates even into this room which is so far from the street, and your sons take delight in the disorders of the heathen ! You do not even withhold them by force from adding to the number of those mad devotees of pleasure !"

" I was young once myself, and I think it no sin to share in the universal rejoicing."

" Say rather the disgraceful idolatry of the worshippers of Dionysus. It is in name alone that you and your children belong to the elect people of God, in your hearts you are heathens !"

" No, Father," exclaimed Apollodorus eagerly. " The
reverse is the case.   In our hearts we are Jews but we
wear the garments of Greeks."

" Why   your   name   is   Apollodorus — the   gift   of
Apollo."

" A   name   chosen   only   to   distinguish   me   from
others.   Who   would   ever   enquire   into   the   meaning
of a .name if it sounds well."

" You, everybody who is not devoid of sense," cried
the Rabbi.   " You think to yourself 'need Zenodotus or
Hermogenes, some Greek you meet at the bath or elsewhere, know at once that the wealthy personage, with
whom he discussed the latest interpretation of the Hellenic myths, is a Jew ?'   And how charming is the man
who asks you whether you are not an Athenian, for
your Greek has such a pure Attic accent !   And what we
ourselves like, we favor in our children, so we choose
names for them too which flatter our own vanity."

" By Heracles !—"

A faint mocking smile crossed Gamaliel's lips and
interrupting the Alexandrian he said :

" Is there any particularly worthy man among our
Alexandrian fellow-believers whose name is Heracles ?"

" No one" cried the Alexandrian " ever thinks of
the son of Alcmene when he asseverates—it only means
'really,—truly—' "

" To be sure you are not fastidiously accurate in the
choice of your words and names, and where there is so
much to be seen and enjoyed as there is here one's
thoughts are not always connected.   That is intelligible
—quite, peculiarly intelligible !   And in this city folks
are so polite that they are fain to wrap truth in some
graceful disguise.   May I, a barbarian from Judea, be

allowed to set it before you, bare of clothing, naked and
unadorned."

" Speak, I beg you, speak."

" You are Jews; but you had rather not be Jews,
and you endure your origin as an inevitable evil.   It is
only when you feel the mighty hand of the Most High
that you recognize it and claim your right to be one of
His chosen people.   In the smooth current of daily life
you proudly number yourselves with his enemies.   Do
not interrupt me, and answer honestly what I shall ask
you.   In what hour of your life did you feel yourself
that you owed the deepest gratitude to the God of your
fathers ?"

" Why should I deny it ?—In the hour when my
lost wife presented me with my first-born son ."

" And you called him ?"

" You know his name is Benjamin."

" Like the favorite son of our forefather Jacob, for in
the hour when you thus named him you were honestly
yourself, you felt thankful that it had been vouchsafed
to you to add another link to the chain of your race—
you were a Jew—you were confident in our God—in
your own God.   The birth of your second son touched
your soul less deeply and you gave him the name of
Theophilus, and when your third male child was born
you had altogether ceased to remember the God of your
fathers, for he is named after one of the heathen gods,
Hephaestion.   To put it shortly : You are Jews when
the Lord is most gracious to you, or threatens to try
you most severely but you are heathen whenever your
way does not lead you over the high hills or through the
dark abysses of life.   I cannot change your hearts—but
the wife of my brother's son, the daughter of Ben Akiba,

must be a daughter of our people, morning, noon, and night. I seek a Rebecca for my daughter and not an Ismene."

"I did not ask you here," retorted Apollodorus. " But if you quit us to-morrow, you will be followed by our reverent regard. Think no worse of us because we adapt ourselves, more, perhaps, than is fitting, to the ways and ideas of the people among whom we have grown up, and in whose midst we have been prosperous, and whose interests are ours. We know how high our faith is beyond theirs. In our hearts we still are Jews; but are we not bound to try to open and to cultivate and to elevate our spirits, which God certainly made of stuff no coarser than that of other nations, whenever and wherever we may? And in what school may our minds be trained better or on sounder principles than in ours—I mean that of the Greek sages? The knowledge of the Most High—"

"That knowledge," cried the old man, gesticulating vehemently with his arms. "The knowledge of God Most High and all that the most refined philosophy can prove, all the sublimest and purest of the thinkers of whom you speak can only apprehend by the gravest meditation and heart-searching—all this I say has been bestowed as a free gift of God on every child of our people. The treasures which your sages painfully seek out we already possess in our scriptures, our law and our moral ordinances. We are the chosen people, the first-born of the Lord, and when Messiah shall rise up in our midst—"

"Then," interrupted Apollodorus, "that shall be fulfilled which, like Philo, I hope for, we shall be the priests and prophets for all nations. Then we shall in truth be a race of priests whose vocation it shall be to call down the blessing of the Most High on all mankind."

"For us—for us alone shall the messenger of God appear, to make us the kings, and not the slaves of the nations."

Apollodorus looked with surprise into the face of the excited old man, and asked with an incredulous smile:

"The crucified Nazarene was a false Messiah; but when will the true Messiah appear?"

"When will He appear?" cried the Rabbi. "When? Can I tell when? Only one thing I do know; the serpent is already sharpening its fangs to sting the heel of Him who shall tread upon it. Have you heard the name of Bar Kochba?"

"Uncle," said Ben Jochai, interrupting the old Rabbi's speech, and rising from his seat: "Say nothing you might regret."

"Nay, nay," answered Gamaliel earnestly. "Our friends here prefer the human above the divine, but they are not traitors." Then turning again to Apollodorus he continued:

"The oppressors in Israel have set up idols in our holy places, and strive again to force the people to bow down to them; but rather shall our back be broken than we will bend the knee or submit!"

"You are meditating another revolt?" asked the Alexandrian anxiously.

"Answer me — have you heard the name of Bar Kochba?"

"Yes, as that of the foolhardy leader of an armed troup."

" He is a hero—perhaps the Redeemer."

"And it was for him that you charged me to load

26

my next corn vessel to Joppa with swords, shields **and**
lance-heads?"

"And are none but the Romans to be permitted to
use iron?"

"Nay—but I should hesitate to supply a friend with
arms if he proposed to use them against an irresistible
antagonist, who will inevitably annihilate him!"

"The Lord of Hosts is stronger than a thousand
legions!"

"Be cautious uncle," said Ben Jochai again in a
warning voice.

Gamaliel turned wrathfully upon his nephew, but
before he could retort on the young man's protest, he
started in alarm, for a wild howling and the resounding
clatter of violent blows on the brazen door of the house
rang through the hall and shook its walls of marble.

"They are attacking my house," shouted Apollodorus.

"This is the gratitude of those for whom you have
broken faith with the God of your fathers," said the old
man gloomily.   Then throwing up his hands and eyes
he cried aloud: "Hear me Adonai!   My years are
many and I am ripe for the grave; but spare these, have
mercy upon them."

Ben Jochai followed his uncle's example and raised
his arms in supplication, while his black eyes sparkled
with a lowering glow in his pale face.

But their prayers were brief, for the tumult came
nearer and nearer; Apollodorus wrung his hands, and
struck his fist against his forehead; his movements were
violent—spasmodic.   Terror had entirely robbed him
of the elegant, measured demeanor which he had acquired among his Greek fellow-citizens, and mingling

heathen oaths and adjurations with appeals to the God of his fathers, he flew first one way and then another. He searched for the key of the subterranean rooms of the house, but he could not find it, for it was in the charge of his steward, who, with all the other servants, was taking his pleasure in the streets, or over a brimming cup in some tavern.

Now the newly-purchased kitchen-slave—the Jew to whom the keeping of the Dionysian feast was an abomination—rushed into the room shrieking out, as he plucked at his hair and beard:

"The Philistines are upon us! save us Rabbi, great Rabbi! Cry for us to the Lord, oh! man of God! They are coming with staves and spears and they will tread us down as grass and burn us in this house like the locusts cast into the oven."

In deadly terror he threw himself at Gamaliel's feet and clasped them in his hands, but Apollodorus exclaimed: "Follow me, follow me up on to the roof."

"No, no," howled the slave, "Amalek is making ready the firebrand to fling among our tents. The heathen leap and rage, the flames they are flinging will consume us. Rabbi, Rabbi, call upon the Hosts of the Lord! God of the just! The gate has given way. Lord! Lord! Lord!"

The terrified wretch's teeth chattered and he covered his eyes with his hands, groaning and howling.

Ben Jochai had remained perfectly calm, but he was quivering with rage. His prayer was ended, and turning to Gamaliel he said in deep tones:

"I knew that this would happen, I warned you. Our evil star rose when we set forth on our wanderings.

26

Now we must abide patiently what the Lord hath determined. He will be our Avenger."

"Vengeance is His!" echoed the old man, and he
covered his head with his white mantle.

"In the sleeping-room—follow me! we can hide
under the beds!" shrieked Apollodorus; he kicked away
the slave who was embracing the Rabbi's feet, and seized
the old man by the shoulder to drag him away with him.
But it was too late, for the door of the antechamber had
burst open and they could hear the clatter of weapons.

"Lost, lost, all is lost!" cried Apollodorus.

"Adonai! help us Adonai!" murmured the old man
and he clung more closely to his nephew, who over-
topped him by a head and who held him clasped in his
right arm as if to protect him.

The danger which threatened Apollodorus and his
guests was indeed imminent, and it had been provoked
solely by the indignation of the excited mob at seeing
the wealthy Israelite's house unadorned for the feast.

A thousand times had it occurred that a single word
had proved sufficient to inflame the hot blood of the
Alexandrians to prompt them to break the laws and
seize the sword. Bloody frays between the heathen inhabitants and the Jews, who were equally numerous in
the city, were quite the order of the day, and one
party was as often to blame as the other for disturbing the peace and having recourse to the sword.
Since the Israelites had risen in several provinces—
particularly in Cyrenaica and Cyprus—and had fallen
with cruel fury on their fellow-inhabitants who were
their oppressors, the suspicion and aversion of the
Alexandrians of other beliefs had grown more intense
than in former times. Besides this, the prosperous

circumstances of many Jews, and the enormous riches
of a few, had filled the less wealthy heathen with envy
and roused the wish to snatch the possessions of those
who, it cannot be denied, had not unfrequently treated
their gods with open contumely.

It happened that just within a few days the disputes
regarding the festival that was to be held in honor of
the Imperial visit had added bitterness to the old
grudge, and thus it came to pass that Apollodorus'
unlighted house in the Canopic way had excited the
populace to attack this palatial residence. And here
again one single speech had sufficed to excite their
fury.

In the first instance Melampus, the tanner, a drunken
swaggerer, who had failed in business, had marched up
the street at the head of a tipsy crew, and pointing
with his thyrsus to the dark, undecorated house, had
shouted:

"Look at that dismal barrack! All that the Jew
used to spend on decorating the street, he is saving up
now in his money chest!" The words were like a
spark among tinder and others followed.

"The niggard is robbing our father Dionysus," cried
a second citizen, and a third, flourishing his torch on
high, croaked out:

"Let us get at the drachmae he grudges the god;
we can find a use for them." Graukus, the sausage-
maker, snatched from his neighbor's hand the bunch of
tow soaked in pitch, and bellowed out, "I advise that
we should burn the house over their heads!"

"Stay, stay," cried a cobbler who worked for Apollodorus'.slaves, as he placed himself in the butcher's
way. "Perhaps they are mourning for some one in

there. The Jew has always decorated his house on former occasions."

" Not they," replied a flute-player in a loud hoarse voice. " We met the old miser's son on the Bruchiom with some riotous comrades and misconducted hussies, with his purple mantle fluttering far behind him."

" Let us see which is reddest, the Tyrian stuff or the blaze we shall make if we set the old wretch's house on fire," shouted a hungry-looking tailor, looking round to see the effects of his wit.

" Ay! let us try!" rose from one man, and then, from a number of others:

" Let us get into the house!"

" The mean churl shall remember this day!"

" Fetch him out!"

" Drag him into the street!"

Such shouts as these rose here and there from the crowd, which grew denser every instant as it was increased by fresh tributaries attracted by the riot.

" Drag him out!" again shrieked an Egyptian slave-driver, and a woman shrieked an echo of his words. She snatched the deer-skin from her shoulders, flourished it round and round in the air above her tangled black hair, and bellowed furiously:

" Tear him in pieces!"

" In pieces, with your teeth!" roared a drunken Mœnad who, like most of the mob that had collected, knew nothing whatever of the popular grudge against Apollodorus and his house.

But words had already begun to be followed by deeds. Feet, fists, and cudgels stamped, drubbed, and thumped against the firmly-bolted brazen door of the darkened house, and a ship's boy of fourteen sprang on

the shoulders of a tall black slave and tried to climb
the roof of the colonnade, and to fling the torch which
the sausage-maker handed up to him into the open
forecourt of the imperilled house.

CHAPTER VI.

THE clatter of arms which Apollodorus and his
guests had heard proceeded not from the Jew's be-
siegers, but from some Roman soldiers who brought
safety to the besieged.

It was Verus, who as he was returning from the
supper he had given his veterans, with an officer of the
Twelfth Legion and his British slaves, had crossed the
Canopic way and had been impeded in his progress by
the increasing crowd which stood before Apollodorus'
house. The praetor had met the Jew at the prefect's
house, and knew him for one of the richest and shrewd-
est men in Alexandria. This attack on his property
roused his ire; still he would certainly not have remained an idle spectator even if the house in danger,
instead of belonging to a man of mark, had been that of
one of the poorest and meanest, even among the Christians. Any lawless act, any breach of constituted order
was odious and intolerable to the Roman; he would
not have been the man he was if he had looked on
passively at an attack by the mob, in times of peace, on
the life and property of a quiet and estimable citizen.
This licentious man of pleasure, devoted to every ener-
vating enjoyment, in battle, or whenever the need arose,
was as prudent as he was brave.

He now first ascertained what purpose the excited crowd had in view, and at once considered the ways and means of frustrating their project. They had already begun to batter the Jew's door, and already several lads were standing on the roof of the arcades with burning torches in their hands.

Whatever he did must be done on the instant, and happily Verus had the gift of thinking and acting promptly. In a few decisive words he begged his companion, Lucius Albinus, to hurry back to his old soldiers and bring them to the rescue; then he desired his slaves to force a way for him with their powerful arms up to the door of the house. This feat was accomplished in no time, but how great was his astonishment when he found the Emperor standing there.

Hadrian stood in the midst of the crowd, and at the instant when Verus appeared on the scene had wrenched the torch out of the hand of the infuriated tailor. At the same time, in a thundering voice, he commanded the Alexandrians—who were not accustomed to the imperial tone—to desist from their mad project. Whistling, grunting, and words of scorn overpowered the mandate of the sovereign, and when Verus and his slaves had reached the spot where he stood, a few drunken Egyptians had gone up to him and were about to lay hands on the unwelcome counsellor. The praetor stood in their way. He first whispered to Hadrian that Jupiter ought to be ruling the world, and might well leave it to smaller folks to rescue a houseful of Jews; and that in a few seconds the soldiers would arrive. Then he shouted to him in a loud voice:

"Away from this Sophist! Your place is in the Museum, or in the temple of Serapis with your books,

and not among the misguided and ignorant. Am
I right Macedonian citizens, or am I wrong?" A
murmur of assent was heard which became a roar
of laughter when Verus, after Hadrian had got away,
went on:

"He has a beard like Caesar, and so he behaves as
if he wore the purple! You did well to let him escape,
his wife and children are waiting for him over their porridge."

Verus had often been implicated in wild adventure
among the populace and knew how to deal with them;
if he now could only detain them till the advent of the
soldiers he might consider the game as won. Hadrian
could be a hero when it suited him; but here where no
laurels were to be won, he left to Verus the task of
quieting the crowd.

As soon as he was fairly gone Verus desired his
slaves to lift him on their shoulders; his handsome
good-natured face looked down upon the crowd from
high above them. He was immediately recognized, and
many voices called out:

"The crazy Roman! the praetor! the sham Eros!"

"I am he, Macedonian citizens, yes, I am he," answered Verus in a clear voice. "And I will tell you a
story."

"Listen, Listen".—"No let us get into the Jew's
house."—"Presently—listen a minute to what the sham
Eros says."—"I will knock your teeth down your
throat boy, if you don't hold your tongue." All the
crowd were shouting in wild confusion.

Curiosity, on the one hand, to hear the noble gentleman's speech, and the somewhat superficial fury of
the mob contended together for a few minutes; at last

curiosity seemed to be gaining the day, the tumult subsided, and the praetor began :

" Once upon a time there was a child who had given
to him ten little sheep made of cotton, little foolish toys
such as the old women sell in the market place."

" Get into the Jew's house, we don't want to hear
children's stories—"

" Be quiet there !"—" Hush now listen; from the
sheep he will go on to the wolves."—" Not wolves—it
will be a she-wolf!" some one shouted in the throng.

" Do not mention the horrid things!" laughed Verus
" but listen to me.—Well, the child set his little sheep
up in a row each one close to the next.   He was
a weaver's son.   Are there any weavers here ?   You ?
and you—ah, and you out there.   If I were not my
father's son I should like to be the son of an Alexandrian weaver.   You need not laugh !—Well, about the
sheep.   All the little things were beautifully white but
one which had nasty black spots, and the little boy
could not bear that one.   He went to the hearth, pulled
out a burning stick and wanted to burn the little ugly
sheep so as only to have pretty white ones.   The lamb-
kin caught fire and just as the flame had begun to burn
the wooden skeleton of the toy a draught from the
window blew the flame towards the other little sheep
and in a minute they were all burned to ashes.   Then
thought the little boy, ' If only I had let the ugly
sheep alone !   What can I play with now ?' and he began to cry.   But this was not all, for while the little rascal was drying his eyes, the flame spread and burnt up
the loom, the wool, the flax, the woven pieces, the whole
house—the town in which he was born, and even, I believe, the boy himself!—Now worthy friends and Mace-

donian citizens, reflect a moment. Any man among you
who is possessed of any property may read the moral
of my fable."

"Put out the torches!" cried the wife of a charcoal
dealer.

"He is right; for by reason of the Jew, we are putting the whole town in danger!" cried the cobbler.

"The mad fools have already thrown in some
brands!"

"If you fellows up there fling any more I will
break your ankles for you," shouted a flax-dealer.

"Don't try any burning," the tailor commanded,
"force open the door and have out the Jew." These
words raised a storm of applause and the mob pressed
forward to the Jew's abode. No one listened to Verus
any more, and he slipped down from his slave's shoulders, placed himself in front of the door and called
out:

"In the name of Caesar and the law I command
you to leave this house unharmed."

The Roman's warning was evidently quite in earnest, and the false Eros looked as if at this moment it
would be ill-advised to try jesting with him. But in the
universal uproar only a few had heard his words, and
the hot-blooded tailor was so rash as to lay his hand on
the praetor's girdle in order to drag him away from the
door with the help of his comrades. But he paid dearly
for his temerity for the praetor's fist fell so heavily on his
forehead that he dropped as if struck by lightning. One
of the Britons knocked down the sausage-maker and a
hideous hand to hand fight would have been the upshot
if help had not come to the hardly-beset Romans from
two quarters at once. The veterans supported by a

number of lictors were the first to appear, and soon after them came Benjamin, the Jew's eldest son, who was passing down the great thoroughfare with his boon-companions and saw the danger that was threatening his father's house.

The soldiers parted the throng as the wind chases the clouds, and the young Israelite pressed forward with his heavy thyrsus fought and pushed his way so valiantly and resolutely through the panic-stricken mob, that he reached the door of his father's house but a few moments later than the soldiers. The lictors battered at the door and as no one opened it, they forced it with the help of the soldiers in order to set a guard in the beleaguered house, and protect it against the raging mob.

Verus and the officer entered the Jew's dwelling with the armed men, and behind them came Benjamin and his friends—young Greeks with whom he was in the habit of consorting daily, in the bath or the gymnasium. Apollodorus and his guests expressed their gratitude to Verus, and when the old Jewish house-keeper, who had seen and heard from a hiding-place under the roof all that had taken place outside her master's house, came into the men's hall and gave a full report of the uproar from beginning to end, the praetor was overwhelmed with thanks; and the old woman embroidered her narrative with the most glowing colors. While this was going on Apollodorus' pretty daughter, Ismene, came in, and after falling on her father's neck and weeping with agitation the house-keeper took her hand and led her to Verus, saying:

"This noble lord—may the blessing of the Most High be on him—staked his life to save us. This beautiful robe he let be rent for our sakes, and every daughter of Israel should fervently kiss this torn chiton, which in the eyes of God is more precious than the richest robe—as I do."

And the old woman pressed the praetor's dress to her lips, and tried to make Ismene do the same; but the praetor would not permit this.

"How can I allow my garment," he exclaimed, laughing, "to enjoy a favor of which I should deem myself worthy—to be touched by such lips."

"Kiss him, kiss him!" cried the old woman, and the praetor took the head of the blushing girl in his hands, and pressing his lips to her forehead with a by no means paternal air, he said gaily:

"Now I am richly rewarded for all I have been so happy as to do for you, Apollodorus."

"And we," exclaimed Gamaliel. "We—myself and my brother's first-born son—leave it in the hands of God Most High to reward you for what you have done for us."

"Who are you?" asked Verus, who was filled with admiration for the prophet-like aspect of the venerable old man and the pale intellectual head of his nephew.

Apollodorus took upon himself to explain to him how far the Rabbi transcended all his fellow Hebrews in knowledge of the law and the interpretation of the Kabbala, the oral and mystical traditions of their people, and how that Simeon Ben Jochai was superior to all the astrologers of his time. He spoke of the young man's much admired work on the subject called Sohar, nor did he omit to mention that Gamaliel's nephew was able to foretell the positions of the stars even on future nights.

Verus listened to Apollodorus with increasing attention, and fixed a keen gaze on the young man, who interrupted his host's eager enconium with many modest deprecations. The praetor had recollected the near approach of his birthday, and also that the position of stars in the night preceding it, would certainly be observed by Hadrian. What the Emperor might learn from them would seal his fate for life. Was that momentous night destined to bring him nearer to the highest goal of his ambition or to debar him from it?

When Apollodorus ceased speaking, Verus offered Simeon Ben Jochai his hand, saying:

" I am rejoiced to have met a man of your learning and distinction. What would I not give to possess your knowledge for a few hours!"

" My knowledge is yours," replied the astrologer. " Command my services, my labors, my time—ask me as many questions as you will. We are so deeply indebted to you—"

" You have no reason to regard me as your creditor," interrupted the praetor, " you do not even owe me thanks. I only made your acquaintance after I had rescued you, and I opposed the mob, not for the sake of any particular man, but for that of law and order."

" You were benevolent enough to protect us," cried Ben Jochai, " so do not be so stern as to disdain our gratitude."

" It does me honor, my learned friend; by all the gods it does me honor," replied Verus. " And in fact it is possible, it might very will be—Will you do me the favor to come with me to that bust of Hipparchus? By the aid of that science which owes so much to him you may be able to render me an important service."

· When the two men were standing apart from the others, in front of the white marble portrait of the great astronomer, Verus asked:

"Do you know by what method Caesar is wont to presage the fates of men from the stars?"

"Perfectly."

"From whom?"

"From Aquila, my father's disciple."

"Can you calculate what he will learn from the stars in the night preceding the thirtieth of December, as to the destinies of a man who was born in that night, and whose horoscope I possess?"

"I can only answer a conditional yes to that question."

"What should prevent your answering positively?"

"Unforeseen appearances in the heavens."

"Are such signs common?"

"No, they are rare, on the contrary."

"But perhaps my fortune is not a common one—and I beg of you to calculate on Hadrian's method what the heavens will predict on that night for the man whose horoscope my slave shall deliver to you early to-morrow morning."

"I will do so with pleasure."

"When can you have finished this work?"

"In four days at latest, perhaps even sooner."

"Capital! But one thing more. Do you regard me as a man, I mean, as a true man?"

"If you were not, would you have given me such reason to be grateful to you?"

"Well then, conceal nothing from me, not even the worst horrors, things that might poison another man's life, and crush his spirit. Whatever you read in the

celestial record, small or great, good or evil. I require
you to tell me all."

" I will conceal nothing, absolutely nothing."

The praetor offered Ben Jochai his right hand, and
warmly pressed the Jew's slender, well-shaped fingers.
Before he went away he settled with him how he should
inform him when he had finished his labors.

The Alexandrian with his guests and children accompanied the praetor to the door. Only Benjamin was
absent; he was sitting with his companions in his father's
dining-room, and rewarding them for the assistance they
had given him with right good wine. Gamaliel heard
them shouting and singing, and pointing to the room he
shrugged his shoulders, saying, as he turned to his host.

"They are returning thanks to the God of our
fathers in the Alexandrian fashion."

And peace was broken no more in the Jew's house
but by the firm tramp of lictors and soldiers who kept
watch over it, under arms.

In a side street the praetor met the tailor he had
knocked down, the sausage-maker, and other ringleaders
of the attack on the Israelite's house. They were being
led away prisoners before the night magistrates. Verus
would have set them at liberty with all his heart, but he
knew that the Emperor would enquire next morning
what had been done to the rioters, and so he forbore.
At any other time he would certainly have sent them
home unpunished, but just now he was dominated by a
wish that was more dominant than his good nature or
his facile impulses.

CHAPTER VII.

WHEN he reached the Caesareum the high-chamber-
lain was waiting to conduct him to Sabina who desired
to speak with him notwithstanding the lateness of the
hour, and when Verus entered the presence of his
patroness, he found her in the greatest excitement. She
was not reclining as usual on her pillows but was pacing
her room with strides of very unfeminine length.

"It is well that you have come!" she exclaimed to
the praetor. "Lentulus insists that he has seen Mastor
the slave, and Balbilla declares—but it is impossible!"

"You think that Caesar is here?" asked Verus.

"Did they tell you so too?"

"No. I do not linger to talk when you require my
presence, and there is something important to be told
just now then—but you must not be alarmed."

"No useless speeches!"

"Just now I met, in his own person—"

"Who?"

"Hadrian."

"You are not · mistaken, you are sure you saw
him?"

"With these eyes."

"Abominable, unworthy, disgraceful!" cried Sabina,
so loudly and violently that she was startled at the shrill
tones of her own voice. Her tall thin figure quivered
with excitement, and to any one else she would have
appeared in the highest degree graceless, unwomanly,
and repulsive: but Verus had been accustomed from his

27

childhood to see her with kinder eyes than other men
and it grieved him.

There are women who remind us of fading flowers,
extinguished lights or vanishing shades, and they are
not the least attractive of their sex: but the large-boned,
stiff and meagre Sabina had none of the yielding and
tender grace of these gentle creatures. Her feeble
health, which was very evident, became her particularly
ill when, as at this moment, the harsh acrimony of her
embittered soul came to light with hideous plainness.

She was deeply indignant at the affront her husband
had put upon her. Not content with having a separate
house established for her he kept aloof in Alexandria
without informing her of his arrival. Her hands trembled with rage, and stammering rather than speaking she
desired the praetor to order a composing draught for her.
When Verus returned she was lying on her cushions,
with her face turned to the wall, and said lamentably:

"I am freezing; spread that coverlet over me. I
am a miserable, ill-used creature."

"You are sensitive and take things too hardly," the
praetor ventured to remonstrate.

She started up angrily, cut off his speech, and put
him through as keen a cross-examination as if he were
an accused person and she his judge. Ere long she had
learnt that Verus also had encountered Mastor, that her
husband was residing at Lochias, that he had taken part
in the festival in disguise, and had exposed himself to
grave danger outside the house of Apollodorus. She
also made him tell her how the Israelite had been rescued, and whom her friend had met in his house, and
she blamed Verus with bitter words for the heedless and
foolhardy recklessness with which he had risked his life

for a miserable Jew, forgetting the high destinies that lay before him. The praetor had not interrupted her, but now bowing over her, he kissed her hand and said:

"Your kind heart foresees for me things that I dare not hope for. Something is glimmering on the horizon of my fortune. Is it the dying glow of my failing fortunes, is it the pale dawn of a coming and more glorious day? Who can tell? I await with patience whatever may be impending—an early day must decide."

"That will bring certainty, and put an end to this suspense," murmured Sabina.

"Now rest and try to sleep," said Verus with a tender fervency, that was peculiar to his tones. "It is past midnight and the physician has often forbidden you to sit up late. Farewell, dream sweetly, and always be the same to me as a man, that you were to me in my childhood and youth."

Sabina withdrew the hand he had taken, saying:

"But you must not leave me. I want you. I cannot exist without your presence."

"Till to-morrow—always—forever I will stay with you whenever you need me."

The Empress gave him her hand again, and sighed softly as he again bowed over it, and pressed it long to his lips.

"You are my friend, Verus, truly my friend; yes, I am sure of it," she said at last, breaking the silence.

"Oh Sabina, my Mother!" he answered tenderly. "You spoiled me with kindness even when I was a boy, and what can I do to thank you for all this?"

"Be always the same to me that you are to-day. Will you always—for all time be the same, whatever your fortunes may be?"

27

"In joy and in adversity always the same; always your friend, always ready to give my life for you."

"In spite of my husband, always, even when you think you no longer need my favor!"

"Always, for without you I should be nothing—utterly miserable."

The Empress heaved a deep sigh and sat bolt upright on her couch. She had formed a great resolve, and she said slowly, emphasizing every word:

"If nothing utterly unforeseen occurs in the heavens on your birth-night, you shall be our son, and so Hadrian's successor and heir. I swear it."

There was something solemn in her voice, and her small eyes were wide open.

"Sabina, Mother, guardian spirit of my life!" cried Verus, and he fell on his knees by her couch. She looked in his handsome face with deep emotion, laid her hands on his temples, and pressed her lips on his dark curls.

A moist brilliancy sparkled in those eyes, unapt to tears, and in a soft and appealing tone that no one had ever before heard in her voice she said:

"Even at the summit of fortune, after your adoption, even in the purple all will be the same between us two. Will it? Tell me, will it?"

"Always, always!" cried Verus. "And if our hopes are fulfilled—"

"Then, then," interrupted Sabina and she shivered as she spoke. "Then, still you will be to me the same that you are now; but to be sure, to be sure—the temples of the gods would be empty if mortals had nothing left to wish for."

"Ah! no. Then they would bring thank-offerings

to the divinity," cried Verus, and he looked up at the
Empress; but she turned away from his smiling glance
and exclaimed in a tone of reproof and alarm:

" No playing with words, no empty speeches or rash
jesting! in the name of all the gods, not at this time!
For this hour, this night is among its fellows what a hallowed temple is among other buildings—what the fervent
sun is among the other lights of heaven. You know not
how I feel, nay, I hardly know myself. Not now, not
now, one lightly-spoken word!"

Verus gazed at Sabina with growing astonishment.
She had always been kinder to him than to any one else
in the world and he felt bound to her by all the ties of
gratitude and the sweet memories of childhood. Even
as a boy, out of all his playfellows he was the only one
who, far from fearing her had clung to her. But to-night!
who had ever seen Sabina in such a mood? Was this
the harsh bitter woman whose heart seemed filled with
gall, whose tongue cut like a dagger every one against
whom she used it? Was this Sabina who no doubt was
kindly disposed towards him but who loved no one else,
not even herself? Did he see rightly, or was he under
some delusion? Tears, genuine, honest, unaffected tears
filled her eyes as she went on:

" Here I lie, a poor sickly woman, sensitive in body
and in soul as if I were covered with wounds. Every
movement, and even the gaze and the voice of most of
my fellow-creatures is a pain to me. I am old, much
older than you think and so wretched, so wretched, none
of you can imagine how wretched. I was never happy
as a child, never as a girl, and as a wife—merciful gods!
—every kind word that Hadrian has ever vouchsafed me
I have paid for with a thousand humiliations."

"He always treats you with the utmost esteem," interrupted Verus.

"Before you, before the world! But what do I care for esteem! I may demand the respect, the adoration of millions and it will be mine.   Love, love, a little unselfish love is what I ask—and if only I were sure, if only I dared to hope that you give me such love, I would thank you with all that I have, then this hour would be hallowed to me above all others."

"How can you doubt me Mother?   My dearly beloved Mother!"

"That is comfort, that is happiness!" answered Sabina. "Your voice is never too loud for me, and I believe you, I dare trust you.   This hour makes you my son, makes me your mother."

Tender emotion, the emotion that softens the heart, thrilled through Sabina's dried-up nature and sparkled in her eyes.   She felt like a young wife of whom a child is born, and the voice of her heart sings to her in soothing tones: "It lives, it is mine, I am the providence of a living soul, I am a mother."

She gazed blissfully into Verus' eyes and exclaimed:

"Give me your hand my son, help me up, for I will lie here no longer.   What good spirits I feel in!   Yes, this is the joy that is allotted to other women before their hair is grey!   But child—dear and only child—you must love me really as a mother.   I am too old for tender trifling, and yet I could not bear it if you gave me nothing but a child's reverence.   No, no, you must be my friend whose heart warns him of my wishes, who can laugh with me to-day, and weep with me to-morrow and who shows that he is happier when his eye meets mine.   You are now my son; and soon you shall have the name of

son; that is happiness enough for one evening. Not another word—this hour is like the finished masterpiece of
some great painter; every touch that could be added
might spoil it. You may kiss my forehead, I will kiss
yours; now I will go to rest, and to-morrow when I
wake I shall say to myself that I possess something
worth living for—a child, a son."

When the Empress was alone she raised her hand
in prayer but she could find no words of thanksgiving.
One hour of pure happiness she had indeed enjoyed,
but how many days, months, years of joylessness and
suffering lay behind her! Gratitude knocked at the door
of her heart but it was instantly met by bitter defiance;
what was one hour of happiness in the balance against
a ruined lifetime?

Foolish woman! she had never sown the seeds of
love, and now she blamed the gods for niggardliness and
cruelty in denying her a harvest of love. And now, on
what soil had the seed of maternal tenderness fallen?

Verus it is true had left her content and full of hope
—Sabina's altered demeanor, it is true, had touched his
heart—he purposed to cling to her faithfully even after
his formal adoption; but the light in his eye was not that
of a proud and happy son, on the contrary it sparkled
like that of a warrior who hopes to gain the victory.

Notwithstanding the late hour, his wife had not yet
gone to bed. She had heard that he had been summoned to the Empress on his return home, and awaited
him not without anxiety, for she was not accustomed to
anything pleasant from Sabina. Her husband's hasty
step echoed loudly from the stone walls of the sleeping
palace. She heard it at some distance, and went to the
door of her room to meet him. Radiant, excited, and

with flushed cheeks, he held out both his hands to her. She looked so fair in her white night-wrapper of fine white material, and his heart was so full that he clasped her in his arms as fondly as when she was his bride; and she loved him even now no less than she had done then, and felt for the hundredth time with grateful joy that the faithless scapegrace had once more returned to her unchangeable and faithful heart, like a sailor who, after wandering through many lands seeks his native port.

"Lucilla," he cried, disengaging her arms from round his neck. "Oh, Lucilla! what an evening this has been! I always judged Sabina differently from you, and have felt with gratitude that she really cared for me. Now all is clear between her and me! She called me her son. I called her mother. I owe it to her, and the purple—the purple is ours! You are the wife of Verus Caesar; you are certain of it if no signs and omens come to frighten Hadrian."

In a few eager words, which betrayed not merely the triumph of a lucky gambler, but also true emotion and gratitude, he related all that had passed in Sabina's room. His frank and confident contentment silenced her doubts, her dread of the stupendous fate which, beckoning her, yet threatening her, drew visibly nearer and nearer. In her mind's eye she saw the husband she loved, she saw her son, seated on the throne of the Caesars, and she herself crowned with the radiant diadem of the woman whom she hated with all the force of her soul. Her husband's kindly feeling towards the Empress and the faithful allegiance which had tied him to her from his boyhood did not disquiet her; but a wife allows the husband of her choice every happiness, every gift

excepting only the love of another woman, and will forgive her hatred and abuse rather than such love.

Lucilla was greatly excited, and a thought, that for
years had been locked in the inmost shrine of her heart,
to-day proved too strong for her powers of reticence.
Hadrian was supposed to have murdered her father, but
no one could positively assert it, though either he or
another man had certainly slain the noble Nigrinus. At
this moment the old suspicion stirred her soul with
revived force, and lifting her right hand, as if in attesta-
tion, she exclaimed:

"Oh, Fate, Fate! that my husband should be heir
of the man who murdered my father!"

"Lucilla," interrupted Verus, "it is unjust even to
think of such horrors, and to speak of them is madness.
Do not utter it a second time, least of all to-day. What
may have occurred formerly must not spoil the present
and the future which belong to us and to our children."

"Nigrinus was the grandfather of those children,"
cried the Roman mother with flashing eyes.

"That is to say that you harbor in your soul the
wish to avenge your father's death on Caesar."

"I am the daughter of the butchered man."

"But you do not know the murderer, and the purple
must outweigh the life of one man, for it is often bought
with many thousand lives. And then, Lucilla, as you
know, I love happy faces, and Revenge has a sinister
brow. Let us be happy, oh wife of Caesar! To-morrow I shall have much to tell you, now I must go to a
splendid banquet which the son of Plutarch is giving in
my honor. I cannot stay with you—truly I cannot, I
have been expected long since. And when we are in

Rome never let me find you telling the children those
old dismal stories—I will not have it."

As Verus, preceded by his slaves bearing torches,
made his way through the garden of the Caesareum he
saw a light in the rooms of Balbilla, the poetess, and he
called up merrily :

" Good-night, fair Muse !"

" Good-night, sham Eros !" she retorted.

" You are decking yourself in borrowed feathers,
Poetess," replied he, laughing. " It is not you but the
ill-mannered Alexandrians who invented that name !"

" Oh! and other and better ones," cried she. " What
I have heard and seen to-day passes all belief !"

" And you will celebrate it in your poems ?"

" Only some of it, and that in a satire which I propose to aim at you."

" I tremble !"

" With delight, it is to be hoped; my poem will em-
balm your memory for posterity."

" That is true, and the more spiteful your verses, the
more certainly will future generations believe that Verus
was the Phaon of Balbilla's Sappho, and that love scorned
filled the fair singer with bitterness."

" I thank you for the caution. To-day at any rate
you are safe from my verse, for I am tired to death."

" Did you venture into the streets ?"

" It was quite safe, for I had a trustworthy escort."

" May I be allowed to ask who ?"

" Why not ? It was Pontius the architect who was
with me."

" He knows the town well."

" And in his care I would trust myself to descend,
like Orpheus, into Hades."

" Happy Pontius ! "

" Most happy Verus ! "

" What am I to understand by those words, charming Balbilla ? "

" The poor architect is able to please by being a good guide, while to you belongs the whole heart of Lucilla, your sweet wife."

" And she has the whole of mine so far as it is not full of Balbilla. Good-night, saucy Muse; sleep well."

" Sleep ill, you incorrigible tormentor ! " cried the girl, drawing the curtain across her window.

CHAPTER VIII.

THE sleepless wretch on whom some trouble has fallen, so long as night surrounds him, sees his future life as a boundless sea in which he is sailing round and round like a shipwrecked man, but when the darkness yields, the new and helpful day shows him a boat for escape close at hand, and friendly shores in the distance.

The unfortunate Pollux also awoke towards morning with sighs many and deep, for it seemed to him that last evening he had ruined his whole future prospects. The workshop of his former master was henceforth closed to him, and he no longer possessed even all the tools requisite for the exercise of his art.

Only yesterday he had hoped with happy confidence to establish himself on a footing of his own, to-day this seemed impossible, for the most indispensable means were lacking to him. As he felt his little money-bag, which he was wont to place under his pillow, he could not forbear smiling in spite of all his troubles, for his fingers sank into the flaccid leather, and found only two coins, one of which he knew alas! was of copper, and the dried merry-thought bone of a fowl, which he had saved to give to his little nieces.

Where was he to find the money he was accustomed to give his sister on the first day of every month? Papias was on friendly terms with all the sculptors of the city, and it was only to be expected that he would warn them against him, and do his best to make it difficult to him to find a new place as assistant. His old master had also been witness of Hadrian's anger against him, and was quite the man to take every advantage of what he had overheard. It is never a recommendation for any one that he is an object of dislike to the powerful, and least of all does it help him with those who look for the favor and gifts of the great men of the world. When Hadrian should think proper to throw off his disguise, it might easily occur to him to let Pollux feel the effects of his power. Would it not be wise in him to quit Alexandria and seek work or daily bread in some other Greek city?

But for Arsinoe's sake he could not turn his back on his native place. He loved her with all the passion of his artist's soul, and his youthful courage would certainly not have been so quickly and utterly crushed if he could have deluded himself as to the fact that his hopes of possessing her had been driven into the remote background by the events of the preceding evening. How could he dare to drag her into his uncertain and compromised position? And what reception could he hope for from her father if he should now attempt to demand her for his wife. As these thoughts overpowered his mind he

suddenly felt as if his eyes were smarting with sand that
had blown into them, and he could not help springing
out of bed ; he paced his little room with long steps, and
he held his forehead pressed against the wall.

The dawn of a new day appeared as a welcome
comfort, and by the time he had eaten the morning porridge which his mother set before him—and her eyes
were red with weeping—the idea struck him that he
would go to Pontius, the architect. That was the life-
boat he espied.

Doris shared her son's breakfast but, contrary to her
usual custom, she spoke very little, only she frequently
passed her hand over her son's curly hair. Euphorion
strode up and down the room, rummaging his brain for
ideas for an ode in which he might address the Emperor
and implore forgiveness for his son. Soon after breakfast Pollux went up to the rotunda where the Queens'
busts stood, hoping to see Arsinoe again, and a loud
snatch of song soon brought her out on to the balcony.
They exchanged greetings, and Pollux signed to her to
come down to him. She would have obeyed him more
than gladly, but her father had also heard the sculptor's
voice and drove her back into the room. Still the mere
sight of his beloved fair one had done the artist good.

Hardly had he got back to his father's little house
when Antinous came sauntering in—he represented in
the artist's mind the hospitable shores on which he might
gaze. Hope revived his soul, and Hope is the sun before which despair flies as the shades of night flee at the
rising of the day-star.

His artistic faculties were once more roused into
play, and found a field for their freest exercise when Antinous told him that he was at his disposal till mid-day,

since his master—or rather Caesar as he was now permitted to name him—was engaged in business. The prefect Titianus had come to him with a whole heap of papers, to work with him and his private secretary. Pollux at once led the favorite into a side room of the little house, with a northern aspect; here on a table lay the wax and the smaller implements which belonged to himself and which he had brought home last evening. His heart ached, and his nerves were in a painful state of tension as he began his work. All sorts of anxious thoughts disturbed his spirit, and yet he knew that if he put his whole soul into it he could do something good. Now, if ever, he must put forth his best powers, and he dreaded failure as an utter catastrophe, for on the face of the whole earth there was no second model to compare with this that stood before him.

But he did not take long to collect himself for the Bithynian's beauty filled him with profound feeling and it was with a sort of pious exaltation that he grasped the plastic material and moulded it into a form resembling his sitter. For a whole hour not a word passed between them, but Pollux often sighed deeply and now then a groan of painful anxiety escaped him.

Antinous broke the silence to ask Pollux about Selene. His heart was full of her, and there was no other man who knew her, and whom he could venture to entrust with his secret. Indeed it was only to speak to her that he had come to the artist so early. While Pollux modelled and scraped Antinous told him of all that had happened the previous night. He lamented having lost the silver quiver when he was upset into the water and regretted that the rose-colored chiton should afterwards have suffered a reduction in length at the hands of his pursuer. An exclamation of surprise, a word of sympathy, a short pause in the movement of his hand and tool, were all the demonstration on the artist's part, to which the story of Selene's adventure and the loss of his master's costly property gave rise ; his whole attention was absorbed in his occupation. The farther his work progressed the higher rose his admiration for his model. He felt as if intoxicated with noble wine as he worked to reproduce this incarnation of the ideal of umblemished youthful and manly beauty. The passion of artistic procreation fired his blood, and threw every thing else— even the history of Selene's fall into the sea, and her subsequent rescue—into the region of commonplace. Still he had not been inattentive, and what he heard must have had some effect in his mind; for long after Antinous had ended his narrative, he said in a low voice and as if speaking to the bust, which was already assuming definite form :

"It is a wonderful thing!" and again a little later; "There was always something grand in that unhappy creature."

He had worked without interruption for nearly four hours, when standing back from the table, he looked anxiously, first at his work and then at Antinous, and then asked him :

"How will that do ?"

The Bithynian gave eager expression to his approbation, and Pollux had, in fact, done wonders in the short time. The wax began to display in a much reduced scale the whole figure of the beautiful youth and in the very same attitude which the young Dionysus carried off by the pirates, had assumed the day before. The incomparable modelling of the favorite's limbs and form was soft but not effeminate ; and, as Pollux had said to himself the day before, no artist in his happiest mood, could conceive the Nysaean god as different from this.

While the sculptor in order to assure himself of the accuracy of his work was measuring his model's limbs with wooden compasses and lengths of tape, the sound of chariot-wheels was heard at the gate of the palace, and soon after the yelping of the Graces. Doris called to the dogs to be quiet and another high-pitched woman's voice mingled with hers. Antinous listened and what he heard seemed to be somewhat out of the common for he suddenly quitted the position in which the sculptor had placed him only a few minutes before, ran to the window and called to Pollux in a subdued voice:

"It is true ! I am not mistaken ! There is Hadrian's wife Sabina talking out there to your mother."

He had heard rightly ; the Empress had come to Lochias to seek out her husband. She had got out of the chariot at the gate of the old palace for the paving of the court-yard would not be completed before that evening.

Dogs, of which her husband was so fond, she detested ; the shrewd beasts returned her aversion, so dame Doris found it more difficult than usual to succeed in reducing her disobedient pets to silence when they flew viciously at the stranger. Sabina terrified, vehemently desired the old woman to release her from their persecution, while the chamberlain who had come with her and on whom she was leaning kicked out at the irrepressible little wretches and so increased their spite. At last the Graces withdrew into the house. Dame Doris drew a deep breath and turned to the Empress.

She did not suspect who the stranger was for she had

never seen Sabina and had formed quite a different idea of her.

" Pardon me good lady," she said in her frank confiding manner. " The little rascals mean no harm and never bite even a beggar, but they never could endure old women. Whom do you seek here mother ?"

" That you shall soon know," replied Sabina sharply. " What a state of things, Lentulus, your architect Pontius' work has brought about. And what must the inside be like if this hut is left standing to disgrace the entrance of the palace! It must go with its inhabitants. —Desire that woman to conduct us to the Roman lord who dwells here."

The chamberlain obeyed and Doris began to suspect who was standing before her, and she said as she smoothed down her dress and bowed low :

" What great honor befalls us illustrious lady ; perhaps you are even the Emperor's wife ? If that be the case—"

Sabina made an impatient sign to the chamberlain who interrupted the old woman exclaiming :

" Be silent and show us the way."

Doris was not feeling particularly strong that day, and her eyes already red with weeping about her son again filled with tears. No one had ever spoken so to her before, and yet, for her son's sake she would not repay sharp words in the same coin, though she had plenty at her command.

She tottered on in front of Sabina, and conducted her to the hall of the Muses. There Pontius relieved her of the duty, and the respect he paid to the stranger made her sure that in fact she was none other than the Empress in person.

28

" An odious woman !" said Sabina, as she went on pointing to Doris, whom her words could not escape.

This was too much for the old woman ; past all self-control she flung herself on to a seat that was standing by, covered her face with her hands and began crying bitterly. She felt as if the very ground were snatched from under her feet.

Her son was in disgrace with Caesar, and she and her house were threatened by the most powerful woman in the world. She pictured herself as already turned into the streets with Euphorion and her dogs, and asked herself what was to become of them all when they had lost their place and the roof that covered them. Her husband's memory grew daily weaker, soon his voice even might fail ; and how greatly had her own strength failed during the last few years, how small were the savings that were hidden in their chest. The bright, genial old woman felt quite broken down. What hurt her was, not merely the pressing need that threatened her, but the disgrace too which would fall upon her, the dislike she had incurred—she who had been liked by every one from her youth up—and the painful feeling of having been treated with scorn and contempt in the presence of others by the powerful lady whose favor she had hoped to win.

At Sabina's advent all good spirits had fled from Lochias, so at least Doris felt, but she was not one of those who succumb helplessly to a hostile force. For a few minutes she abandoned herself to her sorrows and sobbed like a child. Now she dried her eyes, and her eased heart felt the beneficial relief of tears ; by degrees she could compose herself and think calmly.

" After all," said she to herself, " none but Caesar can

command here, and it is said that he gets on but badly
with his spiteful wife, and cares very little what she
wishes.   Hadrian let Pollux feel his power, but he has
always been friendly to me.   My dogs and birds amused
him, and did he not even do me the honor to relish a
dish out of my kitchen ?   No, no, if only I can succeed
in speaking with him alone all may yet be well," and
thus thinking she rose from her seat.

As she was about to quit the anteroom the art-
dealer, Gabinius, of Nicaea, came in, to whom Keraunus
had refused to sell the mosaic in the palace, and whose
daughter had been deprived by Arsinoe of the part of
Roxana.   Pontius had desired him to come to the palace
and he had made his appearance at once, for, since the
evening before, a rumor had been afloat that the Emperor was staying in Alexandria, and was inhabiting
the palace at Lochias.   Whence it was derived, or on
what facts it was supported no one could say.; but there
it was, passing from mouth to mouth in every circle and
acquiring certainty every hour.   Of all that grows on
earth nothing grows so quickly as Rumor, and yet it is a
miserable foundling that never knows its own parents.

The dealer pushed on into the palace with a glance
of astonishment at the old woman, while Doris debated
whether see should seek Hadrian then and there, or return to her little gate-house, and wait till he should at
some time be going out of the palace and passing by her
dwelling.   Before she could come to any decision Pontius appeared on the scene; he had always been very
kind to her, and she therefore ventured to address him
and tell him what had occurred between her son
and the Emperor.   This was no novelty to the architect; he advised her to have patience till Hadrian

28

should have cooled, and he promised her that later he
would do every thing in his power for Pollux, whom he
loved and esteemed.   On this very day he was obliged
by Caesar's command to start on a journey and for a
long absence ; his destination was Pelusium, where he
was to erect a monument to .the great Pompey on the
spot where he had been murdered.   Hadrian, as he
passed the old ruined monument on his way from
Mount Kasius to Egypt, had determined to replace it
by a new one, and had entrusted the work to Pontius
whose labors at Lochias were now nearly ended.   All
that might yet be lacking to the fitting of the restored
palace Hadrian himself wished to select and procure,
and in this occupation so agreeable to his tastes, Gabinius, the curiosity-dealer, was to lend him a helping
hand.

While Doris was still speaking with Pontius, Hadrian and his wife came towards the anteroom.   Hardly
had the architect recognized the tones of Sabina's voice,
than he hastily said in a low voice :

" Till by-and-bye this must do, dame.   Stand aside;
Caesar and the Empress are coming."

And he hastened away.   Doris slipped into the door-
way of a side room, which was closed only by a heavy
curtain, for at that moment she would as soon have met
a raging wild beast as the haughty lady from whom
she had nothing to expect but insult and unkindness.

Hadrian's interview with his wife had lasted barely a
quarter of an hour, and it must have been anything
rather than amiable, for his face was scarlet, while Sabina's lips were perfectly white, and her painted cheeks
twitched with a restless movement.   Doris was too
much excited and terrified to listen to the royal couple,

still she overheard these words uttered by the Emperoı
in a tone of the utmost decision.

"In small matters and where it is fitting I let you
have your way; more important things I shall this time,
as always, decide by my own judgment—my own exclusively."

These words were fraught with the fate of the gate-
house and its inhabitants, for the removal of the "hideous hut" at the entrance of the palace was one of the
"small matters" of which Hadrian spoke. Sabina had
required this concession, since it could not be pleasant
to any one visiting Lochias to be received on the threshold by an old Megaera of evil omen, and to be fallen
upon by infuriated dogs. But Doris so little divined
the import of Hadrian's words that she rejoiced at them,
for they told her how little he was disposed to yield to
his wife in important things, and how could she suspect
that her fate and that of her house should not be included among important matters, nay the most important?

Sabina had quitted the anteroom leaning on her
chamberlain and Hadrian was standing there alone with
his slave Mastor. The old woman would not be likely
to have another such favorable opportunity of supplicating the all-powerful man who stood before her, without the hindrance of witnesses, to exercise his magna-
nimity and clemency towards her son. His back turned
to her; if she could have seen the threatening scowl
with which he stood gazing on the ground she would
surely have remembered the architect's warning and
have postponed her address till a future day.

How often do we spoil our best chances by following an urgent instinct to arrive at certainty as early as

possible, and by not being strong enough to postpone
opening our business till a favorable moment offers
Uncertainty in the present often seems less endurable
than adverse fate in the future.

Doris stepped out of the side door. Mastor, who
knew his master well, and whose friendly impulse was to
spare the old woman any humiliation, made eager signs
to warn her to withdraw and not to disturb Hadrian at
that moment; but she was so wholly possessed by her
anxiety and wishes that she did not observe them. As
the Emperor turned to leave the room she gathered
courage, stood in the doorway through which he must
pass, and tried to fall on her knees before him. This
was a difficult effort to her old joints and Doris was
forced to clutch at the door-post in order not to lose her
balance.

Hadrian at once recognized the suppliant, but to-day
he found no kind word for her; and the glance he cast
down at her was anything rather than gracious. How
had he ever been able to find amusement even in this
woeful old body? Alas! poor Doris was quite a different creature in her little house, among her flowers, dogs
and birds to what she seemed here in the spacious hall
of a magnificent palace. This wide and gorgeous frame
but ill-suited so modest a figure. Thousands of good
people who in the midst of their everyday surroundings
command our esteem and attract our regard give rise to
very different feelings when they are taken out of the
circle to which they belong.

Doris had never worn so unpleasing an aspect to
Hadrian as at this instant, in this decisive moment of
her life. She had followed the Empress straight from
the kitchen-hearth just as she was after passing a sleep-

less night and full of her many anxieties, she had scarcely set her grey hair in order, and her kind bright eyes, usually the best feature of her face, were red with many tears. The neat brisk little mother looked to-day anything rather than smart and bright; in the Emperor's eyes she was in no way distinguished from any other old woman, and he regarded all old women as of evil omen, if he met them as he went out of any place he was in.

"Oh, Cæsar, Great Caesar!" cried Doris throwing up her hands which still bore many traces of her labors over the hearth. "My son, my unfortunate Pollux!"

"Out of my way!" said Hadrian sternly.

"He is an artist, a good artist, who already excels many a master, and if the gods—"

"Out of the way, I told you. I do not want to hear anything about the insolent fellow," said Hadrian angrily.

"But Great Caesar, he is my son, and a mother, as you know—"

"Mastor," interrupted the monarch, "carry away this old woman and make way for me."

"Oh! my lord, my lord!" wailed the agonized woman while the slave pulled her up, not without difficulty. "Oh! my lord, how can you find it in your heart to be so cruel? And am I no longer old Doris whom you have even joked with, and whose food you have eaten?"

These words recalled to the Emperor's fancy the moment of his arrival at Lochias; he felt that he was somewhat in the old woman's debt, and being wont to pay with royal liberality he broke in with:

"You shall be paid for your excellent dish a sum with which you can purchase a new house, for the future your maintenance too shall be provided for, but in three hours you must have quitted Lochias."

The Emperor spoke rapidly as though desirous of bringing a disagreeable business to a prompt termination, and he stalked past Doris who was now standing on her feet and leaning as if stunned against the doorpost.   Indeed if Hadrian had not left her there and had he been in the mood to hear her farther, she was not now in a fit state to answer him another word.

The Emperor received the honors due to Zeus and his fiat had ruined the happiness of a contented home as completely as the thunderbolt wielded by the Father of the gods could have done.

But this time Doris had no tears.   The frightful shock that had fallen in her soul was perceptible also to her body; her knees shook, and being quite incapable just then of going home at once, she sunk upon a seat and stared hopelessly before her while she reflected what next, and what more would come upon her.

Meanwhile the Emperor was standing in a room just behind the antechamber that had only been finished a few hours since.   He began to regret his hardness upon the old woman—for had she not, without knowing who he was, been most friendly to him and to his favorite.

" Where is Antinous ? " he asked Mastor.

" He went out to the gate-house."

" What is he doing there ? "

" I believe he meant—there, perhaps he—"

" The truth, fellow ! "

" He is with Pollux the sculptor."

" Has he been there long ? "

"I do not exactly know."

" How long, I ask you ? "

"He went after you had shut yourself in with Titianus."

"Three hours—three whole hours has he been with that braggart, whom I ordered off the premises!"

Hadrian's eye sparkled wrathfully as he spoke. His annoyance at the absence of his favorite, whose society he permitted no one to enjoy but himself, and least of all Pollux, smothered every kind feeling in his mind, and in a tone of anger bordering on fury he commanded Mastor to go and fetch Antinous, and then to have the gate-house utterly cleared out.

"Take a dozen slaves to help you," he cried. "For aught I care the people may carry all their rubbish into a new house, but I will never set eyes again on that howling old woman, nor her imbecile husband. As for the sculptor I will make him feel that Caesar has a heavy foot and can unexpectedly crush a snake that creeps across his path."

Mastor went sadly away and Hadrian returned to his work-room, and there called out to his secretary Phlegon:

"Write that a new gate-keeper is to be found for this palace. Euphorion, the old one, is to have his pay continued to him, and half a talent is to be paid to him at the prefect's office. Good—Let the man have at once whatever is necessary; in an hour neither he nor his are to be found in Lochias. Henceforth no one is to mention them to me again, nor to bring me any petition from them. Their whole race may join the rest of the dead."

Phlegon bowed and said:

"Gabinius, the curiosity-dealer, waits outside."

"He comes at an appropriate moment," cried the

Emperor.   " After all these vexations it will do me good
to hear about beautiful things."

CHAPTER IX.

AYE, truly! Sabina's advent had chased all good
spirits from the palace at Lochias.

The Emperor's commands had come upon the peaceful little house as a whirlwind comes on a heap of leaves.
The inhabitants were not even allowed time fully to realize their misfortune, for instead of bewailing themselves
all they could do was to act with circumspection.   The
tables, seats, cushions, beds and lutes, the baskets, plants,
and bird-cages, the kitchen utensils and the trunks with
their clothes were all piled in confusion in the court-
yard, and Doris was employing the slaves appointed by
Mastor in the task of emptying the house, as briskly
and carefully as though it was nothing more than a move
from one house to another.   A ray of the sunny brightness of her nature once more sparkled in her eyes since
she had been able to say to herself that all that happened to her and hers was one of the things inevitable,
and that it was more to the purpose to think of the
future than of the past.   The old woman was quite herself again over the work, and as she looked at Euphorion,
who sat quite crushed on his couch with his eyes fixed
on the ground, she cried out to him :

" After bad times, come good ones! only let us keep
from making ourselves miserable.   We have done nothing wrong, and so long as we do not think ourselves
wretched, we are not so.   Only, hold up your head!

Up, old man, up! Go at once to Diotima and tell her that we beg her to give us hospitality for a few days, and house-room for our chattels."

"And if Caesar does not keep his word?" asked Euphorion gloomily. "What sort of a life shall we live then?"

"A bad one—a dog's life; and for that very reason it is wiser to enjoy now what we still possess. A cup of wine, Pollux, for me and your father. But there must be no water in it to-day."

"I cannot drink," sighed Euphorion.

"Then I will drink your share and my own too."

"Nay—nay, mother," remonstrated Pollux.

"Well put some water in, lad, just a little water, only do not make such a pitiful face. Is that the way a young fellow should look who has his art, and plenty of strength in his hands, and the sweetest of sweethearts in his heart?"

"It is certainly not for myself, mother," retorted the sculptor, "that I am anxious. But how am I ever to get into the palace again to see Arsinoe, and how am I to deal with that ferocious old Keraunus?"

"Leave that question for time to answer," replied Doris.

"Time may give a good answer, but it may also give a bad one."

"And the best she only gives to those who wait for her in the antechamber of Patience."

"A bad place for me, and for those like me," sighed Pollux.

"You have only to sit still and go on knocking at the doors," replied Doris, "and before you can look round you Time will call out, 'come in.' Now show

the men how they are to treat the statue of Apollo, and
be my own happy, bright boy once more."

Pollux did as she desired, thinking as he went:
" She speaks wisely—she is not leaving Arsinoe behind.
If only I had been able to arrange with Antinous at
least, where I should find him again; but at Caesar's
orders the young fellow was like one stunned, and he
tottered as he went, as if he were going to execution."

Dame Doris had not been betrayed by her happy
confidence, for Phlegon the secretary came to inform
her of the Emperor's purpose to give her husband half a
talent, and to continue to pay him in the future his little
salary.

" You see," cried the old woman, " the sun of better
days is already rising.   Half a talent! Why poverty has
nothing to do with such rich folks as we are!   What do
you think—would it not be right to pour out half a cup
of wine to the gods, and allow ourselves the other half ?"

Doris was as gay as if she were going to a wedding,
and her cheerfulness communicated itself to her son,
who saw himself relieved of part of the anxiety that
weighed upon him with regard to his parents and sister.
His drooping courage, and spirit for life, only needed
a few drops of kindly dew to revive it, and he once more
began to think of his art.   Before anything else he
would try to complete his successfully-sketched bust of
Antinous.

While he was gone back into the house to preserve
his work from injury and was giving the slaves, whom he
had desired to follow him, instructions as to how it
should be carried so as not to damage it, his master Papias came into the palace-court.   He had come to put
the last touches to the works he had begun, and proposed

to make a fresh attempt to win the favor of the man whom he now knew to be the Emperor. Papias was somewhat uneasy for he was alarmed at the thought that Pollux might now betray how small a share his master had in his last works—which had brought him higher praise than all he had done previously. It might even have been wise on his part to pocket his pride and to induce his former scholar, by lavish promises, to return to his workshop; but the evening before he had been betrayed into speaking before the Emperor with so much indignation at the young artist's evil disposition, of his delight at being rid of him, that, on Hadrian's account, he must give up that idea. Nothing was now to be done, but to procure the removal of Pollux from Alexandria, or to render him in some way incapable of damaging him, and this he might perhaps be able to do by the instrumentality of the wrathful Emperor.

It even came into his mind to hire some Egyptian rascal to have him assassinated; but he was a citizen of peaceful habits, to whom a breach of the law was an abomination and he cast the thought from him as too horrible and base. He was not over-nice in his choice of means, he knew men, was very capable of finding his way up the backstairs, and did not hesitate when need arose to calumniate others boldly, and thus he had before now won the day in many a battle against his fellow-artists of distinction. His hope of succeeding in the tripping of a scholar of no great repute, and of rendering him harmless so long as the Emperor should remain in Alexandria, was certainly not an over-bold one. He hated the gate-keeper's son far less than he feared him, and he did not conceal from himself that if his attack on Pollux should fail and the young fellow should suc-

ceed in proving independently of what ne was capabl.
he could do nothing to prevent his loudly proclaiming
all that he had done in these last years for his master.

His attention was caught by the slaves in Euphorion's
little house, who were carrying the household chattels of
the evicted family into the street. He had soon learnt what
was going forward, and highly pleased at the ill-will manifested by Hadrian towards the parents of his foe, he
stood looking on, and after brief reflection desired a
negro to call Pollux to speak to him.

The master and scholar exchanged greetings with a
show of haughty coolness and Papias said :

"You forgot to bring back the things which yesterday, without asking my leave, you took out of my
wardrobe. I must have them back to-day."

"I did not take them for myself, but for the grand
lord in there, and his companion. If any thing is missing apply to him. It grieves me that I should have
taken your silver quiver among them, for the Roman's
companion has lost it. As soon as I have done here, I
will take home all of your things that I can recover, and
bring away my own. A good many things belonging
to me are still lying in your workshop."

"Good," replied Papias. "I will expect you an
hour before sunset, and then we will settle every thing,"
and without any farewell he turned his back on his
pupil and went into the palace.

Pollux had told him that some of the properties,
which he had taken without asking permission, had been
lost—among them an object of considerable value—and
this perhaps would give him a hold over him by which
to prevent his injuring him. He remained in the palace
scarcely half an hour and then, while Pollux was still

engaged in escorting his mother and their household goods to his sister's house, he went to visit the night magistrate, who presided over the safety of Alexandria. Papias was on intimate terms with this important official, for he had constructed for him a sarcophagus for his deceased wife, an altar with panels in relief for his men's apartment, and other works, at moderate prices, and he could count on his readiness to serve him. When he quitted him he carried in his hand an order of arrest against his assistant Pollux, who had attacked his property and abstracted a quiver of massive silver. The magistrate had also promised him to send two of his guards who would carry the offender off to prison.

Papias went home with a much lighter heart. His pupil, after he had accomplished the easy transfer of his parents, had returned to the palace, and there, to his delight, came across Mastor, who soon fetched him the garments and masks that he had lent the day before to Hadrian and Antinous. The Sarmatian at the same time told him, with tears in his eyes, a sad, very sad story, which stirred the young sculptor's soul deeply, and which would have prompted him to penetrate into the palace at once, and at any risk, if he had not seen the necessity of being with Papias at the appointed hour, which was drawing near, to answer for the valuable property that was missing. Thinking of nothing, wishing nothing so much as to be back as promptly as possible at Lochias, where he was much needed, and where his heart longed to be, he took the bundle out of the slave's hand and hurried away. Papias had sent all his assistants and even his slaves off the premises; he received the breathless Pollux quite alone, and took from him, with icy calmness, the things which had been borrowed from his property-room, asking for them one by one.

"I have already told you," cried Pollux, "that it is not I, but the illustrious Roman—you know as well as I do, who he is—who is answerable for the silver quiver and the torn chiton." And he began to tell him how Antinous had commanded him, in the name of his master, to find masks and disguises for them both. But Papias cut off his speech at the very beginning, and vehemently demanded the restoration of his quiver and bow, of which Pollux could not work out the value in two years. The young man whose heart and thoughts were at Lochias and who, at any cost, did not want to be detained longer than was necessary, begged his master, with all possible politeness, to let him go now, and to settle the matter with him to-morrow after he had discussed it with the Roman, from whom he might certainly demand any compensation he chose. But when Papias interrupted him again and again, and obstinately insisted on the immediate restoration of his property, the artist whose blood was easily heated, grew angry and replied to the attacks and questions of the older man with vehement response.

One angry word led to another, and at last Papias hinted of persons who took possession of other person's silver goods, and when Pollux retorted that he knew of some who could put forward the works of others as their own, the master struck his fist upon the table, and going towards the door he cried out, as soon as he was at a safe distance from the furious lad's powerful fists:

"Thief! I will show you how fellows like you are dealt with in Alexandria."

Pollux turned white with rage, and rushed upon

Papias, who fled, and before Pollux could reach him he had taken refuge behind the two guards sent by the magistrate, and who were waiting in the antechamber.

"Seize the thief!" he cried. "Hold the villain who stole my silver quiver and now raises his hand against his master. Bind him, fetter him, carry him off to prison."

Pollux did not know what had come upon him; he stood like a bear that has been surrounded by hunters; doubtful but at bay. Should he fling himself upon his pursuers and fell them to the earth? should he passively await impending fate?

He knew every stone in his master's house; the anteroom in which he stood, and indeed the whole building was on the ground floor. In the minute while the guards were approaching and his master was giving the order to the lictor, his eye fell on a window which looked out upon the street, and possessed only by the single thought of defending his liberty and returning quickly to Arsinoe he leaped out of the opening which promised safety and into the street below.

"Thief—stop thief!" he heard as he flew on with long strides; and like the pelting of rain driven by all the four winds came from all sides the senseless, odious, horrible cry: "Stop thief!—stop thief!" it seemed to deprive him of his senses.

But the passionate cry of his heart: "To Lochias, to Arsinoe! keep free, save your liberty if only to be of use at Lochias!" drowned the shouts of his pursuers and urged him through the streets that led to the old palace.

On he went faster and farther, each step a leap; the briny breeze from the sea already fanned his glowing cheeks and the narrow empty street yonder he well

29

knew led to the quay by the King's harbor, where he could hide from his pursuers among the tall piles of wood. He was just turning the corner into the alley when an Egyptian ox-driver threw his goad between his legs; he stumbled, fell to the ground, and instantly felt that a dog which had rushed upon him was tearing the chiton he wore, while he was seized by a number of men. An hour later and he found himself in prison, bitten, beaten, and bound among a crew of malefactors and real thieves.

Night had fallen. His parents were waiting for him and he came not; and in Lochias which he had not been able to reach there were misery and trouble enough, and the only person in the world who could carry comfort to Arsinoe in her despair was absent and nowhere to be found.

CHAPTER X.

THE story told by Mastor which had so greatly agitated Pollux and had prompted him to his mad flight was the history of events which had taken place in the steward's rooms during the hours when the young artist was helping his parents to transfer their household belongings into his sister's tiny dwelling. Keraunus was certainly not one of the most cheerful of men, but on the morning when Sabina came to the palace and the gate-keeper was driven from his home, he had worn the aspect of a thoroughly-contented man.

Since visiting Selene the day before he had given himself no farther concern about her. She was not dangerously ill and was exceptionally well taken care of, and the children did not seem to miss her. Indeed, he himself did not want her back to-day. He avoided confessing this to himself it is true, still he felt lighter and freer in the absence of his grave monitor than he had been for a long time. It would be delightful, he thought, to go on living in this careless manner, alone with Arsinoe and the children, and now and again he rubbed his hands and grinned complacently. When the old slave-woman brought a large dish full of cakes which he had desired her to buy, and set it down by the side of the children's porridge, he chuckled so heartily that his fat person shook and swayed; and he had very good reason to be happy in his way, for Plutarch quite early in the morning, had sent a heavy purse of gold pieces for his ivory cup, and a magnificent bunch of roses to Arsinoe; he might give his children a treat, buy himself a solid gold fillet, and dress Arsinoe as finely as though she were the prefect's favorite daughter.

His vanity was gratified in every particular.

And what a splendid fellow was the slave who now —with a superbly reverential bow—presented him with a roast chicken and who was to walk behind him in the afternoon to the council-chamber. The tall Thessalian who marched after the Archidikastes to the Hall of Justice, carrying his papers, was hardly grander than his "body-servant." He had bought him yesterday at quite a low price. The well-grown Samian was scarcely thirty years old; he could read and write and was in a position therefore to instruct the children in these arts; nay, he could even play the lute. His past, to be sure, was not a spotless record, and it was for that reason that he had been sold so cheaply. He had stolen things

29

on several occasions; but the brands and scars which
he bore upon his person were hidden by his new chiton
and Keraunus felt in himself the power to cure him of
his evil propensities.

After desiring Arsinoe to let nothing lie about of any
value, for their new house-mate seemed not to be perfectly honest, he answered his daughter's scruples by
saying:

"It would be better, no doubt, that he should be as
honest as the old skeleton I gave in exchange for him,
but I reflect that even if my body-servant should make
away with some of the few drachmae we carry about
with us, I need not repent of having bought him, since
I got him for many thousand drachmae less than he is
worth, on account of his thefts, while a teacher for the
children would have cost more than he can steal from
us at the worst. I will lock up the gold in the chest
with my documents. It is strong and could only be
opened with a crow-bar. Besides the fellow will have
left off stealing at any rate at first, for his late master
was none of the mildest and had cured him of his pilfer-
ing I should think, once for all. It is lucky that in sell-
ing such rascals we should be compelled to state what
their faults are; if the seller fails to do so compensation
may be claimed from him by the next owner for what
he may lose. Lykophron certainly concealed nothing,
and setting aside his thieving propensities the Samian is
said to be in every respect a capital fellow."

"But father," replied Arsinoe, her anxiety once more
urging her to speak, "it is a bad thing to have a dishonest man in the house."

"You know nothing about it child!" answered Keraunus. "To us to live and to be honest are the same

thing, but a slave!—King Antiochus is said to have de
clared that the man who wishes to be well served must
employ none but rascals."

When Arsinoe had been tempted out on to the balcony by her lover's snatch of song and had been driven
in again by her father, the steward had not reproved her
in any way unkindly, but had stroked her cheeks and
said with a smile: "I rather fancy that lad of the gate-
keeper's—whom I once turned out of doors has had his
eye on you since you were chosen for Roxana. Poor
wretch! But we have very different suitors in view for
you my little girl. How would it be, think you, if rich
Plutarch had sent you those roses, not on his own behalf
but as a greeting on the part of his son? I know that
he is very desirous of marrying him but the fastidious
man has never yet thought any Alexandrian girl good
enough for him."

"I do not know him, and he does not think of a
poor thing like me," said Arsinoe.

"Do you think not?" asked Keraunus smiling. "We
are of as good family, nay of a better than Plutarch, and
the fairest is a match for the wealthiest. What would
you say child to a long flowing purple robe and a chariot
with white horses, and runners in front?"

At breakfast Keraunus drank two cups of strong
wine, in which he allowed Arsinoe to mix only a few
drops of water. While his daughter was curling his hair
a swallow flew into the room; this was a good omen
and raised the steward's spirits. Dressed in his best and
with a well-filled purse, he was on the point of starting
for the council-chamber with his new slave when Sophilus the tailor and his girl-assistant were shown into the
living-room. The man begged to be allowed to try the

dress, ordered for Roxana by the prefect's wife, on the steward's daughter. Keraunus received him with much condescension and allowed him to bring in the slave who followed him with a large parcel of dresses,—and Arsinoe, who was with the children, was called.

Arsinoe was embarrassed and anxious and would far rather have yielded her part to another; still, she was curious about the new dresses. The tailor begged her to allow her maid to dress her; his assistant would help her because the dresses which were only slightly stitched together for trying on, were cut, not in the Greek but in the Oriental fashion.

"Your waiting woman," he added turning to Arsinoe, "will be able to learn to-day the way to dress you on the great occasion."

"My daughter's maid," said Keraunus, winking slily at Arsinoe, "is not in the house."

"Oh, I require no help," cried the tailor's girl. "I am handy too at dressing hair, and I am most glad to help such a fair Roxana."

"And it is a real pleasure to work for her," added Sophilus. "Other young ladies are beautified by what they wear, but your daughter adds beauty to all she wears."

"You are most polite," said Keraunus, as Arsinoe and her handmaid left the room.

"We learn a great deal by our intercourse with people of rank," replied the tailor. "The illustrious ladies who honor me with their custom like not only to see but to hear what is pleasing. Unfortunately there are among them some whom the gods have graced with but few charms, and they, strangely enough, crave the most flattering speeches. But the poor always value it more than the rich when benevolence is shown them."

"Well said," cried Keraunus. "I myself am but indifferently well off for a man of family, and am glad to live within my moderate means—so that my daughter—"

"The lady Julia has chosen the costliest stuffs for her; as is fitting—as the occasion demands," said the tailor.

"Quite right, at the same time—"

"Well, my lord?"

"The grand occasion will be over and my daughter, now that she is grown up, ought to be seen at home and in the street in suitable and handsome, though not costly, clothes.

"I said just now, true beauty needs no gaudy raiment."

"Would you be disposed now, to work for me at a moderate price?"

"With pleasure; nay, I shall be indebted to her, for all the world will admire Roxana and inquire who may be her tailor."

"You are a very reasonable and right-minded man. What now would you charge for a dress for her?"

"That we can discuss later."

"No, no, I beg you sincerely—"

"First let me consider what you want. Simple dresses are more difficult, far more difficult to make, and yet become a handsome woman better than rich and gaudy robes! But can any man make a woman understand it? I could tell you a tale of their folly! Why many a woman who rides by in her chariot wears dresses and gems to conceal not merely her own limbs, but the poverty-stricken condition of her house."

Thus, and in this wise did Keraunus and the tailor converse, while the assistant plaited up Arsinoe's hair with strings of false pearls that she had brought with her, and fitted and pinned on her the costly white and blue silk robes of an Asiatic princess. At first Arsinoe was very still and timid. She no longer cared to dress for any one but Pollux; but the garments prepared for her were wonderfully pretty—and how well the fitter knew how to give effect to her natural advantages. While the neat-handed woman worked busily and carefully many merry jests passed between them—many sincere and hearty words of admiration—and before long Arsinoe had become quite excited and took pleased interest in the needle-woman's labors.

Every bough that is freshly decked by spring seems to feel gladness, and the simple child who was to-day so splendidly dressed was captivated by pleasure in her own beauty, and its costly adornment which delighted her beyond measure. Arsinoe now clapped her hands with delight, now had the mirror handed to her, and now, with all the frankness of a child, expressed her satisfaction not only with the costly clothes she wore, but with her own surprisingly grand appearance in them.

The dress-maker was enchanted with her, proud and delighted, and could not resist the impulse to give a kiss to the charming girl's white, beautifully round throat.

"If only Pollux could see me so!" thought Arsinoe. "After the performance perhaps I might show myself in my dress to Selene, and then she would forgive my taking part in the show. It is really a pleasure to look so nice!"

The children all stood round her while she was

being dressed, and shouted with admiration each time some new detail of the princess's attire was added. Helios begged to be allowed to feel her dress, and after satisfying herself that his little hands were clean she stroked them over the glistening white silk.

She had now advanced so far that her father and the tailor could be called in. She felt remarkably content and happy. Drawn up to her tallest, like a real king's daughter, and yet with a heart beating as anxiously as that of any girl would who is on the point of displaying her beauty—hitherto protected and hidden in her parents' home—to the thousand eyes of the gaping multitude, she went towards the sitting-room; but she drew back her hand she had put forth to raise the latch, for she heard the voices of several men who must just now have joined her father.

" Wait a littte while, there are visitors," she cried to the seamstress who had followed her, and she put her ear to the door to listen. At first she could not make out anything that was going on, but the end of the strange conversation that was being carried on within was so hideously intelligible that she could never forget it so long as she lived.

Her father had ordered two new dresses for her, beating down the price with the promise of prompt pay· ment, when Mastor came into the steward's room and informed Keraunus that his master and Gabinius, the curiosity-dealer from Nicaea, wished to speak with him.

" Your master," said Keraunus haughtily, " may come in; I think that he regrets the injury he has done me; but Gabinius shall never cross this threshold again, for he is a scoundrel."

" It would be as well that you should desire that

man to leave you for the present," said the slave, pointing to the tailor.

"Whoever comes to visit me," said the steward
loftily, "must be satisfied to meet any one whom I permit
to enter my house."

"Nay, nay," said the slave urgently, "my master
is a greater man than you think. Beg this man to leave
the room."

"I know, I know very well," said Keraunus with a
smile. "Your master is an acquaintance of Caesar's. But
we shall see, after the performance that is about to take
place, which of us two Caesar will decide for. This
tailor has business here and will stay at my pleasure.
Sit in the corner there, my friend."

"A tailor!" cried Mastor, horrified. "I tell you he
must go."

"He must!" asked Keraunus wrathfully. "A slave
dares to give orders in my house? We will see."

"I am going," interrupted the artisan who understood the case. "No unpleasantness shall arise here on
my account, I will return in a quarter of an hour."

"You will stay," commanded Keraunus. "This insolent Roman seems to think that Lochias belongs to
him; but I will show him who is master here."

But Mastor paid no heed to these words spoken in
a high pitch; he took the tailor's hand and led him out,
whispering to him:

"Come with me if you wish to escape an evil
hour."

The two men went off and Keraunus did not detain
the artisan, for it occurred to his mind that his presence
did him small credit. He purposed to show himself in
all his dignity to the overbearing architect, but he also

remembered that it was not advisable to provoke un-
necessarily the mysterious bearded stranger, with the big
dog.   Much excited, and not altogether free from anxiety, he paced up and down his room.   To give himself
courage he hastily filled a cup from the wine-jar that
stood on the breakfast table, emptied it, refilled it and
drank it off a second time without adding any water,
and then stood with his arms folded and a strong color
in his face awaiting his enemy's visit.

The Emperor walked in with Gabinius.   Keraunus
expected some greeting, but Hadrian spoke not a word,
cast a glance at him of the utmost contempt and passed
by him without taking any more notice of him than if
he had been a pillar or a piece of furniture.   The blood
mounted to the steward's head and heated his eyes and
for fully a minute he strove in vain to find words to give
utterance to his rage.   Gabinius paid no more heed to
Keraunus than the Roman had done.   He walked on a-
head and paused in front of the mosaic for which he had
offered so high a price, and over which a few days since
he had been so sharply dealt with by the steward.

"I would beg you," he said, "to look at this masterpiece."

The Emperor looked at the ground, but hardly had
he begun to study the picture, of which he quite understood and appreciated the beauty, when just behind him
he heard in a hoarse voice these words uttered with
difficulty :

"In Alexandria—it is the custom, to greet—to say
something—to the people you visit."   Hadrian half
turned his head towards the speaker and said indifferently but with strong and insulting contempt:

"In Rome too it is the custom to greet honest people." Then looking down again at the mosaic he said, " Exquisite, exquisite an inestimable and precious work."

At Hadrian's words Keraunus' eyes almost started out of his head. His face was crimson and his lips pale; he went close up to him and as soon as he had found breath to speak he said:

"What have you—what are your words intended to convey ?"

Hadrian turned suddenly and full upon the steward ; in his eyes sparkled that annihilating fire which few could endure to gaze on and his deep voice rolled sullenly through the room as he said to the miserable man:

"My words are intended to convey that you have been an unfaithful steward, that I know what you would rather I should not know, that I have learned how you deal with the property entrusted to you, that you—"

" That I ?"—cried the steward trembling with rage and stepping close up to the Emperor.

" That you," shouted Hadrian in his face, " tried to sell this picture to this man ; in short that you are a simpleton and a scoundrel into the bargain."

"I—I," gasped Keraunus slapping his hand on his fat chest. " I—a—a—but you shall repent of these words."

Hadrian laughed coldly and scornfully, but Keraunus sprang on Gabinius with a wonderful agility for his size, clutched him by the collar of his chiton and shook the feeble little man as if he were a sapling, shrieking meanwhile:

" I will choke you with your own lies—serpent, mean viper !"

" Madman !" cried Hadrian " leave hold of the Ligurian or by Sirius you shall repent it."

" Repent it ?" gasped the steward. " It will be your turn to repent when Caesar comes. Then will come a day of reckoning with false witnesses, shameless calumniators who disturb peaceful households, while credulous idiots—"

" Man, man," interrupted Hadrian, not loudly but sternly and ominously, "you know not to whom you speak."

" Oh I know you—I know you only too well. But I—I—shall I tell you who I am ?"

" You—you are a blockhead," replied the monarch shrugging his shoulders contemptuously. Then he added calmly, with dignity—almost with indifference :

"I am Caesar."

At these words the steward's hand dropped from the chiton of the half-trottled dealer. Speechless and with a glassy stare he gazed in Hadrian's face for a few seconds. Then he suddenly started, staggered backwards, uttered a loud choking, gurgling, nameless cry, and fell back on the floor like a mass of rock shaken from its foundations by an earthquake. The room shook again with his fall.

Hadrian was startled and when he saw him lying motionless at his feet he bent over him—less from pity than from a wish to see what was the matter with him; for he had also dabbled in medicine. Just as he was lifting the fallen man's hand to feel his pulse Arsinoe rushed into the room. She had heard the last words of the antagonists with breathless anxiety and her father's fall and now threw herself on her knees by the side of the unhappy man, just opposite to Hadrian, and as his distorted and grey-white face told her what had occurred she broke out in a passionate cry of anguish. Her

brothers and sisters followed at her heels, and when
they saw their favorite sister bewailing herself they followed her example without knowing at first what
Arsinoe was crying for, but soon with terror and
horror at their father lying there stiff and disfigured. The
Emperor, who had never had either son or daughter
of his own, found nothing so intolerable as the presence
of crying children. However he endured the wailing
and whimpering that surrounded him till he had ascertained the condition of the man lying on the ground before him.

" He is dead," he said in a few minutes. " Cover
his face, Mastor."

Arsinoe and the children broke out afresh, and Hadrian glanced down at them with annoyance. When his
eye fell on Arsinoe, whose costly robe, merely pinned
and slightly stitched together had come undone with
the vehemence of her movements and were hanging as
flapping rags in tumbled disorder, he was disgusted
with the gaudy fluttering trumpery which contrasted
so painfully with the grief of the wearer, and turning
his back on the fair girl he quitted the chamber of
misery.

Gabinius followed him with a hideous smirk. He
had directed the Emperor's attention to the mosaic
pavement in the steward's room, and had shamelessly
accused Keraunus of having offered to sell him a work
that belonged to the palace, contrasting his conduct with
his own rectitude. Now the calumniated man was dead,
and the truth could never come to light; this was necessarily a satisfaction to the miserable man, but he derived even greater pleasure from the reflection that Arsinoe could not now fill the part of Roxana, and that

consequently there was once more a possibility that it might devolve on his daughter.

Hadrian walked on in front of him, silent and thoughtful. Gabinius followed him into his writing-room, and there said with fulsome smoothness:

"Ah, great Caesar, thus do the gods punish with a heavy hand the crimes of the guilty."

Hadrian did not interrupt him, but he looked him keenly and enquiringly in the face, and then said, gravely, but coolly:

"It seems to me, man, that I should do well to break off my connection with you, and to give some other dealer the commissions which I proposed to entrust to you."

"Caesar!" stammered Gabinius, "I really do not know—"

"But I do know," interrupted the Emperor. "You have attempted to mislead me, and throw your own guilt on the shoulders of another."

"I—great Caesar? I have attempted—" began the Ligurian, while his pinched features turned an ashy grey.

"You accused the steward of a dishonorable trick," replied Hadrian. "But I know men well, and I know that no thief ever yet died of being called a scoundrel. It is only undeserved disgrace that can cost a man's life."

"Keraunus was full-blooded, and the shock when he learnt that you were Caesar—"

"That shock accelerated the end no doubt," interrupted the monarch, "but the mosaic in the steward's room is worth a million of sesterces, and now I have seen enough to be quite sure that you are not the man to save your money when a work like that mosaic is offered

you for sale—be the circumstances what they may.   If
I see the case rightly, it was Keraunus who refused your
demand that he should resign to you the treasure in his
charge.   Certainly, that was the case exactly!   Now,
leave me.   I wish to be alone."

Gabinius retired with many bows, walking backwards to the door, and then turned his back on the
palace of Lochias muttering many impotent curses as
he went.

The steward's new 'body-servant,' the old black
woman, Mastor, the tailor and his slave, helped Arsinoe
to carry her father's lifeless body and lay it on a couch,
and the slave closed his eyes.   He was dead—so each
told the despairing girl, but she would not, could not
believe it.   As soon as she was alone with the old
negress and the dead, she lifted up his heavy, clumsy
arm, and as soon as she let go her hold it fell by his
side like lead.   She lifted the cloth from the dead man's
face, but she flung it over him again at once, for death
had drawn his features.   Then she kissed his cold hand
and brought the children in and made them do the
same, and said sobbing:

"We have no father now; we shall never, never see
him again."

The little blind boy felt the dead body with his
hands, and asked his sister:

"Will he not wake again to-morrow morning and
make you curl his hair, and take me up on his knee?"

" Never, never; he is gone, gone for ever."

As she spoke Mastor entered the room, sent by his
master.   Yesterday had he not heard from the overseer
of the pavement-workers the comforting tidings that after our grief and suffering here on earth there would be

another, beautiful, blissful and eternal life? He went
kindly up to Arsinoe and said :

"No, no, my children ; when we are dead we become beautiful angels with colored wings, and all who
have loved each other here on earth will meet again in
the presence of the good God."

Arsinoe looked at the slave with disapproval.

" What is the use," she asked, " of cheating the children with silly tales ? Their father is gone, quite gone,
but we will never, never forget him."

" Are there any angels with red wings ?" asked the
youngest little girl.

" Oh ! I want to be an angel !" cried Helios, clapping his hands. " And can the angels see ?"

" Yes, dear little man," replied Mastor, "and their
eyes are wonderfully bright, and all they look upon is
beautiful."

" Tell them no more Christian nonsense," begged
Arsinoe. " Ah ! children, when we shall have burned
our father's body there will be nothing left of him but a
few grey ashes."

But the slave took the little blind boy on his knees
and whispered to him :

" Only believe what I tell you—you will see him
again in Heaven."

Then he set him down again, gave Arsinoe a little
bag of gold pieces in Caesar's name, and begged her—
for so his master desired—to find a new abode and, after the deceased was burned on the morrow, to quit
Lochias with the children. When Mastor was gone
Arsinoe opened the chest, in which lay her father's
papyri and the money that Plutarch had paid for the
ivory cup, put in the heavy purse sent by the Emperor,

30

comforting herself while her tears flowed, with the reflection that she and the children were provided at any rate against immediate want.

But where was she to go with the little ones ? Where could she hope to find a refuge at once ? What was to become of them when all they now possessed was spent. The gods be thanked ! she was not forlorn; she still had friends. She could find protection and love with Pollux and look to dame Doris for motherly counsel.

She quickly dried her eyes and changed the remains of her splendor for the dark dress in which she was accustomed to work at the papyrus factory; then, as soon as she had taken the pearls out of her hair, she went down to the little gate-house.

She was only a few steps from the door—but why did not the Graces come springing out to meet her ? Why did she see no birds, no flowers in the window ? Was she deceived, was she dreaming or was she tricked by some evil spirit ? The door of the dear home-like little dwelling was wide open and the sitting-room was absolutely empty, not a chattel was left behind, forgotten—not a leaf from a plant was lying on the ground; for dame Doris, in her tidy fashion, had swept out the few rooms where she had grown grey in peace and contentment as carefully as though she were to come into them again to-morrow.

What had happened here ? Where were her friends gone ? A great terror came over her, all the misery of desolation fell upon her, and as she sank upon the stone bench outside the gate-house to wait for the inhabitants who must presently return, the tears again flowed from her eyes and fell in heavy drops on her hands as they lay in her lap.

She was still sitting there, thinking with a throbbing heart of Pollux and of the happy morning of this now dying day, when a troup of Moorish slaves came towards the deserted house. The head mason who led them desired her to rise from the bench, and in answer to her questions, told her that the little building was to be pulled down, and that the couple who had inhabited it were evicted from their post, turned out of doors and had gone elsewhere with all their belongings. But where Doris and her son had taken themselves no one knew. Arsinoe as she heard these tidings felt like a sailor whose vessel has grounded on a rocky shore, and who realizes with horror that every plank and beam beneath him quivers and gapes. As usual, when she felt too weak to help herself unaided, her first thought was of Selene, and she decided to hasten off to her and to ask her what she could do, what was to become of her and the children.

It was already growing dark. With a swift step, and drying her eyes from time to time on her peplum as she went, she returned to her own room to fetch a veil, without which she dared not venture so late into the streets. On the steps—where the dog had thrown down Selene—she met a man hurrying past her; in the dim light she fancied he bore some resemblance to the slave that her father had bought the day before; but she paid no particular heed, for her mind was full of so many other things. In the kitchen sat the old negress in front of a lamp and the children squatted round her; by the hearth sat the baker and the butcher, to whom her father owed considerable sums and who had come to claim their dues, for ill news has swifter wings than good tidings, and they had already heard of the steward's

30

death. Arsinoe took the lamp, begged the men to wait, went into the sitting-room, passing, not without a shudder, the body of the man who a few hours since had stroked her cheeks and looked lovingly into her eyes.

How glad she felt to be able to pay her dead father's debts and save the honor of his name! She confidently drew the key out of her pocket and went up to the chest. What was this? She knew, quite positively, that she had locked it before going out and yet it was now standing wide open; the lid, thrown back, hung askew by one hinge; the other was broken. A dread, a hideous suspicion, froze her blood; the lamp trembled in her hand as she leaned over the chest which ought to have contained every thing she possessed. There lay the old documents, carefully rolled together, side by side, but the two bags with Plutarch's money and the Emperor's, had vanished. She took out one roll after another; then she tossed them all out on to the floor till the bottom of the chest was bare—but the gold was really gone, nowhere to be found.

The new slave had forced open the lid of the chest and stolen the whole possessions of the orphans of the man who, to gratify his own vanity, had brought him into the house.

Arsinoe screamed aloud, called in her creditors, explained to them all that had occurred and implored them to pursue the thief; and when they only listened to her with an incredulous shrug, she swore that she was speaking the truth, and promised that whether the slave were caught or not she would pay them with the price of her own and her father's personal ornaments. She knew the name of the dealer of whom her father had bought the slave and told it to the unsatisfied dealers, who at last left her to follow up the thief as promptly as possible.

Once more Arsinoe was alone. Tearless, but shivering and scarcely mistress of herself from misery and agitation, she took out her veil, flung it over her head, and hurried through the court and along the streets to her sister.

Verily, since Sabina's visit to the palace all good spirits had deserted it.

CHAPTER XI.

In a perfectly dark spot by the wall of the widow's garden, stood the cynic philosopher who had met Antinous with so little courtesy, defending himself eagerly, but in low tones against the rebukes of another man, who, dressed, like himself in a ragged cloak and bearing a beggar's wallet, appeared to be one of the same kidney.

"Do not deny," said the latter, "that you cling much to the Christians."

"But hear me out," urged the other.

"I need hear nothing, for I have seen you for the tenth time sneaking in to one of their meetings."

"And do I deny it? Do I not honestly confess that I seek truth wherever I may, where I see even a gleam of hope of finding it?"

"Like the Egyptian who wanted to catch the miraculous fish, and at last flung his hook into the sand."

"The man acted very wisely."

"What now !"

"A marvel is not to be found just where everything else is. In hunting for truth you must not be afraid of a bog."

"And the Christian doctrine seems to be very much such a muddy thicket."

"Call it so for aught I care."

"Then beware lest you find yourself sticking in the morass."

"I will take care of myself."

"You said just now that there were decent folks among them."

"A few no doubt. But the others! eternal gods! mere slaves, beggars, ruined handicraftstmen, common people, untaught and unphilosophical brains, and women, for the most part."

"Avoid them then."

"You ought to be the last to give me that advice."

"What do you mean ?"

The other went close up to him and asked him in a whisper:

"Why, where do you suppose I get the money with which I pay for our food and lodging?"

"So long as you do not steal it, it is all the same to me."

"If I had no more, you would ask the question fast enough."

"Certainly not, we strive after virtue and ought to do everything to render ourselves independent of nature and her cravings. But to be sure she often asserts her rights; to return then: where do you get the money ?"

"Why, it burns in the purses of the people in there. It is their duty to give to the poor, and to tell the truth,

their pleasure also; and so week by week they give me
a few drachmae for my suffering brother."

"Bah! you are the only son of your father, and he
is dead."

"'All men are brethren' say the Christians, consequently I may call you mine without lying."

"Join them then for aught I care," laughed the
other. "How would it be if I followed you among the
Christians? Perhaps they would give me weekly
money too, for my suffering brother, and then we could
have double meals."

The cynics laughed loudly and parted; one went
back into the city, the other into the garden belonging
to the Christian widow.

Arsinoe had entered here before the dishonest philosopher and had gone straight to Hannah's house without being detained by the gate-keeper. As she got
nearer to her destination, she tried more and more
earnestly to devise some way in which she might inform
her sister of all the dreadful things that had happened,
and which she must learn sooner or later, without giving
her too great a shock. Her dread was not much less
than her grief. As she reflected on the last few days
and on all that had occurred, it almost seemed as
though she herself had been the cause of the misfortunes
of her family.

On the way to see Selene she could shed no tears,
but she could not help softly moaning to herself now
and then. A woman, who for some distance had kept
pace with her, thought she must be suffering some
severe bodily pain, and when the girl passed her, she
looked after her with sincere compassion, the wailing of
the desolate young creature had sounded so piteous.

True, midway, Arsinoe had suddenly stopped and had
thought that instead of going to Selene for advice, she
would turn round and seek Pollux and ask him to help
her. The thought of her lover forced its way through
all her sorrow and anxiety, through the reproaches she
heaped upon herself and the vague plans floating in the
air which her brain—unaccustomed to any serious
thought, vainly tried to sketch for the future. He was
kind, and would certainly be ready to help her; but
maidenly modesty held her back from seeking him at
so late an hour; besides, how could she discover him
or his parents?

The place where her sister was she was now familiar
with, and no one could judge of their position better or
give sounder counsel than prudent Selene. So she had
not turned round, but had hurried on to reach her destination as soon as possible; and now she was standing
before the little house in the garden. Before opening
the door she once more considered in what way she
could prepare Selene and tell her terrible news, and, as
all that happened stood vividly before her mind's eye,
she began to weep once more.

In front of her, and following her, men and veiled
women, singly or in couples or in larger groups, passed
into Paulina's garden. They came from workshops and
writing-rooms, from humble houses in narrow lanes, and
from the handsomest and largest in the main street.
Each and all, from the wealthy merchant down to the
slave who could not call the coarse tunic or scanty apron
that he wore, his own, walked gravely and with a certain
dignified reserve. All who met within that gate greeted
each other as friends; the master gave a brotherly kiss
to the servant, the slave to his owner; for the congrega-

tion to which they all belonged was as one body, animated and dwelt in by Christ, so that each member was esteemed as equal to the others however different their gifts of body or mind might be, or the worldly possessions with which they were endowed. Before God and his Saviour the rich ship-owner or the grey-haired sage stood no higher than the defenceless widow and the ignorant slave crippled with blows. Still, the members of the community submitted to those more implicitly than to these, for the special talents which graced certain superior Christians were gifts of grace from the Lord, readily acknowledged as such and, so far as they concerned the inner man, deemed worthy of honor.

On Sunday, the day of the Resurrection of the Lord, all Christians, without exception, visited their place of assembly for divine worship. To-day, being the middle of the week, all who could or chose came to the love-feast at Paulina's suburban house. She herself dwelt in the city and she had placed the banqueting hall of her villa, which would hold more than a hundred souls, at the disposal of her fellow Christians in that quarter of the town. The regular service was held in the morning, but after the day's labor was ended the Christians met at one table to have an evening meal in common, or—on other occasions—to partake of the sacramental supper. After sunset the elders, deacons, and deaconesses—most of whom, so long as it was light, had secular work to attend to—met to take counsel together.

Paulina, the widow of Pudeus and sister of Pontius the architect, was a woman of considerable property and at the same time a prudent steward, who did not consider herself justified in seriously impairing her son's

inheritance. This son was residing at Smyrna as a
partner in an uncle's business, and always avoided Alexandria, as he did not like his mother's intercourse with
the Christians. Paulina took the most anxious care not
to make any inroads on the capital intended for him, and
never allowed her hospitality to her fellow-believers to cost
her any more than it did the other wealthy members of
the circle that met at her house. There the rich brought
more than they needed for themselves and the poor
were always welcome; not feeling themselves oppressed
by the benevolence they profited by, for they were often
told that their entertainer was not a mortal, but the
Saviour, who invited each one who followed him faithfully to be his guest.

The hour was approaching which would summon
dame Hannah to join the assembly of her fellow Christians. She could not fail to appear, for she was one of
the deaconesses entrusted with the distribution of alms
and the care of the sick. She noiselessly made her
preparations for going, carefully setting the lamp behind
the water-pitcher so that it should not dazzle Selene,
and she desired Mary to be exact in administering the
medicine to her patient. She knew that the girl had
yesterday attempted to make away with herself, and
guessed the cause; but she asked no questions and disturbed the poor child, who slept a good deal or lay
dreaming with open eyes, as little as possible. The old
physician wondered at her sound constitution, for since
her plunge into the water the fever had left her and
even the injured foot was not much the worse. Hannah
might now hope the best for Selene if no unforeseen
contingency checked her recovery. To prevent this the
unfortunate girl was never to be left alone, and Mary

had gladly agreed with her friend to fill her place whenever she was obliged to leave the house.

The meeting of the elders and guardians had already begun when Hannah took her tablets in her hand, on which was noted the distribution she had made of the money entrusted to her during the last week. She greeted the sick girl and Mary with a kindly look and whispered to the deformed girl:

"I will think of thee in my prayers thou faithful soul. There is some food in the little cupboard—not much, for we must be sparing, the last medicine was so dear.

In the little anteroom a lamp was burning which Mary had lighted as it began to grow dark, and the widow paused for a moment, considering whether she should not extinguish it to save the oil. She had taken up the tongs that hung by it, and was about to put it out, when she heard a gentle tap at the house-door. Before she could enquire who it was that asked admission at so late an hour, the door was opened and Arsinoe entered the little hall. Her eyes were still full of tears and she had great difficulty in finding words to return Hannah's greeting.

"Why what ails you my child?" asked the Christian anxiously when by the dim light, she saw how tearful and sad the girl looked. Arsinoe was long before she could answer. At last she collected herself sufficiently to sob out amid her tears:

"Oh dame Hannah! It is all over with us — my father, our poor father—"

The widow guessed at the blow that had fallen on the sisters and full of anxiety on Selene's account she interrupted the weeping child saying:

" Hush, hush my child—Selene must not hear you.
Come out with me and then you can tell me all."

Once outside the door Hannah put her arm round
Arsinoe drew her towards her, kissed her forehead, and
said :

" Now speak and tell me every thing; think that I
am your mother or your sister.   Poor Selene is still too
weak to advise or help you.   Take courage.   What happened to your poor father ?"

" Struck by apoplexy, dead—dead !" wept the girl.

" Poor, dear little orphan," said the widow in a
husky voice and she clasped Arsinoe closely in her arms.
For some time she allowed the girl to weep silently on
her bosom; then she spoke :

" Give me your hand my daughter and tell me how
it has all happened so suddenly.   Your father was quite
well yesterday and now ?   Yes my girl life is a grave
matter, you have to learn it while you are still young.   I
know you have six little brothers and sisters and perhaps you may soon lack even the necessaries of life.
But that is no disgrace; I am certainly even poorer than
you and yet, by God's help, I hope to be able to advise you and perhaps even to assist you.   Every thing
that I can possibly do shall be done, but first I must
know how matters stand with you and what you need."

There was so much kindness and consolation in the
Christian's tones, so much to revive hope that Arsinoe
willingly complied with her demand and began her story.
At first, to be sure, her pride shunned confessing how
poor, how absolutely destitute they were ; but Hannah's
questions soon brought the truth to light; and when
Arsinoe perceived that the widow understood the misfortunes of their house in their fullest extent, and that

it would be unavailing to conceal how matters stood with her and the children, she yielded to the growing impulse to relieve her soul by pouring out her griefs and described frankly and without reserve the whole position of the family, to the good woman who listened with attention and sympathy. The widow asked about each child separately, and ended by enquiring who, in Arsinoe's absence, was left in charge of the little ones; and when she heard that the old slave-woman to whose care the children were entrusted, was infirm and half-blind, she shook her head thoughtfully.

"Here help is needed and at once," she said decidedly. "You must go back to the little ones presently. Your sister must not at present hear of your father's death; when your future lot is to some extent secure we will tell her by degrees all that has occurred. Now come with me, it is by the Lord's guidance that you came here at the right moment."

Hannah conducted Arsinoe to Paulina's villa, first into a small room at the side of the entrance hall, where the deaconesses took off their veils and their warm wraps in winter evenings. There the girl could be alone, and safe from inquisitive questionings which could not fail to be painful to her. Hannah desired her to await her return, and then joined her colleagues.

In order to do so she had to pass through the room where the elders and deacons were sitting in council. The bishop, who presided over the assembly, sat on a raised seat at the head of an oblong table, and on his right hand and his left sat a number of elderly men, some of whom seemed to be of Jewish or Egyptian extraction but most of them were Greeks. In these the lofty intellectual brow was conspicuous, in those a bright, ecstatic expression particularly in the eyes. Hannah went past the assembly with a reverential greeting into the adjoining room in which the deaconesses sat waiting, for women were not admitted to join or hear the deliberations of the elders. The bishop, a fine old man with a full white beard, raised his kindly eyes as the door closed upon Hannah, fixed them for a few moments on the tips of his fingers that he had raised and then addressed the presbyter who had presented for baptism several candidates who had been grounded during the past year in the Christian faith and doctrine, as follows :

"Most of the catechumens you have presented to me cling faithfully no doubt to the Redeemer. They believe in Him and love Him. But have they attained to that sanctification, that new birth in Christ, which alone can justify us in admitting them through baptism among the lambs of our Good Shepherd ? Let us beware of the tainted sheep which may infect the whole flock. Verily, in these latter years there has been no lack of them, and they have been received among us and have brought the name of Christian into evil repute. Shall I give you an example ? There was an Egyptian in Rhakotis ; few seemed to strive so fervently as he for the remission of his sins. He could fast for many days, and yet no sooner was he baptized than he broke into a goldsmith's shop. He was condemned to death, and before his end he sent for me and confessed to me that in former years he had soiled his soul with many robberies and murders. He had hoped to win forgiveness of his sins by the act of baptism, the mere washing in water, not by repentance and a new birth to a pure and holy life ; and he had gone on boldly in new sin because he confidently hoped that he might again count on the unwearying mercy of the Saviour. Others again, who had been brought up in the practice of the ablutions which have to be performed by those who are initiated into the deeper secrets of the heathen mysteries, regarded baptism as an act of purification, a mystical process of happy augury, or at the best a figurative purification of the soul, and crowded to receive it. Here, in Alexandria, the number of these deluded ones is especially great; for where could any superstition find a more favorable soil than in this seat of philosophical half-culture, or over-culture; of the worship of Serapis, of astrology, of societies of Mystics, of visionaries and exorcisers, and of incredulity—the twin-sister of credulity. Be cautious then to hold back from baptism all those who regard it as a preserving charm or an act of good omen—remembering that the same water which, sprinkled on sanctified hearts, leads them to holy living, brings death to the unclean soul. It is your turn to speak, Irenaeus."

"I only have to say," began the young Christian thus designated, "that I have recently met among the catechumens with some who have attached themselves to us from the basest motives. I mean the idlers who are glad to receive our alms. Have you noticed here a cynic philosopher whose starving brother we maintain? Our deacon Clemens has just ascertained that he is the only son of his father—"

"We will investigate this matter more closely when we discuss the distribution of alms," replied the bishop. "Here we have petitions from several women who desire to have their children baptized; this question we cannot decide here; it must be referred to the next Synod. So far as I am concerned, I should be inclined

not to reject the prayer of the mothers. Wherein does
the utmost aim of the Christian life consist? It seems
to me in being perfectly conformable to the example of
the Saviour. And was not he a Man among men, a
Youth among the young, a Child among children?
Did not His existence lend sanctity to every age, and
especially childhood? He commanded that little children should be brought to Him, and He promised them
the Kingdom of Heaven. Wherefore then should we
exclude them and deny them baptism?"

"I cannot share your views," replied a presbyter
with a high forehead and sunken eyes. "We ought no
doubt to follow the Saviour, but those who tread in His
steps should do so of their own free choice, out of love
for Him, and after He has sanctified their souls. What
is the sense of a new birth in a life that has scarcely begun."

"Your discourse," replied the bishop, "only con-
firms my opinion that this question is one for a higher
assembly. We will now close our discussion of that
point, and go on to the care of the poor. Call in the
women, my good Justinius."

The deaconesses came into the room and took seats
at the lower end of the table, Paulina, the widow of
Pudeus, taking her place opposite the bishop in the
middle of the other women. She had learnt from Selene's kind nurse in what pressing difficulties the children of the deceased steward now found themselves, and
that Hannah had promised to assist them.

The deacons first gave their reports of what their
works had been among the poor; after them the women
were allowed to speak. Paulina, a tall, slight woman
with black hair faintly streaked with gray, drew from

her dress, which was perfectly plain, but made of particularly soft, fine white woollen stuff—a tablet that she placed before her, and slowly raising her eyes and looking at the assembly she said:

"Dame Hannah has a melancholy story to tell you, for which I crave your sympathy. Will you be so good as to allow her to speak?"

Paulina seemed to feel that she was the hostess to her brethren. She looked ill and suffering; a line of pain had settled about her lips, and there were always dark shades under her eyes; still, there was something firm and decisive in her voice, and her glance was anything rather than soft and winning. After her commanding tones Hannah's tale sounded as soft as a song. She described the different natures of the two sisters as lovingly as though they were her own daughters, each in her own way seemed to her so worthy of compassion, and she spoke with pathetic lament of the unprotected, helpless orphans abandoned to misery, and among them a pretty little blind boy. And she ended her speech by saying:

"The steward's second daughter—she is sixteen and so beautiful that she must be exposed to every temptation—has now the whole charge of the nourishment and care of her six young brothers and sisters. Ought we to withhold from them a protecting hand? No, so surely as we love the Saviour we ought not. You agree with me? Well then, do not let us delay our help. The second daughter of the deceased Keraunus is here, in this house; to-morrow early the children must all quit the palace, and now, while I am speaking, are at home alone and but ill tended."

The Christian woman's good words fell on kindly

31

soil, and the presbyters and deacons determined to
recommend the congregation who should assemble at
the love-feast to give their assistance to the steward's
children.

The elders had still much to discuss, so Hannah
and Paulina were charged with the task of appealing to
the hearts of the well-to-do members of the congregation to provide for the orphans. The poor widow first
conducted her wealthy friend and hostess to the little
room where Arsinoe was waiting with growing impatience. She looked paler than usual but, in spite of her
tear-reddened eyes which she kept fixed on the ground,
she was so lovely, so touchingly lovely, that the mere
sight of her moved Paulina's heart. She had once had
two children, an only daughter besides her son. The
girl had died in the spring-time of her maidenhood, and
Paulina thought of her at every hour of her life. It
was for her sake that she had been baptized and devoted
her existence to a series of painful sacrifices. She strove
with all her might to be a good Christian—for surely
she, the self-denying woman who had taken up the
cross of her own free will, the suffering creature who
loved stillness and who had made her country-house,
which she visited daily, a scene of unrest, could not fail
to win Heaven, and there she hoped to meet her innocent child.

Arsinoe reminded her of her Helena, who certainly
had been far less fair than the steward's lovely daughter,
but whose image had assumed new and glorified forms
in the mother's faithful heart. Since her son had left
home for a foreign country she had often asked herself
whether she might not find some young creature to
take into her home, to attach to herself, to bring up as

a Christian, and to bring as an offering to her Saviour's feet.

Her daughter had died a heathen, and nothing troubled Paulina so deeply as that her soul was lost, and that her own struggling and striving for grace could not lead her to the goal beyond the grave. No sacrifice seemed too great to purchase her child's beatitude, and now, standing before Arsinoe and looking at her with deep emotion and admiration, she was seized with an idea which swiftly ripened to resolve. She would win this sweet soul for the Redeemer, and implore Him with ceaseless prayers to save her hapless child as a reward for the work of grace in Arsinoe's soul; and she felt as if she had signed the compact with the Redeemer, when, fully determined on this course, she went up to the girl and asked her:

" You are quite forlorn, quite without relations ?"

Arsinoe bowed her head in assent, and Paulina went on :

" And do you bear your loss with resignation ?"

" What is resignation ?" asked the girl modestly. Hannah laid her hand on the widow's arm and whispered :

" She is a heathen."

" I know it," said Paulina shortly, and then went on kindly but positively :

" You and yours have lost both parents and a home by your father's death. You shall find a new home in my house, with me ; I ask nothing of you in return but your love."

Arsinoe looked at the haughty lady in astonishment. She could not yet feel any impulse of affection towards her, and she did not as yet understand that what was

31

required of her was the one gift which the best will, the most loving heart in the world, could not offer at a command. Paulina did not wait for her reply, but signed to Hannah to follow her to join the congregation now assembled at the evening meal.

A quarter of an hour later the two women returned. The steward's orphans were provided for. Two or three Christian families were ready and willing to take in some of them, and many a kindly house-mother had begged to have the blind child; but in vain, for Hannah had claimed the right to bring up the hapless little boy in her own house, at any rate for the present. She knew how Selene clung to him, and hoped by his presence to be able to work powerfully on the crushed and chilled heart of the poor girl.

Arsinoe did not contravene the arrangements of the two women. She thanked them, indeed, for she felt that she once more stood on firm ground, but she also was immediately aware that it would be strewn with sharp stones. The thought of parting from her little brothers and sisters was terrible and cruel, and never left her mind for an instant, while, accompanied by Hannah in person, she made her way back to Lochias.

The next morning her kind friend appeared again and led her and the little troup to Paulina's town-house. The steward's creditors divided his little possessions; nothing but the chest of papyri followed the girl to her new home. The hour in which the fondly-linked circle of children was riven asunder, when one child was taken here and another there, was the bitterest which Arsinoe had ever experienced or ever could experience through all the after years of her life.

CHAPTER XII.

A LOVELY garden adjoined the Caesareum, the palace in which Sabina was residing. Balbilla was fond of lingering there, and as the morning of the twenty-ninth of December was particularly brilliant—the sky and its infinite mirror the sea, gleaming in indescribably deep blue, while the fragrance of a flowering shrub was wafted in at her window like an invitation to quit the house— she had sought a certain bench which, though placed in a sunny spot, was slightly shaded by an acacia. This seat was screened from the more public paths by bushes; the promenaders who did not seek Balbilla could not observe her here, but she could command a view, through a gap in the foliage, of the path, which was strewn with small shells.

To-day, however, the young poetess was far from feeling any curiosity; instead of gazing at the shrubbery enlivened by birds, at the clear atmosphere or the sparkling sea, her eyes were fixed on a yellow roll of papyrus and she was impressing very dry details on her retentive memory.

She had determined to keep her word to learn to speak, write, and compose verses in the Aeolian dialect of the Greek tongue. She had chosen for her teacher Apollonius, the great grammarian, who was apt to call his scholars "the dullards;" and the work which was the present object of her studies was derived from the famous library of the Serapeum, which far exceeded in completeness that of the Museum since the siege of

Julius Caesar in the Bruchiom, when the great Museum library was burnt.

Any one observing Balbilla at her occupation could hardly have believed that she was studying. There was no fixed effort in her eyes or on her brow; still, she read line for line, not skipping a single word; only she did it not like a man who climbs a mountain with sweat on his brow, but like a lounger who walks in the main street of some great city, and is charmed at every new and strange thing that meets his eye. Each time she came upon some form of structure in the book she was reading that had been hitherto unknown to her, she was so delighted that she clapped her hands and laughed out softly. Her learned master had never before met with so cheerful a student, and it annoyed him, for to him science was a serious matter while she seemed to make a joke of it, as she did of every thing, and so desecrated it in his eyes. After she had been sitting an hour on the bench, studying in her own way, she rolled up the book and stood up to refresh herself a little. Feeling sure that no one could see her, she stretched herself in all her limbs and then stepped up to the gap in the shrubbery in order to see who a man in boots might be who was pacing up and down in the broad path beyond.

It was the praetor—and yet it was not! Verus, under this aspect at any rate, she had never seen till now. Where was the smile that was wont to twinkle in his merry eye like the sparkle of a diamond and to play saucily about his lips—where the unwrinkled serenity of his brow and the defiantly audacious demeanor of his whole handsome person? He was slowly striding up and down with a gloomy fire in his eye, a deeply-lined brow, and his head sunk on his breast: and yet it was not bowed with sorrow. If so, could he have snapped his fingers in the air as he did just as he passed in front of Balbilla, as much as to say: "Come what may! to-day I live and laugh the future in the face!"

But this vestige of his old reckless audacity did not last longer than the time it took to part his fingers again, and the next time Verus passed Balbilla he looked, if possible, more gloomy than before. Something very unpleasant must have arisen to spoil the good humor of her friend's husband; and the poetess was sincerely sorry; for, though she herself had daily to suffer under the praetor's impertinence, she always forgave it for the sake of the graceful form in which he knew how to clothe his incivilities.

Balbilla longed to see Verus content once more, and she therefore came forth from her hiding place. As soon as he saw her he altered the expression of his features and cried out as brightly as ever:

"Welcome, fairest of the fair!"

She made believe not to recognize him, but, as she passed him and bowed her curly head, she said gravely and in deep tones:

"Good day to you, Timon."

"Timon?" he asked, taking her hand.

"Ah'! is it you, Verus?" she answered, as though surprised. "I thought the Athenian misanthrope had quitted Hades and come to take the air in this garden."

"You thought rightly," replied the praetor. "But when Orpheus sings the trees dance, the Muse can turn dull, motionless stones into a Bacchante, and when Bal·billa appears Timon is at once transformed into the happy Verus."

" The miracle does not astonish me," laughed the
girl. " But is it permitted to ask what dark spirit so
effectually produced the contrary result, and made a
Timon of the fair Lucilla's happy husband ?"

" I ought rather to beware of letting you see the
monster, or our joyous muse Balbilla might easily become the sinister Hecate. But the malicious sprite is
close at hand, for he is hidden in this little roll."

" A document from Caesar ?"

" Oh! no, only a letter from a Jew."

" Possibly the father of some fair daughter !"

" Wrongly guessed—as wrong ac possible !"

" You excite my curiosity."

" Mine has already been satisfied by this roll.
Horace is wise when he says that man should never
trouble himself about the future."

" An oracle !"

" Something of the kind."

" And can that darken this lovely morning to you ?
Did you ever see me melancholy ? Yet my future is
threatened by a prophecy—such a hideous prophecy."

" The fate of men is different to the destiny of
women."

" Would you like to hear what was prophesied of
me ?"

" What a question !"

" Listen then ; the saying I will repeat to you came
to me from no less an oracle than the Delphic Pythia :

' That which thou holdest most precious and dear shall be torn from
       thy keeping,
And from the heights of Olympus, down shalt thou fall in the dust.' "

" Is that all ?"

" Nay—two consolatory lines follow."

" And they are— ?"

" Still the contemplative eye discerns under mutable sand drifts
Stable foundations of stone, marble and natural rock."

" And you are inclined to complain of this oracle ?"

" Is it so pleasant to have to wade through dust ?
We have enough of that intolerable nuisance here in
Egypt — or am I to be delighted at the prospect of
hurting my feet on hard stones ?"

" And what do the interpreters say ?"

" Only silly nonsense."

" You have never found the right one; but I—I see
the meaning of the oracle."

" You ?"

" Ay, I! The stern Balbilla will at last descend from
the lofty Olympus of her high-and-mightiness and no
longer disdain that immutable foundation-rock, the adoration of her faithful Verus."

" That foundation — that rock!" laughed the girl.
" I should think it as well advised to try to walk on the
surface of the sea out there as on that rock!"

" Only try."

" It is not necessary; Lucilla has made the experiment for me. Your interpretation is wrong; Caesar
gave me a far better one."

" What was that ?"

" That I should give up writing poetry and devote
myself to strict scientific studies. He advised me to try
astronomy."

" Astronomy," repeated Verus, growing graver.
" Farewell, fair one; I must go to Caesar!"

" We were with him yesterday at Lochias. How
everything is changed there! The pretty little gate-

house is gone, there is nothing more to be seen of all the cheerful bustle of builders and artists, and what were gay workshops are turned into dull, commonplace halls. The screens in the hall of the Muses had to go a week ago, and with them the young scatter-brain who set himself against my curls with so much energy that I was on the point of sacrificing them—"

" Without them you would no longer be Balbilla," cried Verus eagerly. " The artist condemns all that is not permanently beautiful, but we are glad to see any thing that is graceful, and can find pleasure in it with the other children of the time. The sculptor may dress his goddesses after the fashion of graver days and the laws of his art, but mortal women—if he is wise—after the fashion of the day. However, I am heartily sorry for that clever, genial young fellow. He has offended Caesar and was turned out of the palace, and now he is nowhere to be found."

" Oh !" cried Balbilla, full of regret, " poor man—and such a fine fellow ! And my bust ? we must seek him out. If the opportunity offers I will entreat Caesar—"

" Hadrian will hear nothing about him. Pollux has offended him deeply."

" From whom do you know that ?"

" From Antinous."

" We saw him, too, only yesterday," cried Balbilla, eagerly. " If ever a man was permitted to wear the form of a god among mortals, it is he.'

" Romantic creature !"

" I know no one who could look upon him with indifference. He is a beautiful dreamer, and the trace of suffering which we observed yesterday in his countenance is probably nothing more than the outward expression of that obscure regret, felt by all that is perfect, for the joy of development and conscious ripening into an incarnation of the ideal in its own kind, of which he is an instance in himself."

The poetess spoke the last words in a rapt tone, as if the form of a god was then and there before her eyes. Verus had listened to her with a smile, but now he interrupted her, and, holding up a warning finger, he said :

" Poetess, philosopher, and sweetest maiden, beware of descending from your Olympus for the sake of this boy ! When imagination and dreaminess meet half-way they make a pair which float · in the clouds and never even suspect the existence of that firmer ground of which your oracle speaks."

" Nonsense," said Balbilla crossly. " Before we can fall in love with a statue, Prometheus must animate it with a soul and fire from heaven."

" But often," retorted the praetor, " Eros proves to be a substitute for that unhappy friend of the gods."

" The true or the ' sham Eros ? ' " asked Balbilla testily.

" Certainly not the sham Eros," replied Verus. " On this occasion he merely plays the part of a kindly monitor, taking the place of Pontius, the architect, of whom your worthy matron-companion is so much afraid. During the tumult of the Dionysiac festival you are reported to have carried on as grave a discussion as any two gray-bearded philosophers walking in the Stoa among attentive students."

" With intelligent men, no doubt, we talk with intelligence !"

" Aye, and with stupid ones gayly. How much reason have I to be thankful that I am one of the stupid ones. Farewell, till we meet again, fair Balbilla," and the praetor hurried off.

Outside the Caesareum he got into his chariot and set out for Lochias. The charioteer held the reins, while he himself gazed at the roll in his hand which contained the result of the calculations of the astrologer, Rabbi Simeon Ben Jochai; and this was certainly likely enough to disturb the cheerfulness of the most reckless of men.

When, during the night which preceded the praetor's birthday, the Emperor should study the heavens with special reference to the position of the stars at his birth, he would find that, as far as till the end of the second hour after midnight all the favorable planets promised Verus a happy lot, success and distinction. But, with the commencement of the third hour—so said Ben Jochai—misfortune and death would take possession of his house of destiny; in the fourth hour his star would vanish, and anything further that might declare itself in the sky during that night would have nothing more to do with him, or his destiny. The Emperor's star would triumph over his. Verus could make out but little of the signs and calculations in the tables annexed by the Jew, but that little confirmed what was told in the written statement.

The praetor's horses carried him swiftly along while he reflected on what remained for him to do under these unfavorable circumstances, in order not to be forced to give up entirely the highest goal of his ambition. If the Rabbi's observations were accurate—and of this Verus did not for a moment doubt—all his hopes of adoption were at an end in spite of Sabina's support. How should Hadrian choose for his son and successor a man who was destined to die before him ? How could he, Verus, expect that Caesar should ally his fortunate star with the fatal star of another doomed to die ?

These reflections did nothing to help him, and yet he could not escape from them, till suddenly his charioteer pulled up the horses abruptly by the side of the footway to make room for a delegation of Egyptian priests who were going in procession to Lochias. The powerful hand with which his servant had promptly controlled the fiery spirit of the animals excited his approbation, and seemed to inspire him to put a clog boldly on the wheels of speeding fate. When they were no longer detained by the Egyptian delegates he desired the charioteer to drive slowly, for he wished to gain time for consideration.

"Until the third hour after midnight," said he to himself "all is to go well; it is not till the fourth hour that signs are to appear in the sky which are of evil augury for me. Of course the sheep will play round the dead lion, and the ass will even spurn him with his hoof so long as he is merely sick. In the short space of time between the third and fourth hours all the signs of evil are crowded together. They must be visible; but"—and this "but" brought sudden illumination to the praetor's mind, "why should Caesar see them?"

The anxious aspirant's heart beat faster, his brain worked more actively, and he desired the driver to make a short circuit, for he wanted to gain yet more time for the ideas that were germinating in his mind to grow and ripen.

Verus was no schemer; he walked in at the front door with a free and careless step, and scorned to climb the backstairs. Only for the greatest object

and aim of his life was he prepared to sacrifice his inclinations, his comfort and his pride, and to make un-
hesitating use of every means at hand. For the sake of
that he had already done many things which he regretted, and the man who steals one sheep out of the flock
is followed by others without intending it. The first
degrading action that a man commits is sure to be followed by a second and a third. What Verus was now
projecting he regarded as being a simple act of self-
defence; and after all, it consisted merely in detaining
Hadrian for an hour, interrupting him in an idle occupation—the observation of the stars.

There were two men who might be helpful to him
in this matter—Antinous and the slave Mastor. He
first thought of Mastor; but the Sarmatian was faithfully
devoted to his master and could not be bribed.—And
besides!—No! it really was too far beneath him to
make common cause with a slave. But he could count
even less on support from Antinous. Sabina hated her
husband's favorite, and for her sake Verus had never
met the young Bithynian on particularly friendly terms.
He fancied, too, that he had observed that the quiet,
dreamy lad kept out of his way. It was only by intimi-
dation, probably, that the favorite could be induced to do
him a service.

At any rate, the first thing to be done was to visit
Lochias and there to keep a lookout with his eyes wide
open. If the Emperor were in a happy frame of mind
he might, perhaps, be induced to appear during the latter
part of the night at the banquet which Verus was giving
on the eve of his birthday, and at which all that was
beautiful to the eye and ear was to be seen and
heard; or a thousand favoring and helpful accidents

migh. occur—and at any rate the Rabbi's forecast furnished him good fortune for the next few years.

As he dismounted from his chariot in the newly-paved forecourt and was conducted to the Emperor's anteroom he looked as bright and free from care as if the future lay before him sunny and cloudless.

Hadrian now occupied the restored palace, not as an architect from Rome but as sovereign of the world; he had shown himself to the Alexandrians and had been received with rejoicings and an unheard-of display in his honor. The satisfaction caused by the imperial visit was everywhere conspicuous and often found expression in exaggerated terms; indeed the council had passed a resolution to the effect that the month of December, being that in which the city had had the honor of welcoming the 'Imperator,' should henceforth be called "Hadrianus." The Emperor had to receive one deputation after another and to hold audience after audience, and on the following morning the dramatic representations were to begin, the processions and games which promised to last through many days, or—as Hadrian himself expressed it—to rob him of at least a hundred good hours. Notwithstanding, the monarch found time to settle all the affairs of the state, and at night to question the stars as to the fate which awaited him and his dominions during all the seasons of the new year now so close at hand.

The aspect of the palace at Lochias was entirely changed. In the place of the gay little gate-house stood a large tent of gorgeous purple stuff, in which the Emperor's body-guard was quartered, and opposite to it another was pitched for lictors and messengers. The stables were full of horses. Hadrian's own horse, Borysthenes, which had had too long a rest, pawed and stamped impatiently in a separate stall, and close at hand the Emperor's retrievers, boar-hounds and harriers were housed in hastily-contrived yards and kennels.

In the wide space of the first court soldiers were encamped, and close under the walls squatted men and women—Egyptians, Greeks and Hebrews—who desired to offer petitions to the sovereign.   Chariots drove in and out, litters came and went, chamberlains and other officials hurried hither and thither. The anterooms were crowded with men of the upper classes of the citizens who hoped to be granted audience by the Emperor at the proper hour.   Slaves, who offered refreshments to those who waited or stood idly looking on, were to be seen in every room, and official persons, with rolls of manuscript under their arms, bustled into the inner rooms or out of the palace to carry into effect the orders of their superior.

The hall of the Muses had been turned into a grand banqueting-hall.   Papias, who was now on his way to Italy by the Emperor's command, had restored the damaged shoulder of the Urania.   Couches and divans stood between the statues, and under a canopy at the upper end of the vast room stood a throne on which Hadrian sat when he held audience. On these occasions he always appeared in the purple, but in his writing-room, which he had not changed for another, he laid aside the imperial mantle and was no more splendid in his garb than the architect Claudius Venator had been.

In the rooms that had belonged to the deceased Keraunus now dwelt an Egyptian without wife or children—a stern and prudent man who had done good service as house-steward to the prefect Titianus, and the

living-room of the evicted family now looked dreary
and uninhabited. The mosaic pavement, which had in-
directly caused the death of Keraunus, was now on its
way to Rome, and the new steward had not thought it
worth while to fill up the empty, dusty, broken-up place
which had been left in the floor of his room by the removal or the work of art, nor even to cover it over with
mats. Not a single cheerful note was audible in the
abandoned dwelling but the twitter of the birds which
still came morning and evening to perch on the balcony,
for Arsinoe and the children had never neglected to
strew the parapet with crumbs for them at the end of
each meal.

All that was gracious, all that was attractive in
the old palace had vanished at Sabina's visit, and
even Hadrian himself was a different man to what he
had been a few days previously. The dignity with
which he appeared in public was truly imperial and unapproachable, and even when he sat with his intimates
in his favorite room he was grave, gloomy and taciturn.
The oracle, the stars, and other signs announced some
terrible catastrophe for the coming year with a certainty
that he could not evade; and the few careless days that
he had been permitted to enjoy at Lochias had ended
with unsatisfactory occurrences.

His wife, whose bitter nature struck him in all its repellent harshness here in Alexandria—where everything
assumed sharper outlines and more accentuated movement than in Rome—had demanded of him boldly that
he should no longer defer the adoption of the praetor.

He was anxious and unsatisfied; the infinite void in
his heart yawned before him whenever he looked into
his soul, and at every glance at the future of his external

32

life a long course of petty trifles started up before him which could not fail to stand in the way of his unwearying impulse to work. Even the vegetative existence of his handsome favorite Antinous, untroubled as it was by the sorrows or the joys of life, had undergone a change. The youth was often moody, restless and sad. Some foreign influences seemed to have affected him, for he was no longer content to hang about his person like a shadow; no, he yearned for liberty, had stolen into the city several times, seeking there the pleasures of his age which formerly he had avoided.

Nay, a change had even come over his cheerful and willing slave Mastor. Only his hound remained always the same in unaltered fidelity.

And he himself? He was the same to-day as ten years since: different every day and at every hour of the day.

CHAPTER XIII.

WHEN Verus entered the palace Hadrian had returned thither but a few minutes previously from the city. The praetor was conducted through the reception-rooms to the private apartments, and here he had not long to wait, for Hadrian wished to speak with him immediately. He found the sovereign so thoroughly out of tune that he could not think of inviting him to his banquet. The Emperor restlessly paced the room while Verus answered his questions as to the latest proceedings of the Senate in Rome, but he several times interrupted his walk and gazed into the adjoining room.

Just as the praetor had concluded his report Argus set up a howl of delight and Antinous came into the room. Verus at once withdrew into the window and pretended to be absorbed in looking out on the harbor.

" Where have you been ? " asked the Emperor, disregarding the praetor's presence.

" Into the city a little way," was the Bithynian's answer.

" But you know I cannot bear to miss you when I come home."

" I thought you would have been longer absent."

" For the future arrange so that I may be able to find you at whatever time I may seek you. Tell me, you do not like to see me vexed and worried ? "

" No, my lord," said the lad and he raised a supplicating hand and looked beseechingly at his master.

" Then let it pass. But now for something else ; how did this little phial come into the hands of the dealer Hiram ?" As he spoke the Emperor took from his table the little bottle of *Vasa Murrhina* which the lad had given to Arsinoe and which she had sold to the Phœnician, and held it up before the favorite's eyes. Antinous turned pale, and stammered in great confusion. " It is incomprehensible—I cannot in the least recollect—"

"Then I will assist your memory," said the Emperor decidedly. " The Phœnician appears to me to be an honester man than that rogue Gabinius. In his collection, which I have just been to see, I found this gem, that Plotina—do you hear me, boy—that Trajan's wife Plotina, my heart's friend, never to be forgotten, gave me years ago. It was one of my dearest possessions and yet I thought it not too precious to give to you on your last birthday."

32

" Oh, my lord, my dear lord!" cried Antinous in a low tone and again lifting his eyes and hands in entreaty.

" Now, I ask you," continued Hadrian, gravely, and without allowing himself to yield to the lad's beseeching looks, "how could this object have passed into the possession of one of the daughters of the wretched palace-steward Keraunus from whom Hiram confessed that he had bought it ?"

Antinous vainly strove for utterance; Hadrian however came to his aid by asking him more angrily than before :

" Did the girl steal it from you ?   Out with the truth !"

" No, no," replied the Bithynian quickly and decidedly.   " Certainly not.   I remember—wait a minute—yes, that was it.—You know it contained excellent balsam, and when the big dog threw down Selene—the steward's daughter is called Selene—threw her down the steps so that she lay hurt on the stones I fetched the phial and gave her the balsam."

" With the bottle that held it ?" asked the Emperor looking at Antinous.

" Yes, my lord—I had no other."

" And she kept it and sold it at once."

" You know, of course, her father—"

" A gang of thieves !" snarled Hadrian.   " Do you know what has become of the girl ?"

" Yes my lord," said Antinous trembling with alarm.

" I will have her taken by the lictors," asserted the infuriated sovereign.

" No," said the lad positively.   "No, you positively must not do that."

" No—? we shall see !"

" No, positively not, for at the same time you must know that Keraunus' daughter Selene—"

" Well ?"

" She flung herself into the water in despair; yes, into the water, at night—into the sea."

" Oh!" said Hadrian more gently, " that certainly alters the case. The lictors would find it difficult to apprehend a shade and the girl has suffered the worst punishment of all.—But you? what shall I say to your perfidy ? You knew the value of the gem. You knew how highly I valued it, and could part with it to such hands ?"

"It contained the salve," stammered the boy. " How could I think—?"

The Emperor interrupted the boy, striking his forehead with his hand as he spoke:

" Aye, think—we have known unfortunately too long that thinking is not your strong point. This little bottle has cost me a pretty sum; still, as it once belonged to you I give it back to you again; I only require you to take better care of it this time. I shall ask for it again before long! But in the name of all the gods, boy, what is the matter ? Am I so alarming that a simple question from me is enough to drive all the blood out of your cheeks ? Really and truly, if I had not had the thing from Plotina I should have left it in the Phœnician's hands and not have made all this coil about it."

Antinous went quickly up to the Emperor to kiss his hand, but Hadrian pressed his lips to his brow with fatherly affection.

"Simpleton," he said, "if you want me to be pleased with you, you must be again just what you were before

we came to Alexandria.   Leave it to others to do
things to vex me.   You are created by the gods to
delight me."

During Hadrian's last words a chamberlain had
entered the room to inform the Emperor that the deputation of the Egyptian priesthood had arrived to do
homage to him.   He immediately assumed the purple
mantle and proceeded to the hall of the Muses where,
surrounded by his court, he received the high-priests
and spiritual fathers of the different temples of the Nile
Valley, to be hailed by them as the Son of Sun-god, and
to assure them and the religion they cherished his gracious countenance.   He vouchsafed his consent to their
prayer that he would add sanctity and happiness to the
temples of the immortals which they served by gracing
them with his presence, but set aside for the moment
the question as to which town might be permitted to
have the care of the recently-discovered Apis.

This audience took up several hours.   Verus shirked
the duty of attending it with Titianus and the other
dignitaries of the court, and remained sitting motionless
by the window; it was not till Hadrian was gone from
the room that he came forward into it again.   He was
quite alone, for Antinous had left the room with the
Emperor.   The praetor's remaining behind had not
escaped the lad's notice, but he sought to avoid him, for
the domineering, mocking spirit of Verus repelled him.
Besides this the terror which he had gone through, as
well as the consciousness that he had been guilty of a
lie and had daringly deceived his kind master, had upset
a soul hitherto untainted by any subterfuge and had
thrown him off his balance.   He longed to be alone,
for it would have been keenly painful to him at this

moment to discuss indifferent subjects, or to be forced to affect an easy demeanor. He sat in his little room, before a table, with his face buried in his hands that rested on it.

Verus did not immediately follow him, for he understood what was passing in his mind and knew that here he could not escape him. In a few minutes all was still alike in the large room and in the small one. Then the praetor heard the door between the smaller room and the corridor hastily opened and immediately the Bithynian's exclamation:

"At last, Mastor—have you seen Selene?"

With two long, noiseless steps Verus went close to the door leading into the adjoining room, and listened for the slave's answer, though a less sharp ear than that of the praetor might have heard every syllable.

"How should I have seen her?" asked the Sarmatian sharply. "She is still suffering and in bed. I gave your flowers to the deformed girl who takes care of her; but I will not do it again, you may rely upon it, not if you coax even more fondly than you did yesterday and promise me all Caesar's treasure into the bargain! And what can you want with that wretched, pale-faced, innocent creature? I am but a poor slave, but I can tell you this—"

Here the Sarmatian broke off abruptly, and Verus rightly guessed that Antinous had remembered his presence in the Emperor's room and had signed to the slave to be silent.

But the listener had learnt enough. The favorite had told his master a lie, and the suicide of the steward's daughter was a pure romance. Who would have believed that the silent, dreamy lad had so much presence of mind, and such cunning powers of invention ?   The praetor's handsome face was radiant with satisfaction as he made these reflections, for now he had the Bithyn- ian under his thumb, and now he knew how to accom- plish all he wished.   Antinous himself had indicated the right course when he had hastened to the Emperor with a gush of tenderness, in which the warmth was certainly not affected, to kiss his hand.

The favorite loved his master, and Verus could ground his demands on this love without exposing himself, or having to dread the Emperor's avenging hand in case of betrayal.   He knocked at the door of the adjoining room with a firm hand, and then went confidently and composedly up to the Bithynian, told him that he had an important matter to discuss with him, begged him to return with him into the Emperor's room and then said, as soon as they were alone together :

" I am so unfortunate as not to be able to number you among my particular friends ; but one strong senti- ment we have in common.   We both love Caesar."

" I love him, certainly," replied the lad.

" Well then, you must have it at heart to spare him all great sorrow, and to prevent grave apprehensions from paralyzing the pinions of his free and noble soul."

" No doubt."

" I knew I should find a colleague in you.   See this roll.   It contains the calculations and diagrams of the greatest astrologer of our time, and from these it is to be discovered that this night, from the end of the second hour of the morning till the beginning of the fourth, the stars will announce fearful disasters to our Sovereign. Do you understand ?"

" Alas ! perfectly."

" After that the indications of evil disappear. Now if we could only succeed in preventing Hadrian observing the heavens merely during the third hour after midnight we should preserve him from trouble and anxiety, which will torment and spoil his life. Who knows whether the stars may not lie ? But even if they tell the truth, misfortune, when it does come, always comes much too soon. Do you agree with me ?"

" Your suggestion sounds a very sensible one—still I think—"

" It is both sensible and wise," said the praetor, shortly and decidedly, interrupting the boy. " And it must be your part to hinder Hadrian from marking the course of the stars from the end of the second to the beginning of the fourth hour after midnight."

" My part ?" cried Antinous, startled.

" Yours—for you are the only person who can accomplish it."

" I ?" repeated the Bithynian, greatly perturbed. " I—disturb Caesar in his observations !"

" It is your duty."

" But he never allows any one to disturb him at his studies, and if I were to attempt it he would be very angry and send me off in no time. No, no, what you ask is impossible."

" It is not only possible but imperatively necessary."

" That it certainly cannot be," replied Antinous, clasping his forehead in his hand. " Only listen! Hadrian has known for several days past that some great misfortune threatens him. I heard it from his own lips. If you know him at all you must know that he gazes at the stars not merely to rejoice in future happiness, but also to fortify himself against the disasters which threaten

him or the state. What would crush a weaker man
only serves to arm his bold spirit. He can bear all that
may befall, and it would be a crime to deceive him."

"To cloud his heart and mind would be a greater,"
retorted Verus. "Devise some means of taking him
away from his star-gazing for only an hour."

"I dare not, and even if I wished it, it could not be
done. Do you suppose he follows me whenever I
call?"

"But you know him; invent something which will
be sure to make him come down from his watch-
tower."

"I cannot invent or think of any thing."

"Nothing?" asked Verus, going close up to the
Bithynian. "You just now gave striking proof to the
contrary."

Antinous turned pale and the praetor went on :

"When you wanted to rescue the fair Selene from
the lictors your swift invention threw her into the sea!"

"She did throw herself in, as truly as that the
gods—"

"Stay, stay," cried the praetor. "No perjury, at
least! Selene is living, you send her flowers, and if I
should think proper to conduct Hadrian to the house of
Paulina—"

"Oh!" cried Antinous lamentably enough, and
grasping the Roman's hand. "You will not—you cannot. Oh Verus! you will not do that."

"Simpleton," laughed the praetor, slapping the
alarmed youth lightly on the shoulder. "What good
could it do me to ruin you? I have only one thing at
heart just now, and that is to save Caesar from care and
anxiety. Keep him occupied only during the third

hour after midnight and you may count on my friendship; but if out of fear or ill-will you refuse me your assistance you do not deserve your sovereign's favor and
then you will compel me—"

"No more, no more!" cried Antinous interrupting
his tormentor in despair.

"Then you promise me to carry out my wish?"

"Yes, by Hercules! Yes, what you require shall
be done. But eternal gods! how am I to get Caesar—"

"That, my young friend, I leave with perfect confidence to you and your shrewdness."

"I am not shrewd—I can devise nothing," groaned
the lad.

"What you could do out of terror of your master
you can do still better for love of him," retorted the
praetor. "The problem is an easy one; and if after all
you should not succeed I shall feel it no less than my
duty to explain to Hadrian how well Antinous can take
care of his own interests and how badly of his master's
peace of mind. Till to-morrow, my handsome friend—
and if for the future you have flowers to send, my slaves
are quite at your service."

With these words the praetor left the room, but
Antinous stood like one crushed, pressing his brow
against the cold porphyry pillar by the window. What
Verus required of him did not seem to have any harm
in it, and yet it was not right. It was treason to his
noble master, whom he loved with tender devotion as a
father, a wise, kind friend, and preceptor, and whom he
reverenced and feared as though he were a god. To
plot to hide impending trouble from him, as if he were
not a man but a feeble weakling, was absurd and con-
temptible, and must introduce an error of unknown im-

portance and extent into his sovereign's far-seeing pre-
determinations. Many other reasons against the praetor's demands crowded on him, and as each occurred
to his mind he cursed his tardy spirit which never let
him see or think the right thing till it was too late.
His first deceit had already involved him in a second.

He hated himself; he hit his forehead with his fists
and sobbed aloud bitterly again and again, though he
shed no tears. Still, in the midst of his self-accusation,
the flattering voice made itself heard in his soul: "It is
only to preserve your master from sorrow, and it is
nothing wrong that you are asked to do." And each
time that his inward ear heard these words he began
to puzzle his brain to discover in what way it might be
possible, for him to tempt the Emperor, at the hour
named, down from his watch-tower in the palace. But
he could hit on no practicable plan.

"It cannot be done, no—it cannot be done!" he
muttered to himself, and then he asked himself if it were
not even his duty to defy the praetor and to confess to
Hadrian that he had deceived him in the morning. If
only it had not been for the little bottle! Could he
ever confess that he had heedlessly parted with this gift
of all others from his master? No, it was too hard, it
might cost him his sovereign's affection for ever. And
if he contented himself with a half-truth and confessed,
merely to anticipate the praetor's accusation, that Selene
was still living, then he would involve the daughters of
the hapless Keraunus in persecution and disgrace—
Selene whom he loved with all the devotion of a first
passion, which was enhanced and increased by the hin-
drances that had come in its way. It was impossible
to confess his guilt—quite impossible. The longer he

thought, tormenting himself to find some way out of it all, the more confused he became, and the more impotent his efforts at resistance. The praetor had entangled him with thongs and meshes, and at every struggle to escape they only seemed knotted more closely round him.

His head began to ache sadly; and what an endless time Caesar was absent! He dreaded his return, and yet he longed for it. When at last Hadrian came in and signed to Mastor to relieve him of his imperial robes, Antinous slipped behind him, and silently and carefully fulfilled the slave's office. He felt uneasy and worried, and yet he forced himself to appear in good spirits during supper when he had to sit opposite the Emperor.

When, shortly before midnight, Hadrian rose from the table to go up to the watch-tower on the northern side of the palace, Antinous begged to be allowed to carry his instruments for him, and the Emperor, stroking his hair, said kindly:

"You are my dear and faithful companion. Youth has a right to go astray now and then so long as it does not entirely forget the path in which it ought to tread."

Antinous was deeply touched by these words, and he secretly pressed to his lips a fold of the Emperor's toga as he walked in front. It was as though he wanted to make amends in advance for the crime he had not yet committed.

Wrapped in his cloak he kept the Emperor silent company during his studies, till the close of the first hour after midnight. The sharp, north wind which blew through the darkness did his aching head good, and still he racked his wits for some pretext to attract Hadrian from his labors, but in vain. His tormented brain was like a dried-up well; bucket after bucket did he send down, but not one brought up the refreshing draught he needed. Nothing—nothing could he think of that could conduce to his end. Once he plucked up courage and said imploringly as he went close up to the Emperor :

"Go down earlier to-night my lord; you really do not allow yourself enough rest and will injure your health."

Hadrian let him speak, and answered kindly:

"I sleep in the morning. If you are tired, go to bed now."

But Antinous remained, gazing, like his master, at the stars. He knew very few of the brilliant bodies by their names, but some of them were very dear to him, particularly the Pleiades which his father had pointed out to him and which reminded him of his home. There he had been so quiet and happy, and how wildly his anxious heart was throbbing now!

"Go to bed, the second hour is beginning," said Hadrian.

"Already!" said the boy; and as he reflected how soon that must be done which Verus had required of him, and then looked up again at the heavens, it seemed to him as though all the stars in the blue vault over his head had glided from their places and were dancing in wild and whirling confusion between the sky and the sea. He closed his eyes in his bewilderment; then, bidding his master good-night he lighted a torch and by its flaring and doubtful light descended from the tower.

Pontius had erected this slight structure expressly for Hadrian's nightly observations. It was built of timber and Nile-mud and stood up as a tall turret on the

secure foundation of an ancient watch-tower built of
hewn stone, which, standing among the low buildings
that served as storehouses for the palace, commanded
a free outlook over all the quarters of the sky. Hadrian,
who liked to be alone and undisturbed when observing
the heavens, had preferred this erection—even after he
had made himself known to the Alexandrians—to the
great observatory of the Serapeum, from which a still
broader horizon was visible.

After Antinous had got out of the smaller and newer
tower into the larger and older one he sat down on one
of the lowest steps to collect his thoughts and to quiet
his loudly-beating heart. His vain cogitations began
all over again. Time slipped on—between the present
moment and the deed to be done there were but a certain number of minutes. He told himself so, and his
weary brain stirred more actively, suggesting to him to
feign illness and bring the Emperor to his bedside. But
Hadrian was physician enough to see that he was well,
and even if he should allow himself to be deceived, he,
Antinous, was a deceiver. This thought filled him with
horror of himself and with dread for the future, and yet
it was the only plan that gave any hope of success.
And even when he sprang to his feet and walked hastily
up and down among the out-houses he could hit upon
no other scheme. And how fast the minutes flew! The
third hour after midnight must be quite close at hand,
and he had scarcely left himself time to rush back into
the palace, throw himself on his couch, and call Mastor.
Quite bewildered with agitation and tottering like a
drunken man he hastened back into the old tower where
he had left his torch leaning against the wall and looked
up the stone stairs; it suddenly flashed through his mind

that he might go up again to fling himself down them. What did he care for his miserable life.

His fall, his cry, would bring the Emperor down from his observatory and he knew that he would not leave his bleeding favorite uncared for and untended—he could count upon that. And if then Hadrian watched by his bed it would be that, perhaps, of a dying man, but not of a deceiver.   Fully determined on extreme measures, he tightened the girdle which held his chiton above his hips and once more went out into the night to judge by the stars what hour it was. He saw the slender sickle of the waning moon—the same moon which at the full had been mirrored in the sea when he had gone into the water to save Selene.   The image of the pale girl rose before him, tangibly distinct.   He felt as if he held her once more in his arms—saw her once more lying on her bed—could once more press his lips to her cold brow. Then the vision vanished ; instead he was possessed by a wild desire to see her, and he said to himself that he could not die without having seen her once more.

He looked about him in indecision.   Before him lay one of the largest of the storehouses that surrounded the tower.   With his torch in one hand he went in at the open door.   In the large shed lay the chests and cases, the hemp, linseed, straw and matting that had been used in packing the vessels and works of art with which the palace had been newly furnished.   This he knew ; and now, looking up at the stars once more and seeing that the second hour after midnight had almost run to an end, a fearful thought flashed through his mind, and without daring to consider, he flung the torch into the open shed, crammed to the roof with inflammable materials, and stood motionless, with his arms crossed, to watch through the door of the shed the rapidly spreading flame, the soaring smoke, the struggle and mingling of the noiseless wreaths of black vapor from the various combustibles with the ruddy light, the victory of the fire and the leaping flames as they flew upward.

The roof, thatched with palm-leaves and reeds, had begun to crackle when Antinous rushed into the tower only a few paces off crying: " Fire—fire !" and up the stairs which led to the observatory of the imperial star-gazer.

CHAPTER XIV.

THE entertainment which Verus was giving on the eve of his birthday seemed to be far from drawing to an end, even at the beginning of the third hour of the morning. Besides the illustrious and learned Romans who had accompanied the Emperor to Alexandria, the most famous and distinguished Alexandrians had also been invited by the praetor. The splendid banquet had long been ended, but jar after jar of mixed wine was still being filled and emptied. Verus himself had been unanimously chosen as the king and leader of the feast. Crowned with a rich garland, he reclined on a couch strewn with rose-leaves, an invention of his own, and formed of four cushions piled one on another. A curtain of transparent gauze screened him from flies and gnats, and a tightly-woven mat of lilies and other flowers covered his feet and exhaled sweet odors for him and for the pretty singer who sat by his side.

33

Pretty boys dressed as little cupids watched every sign of the 'sham Eros.'

How indolently he lay on the deep, soft cushions! And yet his eyes were every where, and though he had not failed to give due consideration to the preparations for his feast, he devoted all the powers of his mind to the present management of it. As at the entertainments which Hadrian was accustomed to give in Rome, first of all short selections from new essays or poems were recited by their authors, then a gay comedy was performed; then Glycera, the most famous singer in the city, had sung a dithyramb to her harp, in a voice as sweet as a bell, and Alexander, a skilled performer on the trigonon, had executed a piece. Finally a troop of female dancers had rushed into the room and swayed and balanced themselves to the music of the double-flute and tambourine.

Each fresh amusement had been more loudly applauded than the last. With every jar of wine a new torrent of merriment went up through the opening in the roof, by which the scent of the flowers and of the perfume burnt on beautiful little altars found an exit into the open air. The wine offered in libations to the gods already lay in broad pools upon the hard pavement of the hall, the music and singing were drowned in shouts—the feast had become an orgy.

Verus was inciting the more quiet or slothful of his guests to a freer enjoyment and encouraging the noisest in their extravagant recklessness to still more unbridled license. At the same time he bowed to each one who drank to his health, entertained the singer who sat by his side, flung a sparkling jest into one and another silent group, and proved to the learned men who reclined on their couches near to his that whenever it was possible he took an interest in their discussions.

Alexandria, the focus of all the learning of the East and the West, had seen other festivals than this riotous banquet. Indeed, even here a vein of grave and wise discourse flavored the meal of the circle that belonged to the Museum; but the senseless revelry of Rome had found its way into the houses of the rich, and even the noblest achievements of the human mind had been made, unawares, subservient to mere enjoyment. A man was a philosopher only that he might be prompt to discuss and always ready to take his share in the talk; and at a banquet a well-told anecdote was more heartily welcome than some profound idea that gave rise to a reflection or provoked a subtle discussion.

What a noise, what a clatter was storming in the hall by the second hour after midnight! How the lungs of the feasters were choked with overpowering perfumes! What repulsive exhibitions met the eye! How shamelessly was all decency trodden under foot! The poisonous breath of unchecked license had blasted the noble moderation of the Greek nature, and from the vapor of wine which floated round this chaos of riotous topers slowly rose the pale image of Satiety watching for victims on the morrow.

The circle of couches on which lay Florus, Favorinus and their Alexandrian friends stood like an island in the midst of the surging sea of the orgy. Even here the cup had been bravely passed round, and Florus was beginning to speak somewhat indistinctly, but conversation had hitherto had the upper hand.

Two days before, the Emperor had visited the Museum and had carried on learned discussions with the

33

most prominent of the sages and professors there, in the presence of their assembled disciples. At last a formal disputation had arisen, and the dialectic keenness and precision with which Hadrian, in the purest Attic Greek, had succeeded in driving his opponents into a corner had excited the greatest admiration. The Sovereign had quitted the famous institution with a promise to reopen the contest at an early date. The philosophers, Pancrates and Dionysius and Apollonius, who took no wine at all, were giving a detailed account of the different phases of this remarkable disputation and praising the admirable memory and the ready tongue of the great monarch.

"And you did not even see him at his best," exclaimed Favorinus, the Gaul, the sophist and rhetorician. "He has received an unfavorable oracle and the stars seem to confirm the prophecy. This puts him out of tune. Between ourselves let me tell you I know a few who are his superiors in dialectic, but in his happiest moments he is irresistible—irresistible. Since we made up our quarrel he is like a brother to me. I will defend him against all comers, for, as I say, Hadrian is my brother."

The Gaul had poured out this speech in a defiant tone and with flashing eyes. He grew pale in his cups, touchy, boastful and very talkative.

"No doubt you are right," replied Apollonius, "but it seemed to us that he was bitter in discusson. His eyes are gloomy rather than gay."

"He is my brother," repeated Favorinus, "and as for his eyes, I have seen them flash—by Hercules! like the radiant sun, or merry twinkling stars! And his mouth! I know him well! He is my brother, and I will wager

that while he condescended—it is too comical—condescended to dispute with you—with you, there was a sly
smile at each corner of his mouth—so—look now—like
this he smiled."

"I repeat, he seemed to us gloomy rather than gay,"
retorted Apollonius, with annoyance; and Pancrates
added:

"If he does really know how to jest he certainly did
not prove it to us."

"Not out of ill-will," laughed the Gaul, "you do
not know him, but I—I am his friend and may follow
wherever he goes. Now only wait and I will tell you a few
stories about him. If I chose I could describe his whole
soul to you as if it lay there on the surface of the wine
in my cup. Once in Rome he went to inspect the new-
ly-decorated baths of Agrippa, and in the undressing-
room he saw an old man, a veteran who had fought
with him somewhere or other. My memory is greatly
admired, but his is in no respect inferior. Scaurus was
the old man's name—yes—yes, Scaurus. He did not
observe Caesar at first, for after his bath his wounds
were burning and he was rubbing his back against the
rough stone of a pillar. Hadrian however called to
him: 'Why are you scratching yourself, my friend?'
and Scaurus, not at once recognizing Caesar's voice, answered without turning round: 'Because I have no
slave to do it for me.' You should have heard Caesar
laugh! Liberal as he is sometimes—I say sometimes—
he gave Scaurus a handsome sum of money and two
sturdy slaves. The story soon got abroad, and when
Caesar, who—as you believe—cannot jest, a short time
after again visited the bath, two old soldiers at once
placed themselves in his way, scrubbed their backs

against the wall like Scaurus, and called out to him:
' Great Caesar, we have no slaves.'—' Then scratch
each other,' cried he, and left the soldiers to rub themselves."

"Capital!" laughed Dionysius.

"Now one more true story," interrupted the loquacious Gaul. "Once upon a time a man with white hair
begged of him. The wretch was a low fellow, a parasite
who wandered round from one man's table to another,
feeding himself out of other folks' wallets and dishes.
Caesar knew his man and warned him off. Then the creature had his hair dyed that he might not be recognized,
and tried his luck a second time with the Emperor.
But Hadrian has good eyes; he pointed to the door,
saying, with the gravest face: 'I have just lately refused to give your father anything.' And a hundred
such jokes pass from mouth to mouth in Rome, and if
you like I can give you a dozen of the best."

"Tell us, go on, out with your stories. They are all
old friends!" stammered Florus. "But while Favorinus
chatters we can drink."

The Gaul cast a contemptuous glance at the Roman,
and answered promptly:

"My stories are too good for a drunken man."

"Florus paused to think of an answer, but before
he could find one, the praetor's body-slave rushed
into the hall crying out: "The palace at Lochias is
on fire."

Verus kicked the mat of lilies off his feet on to the
floor, tore down the net that screened him in, and
shouted to the breathless runner.

"My chariot—quick, my chariot! To our next
merry meeting another evening my friends, with many

thanks for the honor you have done me. I must be off
to Lochias."

Verus flew out of the hall, without throwing on his
cloak and hot as he was, into the cold night, and at the
same time most of his guests had started up to hurry
into the open air, to see the fire and to hear the latest
news; but only very few went to the scene of the conflagration to help the citizens to extinguish it, and many
heavily intoxicated drinkers remained lying on the
couches.

As Favorinus and the Alexandrians raised themselves
on their pillows Florus cried:

" No god shall make me stir from this place, not if
the whole house is burnt down and Alexandria and
Rome, and for aught I care every nest and nook on the
face of the earth. It may all burn together. The Roman
Empire can never be greater or more splendid than under Caesar! It may burn down like a heap of straw, it
is all the same to me—I shall lie here and drink."

The turmoil and confusion on the scene of the interrupted feast seemed inextricable, while Verus hurried off
to Sabina to inform her of what had occurred. But Balbilla had been the first to discover the fire and quite at
the beginning, for after sitting industriously at her
studies, and before going to bed, she had looked out
toward the sea. She had instantly run out, cried " Fire!"
and was now seeking for a chamberlain to awake
Sabina.

The whole of Lochias flared and shone in a purple
and golden glow. It formed the nucleus of a wide
spreading radiance of tender red of which the extent
and intensity alternately grew and diminished. Verus
met the poetess at the door that led from the garden

into the Empress' apartments. He omitted on this occasion to offer his customary greeting, but hastily asked
her :

"Has Sabina been told ?"

"I think not yet."

"Then have her called. Greet her from me—I must
go to Lochias."

"We will follow you."

"No, stay here; you will be in the way there."

"I do not take much room and I shall go. What a
magnificent spectacle."

"Eternal gods! the flames are breaking out too below the palace, by the King's harbor. Where can the
chariots be ?"

"Take me with you."

"No you must wake the Empress."

"And Lucilla ?"

"You women must stay where you are."

"For my part I certainly will not. Caesar will be in
no danger ?"

"Hardly—the old stones cannot burn."

"Only look! how splendid! the sky is one crimson
tent. I entreat you, Verus, let me go with you."

"No, no, pretty one. Men are wanted down there."

"How unkind you are."

"At last! here are the chariots! You women stay
here; do you understand me ?"

"I will not take any orders; I shall go to Lochias."

"To see Antinous in the flames! such a sight is not
to be seen every day, to be sure !" cried Verus, ironically,
as he sprang into his chariot, and took the reins into
his own hand.

Balbilla stamped with rage.

She went to Sabina's rooms fully resolved to go to the scene of the fire. The Empress would not let herself be seen by any one, not even by Balbilla, till she was completely dressed. A waiting-woman told Balbilla that Sabina would get up certainly, but that for the sake of her health she could not venture out in the night-air.

The poetess then sought Lucilla and begged her to accompany her to Lochias; she was perfectly willing and ready, but when she heard that her husband had wished that the women should remain at the Caesareum she declared that she owed him obedience and tried to keep back her friend. But the perverse curly-haired girl was fully determined, precisely because Verus had forbidden her—and forbidden her with mocking words, to carry out her purpose. After a short altercation with Lucilla she left her, sought her companion Claudia, told her what she intended doing, dismissed that lady's remonstrance with a very positive command, gave orders herself to the house-steward to have horses put to a chariot and reached the imperilled palace an hour and a half after Verus.

An endless, many-headed crowd of people besieged the narrow end of Lochias on the landward side and the harbor wharves below, where some stores and ship-yards were in flames. Boats innumerable were crowded round the little peninsula. An attempt was being made, with much shouting, and by the combined exertions of an immense number of men, to get the larger ships afloat which lay at anchor close to the quay of the King's harbor and to place them in security. Every thing far and wide was lighted up as brightly as by day, but with a ruddier and more restless light. The north-

east breeze fanned the fire, aggravating the labors of the
men who were endeavoring to extinguish it and snatch-
ing flakes of flame off every burning mass.   Each blazing storehouse was a gigantic torch throwing a broad
glare into the darkness of the night.   The white marble
of the tallest beacon tower in the world, on the island
of Pharos, reflected a rosy hue, but its far gleaming light
shone pale and colorless.   The dark hulls of the larger
ships and the flotilla of boats in the background were
afloat in a fiery sea, and the still water under the shore
mirrored the illumination in which the whole of Lochias
was wrapped.

Balbilla could not tire of admiring this varying scene,
in which the most gorgeous hues vied with each other
and the intensest light contrasted with the deepest
shadows.   And she had ample time to dwell on the
marvellous picture before her eyes, for her chariot could
only proceed slowly, and at a point where the street led
up from the King's harbor to the palace, lictors stood
in her way and declared positively that any farther advance was out of the question.   The horses, much scared
by the glare of the fire and the crowd that pressed round
them, could hardly be controlled, first rearing and then
kicking at the front board of the chariot.   The charioteer
declared he could no longer be answerable.   The people
who had hurried to the rescue now began to abuse the
women, who ought to have staid at home at the loom
rather than come stopping the way for useful citizens.

"There is time enough to go out driving by daylight!" cried one man; and another: "If a spark falls
in those curls another conflagration will break out."

The position of the ladies was becoming every instant more unendurable and Balbilla desired the chari-

oteer to turn round; but in the swarming mass of men
that filled the street this was easier said than done. One
of the horses broke the strap which fastened the yoke
that rested on his withers to the pole, started aside and
forced back the crowd which now began to scold and
scream loudly. Balbilla wanted to spring out of the
chariot, but Claudia clung tightly to her and conjured
her not to leave her in the lurch in the midst of the
danger. The spoilt patrician's daughter was not timid,
but on this occasion she would have given much not
to have followed Verus. At first she thought, " A delightful adventure! still, it will not be perfect till it is
over." But presently her bold experiment lost every
trace of charm, and repentance that she had ever undertaken it filled her mind. She was far nearer weeping
than laughing already, when a man's deep voice said
behind her, in tones of commanding decision :

" Make way there for the pumps; push aside whatever stops the way."

These terrible words reduced Claudia to sinking on
to her knees, but Balbilla's quelled courage found fresh
wings as she heard them, for she had recognized the
voice of Pontius. Now he was close behind the chariot,
high on a horse. He then was the man on horseback
whom she had seen dashing from the sea-shore up to
the higher storehouses that were burning, down to the
lake, and hither and thither.

She turned full upon him and called him by his
name. He recognized her, tried to pull up his horse as
it was dashing forward, and smilingly shook his head at
her, as much as to say: " She is a giddy creature and
deserves a good scolding; but who could be angry
with her?" And then he gave his orders to his subor-

dinates just as if she had been a mere chattel, a bale of goods or something of the kind, and not an heiress of distinction.

"Take out the horses," he cried to the municipal guards; "we can use them for carrying water."—"Help the ladies out of the chariot."—"Take them between you Nonnus and Lucanus."—"Now, stow the chariot in there among the bushes."—"Make way there in front, make way for our pumps." And each of these orders was obeyed as promptly as if it was the word of command given by a general to his well-drilled soldiers.

After the pumps had been fairly started Pontius rode close up to Balbilla and said :

"Caesar is safe and sound. You no doubt wished to see the progress of the fire from a spot near it, and in fact the colors down there are magnificent. I have not time to escort you back to the Caesareum; but follow me. You will be safe in the harbor-guard's stone house, and from the roof you can command a view of Lochias and the whole peninsula. You will have a rare feast for the eye, noble Balbilla; but I beg you not to forget at the same time how many days of honest labor, what rich possessions, how many treasures earned by bitter hardship are being destroyed at this moment. What may delight you will cost bitter tears to many others, and so let us both hope that this splendid spectacle may now have reached its climax, and soon may come to an end."

"I hope so—I hope it with all my heart!" cried the girl.

"I was sure you would. As soon as possible I will come to look after you. You Nonnus and Lucanus, conduct these noble ladies to the harbor-guard's house.

Tell him they are intimate friends of the Empress.—
Only keep the pumps going! Till we meet again Balbilla!" and with these words the architect gave his
horse the bridle and made his way through the crowd.

A quarter of an hour later Balbilla was standing on
the roof of the little stone guard-house. Claudia was
utterly exhausted and incapable of speech. She sat
in the dark little parlor below on a rough-hewn wooden
bench. But the young Roman now gazed at the fire
with different eyes than before. Pontius had made her
feel a foe to the flames which only a short time before
had filled her with delight as they soared up to the sky,
wild and fierce. They still flared up violently, as though
they had to climb above the roof; but soon they seemed
to be quelled and exhausted, to find it more and more
difficult to rise above the black smoke which welled up
from the burning mass. Balbilla had looked out for the
architect and had soon discovered him, for the man on
horseback towered above the crowd. He halted now by
one and now by another burning storehouse. Once
she lost sight of him for a whole hour, for he had gone
to Lochias. Then again he reappeared, and wherever
he stayed for a while, the raging element abated its
fury.

Without her having perceived it, the wind had
changed and the air had become still and much
warmer. This circumstance favored the efforts of the
citizens trying to extinguish the fire, but Balbilla ascribed
it to the foresight of her clever friend when the flames
subsided in some places and in others were altogether
extinguished. Once she saw that he had a building
completely torn down which divided a burning granary
from some other storehouses that had been spared, and

she understood the object of this order; it cut off the
progress of the flames.   Another time she saw him high
on the top of a rise in the ground.   Close before him
in a sheet of flame was a magazine in which were kept
tow and casks of resin and pitch.   He turned his face
full towards it and gave his orders, now on this side,
now on that.   His figure and that of his horse, which
reared uneasily beneath him, were flooded in a crimson
glow—a splendid picture!   She trembled for him, she
gazed in admiration at this calm, resolute, energetic
man, and when a blazing beam fell close in front of him
and after his frightened horse had danced round and
round with him, he forced it to submit to his guidance,
the praetor's insinuation recurred to her mind, that she
clung to her determination to go to Lochias because she
hoped to enjoy the spectacle of Antinous in the flames.
Here, before her, was a nobler display, and yet her lively
imagination which often, sometimes indeed against her
will, gave shape to her formless thoughts—called up the
image of the beautiful youth surrounded by the glowing
glory which still painted the horizon.

Hour after hour slipped by ; the efforts of the thousands who endeavored to extinguish the blaze were
crowned by increasing success; one burning mass after
another was quenched, if not extinguished, and instead
of flames smoke, mingled with sparks, rose from Lochias
blacker and blacker—and still Pontius came not to look
after her.   She could not see any stars for the sky was
overcast with clouds, but the beginning of a new day
could not be far distant.   She was shivering with cold,
and her friend's long absence began to annoy her.
When, presently, it began to rain in large drops, she went
down the ladder that led from the roof and sat down by

*he fire in the little room where her companion had gone fast asleep.

She had been sitting quite half an hour and gazing dreamily into the warming glow, when she heard the sound of hoofs and Pontius appeared. His face was begrimed, and his voice hoarse with shouting commands for hours. As soon as she saw him Balbilla forgot her vexation, greeted him warmly, and told him how she had watched his every movement; but the eager girl, so readily fired to enthusiasm, could only with the greatest difficulty bring out a few words to express the admiration that his mode of proceeding had so deeply excited in her mind.

She heard him say that his mouth was quite parched and his throat was longing for a draught of some drink, and she—who usually had every pin she needed handed to her by a slave, and on whom fate had bestowed no living creature whom she could find a pleasure in serving—she, with her own hand dipped a cup of water out of the large clay jar that stood in a corner of the room and offered it to him with a request that he would drink it. He eagerly swallowed the refreshing fluid, and when the little cup was empty Balbilla took it from his hand, refilled it, and gave it him again.

Claudia, who woke up when the architect came in, looked on at her foster-child's unheard-of proceedings with astonishment, shaking her head. When Pontius had drained the third cupful that Balbilla fetched for him he exclaimed, drawing a deep breath :

"That was a drink—I never tasted a better in the whole course of my life."

" Muddy water out of a nasty earthen pitcher !" answered the girl.

"And it tasted better than wine from Byblos out of a golden goblet."

"You had honestly earned the refreshment, and thirst gives flavor to the humblest liquor."

"You forget the hand that gave it me," replied the architect warmly.

.   Balbilla colored and looked at the floor in confusion, but presently raised her face and said, as gayly and carelessly as ever:

"So that you have been deliciously refreshed; and now that is done you will go home and the poor thirsty soul will once more become the great architect. But before that happens, pray inform us what god it was that brought you hither from Pelusium in the very nick of time when the fire broke out, and how matters look now in the palace at Lochias ?"

"My time is short," replied Pontius, and he then rapidly told her that, after he had finished his work at Pelusium, he had returned to Alexandria with the imperial post. As he got out of the chariot at the post-house he observed the reflection of fire over the sea and was immediately after told by a slave that it was the palace that was burning. There were horses in plenty at the post-house; he had chosen a strong one and had got to the spot before the crowd had collected. How the fire had originated, so far remained undiscovered. "Caesar," he said, "was in the act of observing the heavens when a flame broke out in a store-shed close to the tower. Antinous was the first to detect it, cried 'Fire,' and warned his master. I found Hadrian in the greatest agitation; he charged me to superintend the work of rescuing all that could be saved. At Lochias Verus helped me greatly and indeed with so much boldness and judgment that I owe very much to him. Caesar himself kept his favorite within the palace, for the poor fellow burned both his hands."

" Oh !" cried Balbilla with eager regret. " How did that happen ? "

"When Hadrian and Antinous first came down from the tower they brought with them as many of the instruments and manuscripts as they could carry. When they were at the bottom Caesar observed that a tablet with important calculations had been left lying up above and expressed his regret. Meanwhile the fire had already caught the slightly-built turret and it seemed impossible to get into it again. But the dreamy Bithynian can wake out of his slumbers it would seem, and while Caesar was anxiously watching the burning bundles of flax which the wind kept blowing across to the harbor the rash boy rushed into the burning building, flung the tablet down from the top of the tower and then hurried down the stairs. His bold action would indeed have cost the poor fellow his life if the slave Mastor, who meanwhile had hurried to the spot, had not dragged him down the stone stair of the old tower on which the new one stood and carried him into the open air. He was half suffocated at the top of them and had dropped down senseless."

" But he is alive, the splendid boy, the image of the gods ! and he is out of danger ?" cried Balbilla, with much anxiety.

" He is quite well; only his hands, as I said, are somewhat burnt, and his hair is singed, but that will grow again."

" His soft, lovely curls !" cried Balbilla. " Let us go home, Claudia. The gardener shall cut a magnifi-

34

cent bunch of roses, and we will send it to Antinous to
please him."

" Flowers to a man who does not care about them?"
asked Pontius, gravely.

" With what else can women reward men's virtues
or do honor to their beauty?" asked Balbilla.

" Our own conscience is the reward of our honest
actions, or the laurel wreath from the hand of some famous man."

" And beauty?"

" That of women claims and wins admiration, love
too perhaps and flowers—that of men may rejoice the
eye, but to do it honor is a task granted to no mortal
woman."

" To whom, then, if I may ask the question?"

" To Art, which makes it immortal."

" But the roses may bring some comfort and pleasure to the suffering youth."

" Then send them—but to the sick boy, and not to
the handsome man," retorted Pontius.

Balbilla was silent, and she and her companion followed the architect to the harbor. There he parted
from them, putting them into a boat which took them
back to the Caesareum through one of the arch-gates
under the Heptastadium.

As they were rowed along the younger Roman lady
said to the elder:

" Pontius has quite spoilt my fun about the roses—
The sick boy is the handsome Antinous all the same,
and if anybody could think—well, I shall do just as I
please; still it will be best not to cut the nosegay."

CHAPTER XV.

THE town was out of danger; the fire was extinct. Pontius had taken no rest till noonday. Three horses had he tired out and replaced by fresh ones, but his sinewy frame and healthy courage had till now defied every strain. As soon as he could consider his task at an end he went óff to his own house, and he needed rest; but in the hall of his residence he already found a number of persons waiting, and who were likely to stand between him and the enjoyment of it.

A man who lives in the midst of important undertakings cannot, with impunity, leave his work to take care of itself for several days. All the claims upon him become pent up, and when he returns home they deluge him like water when the sluice-gates are suddenly opened behind which it has been dammed up.

At least twenty persons, who had heard of the architect's return, were waiting for him in his outer hall, and crowded upon him as soon as he appeared. Among them he saw several who had come on important business, but he felt that he had reached the farthest limit of his strength, and he was determined to secure a little rest at any cost. The grave man's natural consideration, usually so conspicuous, could not hold out against the demands made on his endurance, and he angrily and peevishly pointed to his begrimed face as he made his way through the people waiting for him.

" To-morrow, to-morrow," he cried; " nay, if necessary, to-day, after sunset. But now I need rest. Rest!
34

Rest! Why, you yourselves can see the state I am in."

All—even the master-masons and purveyors who had come on urgent affairs, drew back; only one elderly man, his sister Paulina's house-steward, caught hold of his chiton, stained as it was with smoke and scorched in many places, and said quickly and in a low tone:

" My mistress greets you; she has things to speak of to you which will bear no delay; I am not to leave you till you have promised to go to see her to-day. Our chariot waits for you at the garden-door."

" Send it home," said Pontius, not even civilly; " Paulina must wait a few hours."

" But my orders are to take you with me at once."

" But in this state—so—I cannot go with you," cried the architect with vehemence. " Have you no sort of consideration? And yet—who can tell—well, tell her I will be with her in two hours."

When Pontius had fairly escaped the throng he took a bath; then he had some food brought to him, but even while he eat and drank, he was not unoccupied, for he read the letters which awaited him, and examined some drawings which his assistants had prepared during his absence.

" Give yourself an hour's respite," said the old housekeeper, who had been his nurse and who loved him as her own son.

" I must go to my sister," he answered with a shrug.

" We know her of old," said the old woman. " For nothing, and less than nothing, she has sent for you before now; and you absolutely need rest. There—are your cushions right—so? And let me ask you, has the humblest stone-carrier so hard a life as you have? Even at meals you never have an hour of peace and comfort. Your poor head is never quiet; the nights are turned into day; something to do, always something to do. It one only knew who it is all for?"

"Aye—who for, indeed?" sighed Pontius, pushing his arm under his head, between it and the pillow. "But, you see, little mother, work must follow rest as surely as day follows night or summer follows winter. The man who has something he loves in the house—a wife and merry children, it may be, for aught I care—who sweeten his hours of rest and make them the best of all the day, he, I say is wise when he tries to prolong them; but his case is not mine—"

"But why is it not yours, my son Pontius?"

"Let me finish my speech. I, as you know full well, do not care for gossip in the bath nor for reclining long over a banquet. In the pauses of my work I am alone, with myself and with you, my very worthy Leukippe. So the hours of rest are not for me the fairest scenes, but empty waits between the acts of the drama of life; 'and no reasonable man can find fault with me for trying to abridge them by useful occupation."

"And what is the upshot of this sensible talk?— Simply this: you must get married."

Pontius sighed, but Leukippe added eagerly:

"You have not far to look! The most respectable fathers and mothers are running after you and would bring their prettiest daughters into your door."

"A daughter whom I do not know, and who might perhaps spoil the pauses between the acts, which at present I can at any rate turn to some account."

"They say," the old woman went on, "that marriage is a cast of the dice. One throws a high number,

another a low one ; one wins a wife who is a match for
the busy bee, another gets a tiresome gnat.   No doubt
there is some truth in it; but I have grown grey with
my eyes open and I have often seen it happen, that how
the marriage turned out depended on the husband.   A
man like you makes a bee out of a gnat—a bee that
brings honey to the hive. Of course a man must choose
carefully."

" How, pray ?"

" First see the parents and then the child. A girl
who has grown up surrounded by good habits, in the
house of a sensible father and a virtuous mother—"

" And where in this city am I to find such a miracle?
Nay, nay, Leukippe, for the present all shall be left to
my old woman. , We both do our duty, we are satisfied
with each other and—"

" And time is flying," said the housekeeper, interrupting her master in his speech. " You are nearly
thirty-five years of age, and the girls—"

" Let them be! let them be! They will find other
men ! Now send Cyrus with my shoes and cloak, and
have my litter got ready, for Paulina has been kept
waiting long enough."

The way from the architect's house to his sister's was
long, and on his way he found ample time for reflection
on various matters besides Leukippe's advice to marry.
Still, it was a woman's face and form that possessed him
heart and soul; at first, however, he did not feel inclined
to feast his fancy on Balbilla's image, lovely as it appeared to him; on the contrary, with self-inflicted
severity he sought everything in her which could be
thought to be opposed to the highest standard of femi-
nine perfections.   Nor did he find it difficult to detect

many defects and deficiencies in the Roman damsel; still
he was forced to admit that they were quite inseparable
from her character, and that she would no longer be
what she was, if she were wholly free from them.   Each
of her little weaknesses presently began to appear as an
additional charm to the stern man who had himself been
brought up in the doctrine of the Stoics.

He had learnt by experience that sorrow must cast
its shadow over the existence of every human being;
but still, the man to whom it should be vouchsafed to
walk through life hand-in-hand with this radiant child of
fortune could, as it seemed to him, have nothing to look
forward to but pure sunshine.   During his journey to
Pelusium and his stay there he had often thought of her,
and each time that her image had appeared to his inward
eye he had felt as though daylight had shone in his soul.
To have met her he regarded as the greatest joy of his
life, but he dared not aspire to claim her as his own.

He did not undervalue himself and knew that he
might well be proud of the position he had won by his
own industry and talents; and still she was the grandchild
of the man who had had the right to sell his grandfather
for mere coin, and was so high-born, rich and distinguished that he would have thought it hardly more
audacious to ask the Emperor what he would take for
the purple than to woo her.   But to shelter her, to warn
her, to allow his soul to be refreshed by the sight of
her and by her talk—this he felt was permissible, this
happiness no one could deprive him of.   And this she
would grant him—she esteemed him and would give
him the right to protect her; this he felt, with thankfulness and joy.   He would, then and there, have gone
through the exertions of the last few hours all over again

if he could have been certain that he should once more
be refreshed with the draught of water from her hand.
Only to think of her and of her sweetness seemed
greater happiness than the possession of any other woman.

As he got out of his litter at the door of his sister's
town-house he shook his head, smiling at himself; for
he confessed to himself that the whole of the long distance he had hardly thought of anything but Balbilla.

Paulina's house had but few windows opening upon
the street and these belonged to the strangers' rooms,
and yet his arrival had been observed.   A window at
the side of the house, all grown round with creepers,
framed in a sweet girlish head which looked down from
it inquisitively on the bustle in the street.   Pontius did
not notice it, but Arsinoe—for it was her pretty face that
looked out—at once recognized the architect whom she
had seen at Lochias and of whom Pollux had spoken as
his friend and patron.

She had now, for a week, been living with the rich
widow ; she wanted for nothing, and yet her soul longed
with all its might to be out in the city, and to inquire
for Pollux and his parents, of whom she had heard
nothing since the day of her father's death.   Her lover
was no doubt seeking her with anxiety and sorrow ; but
how was he to find her ?

Three days after her arrival she had discovered the
little window from which she had a view of the street.
There was plenty to be seen, for it led to the Hippodrome and was never empty of foot-passengers and
chariots that were proceeding thither or to Nicopolis.
No doubt it was a pleasure to her to watch the fine
horses and garlanded youths and men who passed by

Paulina's house; but it was not merely to amuse herself that she went to the bowery little opening; no, she hoped, on the contrary, that she might once see her Pollux, his father, his mother, his brother Teuker or some one else they knew pass by her new home. Then she might perhaps succeed in calling them, in asking what had become of her friends, and in begging them to let her lover know where to seek her.

Her adoptive mother had twice found her at the window and had forbidden her, not unkindly but very positively, to look out into the street. Arsinoe had followed her unresistingly into the interior of the house, but as soon as she knew that Paulina was out or engaged, she slipped back to the window again and looked out for him, who must at every hour of the day be thinking of her. And she was not happy amid her new and wealthy surroundings. At first she had found it very pleasant to stretch her limbs on Paulina's soft cushions, not to stir a finger to help herself, to eat the best of food and to have neither to attend to the children nor to labor in the horrible papyrus-factory; but by the third day she pined for liberty—and still more for the children, for Selene and Pollux. Once she went out driving with Paulina in a covered carriage* for the first time in her life. As the horses started she had enjoyed the rapid movement and had leaned out at one side to see the houses and men flying past her; but Paulina had regarded this as not correct—as she did so many other things that she herself thought right and permissible—had desired her to draw in her head, and had told her that a well-conducted girl must sit with her eyes in her lap when out driving.

* A *Reda*.

Paulina was kind, never was irritable, had her
dressed and waited upon like her own daughter, kissed
her in the morning and when she bid her good-night;
and yet Arsinoe had never once thought of Paulina's
demand that she should love her. The proud woman,
who was so cool in all the friendly relations of life, and
who, as she felt was always watching her, was to her
only a stranger who had her in her power. The fairest
sentiments of her soul she must always keep locked up
from her.

Once, when Paulina, with tears in her eyes had
spoken to her of her lost daughter, Arsinoe had been
softened and following the impulse of her heart, had
confided to her that she loved Pollux the sculptor and
hoped to be his wife.

"You love a maker of images!" Paulina had exclaimed, with as much horror as if she had seen a toad;
then she had paced uneasily up and down and had
added with her usual calm decision:

"No, no, my child! you will forget all this as soon
as possible; I know of a nobler Bridegroom for you;
when once you have learned to know Him you will
never long for any other. Have you seen one single
image in this house?"

"No," replied Arsinoe, "but so far as regards Pollux—"

"Listen to me," said the widow. "Have I not told
you of our loving Father in Heaven? Have I not told
you that the gods of the heathen are unreal beings
which the vain imaginings of fools have endowed with
all the weaknesses and crimes of humanity? Can you
not understand how silly it is to pray to stones? What
power can reside in these frail figures of brass or marble?

idols we call them. He who carves them, serves them
and offers sacrifice to them; aye and a great sacrifice,
for he devotes his best powers to their service. Do you
understand me?"

"No—Art is certainly a lofty thing, and Pollux is a
good man, full of the divinity as he works."

"Wait a while, only wait—you will soon learn to
understand," Paulina had answered, drawing Arsinoe
towards her, and had added, at first speaking gently but
then more sternly: "Now go to bed and pray to your
gracious Father in Heaven that he may enlighten your
heart. You must forget the carved image-maker, and I
forbid you ever to speak in my presence again of such a
man."

Arsinoe had grown up a heathen, she clung with
affection to the gods of her fathers and hoped for happier days after the first bitterness of the loss of her father
and the separation from her brothers and sisters was
past. She was little disposed to sacrifice her young love
and all her earthly happiness for spiritual advantages of
which she scarcely comprehended the value. Her
father had always spoken of the Christians with hatred
and contempt. She now saw that they could be kind
and helpful, and the doctrine that there was a loving
God in Heaven who cared for all men as his children
appealed to her soul; but that we ought to forgive our
enemies, to remember our sins, and to repent of them,
and to regard all the pleasure and amusement which the
gay city of Alexandria could offer as base and worth-
less—this was absurd and foolish.

And what great sins had she committed? Could a
loving God require of her that she should mar all her
best days because as a child she had pilfered a cake or

broken a pitcher; or, as she grew older had sometimes been obstinate or disobedient? Surely not. And then was an artist, a kind faithful soul like her tall Pollux, to be odious in the eyes of God the Father of all, because he was able to make such wonderful things as that head of her mother, for instance? If this really was so she would rather, a thousand times rather, lift her hands in prayer to the smiling Aphrodite, roguish Eros, beautiful Apollo, and all the nine Muses who protected her Pollux, than to Him.

An obscure aversion rose up in her soul against the stern woman who could not understand her, and of whose teaching and admonitions she scarcely took in half; and she rejected many a word of the widow's which might otherwise easily have found room in her heart, only because it was spoken by the cold-mannered woman who at every hour seemed to try to lay some fresh restraint upon her.

Paulina had never yet taken her with her to one of the Christian assemblies in her suburban villa; she wished first to prepare her and to open her soul to salvation. In this task no teacher of the congregation should assist her. She, and she alone, should win to the Redeemer the soul of this fair creature that had walked so resolutely in the ways of the heathen; this was required of her as the condition of the covenant that she felt she had made with Him, it was with the price of this labor that she hoped to purchase her own child's eternal happiness. Day after day she had Arsinoe into her own room, that was decked with flowers and with Christian symbols, and devoted several hours to her instruction. But her disciple proved less impressionable and less attentive every day; while Paulina was speaking Arsinoe was thinking of Pollux, of the children, of the festival prepared for the Emperor or of the beautiful dress she was to have worn as Roxana. She wondered what young girl would fill her place, and how she could ever hope to see her lover again. And it was the same during Paulina's prayers as during her instruction, prayers that often lasted more than hour, and which she had to attend, on her knees on Wednesday and Friday, and with hands uplifted on all the other days of the week.

When her adoptive mother had discovered how often she looked out into the street she thought she had found out the reason of her pupil's distracted attention and only waited the return of her brother, the architect, in order to have the window blocked up.

As Pontius entered the lofty hall of his sister's house, Arsinoe came to meet him. Her cheeks were flushed, she had hurried to fly down as fast as possible from her window to the ground floor, in order to speak to the architect before he went into the inner rooms or had talked with his sister, and she looked lovelier than ever. Pontius gazed at her with delight. He knew that he had seen this sweet face before, but he could not at once remember where; for a face we have met with only incidentally is not easily recognized when we find it again where we do not expect it.

Arsinoe did not give him time to speak to her, for she went straight up to him, greeted him, and asked timidly:

"You do not remember who I am?"

"Yes, yes," said the architect, "and yet—for the moment—"

"I am the daughter of Keraunus, the palace-steward at Lochias, but you know of course—"

"To be sure, to be sure! Arsinoe is your name; was asking to-day after your father and heard to my great regret—"

"He is dead."

"Poor child! How everything has changed in the old palace since I went away. The gate-house is swept away, there is a new steward and there—but, tell me how came you here?"

"My father left us nothing and Christians took us in. There were eight of us."

"And my sister shelters you all?"

"No, no; one has been taken into one house and others into others. We shall never be together again." And as she spoke the tears ran down Arsinoe's cheeks; but she promptly recovered herself, and before Pontius could express his sympathy she went on:

"I want to ask of you a favor; let me speak before any one disturbs us."

"Speak, my child."

"You know Pollux—the sculptor Pollux?"

"Certainly."

"And you were always kindly disposed toward him?"

"He is a good man and an excellent artist."

"Aye that he is, and besides all that—may I tell you something and will you stand by me?"

"Gladly, so far as lies in my power."

Arsinoe looked down at the ground in charming and blushing confusion and said in a low tone:

"We love each other—I am to be his wife."

"Accept my best wishes."

"Ah, if only we had got as far as that! But since my father's death we have not seen each other. I do

not know where he and his parents are, and how are
they ever to find me here?"

"Write to him."

"I cannot write well, and even if I could my messenger—"

"Has my sister had any search made for him?"

"No—oh, no. I may not even let his name pass my
lips. She wants to give me to some one else; she says
that making statues is hateful to the God of the Christians."

"Does she? And you want me to seek your
lover?"

"Yes, yes, my dear lord! and if you find him tell
him I shall be alone to-morrow early, and again towards
evening, every day indeed, for then your sister goes to
serve her God in her country house."

"So you want to make me a lover's go-between.
You could not find a more inexperienced one."

"Ah! noble Pontius, if you have a heart—"

"Let me speak to the end, child! I will seek your
lover, and if I find him he shall know where you are,
but I cannot and will not invite him to an assignation
here behind my sister's back. He shall come openly to
Paulina and prefer his suit. If she refuses her consent I
will try to take the matter in hand with Paulina. Are
you satisfied with this?"

"I must need be. And tell me, you will let me
know when you have found out where he and his parents have gone?"

"That I promise you. And now tell me one thing.
Are you happy in this house?"

Arsinoe looked down in some embarrassment, then
she hastily shook her head in vehement negation and

hurried away. Pontius looked after her with compassion and sympathy.

"Poor, pretty little creature!" he murmured to himself, and went on to his sister's room.

The house-steward had announced his visit, and
Paulina met him on the threshold.   In his sister's sitting-
room the architect found Eumenes, the bishop, a dignified old man with clear, kind eyes.

"Your name is in everybody's mouth to-day," said
Paulina, after the usual greetings.   They say you did
wonders last night."

"I got home very tired," said Pontius, "but as you
so pressingly desired to speak to me, I shortened my
hours of rest."

"How sorry I am!" exclaimed the widow.

The bishop perceived that the brother and sister had
business to discuss together, and asked whether he were
not interrupting it.

"On the contrary," cried Paulina. "The subject
under discussion is my newly-adopted daughter who,
unhappily, has her head full of silly and useless things.
She tells me she has seen you at Lochias, Pontius."

"Yes, I know the pretty child."

"Yes, she is lovely to look upon," said the widow.
".But her heart and mind have been left wholly un-
trained, and in her the doctrine falls upon stony ground,
for she avails herself of every unoccupied moment to stare
at the horsemen and chariots that pass on the way to
the Hippodrome. By this inquisitive gaping she fills
her head with a thousand useless and distracting fancies;
I am not always at home, and so it will be best to have
the pernicious window walled up."

"And did you send for me only to have that done?"

cried Pontius, much annoyed. "Your house-slaves, I
should think, might have been equal to that without my
assistance."

"Perhaps, but then the wall would have to be freshly whitewashed—I know how obliging you always are."

"Thank you very much. To-morrow I will send
you two regular workmen."

"Nay, to-day, at once if possible."

"Are you in such pressing haste to spoil the poor
child's amusement? And besides I cannot but think
that it is not to stare at the horsemen and chariots that
she looks out, but to see her worthy lover."

. "So much the worse. I was telling you, Eumenes,
that a sculptor wants to marry her."

"She is a heathen," replied the bishop.

"But on the road to salvation," answered Paulina.
"But we will speak of that presently. There is still
something else to discuss, Pontius. The hall of my
country villa must be enlarged."

"Then send me the plans."

"They lie in the book-room of my late husband."

The architect left his sister to go into the library,
which he knew well.

As soon as the bishop was left alone with Paulina,
he shook his head and said :

"If I judge rightly, my dear sister, you are going the
wrong way to work in leading this child intrusted to
your care. Not all are called, and rebellious hearts must
be led along the path of salvation with a gentle hand,
not dragged and driven. Why do you cut off this girl,
who still stands with both feet in the world, from all that
can give her pleasure? Allow the young creature to
enjoy every permitted pleasure which can add to the

35

joys of life in youth.   Do not hurt Arsinoe needlessly, do not let her feel the hand that guides her.   First teach her to love you from her heart, and when she knows nothing dearer than you, a request from you will be worth more than bolts or walled-up windows."

"At first I wished nothing more than that she should love me," interrupted Paulina.

"But have you proved her?   Do you see in her the spark which may be fanned to a flame?   Have you detected in her the germ which may possibly grow to a strong desire for salvation and to devotion to the Redeemer?"

"That germ exists in every heart—these are your own words."

"But in many of the heathen it is deeply buried in sand and stones; and do you feel yourself equal to clearing them away without injury to the seed or to the soil in which it lies?"

"I do, and I will win Arsinoe to Jesus Christ," said Paulina firmly.

Pontius interrupted the conversation; he remained with his sister some time longer discussing with her and with Eumenes the new building to be done at her country house; then he and the bishop left at the same time and Pontius proceeded to the scene of the fire by the harbor and in the old palace.

CHAPTER XVI.

PONTIUS did not find the Emperor at Lochias, for Hadrian had moved at mid-day to the Caesareum. The strong smell of burning in every room in the palace had sickened him and he had begun to regard the restored building as a doomed scene of disaster. The architect was waited for with much anxiety, for the rooms originally furnished for the Emperor in the Caesareum had been despoiled and disarranged to decorate the rooms at Lochias, and Pontius was wanted to superintend their immediate rehabilitation. A chariot was waiting for him and there was no lack of slaves, so he began this fresh task at once and devoted himself to it till late at night. It was in vain this time that his anteroom was filled with people waiting for his return.

Hadrian had retired to some rooms which formed part of his wife's apartments. He was in a grave mood, and when the prefect Titianus was announced he kept him waiting till, with his own hand, he had laid a fresh dressing on his favorite's burns.

" Go now, my lord," begged the Bithynian, when the Emperor had finished his task with all the skill of a surgeon: " Titianus has been walking up and down in there for the last quarter of an hour."

" And so he may," said the monarch. " And if the whole world is shrieking for me it must wait till these faithful hands have had their due. Yes, my boy! we will wander on through life together, inseparable comrades. Others indeed do the same, and each one who

35

goes through life side by side with a companion sharing
all he enjoys or suffers, comes to think at last that he
knows him as he knows himself; still the inmost core of
his friend's nature remains concealed from him.   Then,
some day Fate lets a storm come raging down upon
them ; the last veil is torn, under the wanderer's eyes,
from the very heart of his companion, and at last he
really sees him as he is, like a kernel stripped of its
shell, a bare and naked body.   Last night such a blast
swept over us and let me see the heart of my Antinous,
as plainly as this hand I hold before my eyes.   Yes,
yes, yes! for the man who will risk his young and happy
existence for a thing his friend holds precious would
sacrifice ten lives if he had them, for his friend's person.
Never, my friend, shall that night be forgotten.   It gives
you the right to do much that might pain me, and has
graven your name on my heart, the foremost among
those to whom I am indebted for any benefit.—They are
but few."

Hadrian held out his hand to Antinous as he spoke.
The boy, who had kept his eyes fixed on the ground in
much confusion, raised it to his lips and pressed it against
them in violent agitation.   Then he raised his large eyes
to the Emperor's and said :

" You must not speak to me so kindly, for I do not
deserve such goodness.   What is my life after all ?   I
would let it go, as a child leaves go of a beetle it has
caught, to spare you one single anxious day."

" I know it," answered Hadrian firmly, and he went
to the prefect in the adjoining room.

Titianus had come in obedience to Hadrian's orders ;
the matter to be settled was what indemnification was to
be paid to the city and to the individual owners of the

storehouses that had been destroyed, for Hadrian had caused a decree to be proclaimed that no one should suffer any loss through a misfortune sent by the gods and which had originated in his residence. The prefect had already instituted the necessary inquiries and the private secretaries, Phlegon, Heliodorus and Celer, were now charged with the duty of addressing documents to the injured parties in which they were invited, in the name of Caesar, to declare the truth as to the amount of the loss they had suffered. Titianus also brought the information that the Greeks and Jews had determined to express their thankfulness for Caesar's preservation by great thank-offerings.

"And the Christians," asked Hadrian.

"They abominate the sacrifice of animals, but they will unite in a common act of thanksgiving."

"Their gratitude will not cost them much," said Hadrian.

"Their bishop, Eumenes, brought me a sum of money for which a hundred oxen might be bought, to distribute among the poor. He said the God of the Christians is a spirit and requires none but spiritual sacrifices; that the best offering a man can bring him is a prayer prompted by the spirit and proceeding from a loving heart."

"That sounds very well for us," said Hadrian. "But it will not do for the people. Philosophical doctrines do not tend to piety; the populace need visible gods and tangible sacrifices. Are the Christians here good citizens and devoted to the welfare of the state?"

"We need no courts of justice for them."

"Then take their money and distribute it among the needy; but I must forbid their meeting for a general

thanksgiving; they may raise their hands to their great
spirit in my behalf, in private. Their doctrine must not
be brought into publicity; it is not devoid of a delusive
charm and it is indispensable to the safety of the state
that the mob should remain faithful to the old gods and
sacrifices."

"As you command, Caesar."

"You know the account given of the Christians by
Pliny and Trajan?"

"And Trajan's answer."

"Well then let us leave them to follow their own
devices in private after their own fashion; only they
must not commit any breach of the laws of the state
nor force themselves into publicity. As soon as they
show any disposition to refuse to the old gods the respect
that is due to them, or to raise a finger against them, severity must be exercised and every excess must be punished by death."

During this conversation Verus had entered the
room; he was following the Emperor everywhere to-day
for he hoped to hear him say a word as to his observation of the heavens, and yet he did not dare to ask him
what he had discovered from them.

When he saw that Hadrian was occupied he made a
chamberlain conduct him to Antinous. The favorite
turned pale as he saw the praetor, still he retained
enough presence of mind to wish him all happiness on
his birthday. It did not escape Verus that his presence
had startled the lad; he therefore plied him at first with
indifferent questions, introduced pleasing anecdotes into
his conversation and then, when he had gained his purpose, he added carelessly:

"I must thank you in the name of the state and of

every friend of Caesar's. You carried out your undertaking well to the end, though by somewhat overpowering means."

" I entreat you say no more," interrupted Antinous eagerly, and looking anxiously at the door of the next room.

" Oh! I would have sacrificed all Alexandria to preserve Caesar's mind from gloom and care. Besides we have both paid dearly for our good intentions and for those wretched sheds."

" Pray talk of something else."

" You sit there with your hands bound up and your hair singed, and I feel very unwell."

" Hadrian said you had helped valiantly in the rescue."

" I was sorry for the poor rats whose gathered store of provisions the flames were so rapidly devouring, and all hot as I was from my supper, I flung myself in among the men who were extinguishing the fire. My first reward was a bath of cold, icy-cold sea-water, which was poured over my head out of a full skin. All doctrines of ethics are in disgrace with me, and I have long considered all the dramatic poets, in whose pieces virtue is rewarded and crime punished, as a pack of fools ; for my pleasantest hours are all due to my worst deeds ; and sheer annoyance and misery, to my best. No hyena can laugh more hoarsely that I now speak ; some portion of me inside here, seems to have been turned into a hedgehog whose spines prick and hurt me, and all this because I allowed myself to be led away into doing things which the moralists laud as virtuous."

" You cough, and you do not look well. Lie down awhile."

" On my birthday ?   No, my young friend. And
now let me just ask you before I go :   Can you tell me
what Hadrian read in the stars ?"

" No."

" Not even if I put my Perseus at your orders for
every thing you may require of him ?   The man knows
Alexandria and is as dumb as a fish."

" Not even then, for what I do not know I cannot
tell.   We are both of us ill, and I tell you once more
you will be wise to take care of yourself."   Verus left
the room, and Antinous watched him go with much relief.

The praetor's visit had filled him with disquietude,
and had added to the dislike he felt for him.   He knew
that he had been used to base ends by Verus, for Hadrian had told him so much as that he had gone up to
the observatory not to question the stars for himself
but to cast the praetor's horoscope, and that he had informed Verus of his intention.

There was no excuse, no forgiveness possible for the
deed he had done ; to please that dissolute coxcomb, that
mocking hypocrite, he had become a traitor to his master and an incendiary, and must endure to be overwhelmed with praises and thanks by the greatest and
most keen-sighted of men.   He hated, he abhorred himself, and asked himself why the fire which had blazed
around him had been satisfied only to inflict slight injuries on his hands and hair.   When Hadrian returned
to him he asked his permission to go to bed.   The Emperor gladly granted it, ordered Mastor to watch by his
side, and then agreed to his wife's request that he would
visit her.

Sabina had not been to the scene of the fire, but she

had sent a messenger every hour to inquire as to the
progress of the conflagration and the well-being of her
husband. When he had first arrived at the Caesareum
she had met and welcomed him and then had retired to
her own apartments.

It wanted only two hours of midnight when Hadrian entered her room; he found her reclining on a
couch without the jewels she usually wore in the day-
time but dressed as for a banquet.

"You wished to speak with me ?" said the Emperor.

"Yes, and this day—so full of remarkable events as
it has been—has also a remarkable close since I have
not wished in vain."

"You so rarely give me the opportunity of gratifying a wish."

"And do you complain of that ?"

"I might—for instead of wishing you are wont to
demand."

"Let us cease this strife of idle words."

"Willingly. With what object did you send for me?"

"Verus is to-day keeping his birthday."

"And you would like to know what the stars promise
him ?"

"Rather how the signs in the heavens have disposed you towards him."

"I had but little time to consider what I saw. But
at any rate the stars promise him a brilliant future."

A gleam of joy shone in Sabina's eyes, but she
forced herself to keep calm and asked, indifferently:

"You admit that, and yet you can come to no decision ?"

"Then you want to hear the decisive word spoken
at once, to-day ?"

"You know that without my answering you."

"Well, then, his star outshines mine and compels me to be on my guard against him."

"How mean! You are afraid of the praetor?"

"No, but of his fortune which is bound up with you?"

"When he is our son his greatness will be ours."

"By no means, since if I make him what you wish him to be, he will certainly try to make our greatness his. Destiny—"

"You said it favored him; but unfortunately I must dispute the statement."

"You? Do you try too, to read the stars?"

"No, I leave that to men. Have you heard of Ammonius, the astrologer?"

"Yes. A very learned man who observes from the tower of the Serapeum, and who, like many of his fellows in this city has made use of his art to accumulate a large fortune."

"No less a man than the astronomer Claudius Ptolemaeus referred me to him."

"The best of recommendation."

"Well, then, I commissioned Ammonius to cast the horoscope for Verus during the past night and he brought it to me with an explanatory key. Here it is."

The Emperor hastily seized the tablet which Sabina held out to him, and as he attentively examined the forecasts, arranged in order according to the hours, he said:

"Quite right. That of course did not escape me! Well done, exactly the same as my own observations— but here—stay—here comes the third hour, at the be-

ginning of which I was interrupted. Eternal gods!
what have we here?"

The Emperor held the wax tablet prepared by Ammonius at arm's length from his eyes and never parted
his lips again till he had come to the end of the last
hour of the night. Then he dropped the hand that held
the horoscope, saying with a shudder:

"A hideous destiny. Horace was right in saying
the highest towers fall with the greatest crash."

"The tower of which you speak," said Sabina, "is
that darling of fortune of whom you are afraid. Vouch-
safe then to Verus a brief space of happiness before the
horrible end you foresee for him."

While she spoke Hadrian sat with his eyes thoughtfully fixed on the ground, and then, standing in front of
his wife, he replied:

"If no sinister catastrophe falls upon this man, the
stars and the fate of men have no more to do with one
another than the sea with the heart of the desert, than the
throb of men's pulses with the pebbles in the brook. If
Ammonius has erred ten times over still more than ten
signs remain on this tablet, hostile and fatal to the
praetor. I grieve for Verus—but the state suffers with
the sovereign's misfortunes.—This man can never be
my successor."

"No?" asked Sabina rising from her couch. "No?
Not when you have seen that your own star outlives
his? Not though a glance at this tablet shows you
that when he is nothing but ashes the world will still
continue long to obey your nod?"

"Compose yourself and give me time.—Yes, I still
say not even so."

"Not even so," repeated Sabina sullenly. Then,

collecting herself, she asked in a tone of vehement entreaty:

"Not even so—not even if I lift my hands to you in supplication and cry in your face that you and Fate have grudged me the blessing, the happiness, the crown and aim of a woman's life, and I must and I will attain it; I must and I will once, if only for a short time, hear myself called by some dear lips by the name which gives the veriest beggar-woman with her infant in her arms preeminence above the Empress who has never stood by a child's cradle. I must and I will, before I die, be a mother, be called mother and be able to say, 'my child, my son—our son.'" And as she spoke she sobbed aloud and covered her face with her hands.

The Emperor drew back a step from his wife. A miracle had been wrought before his eyes. Sabina—in whose eyes no tear had ever been seen—Sabina was weeping, Sabina had a heart like other women. Greatly astonished and deeply moved he saw her turn from him, utterly shaken by the agitation of her feelings, and sink on her knees by the side of the couch she had quitted to hide her face in the cushions. He stood motionless by her side, but presently going nearer to her:

"Stand up, Sabina," he said. "Your desire is a just one. You shall have the son for whom your soul longs."

The Empress rose and a grateful look in her eyes, swimming in tears, met his glance. Sabina could smile too, she could look sweet! It had taken a lifetime, it had needed such a moment as this to reveal it to Hadrian.

He silently drew a seat towards her and sat down

by her side; for some time he sat with her hand clasped
in his, in silence. Then he let it go and said kindly:

"And will Verus fulfil all you expect of a son?"

She nodded assent.

"What makes you so confident of that?" asked the
Emperor. "He is a Roman and not lacking in brilliant
and estimable gifts. A man who shows such mettle
alike in the field and in the council-chamber and yet
can play the part of Eros with such success will also
know how to wear the purple without disgracing it.
But he has his mother's light blood, and his heart flutters
hither and thither."

"Let him be as he is. We understand each other
and he is the only man on whose disposition I can build,
on whose fidelity I can count as securely as if he were
my favorite son."

"And on what facts is this confidence based?"

"You will understand me, for you are not blind to
the signs which Fate vouchsafes to us. Have you time
to listen to a short story?"

"The night is yet young."

"Then I will tell you. Forgive me if I begin with
things that seem dead and gone; but they are not, for
they live and work in me to this hour. I know that you
yourself did not choose me for your wife. Plotina
chose me for you—she loved you, whether your regard
for her was for the beautiful woman or for the wife of
Caesar to whom everything belonged that you had to
look for—how should I know?"

"It was Plotina, the woman, that I honored and
loved—"

"In choosing me she chose you a wife who was tall
and so fitted to wear the purple, but who was never

beautiful. She knew me well and she knew that I was less apt than any other woman to win hearts; in my parents' house no child ever enjoyed so slender a share of the gifts of love, and none can know better than you that my husband did not spoil me with tenderness."

" I could repent of it at this moment."

" It would be too late now. But I will not be bitter —no, indeed I will not. And yet if you are to understand me I must own that so long as I was young I longed bitterly for the love which no one offered me."

" And you yourself have never loved ?"

" No—but it pained me that I could not. In Plotina's apartments I often saw the children of her relations, and many a time I tried to attract them to me, but while they would play confidently with other women they seemed to shun me. Soon I even grew cross to them—only our Verus, the little son of Ceionius Commodus, would give me frank answers when I spoke to him, and would bring me his broken toys that I might mend their injuries. And so I got to love the child."

" He was a wonderfully sweet, attractive boy."

" He was indeed. One day we women were all sitting together in Caesar's garden. Verus came running out with a particularly fine apple that Trajan himself had given him. The rosy-cheeked fruit was admired by every one. Then Plotina, in fun took the apple out of the boy's hand and asked him if he would not give his apple to her. He looked at her with wide-open puzzled eyes, shook his curly head, ran up to me and gave me— yes, me, and no one else—the fruit, throwing his arms round my neck and saying, ' Sabina you shall have it.'"

" The judgment of Paris."

" Nay, do not jest now. This action of an unselfish

child gave me courage to endure the troubles of life. I knew now that there was one creature that loved me, and that one repaid all that I felt for him, all that I was never weary of doing for him with affectionate liking. He is the only being, of whom I know, that will weep when I die. Give him the right to call me his mother and make him our son."

" He is our son," said Hadrian, with dignified gravity, and held out his hand to Sabina. She tried to lift it to her lips but he drew it away and went on :

" Inform him that we accept him as our son. His wife is the daughter of Nigrinus—who had to go, as I desired to stay and stand firm. You do not love Lucilla, but we must both admire her for I do not know another woman in Rome whose virtue a man might vouch for. Besides, I owe her a father, and am glad to have such a daughter ; thus we shall be blessed with children. Whether I shall appoint Verus my successor and proclaim to the world who shall be its future ruler I cannot now decide ; for that I need a calmer hour. Till to-morrow, Sabina. This day began with a misfortune ; may the deed with which we have combined to end it prosper and bring us happiness."

CHAPTER XVII.

THERE are often fine warm days in February, but those who fancy the spring has come find themselves deceived. The bitter, hard Sabina could at times let soft and tender emotions get the mastery over her, but as soon as the longing of her languishing soul for maternal happiness was gratified, she closed her heart again and extinguished the fire that had warmed it.   Every one who approached her, even her husband, felt himself chilled and repelled again by her manner.

Verus was ill.   The first symptoms of a liver complaint which his physicians had warned him might ensue, if he, an European, persisted in his dissipated life at Alexandria as if it were Rome, now began to occasion him many uneasy hours, and this, the first physical pain that fate had ever inflicted on him, he bore with the utmost impatience.   Even the great news which Sabina brought him, realizing his boldest aspirations, had no power to reconcile him to the new sensation of being ill. He learnt, at the same time, that Hadrian's alarm at the transcendent brightness of his star had nearly cost him his adoption, and as he firmly believed that he had brought on his sufferings by his efforts to extinguish the fire that Antinous had kindled, he bitterly rued his treacherous interference with the Emperor's calculations.   Men are always ready to cast any burden, and especially that of a fault they have committed, on to the shoulders of another; and so the suffering praetor cursed Antinous and the learning of Simeon Ben Jochai, because, if it had not been for them the mischievous folly which had spoilt his pleasure in life would never have been committed.

Hadrian had requested the Alexandrians to postpone the theatrical displays and processions that they had prepared for him, as his observations as to the course of destiny during the coming year were not yet complete. Every evening he ascended the lofty observatory of the Serapeum and gazed from thence at the stars. His labors ended on the tenth of January; on the eleventh the festivities began.   They lasted through many days, and by

the desire of the praetor the pretty daughter of Apollodorus the Jew was chosen to represent Roxana.

Everything that the Alexandrians had prepared to do
honor to their sovereign was magnificent and costly. So
many ships had never before been engaged in any Naumachia as were destroyed here in the sham sea-fight, no
greater number of wild beasts had ever been seen together on any occasion even in the Roman Circus; and
how bloody were the fights of the gladiators, in which
black and white combatants afforded a varied excitement for both heart and senses. In the processions, the
different elements which were supplied by the great central metropolis of Egyptian, Greek and Oriental culture
afforded such a variety of food for the eye that, in spite
of their interminable length, the effect was less fatiguing
than the Romans had feared. The performances of the
tragedies and comedies were equally rich in startling effects; conflagrations and floods were introduced and
gave the Alexandrian actors the opportunity of displaying their talents with such brilliant success that Hadrian
and his companions were forced to acknowledge that
even in Rome and Athens they had never witnessed any
representations equally perfect.

A piece by the Jewish author Ezekiel who, under the
Ptolemies, wrote dramas in the Greek language of which
the subject was taken from the history of his own people,
particularly claimed the Emperor's attention.

Titianus during all this festive season was unluckily
suffering from an attack of old-standing breathlessness,
and he also had his hands full; at the same time he did
his best in helping Pontius in seeking out the sculptor
Pollux. Both men did their utmost, but though they
soon were able to find Euphorion and dame Doris,

36

every trace of their son had vanished. Papias, the
former employer of the man who had disappeared, was
no longer in the city, having been sent by Hadrian to
Italy to execute centaurs and other figures to decorate
his villa at Tibur. His wife who remained at home, declared that she knew nothing of Pollux but that he had
abruptly quitted her husband's service. The unfortunate
man's fellow-workmen could give no news of him whatever, for not one of them had been present when he was
seized; Papias had had foresight enough to have the
man he dreaded placed in security without the presence
of any witnesses. Neither the prefect nor the architect
thought of seeking the worthy fellow in prison, and even
if they had done so they would hardly have found him,
for Pollux was not kept in durance in Alexandria itself.
The prisons of the city had overflowed after the night of
the holiday and he had been transferred to Canopus and
there detained and brought up for trial.

Pollux had unhesitatingly owned to having taken
the silver quiver and to having been very angry at his
master's accusation. Thus he produced from the first
an unfavorable impression on the judge, who esteemed
Papias as a wealthy man, universally respected. The
accused had hardly been allowed to speak at all and
judgment was immediately pronounced against him, on
the strength of his master's accusation and his own
admissions. It would have been sheer waste of time to
listen to the romances with which this audacious rascal
—who forgot all the respect he owed to his teacher and
benefactor—wanted to cram the judges. Two years of
reflection, the protectors of the law deemed, might
suffice to teach this dangerous fellow to respect the
property of others and to keep him from outbreaks

against those to whom he owed gratitude and reverence.

Pollux, safe in the prison at Canopus, cursed his
destiny and indulged in vain hopes of the assistance of
his friends. These were at last weary of the vain search
and only asked about him occasionally. He at first
was so insubordinate under restraint that he was put
under close ward from which he was not released until,
instead of raging with fury he dreamed away his days in
sullen brooding. The gaoler knew men well, and he
thought he could safely predict that at the end of his
two years' imprisonment this young thief would quit his
cell a harmless imbecile.

Titianus, Pontius, Balbilla and even Antinous had
all attempted to speak of him to the Emperor, but each
was sharply repulsed and taught that Hadrian was little
inclined to pardon a wound to his artist's vanity. But
the sovereign also proved that he had a good memory
for benefits he had received, for once, when a dish was
set before him consisting of cabbage and small sausages
he smiled, and taking out his purse filled with gold
pieces, he ordered a chamberlain to take it in his name
to Doris, the wife of the evicted gate-keeper. The old
couple now resided in a little house of their own in the
neighborhood of their widowed daughter Diotima. Hunger and external misery came not nigh them, still they
had experienced a great change. Poor Doris' eyes were
now red and bloodshot, for they were accustomed to
many tears, which were seldom far off and overflowed
whenever a word, an object, a thought reminded her of
Pollux, her darling, her pride and her hope; and there
were few half-hours in the day when she did not think
of him.

36

Soon after the steward's death she had sought out
Selene, but dame Hannah could not and would not
conduct her to see the sick girl, for she learnt from
Mary that she was the mother of her patient's faithless
lover; and on a second visit Selene was so shy, so
timid and so strange in her demeanor, that the old
woman was forced to conclude that her visit was an
unpleasant intrusion.

And from Arsinoe, whose residence she discovered
from the deaconess, she met with even a worse reception. She had herself announced as the mother of
Pollux the sculptor and was abruptly refused admission,
with the information that Arsinoe was not to be spoken
with by her and that her visits were, once for all, prohibited. After the architect Pontius had been to seek
her out and had encouraged her to make another
attempt to see and speak to Arsinoe, who clung faithfully to Pollux, Paulina herself had received her and
sent her away with such repellent words that she went
home to her husband deeply insulted and distressed to
tears. Nor had she resisted Euphorion's decision when
he prohibited her ever again crossing the Christian's
threshold.

The Emperor's donation had been most welcome and
timely to the poor old couple, for Euphorion had completely lost the softness of his voice as well as his memory
through the agitations and troubles of the last few months;
he had been dismissed from the chorus of the theatre and
could only find employment and very small pay of a few
drachmae, in the mysteries of certain petty sectarians or
in singing at weddings or in hymns of lamentation. At
the same time the old folks had to maintain their daughter whom Pollux could no longer provide for, and the

birds, the Graces and the cat all must eat. That it would be possible to get rid of them was an idea which never occurred to either Euphorion or Doris.

By day the old folks had ceased to laugh; but at night they still had many cheerful hours, for then Hope would beguile them with bright pictures of the future, and tell them all sorts of possible and impossible romances which filled their souls with fresh courage. How often they would see Pollux returning from the distant city whither he had probably fled—from Rome, or even from Athens—crowned with laurels and rich in treasure. The Emperor, who still so kindly remembered them, could not always be angry with him; perhaps he might some day send a messenger to seek Pollux and to make up to him by large commissions for all he had made him suffer. That her darling was alive she was sure; in that she could not be mistaken, often as Euphorion tried to persuade her that he must be dead. The singer could tell many tales of luckless men who had been murdered and never seen or heard of again; but she was not to be convinced, she persisted in hope, and lived wholly in the purpose of sending her younger son, Teuker, on his travels to seek his lost brother as soon as his apprenticeship was over, which would be in a few months.

Antinous, whose burnt hands had soon got well under the Emperor's care, and who had never felt a liking and friendship for any other young man but Pollux, lamented the artist's disappearance and wished much to seek out dame Doris; but he found it harder than ever to leave his master, and was so eager always to be at hand that Hadrian often laughingly reproached him with making his slaves' duties too light.

When at last he really was master of an hour to himself he postponed his intention of seeing his friend's parents; for with him there was always a wide world between the purpose and the deed which he never could overleap, if not urged by some strong impulse; and his most pressing instincts prompted him, when the Emperor was disputing in the Museum or receiving instructions from the chiefs of the different religious communities as to the doctrines they severally professed, to visit the suburban villa where, when February had already begun, Selene was still living. He had often succeeded in stealing into Paulina's garden, but he could not at first realize his hope of being observed by Selene— of obtaining speech with her. Whenever he went near Hannah's little house, Mary, the deformed girl, would come in his way, tell him how her friend was, and beg or desire him to go away. She was always with the sick girl, for now her mother was nursed by her sister, and dame Hannah had obtained permission for her to work at home in gumming the papyrus-strips together.

The widow herself was obliged to be at her post in the factory, for her duties as overseer made her presence indispensable in the work-room.

Thus it came to pass that it was always by Mary and never by Hannah that Antinous was received and dismissed. A certain understanding had arisen between the beautiful youth and the deformed girl. When Antinous appeared and she called out to him: "What, again already!" he would grasp her hand and implore her only once to grant his wish; but she was always firm, only she never sent him away sternly but with smiles and friendly admonitions. When he brought rare and lovely flowers in his pallium and entreated her to

give them to Selene in the name of her friend at Lochias,
she would take them and promise to place them in her
room; but she always said it would do neither him nor
her any good at all that Selene should know from whom
they came. After such repulses he well knew how to
flatter and coax her with appealing words, but he had
never dared to defy her or to gain his end by force.
When the flowers were placed in the room Mary looked
at them much oftener than Selene did, and when Antinous had been long absent the deformed girl longed to
see him again, and would pace restlessly up and down between the garden gate and her friend's little house. She,
like him, dreamed of an angel, and the angel of whom
she dreamed was exactly like himself. In all her prayers
she included the name of the handsome heathen and a
soft tenderness in which a gentle pity was often infused,
a grief for his unredeemed soul, was inseparable from all
her thoughts of him.

Hannah was informed by her of each of the young
man's visits, and as often as Mary mentioned Antinous
the deaconess seemed anxious and desired her to threaten
to call the gate-keeper to him. The widow knew full
well who her patient's indefatigable admirer was, for she
had once heard him speaking to Mastor, and she had
asked the slave, who availed himself of every spare moment to attend the services of the Christians, who the
lad was. All Alexandria, nay all the Empire, knew the
name of the most beautiful youth of his time, the spoilt
favorite of Caesar. Even Hannah had heard of him
and knew that poets sang his praises and heathen women
were eager to obtain a glance from his eyes. She knew
how devoid of all morality were the lives of the nobles
at Rome, and Antinous appeared to her as a splendid

falcon that wheels above a dove to swoop down upon it
at a favorable moment and to tear it in its beak and
talons. Hannah also knew that Selene was acquainted
with Antinous, that it was he who had formerly rescued
her from the big dog and afterward saved her from the
water; but that Selene, who was now recovering, did
not know who her preserver had been on this second
occasion was clear from all that she said.

Towards the end of February Antinous had come
on three days in succession, and Hannah now took the
step of begging the bishop, Eumenes, to give the gate-
keeper strict injunctions to look out for the young man
and to forbid his entering the garden, even with force if
it should prove necessary.

But "love laughs at locksmiths" and finds its way
through locked doors, and Antinous succeeded all the
same in finding his way into Paulina's garden. On one
of these occasions he was so happy to surprise Selene,
as, supported on a stick and accompanied by a fair-haired
boy and dame Hannah herself, she hobbled up and down.

Antinous had learnt to regard everything crippled or
defective with aversion, as a monstrous failure of nature's plastic harmony, but to pity it tenderly; but now
he felt quite differently. Mary with her humpback had
at first horrified him; now he was always glad to see
her though she always crossed his wishes; and poor
lame Selene, who had been mocked at by the street boys
as she limped along, seemed to him more adorable than
ever. How lovely were her face and form, how peculiar her way of walking—she did not limp—no, she
swayed along the garden. Thus, as he said to himself
afterwards, the Nereids are borne along on the undu-
lating waves. Love is easily satisfied, nor is this strange,

for it raises all that comes within its embrace to a loftier level of existence. In the light of love weakness is a virtue and want an additional charm.

But the Bithynian's visits were not the widow's only cares; though she bore the others, it is true, not anxiously but with pleasure. Her household had increased by two living souls, and her income was very small. That her patient might not want, she had to work with her own hands while she superintended the girls in the factory, and to carry home with her in the evening papyrus-leaves, not only for Mary, but for herself too, and to gum them together during the long hours of the night. As soon as Selene's condition improved, she too helped willingly and diligently, but for many weeks the convalescent had to give up every kind of employment.

Mary often looked at Hannah in silent trouble, for she looked very pale. After she had, on one occasion fallen in a fainting fit, the deformed girl had gathered courage and had represented to her that though she ought indeed to put out at interest the talent intrusted to her by the Lord, she ought not to spend it recklessly. She was giving herself no rest, working day and night; visiting the poor and sick in her hours of recreation just as she used, and if she did not give herself more rest would soon need nursing instead of nursing others.

"At any rate," urged Mary, "give yourself a little indispensable sleep at night."

"We must live," replied Hannah, "and I dare not borrow, for I may never be able to repay."

"Then beg Paulina to remit your house-rent; she will do so gladly."

"No," said Hannah, decidedly. "The rent of this little house goes to benefit my poor people, and you know how badly they want it. What we give we lend to the Lord, and he taxes no man above his ability."

Selene was now well, but the physician had said that no human skill could ever cure her of her lameness. She had become Hannah's daughter, and blind Helios the son of the house.

Arsinoe was only allowed to see her sister rarely and always accompanied by her protectress, and she and Selene never were able to have any unchecked and open conversation. The steward's eldest daughter was now contented and cheerful, while the younger was not only saddened by the disappearance of her lover, but also, from being unhappy in her new home, she had become fractious and easily moved to shed tears. All was well with the younger orphans; they were often taken to see Selene, and spoke with affection of their new parents.

As she got well her help diminished the strain on her two friends, and in the beginning of March a call came to the widow which, if she followed it, must give their simple existence a new aspect.

In Upper Egypt certain Christian fraternities had been established, and one of these had addressed a prayer to the great mother-community at Alexandria, that it would send to them a presbyter, a deacon and a deaconess capable of organizing and guiding the believers and catechumens in the province of Hermopolis where they were already numbered by thousands. The life of the community and the care of the poor, and sick in the outlying districts required organization by experienced hands, and Hannah had been asked whether she could make up her mind to leave the metropolis and carry on the work of benevolence at Besa in an extended sphere.

She would there have a pleasant house, a palm-garden, and gifts from the congregation which would secure not merely her own maintenance, but that of her adopted children.

Hannah was bound to Alexandria by many ties; in the first place she clung to the poor and sick, many of whom had grown very dear to her, and how many girls who had gone astray had she rescued from evil in the factory alone! She begged for a short time for reflection, and this was granted to her. By the fifteenth of March she was to decide, but by the fifth she had already made up her mind, for while Hannah was in the papyrus-factory Antinous had succeeded in getting into Paulina's garden shortly before sunset and in stealing close up to Hannah's house. Mary again observed him as he approached and signed to him to go, in her usual pleasant way; but the Bithynian was more excited than usual; he seized her hand and clasped her with urgent warmth as he implored her to be merciful. She endeavored at once to free herself, but he would not let her go, but cried in coaxing tones:

"I must see her and speak to her to-day, dear, good Mary, only this once!" And before she could prevent it he had kissed her forehead and had flown into the house to Selene. The little hunchback did not know what had happened to her; confused and almost paralyzed by conflicting feelings she stood shame-faced, gazing at the ground. She felt that something quite extraordinary had happened to her, but this wonderful something radiated a dazzling splendor, and since this had risen for her, for poor Mary, a feeling of pride quite new to her mingled with the shame and indignation that filled her soul. She needed a few minutes to collect

herself and to recover a sense of her duty, and those few
minutes were made good use of by Antinous.

He flew with long steps into the room in which, on
that never-to-be-forgotten night, he had laid Selene on
the couch, and even at the threshold he called her by
her name.   She started and laid aside the book out of
which she was reading to her blind brother.   He called
a second time, beseechingly. Selene recognized him and
asked calmly:

"Do you want me, or dame Hannah?"

"You, you!" he cried passionately.   "Oh Selene, I
pulled you out of the water, and since that night I have
never ceased to think of you and I must die for love of
you.   Have your thoughts never, never met mine on the
way to you? Are you still and always as cold, as passive
as you were then when you belonged half to life and
half to death?   For months have I prowled round this
house as the shade of a dead man haunts the spot where
he had left all that was dear to him on earth, and I have
never been able to tell you what I feel for you?" As he
spoke the lad fell on the ground before her and tried to
clasp her knees; but she said reproachfully:

"What does all this mean?   Stand up and compose
yourself."

"Oh! let me, let me—" he besought her.   "Do not
be so cold and so hard; have pity on me and do not reject me!"

"Stand up," repeated the girl.   "I will certainly not
reproach you—I owe you thanks on the contrary."

"Not thanks, but love—a little love is all I ask."

"I try to love all men," replied the girl, "and so I
love you because you have shown me very much kindness."

"Selene, Selene!" he exclaimed in joyful triumph. He threw himself again at her feet and passionately seized her right hand; but hardly had he taken it in his own when Mary, scarlet with agitation, rushed into the room. In a husky voice, full of hatred and fury, she commanded him to leave the house at once, and when he attempted again to besiege her ear with entreaties she cried out:

"If you do not obey I will call the men in to help us, who are out there attending to the flowers. I ask you, will you obey or will you not?"

"Why are you so cruel, Mary?" asked the blind boy. "This man is good and kind and tells Selene he loves her."

Antinous pointed to the child with an imploring gesture but Mary was already by the window and was raising her hand to her mouth to make her call heard.

"Don't don't," cried Antinous. "I am going at once."

And he went slowly and silently towards the door, still gazing at Selene with passionate ardor; then he quitted the room groaning with shame and disappointment, though still with a look of radiant pride as though he had achieved some great deed. In the garden he was met by Hannah, who immediately hastened with accelerated steps to her own house where she found Mary sobbing violently and dissolved in tears.

The widow was soon informed of all that had occurred in her absence, and an hour later she had announced to the bishop that she would accept the call to Besa and was ready to start for Upper Egypt.

"With your foster-children?" asked Eumenes.

"Yes. It was indeed Selene's most earnest wish to be baptized by you, but as a year of probation is required—"

"I will perform the rite to-morrow morning."

"To-morrow, Father?"

"Yes, Sister, in all confidence.   She buried the old
man in the waves of the sea, and before we were her
teachers she had gone through the school and discipline
of life.   While she was yet a heathen she had taken up
her cross and proved herself as faithful as though she
were a child of the Lord.   All that was lacking to her—
Faith, Love and Hope—she has found under your roof.
I thank thee for this soul thou hast found Sister, in the
name of the Lord."

"Not I, not I," said the widow.   "Her heart was
frozen, but it is not I but the innocent faith of the blind
child that has melted it."

"She owes her salvation to him and to you," replied
the bishop, "and they both shall be baptized together.
We will give the lovely boy the name of the fairest of
the disciples, and call him John.   Selene for the future,
if she herself likes it, shall be known as Martha."

CHAPTER XVIII.

SELENE and Helios were baptized, and two days after
dame Hannah with her adopted children and Mary, escorted by the presbyter Hilarion and a deacon, embarked
in the harbor of Mareotis on board a Nile-boat which
was to convey them to their new home, the town of Besa
in Upper Egypt.   The deformed girl had hesitated as to
her answer to the widow's question whether she would
accompany her.   Her old mother dwelt in Alexandria,
and then—but it was this "then" which helped her

abruptly to cut short all reflection and to pronounce a
decided "yes," for it referred to Antinous.

For a few minutes it had seemed unendurable to
think that she should never see him again, for she could
not help often thinking of the beautiful youth, and her
whole heart ought to belong solely to the One who had
with His blood purchased peace for her on earth and
bliss in the world to come.

The day after being baptized, Selene had gone to
Paulina's town-house, and there, with many tears had
taken leave of Arsinoe. All the affection which bound
the sisters together found expression at this moment of
parting. Selene had heard from Paulina that Pollux
was dead, and she no longer grudged her rival sister
that she grieved for him more passionately than herself,
though at first her peace of mind had more than once
been disturbed by memories of her old playfellow.

She felt it hard to leave Alexandria, where most of
her brothers and sisters were left behind, and yet she
rejoiced to think of a distant home, for she was no longer
the same creature that she had been a few months since,
and she longed for a remote scene of a new and sanctified life.

Eumenes and Hannah were in the right. It was not
the widow but the little blind boy who had won her to
Christianity. The child's influence had proceeded in a
strange course. In the first instance the promises of
the slave Mastor that Helios should some day meet his
father again in a shining realm among beautiful angels
had a powerful effect on the blind child's tender heart
and vivid imagination. In Hannah's house his hopes
had received fresh nurture, and Mary and the widow
told him much about their kind and loving God and His

Son who loved children and had invited them to come
to Him. When Selene began to recover and he was
permitted to talk to her he poured out to her all his delight at what he had heard from the women. At first,
to be sure, his sister took no pleasure in these fanciful
fables and tried to shake his belief and lead back his
heart to the old gods. But while she tried to guide the
child, by degrees she felt compelled to follow in his
path; at first with wavering steps, but dame Hannah
helped her by her example and with many words of
good counsel. She only taught her doctrine when the
girl asked her questions and begged for information.
All that here surrounded Selene breathed of love and
peace, and the child felt this, spoke of it, forced her to
acknowledge it, and, in his own person, was the first
object on which to exercise a wish hitherto unknown to
her, to be herself loving and lovable. The boy's firm
faith, which was not to be shaken by any reasoning or
by any of the myths which she knew, touched her
deeply and led to her asking Hannah what was the real
bearing of one and another of his statements. It had
always seemed a comfort to her that the miseries of our
earthly life would come to an end with death; but Helios
left her without a reply when he said in a sad voice :

" Do you feel no longing, then, to see our father and
mother again ? "

To see her mother again! This thought gave her
an interest in the next world, and dame Hannah fanned
the spark of hope in her soul into flame.

Selene had seen and suffered much misery, and was
accustomed to call the gods cruel. Helios told her that
God and the Saviour were good and kind, and loved
human beings as their children.

"Is it not good and kind," asked he, "of our Heavenly Father to lead us to dame Hannah?"

"Yes, but we have all been torn apart," said Selene.

"Never mind," said the child confidently, "we shall all meet in Heaven."

As she got well Selene asked after each of the children and Hannah described all the families into which they had been received. The widow did not look as if she spoke falsely, and the little ones, when they came to see her, confirmed her report, and yet Selene could hardly believe in the accuracy of the pictures drawn of their lives in the houses of the Christians.

The mother of a Christian family—says a great Christian teacher—should be the pride of her children, the wife the pride of her husband, husband and children the pride of the wife, and God the pride and glory of every member of the household. Love and faith in fact the bond, contentment and virtuous living the law of the family; and it was in just such a pure and beneficent atmosphere, as Selene herself and Helios felt the blessing of in Hannah's house, that each and all of her brothers and sisters were growing up. Her upright sense gave an honest answer when she asked herself what would have become of them all if her father had remained alive and had been dispossessed of his office? They must all have perished in misery and degradation.

And now?—Perhaps in truth the Divine Being had dealt in kindness with the children.

Love, love, and again love, was breathed from all she saw and heard, and yet—was it not love that had caused her greatest sorrows. Wherefore had it been her lot to endure so much through the same sentiment which beautified life to others? Had any one ever had more to suf-

37

fer than she? Aye indeed! A vivacious, eager youth had
duped her and had promised happiness to her sister instead of to her; it had been hard to bear—and yet, the
Saviour of whom Helios had told her, had been far more
severely tried. Mankind, for whom He—the Son of God
—had come down upon earth, to save from misery and
guilt, had rewarded His loving kindness by hanging Him
on the cross.   In Him she could see a companion in
suffering and she asked the widow to tell her all about
Him.   Selene had made many sacrifices to her family—
she could never forget her walk to the papyrus-factory—
but He had let them mock Him and had shed His
blood for His own.   And who was she?—and who was
He? The Son of God.   His image became dear to her;
she was never weary of hearing about His life and fate,
His words and deeds; and without her observing it the
day came when her soul was free to receive the teaching
of Christ with fervent longing.   With faith she acquired
that consciousness of guilt which had previously been
unknown to her. She had been busy and industrious out
of pride and fear, but never from love; she had selfishly
tried to fling from her the sacred gift of life without ever
thinking what would become of those whom it was her
duty to care for.   She had cursed her lovely sister who
needed her protection and care, and even Pollux, her
childhood's playfellow; and a thousand times had she
imprecated the ruler of human destinies.   All this she
now keenly felt with all the earnestness natural to her,
but she was soothed by the tidings that there was One
who had redeemed the world, and taken on Himself the
sins of every repentant sinner.

After Selene had once expressed to the widow her desire to be a Christian, Hannah brought the bishop to see

her. He himself undertook to instruct the girl and he
found in her a disciple anxious and craving for knowledge. Just like those dried-up and dull-colored plants *
which, when they are plunged in water, open out and revive, so did her heart, untimely withered and dry ; and
she longed to be perfectly recovered that she, like Hannah, might tend the sick and exercise that love which
Christ demands of His followers. That which most particularly appealed to her in her new faith was that it did
not promise joys to the rich who could make great sacrifices, but to the miserable sinner who with a contrite
heart yearned for forgivenness, to the poor and abject,
towards whom she felt as though they belonged to the
same family as herself. And her valiant spirit could not
be satisfied with intentions but longed to act upon them.
In Besa she could set to work with Hannah, and this
prospect lightened her grief in quitting Alexandria.

A favoring wind bore the voyagers southward safe
to their destination.

Two days after their departure Antinous once more
stole into Paulina's garden. He went up to the widow's
little house looking in vain for the deformed girl ; the
road was open ; her absence could but be pleasing to
him, and yet it disquieted him. His heart beat wildly
for to-day—perhaps he might find Selene alone. He
opened the door without knocking, but he dared not
cross the threshold, for in the anteroom stood a strange
man, placing boards against the wall. The carpenter,
a Christian to whom Paulina had given this little
house for his family to live in, asked Antinous what he
wanted.

* The Rose of Jericho, *Anastatica hierochuntina ;* a whole plant in
reality not a flower only.

37

"Is dame Hannah at home ?" stammered the Bithyn-ian.

"She no longer lives here."

"And her adopted daughter, Selene ?"

"She is gone with her into Upper Egypt. Have you any message for her ?"

"No," said the lad, quite confounded. "When did they go ?"

"The day before yesterday."

"And they are not coming back."

"For the next few years, certainly not. Later may be, if it is the Lord's pleasure."

Antinous left the garden by the public gate, un-molested. He was very pale, and he felt like a wanderer in the desert who finds the spring choked where he had hoped to find a refreshing draught.

Next day, at the first moment he could dispose of, Antinous again knocked at the carpenter's door to inquire in what town of Upper Egypt the travellers proposed to settle and the artisan told him frankly, "In Besa."

Antinous had always been a dreamer, but Hadrian had never seen him so listless, so vaguely brooding as in these days. When he tried to rouse him and spur him to greater energy his favorite would look at him beseech-ingly, and though he made every effort to be of use to him and to show him a cheerful countenance it was always with but brief success. Even on the hunting ex-cursions into the Libyan desert which the Emperor fre-quently made, Antinous remained apathetic and in-different to the pleasures of the sport to which he had formerly devoted himself with enjoyment and skill.

The Emperor had remained in Alexandria longer than in any other place, and was weary of festivities and ban-

quets, of the wordy war with the philosophers of the
Museum, of conversing with the ecstatic mystics, the
soothsayers, astrologers and empirics with whom the
place swarmed. And the short audiences which he ac-
corded to the heads of the different religious communities,
and the inspection of the factories and workshops of this
centre of industry, began to annoy him. One day he
announced his intention of visiting the southern provinces
of the Nile valley.

The high-priests of the native Egyptian faith had
craved this favor of him, and he was prompted, not only
by his love of information and passion for travelling, but
also by considerations of state-craft, to gratify this desire
of a hierarchy which was extremely influential in those
rich and important provinces. The prospect of seeing
with his own eyes those marvels of Pharaonic times which
attracted so many travellers, was also an incitement, and
his good spirits rose as soon as he observed what a re-
viving effect his determination to visit southern Egypt
had upon Antinous.

His favorite had for the last few weeks expressed not
the smallest pleasure at any single thing. The homage
paid him no less by the Alexandrian than by the Roman
ladies of rank sickened him. At banquets he sat a silent
guest whose neighborhood could not add to anybody's
pleasure, and even the most brilliant and exciting exhibitions in the Circus and the best contests and races in
the Hippodrome had hardly sufficed to attract his gaze.
Formerly he had been an eager and attentive spectator
of the plays of Menander and of his imitators, Alexis,
Apollodorus and Posidippus; but now when they were
performed he stared into vacancy and thought of Selene.

The prospect of going to the place where she was

living excited him powerfully and revived his drooping courage for life.   He could hope once more, and to the man who sees light shining in the future the present is no longer dark.

Hadrian rejoiced in this change in the lad and hastened the preparations for their departure; still, some months passed before he could begin his journey.

In the first place he had to provide for newly colonizing Libya, which had been depopulated by a revolt of the Jews.   Then he had to come to a determination as to certain new post-roads which were to connect the different parts of the empire more nearly, and finally he had to await the formal assent of the Roman Senate to some new resolutions concerning the hereditary reversion of conferred free-citizenship.   This assent was, no doubt a matter of course, but the Emperor never issued an edict without it, and he was very desirous that his decree should come into operation as soon as possible.

In the course of his visits to the Museum the sovereign had informed himself as to the position of the several members of that institution, and he was occupied in making certain regulations which should relieve them of the more sordid cares of life; the condition of the aged teachers and educators of the young had also attracted his observation, and he had endeavored to improve it.

When Sabina represented to him what a large outlay these new measures would entail, he replied:

" We do not allow the veterans to perish who placed their lives, and limbs at the service of the state.   Why then should those who serve it with their intellect be burdened with petty cares ?   Which should we rank the higher, power and poverty or mental wealth ?   The harder I—as the sovereign—find it to answer the question the more positively do I feel it to be my duty to mete out the same measure to all veterans alike, whether officials, warriors or instructors."

The Alexandrians themselves detained him too by a succession of new acts of homage. They raised him to the rank of a divinity, dedicated a temple to him, and instituted a series of new festivals in his honor; partly no doubt to win his partiality for their city and to express their pride and satisfaction in his long stay there, but also because the pleasure-loving community was glad to seize this opportunity as a favorable one for gratifying their own inclinations and revelling in mere unusual enjoyment. Thus the Imperial visit swallowed up millions, and Hadrian, who enquired into every detail and contrived to obtain information as to the sums expended by the city, blamed the recklessness of his lavish entertainers. He wrote afterwards to his brother-in-law, Servianus, his fullest recognition of both the wealth and the industry of Alexandrians, saying, with terms of praise, that among them not one was idle. One made glass, another papyrus, another linen; and each of these restless mortals, said he, is busied in some handiwork. Even the lame, the blind and the maimed here sought and found employment. Nevertheless he calls the Alexandrians a contumacious and good-for-nothing community, with sharp and evil tongues that had spared neither Verus nor Antinous. Jews, Christians, and the votaries of Serapis, he adds in the same letter, serve but one God instead of the divinities of Olympus, and when he asserts of the Christians that they even worshipped Serapis he means to say that they were persuaded of the doctrine of the survival of the soul after death. The dispute as to

which temple should be assigned as the residence of the
newly-found Apis gave Hadrian much to do. From
time immemorial this sacred bull had been kept in the
temple of Ptah at Memphis, but this venerable city of the
Pyramids had been outstripped by Alexandria, and the
temple of Serapis outvied that at Memphis in the province of Sokari, tenfold in size and in magnificence.
The Egyptians of Alexandria, who dwelt in the quarter
called Rhakotis, close to the Serapeum, desired to have
the incarnation of the god in the form of a bull, in their
midst; but the Memphites would not abandon their old
prescriptive rights, and the Emperor had found it far
from easy to guide the contest, which proved a very exciting one to all parties, to a satisfactory issue. Memphis had its Apis, and the Serapeum was indemnified by
certain endowments which had formerly been granted to
the temple at Memphis.

At last, in June, the Emperor could set out. He
wished to traverse the province on foot and on horseback, and Sabina was to follow by boat as soon as the in-
undation should begin.

The Empress would gladly have returned to Rome
or to Tibur, for Verus had been obliged to quit Egypt by
the orders of the physician as soon as the summer heat
had set in. He departed with his wife, as the son of the
Imperial couple, but no word on Hadrian's part had justified him in hoping confidently to be nominated as his
successor to the sovereignty.

The handsome rake's unlimited dissipations were severely checked by his sufferings, but not altogether pre-
vented, and on his return to Rome he continued to
indulge in all the pleasures of life. Hadrian's hesitation
and reluctance often disquieted him, for that imperial

Sphinx had, only too frequently, given the most unexpected solutions to his mystifications. But the fatal end
with which he had been threatened caused him small
anxiety; nay, Ben Jochai's prediction rather prompted
him to enjoy to the utmost every hour of health and ease
that Fate might still allow him.

CHAPTER XIX.

BALBILLA and her companion, Publius Balbinus and
other illustrious Romans, Favorinus the sophist, and a
numerous suite of chamberlains and servants, were to accompany the Empress by water, while Hadrian set forth
on his land journey with a small escort to which he added
a splendid array of huntsmen. Before he reached Memphis, in crossing the Libyan desert, through which his
road lay, he had killed a few lions and many other beasts
of prey, and here he had once more found Antinous the
best of sporting companions. Cool headed in danger,
indefatigable on foot, content and serviceable in all circumstances, the young fellow seemed to Hadrian to be a
comrade created by the gods themselves for his special
delectation. When Hadrian was in the humor to brood
and be silent the whole day long, he never disturbed him
by a word; but in these moods the Emperor found his
favorite's society indispensable, for the mere consciousness
of his presence soothed him.

Antinous too, was happy on these occasions, for he
felt that he was of some use to his venerated master and
could thus alleviate the burden which had never ceased
to weigh on his own soul ever since the crime he had

committed. Besides, he preferred dreaming to talking, and the exercise in the open air preserved him from listless lassitude.

In Memphis Hadrian was detained a whole month, for there he was expected to visit the Egyptian temples with Sabina, who had arrived before him, and to submit to many ceremonials invested with the regalia of the Pharaohs. Sabina often felt as if she must faint when, crowned with the ponderous vulture-headed fillet of the Queens of Egypt, weighed down with long robes and golden ornaments, she was conducted with her husband, in procession, through all the rooms, over the roof and finally into the holiest place of some vast sanctuary. What senseless ceremonials they had to go through in the course of these long circuits, and how many sacrifices had they to attend! When she returned from these visitations she was utterly exhausted, and indeed, it was no small exertion to undergo so many fumigations with incense and so many aspersions, to listen to so many litanies and hymns, to parade through such endless halls and while being elevated to the rank of celestial beings, to be crowned with so many crowns in turn and decorated with all kinds of fillets and symbolic adornments.

Her husband set her a good example, however; through all the ceremonials he displayed the whole grave majesty of his nature, and among the Egyptians behaved as one of themselves. He even took pleasure in the mystical lore of the priests, with whom he often held long conversations.

As at Memphis, so in all the principal temples of the great cities to the southward, the Imperial pair accepted the homage of the hierarchy and the honors due to divinity. Wherever Hadrian granted money for the ex-

tension of a temple, he was required to perform the ceremony of laying a stone with his own hand. But he
always found time to hunt in the desert, to manage the
affairs of state, and to visit the most interesting monuments of past times, and at Memphis especially, the city
of the dead, with the Pyramids, the great Sphinx, the
Serapeum and the tombs of the Apis.

Before quitting the city he and his companions con-
sulted the oracle of the sacred bull. The fairest future
was promised to Balbilla; the bull to whom she had to
offer a cake, with her face averted, had approved of her
gift and had touched her hand with his moist muzzle.
Hadrian was left in ignorance as to the sentence of the
priests of Apis, for it was given to him in a sealed roll
with an explanation of the signs it contained; but he
was solemnly adjured not to open them before at least
half a year had elapsed.

It was only in the cities that Hadrian met his wife,
for he pursued his journey by land and she hers by water.
The boats almost invariably reached their destination
sooner than the land-travellers, and when they at last
arrived, there was always a grand festival to welcome
them, in which however Sabina but rarely took part.
Balbilla proved herself all the more eager to make their
arrival pleasant by some kindly surprise. She sincerely
reverenced Hadrian, and his favorite's beauty had an
irresistible charm for her artist's soul. It was a delight
to her only to look at him; his absence troubled her,
and when he returned she was always the first to greet
him. And yet the bright girl troubled herself about him
neither more nor less than the other ladies in Sabina's
train; only Balbilla asked nothing of him but the
pleasure of looking at him and rejoicing in his beauty.

If he had dared to mistake her admiration for love and
to have offered her his, the poetess would have indignantly brought him to his bearings; and yet she gave
unqualified expression to her admiration of the Bithynian's splendid person, and indeed with rather remarkable demonstrativeness.

When the travellers made their appearance again
after a prolonged absence Antinous would find in the
room in the ship where he was to live flowers, and
choice fruits sent by her, and verses in which she had
sung his praises. He put it all aside with the rest and
only esteemed the donor the less; but the poetess knew
nothing of these sentiments in her beautiful idol, and
indeed troubled herself very little about his feelings. She
had hitherto found no difficulty in keeping within the
limits of what was becoming. But lately there had been
moments in which she had owned to herself that she
might be carried away into overstepping these limits.
But what did she care for the opinion of those around
her, or about the inner life of the Bithynian, whose external perfection of form was all that pleased her. She
did not shrink from the possibility of arousing hopes in
him which she never could nor intended to fulfil, for the
idea did not once enter her mind; still she felt dissatisfied
with herself, for there was one person who might disapprove of her proceedings, one who had indeed in plain
words reprehended her fancy for doing honor to the
handsome boy with offerings of flowers, and the opinion
of that one person weighed with her more than that of
all the rest of the men and women she knew, put together.

This one was Pontius the architect; and yet, strangely
enough, it was precisely her remembrance of him that

urged her on from one folly to another. She had often
seen the architect in Alexandria, and when they parted
she had allowed him to promise to follow her and the
Empress, and to escort them at any rate for a part of
their voyage up the Nile. But he came not, nor had
he sent any report of himself, though he was alive and
well, and every express that overtook them brought
documents for Caesar in his handwriting.

So he, on whose faithful devotion she had built as
on a rock, was no less self-seeking and fickle than other
men. She thought of him every day and every hour;
and as soon as a vessel from the north cast anchor
within sight, she watched the voyagers as they disembarked to detect him among them. She longed for
Pontius as a traveller who has lost his way sighs for a
sight of the guide who has deserted him; and yet she
was angry with him, for he had betrayed by a thousand
tokens that he esteemed and cared for her, that she had
a certain power over his strong will—and now he had
broken his word and did not come.

And she? She had not been unmoved by his devotion, and had been gentler to this grandson of her father's
freed slave than to the best-born man of her own rank.
And in spite of it all Pontius could spoil all the pleasure
of her journey and stay in Alexandria instead of following in her wake. He could easily have intrusted his
building to other architects—the great metropolis was
swarming with them! Well, if he did not trouble himself about her she certainly need care even less about
him. Perhaps at last, at the end of their travels he
might yet come, and then he should see how much she
cared for his admonitions.

But she sighed impatiently for the hour when she

might read him all the verses she had addressed to Antinous, and ask him how he liked them. It gave her a
childish pleasure to add to the number of these little
poems, to finish them elaborately, and display in them
all her knowledge and ability. She gave the preference
to artificial and massive metres; some of the verses were
in Latin, others in the Attic, and others again in the
Aeolian dialects of Greek, for she had now learnt to use
this; and all to punish Pontius—to vex Pontius—and at
the same time to appear in his eyes as brilliant as she
could. She belauded Antinous, but she wrote for Pontius, and for every flower she gave the lad she had sent
a thought to the architect, though with a curl on her
lips of scornful defiance.

But a young girl cannot be always praising the
beauty of a youth in new and varied forms with complete
impunity, and thus there were hours when Balbilla was
inclined to believe that she really loved Antinous. Then
she would call herself his Sappho, and he seemed destined to be her Phaon. During his long absences with the
Emperor she would long to see him—nay, even with
tears; but, as soon as he was by her side again, and she
could look at his inanimate beauty and into his weary
eyes, when she heard the torpid "Yes" or "No" with
which he replied to her questions, the spell was entirely
broken and she honestly confessed to herself that she
would as soon see him before her hewn in marble as
clothed in flesh and blood.

In such moments as these her memory of the architect was particularly fresh, and once, when their ship
was sailing through a mass of lotos leaves, above which
one splendid full-blown flower raised its head, her apt
imagination, which rapidly seized on everything note-

worthy and gave it poetic form, entwined the incident in
a set of verses, in which she designated Antinous as the
lotos-flower which fulfils its destiny simply by being
beautiful, and comparing Pontius to the ship which, well
constructed and well guided, invited the traveller to new
voyages in distant lands.

The Nile voyage came to an end at Thebes of the
hundred gates, and here nothing that could attract
the Roman travellers remained unvisited. The tombs of
the Pharaohs extending into the very heart of the rocky
hills, and the grand temples that stood to the west of the
city of the dead, shorn though they were of their ancient
glory, filled the Emperor with admiration. The Imperial travellers and their companions listened to the famous
colossus of Memnon, of which the upper portion had
been overthrown by an earthquake, and three times in
the dawn they heard it sound.

Balbilla described the incident in several long poems
which Sabina caused to be engraved on the stone of the
colossus. The poetess imagined herself as hearing the
voice of Memnon singing to his mother Eos while her
tears, the fresh morning dew, fell upon the image of her
son, fallen before the walls of Troy. These verses she
composed in the Aeolian dialect, named herself as their
writer and informed the readers—among whom she included Pontius—that she was descended from a house
no less noble than that of King Antiochus.

The gigantic structures on each bank of the Nile
fully equalled Hadrian's expectations, though they had
suffered so much injury from earthquakes and sieges,
and the impoverished priesthood of Thebes were no
longer in a position to provide for their preservation
even, much less for their restoration. Balbilla accom-

panied Caesar on a visit to the sanctuary of Ammon, on
the eastern shore of the Nile.   In the great hall, the
most vast and lofty pillared hall in the world, her impressionable soul felt a peculiar exaltation, and as the
Emperor observed how, with a heightened color she now
gazed upward, and then again, leaning against a towering column, looked at the scene around her, he asked
her what she felt, standing in this really worthy abode of
the gods.

" One thing—above all things one thing !" cried the
girl.   " That architecture is the sublimest of the arts !
This temple is to me like some grand epode, and the
poet who composed it conceived it not in feeble words
but formed it out of almost immovable masses.   Thousands of parts are here combined to form a whole, and
each is welded with the rest into beautiful harmony and
helps to give expression to the stupendous idea which
existed in the brain of the builder of this hall.   What
other art is gifted with the power of creating a work so
imperishable and so far transcending all ordinary stand-
ards ?"

" A poetess crowning the architect with laurels !"
exclaimed the Emperor.   " But is not the poet's realm
the infinite, and can the architect ever get beyond the
finite and the limited ?"

" Then is the nature of the divinity a measurable
unit ?" asked Balbilla.   " No, it is not; and yet this
hall gives one the impression that the very divinity might
find space in it to dwell in."

" Because it owes it existence to a master-mind, which
while it conceived it stood on the boundary line of eternity.   But do you think this temple will outlast the
poems of Homer ?"

" No ; but the memory of it will no more fade away that of the wrath of Achilles or the wanderings of the experienced Odysseus."

" It is a pity that our friend Pontius cannot hear you," said Hadrian. " He has completed the plans for a work which is destined to outlive me and him and all of us. I mean my own tomb. Besides that I intend him to erect gates, courts and halls in the Egyptian style at Tibur, which may remind us of our travels in this wonderful country. I expect him to-morrow."

" To-morrow !" exclaimed Balbilla, and her face fired with a scarlet flush to her very brow.

CHAPTER XX.

SHORTLY after starting from Thebes—on the second day of November—Hadrian came to a great decision. Verus should be acknowledged not merely as his son but also as his successor.

Sabina's urgency would not alone have sufficed to put a term to his hesitancy, especially as it had lately been farther increased by a wish that was all his own. His wife's heart had pined for a child, but he too had longed for a son, and he had found one in Antinous. His favorite was a boy he had picked up by chance, the son of humble though free parents, but it lay in the Emperor's power to make him great, to confer on him the highest posts of honor in the Empire, and at last to recognize him publicly as his heir. Antinous, if any one, had deserved this at his hands, and on no other man could he so ungrudgingly bestow everything that he possessed.

38

These ideas and hopes had now filled his mind for many
months, but the nature and the mood of the young
Bithynian had been more and more adverse to them.

Hadrian had striven more earnestly than his predecessors to raise the fallen dignity of the Senate, and still
he could count securely on its consent to any measure.
The leading official authorities of the Republic had been
recognized and allowed the full exercise of their powers.
To be sure, be they whom they might, they all had to
obey the Emperor, still they were always there; and
even with a weak ruler at its head the Empire might
continue to subsist within the limits established by
Hadrian, and restricted with wise moderation. Nevertheless, only a few months previously he would not have
ventured to think of the adoption of his favorite. Now
he hoped to find himself somewhat nearer to the fulfilment of his wishes. It is true Antinous was still a
dreamer; but in their wanderings and hunting excursions through Egypt he had proved himself gallant and
prompt, intelligent, and, after their departure from
Thebes, even bold and lively at times. Antinous,
under this aspect, he himself might take in hand, and
even name him as his successor in due time, when he
had risen from one post of honor to another. For the
present this plan must remain unrevealed.

When he publicly adopted Verus any idea of a possible new selection of a son was excluded, and he might
unhesitatingly venture to appoint Sabina's darling his
successor, for the most famous of the Roman physicians
had written to Hadrian, by his desire, saying that the
praetor's undermined strength could not be restored,
and that, at the best, he could only have a limited number of years to live. Well, then, Verus might die slowly

and contentedly in the midst of the most splendid
anticipations, and when he should have closed his eyes
it would be time enough to set the dreamer—by that
time matured to vigorous manhood—in the vacant
place.

On the return journey from Thebes to Alexandria
Hadrian met his wife at Abydos, and revealed to her
his intention of proclaiming the son of her choice as his
successor. Sabina thanked him with an exclamation of
"At last!" which expressed partly her satisfaction, but
partly too her annoyance at her husband's long delay.
Hadrian gave her his permission to return to Rome
from Alexandria, and on the very same day messages
were despatched with letters both to the Senate and to
the prefects of Egypt.

The despatch intended for Titianus charged him to
proclaim publicly the adoption of the praetor, to arrange
at the same time for a grand festival, and on that
occasion to grant to the people, in Caesar's name, all
the boons and favors which by the traditional law of
Egypt the Sovereign was expected to bestow at the
birth of an heir to the throne. The whole suite of the
Imperial pair celebrated Hadrian's decision by splendid
banquets, but the Emperor did not himself take part in
them, but crossed to the other bank of the Nile and
went to Antaeopolis in the desert, meaning to penetrate
from thence into the gorges of the Arabian desert and
to chase wild beasts. No one was to accompany him
but Antinous, Mastor, and a few huntsmen and some
dogs.

He meant to rejoin the ships at Besa. He had postponed his visit to this place till the return journey, because he had travelled up by the western shore of the

38

Nile, and the passage across the river would have taken up too much time.

The travellers' tents were pitched one sultry evening in November, between the Nile and the limestone range, in which was arrayed a long row of tombs of the period of the Pharaohs. Hadrian had gone to visit these, for the remarkable pictures on the walls delighted him, but Antinous remained behind, for he had already looked at similar works oftener than he cared for, in Upper Egypt. He found these pictures monotonous and unlovely, and he had not the patience to investigate their meaning as his master did. He had been a hundred times into the ancient rock-tombs, only not to leave Hadrian and not for his own amusement; but to-day— he could hardly bear himself for impatience and excitement, for he knew that a ride, a walk, of a few hours, would carry him to Besa and to Selene. The Emperor would remain absent three or four hours at any rate, and if he made up his mind to it he could have sought out the girl for whom his heart was longing before his return, and still be back again before his master.

But before acting he must reflect. There was the Emperor climbing the hill-side where he could see him, and messengers were expected and he had been charged to receive them. If they should bring bad news, his master must on no account be alone. Ten times did he go up to his good hunter to leap upon his back; once he even took down the horse's head-gear to put on his bridle, but in the very act of slipping the complicated bit between the teeth of his steed his resolution gave way. During all this delay and hesitation the minutes slipped away, and at last it was so late that Hadrian might return and it was folly to think of carrying his plan into execution. The expected express arrived with several letters, but the Emperor did not come back. It grew dark, and heavy rain-drops fell from the overcast sky, and still Antinous was alone. His anxious longing was mingled with regret for the lost opportunity of seeing Selene and alarm at the Emperor's prolonged absence.

In spite of the rain, which began to fall more violently, he went out into the open air, of which the sweltering oppressiveness had helped to fetter his feeble volition, and called to the dogs, with whose help he proposed seeking the Emperor; but just then he heard the bark of Argus, and soon after Hadrian and Mastor stepped out of the darkness into the brightness which shone out from the tent, where lights were burning.

The Emperor gave his favorite but a brief greeting and silently submitted while Antinous dried his hair and brought him some refreshments, and Mastor bathed his feet and dressed him in fresh garments. As he reclined with the Bithynian, before the supper which was standing ready, he said:

" A strange evening! how hot and oppressive the atmosphere is. We must be on the lookout, something serious is brewing."

" What happened to you, my Lord ?"

" Many things. At the door of the very first tomb that I was about to enter I found an old black woman who stretched out her hands against us to keep us out and shrieked out words that sounded horrible."

" Did you understand her ?"

" No—who can learn Egyptian."

" Then you do not know what she said ?"

" I was to find out—she cried out ' Dead!' and again

' Dead !' and in the tomb which she was watching there
were I know not how many persons attacked by the
plague."

" You saw them ?"

" Yes, I had only heard of this disease till then.   It
is frightful, and quite answers to the descriptions I had
read of it."

" But Caesar !" cried Antinous reproachfully and in
alarm.

" When we turned our backs on the tombs," continued Hadrian, paying no heed to the lad's exclamation, " we were met by an elderly man dressed in white
and a strange-looking maiden. She was lame but of remarkable beauty."

" And she was going to the sick ?"

" Yes, she had brought medicine and food to them."

" But she did not go in among them ?" asked Antinous eagerly.

" She did, in spite of my warnings. In her companion I recognized an old acquaintance."

" An old one ?"

" At any rate older than myself. We had met in
Athens when we still were young. At that time he was
one of the school of Plato and the most zealous, nay,
perhaps the most gifted of us all."

" How came such a man among the plague-stricken
people of Besa ?   Is he become a physician ?"

" No. But at Athens he sought fervently and eagerly
for the truth, and now he asserts that he has found it."

" Here, among the Egyptians ?"

" In Alexandria among the Christians."

" And the lame girl who accompanied the philosopher—does she too believe in the crucified God ?"

" Yes. She is a sick-nurse or something of the kind.
Indeed there is something grand in the ecstatic craze of
these people."

" Is it true that they worship an ass and a dove ?"

" Nonsense !"

" I did not want to believe it ; and at any rate they
are kind, and succor all who suffer, even strangers who
do not belong to their sect."

" How do you know ?"

" One hears a great deal about them in Alexandria."

" Alas ! alas !—I never persecute an imaginary foe,
as such I reckon the creeds and ideas of other men ;
still, I cannot but ask myself whether it can add to the
prosperity of the state when citizens cease to struggle
against the pressure and necessity of life and console
themselves for them instead, by the hope of visionary
happiness in another world which perhaps only exists
in the fancy of those who believe in it."

" I should wish that life might end with death," said
Antinous thoughtfully ; " and yet—"

" Well ?"

" If I were sure that in that other world I should
find those I long to see again, then I might long for a
future life."

" And would you really like, throughout all eternity,
to push and struggle in the crowd of old acquaintances
which death does not diminish but rather multiplies ?"

" Nay, not that—but I should like to be permitted
to live for ever with a few chosen friends."

" And should I be one of them ?"

" Yes—indeed," cried Antinous warmly and pressing
his lips to Hadrian's hand.

" I was sure of it—but even with the promise of

never being obliged to part with you my darling, I
would never sacrifice the only privilege which man enjoys above the immortals."

" What privilege can you mean ?"

" The right of withdrawing from the ranks of the
living as soon as annihilation seems more endurable
than existence and I choose to call death to release
me."

" The gods, it is true, cannot die."

" And the Christians only to link a new life on to
death."

" But a fairer and a happier than this on earth."

" They say it is a life of bliss. But the mother of
this everlasting life is the ineradicable love of existence
in even the most wretched of our race, and hope is its
father. They believe in a complete freedom from suffering in that other world because He whom they call
their Redeemer, the crucified Christ, has saved them from
all sufferings by His death."

" And can a man take upon him the sufferings of
others. think you, like a garment or a burden ?"

" They say so, and my friend from Athens is quite
convinced. In books of magic there are many formulas by
which misfortunes may be transferred not merely from
men to beasts, but from one human being to another.
Very remarkable experiments have even been carried
out with slaves, and to this day I have to struggle in
several provinces to suppress human sacrifices by which
the gods are to be reconciled or propitiated. Only think
of the innocent Iphigenia who was dragged to the altar;
did not the gulf in the Forum close when Curtius had
leaped into it ? When Fate shoots a fatal arrow at you
and I receive it in my breast, perhaps she is content with

the chance victim and does not enquire as to whom she has hit."

" The gods would be exorbitant indeed if they were not content with your blood for mine !"

" Life is life, and that of the young is of better worth than that of the old. Many joys will. yet bloom for you."

" And you are indispensable to the whole world."

" After me another will come. Are you ambitious, boy ?"

" No, my Lord."

" What then can be the meaning of this: that every one wishes me joy of my son Verus excepting you. Do you not like my choice ?"

Antinous colored and looked at the ground, and Hadrian went on:

" Say honestly what you feel."

" The praetor is ill."

" He can have but a few years to live, and when he is dead—"

" He may recover—"

" When he is dead, I must look out for another son. What do you think now ? Who is the being that every man, from a slave to a consul, would soonest hear call him ' Father ?' "

" Some one he tenderly loved."

" True—and particularly when that one clung to him with unchangeable fidelity. I am a man like any other, and you, my good fellow, are always nearest to my heart, and I shall bless the day when I may authorize you, before all the world, to call me ' Father.' Do not interrupt me. If you resolutely concentrate your will and show as keen a sense for ruling men as you do for the chase, if you try to sharpen your wits and take in what I teach you, it may some day happen that Antinóus instead of Verus—"

" Nay, not that, only not that!" cried the lad, turning very pale and raising his hands beseechingly.

" The greatness with which Destiny surprises us seems terrible so long as it is new to us," said Hadrian. " But the seaman is soon accustomed to the storms, and we come to wear the purple as you do your chiton."

" Oh, Caesar, I entreat you," said Antinous, anxiously, " put aside these ideas; I am not fit for great things."

" The smallest saplings grow to be palms."

" But I am only a wretched little herb that thrives awhile in your shadow. Proud Rome—"

" Rome is my handmaid. She has been forced before now to be ruled by men of inferior stamp, and I should show her how the handsomest of her sons can wear the purple. The world may look for such a choice from a sovereign whom it has long known to be an artist, that is a high-priest of the Beautiful. And if not, I will teach it to form its taste on mine."

" You are pleased to mock me, Caesar," cried the Bithynian. " You certainly cannot be in earnest, and if it is true that you love me—"

" What now, boy ?"

" You will let me live unknown for you, care for you ; you will ask nothing of me but reverence and love and fidelity."

" I have long had them, and I now would fain repay my Antinous for all these treasures."

" Only let me stay with you, and if necessary let me die for you."

"I believe, boy, you would be ready to make the sacrifice we were speaking of for me!"

"At any moment without winking an eyelash."

"I thank you for those words. It has turned out a pleasant evening, and what a bad one I looked forward to!"

"Because the woman by the tomb startled you?"

"'Dead,' is a grim word. It is true that 'death' —being dead—can frighten no wise man; but the step out of light into darkness is fearful. I cannot get the figure of the old hag and her shrill cry out of my mind. Then the Christian came up, and his discourse was strange and disturbing to my soul. Before it grew dark he and the limping girl went homewards; I stood looking after them and my eyes were dazzled by the sun which was sinking over the Libyan range. The horizon was clear, but behind the day-star there were clouds. In the west, the Egyptians say, lies the realm of death. I could not help thinking of this; and the oracle, the misfortunes that the stars threatened me with in the course of this year, the cry of the old woman—all these crowded into my mind together. But then, as I observed how the sun struggled with the clouds and approached nearer and nearer to the hill-tops on the farther side of the river, I said to myself: If it sets in full radiance you may look confidently to the future; if it is swallowed up by clouds before it sinks to rest, then destiny will fulfil itself; then you must shorten sail and wait for the storm."

"And what happened?"

"The fiery globe burnt in glowing crimson, surrounded by a million rays. Each seemed separate from the rest and shone with glory of its own; it was as though the sinking disc had been the centre of bow-

shots innumerable and golden arrow-shafts radiated to
the sky in every direction.   The scene was magnificent
and my heart beat high with happy excitement, when
suddenly and swiftly a dark cloud fell, as though exas-
.perated by the wounds it had received from those fiery
darts; a second followed, and a third, and sinister Daimons flung a dark and fleecy curtain over the glorious
head of Helios, as the executioner throws a coarse black
cloth over the head of the condemned, when he sets his
knee against him to strangle him."

At this narrative Antinous covered his face with both
hands, and murmured in terror:

" Frightful, frightful! What can be hanging over us ?
Only listen, how it thunders, and the rain thrashes the
tent."

"The clouds are pouring out torrents ; see the water
is coming in already.   The slaves must dig gutters for it
to run off.   Drive the pegs tighter you fellows out there
or the whirlwind will tear down the slight structure."

" And how sultry the air is !"

" The hot wind seems to warm even the flood of
rain.   Here it is still dry; mix me a cup of wine, Antinous.   Have any letters come ? "

" Yes, my Lord."

" Give them to me, Mastor."

The slave, who was busily engaged in damming up
with earth and stones, the trickling stream of rain-water
that was soaking into the tent, sprang up, hastily dried
his hands, took a sack out of the chest in which the
Emperor's despatches were kept and gave it to his master.   Hadrian opened the leather bag, took out a roll,
hastily broke it open, and then, after rapidly glancing at
the contents, exclaimed:

" What is this ? I have opened the record of the oracle of Apis. How did it come among to-day's letters ? "

Antinous went up to Hadrian, looked at the sack, and said :

" Mastor has made a mistake. These are the documents from Memphis. I will bring you the right despatch-bag."

" Stay!" said Hadrian, eagerly seizing his favorite's hand. " Is this a mere trick of chance or a decree of Fate ? Why should this particular sack have come into my hands to-day of all others ? Why, out of twenty documents it contains, should I have taken out this very one ? Look here.—I will explain these signs to you. Here stand three pairs of arms bearing shields and spears, close by the name of the Egyptian month that corresponds to our November. These are the three signs of misfortune. The lutes up there are of happier omen. The masts here indicate the usual state of affairs. Three of these hieroglyphics always occur together. Three lutes indicate much good fortune, two lutes and one mast good fortune and moderate prosperity, one pair of arms and two lutes misfortune, followed by happiness, and so forth. Here, in November, begin the arms with weapons, and here they stand in threes and threes, and portend nothing but unqualified misfortune, never mitigated by a single lute. Do you see, boy ? Have you understood the meaning of these signs ?"

" Perfectly well; but do you interpret them rightly ? The fighting arms may perhaps lead to victory."

" No. The Egyptians use them to indicate conflict, and to them conflict and unrest are identical with what we call evil and disaster."

" That is strange !"

" Nay, it is well conceived; for they say that every-thing was originally created good by the gods, but that the different portions of the great All changed their nature by restless and inharmonious mingling. This explanation was given me by the priest of Apis, and here—here by the month of November are the three fighting arms—a hideous token. If one of the flashes which light up this tent so incessantly, like a living stream of light were to strike you, or me, and all of us—I should not wonder. Terrible—terrible things hang over us! It requires some courage under such omens as these, to keep an untroubled gaze and not to quail."

" Only use your own arms against the fighting arms of the Egyptian gods; they are powerful," said Antinous; but Hadrian let his head sink on his breast, and said, in a tone of discouragement:

" The gods themselves must succumb to Destiny."

The thunder continued to roar. More than once the storm snapped the tent-ropes, and the slaves were obliged to hold on to the Emperor's fragile shelter with their hands; the chambers of the clouds poured mighty torrents out upon the desert range which for years had not known a drop of rain, and every rift and runlet was filled with a stream or a torrent.

Neither Hadrian nor Antinous closed their eyes that fearful night. The Emperor had as yet opened only one of the rolls that were in the day's letter-bag; it con-tained the information that Titianus the prefect was cruelly troubled by his old difficulty of breathing, with a petition from that worthy official to be allowed to retire from the service of the state and to withdraw to his own estate. It was no small matter for Hadrian to dispense for the future with this faithful coadjutor, to lose the man on whom he had had his eye to tranquillize Judaea—where a fresh revolt had raised its head, and to reduce it again to subjection without bloodshed. To crush and depopulate the rebellious province was within the power of other men, but to conquer and govern it with kindness belonged only to the wise and gentle Titianus. The Emperor had no heart to open a second letter that night. He lay in silence on his couch till morning began to grow gray, thinking over every evil hour of his life—the murders of Nigrinus, of Tatianus and of the senators, by which he had secured the sovereignty—and again he vowed to the gods immense sacrifices if only they would protect him from impending disaster.

When he rose next morning Antinous was startled at his aspect, for Hadrian's face and lips were perfectly bloodless. After he had read the remainder of his letters he started, not on foot but on horseback, with Antinous and Mastor for Besa, there to await the rest of the escort.

CHAPTER XXI.

THE unchained elements had raged that night with equal fury over the Nile city of Besa. The citizens of this ancient town had done all they could to give the Imperial traveller a worthy reception. The chief streets had been decked with ropes of flowers strung from mast to mast and from house to house, and by the harbor, close to the river shore, statues of Hadrian and his wife had been erected.   But the storm tore down the masts and the garlands, and the lashed waters of the Nile had beaten with irresistible fury on the bank; had carried away piece after piece of the fertile shore, flung its waves, like liquid wedges into the rifts of the parched land; and excavated the high bank by the landing-quay.

After midnight the storm was still raging with un-heard-of fury; it swept the palm thatch from many of the houses, and beat the stream with such violence that it was like a surging sea.   The full unbroken force of the flood beat again and again on the promontory on which stood the statues of the Imperial couple.   Shortly before the first dawn of light the little tongue of land, which was protected by no river wall, could no longer resist the furious attack of the waters; huge clods of soil slipped and fell with a loud noise into the river and were followed by a large mass of the cliff, with a roar as of thunder; the plateau behind sank, and the statue of the Emperor which stood upon it began to totter and lean slowly to its fall.   When day broke it was lying with the pedestal still above ground, but the head was buried in the earth.

At break of day the citizens left their houses to in-quire of the fishermen and boatmen what had occurred in the harbor during the night.   As soon as the storm had abated, hundreds, nay thousands, of men, women and children thronged the landing-place round the fallen statue—they saw the land-slip and knew that the cur-rent had torn the land from the bank and caused the mischief.   Was it that Hapi, the Nile-god, was angry with the Emperor? At any rate the disaster that had befallen the image of the sovereign boded evil, that was clear.

The Toparch, the chief municipal authority, at once set to work to reinstate the statue which was itself uninjured, for Hadrian might arrive in a few hours. Numerous men, both free and slaves, crowded to undertake the work, and before long the statue of Hadrian, executed in the Egyptian style, once more stood upright and gazing with a fixed countenance towards the harbor. Sabina's was also put back by the side of her husband's and the Toparch went home satisfied. With him most of the starers and laborers left the quay, but their place was taken by other curious folks who had missed the statue from its place, where the land had fallen, and now expressed their opinions as to the mode and manner of its fall.

"The wind can never have overturned this heavy mass of limestone," said a ropemaker: "And see how far it stands from the broken ground."

"They say it fell on the top of land-slip," answered a baker.

"That is how it was," said a sailor.

"Nonsense!" cried the ropemaker. "If the statue had stood on the ground now carried away, it must have fallen at once into the water and have sunk to the bottom—any child can see that other powers have been at work here."

"Very likely," said a temple-servant who devoted himself to the interpretation of signs:. "The gods may have overset the proud image to give a warning token to Hadrian."

"The immortals do not mix in the affairs of men in our day," said the sailor; "but in such a fearful night as

39

this peaceful citizens remain within doors and so leave a fair field for Caesar's foes."

"We are all faithful subjects," said the baker indignantly.

"You are a pack of rebellious rabble," retorted a Roman soldier, who like the whole cohort quartered in the province of Hermopolis, had formerly served in Judaea under the cruel Tinnius Rufus. "Among you worshippers of beasts squabbles never cease, and as to the Christians, who have made their nests out there on the other side of the valley, say the worst you can of them and still you would be flattering them."

"Brave Fuscus is quite right!" cried a beggar. "The wretches have brought the plague into our houses; wherever the disease shows itself there are Christian men and women to be seen. They came to my brother's house; they sat all night by his sick children and of course both died."

"If only my old governor Tinnius Rufus were here," growled the soldier, "they would none of them be any better off than their own crucified god."

"Well, I certainly have nothing in common with them," replied the baker. "But what is true must continue true. They are quiet, kind folks and punctual in payment, who do no harm and show kindness to many poor creatures."

"Kindness?" cried the beggar, who had received alms himself from the deacon of the church at Besa, but had also been exhorted to work. "All the five priests of Sekket of the grotto of Artemis have been led away by them and have basely abandoned the sanctuary of the goddess. And is it good and kind that they should have poisoned my brother's children with their potions?"

"Why should they not have killed the children ?" asked the soldier. "I heard of the same things in Syria; and as to this statue, I will never wear my sword again—"

"Hark! listen to the bold Fuscus," cried the crowd. "He has seen much."

"I will never wear my sword again if they did not knock over the statue in the dark."

"No, no," cried the sailor positively. "It fell with the land that was washed away ; I saw it lying there myself."

"And are you a Christian, too ?" asked the soldier, "or do you suppose that I was in jest when I swore by my sword ? I have served in Bithynia, in Syria, and in Judaea. I know these villains, good people. There were hundreds of Christians to be seen there who would throw away life like a worn-out shoe because they did not choose to sacrifice to the statues of Caesar and the gods."

"There, you hear!" cried the beggar. "And did you see a single man of them among the citizens who set to work to restore the statue to its place ?"

"There were none of them there," said the sailor, who was beginning to share the soldier's views.

"The Christians threw down the Emperor's statue," the beggar shouted to the crowd. "It is proved, and they shall suffer for it. Every man who is a friend of the divine Hadrian come with me now and have them out of their houses."

"No uproar!" interrupted the soldier to the furious man. "There is the tribune, he will hear you."

The Roman officer, who now came past with a troop of soldiers to receive the Emperor outside the city, was greeted by the crowd with loud shouting. He com-

39

manded silence and made the soldier tell him what had
so violently excited the people.

"Very possibly," said the tribune, a sinewy and
stern-looking man, who, like Fuscus, had served under
Tinnius Rufus, and had risen from a sutler to be an
officer, "Very possibly—but where are your proofs?"

"Most of the citizens helped in reerecting the statue,
but the Christians held aloof from the work," cried the
beggar. "There was not one to be seen. Ask the
sailor, my lord; he was by and he can bear witness to
it."

"That certainly is more than suspicious. This matter must be strictly inquired into. Pay heed, you people."

"Here comes a Christian girl!" cried the sailor.

"Lame Martha; I know her well," interrupted the
beggar. "She goes into all the plague-stricken houses
and poisons the people. She stayed three days and
three nights at my brother's turning the children's pillows till they were carried out. Wherever she goes
death follows."

Selene, now known as Martha, paid no heed to the
crowd, but with her blind brother Helios, now called
John, went calmly on her way which led from the raised
bank down to the landing-quay. There she wished to
hire a boat to take her across the stream, for in a village
on the island over against the town dwelt some sick
Christians to whom she was carrying medicines and
whom she was intending to watch. For months past
her whole life had been devoted to the suffering. She
had carried help even into heathen homes, and shrunk
from neither fever nor plague. Her cheeks had gained
no color, but her eyes shone with a gentler and purer

light which glorified the severe beauty of her features. As the girl approached the captain he fixed his eyes on her, and called out:

"Hey! pale-face—are you a Christian?"

"Yes, my lord," replied Selene, and she went on quietly and indifferently with her brother.

The Roman looked after her, and as she passed by Hadrian's statue, and, as she did so, dropped her head rather lower than before, he roughly ordered her to stop and to tell him why she had averted her face from the statue of Caesar.

"Hadrian is our ruler as well as yours," answered the young girl. "I am in haste for there are sick people on the island."

"You will bring them no good!" cried the beggar. "Who knows what is hidden there in the basket?"

"Silence!" interrupted the tribune. "They say, girl that your fellow-believers overthrew the statue of Caesar in the night."

"How should that be? We honor Caesar no less than you do."

"I will believe you, and you shall prove it. There stands the statue of the divine Caesar. Come with me and worship it." Selene looked with horror in the face of the stern man, and could not find a word of reply.

"Well!" asked the captain, "will you come? Yes or no?"

Selene struggled for self-possession, and when the soldier held out his hand to her she said with a trembling voice:

"We honor the Emperor but we pray to no statue—only to our Father in Heaven."

"There you have it!" laughed the beggar.

"Once more I ask you," cried the tribune. "Will
you worship this statue, or do you refuse to do so?"

A fearful struggle possessed Selene's soul. If she resisted the Roman her life was in danger, and the fury of
the populace would be aroused against her fellow-believers—if, on the other hand, she obeyed him, she
would be blaspheming God, breaking her faith to the
Saviour who loved her, sinning against the truth and her
own conscience. A fearful dread fell upon her, and deprived her of the power to lift her soul in prayer. She
could not, she dared not, do what was required of her,
and yet the overweening love of life which exists in every
mortal led her feet to the base of the idol and there
stayed her steps.

"Lift up your hands and worship the divine Caesar,"
cried the tribune, who with the rest of the lookers-on
had watched her movements with keen excitement.

Trembling, she set her basket on the ground and
tried to withdraw her hand from her brother's; but the
blind boy held it fast. He fully understood what was required of his sister, he knew full well, from the history of
many martyrs that had been told him, what fate awaited
her and him if they resisted the Roman's demand; but
he felt no fear and whispered to her:

"We will not obey his desires Martha; we will not
pray to idols, we will cling faithfully to the Redeemer.
Turn me away from the image, and I will say 'Our
Father.'"

With a loud voice and his lustreless eyes upraised to
Heaven, the boy said the Lord's prayer. Selene had first
set his face towards the river, and then she herself turned
her back on the statue; then, lifting her hands, she followed the child's example.

Helios clung to her closely, her loudly uttered prayer was one with his, and neither of them saw or heard anything more of what befell them.

The blind boy had a vision of a distant but glorious light, the maiden of a blissful life made beautiful by love, ·as she was flung to the ground in front of the statue of Hadrian, and the excited mob rushed upon her and her faithful little brother. The military tribune tried in vain to hold back the populace, and by the time the soldiers had succeeded in driving the excited mob away from their victims, both the young hearts, in the midst of the triumph of their faith, in the midst of their hopes of an eternal and blissful life, had ceased to beat for ever.

The occurrence disturbed the captain and made him very uneasy. This girl, this beautiful boy, who lay before him pale corpses, had been worthy of a better fate, and he might be made to answer for them; for the law forbade that any Christian should be punished for his faith without a judge's sentence. He therefore commanded that the dead should be carried at once to the house to which they belonged, and threatened every one, who should that day set foot in the Christian quarter, with the severest punishment.

The beggar went off, shrieking and shouting, to his brother's house to tell the mistress that lame Martha, who had nursed her daughter to death, was slain; but he gained an evil reward, for the poor woman bewailed Selene as if she had been her own child, and cursed him and her murderers.

Before sundown Hadrian arrived at Besa, where he found magnificent tents pitched to receive him and his escort. The disaster that had befallen his statue was kept a secret from him, but he felt anxious and ill. He

wished to be perfectly alone, and desired Antinous to go
to see the city before it should be dark.   The Bithynian
joyfully embraced this permission as a gift of the gods;
he hurried through the decorated high streets, and made
a boy guide him from thence into the Christian quarter.
Here the streets were like a city of the dead; not a door.
was open, not a man to be seen.

Antinous paid the lad, sent him away, and with a
beating heart went from one house to another.   Each
looked neat and clean, and was surrounded by trees and
shrubs, but though the smoke curled up from several of
the roofs every house seemed to have been deserted. At
last he heard the sound of voices. Guided by these he
went through a lane to an open place where hundreds of
people, men, women and children, were assembled in
front of a small building which stood in the midst
of a palm grove.

He asked where dame Hannah lived, and an old
man silently pointed to the little house on which the attention of the Christians seemed to be concentrated.
The lad's heart throbbed wildly and yet he felt anxious
and embarrassed, and he asked himself whether he had
not better turn back and return next morning when he
might hope to find Selene alone.

But no! Perhaps he might even now be allowed to
see her.

He modestly made his way through the throng,
which had set up a song in which he could not determine whether it was intended to express feelings of sadness or of triumph.   Now he was standing at the gate
of the garden and saw Mary the deformed girl. She
was kneeling by a covered bier and weeping bitterly. Was dame Hannah dead? No, she was alive, for

at this moment she came out of her house, leaning on
an old man, pale, calm and tearless. Both came forward, the old man uttered a short prayer and then stooping down, lifted the sheet which covered the dead.

Antinous pushed a step forward but instantly drew
two steps back—then covering his eyes with his hand he
stood as if rooted to the spot.

There was no vehement lamentation. The old man
began a discourse. All around were sounds of suppressed weeping, singing and praying but Antinous saw
and heard nothing. He had dropped his hand and
never took his eyes off the white face of the dead till
Hannah once more covered it with the sheet. Even
then he did not stir.

It was not till six young girls lifted Selene's modest
bier and four matrons took up that of little Helios on
their shoulders and the whole assembly moved away after them, that he too turned and followed the mourning
procession. He looked on from a distance while the
larger and the smaller coffins were carried into a rock-
tomb, while the entrance was carefully closed, and the
procession dispersed some here and some there.

At last he found himself alone and in front of the
door of the vault. The sun went down, and darkness
spread rapidly over hill and vale. When no one was
to be seen who could observe him, he threw up his arms,
clasped the pillar at the entrance of the tomb, pressed
his lips against the rough wooden door and struck his
forehead against it while his whole body trembled with
the tearlesss anguish of his spirit.

For some minutes he stood so and did not hear a
light step which came up behind him. It was Mary,
who had come once more to pray by the grave of her

beloved friend.   She at once recognized the youth and softly called him by his name.

"Mary," he answered, clasping her hand eagerly. "How did she die ?"

"Slain," she said, sadly.   "She would not worship Caesar's image."

Antinous shuddered at the words, and asked :

"And why would she not ?"

"Because she was faithful to our belief, and so hoped for the mercy of the Saviour.   Now she is a blessed angel."

"Are you sure of that ?"

"As sure as I live in hope of meeting the martyr who rests here, again in Heaven !"

"Mary."

"Leave go of my hand !"

"Will you do me a service, Mary ?"

"Willingly, Antinous — but pray do not touch me."

"Take this money and buy the loveliest wreath that is to be had here.   Hang it on this tomb, and say as you do so—call out—'From Antinous to Selene.'"

The deformed girl took the money he gave her and said :

"She often prayed for you."

"To her God ?"

"To our Redeemer, that he might give you also joy. She died for Christ Jesus ; now she is with him, and he will grant her prayers."

Antinous was silent for a while, then he said :

"Once more give me your hand, Mary, and now farewell.   Will you sometimes think of me, and pray for me too, to your Redeemer ?"

" Yes, yes, and you will not quite forget me, the poor cripple ?"

" Certainly not, you good, kind girl! Perhaps we may some day meet again." With these words Antinous hurried down the hill and through the town to the Nile.

The moon had risen and was mirrored in the rough water. Just so had its image played upon the waves when Antinous had rescued Selene from the sea. The lad knew that Hadrian would be expecting him, still he did not seek his tent. A violent emotion had over-powered him ; he restlessly paced up and down the river-bank rapidly reviewing in his memory the more prominent incidents of his past life. He seemed to hear again every word of the dialogue that had taken place yesterday between Hadrian and himself. Before his in-ward eye he saw once more his humble home in Bithyn-ia, his mother, his brothers and sisters whom he should never see again. Once more he lived through the dread-ful hour when he had deceived his beloved master and had been an incendiary. An overmastering dread fell upon him as he thought of Hadrian's wish to put him in the place of the man whom the prudent sovereign had chosen as his successor—a choice that was perhaps the direct outcome of his own crime. He, Antinous, who to-day could not think of the morrow, who always kept out of the way of the discourse of grave men because he found it so hard to follow their meaning, he who knew nothing but how to obey, he who was never happy but alone with his master and his dreaming, far from the bustle of the world—he, to be burdened with the purple, with anxiety, with a mountain-load of responsibility !

No, no ; the idea was unheard-of—impossible ! And

yet Hadrian never gave up a wish he had once expressed in words. The future loomed before his soul like some overpowering foe. Suffering, unrest, and misfortune stared him in the face, turn which way he would.

What was the hideous fatality that threatened his sovereign? It was approaching, it must come if no one—aye, if no one should be found to stand between him and the impending blow, and to receive in his own breast—in his own heart, bared to receive the wound—the spear hurled by the vengeful god. And he—he, and he alone was the one who might do this.

The thought flashed into his mind like a sudden blaze of light; and if he should find the courage to devote himself to death for his dear master all his sins against him would be expiated; then—then—oh, how lovely a thought!—then might he not find entrance into the gates of that realm of bliss which Selene's prayers had opened to him? There he would see his mother again and his father, and by and bye his brothers and sisters—but now, at once in a few minutes Her whom he loved and who had trodden the ways of death before him.

An exquisite sense of hope such as he had never felt before flooded his soul. There lay the Nile—here was a boat. He gave it a strong push into the stream and with a powerful leap, as when hunting he had often sprung from rock to rock, he jumped into the boat. He had just seized an oar when Mastor, who had been desired by the Emperor to seek him, recognized him in the moonlight and desired him to return with him to the tents.

But Antinous did not obey. As he pushed out into the stream he called out:

"Greet my Lord from me—greet him lovingly, a thousand times, and tell him Antinous loved him more than his life. Fate demands a victim. The world cannot dispense with Hadrian, but Antinous is a mere nonentity, whom none will miss but Caesar, and for him Antinous flings himself into the jaws of death."

"Stay—stop! hapless boy, come back!" shouted the slave, and leaping into a boat he followed that of the Bithynian, which, impelled by strong and steady strokes, flew away into the current.

Mastor rowed with all his might, but he could not gain upon the boat he was pursuing. Thus in a wild race both reached the middle of the stream. There, the slave saw Antinous fling away his oar, and an instant later he heard Antinous call loudly on the name of Selene, and then, in helpless inactivity, he saw the lad glide into the waters, and the Nile swallowed in its flood the noblest and fairest of victims.

CHAPTER XXII.

A NIGHT and a day had slipped away since the death of the Bithynian. Ships and boats from every part of the province had collected before Besa to seek for the body of the drowned youth, the shores swarmed with men, and cressets and torches had dimmed the moonlight on river and shore all through the night; but they had not yet succeeded in finding the body of the beautiful youth.

Hadrian had heard in what way Antinous had perished. He had required Mastor to repeat to him more than once the last words of his faithful companion and neither to add nor to omit a single syllable. Hadrian's accurate memory cherished them all and now he had sat till dawn and from dawn till the sun had reached the meridian, repeating them again and again to himself. He sat gloomily brooding and would neither eat nor drink. The misfortune which had threatened him had fallen—and what a grief was this! If indeed Fate would accept the anguish he now felt in the place of all other suffering it might have had in store for him he might look forward to years free from care, but he felt as though he would rather have spent the remainder of his existence in sorrow and misery with his Antinous by his side than enjoy, without him, all that men call happiness, peace and prosperity.

Sabina and her escort had arrived—a host of men; but he had strictly ordered that no one, not even his wife, was to be admitted to his presence. The comfort of tears was denied him, but his grief gripped him at the heart, clouded his brain and made him so irritably sensitive that an unfamiliar voice, though even at a distance, disturbed him and made him angry.

The party who had arrived by water were not allowed to occupy the tents which had been pitched for them not far from his, because he desired to be alone, quite alone, with his anguish of spirit. Mastor, whom he had hitherto regarded rather a useful chattel than as a human creature, now grew nearer to him—had he not been the one witness of his darling's strange disappearance. Towards the close of this, the most miserable night he had ever known, the slave asked him whether he should not fetch the physician from the ships, he looked so pale; but Hadrian forbade it.

"If I could only cry like a woman," he said, "or like other fathers whose sons are snatched away by death, that would be the best remedy. You poor souls will have a bad time now, for the sun of my life has lost its light and the trees by the way-side have lost their verdure."

When he was alone once more he sat staring into vacancy and muttered to himself:

"All mankind should mourn with me for if I had been asked yesterday how perfect a beauty might be bestowed on one of their race I could have pointed proudly to you, my faithful boy and have said, 'Beauty like that of the gods.' Now the crown is cut off from the trunk of the palm and the maimed thing can only be ashamed of its deformity; and if all humanity were but one man it would look like one who has had his right eye torn out. I will not look on the monsters, lean and fat, that they may not spoil my taste for the true type! Oh faithful, lovable, beautiful boy! What a blind, mad fool have you been! And yet I cannot blame your madness. You have pierced my soul with the deepest thrust of all and yet I cannot even be angry with you. Superhuman! godlike was your faithful devotion. Aye, indeed, it was!" As he thus spoke he rose from his seat and went on resolutely and decidedly:

"Here I stretch out this my right hand—hear me, ye Immortals! Every city in the Empire shall raise an altar to Antinous, and the friend of whom you have robbed me I will make your equal and companion. Receive him tenderly, oh, ye undying rulers of the world! Which among you can boast of beauty greater than his? and which of you ever displayed so much goodness and faithfulness as your new associate?"

This vow seemed to have given Hadrian some comfort. For above half an hour he paced his tent with a firmer tread, then he desired that Heliodorus his secretary might be called.

The Greek wrote what his sovereign dictated. This was nothing less than that henceforth the world should worship a new divinity in the person of Antinous.

At noonday a messenger in breathless haste came to say that the body of the Bithynian had been found.

Thousands flocked to see the corpse, and among them Balbilla, who had behaved like a distracted creature when she heard to what an end her idol had come. She had rushed up and down the river-bank, among the citizens and fishermen, dressed in black mourning robes and with her hair flying about her. The Egyptians had compared her to the mourning Isis seeking the body of her beloved husband, Osiris. She was beside herself with grief, and her companion implored her in vain to calm herself and remember her rank and her dignity as a woman. But Balbilla pushed her vehemently aside, and when the news was brought that Nile had yielded up his prey she rushed on foot to see the body, with the rest of the crowd.

Her name was in every mouth, everyone knew that she was the Empress' friend, and so she was willingly and promptly obeyed when she commanded the bearers who carried the bier on which the recovered body lay to set it down and to lift up the sheet which shrouded it.

Pale and trembling, she went up to it and gazed down at the drowned man; but only for a moment could she endure the sight. She turned away with a shudder, and desired the bearers to go on. When the funeral procession had disappeared and she could no longer hear the shrill wailing of the Egyptian women, and no longer see them streaking their breast, head, and hair with damp earth and flinging up their arms wildly in the air, she turned to her companion and said calmly: "Now, Claudia, let us go home."

In the evening at supper she appeared dressed in black, like Sabina and all the rest of the suite, but she was calm and ready with an answer to every observation.

Pontius had travelled with them from Thebes to Besa, and she had spared him nothing that could punish him for his long absence, and had mercilessly compelled him to listen to all her verses on Antinous.

He meanwhile had been perfectly cool about it, and had criticised her poems exactly as if they had referred not to a man of flesh and blood but to some statue or god. This epigram he would praise, the next he would disparage, a third condemn. Her confession that she had been in the habit of complimenting Antinous with flowers and fruit he heard with a shrug of the shoulders, saying pleasantly: "Give him as many presents as you will; I know that you expect no gifts from your divinity in return for your sacrifices."

His words had surprised and delighted her. Pontius always understood her, and did not deserve that she should wound him. So she let him gaze into her soul, and told him how much she loved Antinous so long as he was absent. Then she laughed and confessed that she was perfectly indifferent to him as soon as they were together.

When, after the Bithynian's death, she lost all self-control he simply let her alone, and begged Claudia to do the same.

40

The same day that the body was found it was burnt
on a pile of precious wood. Hadrian had refused to see
it when he learnt that the death by drowning had terribly distorted the lad's features.

A few hours after the ashes of the Bithynian had
been collected and brought in a golden vase to Hadrian,
the Nile fleet was once more under sail, this time with
the Emperor on board one of the boats, to proceed
without farther halt to Alexandria.

Hadrian remained alone with only his slave and his
secretary on the boat that conveyed him; but he several
times sent to Pontius to desire him to come from the
ship on which he was and visit him on his. He liked to
hear the architect's deep voice, and discussed with him
the plans which Pontius had sketched for his mausoleum
in Rome and the monument to his lost favorite which
he proposed to have erected from designs of his own in
the large city which he intended should stand on the
site of the little town of Besa, and which he had already
named Antinoë. But these discussions only took up a
limited number of hours, and then the architect was at
liberty to return to Sabina's boat, on which Balbilla also
lived.

A few days after they had quitted Besa he was sitting alone with the poetess on the deck of the Nile
boat which, borne by the current and propelled by a
hundred oars, was rapidly and steadily nearing its destination. Ever since the death of the hapless favorite
Pontius had avoided mentioning him to her. She had
now become as observant and as talkative as before,
and in her eyes there even shone at times a ray of the
old sunny gayety of her nature. The architect thought
he comprehended the characteristic change in her senti-

ments, and would not allude to the cause of the violent but transient fever under which she had suffered.

"What did you discuss with Caesar to-day?" asked Balbilla of her friend. Pontius looked down at the ground and considered whether he could venture to utter the name of Antinous before the poetess. Balbilla observed his hesitation and said:

"Speak on; I can hear anything. That folly is past and over."

"Caesar is at work at the plans for a new town to be built and called Antinoë, and a sketch for a monument to his ill-fated favorite," said Pontius. "He will not accept any help, but I have to teach him to discriminate what is possible from what is impossible."

"Ah! he is always gazing at the stars and you look steadily at the road on which you are walking."

"An architect can make no use of anything that is unsteady or that has no firm foundation."

"That is a hard saying, Pontius. It is true that during the last few weeks I have behaved like a fool."

"I only wish that every tottering structure could recover its balance as quickly and as certainly as you! Antinous was a demigod for beauty, and a good faithful fellow besides."

"Do not speak of him any more," exclaimed Balbilla shuddering. "He looked dreadful. Can you forgive me for my conduct?"

"I never was angry with you."

"But I lost your esteem."

"No, Balbilla. Beauty, which is dear to us all, and which the Muse has kissed, attracted your easily moved poet's soul and it fluttered off at random. Let it fly! My friend's true womanly nature was never carried

40

away by it. She stands on a rock, that I am sure of."

" How good and kind in you to say so—too good, too kind! for I am a feeble creature, turned by every breeze that blows, a vain little fool who does not know one hour what she may do the next, a spoilt child that likes best to do the thing it ought to leave undone, a weak girl who finds a pleasure in doing battle with men. For all in all—"

" For all in all a darling of the gods who to-day can climb the rocks with a firm step and to-morrow lies dreaming in the sunshine among flowers—for all in all a nature that has no equal and which lacks nothing, nothing whatever that constitutes a true woman excepting—"

" I know what I lack," cried Balbilla. " A strong man on whom I can depend, whose warnings I can respect. You, you are that man; you and none other, for as soon as I feel you by my side I find it difficult to do what I know to be wrong. Here I am, Pontius! Will you have me with all my moods, with all my faults and weaknesses ?"

" Balbilla!" cried the architect, beside himself with heartfelt agitation and surprise, and he pressed her hand long and fervently to his lips.

" You will ? You will take me ? You will never leave me, you will warn, support me and protect me ?"

" Till my last day, till death, as my child, as the apple of my eye, as—dare I say it and believe it ?—as my love, my second self, my wife."

" Oh! Pontius, Pontius," she exclaimed, grasping his broad, right hand in both her own. " This hour restores to the orphaned Balbilla, father and mother and gives her besides the husband that she loves."

"Mine, mine!" cried the architect. "Immortal gods! During half a lifetime I have never found time, in the midst of labor and fatigue, to indulge in the joys of love and now you give me with interest and compound interest the treasure you have so long withheld."

"How can you, a reasonable man, so over-estimate the value of your possession? But you shall find some good in it. Life can no longer be conceived of as worth having without the possessor."

"And to me it has so long seemed empty and cold without you, you strange, unique, incomparable creature."

"But why did you not come sooner, and so give me no time to behave like a fool?"

"Because, because," said Pontius, gravely, "such a flight towards the sun seemed to me too bold; because I remember that my father's father—"

"He was the noblest man that the ancestor of my house attracted to its greatness."

"He was—consider it duly at this moment—he was your grandfather's slave."

"I know it, but I also know, that there is not a man on earth who is worthier of freedom than you are, or whom I could ask as humbly as I ask you: Take me, poor, foolish Balbilla, to be your wife, guide me and make of me whatever you can, for your own honor and mine."

The brief Nile voyage brought days and hours of the highest happiness to Balbilla and her lover. Before the fleet sailed into the Mareotic harbor of Alexandria, Pontius revealed his happy secret to the Emperor. Hadrian smiled for the first time since the death of his favorite, and desired the architect to bring Balbilla to him.

"I was wrong in my interpretation of the Pythian oracle," said he, as he laid the poetess's hand in that of Pontius. "Would you like to know how it runs Pontius —do not prompt me, my child. Anything that I have read through once or twice I never forget. Pythia said

> That which thou holdest most precious and dear shall be torn from thy keeping,
> And from the heights of Olympus, down shalt thou fall in the dust;
> Still the contemplative eye discerns under mutable sand-drifts
> Stable foundations of stone, marble and natural rock.'

You have chosen well girl. The oracle guaranteed you a safe road to tread through life. As to the dust of which it speaks, it exists no doubt in a certain sense, but this hand wields the broom that will sweep it away. Solemnize your marriage in Alexandria as soon as you will, but then come to Rome, that is the only condition I impose. A thing I always have at heart is the introduction of new and worthy members into the class of 'Knights,' for it is in that way alone that its fallen dignity can be restored. This ring, my Pontius, gives you the rank of *eques*, and such a man as you are, the husband of Balbilla and the friend of Caesar may no doubt by-and-bye find a seat in the Senate. What this generation can produce in stone and marble, my mausoleum shall bear witness to. Have you altered the plan of the bridge?"

CHAPTER XXIII.

In Alexandria the news of the nomination of the
"sham Eros" to be the Emperor's successor was hailed
with joy, and the citizens availed themselves gladly of
this fresh and favorable opportunity to hold one festival
after another. Titianus took care to provide for the due
performance of the usual acts of grace, and among
others he threw open the prison-gates of Canopus, and
the sculptor Pollux was set at liberty.

The hapless artist had grown pale, it is true, in durance vile, but neither leaner nor enfeebled in body; on
the other hand all the vigor of his intellect, all his bright
courage for life and his happy creative instinct, seemed
altogether crushed out of him. His face, as in his dirty
and ragged chiton, he journeyed from Canopus to Alexandria, revealed neither eager thankfulness for the unexpected boon of liberty, nor happiness at the prospect of
seeing again his own people and Arsinoe.

In the town he went, unintelligently dreaming as he
walked, from one street to another, but he was familiar
with every stone of the way, and his feet found their
way to his sister's house. How happy was Diotima,
how her children rejoiced, how impatient was each one
to conduct him to the old folks! How high in the air
the Graces frisked and leaped in front of the new little
home to welcome the returned absentee! And Doris,
poor Doris, almost fainted with joyful surprise and her
husband had to support her in his arms when her long
vanished son, whom she had never given up for lost,

however, suddenly stood before her and said : "Here am I." How fondly she kissed and caressed her dear, cruel, restored fugitive. The singer too loudly expressed his joy alike in verse and in prose, and fetched his best theatrical dress out of the chest to put it on his son in the place of his ragged chiton.

A mighty torrent of curses and execrations flowed from the old man's lips as Pollux told his story. The sculptor found it difficult to bring it to an end, for his father interrupted him at every word, and all the while he was talking his mother forced him to eat and drink incessantly, even when he could no more. After he had assured her that he was long since replete, she pushed two more pots on to the fire, for he must have been half-starved in prison, and what he did not want now he would find room for two hours hence. Euphorion himself conducted Pollux to the bath in the evening, and as they went home together he never for an instant left his side; the sense of being near him did him good and was like some comfortable physical sensation.

The singer was not usually inquisitive, but on this occasion he never ceased asking questions till Doris led her son to the bed she had freshly made for him. After the artist had gone to rest, the old woman once more slipped into his room, kissed his forehead, and said:

"To-day you have still been thinking too much of that hideous prison—but to-morrow my boy, to-morrow you will be the same as before, will you not?"

"Only leave me alone mother; I shall soon be better," he replied. "This bed is as good as a sleeping-draught; the plank in the prison was quite a different thing."

"You have never asked once for your Arsinoe," said Doris.

"What can she matter to me? Only let me sleep."

But the next morning Pollux was just the same as he had been the previous evening, and as the days went on his condition remained unchanged. His head drooped on his breast, he never spoke but when he was spoken to, and when Doris or Euphorion tried to talk to him of the future, he would ask: "Am I a burden to you?" or begged them not to worry him.

Still, he was gentle and kind, took his sister's children in his arms, played with the Graces, whistled to the birds, went in and out, and played a valiant part at every meal. Now and again he would ask after Arsinoe. Once he allowed himself to be guided to the house where she lived, but he would not knock at Paulina's door and seemed overawed by the grandeur of the house. After he had been brooding and dreaming for a week, so idle, listless, and absent that his mother's heart was filled with anxious fears every time she looked at him, his brother Teuker hit upon a happy idea.

The young gem-cutter was not usually a frequent visitor to his parents' house, but since the return of the hapless Pollux he called there almost daily. His apprenticeship was over and he seemed on the high-road to become a great master in his art; nevertheless he esteemed his brother's gifts as far beyond his own and had tried to devise some means of reawakening the dormant energies of the luckless man's brain.

"It was at this table," said Teuker to his mother, "that Pollux used to sit. This evening I will bring in a lump of clay and a good piece of modelling wax. Just put it all on the table and lay his tools by the side of it; perhaps when he sees them he will take a fancy again to work. If he can only make up his mind to model even a doll for the children he will soon get into the vein again, and he will go on from small things to great."

Teuker brought the materials, Doris set them out with the modelling tools, and next morning watched her son's proceedings with an anxious heart. He got up late, as he had always done since his return home, and sat a long time over the bowl of porridge which his mother had prepared for his breakfast. Then he sauntered across to his table, stood in front of it awhile, broke off a piece of clay and kneaded and moulded it in his fingers into balls and cylinders, looked at one of them more closely and then, flinging it on the ground, he said, as he leaned across the table supporting himself on both hands to put his face near his mother's:

"You want me to work again; but it is of no use— I could do no good with it."

The old woman's eyes filled with tears, but she did not answer him. In the evening Pollux begged her to put away the tools.

When he was gone to bed she did so, and while she was moving about with a light in the dark, lumber-room in which she had kept them with other disused things, her eye fell on the unfinished wax model which had been the last work of her ill-starred son. A new idea struck her. She called Euphorion, made him throw the clay into the court-yard and place the model on the table by the side of the wax. Then she put out the very same tools as he had been using on the fateful day of their expulsion from Lochias, close to the cleverly-sketched portrait, and begged her husband to go out with her quite early next morning and to remain absent till mid-day.

"You will see," she said, "when he is standing face to face with his last work and there is no one by to disturb him or look at him, he will find the ends of the threads that have been cut and perhaps be able to gather them up again and go on with the work where it was interrupted."

The mother's heart had hit upon the right idea.

·When Pollux had eaten his breakfast he went to his table exactly as he had done the day before; but the sight of the work in hand had quite a different effect to the mere raw clay and wax. His eyes sparkled; he walked round the table with an attentive gaze examining his work as keenly and as eagerly as if it were some fine thing he saw for the first time. Memory revived in his mind. He laughed aloud, clasped his hands and said to himself, "Capital! Something may be made of that!"

His dull weariness slipped off him, as it were; a confident smile parted his lips and he seized the wax with a firm hand. But he did not begin to work at once; he only tried whether his fingers had not lost their cunning, and whether the yielding material was obedient to his will. The wax was no less docile to his touch than in former days, as he pinched or pulled it. Perhaps then the tormenting thought that blighted his life, the dread that in the prison he had ceased to be an artist, and had lost all his faculty was nothing more than a mad delusion! He must at any rate try how he could get on at the work.

No one was by to observe him—he might dare the attem t at once. The sweat of anguish stood in large

beads on his brow as he finally concentrated his volition, shook back the hair from his face and took up a
lump of the wax in both hands. There stood the portrait of Antinous with the head only half-finished.
Now—could he succeed in modelling that lovely head
free-hand and from memory ?

His breath came fast, and his hands trembled as he
set to work ; but soon his hand was as steady as ever, his
eye was calm and keen again, and the work progressed.
The fine features of the young Bithynian were distinct to
his mind's eye, and when, about four hours after, his
mother looked in at the window to see what Pollux was
doing, whether her little stratagem had succeeded, she
cried out with surprise, for the favorite's bust, a likeness
in every feature, stood on a plinth side by side with the
original sketch. Before she could cross the threshold
her son had run to meet her, lifted her in his arms, and
kissing her forehead and lips he exclaimed, radiant with
delight :

" Mother, I still can work. Mother, mother, I am
not lost !"

In the afternoon his brother came in and saw what
he had been doing, and now—and not till now—could
Teuker honestly be glad to have found his brother again.

While the two artists were sitting together, and the
gem-cutter was suggesting to the sculptor, who had com-
plained of the bad light in his parent's house, that he
should carry the statue to his master's workshop—which
was much lighter—to complete it, Euphorion had quietly gone to some remote corner' of his provision-shed and
brought to light an amphora full of noble Chian wine
which had been given to him by a rich merchant, for
whose wedding he had performed the part of Hyme-

naeus with a chorus of youths. For twenty years had he still preserved this jar of wine for some specially happy occasion. This jar and his best lute were the only objects which Euphorion had carried with his own hand from Lochias to his daughter's house and then again to his own new abode. With an air of dignified pride the singer set the old amphora before his sons, but Doris laid hands upon it at once and said:

"I am glad to bestow the good gift upon you, and would willingly drink a cup of it with you; but a prudent general does not celebrate his triumph before he has won the battle. As soon as the statue of the beautiful lad is completed, I myself, will wreathe this venerable jar with ivy, and beg you spare it to us, my dear old man—but not before."

"Mother is right," said Pollux. "And if the amphora is really destined for me, if you will allow it, my father shall not remove the pitch wig from its venerable head, till Arsinoe is mine once more!"

"That is well my boy," cried Doris, "and then I will crown, not merely the jar but all of us too, with nothing but sweet roses."

The next day Pollux, with his unfinished statue, removed to the workshop of his brother's master. The worthy man cleared the best place for the young sculptor, for he thought highly of him and wished to make good, as far as lay in his power, the injustice the poor fellow had suffered from the treachery of Papias. Now, from sunrise till evening fell, Pollux was constant to his work. He gave himself up to the resuscitated pleasure and power of creation with real passion. Instead of using wax he had recourse to clay, and formed a tall figure which represented Antinous as the youthful Bac-

chus, as the god might have appeared to the pirates. A
mantle fell in light folds from his left shoulder to his
ankles, leaving the broad breast and right arm entirely
free; vine-leaves and grapes wreathed his flowing locks,
and a pine-cone, flame-shaped, crowned his brow. The
left arm was raised in a graceful curve, and his fingers
lightly grasped a thyrsus which rested on the ground
and stood taller than the god's head; by the side of this
magnificent figure stood a mighty wine-jar, half hidden
by the drapery.

For a whole week Pollux had devoted himself to this
task during all the hours of daylight with unflagging zeal
and diligence.   Before night fell he was accustomed to
leave his work and walk up and down in front of
Paulina's house, but for the present he refrained from
knocking at the door and asking after the girl he loved.
He had heard from his mother how anxiously she was
guarded from him and his; still Paulina's severity would
certainly not have hindered the artist from making the
attempt to possess himself of his dearest treasure. What
held him back from even approaching Arsinoe, was the
vow he had made to himself never to tempt her to quit
her new and sheltered home till he had acquired a firm
certainty of being once for all an artist, a true artist, who
might hope to do something great, and who might dare
to link the fate of the woman he loved, with his own.

When, on the eighth morning of his labors, he was
taking a few minutes rest, his brother's master came past
the rapidly advancing work, and after contemplating it
for some time exclaimed:

"Splendid, splendid! Our time has produced nothing
to compare with it!"

An hour later Pollux was standing at the door of

Paulina's town-house, and let the knocker fall heavily on
the door. The steward opened to him and asked him
what he wanted. He asked to speak with dame Paulina,
but she was not at home. Then he asked after Arsinoe,
the daughter of Keraunus, who had found a home with
the rich widow. The servant shook his head.

"My mistress is having her searched for," he said.
"She disappeared yesterday evening. The ungrateful
creature! She has tried to run away several times before
now."

The artist laughed, slapped the steward on the back,
and said:

"I will soon find her!" and he sprang away down
the street, and back to his parents.

Arsinoe had received much kindness in Paulina's
house, but she had also gone through many bad hours.
For months she had been obliged to believe that her
lover was dead. Pontius had told her that Pollux had
entirely vanished and her benefactress persisted in always speaking of him as of one dead. The poor child
had shed many tears for him, and when the longing to
talk of him with some one who had known him had
taken possession of her she had entreated Paulina to
allow her to go to see his mother or to let Doris visit
her. But the widow had desired her to give up all
thought of the idol-maker and his belongings, speaking
with contempt of the gate-keeper's worthy wife. Just
at that time Selene also left the city, and now Arsinoe's
longing for her old friends grew to a passionate craving
to see them again.

One day she yielded to the promptings of her heart
and slipped out into the street to seek Doris; but the
door-keeper, who had been charged by Paulina never

to allow her to go outside the door without his mistress's express permission, noticed her and brought her back to her protectress—not this time only, but on several subsequent occasions when she attempted to escape.

It was not merely her longing to talk about Pollux which made her new home unendurable to Arsinoe, but many other reasons besides. She felt like a prisoner; and in fact she was one, for after each attempt at flight her freedom of movement was still farther impeded. It is true that she had soon ceased to submit patiently to all that was required of her and even had often opposed her adoptive mother with vehement words, tears and execrations, but these unpleasant scenes, which always ended by a declaration on Paulina's part that she forgave the girl, had always resulted in a long break in her drives and in a variety of small annoyances. Arsinoe was beginning to hate her benefactress and everything that surrounded her, and the hours of catechising and of prayer, which she could not escape, were a positive martyrdom. Ere long the doctrine to which Paulina sought to win her was confounded in her mind with that which it was intended to drive out, and she defiantly shut her heart against it.

Bishop Eumenes, who had been elected in the spring Patriarch of the Christians of Alexandria, visited her oftener than usual during the summer when Paulina lived in her suburban villa. Paulina, it is true, had fancied she could do without his help, and that she could and must carry her task through to the end by herself; but the worthy old man had felt sympathetically drawn to the poor ill-guided child, and sought to soothe and calm her mind and show her the goal, towards which Paulina desired to lead her, in all its beauty. After such

discourses Arsinoe would be softened and felt inclined
to believe in God and to love Christ, but no sooner had
her protectress called her again into the school-room
and put the very same things before her in her own
way than the girl's heartstrings drew close again ; and
when she was desired to pray she raised her hands, indeed, but out of sheer defiance, she prayed in spirit to
the Greek gods.

Frequently Paulina received visits from heathen acquaintances in rich dresses and the sight of them always
reminded Arsinoe of former days. How poor she had
been then ! and yet she had always had a blue or a red
ribbon to plait in her hair and trim the edge of her
peplum. Now she might wear none but white dresses
and the least scrap of colored ornament to dress her
hair or smarten her robe was strictly forbidden. Such
vain trifles, Paulina would say, were very well for the
heathen, but the Lord looked not at the body but at
the heart.

Ah! and the poor little heart of the hapless child
could not offer a very pleasing sight to the Father in
Heaven, for hatred and disgust, sadness, impatience, and
blasphemy seethed in it from morning till night. This
young nature was surely formed for love and contentment, and both had left her weeping. Still Arsinoe
never ceased to yearn for them.

When November had begun and another attempt to
run away during their move back to the town-house
had failed, Paulina tried to punish her by never speaking a word to her for a fortnight, and forbidding even
the slave-women to speak to her. In these two weeks
the talkative girl was reduced almost to desperation,
and she even thought of throwing herself off the roof

41

down into the court-yard. But she clung too dearly to life to carry this horrible project into execution. On the first of December Paulina once more spoke to her, forgave her ingratitude, as usual in a long, kind speech, and told her how many hours she had spent in praying for her enlightenment and improvement.

Paulina spoke the truth, and yet but half the truth, for she had never felt a real love for Arsinoe, and had now for a long time watched her come and go with actual dislike; but she required her conversion in order that the warmest wish of her heart might find fulfilment. It was for the happiness of her daughter, and not for the sake of her recalcitrant companion, that she prayed for her enlightenment and never ceased in her efforts to open the callous heart of her adopted child to the true faith.

In the afternoon preceding that morning when Pollux had at last knocked at the Christian widow's door, the sun shone with particular brilliancy, and Paulina had allowed the girl to go out with her. They spent some little time with a Christian family who dwelt on the shore of Lake Mareotis, and so it fell out that they did not return home till late in the evening. Arsinoe had long learnt, while she sat apparently gazing at the ground, to keep her eyes out of the carriage and to see everything that was going on around her; and as the chariot turned into their own street she spied in the distance a tall man who looked like her long-wept Pollux. She fixed her eyes upon him, and had some difficulty in keeping herself from calling out aloud, for he it was who walked slowly down the street. She could not be mistaken, for the torches of two slaves who were walking in front of a litter had broadly lighted up his face and figure.

He was not lost—he was living, and seeking her. She could have shouted aloud for joy, but she did not stir till Paulina's chariot was standing still in front of her house. The door-keeper bustled out as usual to help his mistress to step out of the high-slung vehicle. Thus Paulina for an instant turned her back, and in that moment Arsinoe sprang out of the opposite side of the chariot, and was flying down towards the street where she had seen her lover. Before Paulina could discover that she was gone the runaway found herself in the midst of the throng which, when the day's work was over, poured out from the workshops and factories on their way home.

Paulina's slaves, who were sent out at once to seek the fugitive, had to return home this time empty-handed; but Arsinoe, on her part, had not succeeded in finding him she sought. For an hour she looked round and about her in vain; then she perceived that her search must be unsuccessful, and wondered how she might find her way to his parents' house. Rather than return to her benefactress she would have joined the roofless crew who passed the night on the hard marble pavement of the forecourts of the temple.

At first she rejoiced in the sense of recovered liberty, but when none of the passers-by could tell her where Euphorion, the singer, lived, and some young men followed her and addressed her with impudent speeches, terror made her turn aside into a street which led to the Bruchiom; her persecutors had not even then ceased to follow her, when a litter, escorted by lictors and several torch-bearers, was carried past. It was Julia, the kind wife of the prefect, who sat in it; Arsinoe recognized her at once, followed her, and reached the door of her resi-

41

dence at the same moment as she herself. As the matron got out of her litter she observed the girl who placed herself modestly, but with hands uplifted in entreaty, at the side of her path. Julia greeted the pretty creature in whom she had once taken a motherly interest with affectionate sympathy, beckoned Arsinoe to her, smiled as she listened to her request for a night's shelter, and led her with much satisfaction to her husband.

Titianus was ill; still he was glad once more to see the ill-fated palace-steward's pretty daughter; he listened to her story of her flight with many signs of disapprobation, but kindly withal, and expressed the warmest satisfaction at hearing that the sculptor Pollux was still in the land of the living.

The grand and lordly bed in one of the strangers' rooms in the prefect's house had held many a more illustrious guest, but never one whose sleep was brightened by happier dreams than the poor orphaned " little fugitive," who, no longer ago than yesterday, had cried herself to sleep.

CHAPTER XXIV

ARSINOE was up betimes on the following morning; much embarrassed by all the splendor that surrounded her, she walked up and down her room thinking of Pollux. Then she stopped to take pleasure in her own image displayed in a large mirror which stood on a dressing-table, and between whiles she compared the couch, on which she lay down again at full length, with those in Paulina's house. Once more she felt herself a

prisoner, but this time she liked her prison, and presently, when she heard slaves passing by her room, she flew
to the door to listen, for it was just possible that Titianus might have sent to fetch Pollux, and would allow
him to come to see her. At last a slave-woman came
in, brought her some breakfast, and desired her from
Julia to go into the garden and look at the flowers and
aviaries till she should be sent for.

Early that morning the news had reached the prefect that Antinous had sought his death in the Nile, and
it had shocked him greatly, less on account of the hapless youth than for Hadrian's sake. When he had given
the proper officials orders to announce the melancholy
news and to desire the citizens to give some public expression of their sympathy with the Emperor's sorrow, he
gave audience to the Patriarch Eumenes.

This venerable man, ever since the transactions
which he had conducted with reference to the thanksgiving of the Christians for the safety of the Emperor
after the fire, had been one of the most esteemed friends
of Titianus and Julia. The prefect discussed with the
Patriarch the inauspicious effects that the death of the
young fellow might be expected to have on the Emperor, and as a result, on the government, although the
favorite had had no qualities of mind to distinguish him.

"Whenever Hadrian," continued Titianus, "would
give his unresting brain an hour's relaxation, and release
himself from disappointment and vexation and the
severe toil and anxiety of which his life is overfull,
he would go out hunting with the bold youth or would
have the handsome, good-hearted boy into his own
room. The sight of the Bithynian's beauty delighted
his eye, and how well Antinous knew how to listen to

him—silent, modest and attentive! Hadrian loved him
as a son, and the poor fellow clung to his master in return with more than a son's fidelity; his death itself
proved it.   Caesar himself said to me once: 'In the
midst of the turmoil of waking life, when I see Antinous a feeling comes over me as if a beautiful dream
stood incorporate before my eyes.'"

"Caesar's grief at losing him must indeed be great,"
said the Patriarch.

"And the loss will add to the gloom of his grave
and brooding nature, render his restless scheming and
wandering still more capricious, and increase his suspi-
ciousness and irritability."

"And the circumstances under which Antinous perished," added Eumenes, "will afford new ground for his
attachment to superstitions."

"That is to be feared. We have not happy days be-
· fore us; the revolt in Judaea, too, will again cost thousands of lives."

"If only it had been granted to you to assume the
government of that province."

"But you know, my worthy friend, the condition I
am in. On my bad days I am incapable of commanding a thought or opening my lips. When my breathlessness increases I feel as if I were being suffocated.   I
have placed many decades of my life at the disposal of
the state, and I now feel justified in devoting the diminished strength which is left me to other things.   I and
my wife think of retiring to my property by lake Larius,
and there to try whether we may succeed, she and I, in
becoming worthy of the salvation and capable of ap-
prehending the truth that you have offered us. You are
there Julia?   As the determination to retire from the

world has matured in us, we have, both of us, remembered more than once the words of the Jewish sage, which you lately told us of. When the angel of God drove the first man out of Paradise, he said: 'Henceforth your heart must be your Paradise.' We are turning our backs on the pleasure of a city life—"

"And we do so without regret," said Julia, interrupting her husband, " for we bear in our minds the germ of a more indestructible, purer, and more lasting happiness."

" Amen !" said the Patriarch. "Where two such as you dwell together there the Lord is third in the bond."

" Give us your disciple Marcianus to be our travelling-companion," said Titianus.

" Willingly," said Eumenes. "Shall he come to visit you when I leave you ?"

" Not immediately," replied Julia. "I have this morning an important and at the same time pleasant business to attend to. You know Paulina, the widow of Pudeus. She took into her keeping a pretty young creature—"

" And Arsinoe has run away from her."

" We took her in here," said Titianus. " Her protectress seems to have failed in attracting her to her, or in working favorably on her nature."

" Yes," said the Patriarch. " There was but one key to her full, bright heart—Love—but Paulina tried to force it open with coercion and persistent driving. It remained closed—nay, the lock is spoiled.—But, if I may ask, how came the girl into your house ?"

" That I can tell you later, we did not make her acquaintance for the first time yesterday."

" And I am going to fetch her lover to her," cried the prefect's wife.

" Paulina will claim her of you," said the Patriarch.
" She is having her sought for everywhere ; but the child
will never thrive under her guidance."

" Did the widow formally adopt Arsinoe ?" asked
Titianus.

" No ; she proposed doing so as soon as her young
pupil—"

" Intentions count for nothing in law, and I can protect our pretty little guest against her claim."

" I will fetch her," said Julia. " The time must certainly have seemed very long to her already. Will you
come with me, Eumenes ?"

" With pleasure," replied the old man, "Arsinoe and
I are excellent friends; a conciliatory word from me will
do her good, and my blessing cannot harm even a
heathen. Farewell, Titianus, my deacons are expecting
me."

When Julia returned to the sitting-room with her
protégée, the child's eyes were wet with tears, for the
kind words of the venerable old man had gone to her
heart and she knew and acknowledged that she had experienced good as well as evil from Paulina.

The matron found her husband no longer alone.
Wealthy old Plutarch with his two supporters was with
him, and in black garments, which were decorated
with none but white flowers, instead of many colored
garments; he presented a singular appearance. The old
man was discoursing eagerly to the prefect; but as soon
as he saw Arsinoe he broke off his harangue, clapped
his hands and was quite excited with the pleasure of
seeing once more the fair Roxana for whom he had
once visited in vain all the gold-workers' shops in the
city.

"But I am tired," cried Plutarch, with quite youthful vivacity, "I am quite tired of keeping the ornaments for you. There are quite enough other useless things in my house. They belong to you, not to me, and this very day I will send them to the noble Julia, that she may give them to you. Give me your hand, dear child; you have grown paler but more womanly. What do you think, Titianus, she would still do for Roxana; only your wife must find a dress for her again. All in white, and no ribband in your hair!—like a Christian."

"I know some one who will find out the way to fitly crown these soft tresses," replied Julia. "Arsinoe is the bride of Pollux, the sculptor."

"Pollux!" exclaimed Plutarch, in extreme excitement. "Move me forward, Antaeus and Atlas, the sculptor Pollux is her lover? A great, a splendid artist! The very same, noble Titianus, of whom I was just now speaking to you."

"You know him?" asked the prefect's wife.

"No, but I have just left the work-shop of Periander, the gem-cutter, and there I saw the model of a statue of Antinous that is unique, marvellous, incomparable! The Bithynian as Dionysus! The work would do no discredit to a Phidias, to a Lysippus. Pollux was out of the way, but I laid my hand at once on his work; the young master must execute it immediately in marble. Hadrian will be enchanted with this portrait of his beautiful and devoted favorite. You must admire it, every connoisseur must! I will pay for it, the only question is whether I or the city should present it to Caesar. This matter your husband must decide."

Arsinoe was radiant with joy at these words, but she stepped modestly into the background as an official came in and handed Titianus a dispatch that had just arrived.

The prefect read it; then turning to his friend and his wife, he said:

" Hadrian ascribes to Antinous the honors of a god."

" Fortunate Pollux!" exclaimed Plutarch. " He has executed the first statue of the new divinity. I will present it to the city, and they shall place it in the temple to Antinous of which we must lay the first stone before Caesar is back here again. Farewell, my noble friends! Greet your bridegroom from me, my child. His work belongs to me. Pollux will be the first among his fellow-artists, and it has been my privilege to discover this new star—the eighth artist whose merit I have detected while he was still unknown. Your future brother-in-law too, Teuker, will turn out well. I am having a stone cut by him with a portrait of Antinous. Once more farewell ; I must go to the Council. We shall have to discuss the subject of a temple to the new divinity. Move on you two!"

An hour after Plutarch had quitted the prefect's house Julia's chariot was standing at the entrance of a lane, much too narrow to admit a vehicle with horses, and which ended in a little plot on which stood Euphorion's humble house. Julia's outrunners easily found out the residence of the sculptor's parents, led the matron and Arsinoe to the spot, and showed them the door they should knock at.

" What a color you have, my little girl!" said Julia. " Well, I will not intrude on your meeting, but I should like to deliver you with my own hand into those of your future mother. Go to that little house, Arctus, and beg dame Doris to step out here. Only say that some one wishes to speak with her, but do not mention my name."

Arsinoe's heart beat so violently that she was incapable of saying a word of thanks to her kind protectress.

" Step behind this palm-tree," said the lady. Arsinoe obeyed; but she felt as though it was some outside volition, and not her own, that guided her to her hiding-place. She heard nothing of the first words spoken by the Roman lady and Doris. She only saw the dear old face of her Pollux's mother, and in spite of her reddened eyes and the wrinkles which trouble had furrowed in her face, she could not tire of looking at it. It reminded her of the happiest days of her childhood, and she longed to rush forward and throw her arms round the neck of the kindly, good-hearted woman. Then she heard Julia say :

" I have brought her to you. She is just as sweet and as maidenly and lovely as she was the first time we saw her in the theatre."

" Where is she ? Where is she ?" asked Doris in a trembling voice.

Julia pointed to the palm, and was about to call Arsinoe, but the girl could no longer restrain her longing to fall on the neck of some one dear to her, for Pollux had come out of the door to see who had asked for his mother, and to see him and to fly to his breast with a cry of joy had been one and the same act to Arsinoe.

Julia gazed at the couple with moistened eyes, and when, after many kind words for old and young alike, she took leave of the happy group, she said :

" I will provide for your outfit my child, and this

time I think you will wear it, not merely for one transient hour but through a long and happy life."

Joyful singing sounded out that evening from Euphorion's little home. Doris and her husband, and Pollux and Arsinoe, Diotima and Teuker, decked with
garlands, reclined round the amphora which was wreathed
with roses, drinking to pleasure and joy, to art and love,
and to all the gifts of the present. The sweet bride's
long hair was once more plaited with handsome blue
ribbons.

Three weeks after these events Hadrian was again in
Alexandria. He kept aloof from all the festivals instituted in honor of the new god Antinous, and smiled
incredulously when he was told that a new star had appeared in the sky, and that an oracle had declared it to
be the soul of his lost favorite.

When Plutarch conducted the Emperor and his
friends to see the Bacchus Antinous, which Pollux had
completed in the clay, Hadrian was deeply struck and
wished to know the name of the master who had executed this noble work of art. Not one of his companion's had the courage to speak the name of Pollux in
his presence; only Pontius ventured to come forward
for his young friend. He related to Hadrian the hapless artist's history and begged him to forgive him. The
Emperor nodded his approval, and said:

"For the sake of this lost one he shall be forgiven."

Pollux was brought into his presence, and Hadrian,
holding out his hand said as he pressed the sculptor's:

" The Immortals have bereft me of his love and faithfulness, but your art has preserved his beauty for me and for the world—"

Every city in the Empire vied in building temples and erecting statues to the new god, and Pollux, Arsinoe's happy husband, was commissioned to execute statues and busts of Antinous for a hundred towns; but he refused most of the orders, and would send out no work as his own that he had not executed himself on a new conception. His master, Papias, returned to Alexandria, but he was received there by his fellow-artists with such insulting contempt, that in an evil hour he destroyed himself. Teuker lived to be the most famous gem-engraver of his time.

Soon after Selene's martyrdom dame Hannah quitted Besa; the office of Superior of the Deaconesses at Alexandria was intrusted to her, and she exercised it with much blessing till an advanced age. Mary, the deformed girl, remained behind in the Nile-port, which under Hadrian was extended into the magnificent city of Antinoë. There were there two graves from which she could not bear to part.

Four years after Arsinoe's marriage with Pollux, Hadrian called the young sculptor to Rome; he was there to execute the statue of the Emperor in a quadriga. This work was intended to crown and finish his mausoleum constructed by Pontius, and Pollux carried it out in so admirable a manner, that when it was ended, Hadrian said to him with a smile:

" Now you have earned the right to pronounce sentence of death on the works of other masters."

Euphorion's son lived in honor and prosperity to see his children, the children of his faithful wife Arsinoe—

who was greatly admired by the Tiber—grow up to be worthy citizens. They remained heathen; but the Christian love which Eumenes had taught Paulina's foster-daughter was never forgotten, and she kept a kindly place for it in her heart and in her household. A few months before the young couple left Alexandria, Doris had peacefully gone to her last rest, and her husband died soon after her; the want of his faithful companion was the complaint he succumbed to.

On the shores of the Tiber, Pontius was still the sculptor's friend. Balbilla and her husband gave their corrupt fellow-citizens the example of a worthy, faithful marriage on the old Roman pattern. The poetess's bust had been completed by Pollux in Alexandria, and with all its tresses and little curls, it found favor in Balbilla's eyes.

Verus was to have enjoyed the title of Caesar even during Hadrian's lifetime, but after a long illness he died the first. Lucilla nursed him with unfailing devotion and enjoyed the longed-for monopoly of his attentions through a period of much suffering. It was on their son that in later years the purple devolved.

The predictions of the prefect Titianus were fulfilled, for the Emperor's faults increased with years and the meaner side of his mind and nature came into sharper relief. Titianus and his wife led a retired life by lake Larius, far from the world, and both were baptized before they died. They never pined for the turmoil of a pleasure-seeking world or its dazzling show, for they had learnt to cherish in their own hearts all that is fairest in life.

It was the slave Mastor who brought to Titianus the news of the sovereign's death. Hadrian had given

him his freedom before he died and had left him a handsome legacy.

The prefect gave him a piece of land to farm and
continued in friendly relations with his Christian neighbor and his pretty daughter, who grew up among her
father's co-religionists.

When Titianus had told his wife the melancholy
news he added solemnly:

" A great sovereign is dead. The pettinesses which
disfigured the man Hadrian will be forgotten by posterity, for the ruler Hadrian was one of those men
whom Fate sets in the places they belong to, and who,
true to their duty, struggle indefatigably to the end.
With wise moderation he was so far master of himself
as to bridle his ambition and to defy the blame and pre-
judice of all the Romans. The hardest, and perhaps
the wisest, resolution of his life was to abandon the provinces which it would have exhausted the power of the
Empire to retain. He travelled over every portion of
his dominion within the limits he himself had set to it,
shrinking from neither frost nor heat, and he tried to be
as thoroughly acquainted with every portion of it as if
the Empire were a small estate he had inherited. His
duties as a sovereign forced him to travel, and his love
of travel lightened the duty. He was possessed by a
real passion to understand and learn everything. Even
the Incomprehensible set no limits to his thirst for knowledge, but ever striving to see farther and to dig deeper
than is possible to the mind of man, he wasted a great
part of his mighty powers in trying to snatch aside the
curtain which hides the destinies of the future. No one
ever worked at so many secondary occupations as he,
and yet no former Emperor ever kept his eye so uner-

ringly fixed on the main task of his life, the consolida-
tion and maintenance of the strength of the state and
the improvement and prosperity of its citizens."

(2)

THE END.

www.ingramcontent.com/pod-product-compliance
Lightning Source LLC
Chambersburg PA
CBHW030738030726
47497CB00001B/32